RED RAIN

VOL.3

RED RAIN

VOL.3

RACHEL NEWHOUSE

CONTENTS

JONAH

RED RAIN #7

JULY 2076

1: NIC

I should have known my ex-girlfriend would try to kill me.

To her credit, she'd set the stage beautifully. She'd trapped us on the Bridge of Seventeen Arches, where the moonlit water prevented any heroic escape. A pair of guards stood behind her on the west bank, while another set approached from across the bridge. On the other side of the lake, Beijing's iconic Summer Palace sprawled on the hill, aglow with the light and music of the annual United state dinner. It was a stunning backdrop for a crime of passion.

She slithered towards us, the clack of her stilettos on the brick more irritating than threatening. "Dr. Von Nieuwenhuyse, you're under arrest."

I took a step back, mostly to avoid her overpowering perfume. "You've been saving up for that one, haven't you, Asia?"

She flicked her tongue like she had hair in her mouth. "You can call me Min," she said, referring to one of three of her given names.

"I could call you a lot of things, but there are children present," I returned. I shoved Philadelphia, my ward, behind me, even though I knew it was a wasted gesture.

Phil glanced rapidly between us, as if the motion could help her sheltered seventeen-year-old brain catch up. "Are you two—"

I put my hand up. "*Were*. Whatever you were about to say, it's past tense."

"Nic," Asia scolded, "you didn't even give me a chance."

"If you wanted a chance, you shouldn't have led with 'you're under arrest.' I have standards."

"I got desperate," Asia said in a tone that suggested she was anything but.

"I just never pictured you as someone who would be in a relationship. Ever," Phil commented, eyeing me like this revelation changed everything.

"And you wonder why." I gestured at Asia.

She took it as a compliment. "We have so much to catch up on. I've been waiting eight years for you to accept my invitation." She beckoned to her guards, who advanced like a noose cinching.

I stuck both of my arms out to stop them. "Hold on, let's get one thing straight. I'm Andromeda's plus one, *not* yours," I said, using Phil's legal name.

"Wait, you've been waiting *eight years*?" Phil shoved my arm aside and faced Asia. "Why didn't you just arrest him while he was on Mars?"

"An excellent observation," I praised. I folded my arms and glared at Asia. "If you're so madly in love with me, why didn't you propose before now? You knew exactly where I was."

I remembered, despite my best attempts, the day we broke up. Asia had been just as wealthy and powerful then as she was now; she could have easily had me arrested, or defunded my science station on Mars, or employed any number of threatening tactics. But she hadn't. She'd accepted her defeat and slunk into the shadows, and the only contact I received from her was an annual invitation to the state gala. It wasn't until recently that I realized she'd even been paying attention to what I was experimenting with on Mars.

Asia stroked one of the marble dragons that capped the bridge's railing. "You don't think this is the perfect place to get engaged?"

"As much as I appreciate the effort that went into this elaborate set-up, no, this seems ill thought out." It made no sense for Asia to wait so long, only to confront me in a public place. Even though there was no one else on the bridge, there were still people nearby. People that might ask questions—or worse, tell Asia's father.

General Secretary Mong, the supreme leader of the United, had not been privy to my romance with Asia—or the various illegal schemes she and I had attempted together. I'm sure he'd be fascinated to know that his own daughter had helped me create a world-ending superweapon designed to bring his empire to its knees.

No, nothing about this macabre play made sense for Asia, and that was what I found most threatening.

"Why now, Asia?" I demanded.

She giggled, a disgusting little sound. "Isn't it obvious?"

"No," I admitted, knowing full well I was about to lose.

Asia strolled over and grabbed Phil's arm. I reacted, but the guards were faster. I heard the distinct sound of an electric gun powering up and froze.

And that's when I remembered I was also carrying.

Asia pulled Phil towards her. Phil stopped breathing, her panicked blue eyes begging me to help. I could only watch as Asia ran her deadly manicured nails through Philadelphia's ashy blonde curls.

"It's been so long since the great Dr. Von Nieuwenhuyse has cared about anyone but himself…" Asia cooed. She hooked one finger under the pearl necklace Philadelphia wore—the necklace I had given Asia as a gift so many years ago. Asia yanked on the chain, and Phil gasped, clutching her throat.

Asia held her there and looked up at me, bloodred lips curled in a sneer. "I simply couldn't waste the opportunity."

Suddenly, Asia's eight years of silence made sense. Philadelphia changed everything, as she had an annoying habit of doing. Three months ago, Phil had been my enemy, an incessant reminder of my failure. But somewhere in the process of escaping from prison, destroying my own superweapon, and generally doing our best to get ourselves killed, we'd mutually agreed to update our status. I'd signed a paper making her my legal dependent, and that paper gave Asia the card she needed to play her hand.

For the first time in years, I was a man with something to lose.

"You're right," I admitted. "That should have been obvious."

Asia let Phil go, and she jerked away. "You've been using me?" she screeched at Asia.

"Catch up, darling," I admonished. "It's basic blackmail."

"Was this your plan the whole time?" Phil demanded.

"If you mean to imply that I orchestrated this whole 'thunderbird' revolution as bait to lure Nic back to Earth…" Asia flicked her fingers, as if the resistance movement was no more inconvenient than a crumb to be brushed off the table. "Then no. I had nothing to do with your adorable little videos trending. I just know an opportunity when I see one."

Phil slid behind me, even though she probably would have been safer literally anywhere else. "You're disgusting."

"Now you know why we broke up." I took a rallying breath. "Any other clarifying questions? Because we should probably speed this up. That party isn't going to last forever, and eventually other people are going to want to use this bridge for something other than a standoff."

"I'm ready to go if you are. Shall we?" Asia nodded at the west bank, where her guards waited.

I took a step towards her. Phil grabbed my arm. "Nic, you can't!"

"Honey, were you not listening to her evil monologue?" I grabbed Phil's wrist and pried her hand off my jacket. "If I don't do as she says, she'll kill you or something equally pedantic."

Asia cackled. "I usually warm up with some light torture. Give me some credit."

"Well, today's your lucky day, because I don't feel like listening to Andi scream. It's a horribly irritating sound, and I already have a headache." I strode up to Asia, folded one hand behind my back, and bowed. "Shall we go get a coffee? I'll buy."

She jerked back. "Beg pardon?"

"I said, let's go get coffee. Hang on, let me make sure I brought my phone so I can pay." I patted my pockets. As I did so, I subtly pressed the button on the pistol I had holstered under my jacket.

I grunted to cover the whir of it powering on. "Okay, good to go. You, me, date." I looked back up at Asia and held out my hand.

She eyed it like a dead fish.

"That's what you want, isn't it? Us, together. If I go with you, there's no reason Andi can't go home, right? Or did I miss something?"

"There are a couple of other things I want, but…" Asia grasped my hand and pulled me towards her. "This is a good place to start, if you're offering."

Phil finally found her voice. "Nic, don't—"

"Shh," I hissed over my shoulder, "the adults are talking."

I leaned into Asia, pushing her against the railing. Her guards shifted, but Asia put her hand up. "I can handle this one," she crooned, her dark eyes mocking me.

I put my lips close to hers, then stopped. I watched out of my peripheral until I saw one of the guards power off his weapon and slide it into his holster.

"Min," I whispered quietly enough that only she could hear. "There's something I should tell you."

"Yes?" she begged.

I took a deep breath. "I'm *not* sorry it had to be this way."

And then I grasped her shoulders and shoved her over the railing.

She tumbled into the water with a shriek and a very satisfying splash. The guards on the bank reacted immediately, diving into the lake after her.

The two on the bridge were slower on the draw. "Aren't you going to rescue your boss?" I taunted.

They fumbled with their weapons.

"No? Then you're fired." I whipped my warmed-up pistol out of my jacket and shot them both.

Phil screamed. So much for avoiding that ear-splitting sound.

"Run!" I shouted unnecessarily. She kicked off her shoes and raced after me, abandoning her heels in the middle of the bridge like Cinderella.

Asia got her head above water long enough to shout something wholly inappropriate after us.

It was a stupidly long bridge, and I cursed every one of its ostentatious arches as we passed. At this rate, they'd have Asia fished out of the water before we got to the other side.

A few guards were posted on the east bank, checking invitations like some imperial bouncers. They rushed to meet us at the foot of the bridge, no doubt drawn by the distant sound of Asia's enraged yelling.

"There's been a fight!" I exclaimed before they could ask. "Some lady fell in the water—you have to help her!"

The promise of a damsel in distress did the trick. The guards raced onto the bridge, shouting orders at each other. Attempting to look casual, I hooked my arm with Phil's and hurried her across the courtyard to the street, where a throng of enterprising cab drivers waited to feast on drunk party guests.

One hapless lad ran ahead of the others and got to me first. "Do you need a ride, sir?" he begged in broken English.

"More than you know." I gestured for him to lead the way.

He darted to his car on the curb and opened the door. I waited until he had helped Phil into the back seat, then pulled my gun on him.

"Keys," I demanded.

The driver barked his disagreement in Mandarin, so I turned and shot the person standing closest to us to reinforce my point.

"Nic!" Phil screamed, and several other passersby joined her.

The driver wisely decided the vehicle wasn't worth his life. He threw his keyring at me, shouting about how he was going to report this.

"Asia's way ahead of you," I droned, and shot him to end the conversation.

The crowd devolved into a panic as everyone graciously got out of my way. I ran to the driver's door and jumped in. I jammed the key in the ignition and swiped commands onto the car's overly complicated control panel. Thankfully, it was a cheap vehicle and didn't have any inconvenient safety features like face recognition, so it started on the first turn. I slammed on the gas, clipping the rear of the car ahead of me as I jerked away from the curb.

Phil squealed in tune to the crunching metal. "Nic, what are you doing?"

"Don't worry, it was set on stun." I navigated out of the parking lot, slowing down just long enough to make an inconspicuous turn into traffic. I waited until we were a few blocks away before checking the mirrors; there were no flashing lights in my peripheral.

I sped up as much as I could without drawing attention to ourselves. "Turn off your phone," I barked at Phil.

"J-Jayde has my phone," she returned, voice warbly from adrenaline.

I shot her an incredulous glance in the rearview mirror. She shrugged. "This dress doesn't have pockets."

"Well, I guess that will give them a beacon to find his body." We'd left Jayde back at the palace, lying unconscious on the third-floor balcony of the Tower of Incense. He was Phil's former ally in the underground—strong emphasis on *former*. He had blackmailed Phil into going to this cursed party as part of an absurd assassination plot. I could only hope the government would find him and make him regret his life choices.

Keeping one eye on the crowded road, I fished my phone out of my pocket and turned it off. "Asia will have our files flagged as soon as she gets dried off. If we stay offline, it will buy us some time."

I glared at the darkened screen of my device as my own words sank into me. I'd never been friends with the law, but I'd always had my clean identity—and my secluded science station on Mars—to fall back on. At any point, I could have shut up, minded my own business, and lived happily ever after in my castle in the stars.

Not anymore. With a few keystrokes, Asia would turn me and Andromeda Nolan—Philadelphia's legal identity—into the United's most wanted criminals. We wouldn't be able to even check our email without alerting the authorities, much less buy a transit ticket off the planet.

"So much for going back to Mars," I grunted, hurling my phone onto the passenger seat.

Phil said nothing. As much as silence was my preferred mode of conversation, I was smart enough to know that no reaction to circumstances as dire as ours was a bad sign. I looked at her in the rearview mirror and saw all the telltale signs of a panic attack. Her whole body was rigid as she gripped the door handle. She stared out the window with glassy eyes, her shoulders heaving with shallow breaths.

"You need to breathe slowly," I commanded. "Try to lower your heart rate by at least fifty beats per minute."

She glared at me. "Is that your way of telling me to calm down?"

I shrugged. "I figured the specific directions were more helpful."

She grimaced. With great effort, she pried her hand off the door handle and clenched it in her lap. "I don't… know if I can calm down," she admitted.

"Keep practicing," I deadpanned. "You're going to need the calories."

She frowned.

I turned my attention back to the road. "We're going to be running for a very long time."

2: PHILADELPHIA

So much for going back to Mars.

I struggled to obey Nic's instructions, but the more I tried to breathe slowly, the more I felt my throat cinching shut. I was painfully aware of my pulse as my heart slammed into my ribs. My head was buzzing, and the only thing I could hear were the echoes of a hundred accusations.

This was all my fault, again. I'd known for a while that I could never go back to a quiet life on Mars; I'd made that choice when I accepted the title of "Blue Fire." I thought I could lead a revolution—I thought *God* wanted me to lead a revolution.

But I was an idiot. I made a mistake by going to Beijing, and now everything was ruined. My file was marked, the revolution was in shambles, and Jayde had tried to kill me.

Nic had saved me from getting thrown off a balcony, but now he was stuck on Earth with me. I had made us both criminals, and if the United investigated Nic's file, the base on Mars would be the next to fall. What would happen to my brother Ephesus and Nic's sister, Cea? Ephesus had just gotten back to Mars, and he was an accomplice in as many crimes as I was. The government wouldn't hesitate to arrest him—or worse—when they found out where he was hiding. And what of the base's other residents, like the Sardises? They had been nothing but kind to me, and now I was putting them all in danger.

All because I didn't listen to Nic when he told me to come home.

You are not a hero, Andromeda.

"We need a place to go," Nic interrupted my inner monologue. "At least to get some supplies and a change of clothes. You won't last twenty-four hours on the street in that dress."

I looked down at the crumpled layers of silk around my waist. He was right, and he would fare only marginally better in his white suit jacket and slick pants.

Unfortunately, I'd only been in Beijing for four days and didn't know anything about the city. We couldn't go back to my house. The Nolans, my adopted family, had a gorgeous estate with everything we could possibly need, but Asia would have it locked down within the hour. There was only one other person in this entire country that I knew by name, and there was no guarantee she'd be at her studio.

"Narissa," I offered. "My stylist."

Nic arched an eyebrow. "Do you trust her? She worked for Thames."

"I do," I said, and then tried to quantify why. "She knew what I was planning on doing."

I rubbed my right palm and felt the tiny computer chip that was buried just beneath my skin. Even though I couldn't see it, I knew there was a network of wires woven through my fingers that turned my palm into a weapon. If I had shaken the Secretary General's hand back at the party, the computer in my skin would have reacted to his DNA and sent him into cardiac arrest with an electromagnetic shock. It would have been the perfect assassination.

And I almost went through with it.

I resisted the urge to crush the chip. The last thing I needed was for the wiring to short circuit and electrocute me.

"Narissa knew what was going on," I said, forcing my attention back to the present. "She didn't have all the details, but she knew Jayde and I were planning something and wanted to help. She made the dress." I fingered the jagged silver embroidery that decorated my skirt like lightning, turning me into a living thunderbird.

"I don't see what a costume change has to do with it," Nic commented, "but hopefully she still likes you more than the United."

I swallowed. Narissa's motivations were a mystery to me, but she'd been willing to die to help me become Blue Fire. Hopefully, that generosity would extend a little further—if she was even home.

I gave Nic the name of Narissa's studio, and he keyed it into the cab's navigation system. Thankfully, it was only fifteen minutes away.

"We're going to have to ditch the car a few blocks away and walk in," Nic said as he turned into an abandoned alley. The vehicle pitched as we rolled over water-filled potholes. "As soon as the driver wakes up and turns in a report, they'll start tracking the cab."

Nic parked behind an apartment building with a cluster of other sketchy cars. I opened the cab door and instantly remembered I was barefoot. I gingerly stepped onto the cold concrete, swallowing a wince. Now that the adrenaline was wearing off, my bloody heels were screaming in agony.

Nic had the grace to slow down and wait for me as I picked my way around trash and sharp pieces of gravel. We skirted the backs of buildings until we came to Narissa's shop. The alley lights were not on; I prayed that meant we couldn't be easily seen on any security cameras.

"What's your plan if she's not home?" Nic asked as we climbed the steps to the rear door.

"Pray and ask God for a brilliant idea," I replied.

He snorted. I didn't bother to tell him that was my actual plan.

Thankfully, Plan B wasn't necessary. I rapped on the door with my knuckles, and it opened instantly.

Narissa stood there. She took in my scuffed heels and muddy hem with her sharp eyes. "I thought you said you weren't going to be running."

"There was a change of plans," I confessed.

"I know, I saw the news." She held the door open and waved us inside.

Mercifully, her shop was deserted. The shades were drawn, and all the lights were dark. The waterfall that decorated the rear wall was off, a few drips of water still glinting on the glass. "I'm surprised you're still at work," I commented.

She locked the door behind us. "I wasn't. But when I saw that your appearance at the party was surprisingly uneventful, I figured something had gone wrong, and you might need me."

I took in her appearance. This was the most casual I'd ever seen her; she had no makeup on, and she wore loose sweats that seemed completely out of character. "Thank you for coming back," I said, and directed the same at Jesus.

She turned to Nic and offered her hand. "I assume you're the wild card of the night. Q, is it? Pleased to finally make your acquaintance."

After a flicker of hesitation, he accepted the handshake. "Just Nic, please."

She snorted. "You'd better get used to the nickname, Q. Sounds like you two will be going back to codenames for a while. This way." She flicked her fingers and led us towards the elevator.

We descended two floors beneath the building to Narissa's private studio. I let her get off the elevator first, then grabbed Nic's sleeve to hold him back. "Be careful what you say around her," I hissed.

"I thought you said you trusted her!" he snapped, shrugging me off.

"I do, but she's got eye implants. The algorithm hears everything." I remembered when Narissa had taken out her contacts and shown her robotic eyes to me. The implants had cured her of blindness, and she could take measurements, manipulate dress patterns, and match the perfect foundation shade, all just by thinking about it. But in exchange, the government saw everything she saw and heard everything she heard—the perfect form of control.

Nic muttered something foul. "Well, hopefully the government hasn't updated its search parameters yet," he grunted and stepped off the elevator.

Narissa clapped her hands. The lights in the studio flickered on, revealing the futuristic dress fabricator that dominated the floor. Its robotic needles were frozen in mid-air, the unfinished form of a bodice abandoned on the cutting board.

I walked up and looked inside the glass at the sleek black garment. The material was stiff but had an otherworldly sheen to it, like it was a cross between leather and silk. Complex embroidery flared from the neckline; the layered stitching made the sleeve look like it was made of feathers.

"The design's not finished. I need to start over." Narissa grasped my shoulders and steered me away. "There are men's clothes in the closet over there—take what you need. I can fit them if necessary," she said to Nic. "You, on the other hand, should be glad you left your change of clothes here this morning. I don't carry many practical women's outfits." She grabbed a pile of clothes off a drafting table and pushed me into a fitting room, shutting the door behind us.

I obediently turned around and let her unzip my dress. "Thank you for helping us."

"I don't want to know the details. Just tell me one thing." She paused, her eyes finding mine in the mirror. "Did something go wrong, or did you change your mind?"

I swallowed. "I changed my mind." *Too little too late.*

She grunted and helped me step out of the dress. "Well, at least you made a good impression on Mong."

She wasn't wrong. Instead of shaking the General's hand, I'd bowed. He'd been pleased with my show of humility and had taken a shining to me, although I think that had more to do with the Holy Spirit than any charisma of mine. I'd even invited him over for dinner—and he'd accepted.

Not that the social capital would do me any good after Asia flagged my file.

"What are you going to do with the dress?" I asked.

Narissa held the cloud of gray-blue silk up to the light and examined a seam. "I'll wash and mend it. You're going to need it again."

It was said with finality, so I didn't argue, even though I highly doubted I'd have an occasion to dress up for a ball again. My days as an elite Nolan were over.

I grabbed the stack of clothes off the stool. It was the outfit I'd changed out of this morning, along with my little black backpack. My heart lurched at the sight of it. There was nothing of monetary value in there, but at least I would have the leather-bound Bible my boyfriend Stanyard had given me.

I shivered as I quickly changed into my ripped jeans, nondescript t-shirt, and black leather jacket. What would Stanyard say when he found out what happened? Jayde had threatened to kill him if I didn't go to Beijing and complete the assassination, which we'd codenamed "Operation Thunderbird." Nic said he'd taken care of it and gotten Stanyard to safety. I believed him, but that didn't change the fact that I'd lied to my best friend.

The last time I'd seen Stanyard, he'd convinced me not to go along with the operation. He'd also told me he loved me—and instead of saying "I love you, too" like a normal person, I'd kissed him.

Then, not six hours later, I'd dropped off the grid and boarded a flight to Beijing, apparently going back on everything I'd just said. What must he think of me? I knew Stanyard well enough to trust that he'd forgive me in time. But what would he say when he found out I'd almost started a war and sacrificed millions of people just to save him?

My dad had done the same thing when he created Red Rain, Nic's chemical superweapon. He'd given the government the keys to the apocalypse in exchange for my life. When I'd learned the truth, I'd felt enraged, betrayed, and abandoned.

I had no doubts Stanyard would feel the same.

I shrugged the backpack on, feeling the weight settle between my shoulders along with the heaviness in my heart. *Jesus, I'm so sorry. I should have trusted You.*

Narissa opened the fitting room door. I quickly pulled on my boots and walked back out into the studio. Nic, in typical male fashion, had clearly gotten dressed in thirty seconds and spent the rest of the time pacing the room. He now wore jeans, a plain button-up, and a light windbreaker. I missed his perpetual lab coat already, although I would never have admitted that to him.

"I need to get online before they flag my file," he declared as soon as we came out of the fitting room.

Narissa gestured at a laptop that was precariously balanced on a stack of fabric bolts. Nic took it, sat down cross-legged on the floor, and started typing rapidly.

"Me too. I need to send a message to Stanyard. Is it safe to text him?" I looked to Nic for permission. The last thing I wanted to do was get someone killed because I spoke too soon.

"You can text whoever you want before they flag your file," he said, clearly not listening to me. He pulled his phone out of his pocket, powered it on, and tossed it at me.

I caught it gracelessly. I opened the encrypted messaging app and saw that Stanyard—or "Aurelius," as he went by online—was a pinned contact. He was not online.

I started a new chat and hesitated with my thumbs over the screen. How could I cram a heartfelt apology and an explanation of a near-death experience into one message?

"Just tell him you're going offline so he doesn't worry," Nic offered, apparently noticing the fact that my fingers weren't moving.

I chewed my lip and tried to follow his advice.

HEY. IT'S BLUE FIRE. I'M SAFE, Q'S WITH ME. WE HAVE TO GO OFFLINE FOR A WHILE. I WILL CALL WHEN I CAN. I LOVE YOU.

I hit send, then added:

I'M SO SORRY

3: NIC

I watched out of the corner of my eye as Phil stood there, staring dumbly at the phone in her hand. No doubt she was hoping Pizza Boy would come online and call her. When he didn't, she handed the device back to me with a sigh.

I took it and leaned it against the laptop's screen to pair the devices. "You need to wash your makeup off. Your eyeliner is running."

She glared at me, but there was nothing to be offended about. It was a factual statement.

"There's makeup wipes in the bathroom. Here, let me take your extension out." Narissa held Phil still with one hand and used the other to remove a clip of fake curls from her hair. Phil's bleached locks fell to her shoulders, tired and stringy—not unlike the girl they were attached to.

Narissa herded her into the bathroom and shut the door after her. I turned my attention back to the laptop. I'd remotely logged into my private server on Mars. I tabbed through the database and started downloading as many files as I could to my phone. Contacts, music, blackmail—anything I might need while we were on the move for the next several weeks.

Narissa approached me. "Where are you going to go?"

"I know some safe houses," I lied. The truth was that both of my safe havens—the base on Mars and my parents' house—would become death traps once Asia staked them out. But anywhere would be preferable to Beijing, and if I could get out of the city and call Ephesus on a secured line, we could figure something out.

Probably.

Narissa wisely didn't ask for more details. She grabbed a backpack off the floor and dumped the contents onto a cutting table. "I don't have much by way of survival supplies here, but what I have you're welcome to." She walked over to her mini fridge and started stuffing water bottles and snacks into the bag.

"Thank you," I said with as much sincerity as I knew how to convey. My phone screeched at me, complaining about its storage being full. I cancelled the remaining downloads with a grunt. "I'd recommend copying what you need off this laptop and doing a factory reset. Then they won't be able to catch you with any incriminating files. Some of the info I downloaded isn't exactly legal."

"Keep the laptop." She yanked a bolt of wool out of the middle of a stack of fabric, causing the rest of the bolts to tumble onto the floor. "Just reregister it under your name—please."

I nodded and navigated to the settings. "What's your plan when Asia shows up? They'll know I accessed your Wi-Fi."

"Don't worry about me." She threw the wool on the cutting board and measured out a generous portion. "I've got as much dirt on Asia as she has on me. We're in this together. Besides, she knows you trust me. She's better off leaving me alone and hoping you'll come back, looking for help." She slid her scissors down the groove in the cutting board with deadly swiftness. "So don't come back."

"Wasn't planning on it." I hesitated on the laptop's registration page, debating. Then, with a couple of clicks, I changed the ownership to Andromeda.

Narissa dropped the backpack on the floor next to me. "I wasn't worried about you."

Just then, Phil came out of the bathroom. With her makeup gone and her hair down, she'd transformed from a manicured princess back into a sullen teenager. Her eyes were swollen and bloodshot, and I could tell the night was catching up to her. We'd be lucky if we made it three blocks before she collapsed, which meant we needed to get moving.

I powered off my devices and stuffed them in the backpack. "Any recommendations for someone who can get us out of the country?" I asked Narissa.

She rolled up the makeshift blanket and helped me strap it to the backpack. "You don't need to get out of the country. You need to get off the grid."

I didn't disagree, but that was a tall order in the world's most heavily surveilled and technologically advanced country. "Any recommendations?" I countered.

I wasn't expecting an answer, but to my surprise, Narissa had one. "Jael."

I looked up at her. "Who?"

Narissa put her palms forward. "I haven't met her, but I've heard of her. They say she's got connections in the tech world and can get anyone off the grid."

"That sounds too good to be true," I intoned.

Narissa shrugged. "She once hid an entire church congregation and broke the pastor out of jail hours before his execution—all without leaving a trace. They say she hacked into the police chief's cell phone and even remotely edited the security footage."

That sounded like a straight-up fairytale, but the notion of Christians getting romantically rescued from death was enough to convince Phil that this mystical woman was our savior. "Where can we find her?" she said, eyes wide with gullible wonder.

"Even if I knew where she was, I wouldn't tell you." Narissa tapped her temple, reminding us all of her implants. "But you don't just *find* Jael. You have to find someone who knows her, and they'll take you to her."

I stood up and shouldered the backpack. "And where, exactly, do these followers of Jael like to congregate?"

Narissa must not have liked my tone of voice, because she gave me a frown that could have curdled butter. "Your best bet is to find someone who attends *jiating jiaohui.*"

"What?" Phil asked.

"House church," I answered, and then regretted it when Narissa whipped her head to stare at me. She arched an eyebrow, the thin line of plucked hairs curling like a cat's tail.

In her defense, I probably shouldn't have known what that phrase meant. But being a highly educated individual—and hanging out with elites like Asia—had taught me some functional Mandarin, and I was more versed in religious terminology than I cared to admit. But the fact that I had personal experience with the Chinese Christian community was not information Phil needed to have right now, so I kept the conversation moving.

"That will be easier said than done," I muttered. "It's an underground church for a reason."

Associating with anything but the Chinese state religion had been risky fifty years ago. Now even the state religion was illegal, and claiming to be Protestant was a swift way to meet Jesus.

None of this deterred Phil. "Any idea where to look? Surely you know someone."

Narissa opened her mouth, but the trill of an alarm spared her the trouble. "That would be Asia." She strode over to a computer terminal and brought up a security feed. Sure enough, Asia and half a dozen guards stood outside, pounding on the front door.

I cursed. I knew our luck was too good to last.

"She was quick." Narissa squinted at the screen. "Why is her hair wet? She never goes out without styling her hair."

"Consolation prize," I grunted. "How do we get out of here?"

Narissa ran to the corner of the room and pressed on one of the flatscreens that lined the wall. It popped away from the plaster and swung open on hinges, revealing an ominous rusted metal door.

Narissa dragged it open with both hands. The neglected hinges squealed like the jump scare in a cheap movie. The unlit stairwell beyond certainly looked like a place you'd get murdered.

"This goes to the storage on the second floor. Take the balcony all the way to the north end of the building. There are stairs that lead back to the street, and the subway entrance is right around the corner. I'll stall them as long as I can," Narissa explained.

"Perfect," I said, and ran for the stairs.

Phil tightened the straps on her backpack and followed. As she passed, Narissa grabbed her arm and held her back. "Ask for Jael. I promise she's your best bet."

I cleared my throat. It wasn't Phil who needed to be convinced.

Phil searched the woman's face. "Should I tell her you sent me?"

Narissa snorted and shoved her towards the stairs. "You don't need to namedrop me. You're Blue Fire." And then she slammed and latched the door, shutting us in the darkness.

I grabbed the railing and started up the steps, glad Phil couldn't see my expression in the shadows. Identifying herself as Blue Fire was the last thing she should be doing on the streets of Beijing. I'd find us another way out of this country, even if we had to walk to Tibet.

And if I had any say, Phil would never identify herself as Blue Fire again.

The storage room above the shop was uninhabited except for Narissa's fabric hoard. I wove around the heaps of bolts to the back entrance. After checking the peephole, I slowly lifted the deadbolt and cracked open the door.

The alley behind the building was quiet. Narissa's shop lights were still off, making the only source of light the yellowed streetlamp. I crept onto the balcony and gestured for Phil to follow. I slid along the building, careful to stay in the shadows under the awning.

A shout pierced the night. Phil choked on a gasp, slapping her hand over her mouth. I flattened myself against the building and watched. Two guards entered the far end of the alley, muttering to each other in Mandarin.

"What do we do?" Phil hissed.

"Stay quiet for starters," I reprimanded. Looking around, I spotted an abandoned brick. Moving slowly to avoid drawing attention, I shoved the brick over the edge of the balcony. It crashed onto a car below with a symphony of shattering glass.

Hopefully that wasn't Narissa's car.

The guards shouted and ran under the balcony to investigate. Taking advantage of their distraction—and the wailing car alarm—I took off at a run. "Come on!"

We raced to the north end of the building. I grasped the railing and leapt down the short metal stairs, skipping most of the steps. I didn't dare look back as we darted across the alley and around the corner, briefly exposing ourselves to the streetlights and security cameras. If we could get into the subway, we could lose them.

Phil struggled to keep up. "Don't we need a ticket?"

I shoved past a cluster of late-night commuters. "No, communism has its perks."

Phil tried to be more polite and walk around the passersby, almost losing me in the process. "But don't they scan your electronics at the gates?" she panted.

"Sure—if your devices are turned on." I led the way down the steps into the underground station, using my long legs to take two at a time. Phil clattered after me.

I shoved through the turnstile. The dead ticket scanners glared up at me wearily, their obsolete screens dark. I hurried down the long queue to the platform. The subway was closing within the hour, and the crowd on the tile was thinning. But it was still enough of a throng to get lost in.

Phil caught up to me just as the next train screeched into the station. Not trusting her to make it through the crowd, I grabbed her shoulders and pushed her onto the car ahead of me. I shoved past the other passengers and navigated to vacant seats in the far corner.

Shrugging my backpack off, I sat down. I gratefully closed my eyes and leaned my head against the window, hoping to summon a moment of silence.

Phil was oblivious to my social cues. She slid uncomfortably close to me as the train lurched away from the station. "Doesn't it trip the algorithm if you board without a device?" she hissed. She tried to lower her voice, but she only succeeded in making the pitch more irritating.

I opened my eyes for the sole purpose of rolling them dramatically. "This isn't like Boston. Fifteen million people ride the subway in Beijing every day. Even if they did try to stop you at the gate, it would be incredibly hard to determine who set off the alarm, and you could easily disappear in the crowd."

Overpopulation was the enemy of control, and Beijing's beleaguered public transportation system couldn't keep up. China didn't have the luxury of getting bogged down in paperwork and scanners like America did. That meant the subway was truly free to ride.

Of course, that grace would run out as soon as we needed to do something that involved actual money. Like buy food.

Phil accepted that explanation and scooted away, mercifully restoring some personal space. "At least we won't have any trouble getting around."

Getting around the city wasn't a problem. It was crossing the border—or worse, trying to board a plane or transit—that would take a miracle.

Phil fidgeted with her backpack straps. "Where are we going?"

I closed my eyes again and folded my arms across my chest. "Far away from here."

And that's exactly what we did. We rode the train to the end of the line, then switched to a different one and repeated the process. By the time the rails shut down, we were on the other side of the province.

We emerged into the night and walked for another half-mile. The neighborhood we found ourselves in was on the bleeding edge of modernism. The pavement was crumbling, and the storefronts were dimly lit, their cold neon signs the victims of power shortages. Up ahead, a shantytown had been razed to make room for a new trio of apartment complexes. The remains of the slum were still piled in a heap on the edge of the lot like a headstone.

Phil wisely stayed close to me as we approached the chain-link fence that blocked off the construction site. The site was not active; I could tell by the gaps in the fence and the trash blowing around the yard. Failed construction projects were a common sight in China, especially after over a hundred years of communism, and tonight that would be our salvation. An abandoned site meant no power to the security cameras.

We found a place where the fence had been cut. I held the chain link aside so Phil could slip through, then ducked in after her. I listened for signs of trouble as we hurried across the shadowy lot, but the night was quiet except for the omnipresent hum of the surrounding city.

The building was nothing more than a concrete skeleton, with no glass in the windows. A glance at the heaps of soiled blankets in the empty lobby suggested we were not the only vagrants using the shelter, but no one else was in sight. We climbed the steps to the fifth floor and claimed the first empty room. It was hardly a secure position, but at least if anyone gave us trouble, we could make a quick exit.

The room was coated in dust and littered with a few pieces of trash, but nothing obscene. I grabbed an abandoned tarp off a stack of lumber. Phil helped me shake it out and lay it in the corner, where it was sheltered from the wind.

I unclipped the wool from the backpack and handed it to her. "Get as much sleep as you can. I need you ready to run tomorrow. I'll keep watch."

She didn't argue, but her haunted eyes searched me, her pale face ghostly in the darkness. "What about you?"

I shrugged and sat down next to the doorframe. "I'm a scientist. I'm an expert at running on no sleep."

She lay down on the tarp and wrapped herself in the blanket. I stretched my long legs out, folded my arms behind my head, and propped myself on the lumpy backpack. I closed my eyes, knowing I was in no danger of falling asleep in these conditions.

Phil let me enjoy about five minutes of silence before she shattered it. "Nic?"

I didn't bother to open my eyes. "What?"

There was a pause, her breathing audible. When she spoke again, her voice was weak and labored. "I'm sorry."

I looked up and glared at the ceiling. What was I supposed to say to that? *"It's not your fault," "I forgive you," "We'll figure it out"*? None of those statements were true, and I at least had the decency not to lie to her.

I settled into the backpack. "Just get some sleep."

4: PHILADELPHIA

"Get up, we have to move!"

I started awake, although calling what I had been doing "sleeping" was perhaps being overly generous. I'd lain awake for what must have been hours, trying and failing to find the courage to talk to Nic. There was so much I wanted—needed—to say, but I knew he wasn't in the mood to hear it. So I'd put my back to him and pretended to sleep while the unspoken words cycled over and over in my head, echoing on top of one another like pressure building in a closed pot. Eventually, I'd passed out, but my emotions just turned themselves into nightmares, most of which were unembellished memories.

So when Nic shook my shoulder and yelled in my ear, I jerked into reality with a shriek and a flood of adrenaline. I nearly smacked him in the face before I realized it was him.

He saw it coming and ducked. "We need to move, now!"

"Why?" I gasped, waiting for my breathing, heart rate, vision, or literally *any* part of my body to function within normal parameters.

He yanked the blanket away from me and wadded it into a ball. "I need to get online immediately, or we're in huge trouble."

I had several follow-up questions—like how we could possibly be in any more trouble than we already were—but I knew I'd better not argue. I stumbled up and nearly fell back down again. Sleeping on concrete was making me feel like a doll whose joints had been bent out of shape by a cruel child.

Nic didn't wait for me to get it together. He slung our backpacks over his shoulder and ran for the stairs, expecting me to keep up. I tripped over debris as I crashed down the stairwell after him. When we got to the lobby, I saw movement and smelled what could have been food cooking, but Nic didn't pause to say hello. I nearly stepped on some poor old lady sleeping in a heap of plastic bags as I struggled to catch up to him.

The sky was bathed in the pale yellow of a smog-diffused sunrise. The hum of the city was louder now, like an engine without a muffler. Nic paused for only a breath to scan the yard, then darted to the hole in the fence. He slid through first, backpacks and all, and held the wire aside for me. I crawled through much less nimbly. He took off running again before I was even on my feet.

"Nic, wait!" I yelled. I willed my sluggish body to move and ran after him.

"We need to get to a shop with Wi-Fi!" he shouted back, not slowing down at all.

He whipped around the corner. I followed—and ran straight into the path of a bicycle.

The rider yelped in Mandarin and swerved. I stumbled back into the building behind me, narrowly avoiding getting my toes run over. I mumbled an apology, although I doubted the man understood me. He gave me a suspicious glare, then adjusted the sacks he had precariously balanced on his handlebars and kept moving.

Catching my breath, I looked around—and realized Nic was nowhere in sight.

Oh Jesus, help! I prayed as the panic returned like a bout of nausea. Where was he? It was early morning, but the street was already crowded. A line of several dozen commuters waiting for the bus clogged the sidewalk. Vendors congested the road with their carts, and bicyclists narrowly swerved through the mess. All around there were horns honking and signs flashing and people shouting in a language I couldn't understand—and not one of them was tall with blond hair.

"Nic!" I screeched, but it was useless. I could barely hear myself over the din.

I pressed myself against the wall as a cluster of schoolkids shoved past me. I couldn't get lost. I wouldn't last a night on my own; I didn't even have a device on me. *Where would he go? Why would he—*

The Holy Spirit breathed on me with a whisper of wisdom, causing me to stop. Nic would do exactly what he said he'd do: find a shop with public Wi-Fi. He'd look for the closest one, preferably a business where it wouldn't seem suspicious if he sat down and pulled out his laptop.

Like a café.

Thanking the Holy Spirit, I took a brave step off the curb and looked around. I couldn't read any of the signs, but it was easy to tell which stores sold food. The first two on the street were little more than kiosks with an order counter, their faded backlit menu signs nearly identical to restaurants back home. I ventured further down the road, straining to see the shops through the throng of people. *There*—I spotted a short metal fence and a cluster of rickety plastic chairs. An eatery of some kind.

I looked both ways and darted across the street. Sure enough, Nic sat at a table in an inconspicuous corner of the patio, his laptop open in front of him.

"Nic!" I shoved a vacant chair out of my way and ran to his side. I wasn't sure whether to hug him or hit him.

He barely looked up, his fingers not missing a beat as they continued to type. "Don't yell my name in public places."

"Then don't leave me behind in a public place," I snapped. The urge to hit was winning. "I almost got lost."

"*You* may have gotten lost, but I was in no danger of losing *you*." He squinted at the screen, scrolling with his finger. "You were five yards away. I was watching."

He said it like a parent supervising a toddler on the playground, and I realized that's what the whole situation must feel like to him. Except this "playground" was Beijing, and we were both wanted criminals.

"Yeah, but *I* didn't know you were watching," I argued. "I was scared."

He wasn't stirred by my emotional transparency. "You need to learn not to panic," he scolded, as if it were as simple as mastering basic multiplication. "Just slow down and think a little."

I *had* done that, not that he'd appreciate my maturity. "Well, maybe I wouldn't panic if you didn't leave me behind in Beijing!" I sighed. It was no use; he wasn't even looking at me. I pointed at the laptop. "What was so urgent, anyway?"

"Believe it or not, I have to turn in a tax form."

I didn't believe that for a second. "I thought you hated paperwork."

He hit enter. "My point exactly."

None of this made any sense. Since when were taxes urgent? What government form could possibly be so important that he'd risk going online? Surely our files were marked by now.

"Never mind," I said aloud, in case he was thinking about being forthcoming with more information. "If you're going to make a mark online, I might as well buy some food."

"Excellent idea." He pulled his phone out of his pocket and tossed it at me. "Go to the shop next door. Get some packaged food, fruit—anything that will travel well."

"Sure." I slung my little black backpack over my shoulder—just in case—and unzipped the bag Narissa had given us. I spied an empty shopping sack made of silk remnants and a metal canteen and grabbed both.

"Don't turn the phone on until you're ready to pay," Nic continued his safety lecture, "and then come straight back here." His eyes left his screen for a minute. "I promise I'm watching."

I didn't grace that with a response. I turned and navigated around the metal fence to the shop next door. It was a little corner store, its front display crammed to the overflowing with ramen. I stepped through the open door and blinked. The place was surreally bright, washed out by the white walls and the blinding lights from the row of refrigerator cases. I wandered up the aisles, scanning the colorful packages decorated with cute cartoons. I couldn't read any Mandarin, but thankfully most of the labels had pictures—some were even written in English. I filled my bag with a variety of ready-to-eat food and hoped Nic wouldn't criticize my shopping skills.

I reached the back of the store and saw the drink station. There was a soda fountain and a futuristic smoothie maker—and a carafe of fresh coffee. I grinned, twisted the cap off my canteen, and filled it to the brim.

The clerk, a gentle-looking old man, put his tablet down when I approached. I offered him a smile and unloaded my purchases on the counter. I hoped he wouldn't think me rude for not talking.

I put my canteen on the counter. He nodded at it. "Coffee?" he asked.

"Yes, please," I said, taking advantage of the moment to speak in English.

He winked and hit a key on his terminal. The payment kiosk on the edge of the counter flickered to life, a total displayed on the screen.

I powered on Nic's phone. The payment app—the universal way to legally transfer money in the United—was right on the home page. I held my phone over the kiosk and hesitated. As soon as I made this purchase, Asia, if she was watching Nic's file, would know exactly where we were. But we needed food, so there was no way around it.

I tapped the phone to the kiosk and braced myself, subconsciously expecting it to cough up an error. It didn't. The screen turned green, and a happy smiling face appeared, praising me for my responsible citizenship.

The clerk started to hand my purchases back to me—then stopped. He squinted at his terminal. "Is not your phone."

I couldn't tell whether he meant it as a question or a statement, but I didn't know how to answer him. How did he know it wasn't my phone? Did it pull up Nic's ID on his screen? Some stores in America could see your ID after you paid. If that was the case, there was no way I'd pass for mustached Dr. Nic Von Nieuwenhuyse, so I decided to opt for a half-truth.

"No, it's my… dad's," I managed, and grimaced. I held the phone below the counter and powered it off.

The clerk squinted at me, then relented. He shoved the rest of my packages across the counter towards me. I shoveled them into my bag, thanked him, and ran out the door, almost forgetting my canteen.

Nic was still typing aggressively on his laptop. "Yay, you survived," he deadpanned.

I ignored the shot. "Are you ready to go?" I asked, standing uncomfortably close to his chair. Maybe if I hovered in his bubble, he'd catch my sense of urgency.

He elbowed me away. "Almost. I forgot how many forms were involved in this. It's been a long time since I married someone."

I dropped the canteen. It hit the brick with a loud *thunk* and rolled under the table. "You got *married?*"

"Sorry, poor choice of words." He kicked the canteen back towards me. "I meant I *officiated* a wedding."

That was no less shocking. Nic was the least romantic person in the galaxy, and when would he have had time to officiate a wedding? Who in the world that we knew was getting married right now? "Who—"

I didn't get to finish the question. Just then, the clerk from the corner store approached us—followed by several younger, bigger, meaner-looking men.

The clerk gave me a reproachful frown, like I'd stolen a candy bar. "This is your dad?" He nodded at Nic.

Nic slammed the laptop shut and glared at me. "What did you tell him?"

Now did not seem like the time to explain. I grabbed the canteen off the ground and backed away. "Sorry, sirs, we were just going."

Nic took the cue and started to stand up. One of the younger men clamped a hand on his shoulder and pushed him back down.

The clerk folded his arms and barked something in Mandarin. I was more than a little surprised when Nic spat back in the same language.

"What did he say?" I asked.

Nic rolled his eyes, as if this was a perfectly normal exchange to have with strangers. "They're performing a citizen's arrest on me."

5: NIC

Phil tried and failed to land a reaction to that.

"And what did you say?" she finally managed.

"Over my dead body."

I swung my long legs and knocked the clerk flat on his back. His old bones cracked on the brick, drawing gasps from the passersby, but there was no time to waste on sympathy. The young grunts he had with him tried to hold me down, but I whipped my holstered gun from underneath my jacket.

The weapon wasn't on, but the boys wisely didn't take the time to find out. They scattered, cursing. I returned the sentiment as I stood up and kicked my chair at them. At least that would give them something to trip over.

Phil, to her credit, turned and ran without being told. I grabbed my laptop and backpack and caught up to her in three strides.

We darted across the street. The noise of the crowd changed pitch as bystanders registered what was happening. A path cleared in front of us thanks to my brandished gun, but there were shouts and screams in our direction. I saw the flash of a cellphone camera and knew we had to get out of sight before the entire internet knew we were here.

"Should we take the subway?" Phil yelled.

"No, it's rush hour—we'll get stuck in the line. This way!" I concealed my gun and pointed towards the next row of shops. We jumped up on the sidewalk, narrowly missing a bus as it screeched to a stop. I shoved my way through the line of commuters, eliciting complaints. Phil stumbled along in my wake.

I darted through the nearest gap in the buildings to the alleyway behind. It was almost as busy as the street itself, with neighbors gossiping in back doorways and several rear-facing shop entrances. I kept one eye on the uneven road as I led us around tent signs and abandoned mopeds. Phil clutched her shopping bag to her chest and managed to keep up.

We ran to the end of the row, then slipped between the buildings to the next street over. We repeated this process, zigzagging between blocks, until we were at least a mile from our original location.

I halted when I reached the end of the street. Phil rear-ended me. "What are you doing?" she hissed.

"Acting natural," I returned. I smoothed my hair and strolled onto the main road like I had nowhere to be. Phil imitated me, albeit poorly. I paused at the first shop and pretended to browse the wares, even as my eyes scanned the street. The crowd flowed around us calmly. There were no stares or cameras being aimed in our direction, and I couldn't hear any commotion over the normal din of traffic. So far, this side of town was none the wiser to our disturbance.

We'd gotten lucky. But luck had a nasty habit of refusing to repeat itself.

I shouldered my backpack and continued walking. "Keep up."

She scampered to obey. "Why did they try to arrest you?"

"Besides my criminal good looks? That's an excellent question. What in the world happened in there?" I glared down at her. She had barely been out of my sight for five minutes, and she'd managed to blow our cover while buying potato chips. I knew Phil wasn't very street-smart, but that level of incompetence was stupendous even for her.

"I don't know!" She almost dropped the canteen as she struggled to hold on to her purchases. "Everything went fine. I paid without issue, and he seemed nice. He even spoke English."

"So what, you struck up a conversation about how I'm an amazing parent?" The very word left a bad taste in my mouth. "Did you really tell the guy I was your father?"

She stopped in the middle of the sidewalk. "*That's* what you're worried about?"

I turned to face her. "Obviously, or I wouldn't be asking."

She must be getting hungry, because her tolerance for sarcasm was even lower than usual. "You're the one who called me your 'daughter' in front of Jayde," she snapped.

I didn't need to be reminded. "I was going for dramatic." I'd been trying to strike the fear of God into my enemies—and I'd succeeded quite well, judging by the fact that Jayde had immediately lost control of the situation.

"Well, I was going for believable." She crossed her arms and pouted. "He asked me if the phone was mine, and I figured it must have pulled up your ID or something. So I lied. And legally, that wasn't a lie."

It wasn't, but I didn't need to be reminded of that either. "The technical term is 'legal guardian,' but..." I sighed. In her defense, she'd handled the situation as well as could be expected, but this little revelation confirmed the worst. "Well, at least that explains one thing."

"What?" she asked.

After glancing around to make sure no passersby had suddenly become interested in our conversation, I confessed: "Asia must have flagged my file as a national security risk."

She gaped at me with that stupid bug-eyed expression I hated so much. "Meaning?"

"Meaning that if I check in anywhere, not only will it alert the government, but it will also alert nearby citizens and authorize them to detain me. It's a security code normally used for terrorists and escaped convicts—or people you really want to catch."

To be fair, according to Asia, I fit all three of those categories.

Phil bit her lip so hard it flushed white. "So no more buying food."

"So no more buying food." Or making phone calls. Or crossing any checkpoint that required a thumb scan. I knew we'd have to be sparing with our online activity; Asia was undoubtedly watching our files like a hawk, waiting for us to give her a pinpoint so she could pounce. Now, she wouldn't even have to hurry. If we checked in anywhere, the patriotic citizens of Beijing would detain us until she got there.

And as much as I believed in the power of a good gun, even I knew that "eat, shoot and leave" wasn't a long-term solution.

"I'm sorry," Phil mumbled.

I rubbed my neglected mustache. There were plenty of things about our situation that I could blame Phil for, but this wasn't one of them. I should have checked my file before logging in at a crowded place.

My thought trailed off when I realized the math of the situation wasn't adding up. Why had it taken the crowd so long to notice us? No one had been suspicious until Phil paid using my phone. I'd been online with the laptop for a good ten, maybe fifteen minutes, and no one had said anything. If Andromeda's file was flagged as mine was, then the owner of the shop whose Wi-Fi I borrowed—as well as all the patrons at nearby tables—should have gotten an alert.

Unless...

I ducked into the shadows of the nearest alley, sat down on a back step, and pulled out my laptop.

"What are you doing?" Phil screeched at a delightful pitch. She darted to my side and hovered in my bubble like she always did when she was nervous. "You just said we couldn't go online."

"*I* can't. But you..." The shop's Wi-Fi was just strong enough for me to connect from the alley. I pulled up Andromeda's file and proved myself right: She hadn't been flagged, at least not with any public alerts. Asia was no doubt tracking her, but as far as the rest of the world was concerned, Andromeda was still a citizen in good standing.

I angled the screen so Phil could see. Her jaw went slack like she'd been stabbed with a needle. "That doesn't make any sense."

I agreed, it didn't—and I hated when things didn't make sense. Most of my enemies could be decoded, their behavior reduced to an algorithm dependent on what they had to win or lose. But there was nothing more dangerous than a villain with hidden motivations. People like that could not be controlled, and when I couldn't control the game, I almost always lost.

I'd never been able to control Asia. And to think a younger, more idealistic version of myself had found that attractive.

"Maybe she's hoping I'll keep checking in online so she can use me to find you," Phil suggested.

"You're not that stupid," I countered, and hoped she wouldn't prove me wrong. "It would be much faster to flag your file and let the authorities find you. Then she could just torture you until I got bored of listening to you scream and turned myself in."

"Classy," Phil grunted, and she wasn't wrong. Asia truly had created the perfect trap. Even if I wanted to send Phil home and flee on my own—something I would do in a heartbeat—I couldn't. Asia would find Phil and use her as bait to lure me in.

But if Phil was supposed to be the lump of peanut butter in the mousetrap, why not flag her file? It would be so much more efficient to let Beijing's surveillance state do the heavy lifting. Asia didn't like getting dirt under her fingernails; all this manual labor was not her style.

No, if Asia was going to the trouble of keeping Phil's file clean, that meant she had a very specific reason for doing so. She needed Phil for something.

I froze when I realized my fatal error. Phil wasn't the bait in the mousetrap.

I was.

6: PHILADELPHIA

Nic glared at the screen in silence, long enough that I began to worry. Admittedly, with how frayed my nerves were, it was a short trip.

"Is something wrong?" I prodded.

He slammed the laptop shut and stood up. "Give me the phone," he demanded, ignoring the question.

I fished it out of my pocket. He took it and typed with both thumbs. "I'm registering this phone to you, so we can at least buy food without getting arrested. But Asia is watching your file, so we can only check in if absolutely necessary."

"What if Asia updates my security code?"

"She won't," he declared unequivocally.

He was probably right, but that still raised several insidious questions. Nic might disagree, but I knew Asia was keeping my file clean to try to bribe me into coming home. That had been her M.O. since we'd met. She would ignore any sin and bend any law as long as I agreed to be Andromeda Nolan.

Had she really done all that just to trap Nic? I wasn't sure I believed that. She'd gone to an awful lot of trouble to induct me into high society, even going so far as to decorate my bedroom at the Nolans' Beijing estate. Hiring an interior designer seemed like an excess if all she wanted was her ex-boyfriend back.

But then again, I had no idea what her history was with Nic. Surely, she wanted a lot more than romance from him, but now was definitely not the time to ask Nic about his love life.

The device screeched at him. "I'm taking this offline so we can turn it on without triggering an alert. I want you to keep it on you in case we get separated, but do *not* bring it online unless I give you express permission."

I nodded. "Right."

He held the phone out. I went to take it, but he refused to let go, forcing me to look up at him.

He stared at me for a beat before speaking. "I'm trusting you."

"I know." I met his gaze.

His gray eyes darkened like an impending storm. "Really? Because the last time we had a bonding moment like this, you immediately turned around and ignored all my advice."

I looked at my muddy boots as his words dragged my spirits down like a rock under water. "Nic…" I started, but there was nothing to say. He'd made himself clear. He said he trusted me—but he didn't.

He let go of the phone. I stared at my reflection on the dark screen as the weight settled in my hands like a live bomb.

"We need to keep moving—they'll know we checked in here." He turned and led the way down the alley.

I pocketed the phone and followed him. I waited until we'd reached the end of the block before attempting conversation. "Where are we going?"

"Out of the city. We need to get somewhere rural where there isn't as much surveillance."

I quickened my pace to match his long strides. "But what about Jael?"

He gave that tired groan that made me regret I'd said anything. "I'm sure she's a charming individual, but I am not in the mood for a ghost hunt."

"But Narissa said—"

"Narissa hasn't even met her." Nic looked down at me, but the condescending expression on his face made me wish he wouldn't. "Andi, we are not risking our lives for a phantom. We know nothing about this woman, if she even exists. And you of all people know what happens when you trust someone you don't know."

I turned my attention to the cluttered street ahead of us so he couldn't see the tears that abruptly stung my eyes. Maybe it was because I was hungry, and everything still hurt, and I had a headache, and I probably should have stopped to drink water seventeen blocks ago—but suddenly, I just wanted this conversation to be over. I didn't want to be reminded that we were in this mess because I trusted someone I shouldn't have.

And yet, even as I tried to wade through the guilt, I knew I wouldn't be alive right now if I hadn't trusted certain people along the way: Cea, Stanyard, John and Dowe, even Nic. *Especially* Nic. A few months ago, I'd had every reason not to trust Nic. But I'd given him a chance, and he'd never made me regret that choice. Even now, when he was being tactless and cold, I still didn't regret letting him into my life.

What was the difference? What separated Nic from someone like Jayde? Neither of them knew Jesus, at least not in any appreciable way. Nic had walked away from his parents' faith years ago and never looked back. He'd also kidnapped my brother, threatened my father, tried to invent a superweapon, and various other sundry crimes. So why could I trust him and not Jayde? How was I supposed to know who to trust in the future? What was I supposed to be looking for?

Unfortunately, Nic didn't seem interested in educating me on the nuances. He strode into the intersection, barely pausing to look for oncoming traffic. "If we can get somewhere rural," he continued seamlessly, "I should be able to make a call without giving Asia a direct pinpoint—or I might be able to find someone who's willing to help us launder money so I can buy fake prints. If I can just get online without tipping Asia off, I can call your brother or that boyfriend of yours and—"

"Stanyard!" I gasped, causing Nic to jump. I hadn't meant to shout, but I'd just remembered that I'd texted Stanyard the night before. Surely, he'd replied by now.

I stepped up on the sidewalk and pulled the phone out. "What are you doing?" Nic demanded, reaching for me.

I jerked back. "I'm just seeing if he replied. If there are any new messages, they would have downloaded while you were online. I'm not going to text him back—Nic, do you really think I'm that stupid?"

He folded his arms. "You're a teenage girl in love. Yes, I think you're that stupid."

I growled and turned away from him. My relationship with Stanyard was one of the few good things that had happened since I'd come back to Earth. Why did Nic have to be so mean about it?

Why did he have to be so mean about everything?

I opened the messaging app and was rewarded with a dozen messages from Stanyard. The first few were the usual somersault of *you're okay I was so worried I miss you I'm so sorry this happened I love you.* I couldn't help but smile even as my heart ached; Stanyard always rambled when he panicked.

When he realized I wasn't online and responding, he'd slowed down and started using fewer words. He confirmed he was safe and told me to take care of myself and not worry about him. Then he sent the message I really needed to hear:

I KNOW WHY YOU WENT. I WANT YOU TO KNOW I FORGIVE YOU.

The screen blurred as my eyes swam with tears, welcome ones this time. I'd known, factually, that he would forgive me. We'd been through too much over the past two months, had too many fallouts and apologies, for this to be the last straw. He'd forgiven me even when I couldn't forgive myself.

I could only hope he still loved me even though I absolutely didn't love myself.

I scrolled to the last message.

I SAW THE LIVESTREAM. I'M PROUD OF YOU.

I closed my eyes and took a deep breath, letting his words put a period on my anxiety. At least *someone* thought I did the right thing.

I looked up to find Nic still staring at me. "What? Do you want to read the messages?" I shook the device at him.

He put his hands up. "No thank you. I've got enough on my plate dealing with Asia's unrequited love—I don't need to add your teenage hormones to the list."

"Good, I didn't want your opinion anyway," I returned, then regretted it. It was a rude thing to say—and it wasn't even true. I *did* want Nic's opinion. I just didn't want the biting sarcasm and cruel disinterest that usually came with it.

Nic gracelessly changed the subject. "What's for breakfast?"

More like brunch at this point. I shoved the shopping bag at him.

He took it and riffled through the contents. "Let's find a place to sit—I need to plan our route."

We turned the corner and found ourselves in an arts district. Bronze statues cluttered the sidewalk, and carefully curated graffiti coated every available wall. Across the square, a series of historic brick buildings had been converted into a gallery. The roofs were a strange scallop design paneled with glass, and the remains of a smokestack stuck into the sky—a decommissioned factory of sorts. I could tell at a glance that much of the art was brazenly political, praising the United and its communist predecessors, but at least the place was a tourist trap. It was decently busy, with plenty of Americans milling around, so we wouldn't stand out.

We found a secluded park bench and sat with our backs to a brick wall. Nic unwrapped a protein bar and started gnawing on it, propping both elbows on his knees and staring into space like he always did when he was processing.

I fished out the canteen. The metal was still slightly warm to the touch, making me hope the contents were still hot. I unscrewed the lid and took a slow sip. It tasted different from the coffee Mrs. Von, Nic's mom, made, but it was still coffee. It was familiar, normal—and normalcy was something I desperately needed right now.

I inhaled the earthy steam and tried to imagine myself back in Boston. Normally at this time, I'd be sitting at the Vons' kitchen island, listening to Mr. Von's good-natured chatter while a mundane sitcom droned on the TV in the background. Mrs. Von would be bustling about the kitchen, opening every cabinet in the room until she found the plates that had been on the same shelf for the last twenty years.

Thanks to a botched neurosurgery—another cruel government attempt to crush the unassimilated—the Vons had the object permanence of a six-month-old. They forgot everything as soon as it was out of sight. No doubt they'd forgotten about me by now, moved on and created a new daily routine as if I'd never existed.

I'd give anything for the pleasure of reintroducing myself.

Would I ever see them again? Going back to Boston seemed impossible. The government was just as controlling there as it was here, and I couldn't trust the underground, not after what happened with Jayde. The assassination had been a blackout mission; only a handful of people even knew I was in Beijing. But I had no way of knowing who was on Jayde's side and who was on mine. And if Jayde managed to get out of Beijing alive, he may very well poison the rest of them against me.

I reached up and instinctively rubbed my right shoulder, where my thunderbird tattoo was hidden under my sleeve. What did the internet think of me now? A week ago, I'd been a trending celebrity, the figurehead of a revolution. My videos raked in millions of views as Jayde used my image—the thunderbird—to coordinate Operation Blue Fire.

We'd been months away from staging a global demonstration designed to wake the public from their stupor, but now what? In my last video, I'd told my followers I was going offline while some stuff blew over. I'd intended to reveal myself to the world when I killed the General. What would people say if I didn't come online for weeks? Would Operation Blue Fire still happen without me?

The unassimilated—social noncompliants who refused to deny their religious and national identities and sign the file—were still in danger. The leadership in Beijing was planning to deport all the unassimilated to work camps in China, a certain one-way trip. If Operation Blue Fire didn't succeed, what would happen to my people—the Christians, the Jews, the rejects? If we lost the momentum of the revolution, there would be no getting it back. And if my feud with Jayde divided us from the inside, we'd be worse off than when we started.

And it would, as always, be my fault.

7: NIC

I'd get so much more done if I didn't spend half my waking hours saving Phil from her own thoughts.

She'd gone silent—the kind of silence where she forgets to breathe—disrupting the atmospheric pressure and jerking me out of my mind palace. I looked up and saw that she was two beats away from a meltdown. Her shoulders were hunched and her face was pinched like she was caving in on herself. I could tell by the look in her eyes that she was trapped in a cycle of guilt and unanswered questions. I knew what would happen if she crashed at the bottom, and I was not about to spend the rest of my day putting her back together.

"What's in the canteen?" I interrupted.

She abruptly relaxed her grip, almost dropping it. She held it out to me.

I got a whiff of the contents, and suddenly, life became significantly less horrible.

I snatched the canteen and gulped the coffee like it was oxygen itself. The rich, still-warm liquid hit my throat, putting my soul back in my body. I felt my humanity returning; maybe I could actually get through today without murdering something.

I came up for air with a satisfied sigh. "You're hired."

She regarded me with amusement. "For what?"

"My assistant."

She paused and gave my offhand comment way too much thought. "That's actually a job I could probably handle."

"Well, we've already established you can fetch coffee." That was half the job description. "Can you reply to emails and manage a calendar?"

She shrugged. "I mean, sure."

"And can you keep secrets from the government?"

"With pleasure."

I gave her a sideways glance. "Except for that one time you turned my entire base over to Ambrose."

It took her so long to get the joke that I almost regretted making it.

"Wow," she finally managed after she'd gaped at me for a solid minute.

"What? Too soon?"

"No, I… I'm just surprised you know how to tease." She leaned away, as if she were afraid I was going to take it back.

I shrugged and took another drink of coffee. "It's just sarcasm but nicer."

She grinned and held out her hand for the canteen.

I passed it to her in surprise. "You like black coffee?"

She tipped the canteen back and chugged like a drunk pirate. "Is there another way to take it?"

There wasn't—and there was only one person who could have taught her that.

Her dad didn't drink the stuff. Her brother used enough cream that he may as well start with a gallon of milk and add a splash of coffee to it. Even my dad took some sugar with his.

No, she definitely learned this important life skill from me. And, if she was picking up on my sense of humor and coffee drinking habits, logical deduction assumed that she was also learning other things from me.

It took me a full five minutes to reboot my universe around that unfortunate fact.

We ate in silence for a while. Phil nibbled on a bag of trail mix, eating one piece at a time like she had to make it last. I chewed on another protein bar, struggling to keep my thoughts on our present predicament.

Normally, I possessed an inhuman ability to hyperfocus on a problem until I found a solution. But no matter how many times I started over at the beginning and tried to trace our next steps, my mind kept wandering off like an untrained dog. Asia, my parents, the base on Mars, the fragile teenage girl sitting next to me—my thoughts insisted on focusing on anything *but* the most immediate problem.

Perhaps it was because I subconsciously knew there was no solution. At least no solution that I liked.

After about ten minutes, I could tell Phil wanted to break the silence, so I let her. "What's wrong?" I said by way of invitation.

She drummed her fingers on the bench. "Can I tell you something?"

Always would have been the correct answer, but I opted to be a little less sappy. "That's certainly preferable to keeping it stuffed up inside."

She snorted, then paused to parse her words. "Sometimes… sometimes I wish I hadn't blown up that lab in Wing 74."

I blinked. When I didn't respond for a long moment, she arched an eyebrow. "Sorry," I coughed, "that was just a deeper personal revelation than I was prepared for. Run that by me again?"

"I mean... I know it was the right thing to do. I don't *regret* it. But like... sometimes I think about how living in Wing 74 would have been so much easier than dealing with all this. Putting up with you would have been... easy."

"Solid burn. Thank you for confirming that I utterly failed as an evil overlord."

She giggled, and the sound was less annoying than I would have expected. "I guess... I just finally understand how Ephesus could do it. How he could put up with that for two years, you know?"

I did know, partially because I'd designed it that way. But I also knew that compromise like that led down a very dangerous path. Compromise had made her brother a coward. It had killed her father. And it had turned me into the kind of man who would kidnap, murder, and set the world on fire.

I tapped my foot and ordered my words carefully. "You want to hear something equally personal and awkward?"

She looked up at me and waited.

I met her gaze. "I'm glad you blew up that lab."

Her whole face lit up—probably, I noted in retrospect, because she had been waiting to hear those words for a very long time. "Really?"

I nodded. "If you hadn't, your father would have created Red Rain, and I would have given it to Carnegie, who would have given it to Thames, and Asia would have gotten what she wanted all along."

It was the truth. But as I stared at Philadelphia, with her big, watery doe-eyes that I used to hate so much, I realized that might not be the only reason.

She smiled, but the warm fuzzy feelings were short-lived. "So, you and Asia..."

"Oh, here we go," I groaned. I rubbed my temples and tried to psych myself up for the conversation I'd been avoiding for nearly a decade. "Let's just get this all out of the way. Yes, we dated once. No, we were never married. Yes, she was just as terrible a person then as she is now. And no, I'm not still in love with her. End of story."

"Okay, but you did love her once," Phil clarified.

"I should have known that's the part of the story you'd get hung up on."

"I just don't understand... *how*. Why?"

"Why? Besides the fact that she was an attractive woman?" *Still is, unfortunately.*

"Nic," Phil scolded.

"What? I was a young man once, believe it or not."

She folded her arms and glared at me. I knew she wouldn't leave me alone until I gave her the full story, so I relented and leaned back against the wall. "She was powerful… and rich. She could bend laws, forge files, and get any paperwork approved."

"And?" Phil prodded.

"And what?" I sighed. This story was going to go on forever if she kept questioning my answers.

"And there has to be something more. You're not that shallow."

It was almost a compliment if I thought about it hard enough. "I was then."

I begrudgingly dredged up the memories and tried to resurrect the boy I'd been when I'd met Asia nearly fifteen years ago. It wasn't as difficult as I would have liked. He was still there, lurking in the back of my mind like a deadbeat in his parents' basement. I'd suffocated him over the years with sarcasm and plans of world domination, but he was still very much alive.

"I was trying to create Red Rain and needed someone to cut the red tape. Asia gave me everything I wanted: unlimited funding and complete freedom from government scrutiny. All in exchange for the low, low price of love and companionship."

Phil twitched her nose like a rabbit as she chewed on that information. "Why? Did she really like you that much?"

So much for giving me compliments. "I think she wanted to watch the world burn as much as I did." Asia had made it very clear that she wanted to break the system. My mistake was believing that she wanted to do it for the same reasons.

"And you?"

I stared up at the sky as that foolish little boy reared his head out of the basement. "I believed it could be done."

I'd truly believed that Red Rain could change the system—and that Asia was the one to do it with me. We'd been unstoppable in our heyday. With her connections and influence, and my charisma and science, there was no sponsor we could not win, no official we could not manipulate. We could have done it. We could have saved the world.

Of course, back then there was still something—someone—in the world worth saving.

There was a pause, and then Phil asked the question I'd been dreading most of all. "What happened?"

I took a deep breath, knowing full well this revelation would fundamentally alter her opinion of me in a way I wasn't sure I was ready for. "I refused to give her Red Rain."

Phil jerked upright and nearly fell off the bench. "You—what?"

"Surprise," I droned. "I wanted to abandon the project, but she wouldn't have it."

Phil tried and failed to adjust to this new reality. "But how... why... You literally faked people's deaths to keep this project a secret. That makes no sense for you."

"It didn't then, either."

"But... what changed your mind?"

"My dad."

The same person who had always possessed the power to change my mind—the one catalyst who had repeatedly disrupted the chemical equation of my life.

Her expression brightened at the mention of him, then immediately fell again. "He knew?"

"Dads know everything," I muttered, a fact she hadn't quite figured out yet. "He tried to convince me to stop—told me there was a better way."

"There is a better way," Phil echoed.

I turned away and stared at one of the uninspired statues across the plaza. There were many reasons why I'd never wanted to have this conversation with Phil, but that was at the top of the list. I knew she'd say the same things my dad used to, partly because they were practically the same person.

After all, Phil was the only other person who had ever convinced me to change my mind about Red Rain.

With an uncharacteristic amount of discretion, Phil decided not to push it. She stared at her lap, tracing the scratches in the metal canteen with her chipped fingernail. I knew she was running the numbers and searching for the missing piece in my tragic life story.

I waited. She'd get there in a second.

"Asia was the one who did it," she declared after a moment. She looked up at me for confirmation. "Asia put your parents under."

"Bingo. She thought it would convince me why we needed Red Rain. I think she was hoping it would be my villain origin story."

I winced. Even I could tell that there was too much pain in my voice for the sarcasm to be effective, so I gave up. "Unfortunately for her, I hacked into the medical records and found out who authorized the procedure."

I remembered the blinding rage, the nauseous grief, the shattering of ceramic as I'd hurled my coffee mug into the wall. And through it all, a seeping tidal wave of guilt as I realized I was a complete and utter failure.

Phil hesitated. She regarded me nervously, her jaw set on edge like she always did when she was afraid to tell me something. "What?" I said, even though I was quite sure I didn't want to know.

"She succeeded," she whispered.

"Who did?"

"Asia. She won." Phil swallowed and pushed the rest of the words out. "Putting your parents through surgery *did* inspire you to finish Red Rain. She got what she wanted."

My vision flashed black and blue as I realized she was right. It may not have gone the way she'd hoped, but Asia had still won in the end. She'd faded into the shadows and waited patiently for eight years while I created Red Rain for her.

It was my fault for not realizing she was still watching. In truth, she'd never left. She'd given me some space, letting my former assistant Carnegie and her cohort Thames run the show so I wouldn't think it was her. But she'd always been there, waiting, playing the long game, keeping the government off my scent so I could give her the keys to the apocalypse.

I'd always known I was a fool for getting involved with Asia. But it wasn't until now that I realized what an idiot I truly was.

Phil interrupted my self-flagellation. "Do you think she still wants Red Rain?"

I shook my head. "If she did, she'd have it already. She's known about 'Andromeda' this whole time. If she wanted to use you as blackmail to bribe your father, she would have done that two months ago. Even now, if she really wants the formula, she can just run a brain scan on him."

"But…" Phil started, not as an argument, but as a plea for reassurance that her father was safe.

I wasn't about to lie to her. "We've been over this. If any of your father's memories are intact, that includes Red Rain. All she has to do is hook him up to a synaptic device, and she can download everything she wants to know."

That had probably been Asia's plan all along. Dr. Smyrna was Phil's biological father and the real scientist responsible for making Red Rain a reality. My former assistant Carnegie had kidnapped him and had him cryogenically frozen—one of the many preventable tragedies that had happened because Phil ignored my advice. Carnegie had been planning to sell the body—and the formula for Red Rain—to Asia.

And then, inexplicably, Asia's plans had changed. Phil had interrupted the deal and made a mess of things, as she often did, but it was nothing Asia couldn't have fixed. If Asia wanted Dr. Smyrna's body, she could have procured it by now. She'd been watching Phil and knew she'd been staying with my parents; all Asia would have had to do was send a car to follow Phil, and she could have snatched the old man like taking an egg out of a nest.

No, I believed Asia when she said she didn't need Red Rain anymore, and that was the most insidious revelation about this whole ordeal. Red Rain had outlived its usefulness. Asia had a new plan, and all I knew was that her plan involved Philadelphia.

Unfortunately for her, Philadelphia was the one thing I wouldn't let her have.

8: PHILADELPHIA

Nic fell silent. Without even finishing his last thought, he propped his elbows on his knees and returned to the depths of his mind.

I let him go. I turned my focus back to my forgotten lunch and tried to find the center of my own thoughts in the bottom of the trail mix bag.

Like a finished jigsaw puzzle, Nic's story explained everything. All the events and characters that had intersected our lives over the last nine months lined up like pieces on a chess board. Clearly, Asia had been controlling this game of chess for a very long time, and my family and I were just the latest pawns in her army.

And yet, the truth of Nic's past was completely dissonant from the caricature I'd built in my mind. Perhaps without realizing it, I'd written my own explanation to Nic's behavior, a twisted backstory that helped me justify the mad scientist who had become my ally.

I'd assumed until today that Nic had always been amoral, a man without a compass or regard for human life. That's how Ephesus had described him, although my brother had definitely seen Nic at his worst. But even Cea had made it sound like her brother had always been this way—aloof, coldhearted, and willing to sacrifice those he loved.

But maybe neither of them had ever met the real Nic. The Nic who listened to his father's advice. The Nic who wasn't afraid to stand up to Asia. The Nic who abandoned Red Rain because he believed there was a better way.

That was the Nic I knew.

It made me wonder if Nic knew more about God than he cared to admit. After all, Nic's parents were diehard Christians; the apple can only fall so far from the tree, even if that apple is actively trying to roll away down the hill. I also knew Nic had a soft side, however much he hated it. For someone who had been bent on starting WWIV less than a year ago, he hadn't been very hard to convert.

If I of all people could convince Nic to change his mind, then it must have been a short trip.

There was so much I wanted to ask him, but I figured I had exhausted his emotional transparency for one day, so I held my tongue. Instead, I closed my eyes and did something I probably should have been doing all along: I prayed for him.

Nic crumpled his wrapper and stood up. "We should keep moving."

I groaned. I was already starting to hate that phrase, and it wasn't even noon.

We deposited our trash and left the arts district. Nic offered to carry the shopping bag, so I let him. The sun was now high overhead, blanketing the city in a layer of mugginess that was almost as thick as the smog itself. I stripped my leather jacket and tied it around my waist. I felt sorry for Nic; he rolled up the sleeves of his windbreaker, but he couldn't take it off unless he wanted to cause a scene with his holstered gun. I could tell he was uncomfortable, with a line of sweat dampening the edge of his greasy blond hair.

Descending into the subway tunnel brought us some relief. Rush hour had dwindled, so while there was still a sizable queue clogging the platform, the line at least appeared to be moving. We waited until three trains had come and gone before we finally found room on a car.

I grabbed the hem of Nic's jacket as the crowd squeezed us onto the train. It felt like we were being carried along, like a branch dragged with the current. People bustled against me on all sides, rubbing against my arm and digging my backpack into my shoulder blades. It was hot and noisy, and all I could see was a blur of foreign faces. I held my breath, afraid that if I let it out, there wouldn't be enough air for me to get another.

Suddenly, we broke through a gap to the interior of the car. I stumbled into Nic as the train lurched into motion. Thankfully, he was tall enough to grab the top bar, so I held onto him as he stood steady. I refused to let go as he weaseled our way further into the car; every time someone would move, he'd slide in to take their place.

After about fifteen minutes, we managed to snatch a seat in the corner. There was only one, and Nic all but shoved me into it when the occupier got up to make their stop.

"Thanks," I said, reaching to take the shopping bag from him.

He just nodded as he stationed himself in front of me, grabbing the bar above my head.

I watched out the window as the train sped up. The lights of the tunnel blurred into a streak, then abruptly came back into focus again as the train slowed at the next platform. I waited until we'd passed three more stops before speaking again.

"End of the line?" I ventured.

He grunted. "This line goes all the way to the west side of the province. We'll get off there, see about catching a bus out of the district."

I traced the embroidery on the silk bag and didn't respond. I didn't want to question him, but I wasn't sure getting out of the city would do us any good. Nic couldn't log in anywhere, and if I went online, it would give Asia a beacon to find us both. Even if the location wasn't precise, it would still tell her what village we were in, and it might be more difficult for us to hide in the country than it was in the city. The further we got into the rural areas, the fewer Americans there would be, and the more we'd stand out. Especially Nic—even in the subway car, he was at least a head above most of the other riders.

But even if we could get online, what then? Thanks to the inheritance Thames Nolan had left to me, I was rich, but I couldn't spend a penny without leaving a digital trail. We needed to launder money, but I doubted some poor rice farmer in the middle of the mountains could—or would—help us with that. Nic said he was going to call Ephesus, but what could my brother do? He was a hundred million miles away on Mars.

I winced. What must my brother think? I hadn't involved him in any of this. He'd been offline on a transit to Mars during this whole ordeal. He'd been supportive of my role as Blue Fire, just like he had supported me my entire life, but I could tell he didn't like the idea of me leading a revolution any more than Nic did. I'm sure he was horrified when he found out I'd gone to China with the intent of murdering a man. And now I'd dropped off the grid completely; I hadn't even sent him a text when I was last online.

I looked up at Nic. "Have you talked to Ephesus?"

The glazed look in his eyes shattered. "Oh—" He started to swear, then caught himself just in time.

I stiffened, instantly resuming panic mode. "What?"

He aggressively rubbed his face with his hand. "There's something you should know."

I tried to swallow, but it caught in my throat. "I hate it when you say that."

"You and me both."

I braced my feet on the floor as the subway screeched to a stop at the next platform. "Is Ephesus okay?"

"Oh, he's doing *fantastic*." The bitterness in Nic's voice was so palpable that you could have snapped a piece off like peanut brittle.

I took a deep breath and tried to remind my heart that things really couldn't get any worse at this point. "Well, just as long as no one's dead, getting adopted, or changing their name."

Nic grimaced. "We're good on the first two. But there might be a name change involved."

"What?" Abruptly, the events of this morning snapped into focus. "Wait, does this have something to do with the paperwork you had to fill out?"

"Regrettably."

My cheeks started buzzing like I'd been slapped in the face. "No. He didn't."

"Against my advice to the contrary, he did."

A ringing in my ears joined the chaos. "He can't."

"Trust me, I don't like it any more than you do."

A dozen violent feelings fought for dominance, but disbelief was winning. "To whom?"

Nic rolled his eyes. "Who do you think?"

"Cea!" I dropped the shopping bag and grabbed both sides of my face. Of course, it was Cea. Ephesus had been sweet on Nic's sister for a while, but I had no idea they were thinking of getting *married*.

Nic stooped to grab a protein bar that had tumbled to the floor. "Eyup. Welcome to the family, sis. Thanks to that tax form I just turned in, we're now legally related in more than one way, so that's weird."

"Weird" didn't even begin to describe it. "But—why? How?"

"I called the base as soon as I landed. I caught him proposing, and instead of being embarrassed like normal people, they asked me to marry them."

"And you said *yes*?"

Nic gestured with the protein bar, almost smacking the rider next to him. "I couldn't say no! She's my sister!"

"Never stopped you before." Oddly, I felt more betrayed by Nic than anyone else; surely, he was on my side with this one.

"Fair point, but only a fool messes with a woman's wedding."

I yelled as anger suddenly overtook my other emotions. "I can't believe him! Sorry," I added when the person on the bench next to me gave me a terrified look. She decided she'd rather ride elsewhere and got up. Nic quickly took her spot.

I slumped back against the window as the reality of my new family tree sank into me. My own brother got married—*without me*. "I can't believe he would do this to me," I repeated, this time at an appropriate decibel.

"Honestly, same," Nic agreed.

"He's my only sibling! He's literally the only close family I have left. And he didn't even tell me he was going to propose." I wanted to be happy for them, I really did. I loved both of them, and they deserved happiness— especially my brother, after all he'd been through. But to get married on a whim and not even mention it to me? That was adding insult to injury when I was already approaching crush depth with anxiety and stress.

I tried to release my frustration and just ended up making a weird growling sound. "I'm going to kill him when we get back."

It was an exaggeration, but Nic was on board with the plan. "I'll hold, you punch."

I couldn't help but laugh. My anger melted as I realized the absurdity of the whole situation. "Well, I guess I could start telling people you're my brother, if you like that better."

He turned to me with a gaze so dead that his face might as well have been stone. "I don't."

I smirked.

We spent the rest of the ride in relative silence. Nic scrolled through an offline map on his phone, searching for bus routes. I kept my mind busy by praying for Ephesus and Cea and watching the TV that was mounted at the top of the wall. Some talk show was playing. The subtitles were in simplified Chinese, but I enjoyed trying to guess what they were saying based on their hand gestures and facial expressions.

And then the news came on.

It was a replay of last night's gala. I stiffened as I recognized the palace, the guests—and General Secretary Mong. He smiled benevolently as he gave a gracious bow to the camera.

"Nic," I hissed, poking him.

He looked up. His face folded in a frown as the screen flashed to clips of the various celebrities and political giants that had been in attendance. There were several staged shots as Mong and foreign diplomats posed for the camera, faking smiles and embracing each other as if a good photo could prove that all was well with the world.

Suddenly, I appeared.

I sucked in my breath as my own face filled the screen. My dress glittered in the flash of a thousand camera bulbs as I lifted my skirts and bowed. I was surprised at how smooth and elegant the motion looked; my face was calm, like I had rehearsed this moment a thousand times. The camera was zoomed in too close to see the reaction of the crowd; was that by accident or design? Nevertheless, the pleasure on the General's face was evident as he returned the gesture.

Some Mandarin characters flashed across the screen, and then the clip was gone as quickly as it had appeared. "What did it say?" I whispered to Nic.

He shook his head—although whether that was because he couldn't read it or because he didn't want to tell me, I'll never know. "Keep your head down," he hissed.

I glanced around the subway car, but no one was paying us any mind. Hopefully, without my manicured makeup, extra curls, and sparkling dress, I wouldn't attract attention. But I still tucked my bleached hair behind my ear as I sank into the seat.

It took over two hours for us to reach the end of the line. I fought to keep up with Nic as he shoved his way through the mid-afternoon shopping crowd to the nearest bus stop. The shelter roof was modeled after a traditional tile design, and the stained concrete walls had been retrofitted with a chaotic array of digital signboards. Nic planted himself in front of one and studied the scrolling text. After a minute, he started tugging on his mustache.

I knew what that meant. He had no idea where to go.

I sat down on a nearby bench and started praying, hard. There had to be another solution besides fleeing to the mountains. Weren't there safe houses, black markets, places outside the law? There were almost thirty million people in this province; we couldn't be the only criminals on the run. Surely there were people willing to do things under the radar for the right price— like Andes, the technician and tattoo artist I used back in Boston.

The question was how to find people outside the law. I'd needed a referral to get to Andes, and I didn't know anyone here. Would Nic know someone? He had obviously spent time in Beijing in the past; he had dated Asia of all people. But that had been years ago; all of his contacts may have gone cold.

My eyes wandered around the shelter, searching for answers—and that's when I saw it.

It was small and disfigured; the resemblance was so crude that you wouldn't know what it was unless you were already looking for it. I stood and walked over for a closer look. It was drawn on the underside of the roof near the corner. It was nearly lost amongst the collage of other graffiti and coarse sayings that had been added by rebellious teens over the years. But I knew what it was.

A thunderbird.

9: NIC

"Nic," Phil hissed.

Her clammy fingers brushed my arm. I grimaced and shrugged her off. Physical contact wasn't my favorite thing, and she'd reached for me with her right hand—the hand that still contained an active bomb. Supposedly, it would only detonate for its intended target, but I didn't particularly trust Jayde's programming skills. Until we could get the wires in her hand removed, I'd just as soon avoid getting all touchy-feely.

"What?" I sighed and glanced back at her.

"Look." She attempted to subtly point at the roof of the bus stop. Almost nothing Phil did was subtle; it looked like she was having a seizure as she jerked her head and rolled her eyes upward.

I followed her gaze, saw what it was, and immediately knew we had to leave.

"Let's go." I shouldered my backpack and spun on my heels.

She did the exact opposite, planting herself in front of the signboard in a way that looked anything but nonchalant. "No, wait, I think this can help us. What do the characters say?"

There were a handful of simplified Chinese characters scribbled next to the thunderbird; I could tell they had been added at the same time due to the fading of the ink. They were numbers—a bus route, probably. All the more reason we should get far away from this stop.

"We need to get out of here." I made a second attempt to leave.

"Nic, wait!"

I did no such thing. I shoved past a group of commuters and hurried down the street, knowing she'd keep up out of fear of being left behind.

It took her a block to catch up. "Nic, stop, please!"

"We're not safe here." I turned into an alley, eager to get out of sight.

She found a burst of energy and darted ahead of me. She halted and attempted to block the way. "But what if we are? What if—what if that's the solution?"

I knew exactly what she was suggesting, and it was a terrible idea. "Absolutely not—"

"No, don't you see?" she blathered on. "There's an underground here, and they know me. If we can find a safe house or a point of contact and tell them I'm here, they'll take care of us."

The Chinese underground was the last thing she should be getting involved with. "No," I repeated, louder, hoping the volume would get her attention. "We're going to get out of the city and call your brother."

My attempt to regain control of the situation backfired; she just raised her volume to match mine. "But what can he do? Surely Asia's watching the activity on base. We need temp files—and the underground can get us those."

"That would be great, if it weren't for two inconvenient complications." I spelled it out for her, even though she really should have been smart enough to see how foolish her plan was. "If we waltz in there and announce ourselves, not only will they know we're in Beijing, but they'll also know what our temporary identities are. Both of those are pieces of information I'd like to keep to ourselves."

"No, Nic, you don't understand," she cried, even though I definitely did. "It's not like that. I'm Blue Fire."

The very sound of the forbidden callsign made my blood run cold. *No, you're not,* I thought. *You're just a dumb teenage girl, and you have no idea who you're dealing with.*

She mistook my silence as consent. "They trust me—I'm their leader. If we tell them I'm here, they can help us."

I was sure they would—and then we'd be right back where we started, with Philadelphia in the middle of a war she didn't understand. "Enough," I demanded, and shoved her out of the way. "I've made up my mind."

She stumbled and almost fell over. "No, Nic, just listen to me, please!" She regained her balance and grabbed my jacket sleeve. "You have to trust me! I can do this—I can fix this!"

Her pitiful statement pierced a memory, and I snapped. "No, you can't!"

My shout ricocheted off the dumpster beside us, finally silencing her. She let go of my sleeve. I took a deep breath and lowered my voice, but only for the benefit of any eavesdroppers.

"No, you can't fix this, *Andromeda*," I slurred the name into a warning, "and you know why?"

She did—we both did—but I stated it for the court anyway.

"Because you got us into this mess. We're stranded in Beijing without any way to get online, hunted by the worst woman in history, because you thought you were a hero. You got mixed up with people and politics you didn't understand, and you almost started a war and got us all killed."

My anger wavered, but not because there wasn't plenty of it to go around. No, I abruptly realized that it wasn't her ignorance that bothered me. It wasn't the fact that she'd gotten tangled up in a petty revolution that made me so furious.

It was the fact that I'd tried, again and again, to reason with her. And yet, after all I'd done for her, she still wasn't listening.

I was done bargaining with her. I hadn't come all the way back to Earth and risked my life to save her just to have her throw it all away. I was going to get us off this planet alive if it was the last thing I did, and if that meant I had to play the bad guy for a while, so be it.

"Look, I came back for you because, believe it or not, I don't want you dead. But I'm sick and tired of having my decisions questioned after all I've done to try to help you." I kept my back to her as I continued. "So from now on, you will let me be the adult. We're going out of the city so I can find someone who can help us get online. You will let me do the talking, and I don't want to hear another word about the underground. Have I made myself clear?"

She was silent. I turned and looked back at her.

Her eyes were on the ground as she gripped her chest with both arms. "Yessir," she mumbled, and I heard in her voice the shake that told me the argument was over.

"Good," I said with palpable relief, even though I wondered how long our impasse would last. "Now come on."

I led the way down the alley in the opposite direction of the bus stop—even though I knew that was neurotic. Just because the underground was using the bus didn't mean we couldn't. They didn't know Phil was in Beijing, and even if they did, they likely wouldn't recognize her with her blue contacts and bleached hair.

But by the time I admitted to myself that I was overreacting, we'd already walked a mile in the wrong direction. Although "wrong" was a relative term when I didn't really know where we were going. I knew I wanted to get out of the city, into the country where the surveillance was hopefully lighter, but that was easier said than done when the free public transportation system only went so far.

Still, I would rather spend the night in a village than the sewers of the inner city, so I took us to another bus stop and doubled back to where we came from, hoping Phil wouldn't question it. By then, rush hour had started, so we waited in line for over an hour before we caught a bus out of town.

And that's about when I realized I was in deep trouble. Phil wasn't talking. At all.

In fact, she didn't say a word the entire trip. Several times, I glanced back to make sure I hadn't lost her. She stayed close and didn't complain, but she didn't once turn to look up at me.

We finally managed to squeeze onto a bus, although it was standing room only. We rode the line as far as it would take us, out into the suburbs of Beijing. Of course, given the intensity of China's urban sprawl, "suburb" was a bit of a loose term. The area we found ourselves in was almost as densely packed as the inner city. The only difference was that everything was newer and more orderly, to the point of being bland. Endless rows of apartments were laid out in perfect squares like prison cells. A deliberate attempt had been made to leave room for grass in between the buildings, but it did little to soften the severity of concrete and tile.

By then it was nearly dark, and Phil still wasn't talking. I was contemplating doing the unthinkable and initiating conversation when I got a cruel reminder that we weren't alone in the universe.

It started to rain.

I sensed the shift in the wind and knew we only had minutes before it turned into a downpour. We were still in the shopping district where the bus had let us off, so I figured our best bet was to find shelter in an alley. I led us behind the buildings and ran until I found an abandoned corner void of any prying eyes.

The strip of shops had been closed down, making me hope the apartments above were empty as well. I climbed the metal staircase and peeked through the iron grates into the grimy windows; everything was dark and uninhabited. I tried the doors, but they were all locked. I contemplated kicking one down, but there was still power going to the building, which meant the alarm system could be online. By now the rain was coming down in torrents, so I decided not to press our luck and accepted the relative shelter of the awning.

We set up camp in the middle of the building, shielded from the wind by some forgotten boxes. The air was still damp and chilly, but at least the concrete was dry. I divvied up our dinner, then stared at the contents of the bag and appreciated the severity of our situation. We could stretch the food for a few more days if needed, but the water would run out tomorrow. Unless I could find a sanitary place to refill our bottles, I'd have to send Phil to buy more—and then we would start all over with our deadly game of hide-and-seek with Asia.

Before I could work out a solution to that problem, our solitude was rudely interrupted. A crash came from the far end of the building, loud enough to be heard over the rain pounding on the concrete. I dropped the bag and whipped around, but there was nothing to see. There were no lights in the alley except the streetlamp at the end of the block, and the only movement was the water pouring off the gutter.

Phil sat up straight. "I'll go check," I assured her, even though she hadn't said anything.

I crept to the end of the building. As I neared the last apartment, I heard it again. This time, it was more of a scratch and a rustle, and it was clearly coming from the pile of boards and trash that was heaped on the edge of the balcony.

I really hope there's not a homeless person under here, I thought to myself, then grabbed the topmost board and flung it aside.

It wasn't a person. It was a cat.

It was a scrawny, pathetic little thing. It huddled against the building, mewing pitifully and staring up at me with yellow eyes that were too big for its stunted body. Its dark gray fur was sopping wet, and its eyes were crusted almost shut with gunk. The stupid animal looked like it had already expended eight of its lives, and I wondered if it would survive the night.

Suddenly, Phil found her voice. "Kitty!"

I sighed loudly in relief. She gave me a funny look.

"Never mind," I said. "And no, you can't keep it."

"But why not?" She walked over and knelt beside me. She held out her hand and clucked encouragingly. The cat answered the summons. It got up— and came straight to me.

I jerked back as it tried to wrap itself around my ankle. "Because it'll do stuff like *that*. Also, it might belong to somebody."

Phil pried the cat off my pant leg and cuddled it in her arms. "I doubt he has an owner. Look at him."

She was probably right. If the poor animal did have owners, they weren't feeding him. But that didn't mean *I* was going to pick up the slack. "And what exactly are *you* going to feed him? He can't eat trail mix, even if I was willing to share."

She scratched him behind the ears. He accepted the attention and settled in her arms, even though he kept his fat eyes on me. "I don't have to feed him—he'll eat mice or whatever."

"Well, he might starve for lack of ambition," I commented, noting how skinny he was.

Phil was not deterred in the slightest. She skipped back over to our backpacks and unclipped the blanket. She sat cross-legged on the floor, made a nest with the blanket, and tucked the cat in her lap. He immediately started purring like he was king of the universe.

"I'm going to name him Tommy," she announced.

"Why, because it's a tom cat?" I snarked.

She wrinkled her nose at me. "No, after my dad."

I heard the clip in her voice and saw the flicker in her eyes—grief over the loss of a parent. I knew that grief all too well.

And that's when I remembered that Phil had suffered through her own special kind of purgatory since coming back to Earth. She'd been punished enough for her mistakes; she really didn't need me to yell at her.

I sat down next to her, leaning against the building and folding my long legs to keep them out of the rain. "Look… I'm sorry I yelled at you."

I expected her to perk up, like she usually did any time I was a decent human being. But she didn't. Instead, she looked down and turned red with shame. "No, you're right," she mumbled. "I never should have become a Nolan."

It was an abrupt declaration that, as far as I was concerned, had nothing to do with what we'd been discussing earlier. "I'm going to need more context, because I wasn't privy to the five hours of internal monologue that led up to that statement."

I meant it as a joke and an invitation. I failed at both objectives.

"I was never supposed to be a Nolan," she repeated, which literally gave me no additional information.

"Explain," I prodded.

Instead of answering, she started petting the cat more aggressively. He didn't appreciate her anxious hand movements and opened one eye to squint at me, as if expecting me to commiserate.

"Philadelphia." I elbowed her to get her to stop. "Talk to me."

"I'm not supposed to be here!" she shrieked. Tears filled her eyes at the same time a rare emotion made it onto her face: anger. "I never should have met the General, I never should have come to Beijing, I never should have agreed to be Blue Fire, I never should have come back to Earth, I never should have a recorded any videos, and I never should have taken the Nolans' name."

That was a whole lot of conjecture—and at least one of those statements was empirically false.

Tears were winning the battle for her emotions. She scooped the stupid cat up and buried her face in his neck, sobbing into his already-wet fur. "You were right, you were right about everything. I'm not a hero, I'm not Blue Fire, and I'm not Andromeda Nolan. I should have just stayed Philadelphia Smyrna."

"I never said that," I argued, and as soon as the words left my mouth, I knew.

She *was* supposed to be Andromeda Nolan. She was supposed to go back to Earth, record videos, and lead the revolution. She was supposed to be Blue

Fire. She was supposed to be here, in Beijing. And she absolutely was supposed to meet the General.

She just wasn't supposed to kill him.

I saw it all, clear as day, as if it were a reality that had already happened. The details were sharp and precise, and the picture felt almost more real than the damp alley in front of me. It had been years since I'd had a vision like that, but I knew what it was and where it came from.

And I wanted absolutely nothing to do with it.

I didn't want to live in that world: a world where Philadelphia truly was a Nolan. A reality where she lived amongst the elites in Beijing and played politics with her wealth and influence. That was the life I'd had ten years ago.

I didn't want to go back to that life. And I didn't want that life for her, either.

Phil, thankfully, saw none of that for herself. She just sat there, sniveling into that stupid cat, crushed under the weight of her teenage failures. I knew that if I didn't get her out of the pit, she'd spend all night crying.

"Hey."

She didn't look up at me, but I waited until her breathing had slowed before continuing.

"I promise I'll get us out of this. I will get us home, and you won't have to worry about any of that ever again. Okay?"

"Okay," she repeated. She gave an ugly sniff and lifted her head, mercifully allowing the cat to breathe again. He gave a disgruntled mew but didn't seem motivated enough to vacate his warm nest in the blankets.

With her emotional crisis averted, my mind immediately went back to processing bigger problems. I needed some peace and quiet, but that meant I had to distract her. "Here." I reached into my backpack and fished out the pair of earbuds Narissa had given us. I tossed them at Phil. "I downloaded part of my music archive to the phone."

Something close to a smile warmed her face; she knew what I meant. She put the earbuds in and pulled the phone out of her backpack. She scrolled through the menus until she found one of the old worship albums I had downloaded for just such an emergency. She leaned against the wall and pulled her knees to her chest, stroking the cat's fur. The stupid animal accepted his fate and started purring.

I waited until Phil had zoned out and closed her eyes before getting up and moving to the end of the balcony. I sat on the top step, careful to stay under the protection of the awning, and tented my arms on my knees. I stared out at the pouring rain and tried to rouse my inner genius.

We needed new files—especially Phil. That was apparent to me now. Andromeda Nolan had become just as much of a curse as Philadelphia

Smyrna, and if she had any hope of avoiding the underground—let alone Asia—she needed to become a new person. I didn't relish the idea of walking her through another identity crisis, but it was necessary.

Unfortunately, clean files were not easy to come by. Andes could do it, but going to him was too risky; both Jayde and Asia knew about him. Besides, we needed clean files before we were going to be able to get out of the country. That meant we needed a contact in China, someone who could launder money so effectively that even Asia wouldn't be able to find the electronic trail.

And there was only one person I'd heard of who could do that. If she was even a real person.

I groaned and raked my hand over my untrimmed beard. I didn't like it one bit, especially since it involved admitting to Phil that I changed my mind, but we were running out of options.

If it would keep Phil safe, this was a risk I was going to have to take.

10: PHILADELPHIA

The sun was high overhead when I awoke the next morning. It took a full minute of me squinting at the bright ball of gas before I processed what that meant.

I'd overslept.

I jerked upright, fighting to get out of the blanket. My cat squealed as I accidentally dumped him on the concrete. "Nic!"

"Good morning, princess," he chirped from where he sat on the top step. "Someone slept well."

I paused to assess my five senses and realized he was right—it had been a good night's sleep. My joints were stiff from sleeping on concrete for the second night in a row, but my head felt clear. How I had been able to sleep so well on the street in the rain was beyond me; I could only imagine the worship music had played a factor.

I removed the earbuds and tucked them in the pocket of Nic's backpack. "Why didn't you wake me up?"

"I figured you needed the sleep." He chucked a protein bar at me.

I was in no frame of mind to catch it, so it plunked off my shoulder and fell on the ground. Tommy pounced on it and began clawing at the shiny plastic. "Yeah, but I thought we had to 'keep moving.'"

The glare he shot me over his shoulder told me I'd better watch my attitude. "We do, but I'm in absolutely no rush to get where we're going. Besides, service doesn't start until five."

"Service?"

He took a deep breath. "We're going to find Jael."

My universe stopped and rebooted when I realized what that meant. "Really? Why? How?"

He groaned and closed his eyes, as if he were already regretting his decision. "Which question do you want an answer to? Because I only have the mental capacity for one."

I paused to consider that. I really wanted to know why—what had happened overnight to convince him to change his mind? Was it something I said? Did he finally agree with me? I didn't even need a replay of his whole thought process; I really just wanted an apology.

But I didn't need one.

After pausing to cast a prayer up at God, I turned back to Nic. "Let's go with 'how.'"

"If Narissa is telling the truth, then it sounds like most of the Christians around here know who she is. Our best bet is to find a church and ask them to refer us."

Now that was a plan I could get behind—except I had absolutely no idea how to find a church in Beijing. Christianity had been illegal here even longer than it had been in America. Narissa might know of a congregation, but it wasn't safe to contact her.

I looked up at Nic. "I don't suppose *you* know of any churches," I deadpanned.

"Unless they've all been rounded up and executed, there's a group that used to meet every night in a factory on the river," he declared without batting an eyelash.

"Wait, *what*?"

He ignored my implied disbelief. "But it's all the way on the south side of the province, so we've got some walking to do." He stood and stretched. "Rise and shine, sleeping beauty. It's time to move. And don't you dare bring that cat."

I had so many questions, but Nic seemed determined to avoid them. After we argued for several minutes about my cat, he hustled me down to the square. Tommy followed of his own accord, making the whole argument moot.

Nic sent me into the nearest store to buy more food and water. We were about to head to the other side of the province; we might as well make a mark online and send Asia in the opposite direction. I refilled our bag, picked up a battery pack for the phone and some canned food for Tommy, and ordered two large coffees. I paid without issue; the clerk barely even made eye contact.

I stole a glance at the messaging app as I hurried back to Nic. It was still signed in under his username, so most of the unread messages were from people I didn't know. But I did recognize the top two users. Ephesus had sent a "thank you," followed by:

PLEASE TELL BLUE FIRE TO CALL ME AS SOON AS YOU CAN SAFELY GET ONLINE

I swallowed a nip of guilt and switched over to the chat with Stanyard. In his usual fashion, he'd sent a message every few hours. Most of them were reminders that he was praying for me, but the most recent message was less encouraging:

FYI, GREEN DRAGON HAS NOT CHECKED IN. NO ONE KNOWS WHERE HE IS. BE CAREFUL

I paused on the sidewalk outside of the store and worked my jaw. That meant one of two things: Either Jayde had gotten arrested at the party, or he had escaped and was still in Beijing. Seeing as there was no mention of an arrest on the news—or, apparently, on Jayde's file—I had a sinking feeling it was the latter.

I clicked in the box and prepared to send Stanyard a quick message, but before I could figure out what to say, a text came through.

It was from Asia.

YOU MUST BE SO TIRED AND HUNGRY

I froze. She knew I was online; she must have been watching my file and saw the purchase.

YOU DON'T HAVE TO DO THIS. YOU KNOW I WON'T HURT YOU.

Do I know that? I wondered. She sent one final plea.

JUST COME HOME. I'M WORRIED ABOUT YOU.

I quickly took the phone offline and hid it in my backpack.

I joined up with Nic where he waited on a nearby bench. He was trying and failing to keep Tommy out of his lap. Knowing we'd get complaints if I took a cat on the bus, I convinced Tommy to climb in my backpack; he was so scrawny that he fit even with the Bible and other objects stashed in there.

With my new pet safely hidden, we ran to the closest bus stop. It was midday, and the lines weren't long. We were able to fit on the next bus. We rode it across the neighborhood to the subway line that would carry us south.

I daren't talk about an illegal religion while we were crammed in a train with dozens of other people, so I let Nic savor his coffee in silence. We cut across the province, then jumped on another bus that took us deep into the heart of a riverside district.

The neighborhood was old, but not in the smoggy, over-processed way of the inner city. As I watched out the window at the passing streets, it was like time was getting stripped away in layers, revealing the ancient civilization that had once thrived in this valley. The skyrises faded into the background, replaced by narrow two- and three-story homes that crowded the riverbank. Their foundations dipped into the canal, and stains on their white-washed walls revealed the height of past floods. Willows crowded for space in between the houses, their lacy leaves dragging in the water, and red-and-gold lanterns dangled from the gray roofs. The whole town was peaceful and strangely quiet, as if time moved as slowly as the ripples on the water.

The bus let us off on a street corner. We crossed a bridge to the other side of the river, and I paused in the middle and appreciated the view of the sunlight warming the greenish water. "It's beautiful," I commented, and turned to Nic for confirmation.

He barely gave it a passing glance. "Come on."

We found a secluded park and stopped under the shade of a mulberry tree to eat. I let Tommy out of my backpack and gave him a can of food, which he licked clean.

Meanwhile, I tried to muster up the courage to consume another protein bar. After two days of wandering, the sugary packaged food wasn't cutting it. As much as I hated to admit it, Asia was right; I *was* tired and hungry. If I didn't have any sense, it would be tempting to go back to the Nolan estate.

I told Nic about the text messages. He grunted and crushed his empty water bottle. "Hopefully this Jael character can get us temporary files—or has access to a secured line. We're not going anywhere until we can get online without Asia knowing."

I reached down to stroke Tommy's back and weighed my words carefully. "So… how *do* you know about this church, anyway?"

Nic didn't fall for it. "I told you that you only got to ask one question, and you've expended that credit for the day."

Unfortunately for him, I was feeling equally stubborn. "You know I'm just going to keep bugging you until you answer me, right?"

He grumbled, but it was the kind of grumble that told me I was about to get my way. "It's not rocket science," he said without looking at me. "You've met my parents."

"Yeah, and I've also met you."

He turned to stare at me, making me wonder if my comment had cut deeper than intended.

He shifted his attention back to the uneven brick road. "My dad used to come to Beijing for business once or twice a year. The factory owner is—was—a partner of his. Dad encouraged him to let people meet in his building. In exchange, Dad granted him an exclusive contract to produce a patented part for his science stations."

"He bribed him," I clarified.

Nic blinked, as if he'd never thought of it that way. "I guess so."

I chewed the last bite of my protein bar as this information cast new light on the gentle, innocent man I'd met back in Boston. I knew Mr. Von had been another person before the neurosurgery, but this story painted an entirely different picture than the one I'd been imagining. This Mr. Von was intelligent, powerful, cunning—not unlike his son.

It also made me think of the massive bank account I had sitting at home. For the first time, I wondered if there was more I should be doing with my money.

Nic continued his story before I could fully process the thought. "When I was a teenager, he used to bring me along on his trips whenever he could, so I've been there several times. If they're still meeting at the factory, hopefully they'll remember Dad's name and let us in."

"And if they're not still meeting there?"

"Then we're no worse off than we started—and maybe they know where another meeting place is." Nic shrugged, but I could tell the gesture was forced. His voice was so artificially calm that it sounded robotic. "They were still meeting there when I came back in college."

I tried to pinpoint where that fit in the timeline of Nic's life. "What happened?"

"What do you mean?" he returned, but his eyes were avoiding mine.

I leaned forward, trying to get in his line of vision. "Nic, I'm not stupid."

"I didn't say you were."

He actually had—several times—but that was beside the point. "I can do basic math. If you went to church in college, that means you were going without your dad. Which kind of implies you wanted to go."

He swiveled to face me. "What is it you want, Phil? What do you want me to say?"

Tact was getting me nowhere, so I decided to come right out with it. "I want to know why you're not a Christian anymore."

He drew back from me, putting as much distance between us as he could without getting up and walking away. "If you're looking for a Judas Iscariot moment so you can make my tragic backstory fit in your tidy little sense of morality, then you're not going to find it. Stop trying to justify me."

"I'm not," I snapped, because that truly *wasn't* what I wanted. It didn't have to make sense, and I certainly didn't have to agree. I just wanted to understand.

"Then why do you care?" he challenged.

"Because I care about you."

The words slipped out before I could filter them, but I didn't take them back. They were true.

The anger evaporated from his face, leaving a void in his expression. I took advantage of his silence and forged ahead. "Look, I know this concept makes you want to throw up or whatever, but I care about you. You saved my life at the party. And before that, you tried to help me with my dad. You even 'adopted' me. For these past few months, you've… you've been there for me."

As I rambled on, my voice began to shake. Not because I was nervous, but because I was terrified of how true my words really were. Ever since Rott, Nic *had* cared about me—in his own sarcastic, socially inept way. To the best of his ability, he was trying to protect me.

And I owed him an apology.

He grimaced and looked royally uncomfortable. "Phil, look—"

I put up my hand and cut him off. I wasn't going to let him avoid the conversation, not this time. "No, just listen. I need you to hear this. I need you to know that I'm sorry. For what I said on the phone."

I flinched as the memories of that heated, hurtful conversation echoed in my ears. I swallowed and forced as much intention into my voice as I could, struggling to rebuild the wall I'd torn down with my words.

"I don't think you're a coward. I think you're brave, and I know you risked your reputation and the base when you agreed to become my legal guardian. Let alone when you came back to Earth to save me."

Tommy wrapped himself around Nic's ankles, as if agreeing with my assessment of his character. Nic shoved him away. "Philadelphia—"

"Just listen, please," I begged. "I know you care about me. And… it was wrong of me to say that you don't understand what it's like to be unassimilated. I see that now. With everything you told me about Asia and your parents… You do understand."

As soon as the words left my mouth, I realized I'd answered my own question. *That's* what had happened: Asia. Asia was the wedge that had come between Nic and the Lord. I tried to imagine what he must have felt. He had done what he thought was right—made the courageous choice to delete Red Rain—only to have the woman he loved kill his parents in retaliation. If that had happened to me, I would have questioned my ethics, too.

Or maybe that wasn't what happened. Maybe I was completely wrong about him.

Maybe… it didn't matter.

I looked up at him. He'd gone eerily silent. He was still staring at me, his eyebrows twisted in a gesture I didn't have a translation for.

I had no idea how to end this awkward conversation I'd started, so I settled for repeating myself. "I just… want you to know I'm sorry. I apologize for the things I said, and I don't think of you like that."

He looked down at my cat, who was attacking a fallen leaf. "I know you don't," he said after a minute, and I realized, in retrospect, that was the best reaction I could have hoped for in the situation.

We waited in the park until it was nearly five o'clock, then walked the rest of the way to the factory. It was situated on the outskirts of town, where the river widened and picked up enough energy to power the industry. The building had aged a little less gracefully than the town; its pipes and smokestacks were bleeding rust, and the windows were clouded, with many boarded over. But the factory was still in full operation, with steam chugging into the sky and the omnipresent grind of machinery filling the air, which I hoped was a good sign.

Nic explained that service happened at five o'clock, with shift change concealing the flow of people in and out of the building. The dock gates were open, and a stream of people converged towards the security checkpoint like a dammed river. Most of them wore the blue uniforms and white hardhats of factory workers, but I caught a few civilians and office staff mixed in, their coats pulled up and their hats pulled down to conceal their faces. I hid Tommy in my backpack and stayed close to Nic.

He waited until the crowd had dwindled and then joined the back of the line. We were almost the last ones to approach the gate.

An exhausted teenager who looked far too young to have a job like this squinted at us through the glass of the security booth. "Name?"

"Von Nieuwenhuyse," Nic said, enunciating carefully.

I couldn't see the kid's expression behind the face mask he wore, but I could see the twitch of his bushy eyebrows. He looked down at his desk. He pushed his tablet aside, revealing a water-stained ledger that was nearly buried under the other paraphernalia on the desk. I could see the list held a mix of Mandarin and English surnames.

The teen scanned the paper with his finger. "I don't see you on tonight's shift," he said, English poor but translatable.

"Maybe you don't understand me." Nic leaned closer to the speaker in the glass. "I said Von Nieuwenhuyse, as in Dr. Paul Von Nieuwenhuyse."

I held my breath while the kid recalibrated, and then his eyes lit up. He tapped his tablet, and the keypad on the outside of the security booth lit up. "Fingerprints, please," he instructed.

My heart stopped. *No, God, no.*

Nic took a step back, and the teenager misinterpreted his hesitation. "For internal records only," he assured. "You understand."

I did understand—except that Nic's fingerprint would set off a security warning and alert everyone that he was wanted criminal, internal system or not.

"He's with me," I volunteered, and shoved my way forward. I pressed my thumb to the keypad before Nic could stop me.

The screen chirped, and the teenager nodded. "You're good. Now you, please, sir."

Nic put his hands up. "Look, I really just need to speak to your manager. It won't take long. He's a friend of my father's."

The teen finally picked up on the fact that something was wrong. I saw the shift in his posture—the straightening of his back, the narrowing of his eyes. "I'm sorry, sir, but I can't do that."

"It's important," Nic insisted, and even I could tell that he was getting desperate. "You don't understand—my father sent me."

"I'm sorry, sir," the kid repeated. He slid his hand beneath the desk. "But I don't know you."

I saw what he was reaching for—a panic button—and knew I had to do something before we caused a scene.

"Then tell him *I* want to see him," I declared, putting myself in front of Nic.

The teen hesitated, his finger over the button. "And who are you?"

"Andromeda—" Nic threatened, reaching for me.

I shrugged out of his grasp and glanced around to make sure no one was watching. I knew what I was about to do was dangerous, but we didn't have a choice. We had to get in and see Jael. She was our only hope.

I faced the kid and rolled up my right sleeve, revealing my thunderbird tattoo. "I am Blue Fire."

11: NIC

The ticket boy squinted at Phil like he didn't believe her, and for a desperate second, I prayed that he wouldn't.

But before I could regain control of the situation, Phil reached up and popped her blue contacts out, revealing her natural brown eyes. The kid uttered an oath in Mandarin.

I copied him, swearing loudly in English and hoping everyone, especially Phil, heard.

The kid yanked his face mask off and threw it on the counter. "Hurry—this way."

I was just about to grab Phil's arm and pull her in the opposite direction when the kid punched a button on the wall of the control booth. I heard the squeak and groan of tired hinges and turned to see the massive dock gates closing.

I swore again, not that anyone was deterred by my objections.

The kid scrambled out of the control booth and took off across the yard at a run, waving at us to follow. He shouted in Mandarin at the guards loitering around the lot. His words were too urgent for me to translate, but I understood the gist when the guards fell into step beside us, weapons ready.

Phil, for once in her life, seemed wholly unafraid.

The kid led us around the back of the factory to a shipping entrance. The garage door stood open, as if they'd been waiting to receive us this entire time. The grind of the factory was unfiltered now, made worse by the dissonant chatter of workers. We ran up the dock and past the endless rows of lockers, where a few straggling employees were suiting up.

I tried to grab Phil's shoulder and hold her back. "What in the world are you—"

I stopped when I saw one of the guards glance at me. I read the frown on his face and saw his finger slide into position on the trigger and knew I'd better not try anything here.

We followed the kid up a flight of stairs and across a catwalk that overlooked the production floor. Rows of blindingly lit workstations lined the cavernous concrete room. Several hundred gloved workers labored in tandem with bright yellow robotic arms, manipulating trays of circuitry. I was extremely familiar with the blueprint for the machinery and could tell that it had changed little in the last decade; clearly, the factory was still producing the coveted part for interstellar space stations.

I swallowed an irrational burst of rage. Apparently, Tang, the factory owner, had fared better than my father.

We descended in an elevator to the basement, where the mess hall was located. I struggled to stay in control of my faculties as unwelcome muscle memory kicked in. I remembered everything. The slight jerk as the rusty elevator hit the bottom. The smell of bland, over-processed food and hot plastic. And the moan of collective prayer in several languages, one of which I wish I didn't understand.

The elevator doors ground open, revealing a service in full swing. The stuffy, fluorescent-lit hall was packed, even more so than it would be during lunch hour. People of all ages and races crowded the aisles in between the yellowed plastic tables, while parents balanced their little children on the pea-green chairs so they could get a better view. I noted that attendance had at least doubled, if not tripled, since the last time I visited. I would have expected the opposite trend.

At the far end of the hall, on the podium normally used for announcements, a couple of pastors paced back and forth, reading from contraband Bibles while they joined the throng in prayer. I scanned the crowd for familiar faces, searching for anyone I even remotely trusted, but saw no one.

A few guards stood watch inside the entrance. The ticket boy grabbed one of them and whispered in his ear. The soldier snapped to attention and turned to Phil. After a moment of regarding her in wonder, he saluted. His partners copied the gesture.

I felt my blood boil at the same time my skin went cold with fear.

One of the guards gestured for Phil to follow him. Before I could object, she stepped forward, and he led her away. I quickly lost sight of her as they wove through the congested crowd. I sensed the shift in the atmosphere—the worship tapering off as people took notice of the stranger and began to whisper. I felt eyes looking in my direction and backed up, but the guards blocked the hall to the elevator.

Suddenly, Phil appeared on the podium at the opposite end of the room. The guard bent and spoke to her, and she obliged, taking off her backpack and rolling up her right sleeve.

"Phil, don't!" I yelled, not realizing until too late that I'd spoken aloud. Several people turned to me, but I was quickly forgotten when one of the pastors took a mic and called for attention.

As if Jesus had just commanded the storm to cease, the whole room stilled. In the brief second of silence, I tried to catch Phil's gaze.

Don't do this!

She didn't see me. The pastor cupped the microphone and announced something in Mandarin. A murmur washed over the crowd, punctuated by several shrieks of surprise.

Phil frowned at the pastor, not understanding. He grinned and repeated himself in English.

"Blue Fire has returned!"

Then he stepped aside, leaving her center stage, her tattoo bared for all the world to see.

The crowd devolved into a tornado of cheers, claps, and stomps. The guards on the sidelines shouted military slogans and saluted. A small child near me started jumping up and down on the table and squealing about the "thunderbird," at the encouragement of her older siblings.

Phil stared at the crowd, petrified. For one final moment, she was the scared, pitiful teenage girl I thought I knew.

And then she smiled.

The pastor handed her the microphone. She took it and strode to the edge of the podium like she had been preparing for this moment her entire life. The crowd hushed unbidden, a few excited whispers escaping as they waited, no doubt expecting some great speech.

I was horrified when she opened her mouth and gave them one.

"God is for you."

The words were quiet, hesitant, as if she were testing the ice with them. She let them hang there while she frowned in thought, no doubt giving the voice in her head time to catch up. When she spoke again, I could tell the words were not her own.

"He sees you. He knows your faithfulness. He knows how much you have risked to be here, and He wants you to know that He is *for* you. And greater is He that is in us than he that is the world!"

Her volume skyrocketed, just in time to avoid getting drowned out by the applause and cheers of *Amen!* that erupted. She rattled on without waiting for them to quiet down.

"Because *His* is the name that's above every other name, every government, every spirit, every demonic force. He is above the United, above communism, above socialism, above war—and He will *always* be victorious!"

Such grand words from a little girl who had no strength or power to back them up, and the people were delirious over them. She leaned out over the crowd, so far she was in danger of falling off the podium. "He is for you, and He will fight for you. Now is not the time to back down. Now is not the time to surrender!"

I winced. I knew she didn't mean for her words to be political, but I could tell that the better part of the crowd—especially the teenagers—took them that way. I saw the soldiers exchanging nods and slaps on the back while the youth pumped fists. The damage had been done.

Phil abruptly came off her spiritual high. She blinked, like she'd returned to this reality and remembered who she was and where she was. She backed away from the edge of the podium and flushed bright red, but the smile remained on her face.

She turned to hand the microphone back to the pastor. He didn't take it. Instead, he put his hands out in front of him, one on top of the other, and bowed.

The room fell silent as the rest of the leadership on the platform followed suit. Slowly, like a wave rolling into the shore, the crowd copied. One by one, everyone, even the little children, stacked their hands and bent their backs, until the entire room was bowing.

Except me.

She finally caught my eye over the dipped heads of the crowd. I glared at her, knowing my opinion was clearly written on my face.

You have no idea what you've done.

"Von?"

I turned. A Chinese man about my age pushed his way towards me as the crowd began to disperse. He halted and frowned at me.

"Sorry," he said, blinking as if he'd seen a ghost. "You just look so much like your father. Nic, was it? May I call you that?"

"Please don't call me anything longer," I returned, and accepted the handshake he offered. I felt at a sore disadvantage since I couldn't return the favor of name recognition.

He mercifully helped me out. "Tang Lanzhou."

Tang—the factory owner's surname. Vague recollections of a younger Tang shadowing meetings with my father came back to me, and I realized this must be the factory owner's son. We were comparable in age, which meant we'd shared an assumed companionship while our fathers talked business and civil disobedience. To call him a "friend" would have been much too forward, but if he remembered my father, that was a step in the right direction.

"What are you doing here?" Lanzhou dropped his voice to a volume intended only for me to hear.

"Trying and failing to keep my legal dependent from starting a war" would have been the correct answer. I glanced back at the podium. The crowd had come back to life and was now swarming the platform, chattering and calling out to Phil. Everyone, especially the teenagers, was clamoring to shake her hand. Phil seemed to have forgotten that she was a walking bomb and accepted the friendship enthusiastically.

Lanzhou followed my gaze. "How do you know Blue Fire?"

I groaned. "My enemies call me 'Q,'" I admitted, and hoped that would be enough. My full involvement in Blue Fire's history—namely, that I was the nameless "governor" who had invented Red Rain—was not information I was eager to divulge.

Thankfully, Lanzhou didn't ask for more details. "And what are you two doing in Beijing?"

"Mission gone awry," I grunted, which was actually the complete truth.

He paled at the implications. "She shouldn't be here. The entire Council wants her dead."

I couldn't agree more—although, I realized in a cruel irony, it wasn't an entirely accurate statement. The rest of the Beijing leadership might want Phil to hang, but Asia wanted her alive, which was even worse.

"That's actually why we're here," I said, seizing the opportunity to shift the conversation. I glanced around to make sure no one was eavesdropping before confessing, "We need to get off the grid. We're looking for Jael."

The way his eyes flickered told me I'd hit the jackpot. At least Jael *was* a real person—that was a start.

"Who told you that name?" he demanded, but not unkindly.

"Narissa."

If he knew her, he didn't let it on. "Jael's not in town right now," he said, cautiously, his eyes also taking a warning lap around the room. "But I can call one of her people."

I wasn't thrilled about the prospect of being run through this mystical woman's secretary, but it was better than anything else I had to go on at this point. "Can she help?"

"She's probably the only person who can help you." The bitter tone of his voice told me that our situation was as dire as I feared. "And for Blue Fire, she will," he added, answering my other unspoken question. Phil had been right about one thing—these people did love her.

You're all fools.

"We need to get you out of sight before she causes a scene," Lanzhou hissed.

We were well past that stage, in my opinion. I looked up and watched as a woman bowed before Phil and held out a gift; it looked like a piece of jewelry of some kind. Phil accepted the offering reverently.

"You can stay at my house. There's plenty of room." Lanzhou touched my shoulder.

I made no attempt to be polite as I shrugged out of his grasp. "We're fine, thank you. Just tell us when and where to meet Jael."

"Nic, please, I can tell you're not fine. I don't know what happened out there, but you look terrible. When was the last time you slept?"

I'd snatched a few hours last night, which might have been enough, had I not been sleeping outside, on concrete, and in the rain. I instinctively reached up to touch my unshaven chin and realized he had a point. We couldn't spend another night on the street. We needed showers and a full meal, and I needed to borrow a device so I could get online and call Ephesus.

"Fine. And thank you," I added for the sake of decorum, even though I was feeling anything but grateful.

He beamed. "It would be an honor to host you and Blue Fire."

I'm sure it would, I thought as I forced a smile.

He turned. "Come on—this way."

One night, I promised myself as I followed him through the crowd. We would stay one night so we could get online, make arrangements with Jael, and rest. Then we were leaving before Phil caused any more damage.

I looked back to see a guard hustling her off stage. *Just one night*, I repeated, *and then Blue Fire is retiring for good.*

12: PHILADELPHIA

My head swam as I received an endless stream of handshakes, bows, and salutes. It wasn't that I wasn't present in the moment; in fact, it was almost like I was *too* present. The people in front of me seemed larger than life, and all I could focus on was the expressions on their faces and the inflections in their voices—things they probably didn't even notice about themselves.

All the while, the words I'd spoken into the mic kept echoing around in my head, louder than ever, as if the Holy Spirit never stopped talking. All I could think about was how much God *loved* these people, and how precious they were to Him, and how much He wanted to protect and prosper them. I wanted to tell them all that, look each of them in the eye and remind them who their God was. But the crowd was so thick and excited that I couldn't have gotten a word in had I wanted to, so I just accepted their affection as my spirit continued to spin out of my control.

I jerked out of my stupor when a lady pressed something cold into my hands. I looked down at it: It was a beautiful bangle made of solid jade.

My heart went to my throat. "No, please," I said, pushing it back.

She smiled and closed my fingers around the jewelry. "It's a symbol of protection," she insisted. "So, when you wear it, remember that we're all praying for you."

I squeezed the bracelet over my hand and felt the weight settle on my wrist. "Thank you," I whispered, suddenly too overwhelmed to say more.

There was an eruption of chatter from the other women standing by, and I saw several pull their own bangles off their wrists. One by one, women walked up to the platform and laid their jewelry at my feet: bracelets, pendants, even earrings. My refusals fell on deaf ears. All I could do was stare at the growing pile of precious green stone and murmur endless thank you's as my emotions caved in on me like a breaking wave.

A voice came from behind me. "Blue Fire?"

I turned to see one of the pastors bowing to me. It was the one who had handed me the microphone. He was perhaps forty, with a youthful charm to his expression that wholly disagreed with his slightly grayed hair. "Tang Bowen. Do you prefer Blue Fire or Miss Smyrna?"

"Just Philadelphia, please," I said. If these people knew my secret identity, I was going to take the rare opportunity to use my birth name.

He smiled warmly. "You're to be a guest at my family's house tonight. This way, please. Don't worry, I'll send someone to collect your things."

I turned to follow him. A guard flanked me and hustled me off the stage, eliciting several cries of protest from the crowd.

Nic met us backstage, along with several more guards and another Asian businessman. One of the soldiers held out my jacket and backpack. "Your bag, miss..." He hesitated. "It's... meowing."

"Tommy!" I cried, remembering. Figuring I could get away with just about anything at this point, I unzipped my bag and took my cat into my arms. He howled in protest and tried to lunge towards Nic. I hissed a reprimand and adjusted my grip on his bony frame.

The Asian man laughed. "I see we need to set out three extra places tonight. Tang Lanzhou." Since my hands were full, he forewent a handshake and bobbed his head instead. "Our family is old friends of the Vons."

I remembered what Nic had said about the factory owner and deduced that these men must be related. The family resemblance between Bowen and Lanzhou was slight but noticeable, making me wonder if they were cousins. The knowledge that they knew Mr. Von instantly made me feel more at peace. "Very pleased to meet you," I said.

"The honor is all ours," Lanzhou returned with a smile. "Come on—you must be exhausted from your journey."

It was phrased tactfully, but I was sure our situation must be apparent. If nothing else, the pungent smell of my muddy clothing must have given it away.

The thought of a warm bath, a full meal, and a real bed made my heart dizzy. I turned to Nic as we followed the guards down the hallway. "See?" I whispered after Lanzhou and Bowen had gotten a step ahead of us. "I told you they would help us."

He didn't answer. I searched his face for a reaction, but there was none. His expression was completely blank, which either meant he'd given up—or he'd made a deliberate effort to mask his emotions.

I shook off a shiver of nervousness. We would talk later, I was sure, but even he couldn't deny that I was right. No one could deny what happened back there.

We followed the Tangs out to the docks, where I paused to hide my tattoo and put my blue contacts back in, just in case. They led us down the narrow boardwalk that flanked the river, back into the residential district.

The sun was still warm in the sky, but it had dipped below the houses, silhouetting the whole street in soft pink and orange. Shutters were opened to the cooling air, and families gathered in laughing clusters on their verandas. I heard plates clattering and smelled foreign spices and was suddenly reminded how hungry I was. Tommy mewed and struggled to get down.

The Tangs led us under a quaint stone arch that opened to a small courtyard. It was a stunning traditional residence in immaculate condition. A ring of two-story wooden homes boxed in the patio. The shutters were carved with traditional geometric designs, and the balconies on the upper floors were decorated with lanterns and ornate railings. A covered veranda overlooked the canal. It held a long table, around which were gathered at least a dozen people.

"Ba!" Lanzhou called, darting ahead of us. "You won't believe who I've brought you."

The elderly man at the head of the table rose and came to meet us. Lanzhou took his hands and guided him to Nic. "This is Nic Von Nieuwenhuyse, Von's son—you remember?"

Mr. Tang's face exploded in a grin that seemed too big for his slight frame to contain. "If I didn't, that mustache would remind me. You're a spitting image—it's like he's back from the dead."

Nic hesitated, clearly waffling between familiarity and formality. He finally settled on a half bow. "Tang *Xiansheng*."

"None of that," the man snorted. He reached out and yanked Nic into a hug that looked surprisingly strong. I choked back a laugh as every muscle in Nic's body went rigid.

Mr. Tang gave him a firm pat on the back. "You have our condolences. Your father is sorely missed."

"Thank you," Nic said, and relaxed—just a little.

Mr. Tang released him. "It's wonderful to have you back. What brings you to Beijing?"

Nic put up his hand. "We're not staying long—"

Bowen spoke on top of him. "That's our other surprise." He gently shoved me forward. "Blue Fire has come to honor our house tonight."

The other family members clustered around with a whisper of surprise. "Hi," I managed, having no idea what etiquette would be appropriate. "Honored to meet you."

The senior Tang beamed. "The honor is all ours," he said, and bowed. His family copied him.

"Please, that's not necessary," I begged. I was a little miffed that Nic, the one person who *didn't* want a hug, was the only one who got one. I squeezed

Tommy for consolation—a little too hard for his tastes. He yelped and dug all of his claws into my arm. I instinctively let go, and he leapt to the ground and darted across the courtyard.

"Tommy!" I cried. Logically, I knew he was just a stray, but it still hurt to be rejected so quickly.

"Don't worry, he'll come home when he's ready," Lanzhou assured me with a chuckle.

"Which is hopefully never," Nic muttered. I glared at him, but he intentionally looked elsewhere.

An elegant older woman—Mrs. Tang, I assumed—stepped forward. "Come," she said to me while beckoning at two other female family members. "Let's get you cleaned up."

They led me upstairs to a bathroom, where I took an absolutely heavenly shower. Despite the fact that the bathroom was ancient—the water was slightly cold and tasted metallic—I'd never been so grateful for running water in my life. While I scrubbed and conditioned my hair, Mrs. Tang threw my disgraced outfit in the wash and sent a niece to scrounge up a change of clothes for me. The shorts and t-shirt she brought barely fit, but I was thrilled to be wearing something that smelled of soap instead of sweat. I slid on the borrowed pair of house shoes and went to join the family on the veranda.

Night was falling, and a cool breeze swept across the open deck. The canal glowed orange-red with the light from a hundred lanterns. The windows on almost every house along the block were open, allowing the laughter and chatter of the neighbors to mingle with ours.

We all crammed around the long wooden table while Mrs. Tang served a vibrant feast that never seemed to end. There were heaps of steamed rice, mounds of colorful sauteed vegetables, and crispy chunks of tofu simmering in red-hot sauce. There were more dumplings than I could count and a fish that had been broiled whole. I sat between two of the Tang daughters, who giggled and showed me how to use chopsticks while we all ate from the same bowls in communal harmony.

Nic, for his part, looked significantly less grumpy with his hair washed and his mustache and goatee returned to their natural order. He wasn't very talkative; he only engaged when Lanzhou cornered him with a question. But he ate enthusiastically and seemed less annoyed with the world (and me) than usual.

Conversation at the table steered mercifully clear of politics, in part because we were outside within potential earshot of the neighbors. But as soon as the younger family members had wandered off, Bowen lured me into the kitchen under the pretense of washing dishes.

"Is everything all right?" he said in a tone barely loud enough to be heard over the water running in the sink.

I switched the faucet off and plunged my hands into the soapy water. "You're going to need to be more specific."

"With Operation Blue Fire." He dropped another plate into the sink, causing a tuft of bubbles to float away. "I saw your last video, and it's been over a week since you were online. Is there something we should know?"

I wished I had an answer for him, but the truth—that my allies had tried to kill me and we were on the run from the most powerful woman in China— seemed like information I shouldn't reveal yet. "Everything's under control," I said, which was probably the biggest lie I'd ever told.

"What in the world are you doing? Get out of the kitchen! You're our guest!" Lanzhou appeared in the doorway with a stack of bowls.

"I don't mind," I protested. In fact, doing mundane chores sounded relaxing.

He wasn't having it and elbowed me out of the way. "Let me handle this. I can do the dishes—we need you to focus on other things."

Bowen handed me a towel. "He's right. You need to record a video. People are talking."

I looked down at my hands and took my time wiping away every last trace of soap. "What are they saying?"

"That you quit." Bowen's statement was factual, without any accusation, but I could hear the uncertainty in his voice. "They're saying you got scared and the operation is canceled."

My heart shattered as he confirmed my worst fears. The movement was failing—and it was all because of me. All because I listened to Jayde instead of the Holy Spirit.

But it wasn't too late, was it? "The operation's still on," I insisted, and desperately hoped it was true.

"Then tell them that. Please," Bowen pleaded. "They need to hear from you. I... need to hear from you."

I looked up to find him staring at me. Abruptly, he chuckled.

"What?" I prodded.

He grinned boyishly. "Sorry, I just still can't believe *Blue Fire* is in my kitchen."

"And you almost made her wash the dishes," Lanzhou chided.

"I volunteered," I reminded him, and we all shared a laugh.

Bowen sobered and leaned against the cold oven. "Why are you really in Beijing? I know Nic didn't come just to see us."

That's an understatement. I swallowed and struggled to come up with a plausible excuse.

"Nic said it was a mission gone awry," Lanzhou volunteered when I went silent for too long.

That was certainly one way to put it. "I can't tell you," I managed, which was, regrettably, the truth.

"We understand," Lanzhou said. His voice was slow and gentle, as if I was a scared rabbit that might bolt. "We just want to help if we can."

"You can trust us—you can trust all of us," Bowen added, too quickly. "My entire congregation supports the operation. I've got six more churches across the city willing to move, and several more in nearby provinces. All you have to do is say the word."

My heart started beating fast but steady, like my pulse had slipped into a higher gear. The thought that there were churches in Beijing—whole congregations of people I'd never met—that supported me made my head spin. Jayde had told me that the operation had global support, but it was just a statistic, the faceless analytics on my videos. Now I had seen it with my own eyes.

I twirled the jade bangle around my wrist. These people were willing to risk their lives for a cause *I* started. Was I really going to drop off the grid and leave them all behind? Did God really give me all of this influence and power just to have me throw it away? Was Blue Fire really a mistake?

Bowen didn't seem to think so. "Please, if there's ever anything you need, just say so."

What I needed was to talk to somebody. Someone who understood me and believed I was destined to do good in the world. Someone who believed that God had been working miraculously in my life.

And that person was not Nic.

"I need to get online," I said, looking up. "And I can't make a mark on my file. Do you have a device I can borrow?"

"Of course. Follow me." Bowen turned and led the way out of the kitchen.

The night had grown dark, and the rest of the family had retired to bed—as had Nic, apparently. Both the veranda and the courtyard were empty as I followed Bowen to the hall that faced the street. He fetched a tablet from a locked drawer in Mr. Tang's study, then led me up the stairs to the second floor. The narrow corridor was divided into several small bedrooms, but the cramped space was no less elegant than the rest of the house. The dark wood paneling, silkscreen doors, and carved shutters gave the dimly lit hallway the air of a temple.

"I put your belongings in here." Bowen opened the door closest to the stairs. "I believe Nic's staying at the end of the hall."

I glanced down the hallway. There was no light shining from under the door; had he fallen asleep already?

"Thank you," I said, turning back to Bowen. "For everything."

He beamed. "Anything for Blue Fire. Most of the family sleeps in the hall on the other side of the courtyard—come get us if you need anything."

I smiled gratefully. He gave a slight bow and descended the stairs.

I stepped into the bedroom and shut the door behind me. The room was narrow but beautifully decorated. The modest shelf bed was carved with silhouettes of dragons and clouds, and the nightstand and wardrobe were solid dark mahogany. The linens were muted shades of blue and turquoise, making the pile of pillows look like a pool of water. The silkscreen door to the tiny private balcony was open, filling the room with cool night air and the steady sound of the river.

I took a deep breath and let the peace of the quiet room wash over me. I felt my jaw unclench while the muscles all along my spine relaxed. It was as if my body, for the first time in three days, abruptly realized that we could stop running. We would be safe here—at least for tonight. *Thank you, Jesus.*

I sank down on the edge of the bed. Instantly, the cocoon of silk and cotton threatened to pull me in. I would have fallen asleep right then if my mind weren't fixated on more pressing matters.

I turned on the tablet, installed the messaging app Nic always used, and created a dummy profile. Thankfully, I had Stanyard's username memorized. I had no idea who this tablet was registered to or how good the Tangs' internet protection was, so I sent a generic message and hoped he wouldn't ignore the unfamiliar username.

IT'S ME. IS IT SAFE TO TALK?

I gripped the device, praying. Almost immediately, his avatar flashed green, and the device trilled.

I answered. "Stanyard!" I gasped, almost before my audio and video had connected.

"Philadelphia! Oh, praise God." His video came on, bringing me face to face with my best friend. He shoved his headphones back, causing his wild brown hair to spring up in all directions. It was so cute that I almost cried. "You're okay," he said, the inflection somewhere between a statement and a question.

"Yes, I promise. We're in a safe place, and Nic's with me." I searched his image, wishing he wasn't so far away. Stanyard would give me the hug I so desperately needed—and a kiss, if I were so inclined. "Are you okay? Where are you?"

"I'm fine," he insisted. "I'm on base right now."

I gasped. Base was the last place he should be. "Stanyard! You need to get out of there! Jayde—"

Someone else spoke in the background. "Is that her?"

I stiffened; I knew that Russian accent all too well. "Get away from him!"

He did the exact opposite. Lev shoved his way into the frame, leaning over Stanyard's shoulder and practically pushing my boyfriend out of the shot.

My blood ran hot and cold as I vacillated between betrayal and anger. Lev was Jayde's lackey, the very person who was supposed to pull the trigger if I failed the mission. Of all the people on base, he was the one I trusted the least; I knew where his loyalties lay. "Don't touch him!" I hissed.

Lev tipped his head to the side and squinted his faded blue eyes in that lost, pitiful expression that used to make me feel sorry for him. "But I wasn't—"

"No," I snapped. "You know what you did. How could you?"

"Whoa, Phil, it's okay." Stanyard put himself back in the center of the camera and tried to regain control of the situation. "He's with me. He told me everything."

"What?"

"As soon as you guys left, he told me what was going on. He would never have hurt me, Phil."

"But..." That revelation should have made me feel relieved—and it did—but it also made me more confused. "Why didn't he stop Jayde? He could have prevented all of this."

Lev answered for himself. "I didn't know what Jayde would do to you."

I swallowed. Stanyard handed him the device so I could see Lev's face as he continued. "He's a violent man, and I didn't know what he would do if I defied him. So I waited until you were gone."

"He sent false reports to Jayde so he would think everything was under control," Stanyard added. "It bought us time so Nic could get to you."

I took a deep breath as one of the fractured pieces of my life was made whole again: Lev *did* care, and he was every bit the innocent youth I thought he was. "Thank you," I said with as much sincerity and respect as I could.

His face twitched in a small smile. "I'm loyal to you, thunderbird," he said, and saluted.

Stanyard took the device back. I waited until Lev had walked away before speaking. "Does everybody know?"

Stanyard nodded. "The entire base knows what happened. Tower didn't tell them all the details, but he made it clear that Jayde forced you into a rogue mission against your will. Everyone's on your side."

I leaned my head against the bedpost as this new reality coalesced. Operation Blue Fire truly *was* still on schedule. Nothing had changed, not really. Jayde was dangerous, yes, but he was one man with limited supporters. If I released a statement before he did, I could remove him from power and pick the movement up where it left off.

"I need to record a video," I declared, sitting up.

"I agree," Stanyard said, but his voice had that slow pitch to it that told me he had reservations. "But what are you going to say?"

"That the operation is still on schedule. That Blue Fire is back. Don't you see? We can still do this." I searched his face, desperately hoping I wouldn't see doubt and disappointment. I got enough of that from Nic.

There wasn't any, but he still looked nervous as he replied, "I do see. But Phil—you're in Beijing. It's *not* safe there."

Maybe it wasn't—but that didn't mean I was without help. "I know, but Stanyard, there's *thousands* of people who support me here. I met a pastor today; he says he's got a dozen churches ready to move. And he's just the first person I talked to."

Stanyard's compassionate brown eyes went wide with the reverence that statement deserved. "What are you suggesting?"

I chewed my lip as the excitement swirled around in my head with nowhere to land. "I don't know. I just know this can't all be a mistake."

"I don't think it is," he agreed.

I struggled to detangle my thoughts from the guilt and shame that tainted them. "I know Nic thinks I should never have gone back to Earth, but... I just can't believe that God set this all up for nothing. I know trying to kill the General was a mistake, but... what if the rest wasn't?"

It had been Jayde's idea to assassinate the General, but all the events leading up to that had been out of his control. Andromeda Nolan, Asia, the invite to the party. Even now, I questioned whether Asia was truly interested in Nic's affections. Surely, there was more to her role in this; what if God had been pulling the strings the entire time?

Stanyard was silent for a long moment as we both let those thoughts run their course. "What are you saying?" he prodded.

It wasn't an accusation; it was an invitation. He knew what I was thinking, but I had to say it for myself.

"I'm saying... maybe I am supposed to be in Beijing."

I pinched my eyes shut as that admission caused the events of the past few weeks to warp and refocus, this time with entirely different colors.

"I don't know," Stanyard admitted with gentle honesty. "But whatever you do, I'll support you."

I opened my eyes and looked down at the screen. "Thank you." *This is why I love you.*

"Just promise me one thing. Before you do anything, talk to Nic."

I cringed, and he saw. "I know he's a pain sometimes, but he knows more about Beijing politics than the rest of us put together. He knows what you're dealing with, and he knows the city."

"I know, and I want to talk to him," I said, and it was the truth. "It's just… I feel like he hates everything about the revolution. And he certainly doesn't believe God's involved."

My heart ached at my own words. If only Nic would give God another chance, then, surely, he'd see what I saw.

"I know," Stanyard echoed. "But he cares about you."

I sighed. I couldn't deny that.

"I'm not saying take his word as the gospel, but… he wouldn't have come all the way back to Earth to save you if he didn't care. He sees something in you—even if it's not what you see."

I let the silence hang as I considered that.

"Plus… I'd feel a lot better if you talked to him."

I looked back down at the screen. Stanyard was smiling, but I could see the pain etched in the creases around his lips. "I'm sorry, Stanyard," I whispered. "For lying and leaving you out of the conversation."

"I know you are."

"Are you… mad?" I braced myself for his answer.

"It's fine," he said, but the look in his eyes told me he was holding back just because he didn't want to hurt me.

"No, tell me, please." I didn't really want to hear it, but I had to know. I couldn't live with open wounds between Stanyard and me. Not like I did with my father.

"I'd be lying if I said it didn't hurt when I found out you changed your mind literally *ten minutes* after we'd talked about it." Some of the pain slipped into his voice, and he took a breath, long and deep. "But that's between me and the Lord. It's not your job to manage my feelings."

I struggled to accept that as I marveled, yet again, at the work Jesus had done in Stanyard's life. This was not the same bitter teen I'd known in high school.

"Do you forgive me?" I asked after a moment.

"Yes," he said without hesitation, bringing our relationship full circle as we traded places. "Of course, I do."

I sank back against the pillows and let the strength of our relationship break my fall—again. "I love you so much. And I miss you."

"You have *no* idea how much I miss you." His eyes danced as he allowed a broad grin to take over his face. "When you get back, you owe me a first date. Like a real one."

I sucked in my breath as the butterflies did their elated dance in my stomach. A date? I tried to imagine what it would be like to eat at a candlelit table, or go to the movies, or walk in the park—but the images seemed fuzzy, like a watercolor illustration. Our relationship had been so plagued by fear and terror and pain—not to mention that one time I almost shot him in the face—that I couldn't even imagine what it would be like to just *date*. To just enjoy life.

"Deal," I said, and found myself blushing. The smile he was giving me wasn't making it easy for me to keep my composure.

Abruptly, I remembered who else was back in Boston. I sat up. "How's Dad?"

Stanyard hesitated, and I panicked. "What's wrong?"

"Nothing," he said, putting a hand up. "That's just it. He's doing *great*. Mrs. Nolan woke him up a few days ago, and he's making excellent progress."

"Really?" I gasped. All the air was choked out of my lungs as a hundred forgotten hopes suddenly resurrected in my soul. Was it possible that my dad might get to live a normal life? Had God given me my father back?

"He doesn't remember any people," Stanyard quickly clarified, "but he's gotten a lot of his vocabulary back, and he's flying through physical therapy. Andes installed some kind of brain implant, and he's been working with... what's his name? Data? I think he's the one who programmed your chip."

I flinched but nodded. Data was one of the many members of the Boston underground—a prominent one, judging by how active he had been on the radio. He was also a powerful programmer and was the one who had procured the General Secretary's DNA and coded the kill chip in my palm.

Stanyard didn't seem bothered by the man's resume. "They've both been working with him, and whatever they're doing is really helping. He was a different person this morning."

That was great news to me, but I caught the hitch in Stanyard's voice. "What is it?"

His eyes took a lap around the room, like they always did when he was hesitant to admit something. "I don't know. It's kind of scary how fast he's improving. Mrs. Nolan doesn't like it."

"Well, she doesn't believe in miracles." I did. *Thank you, Jesus.* "Can I see him?"

Stanyard grimaced. "I don't think that's a good idea tonight. He won't remember you, and he's still very disoriented. He was kind of... surly when I talked to him earlier."

My soul ached, but I didn't blame my father for his attitude. After all, he had just been raised from the dead and had no idea who he was, let alone who any of the people around him were. That would be terrifying, lonely, and frustrating.

I knew it was going to take time to put my father back together, even with all this progress. Would he ever regain his memories? I dared, for the first time in weeks, to hope that might be possible. But even if he didn't, at least he would have a chance at a dignified life. And that was all I could ask for.

"Tell him I love him," I said, blinking away tears that weren't quite happy. "Even if he doesn't know who I am."

Stanyard nodded.

I heard footsteps creaking in the hall and stood up. "I think Nic's awake—I'm going to go talk to him."

Stanyard nodded approvingly. "When can you call me again?"

"I don't know how long we're staying here, but it's definitely for tonight. I can call you when I get up."

"I'd like that a lot. I love you, Philadelphia."

I savored the sweet tone of his voice before returning the affection. "I love you too."

13: NIC

For a few surreal hours, it was as though the last twenty years had never happened.

Without waiting for permission, the Tangs assimilated me back into the fold. Lanzhou peppered me with questions as if we were under a moral obligation to catch up, while Mr. Tang treated me exactly as he would my father. They inquired about my work on Mars, and Mrs. Tang was mortified to learn that I was still romantically unattached. There was teasing and reminiscing and altogether too much laughter. The whole family acted as if nothing had changed.

As if I hadn't changed.

I excused myself as soon as I could without arousing suspicion. I pulled Lanzhou aside, out of earshot of his younger relatives. "I need to borrow a device."

He nodded and led me across the courtyard to his father's study. "Is your file marked?" he guessed, not easily fooled.

"Let's just say some people aren't happy about my involvement with Blue Fire."

He grunted and stooped to unlock the secret drawer hidden at the bottom of his father's massive desk. "I talked to Jael. She said it might be a few days before she can get here herself, but she's sending her people tomorrow."

A few days? There was no way I was staying in one place for that long. A thousand starry-eyed churchgoers knew Philadelphia was in the area; it was only a matter of time before word got out and Asia made her move. I wasn't going to leave the lights on for her.

My objections must have made it onto my face, because Lanzhou looked up and spoke emphatically. "I promise you're safe here."

"I might be," I said by way of concession, "but keeping Phil quiet is like trying to hide a cackle of starved hyenas. Trust me, I've tried."

He was not deterred by my visceral metaphor. "My father has bought off half the local police force to keep the church safe. He can cover Blue Fire for a couple of nights." He pulled out a tablet and locked the drawer. "I asked a few of the guards from the factory to come watch the house tonight if that makes you feel better."

It did, actually. But I wasn't about to admit it, so I changed the subject. "How protected is your internet traffic?"

"Well enough." He turned the tablet on and held it out to me. "Jael has 'tweaked' our router as a thank-you for what we're doing for the church, so most of our traffic bypasses the algorithm. Don't go logging into any government sites, but as long as you use this device, your calls won't be recorded."

That was all I needed to hear. I took the device, nodded a goodnight, and went to my room on the second floor. It was at the end of the hall, as far away from other people as possible—just where I liked it.

Phil hadn't made it up to her room at the top of the stairs yet. She was probably still in the kitchen, soaking up the companionship like a well-adjusted human. She and I needed to have a talk, but not before I called Ephesus.

I shut and latched my bedroom door and turned off the lights, hoping that would deter any intrusion. I had a suspicion that Asia knew about all my accounts, even the encrypted ones, so I installed a messaging app and created a dummy profile. I sent Ephesus a message and sat back to wait. If my calculations were correct, it should be about the same time at the base on Mars as it was in Beijing, which meant he was hopefully awake and paying attention to his phone.

It took him long enough—about fifteen minutes—but he eventually called me back. "Taking the night off?" I chided, not being shy with my annoyance.

"No, but I have a base to run." There was a beat before he enabled video, as if he wasn't sure if he wanted to see my face.

"Is everything all right? Have you had any trouble? Have you checked on the ionators in Wing 56 recently? They've been buggy—and don't forget the gravity augmenter in Wing 43 needs to be manually calibrated every six weeks."

Ephesus blinked. "Miss me, huh?"

"You? No. The base, yes." This was more emotional transparency than I was comfortable sharing with Ephesus, but I would have given anything to be sitting at my desk on Mars and slogging through mundane emails right now. I would have even volunteered to do paperwork.

"The base is fine," Ephesus insisted as he settled down in a desk chair. "As is Cea, in case you were going to ask."

"I wasn't. I'm quite confident that you're taking *excellent* care of her."

He smiled, as if he took that as a compliment. In a way, it was.

"Where's Phil?" he demanded after he'd stopped daydreaming about his new wife.

As if in answer, I heard a door shut further down the hall, and muffled voices came through the thin paneling. "Sounds like she's in the other room making kissy faces at her boyfriend."

"Stanyard?"

I rolled my eyes. As if Phil would give the time of day to literally anyone else.

"Well, tell her to call me."

I murmured to myself as the facts of the situation made themselves apparent. "Fascinating."

"I think what you meant to say was, 'Of course, brother-in-law.'"

"First of all, I don't care what the paper says; I'm not calling you that. Second of all, I just made the unfortunate deduction that she must *really* be in love with him."

"Well yeah," Ephesus fussed. "They've known each other since like the first grade. I'm not surprised—"

"Not that," I cut him off with a groan. Ephesus's innocence would be adorable—if he weren't a full-grown man. "I mean, she's only been online twice in the last seventy-two hours, and both times, she's chosen to call him instead of you."

We both let that fact marinate in the silence. Ephesus, because he was stunned by my flawless tact. Me, because I finally realized that this relationship *was* serious. And if I didn't want Phil to run off and elope without involving me—like her brother did—I'd better start taking it seriously.

Ephesus recovered from the slight. "Do me a favor and stay on Earth."

I sighed and brought my focus back to more immediate problems. "I may not have a choice."

Using as few gory details as possible, I briefed Ephesus on the issues regarding my file and my involvement with Asia.

He, naturally, took the opportunity to antagonize me. "Wow, didn't realize you were such a heartthrob."

"It's the facial hair. You should try it sometime," I returned, even though I was aware of the irony. My mustache was the one part about me that Asia *didn't* like. "But, even though I'm sure she's already started picking out curtains, I don't think it's me she wants. I think it's your sister."

Ephesus knotted his eyebrows together and waited for me to elaborate.

"I think she's using me as leverage to make sure Phil doesn't leave the city. The Nolans, the party invite—I think this was all an elaborate set-up to get Phil to Beijing."

"I have to admit that makes a lot more sense than her wanting revenge for unrequited love," Ephesus consented. "But what could she possibly want Phil for?"

"That's what I haven't figured out yet."

"I'm shocked," Ephesus said in a tone that suggested he actually was.

"I've been a little preoccupied with not dying."

"Then let's put our brains together. What do you know about Asia?"

"A lot of things I'd rather forget," I admitted. "But first and foremost, she's not stupid. She knows about Phil's multiple personalities, and she knows Jayde is with the underground. I'm sure she realized Phil had ulterior motives for coming to Beijing."

"She was going to let it happen," Ephesus surmised. "But why? What does she have to gain?"

Everything.

As soon as he said it, I knew.

"She wanted Phil to pull the trigger," I explained, spelling it out for both of us. "She wanted her father to die. She wants war."

Asia wanted power—she always had. But if she had tried to depose the General directly, she would have ignited resistance from the Council and her father's loyalists. She would have risked weakening the entire government, never mind the heyday the press would have had with her reputation. But if she could get Phil to start a war—or, better yet, assassinate the General—then she could seize power while barely lifting a finger. All the while, she could unite the government and the press against those pesky "unassimilated."

After all, if there was one thing Asia hated, it was an unnecessary mess.

Ephesus broke the heavy silence. "We need to get Phil off that planet."

"I couldn't agree more, but that's going to be easier said than done when Asia isn't the only one who wants her to start a war."

His eyes darkened. "Do you think the underground will try to keep her there?"

I glanced out the window at the shadowy street, reassuring myself that no one was within earshot. "I don't know, but they certainly won't be happy when they find out she's retiring for good."

And neither will the Lord, I abruptly remembered with a punch to the gut.

"What can I do to help?" Ephesus unwittingly interrupted.

"Sadly, probably nothing." I tried to turn my thoughts back to the conversation at hand, but it was like slogging through wet concrete. "There's a woman here who can supposedly get us new files without Asia knowing. I'm not optimistic, but I'm going to at least give her until tomorrow."

"And if she fails to deliver?"

"Then I need you working on backup plans. Money isn't the problem—Phil could buy the entire planet of Mars if she wanted." I snorted at the irony of that. "The problem is figuring out a way to transfer the money so that there is absolutely no electronic trail linking our old files to our new ones. Asia's watching our accounts like a hawk—if we transfer even a penny, she's going to investigate."

"So you need a creative programmer," Ephesus suggested.

"No, I need a *genius* programmer." I arched my eyebrow and waited for him to take the invitation.

He beamed. "I'm flattered."

"Don't let it go to your head. We also need a technician who's good about covering his tracks. We can't use Andes; Asia knows we've worked with him before."

"I'm on it," Ephesus declared. I saw him start typing in the background.

"Thank you," I said, and meant it. I paused and leaned my ear towards the wall; I could still hear Phil chattering away. I'd better go in there and get my obligatory lecture out of the way before she fell asleep. "I need to go," I announced to Ephesus.

"Call me tomorrow with an update," he said, sounding uncannily like me.

I figured our relationship had progressed to the point where we didn't need to bother with paltry etiquette like goodbyes, so I hung up.

Setting the tablet aside, I opened my door and started down the hall. Phil must have been hit with the same brain wave, because at that moment she came out of her room.

"Nic." She darted over and met me halfway. "Can we talk?"

"We're about to."

She looked down and fidgeted, apparently losing her nerve. "It's about today."

How nice of her to volunteer the subject. "Yes, about that." I crossed my arms, bracing myself for her pitiful excuses. "You deliberately disobeyed me."

She riffled through her repertoire of arguments and settled on the weakest one. "But I didn't... I didn't mean to."

"I'm going to need you to backspace that sentence and try again, because there was nothing unintentional about what you did. I explicitly told you not to identify yourself as Blue Fire. Do you have any idea how dangerous that was?" I fought to keep the pain out of my voice. Why couldn't she just listen to me for once? Did she really not see how much danger she was putting both of us in?

"I know, I know, I just… didn't want him to pull up your file and cause a scene."

"So you went and caused a bigger scene? Phil, you just identified yourself in front of a thousand people, and we don't know a single one of them. How do you know one of them isn't going to tell the police? And don't say it's because they all go to church."

The way she snapped her mouth shut told me that's exactly what she had been planning to say.

I rubbed my temples; I could already feel the pressure headache coming on, and we'd only been talking for sixty seconds. "Phil, you can't trust someone just because they go to church—or because they claim to be part of the underground."

"Maybe." She swallowed and made her voice calm and strong, as if that would impress me. "But that doesn't mean we're not in this together."

"No, that's *exactly* what that means."

"No, Nic, you don't understand! This is real—the revolution is real. They really believe in me."

"It's their funeral."

She clenched her fists, and her ears flushed red. "Nic, this isn't a joke! They trust me, and they *will* follow me. All I have to do is say the word."

"Which is exactly why you should keep your mouth shut." I stopped when I realized this conversation was starting to sound exactly like the arguments we'd had a dozen times before. And as a scientist, I knew firsthand that the quickest way to prove yourself an idiot was to do the same actions and expect a different result.

I took a deep breath and decided to try something revolutionary: softening my voice. "Phil, I'm not denying that the movement exists. I'm saying you need to put a stop to it before it gets out of hand."

She started to speak, but I put up a hand to stop her. "I know you think this is the solution, but it's not. You won't save a single Christian by starting a rebellion. The only person who will benefit from war is Asia."

She went silent, staring at the floor as if she were, for once, considering my words. I tried to close and lock the door while I had the opportunity. "She's using you, Phil. You are not in control. She is."

"No. She's not," Phil said, barely a whisper. She looked up. "God is."

I gaped at her. I couldn't decide which was more astounding: the fact that she was ignoring everything I said, or the fact that she'd just pulled the God-card on me.

She prattled on before I could recover. "I know you don't see the world the way I do, but there's no way this can't be God. There's just too much that has happened for this to be a crazy accident. Maybe that's not how you see it, but that's what I believe."

What a basal thing to accuse me of. The problem wasn't that I didn't see. The problem was that I saw too much.

"I think… I believe that God wanted this to happen. I believe He wants me to be Blue Fire." She straightened, her voice full of sickening confidence. "Everything that's happened these last six months has lined up to bring me here—my dad, Wing 74, Thames, even the invite to that stupid party."

I wanted to refute her, to knock the legs out from under her bravado before she did something foolish. But I couldn't come up with the words fast enough. Not when I knew she was right.

"I know trying to kill the General was a mistake, but… what if the rest wasn't? What if I am supposed to be Blue Fire? What if I am supposed to be on Earth? What if this operation is the right thing to do? What if… what if I was supposed to come to Beijing?"

She hesitated, and I could see the gears turning, her face twitching as she followed the thoughts to their logical conclusion. I knew that if I didn't shut her down right now, she'd see what I saw: that she was supposed to go to Nineveh.

And I would rather spend a hundred years in the belly of a whale than risk my life—or hers—trying to save this cursed city.

Unfortunately, I knew Phil lacked a healthy fear of death, so scaring her into quitting wouldn't work. If I wanted her to give up, I had to convince her that this *wasn't* the right thing to do.

For better or for worse, I knew exactly how to accomplish that.

"No, Phil," I said, drawing myself to my full height. "You weren't."

She started to retaliate, but I cut her off. "I know you think this is God, but do you know what I see?" I spoke slowly and deliberately, laying each word out in the open so that there would be no room for debate. "I see a foolish, impulsive teenage girl who's being used by the government to start a war. All those 'miracles' you talk about? They're just proof that Asia has been controlling the game for a very long time. She brought your family to Mars. She convinced the Nolans to adopt you. She invited you to the party. She let you play out your thunderbird fantasy—and you know why? Because she wanted you to do it."

Phil slowly shut her mouth and clenched her jaw.

I dug the grave deeper. "She wanted you to kill her father because she wanted to take his place. Your little insurrection would have given her the perfect excuse to seize power without even having to get up from her desk. She would have become the next dictator and rewritten the laws the way she wants them—and I guarantee you there isn't room for Christians in her perfect world."

I laughed joylessly when I realized how true that was. "Asia would have killed them all. She would have ended the reassimilation program for good—and your violent rebellion would have given her the perfect excuse. She would have slaughtered them. Do you really think that's what God wanted you to do?"

I saw the tears well up in Phil's eyes and knew I had won. Not wanting to take chances, I braced myself and drove the last nail in the coffin.

"I said it once, and I'll say it a dozen times until you finally get it through your head: You are not a hero. God did not choose you for anything. He had nothing to do with you becoming 'Blue Fire.' You made that up. You let your moment of fame go to your head, and you almost got us all killed. You're a fool, Philadelphia, and you'd be dead if I hadn't come to rescue you."

A sob escaped her lips. She slapped her hands over her mouth and stared down at the ground as her whole body started to shake.

I looked away. The deed was done.

"Go to your room," I ordered.

She obeyed me, a little too literally. She turned and ran down the hall, slamming the door so hard the whole house seemed to groan.

Something meowed. I looked down to see that stupid cat tangling himself around my legs.

Of course, of all the things I *didn't* want to follow me home.

I kicked him away. "Go comfort her," I snapped. Then I turned and locked myself in my room.

I closed my eyes and leaned against the door, but no sooner had the silence returned than it was broken by the sound of pitiful sobbing from outside.

I unwillingly walked to the window. Phil was on her balcony, crying. She huddled against the railing with her face on her knees, doing a terrible job of muffling her sobs.

I slammed and latched my shutters, dampening the sound. Fishing my laptop and a pair of earbuds out of my backpack, I returned to the bed. I plugged in and queued up an album I'd stealthily downloaded while at Narissa's shop. The comforting sound of Bruno Mars instantly drowned out the world.

I leaned back on the pillow and closed my eyes. Phil would get over herself. She just needed a few hours to cry it off, like she always did, and then she'd see the truth of what I was saying. We'd meet with Jael's people tomorrow, and if they couldn't help us, I'd steal a device from the Tangs and head to the country. I'd have to be careful, but as long as I didn't let my distrust slip at breakfast, I was confident I could fool them long enough to get Phil out of town.

And then we could finally leave Earth—and the revolution—behind for good.

14: PHILADELPHIA

I didn't want to cry, but I didn't know what else to do. There was nothing I could say, nothing I could do, that would make anything right in the world.

So I huddled on the balcony, my back to the cold wooden wall, and sobbed while my universe collapsed. All the camaraderie I thought I'd developed with Nic over the past few days went up in smoke like matchsticks, lit on fire with a few choice words.

I knew what he thought of me. No matter how many times I apologized, no matter how many times I tried to make it right, I would always be the stupid, petulant teenager who ruined his life. I was foolish, arrogant, and good for nothing. I was dead weight, a burden he'd decided to shoulder because he felt sorry for me.

And nothing I could ever do or say would change that.

I finally understood what Stanyard meant when he said he was "giving me his weapons." He needed to know that I was truly forgiving him and wouldn't throw his past betrayal in his face every time he slipped up.

Now Nic was doing the same thing. He had all my weapons, and he wasn't afraid to use them. He hadn't forgiven me.

And, if today was any indication, he never would.

But even worse than the rejection was the cold, slippery feeling that was seeping into the corners of my mind. It was like a shadow, bleeding into my subconscious and breaking my reality apart at the edges like a cliff crumbling into the sea.

What if… what if Nic is right? What if this isn't God?

Something creaked behind me. I jumped and whipped around, but there was nothing there. The bedroom was dark and empty, the open door to the hallway drifting in the breeze.

Wait. My blood froze as I processed what I was seeing. I'd closed the door when I'd come in.

Before I could register what that meant, a large hand closed around my arm.

I started to scream, but another hand slapped over my mouth and stifled the sound. Someone big and bulky with clomping footsteps hauled me up and dragged me back into the room. Several large figures—men—crowded around me, but I couldn't make out any faces in the darkness. I shouted and squirmed against the man who held me, but it didn't do any good.

One of them wrestled my arm out of my jacket sleeve. I flinched as something sharp stabbed my upper arm. I twisted my head just in time to see one of the men yank a syringe out of my shoulder.

Blood pounded in my ears and made the room flash wild colors. *Oh God, oh God, help me!*

Someone started counting down ominously under his breath. At first, nothing happened, so I used my last window of sanity to slam my heel into my captor's shin. His hold loosened as he grunted. I managed to wrench away—just as the first wave of dizziness hit.

I tripped over the stool at the foot of the bed and crashed to the floor. I struggled to brace my hands on the wood and push myself up, but the room was spinning, spinning. I vomited without warning. I managed to roll away, but the world continued to tumble even after I stopped moving, like a can rolling downhill.

"Nic," I managed, but my voice came out weak, slurred.

"Nic can't help you now, princess," one of them grunted. There were footsteps pounding in all directions, and whispered orders, and cold hands sliding under me and picking me up. I tried to fight, but none of my nerves responded. All I could feel was a dense darkness overtaking me, like an ocean wave sweeping me under.

The last thing I registered before the world went black was a male voice I thought I recognized. "Welcome back, Blue Fire."

15: NIC

I woke to the sound of that stupid cat scratching at my bedroom door.

I knew that's what it was before I even came to full consciousness. The irritating sound of his outstretched nails grinding on the wood ripped into my sleep and shredded it like a napkin. It wasn't a light scratching, either; it sounded like he was peeling off chunks of the door with his claws.

I rolled over and put my arm over my ear. I never should have let Phil keep the dumb thing. Hopefully our hosts wouldn't charge us damages.

There was a brief respite, as if the cat had heard the bed creak and was waiting for me to get up. When the door did not open, he resumed his demands. This time, he added incessant meowing. Actually, *howling* would be a more accurate description of the blood-curdling sound the animal was producing.

I threw the blanket aside and stood up with a curse. I slammed the door open. "Get lost," I shouted, using colorful language I hoped he would appreciate.

He blinked up at me, tail flicking like a question mark. Then, as if satisfied I was fully awake, he took off.

I leaned out and watched him tear down the hallway. He nearly collided into Phil's door, which stood open.

I sighed. If Phil was up, I may as well be up. Time to face each other, get her morning dose of teenage angst out of the way, and then talk to Lanzhou about setting up a meeting with Jael. The sooner we could get new files, the sooner we could get out of here.

I returned to my bedroom and took sixty seconds to cull my mustache, straighten my hair, and put on a pair of house shoes. Then I strapped my holster under my arm and concealed it beneath my jacket. I knew I wouldn't need my gun at breakfast, but I wasn't about to leave the weapon unattended.

The house was oddly silent as I walked down to Phil's room. The only sound in the hallway was my footsteps creaking on the ancient boards.

I stood behind the open door and rapped it with my knuckles. No answer.

"Phil?" I ventured.

Still nothing. I pushed the door aside and saw that the room was empty. In fact, it looked like it hadn't been slept in at all. The bedsheets were still neatly tucked into the mattress, and the pillows were all fluffed. Had she cried herself to sleep on the balcony? I wouldn't put it past her.

I took a step into the room. The door to the balcony was open, but she wasn't outside. A quick scan revealed that her little black backpack was sitting on the nightstand.

I picked it up and unzipped it. Everything was in there, including the phone.

Something rolled on the floor behind me. I turned to see that stupid cat playing with something in the corner. He batted it back and forth as he sprang about, tail hairs on end.

I walked over and scooped the cat up with one hand and the object up with the other. As soon as my fingers closed around it, I knew what it was. I'd used one many times in the past, and never for good reason.

It was the plastic cap to a syringe.

I whipped back around and studied the room again. This time, I caught all the sinister nuances that told me something was wrong: the stool shoved away from the foot of the bed, the muddy bootprint near the balcony door. The faint scent of vomit hung in the air, and a patch of the wood floor was shiny, as if someone had hastily tried to clean it.

The pieces snapped together in one horrifying puzzle. Phil was in trouble.

Guilt mangled with rage flashed through me. The cat mewed pitifully, and this time, I agreed with him. I knew we shouldn't have stayed the night.

I dropped the cat and ran for the stairs. I burst into the courtyard and heard talking and clattering dishes coming from the veranda that overlooked the canal. Most of the family was already gathered around the long table, gossiping over bowls of rice porridge. I brushed past them and shoved my way into the kitchen.

Lanzhou, Bowen, and several others bustled about the cramped space. Lanzhou stood over one of the giant iron woks that was inlaid in the vintage brick stove. *"Zǎo!"* he greeted me warmly.

I forwent all the rules of etiquette. "Has anyone seen Philadelphia?"

The chatter ceased as everyone turned to look at me. Their stunned silence gave me the answer I needed.

Lanzhou dropped his *chuan*. "What's wrong?"

I held the syringe cap out to him. "What did you do to her?"

Lanzhou had the decency to look horrified, but Bowen wasted no time in going on the defensive. "What do you mean, 'what did we do to her'? Where is she?"

"That's what I'd like to know," I shot back. "She's gone, and it looks like there's been a break-in."

Lanzhou turned and called to his nephew, who was standing across the kitchen. "I want a perimeter check, now. Search the entire house. Send someone down to the square and make sure she's not there."

The young man darted off to obey.

Bowen couldn't muster the energy to be worried. "Are we sure she didn't just wander off? She's a teenager."

"Of course, she didn't just 'wander off.'" I mocked him with air quotes. "First, she's too terrified to go anywhere without me. Second, she didn't take her phone."

Bowen shrugged. "She doesn't need it if she's not planning on checking in online. Maybe she just needed some time away from you."

"He's right." Lanzhou physically put himself between us, which was probably the only thing that stopped me from punching Bowen in the nose. "Let's not lose our heads just yet. She might have just gone to the—"

"Don't argue with me about Philadelphia!" I yelled. "I know her better than all of you put together. She would not leave without me. Go check the room if you want, but I'm telling you, she's in trouble, and I want answers."

Bowen correctly assumed that the accusation in my voice was aimed at him. "What makes you think we know anything?"

"She's *your* Blue Fire," I threatened. "You're supposed to be protecting her."

Lanzhou laid a warning hand on my arm, but it did nothing to ground me. "We had guards posted outside the house all night," he said, voice deliberately calm. He turned to Bowen. "Did they say anything when you relieved them this morning?"

Bowen shook his head. "Nothing to report."

"Unless they were bribed," I hissed.

Bowen's gaze darkened. "Exactly what are you suggesting?"

Lanzhou pinched me, but I shrugged him off. "Exactly what you think I'm suggesting."

Bowen's biceps tensed. "Why would we kidnap her? She's one of us."

She *wasn't* one of them, but he had a point. They had no reason to kidnap her while she was sleeping under their roof—unless they'd overheard our argument last night and knew we would be leaving.

But even then, threatening her would have been inefficient. She wasn't the unknown in this equation; I was. If they wanted to convince Phil to stay on Earth and lead the revolution, I was the one they needed to get out of the way.

As if sensing my thoughts, Bowen turned the interrogation back on me. "What about you? Your room was close to hers. Did you hear anything last night?"

"No…" I didn't even finish the thought before I realized my mistake. I hadn't heard anything last night. I'd put my headphones in so I wouldn't have to listen to her cry—never realizing that was when she would need me the most.

I spun towards the door. "I'm going to find her."

"Nic, stop." Lanzhou blocked my path. "If she really is in trouble, we're going to need help. Let us search the house, talk to the guards who were on shift last night. If we can't find her, we'll send out a search party."

Bowen finally decided to take the situation seriously. "I'll call them right now." He strode out of the room.

I appreciated that he was making himself useful, but I wasn't going to wait around while they ran through their petty due process. "We don't have time for this! She's the most wanted woman on Earth right now."

"Who do you think might have taken her?" Lanzhou asked. "Think. Is there anyone I should know about?"

I shook my head; I had absolutely no idea who would want to kidnap her. Bowen was right; it probably wasn't one of them. And it definitely wasn't Asia; she would have just burned the whole house down. Asia was not one to be subtle, and she had no reason to work secretly in the dark. If the government had found Phil, they would have taken both of us and raided the entire house while they were at it.

No, process of elimination suggested that whoever had kidnapped her was acting outside the rule of both the United and the underground. They answered to no one, which meant they had no incentive to keep her in one piece. Whatever their plan was, they would not be kind to her.

The realization filled me with such anger and dread that I almost wished it *was* Asia who had taken her. At least I could trust Asia to be civil.

Lanzhou steadied me with a hand to the shoulder. "You need to sit down."

That was the exact opposite of what I should be doing. "No, I'm going to look for her." I tried to shove past him.

Lanzhou sighed and pushed me back. "Nic, seriously, think this through. What are you going to do? Start going door to door? You don't even have a functioning phone."

He was right, and that just made me hate myself even more. Not that I needed any help in that department.

"Look, I promise we will find her. You have the entire underground on your side. I just talked to Jael's people—they'll be here any minute. She can help; she's got access to the algorithm."

"Good for her, but that won't help us. Phil doesn't have any electronics on her."

"No, but whoever took her might. Please, just wait for Jael. We'll figure this out together."

I grunted my consent. Jael was the last person I wanted to involve, but if she truly was as powerful as everyone said, then she was Phil's best bet. I certainly didn't have any better ideas.

Lanzhou took advantage of my silence to shove a bowl of porridge into my hand. "Sit, eat something. I'll go get the rest of the family together."

He pushed me out of the kitchen and steered me towards the now-vacant table on the veranda. I unwillingly slumped down on the bench. After waiting to make sure I was going to stay put, Lanzhou took off, shouting across the courtyard in Mandarin.

I glared at the soupy contents of my bowl. I had no desire to eat any of it, but I didn't have anything better to do. Lanzhou was right; there was nothing I could do. I couldn't get online, I couldn't track her, and I didn't know anything about the area. I hadn't been this useless since Phil and I were trapped in Wing 74.

Abruptly, I remembered watching her final stream and hearing the gunshot and the shriek as the camera went black—and realizing that she'd just sacrificed herself to save everyone. She'd risked her life to do what was right after my choices had put her in danger. Again.

I roared and hurled my bowl onto the deck. The porcelain shattered with a crash as hot rice splattered up my leg. I welcomed the brief flash of pain.

A gasp came from behind me. "Whoa, dude, wasting food is not cool."

I froze. I knew that voice. *Dear God, anyone but them.*

Unsurprisingly, God wasn't interested in granting my sacrilegious requests. A second voice joined the conversation. "Yeah, I would have eaten that!"

Yup, there was the other one. I begrudgingly turned around.

It was John and Dowe.

16: PHILADELPHIA

The world was still spinning when I came to.

The first thing I registered was a nauseous wave of dizziness, that endless swirling that told me I'd be better off asleep than awake. I tried to push past it, searching for solid ground, any feeling I could grab and center my senses on. I opened my eyes, but all I could see was darkness and flashing colors that I wasn't sure were real or imagined. I tried to speak but couldn't; my breath caught on something painful and sticky, jamming the air in my throat. I tried to move my hands but couldn't do that either; sharp metal bit into my wrists, and my back was pressed against something cold. I twisted but nothing budged, I screamed but no sound came out, and all the while the colors in the room were burning brighter and brighter until I could practically hear them ringing in my ears.

Jesus, Jesus, Jesus...

Breathe. Breathe.

I pinched my eyes shut again. I forced myself to hold still and start praying. The words were nonsense, but I repeated them over and over until I reconnected with the feeling that I wasn't alone in the world. I waited until I could count to three between each breath, then opened my eyes again.

I took stock of my senses—slowly this time. I was sitting on a soggy dirt floor in a dark room. My hands were cuffed behind my back, and I felt a metal pole between my shoulder blades. A thick piece of tape was slapped over my mouth, pulling on loose hairs that had fallen out of my ponytail. And everything—*everything*—hurt.

I struggled to swallow my heart as a blanket of fear dropped over me. I was no stranger to fear; I'd stared down guns, fallen from great heights, and danced with death more than once. But this was different. This wasn't the jolt of terrified energy that shot through me when my flight-or-flight response kicked in. This was slow and heavy, a weight that settled in my lungs like the oxygen had gotten sucked out of the room. This was a dread, the realization that something very bad was about to happen.

And I could do nothing to stop it.

Holy Spirit, I need You now.

I didn't feel any peace, but I banked on the trust that He was there. I looked around and tried to figure out where I was. As my eyes adjusted to the darkness, I could tell I was in a small room. All the windows were boarded up, so the only light came from holes and gaps in the wood. There were heaps of trash piled against the walls, making me wonder if the garbage was the only thing keeping the house from caving in. The whole place smelled rancid and musty, like the dirt floor never fully dried in between rains.

I twisted and looked behind me. I was cuffed to the frame of what had, at some point, been a bunk bed. So many of the crossbars were broken or missing that you probably couldn't have put a mattress on it even if you wanted to, but it was still heavy enough that I had no hope of dragging it.

Before I could formulate any more questions, noise erupted outside. Gruff comments were exchanged, and then the gap of light underneath the door was blocked out. I sat up straight and summoned all my defenses as a key rattled in the lock. The door swung open, revealing a flood of morning light and the silhouette of a man.

He stood there, staring, waiting until my vision adjusted to the light and I could focus on his face.

Jayde.

Suddenly, all my questions were answered. I knew exactly what was going on. In spite of myself, I began to tremble as I accepted the inevitable.

Jayde was going to kill me. The only wonder was why he hadn't done it already.

He kicked the door mostly shut, leaving a shaft of light just barely enough to see by. He squatted next to me and studied me, arms propped on his knees. I searched his face for any emotion, but there was none, not even anger. He was calm, controlled. He looked just like he did any other day, like this was a regular staff meeting in the office.

He reached up and grabbed the back of my head. I shuddered as his calloused fingers brushed my neck. He used his other hand to rip the gag off in one sharp yank. I gasped for air as my eyes watered and my face burned.

He wadded the tape up and tossed it across the room. He seemed content with the silence, as if waiting for me to speak first. I had nothing to say and absolutely no desire to talk to him.

He finally got bored of waiting. "No questions?"

I took a deep breath. If he was going to make me talk, I might as well get some information. "How'd you find me?" I ventured, and winced when I realized how dry and cracked my voice was. I swallowed fruitlessly.

He gave a hollow laugh. "I didn't have to 'find' you, Phil. The entire Chinese underground knows you were at church. I have a friend who works at that factory. He volunteered to be on guard at the house last night."

I clenched my fists behind my back. This was why Nic hadn't wanted me to reveal myself. As always, he'd been right—right about everything.

"And I suppose you're here to finish the job," I returned.

He snorted. "I wish."

I felt annoyance flare up in me. All my adrenaline was tired of cycling around my nerves with nowhere to go. "Just get it over with. If you think I'm going to beg and plead, you'll be disappointed. I'm not bargaining with you."

The bravado in my voice was weak, but the threat was real. He'd get nothing from me.

He shook his head. "Sounds fun, but not today. We've got other business to attend to."

Suddenly, my panic found something to focus on, and a fresh wave of terror washed over me. "What?"

He fingered his holstered gun. "Look, you have no idea how much I'd love to kill you right now…"

I have an inkling, I thought but wasn't dumb enough to say.

"But thankfully for you, a mutual friend has convinced me that you're still worth more alive than dead."

"Who?" Who was Jayde talking to that would argue for my life? Only a handful of people knew Jayde and I were in Beijing. Was it my uncle? My uncle Tower had known about the assassination; surely, he would fight for me, if he knew what was happening. But would Jayde tell him what was going on?

Jayde wasn't forthcoming with the information. "Since Operation Thunderbird was conveniently top secret, there are only a handful of people who know you failed. As far as the rest of the underground knows, you're just hiding out waiting for stuff to blow over. All you have to do is record a video saying you're back in command, and this all goes away. You go back to being the pretty face of the revolution, and Operation Blue Fire continues as scheduled."

That explained a lot. Jayde was still planning to launch a revolution, and he wanted me to lead. I was still his Blue Fire—except he didn't realize that he wasn't in charge anymore.

"It won't work," I challenged. "They won't listen to you. They're loyal to me."

Unfortunately, this was not news to him. "Oh yes, I know all about Lev's little mutiny." The slithering tone of his voice made my blood run cold. "But this isn't a numbers game, princess. It doesn't matter whether they're loyal to me or not. Whoever controls the thunderbird controls the war."

You don't control me. I shoved him away with my foot. "I'm not recording anything for you."

He hit me. Drew his arm back and slapped me across the face. I gasped as the room spun like a kaleidoscope.

"If I have to cuff you to a chair in front of a camera, I will," he declared. His voice was steady, almost bored, as if he'd rehearsed this whole exchange. "But I'm sure we can come to an agreement. You're easy to motivate."

I had been—once. But his collateral, Stanyard, was safely out of reach. There was no one else he could threaten—

He spoke before I finished the thought. "I still have your father."

"But he's gone," I argued, before realizing I was playing right into his hand. My father was alive, and according to Stanyard, he was doing well physically. But he had lost all his memories; he didn't even know me.

"If that mattered to you, you never would have thawed him out." Jayde read my mind. "But you're right, threatening to kill him is a bit passé. It would be much more fun to play with his memories. Perhaps, give him some new ones—about you."

Is that possible? I thought but daren't ask. I tried to deflect the panic; there was no way Mrs. Nolan, Thames's wife, would let Jayde touch my father. She was supervising my father's therapy and had promised to keep him safe until I returned—but if Jayde had enough people on his side, there might not be anything she could do to stop him.

As if that wasn't threatening enough, Jayde autofilled several other insidious possibilities. "Or, if that doesn't work, I know where your brother is. Or the Vons. You're such a kind, caring person, Philadelphia Smyrna—you give me so much material to work with."

I won't do it. The determination formed in my mind, but I couldn't find the words. I wouldn't—would I? We'd been through this whole song and dance before. I knew what could happen if I ignored the Lord and compromised instead of trusting Him to protect the ones I loved. I wouldn't make the same mistake, not this time.

Except, I still wasn't convinced that leading the revolution *was* a mistake.

Jayde didn't wait for me to find my moral compass. "You think about it and let me know whose life you'd like to play with. But in the meantime, as far as anyone else knows, you never went to Beijing, there was no Operation Thunderbird, and we're still the best of friends—got it?"

"And how do you want me to explain the bruise you just gave me?" I snarled.

He drew his hand back like he was going to give me another one. I pinched my eyes shut and braced myself. *Jesus, help.*

After a moment's hesitation, Jayde grunted. "You're right, I'd better not mess up that pretty face of yours. There's only so much makeup can fix."

I opened my eyes and waited.

"We leave for Boston in a few hours. In the meantime, I *don't* trust you to sit still, so hopefully this helps."

Jayde pulled a roll of duct tape from the pocket of his cargo pants and tore off a generous strip. The hideous sound of the tape unwinding sent my panic into overdrive. I barely managed to swallow a cry of pain as Jayde grabbed my chin and gagged me with more force than was necessary.

Holy Spirit, please don't leave me.

Jayde rose and walked to the door. I tried to look past him as he opened it, but all I could see was what looked like a stone courtyard and a few more guards.

Jayde hesitated in the doorway with his back to me. "Do you know why I hate you so much, Phil?"

I didn't particularly want to know, but he volunteered the answer. "Because you have what so many people have *died* trying to get, and you're willing to throw it all away."

He looked back at me. When he spoke, his voice was quiet, transparent—almost like we were equal partners again. "Hundreds of people have tried over the years to start a revolution or change the law—and they've all failed. They've all been killed or swept under the rug, and the United only got more powerful. Then you come along, and suddenly, you have an entire army following you. Overnight you've managed to create an entire freedom movement—do you understand how improbable that is?"

I did. I would have called it a miracle, because it was one.

Even if Nic didn't think so.

Jayde's calm demeanor broke. I couldn't read his facial expression against the backlight of the morning sun, but I could hear the emotion in his voice. He sounded confused. Sad. In pain. "I still don't know how you did it. I don't know what it is about you that everyone loves. But you have *everything*—you, and only you, can do this. You could save the world. But you won't."

He took a deep breath, and I saw the anger returning to his posture. "I'll never understand you," he muttered, and punctuated with some foul terms. "But we're going to do this whether you like it or not. So the choice is yours: You can be an army general, or you can be a prisoner of war. Hopefully, a little more time locked in here will help you decide which one."

Then he slammed and latched the door, leaving me with that final threat.

I waited until the voices had faded outside before putting my face to my knees. My head spun, but this time, it wasn't because I was dizzy. No, my mind was reeling because I knew Jayde was right.

I did have everything—but it wasn't because I was anyone special. All I'd done was help Nic destroy a factory of Red Rain. That video had leaked to the internet, where it had trended instantly. Thames had added fuel to the fire by forcing me to record more videos recounting my life story, but I knew he wasn't responsible for making me the figurehead of a revolution. Only one person could be responsible for that.

God.

No matter what Nic said, I genuinely believed God had turned me into Blue Fire. Maybe Nic was right about some things; maybe Asia had invited me to the party because she wanted me to kill her father. Maybe she was using my image to start her own war. But that still didn't explain why my videos had trended in the first place. Even Asia herself admitted she had nothing to do with that. And if that wasn't God, then who was it? If God didn't want me to change the world, then why was I here?

And I still believed in the rebellion, didn't I? Jayde was a monster, and I wanted nothing to do with him—but revolution was the right thing to do, wasn't it? I still believed the United was evil. I still wanted to save the unassimilated and rescue everyone who had suffered in a containment camp like I did. I still intended to fight for freedom. I was still Blue Fire—even if I wasn't the Blue Fire Jayde wanted me to be.

But could there be a revolution as long as Jayde was involved? I didn't trust him; frankly, I didn't trust most of the underground. And maybe that was the real problem: Even if Operation Blue Fire did succeed, who would end up on top? Would the new world be any better than the last?

It wouldn't be if people like Jayde were in charge. Jayde had proven he was willing to sacrifice all morals to win. I had no doubt that he'd apply the same logic to a reformed government, whatever that might look like.

No, the more I learned about Jayde and the underground, the more I was convinced that the rebels couldn't be trusted with the government any more than the Beijing leadership could. My chest tightened when I realized that's what Nic had been trying to tell me all along. That's why he'd wanted me to come home.

Had he been right? Were we supposed to run back to Mars and hide—until what? Until the perfect leader came along? The perfect leader didn't exist. There was no such thing as the perfect opportunity, the perfect government, the perfect moment in time. Unless Jesus came back tomorrow, there was no way to reform the world overnight. No matter who did it or how it happened, change would be a slow process. A slow, painful, potentially bloody process.

Was I still the person God had called to start that change? Or was Nic right? What if God didn't call me at all? What if I really hadn't heard from the Lord?

I searched for an answer, but there was none. If I blocked out the rattle of fear, I could sense the Holy Spirit nearby, like He was sitting in the room with me. But He was eerily silent. I felt no unction, no wisdom, no push in any direction. It felt like *none* of the options were right—which led me to suspect that none of them were.

I twisted my wrists and felt the jade bangle slide on my arm. I hoped that lady had been telling the truth when she said the church was praying for me, because right now, I didn't have any other options. I'd been able to blast my way out of a lot of prisons, but Jayde had been smart this time. I groaned and tried to shift my position, but I just succeeded in pinching my skin in the cuffs. I winced as the will to cry shoved to the forefront of my mind. I wasn't going anywhere—and Nic, the one person who could possibly rescue me, had no idea where I was.

I trusted that Nic knew me well enough to realize I didn't just run off. He would know something was wrong, but he had no way of knowing Jayde was involved. There was no way to track me; I didn't have any electronics that would give away my position. No, by the time Nic had any inkling of what was going on, Jayde and I would be back in Boston.

And then, if Jayde had his way, even Asia wouldn't be able to find me.

17: NIC

"Man, are we happy to see you, Q!"

The feeling was not mutual. I stood up and backed away so I could study the pair from a safe distance. John and Dowe had been my prison mates on Rott, and like everything else from my time in jail, I would have preferred to leave them in the past.

It wasn't that they were terrible people; in fact, they met all the criteria to be classified as friends. But while they had been valuable allies, their personalities seemed uniquely designed to torment me. They had no social skills, no shame, and no concept of an "indoor voice." They were also obnoxious to look at; they were so very nearly identical that it looked like God had gone CTRL+C, CTRL+V. And yet, as far as I was aware, they weren't related—not that I'd wasted much brain power trying to unravel the mystery that was John and Dowe.

I certainly didn't have any mental energy to deal with them today. "What are you doing here?" I demanded in a way that I hoped came off as unwelcoming.

They were not deterred. "We're here to see you! Why else would we come to Beijing?" Dowe replied.

"Yeah!" John echoed. "We came as soon as we heard Blue Fire was here!"

"Wait." I put up my hand to pause the conversation while I did the math. "How did you get here?"

"Same way we always get to China," Dowe deadpanned.

"No, I mean, a flight to China takes at least thirteen hours. We just checked in last night. How'd you get here so fast?"

John looked like he was prepared to mouth off, then hesitated. He turned to Dowe. "How *did* we get here so fast?"

Dowe looked as astounded as the rest of us. "You're right, by all accounts it doesn't make sense."

"John, Dowe, you made it!" Lanzhou darted onto the veranda. "It's so great to see you. Welcome back." He offered them both a hug and a slap on the back, which they reciprocated with far too much enthusiasm.

"You know these guys?" I exclaimed.

"Doesn't everybody know a John Dowe?" Lanzhou returned with a wink. He turned to me. "Sorry to break up the reunion…"

"No, please do," I groaned.

Lanzhou ignored the comment. "I've got Jael on the line in the other room. She wants to speak with you."

Finally, we can make some real progress. I nodded at Lanzhou to lead the way, then followed him across the courtyard to his father's study. John and Dowe scampered behind like lost puppies.

Bowen and the rest of the family were already crammed around the massive desk, talking to someone on the computer. They cleared the way so I could stand in front of the monitor.

A black woman about my age was on the screen. Everything about her could be described as *imposing*, from her fierce glare to the wildly embroidered turban that was wrapped around her head like a crown. She certainly carried herself like a queen; she sat up straight and looked down at the camera at a slight angle, as if we were all subjects in her courtroom.

"Q," she said, dipping her head in greeting. "Pleased to make your acquaintance." Her voice was seasoned with a rich Hausa accent, which somehow made her sound all the more imperial.

"The pleasure is all mine, I'm sure," I returned. "Your reputation precedes you."

She arched one cat-like eyebrow. "I shall endeavor to live up to it. I'm sorry I can't be there in person, but my flight won't land for another three hours."

As if corroborating her statement, her camera jolted, like her plane was going through turbulence. *At least someone has to obey the laws of physics.*

"Amateur," Dowe smirked, loud enough for everyone to hear.

Jael wasn't having it. Her entire demeanor changed. "John. Dowe. Front and center. *Now.*"

They elbowed their way up to the desk, which put them much too close to me. Jael drew herself up higher until her forehead was grazing the top of the frame. "Do not backtalk me," she ordered. "The whole reason Blue Fire is in this mess is because you failed the mission. If she gets hurt, I *will* court martial you."

There were several important pieces of information in that sentence, and I tried to quickly sort them by relevance. "Mission?"

"Yeah!" John squealed like it was bring-your-kid-to-work day. "That's our boss!"

I wasn't sure whether that doubled or halved my respect for the woman. "I am so sorry," I said, looking back at the screen.

She dipped her head. "Thank you for your condolences."

"And what, exactly, was this mission, and how does it involve Philadelphia?" I continued before John or Dowe could mouth off.

"Doctor, I've known about 'Operation Thunderbird' the whole time," Jael said, voice dripping with patronizing benevolence. "Tower has been in contact with me."

I paused while my brain categorized that data. "Well, at least he's not a total deadbeat of an uncle."

Jael almost smiled. "I had intended to intercept Blue Fire before she got to the General. Unfortunately, my agents missed the date." Her voice hardened over with accusation.

John paled. "The birthday party's *today*?"

"It was Saturday," Jael deadpanned.

"Wait, you were supposed to be there?" I yelled. "And you *forgot the date*?" I wasn't sure which I found more shocking: The fact that someone else had tried to save Phil, or the fact that they'd failed because they couldn't keep a calendar.

Dowe shrugged sheepishly. "I could've sworn Andi said it was July 4th..."

"That was three weeks ago," Lanzhou pointed out.

"So?" Dowe frowned, as if going back in time was something he had been planning to do all along.

John was still panicking. "I left my gift at home..."

I slapped my hands down on the wooden desk. "Would someone other than John and Dowe like to explain what's going on?"

"I promise all your questions will be answered, doctor," Jael insisted, which sounded weirdly like a threat. "But at the moment, it sounds like we have a more immediate crisis. Lanzhou?"

He leaned over my shoulder so she could see him. "Blue Fire is gone, and I agree with Nic—it looks like foul play. We've searched the house and the square, but there's no sign of her."

"The guard who was on duty last night is conveniently not answering my calls," Bowen added, and had the decency to look ashamed.

"Well, luckily for us all, his phone is still online—which tells me everything I need to know." Jael paused for unnecessary drama. "Jayde has our Blue Fire."

John and Dowe gasped in unison, supplying the disgust I was too tired to express. That little revelation answered all my questions and confirmed my worst fears. Of all the people who wanted to hurt Philadelphia, Jayde would be the cruelest.

"Well, you'd better hope she's not dead already," I snapped.

"She's not," Jael declared with a confidence that came off as heartless. "I have every reason to believe that Jayde needs Blue Fire alive as much as the rest of us do."

I did not appreciate the content of her sentence or the attitude she used to punctuate it. "What do you mean?"

The rings on her fingers flashed as she flicked her hand across the screen. "Jayde's recent texts and calls make it very clear he's still planning to launch a revolution, and for that, he needs a living thunderbird."

That's what I'm afraid of. "And how do you know he has her?" I challenged.

"I've been tracking his cell phone activity." She sounded almost bored by the question, as if I ought to have known the answer already. "For the past few days, he's been trailing you two. Every time you checked in, he showed up to the same place a few hours later. And last night, he was at the house, along with several of his friends. His phone registered on the Tangs' router."

I gripped the edge of the desk as rage rolled through me. Jayde had simply waltzed in and snatched Philadelphia right off her balcony—all the while I'd been just a few doors away, lost in my own conceit.

Lanzhou spoke before I could get too invested in self-laceration. "And who is this Jayde, exactly?"

"You may know him as the Green Dragon," Jael explained. "He's, shall we say, a former friend of Philadelphia's from Boston."

Lanzhou glanced at me. "So when you say you had a mission go awry…"

"I'll debrief you later," Jael interrupted. "For now, our focus is getting Philadelphia back before Jayde tries to leave the city. I attempted to reach out and *introduce* myself," she stretched the word into a threat, "but he's not returning my calls. So we'll have to do this the hard way."

I took a deep breath and stuffed my emotions back in the closet. "And that is?"

"Jayde's cell phone activity puts him in a neighborhood across town. He's been there since late last night. If Philadelphia is still alive, she's there. We're going to go get her out."

I straightened. "Excellent. When do we leave?"

"Immediately." Jael straightened, and her voice took on a militaristic edge. "Lanzhou, you're in charge of this mission."

At least that was a decision I could agree with. "I'm with him," I declared, and was somewhat surprised when no one argued.

Jael nodded. "Bowen, you too. I want four more."

"Us!" John and Dowe shrieked in unison.

"No," I snapped.

"Yes," Jael countered me. "This is their mission, and they're going to finish it."

I had several follow-up arguments—the primary one being that Phil was in this mess partially because of John and Dowe's earlier failure. But Jael continued barking orders before I could voice my concerns. "I need two more volunteers."

"I can pull some men off the line at the factory," Bowen offered. "They can get here in fifteen minutes."

"Perfect," Jael agreed.

I added the numbers. "Only seven?"

"Any more, and we'll likely attract attention moving in a pack," Lanzhou explained.

That was a fair point, but it didn't inspire confidence. "You'd better hope Jayde doesn't have more than six friends with him," I muttered.

"He doesn't, not according to the cellular traffic in that area." The glare of a backlit screen flickered across Jael's face, like she was verifying her findings as she talked. "I've analyzed all the registered devices that have connected to that cell tower in the last twelve hours. Of them, only a handful are people I suspect are associated with Jayde. Of course, the algorithm isn't perfect, but it's a risk we're going to have to take if we want to be discreet. I'd like to avoid getting the real police involved if possible."

"Don't have to tell me twice," I muttered, but cast a wary glance at John and Dowe.

"I'd also like to avoid causing a commotion in the underground until I know what Jayde is planning." Jael swiveled her eyes in a firm, nonnegotiable glare that seemed to include everyone in the room, even though she was confined to the monitor. "The operation is hanging by a thread as it is. If we can keep this *indiscretion* between us, I may still be able to reason with Jayde without causing factions. So I want weapons set on stun, and we're not taking any prisoners—am I understood?"

I grunted. I couldn't care less about Jayde's feelings, and the entire revolution could crash and burn for all I cared. If I got a shot at that monster, I was taking it.

"That includes you, doctor."

I looked up to find Jael arching her eyebrows. It was a patronizing stare, like she knew she was in control of the entire situation even though she was however-many miles away.

I folded my arms. I wasn't about to apologize for my protectiveness of Phil.

"Unless..." She shifted back from the camera, as if my very existence was beneath her. "You'd like to stay home while my team does the rescuing."

I looked at the dozen family members gathered around me. There was an audible shift in the room, and Lanzhou pinched my arm warningly. Even Dowe shook his head at me, and he was not subtle about it.

I didn't care want any of them thought, but I was one man against ten. Worse, I was the outsider here. The Tangs might know my father, but they were more loyal to Jael than me. I wasn't about to try my luck with those odds.

I unzipped my jacket and made a dramatic scene of pulling out my gun and changing the setting. I jammed it back in its holster and deferred to Jael with a mocking bow.

She smirked, revealing the tiniest sliver of her white teeth that stood out like diamonds on her dark face. "Let's move out."

✳

Jayde's current location put him at the heart of the city, which meant rush hour was our greatest enemy. Public transportation was out of the question, and it would take hours for us to crawl through the standstill on the highway.

Thankfully, Bowen had a solution: motorbikes. I hadn't ridden one since college, but muscle memory kicked in after a few wobbly laps around the alley. I wasn't about to buddy ride with someone else, even though John graciously offered.

After suiting up with helmets and an ample amount of weapons, we headed out. Lanzhou led the way, following the directions Jael sent him. We rode single file along the riverbank until we reached the end of the dock. Then Lanzhou led us on a twisted tour of the city, crisscrossing alleyways, cutting across courtyards, and skirting sidewalks in a way that was probably illegal. We reached our destination in thirty minutes, a herculean record for rush hour.

I could only hope we weren't thirty minutes too late.

The neighborhood Jael sent us to was definitely a slum. It was a *hutong*, a network of alleys created by interlocking courtyard homes. Several centuries ago, the brick structures would have represented the crown of old Beijing's culture and history. But the United had no taste for culture or history, and the neighborhood had been left to rot.

Several streets had been demolished and the debris left heaped along the road, the marker of a failed urban renewal project. Many of the remaining homes had been condemned and abandoned; their tile roofs were crumbling, exposing rotting beams. The seamless brick walls blended into a blur of tired gray, decorated only by irreverent graffiti.

But despite the stench of death that hung over the neighborhood, it was evident that people still lived there. Rusty bikes collapsed beside backdoors, while retrofitted window units struggled against the summer heat. Laundry hung from every awning, and a few food vendors struggled to eke out a living on the street corners. All the residents I saw looked as tired and worn down as the buildings themselves, like they were one breath away from collapsing.

We ditched the bikes on the outskirts of the neighborhood. Bowen bribed a wrinkled old man into letting us park in his courtyard and assigned one of the young men from the factory to guard them.

I yanked my helmet off and tossed it on the ground. "What now?" I hissed to Lanzhou, and hoped the homeowner didn't understand much English.

"We split up, two and two. Jayde is still in the neighborhood—Jael says he made a call two minutes ago." Lanzhou scrolled on his device.

"And she can't give us a more precise pinpoint?"

Lanzhou shrugged. "He hacked his device to disable location services. All she knows is what cell tower he's pinging off of."

I groaned. Where was the surveillance state when you needed it?

Lanzhou tried to comfort me with a pat on the arm, which had the opposite effect on my nerves. "I promise she's still here. Jayde won't leave without her. So either we'll find her, or we'll find Jayde."

He turned to the rest of the team. "We'll start at the west end and work our way east. Check every abandoned building, ask the residents if they saw anything suspicious last night."

I doubted anyone had seen anything; that's why Jayde had chosen this neighborhood as a hideout. It was a sketchy part of town. No one would question a suspicious vehicle or a couple of thugs passing through.

"If you find anything, radio." Bowen passed a walkie talkie to each member of the group. "Don't go in alone."

The latter admonition was directed at me. I glared at him as I snatched the radio from his hand.

"And remember, keep it down!" Dowe urged in a voice that was the exact opposite of quiet.

"Be discreet. Blend with the surroundings," John added.

If we wanted to be discreet, we shouldn't have brought you, I thought. Dowe looked normal enough, but John wore a bulky parka that was completely inappropriate for the season. His pockets were clearly loaded with contraband; his jacket was so lumpy that he looked like a stupid inflatable at a used car lot. We'd be lucky if he didn't get reported as a "suspicious package."

As if hearing my thoughts and deciding to punish me for them, Lanzhou announced, "Nic and John, you're together."

"What?" we both screeched at the same time.

"I wanted to go with Dowe," John pouted.

Wow, rejected by John. This was a new low in my life.

"Don't shoot the messenger, these are Jael's assignments." Lanzhou shrugged, but even he was frowning at his phone skeptically. "Dowe, you're with me. Bowen, take Haoyu. Let's roll!"

We split up, each team taking a street. I ran down the block and hoped John would keep up. I didn't even bother to look at the first few buildings; this end of the neighborhood was too busy, with several stores and a bus stop. There was no way Jayde could hide here.

John huffed and panted from behind me. "Whoa, Q, aren't you going to stop and look for evidence?"

I wasn't about to waste time explaining my logic to him. I kept running, scanning the shuttered buildings for anything out of the ordinary. But in truth, I had no idea what I was looking for. The neighborhood was huge, and we were dealing with a semi-professional. Jayde wasn't brilliant, but he wasn't sloppy. He would have covered his tracks. And meanwhile, the locals were already giving us—well, mostly John—suspicious looks. If we wanted to stay under the radar, banging down doors and asking people if they'd seen a red-haired military brat seemed ill-advised.

I halted in the middle of the road and let the wave of hopelessness catch up to me. We would never find her in here, and if we created too big of a stir, Jayde would bail—or just shoot Philadelphia to bury the evidence.

It took John a full thirty seconds to reach me. He staggered and braced himself against the nearest wall. "How... do..." He gulped in air and tried again. "How do... you live this way? Whew..."

"What do you mean?" I asked, not that I really cared.

"All this running."

As often was the case with John and Dowe, it was a strangely metaphorical statement. I hated it when they waxed philosophical.

"One sec, I'm almost ready." John raised one finger, took a deep breath, and meowed.

I jerked back. Even he looked surprised by the sound that had come from his lips. He cleared his throat and opened his mouth to try again. There was another mew—but this time, I could clearly tell it was coming from inside his jacket.

My mathematical brain instantly put two and two together. "You didn't."

John turned red all the way up to the edge of his receding hairline. "How could I say no? He was begging to come with..."

He unzipped his jacket, and that stupid cat popped his head out. John reached down and scratched behind the cat's ears. "Besides, he's *so cute.*"

That was the last word I would have used to describe the animal. I groaned and pinched my temples. "Look, John, I appreciate that you're trying to help…" I patronized him, even though neither half of that statement was true. "But I don't feel like you're grasping the severity of the situation. Need I remind you that Philadelphia could *die*?"

All of my frustration came out in a shout, which neither the cat nor John appreciated. John gasped, and the cat took off. He wiggled out of John's coat, clawed up on his shoulder, and jumped. He landed on the roof of the house behind us and started scampering along the edge.

"Come back, kitty!" John cried, standing on his toes and swiping at the animal. "Oh no, Phil's gonna kill me if I lose her cat…"

"Wait." I grabbed his arm and held him back. The cat paused at the end of the house and turned to look at me, glassy eyes blinking. Then he flicked his tail and kept moving.

Suddenly, I knew what to do. It was a dumb idea, spoken by a voice I hadn't talked to in years, but I decided to take the bait.

"You'd better not make me look like an idiot," I muttered aloud.

"Who are you talking to?" John asked.

"Not you," I intoned. I pointed. "We have to follow that stupid cat!"

John needed no encouragement and took off at a run.

We barreled down the alley, avoiding piles of trash and fallen bricks while we kept one eye on the cat. He slinked along the edge of the interconnected roofs, slipping under the power lines that hung dangerously low. He led us down a narrow passageway to the next street over and then back again, occasionally pausing on the corner to sniff the air.

Abruptly, he stopped in the middle of a roof. He climbed up to the peak and glanced back at me, whiskers twitching. Then he leapt over the edge and disappeared into the courtyard beyond.

"This has to be it—she's here." I scanned the alley. The house and the ones on either side of it were abandoned, the perfect place for a handful of criminals to hide out for the night. We were on the backside of the building, and the rear door and all the windows were boarded up.

"This way," John whispered. He squeezed into the narrow passageway between the two houses. I followed, squatting to make sure I stayed out of sight of the windows. John found a place where the courtyard wall sagged low because several rows of brick were missing. He jumped up on an abandoned barrel with an agility that belied his age and peered into the courtyard.

"It's him—there's Jayde."

I let out my breath and thanked the voice in my head—and that stupid cat. "How many people does he have with him?" I asked, making sure to keep my voice low.

John counted off on his fingers. "Three in the courtyard."

I reached inside my jacket and powered on my gun, then hesitated. I could easily take the four of them out from over the courtyard wall, but there could be more guarding the main gate. We had no way of knowing how many there were or what kind of backup they had. As much as I wanted to drop Jayde in his tracks, if we wanted to avoid causing a commotion, we'd be better off luring them away from the house and sneaking Phil out the back.

"We need a distraction," I thought aloud.

"Say less," John crowed.

"A *small* one," I added when I remembered who I was talking to.

He slid a can of silly string back inside his coat. "Killjoy."

"Radio the others—get them to meet you out front. We need to draw them away from the main gate." I pictured the layout of the neighborhood in my mind as the pieces of the plan fell into place. "I'll jump the wall and get Phil out. Tell Lanzhou to meet me in the alley—we'll take Phil out through the back and be gone before they return."

We'd be safe as long as we could get to the more populated streets. Jayde couldn't risk causing a scene any more than we could.

"Genius," John said, and went for a high-five that I ignored. He shrugged it off and continued down the passageway, whispering into his radio.

I took the spot he had vacated and scanned the courtyard. Only one of the halls was still standing. Two burly young men armed with military rifles blocked the doorway. They were mere yards away from me, well within range of my electric pistol.

Suddenly, Jayde strode into view. He strutted about the courtyard, looking like a rooster with his shock of red hair. He barked something to the guards at the door.

I pulled my gun out of its holster and leveled it. I had a clear shot right at Jayde's head. I put my finger on the setting button.

Just then, a shout, a crash, and a squawk came from the next street over. At least, *squawk* was the best way I could describe the sound; it sounded like a startled chicken. And since John and Dowe were involved, I knew better than to ask questions.

Someone yelled for Jayde. He swore and turned to one of the boys guarding the door. "Do *not* move. You, with me." He ran out the main entrance, taking two of the other soldiers with him. The third planted himself in front of the door to the north hall.

I licked my lips in glorious anticipation. At least I'd get to shoot *something* today.

I waited until the shouts and squawking had faded into the distance, then took aim and fired. The electric bullet sapped the breath from the kid's lungs, and he slumped over without a sound.

Holstering my gun, I scrambled over the wall and dropped into the courtyard. I grabbed the guard's rifle and slammed it against the mulberry tree, bending the barrel and rendering it temporarily unusable. Then I rolled his body over. I patted down his pockets until I found what I was looking for: a keyring.

The key to the door was easy to spot; it was just as old and tarnished as the house itself. After glancing to make sure Jayde and his cronies hadn't come back yet, I unlocked the deadbolt and threw the door open.

There she was, huddled in the dark amongst piles of trash like unwanted merchandise. She was cuffed to the rusted skeleton of a bunk bed and gagged with a piece of tape. She groaned and lifted her head when I opened the door. She blinked at me, squinting in the light.

"Philadelphia. It's me." I enunciated slowly, knowing I would be nothing more than an imposing silhouette thanks to the dramatic backlighting.

She instantly came alive, jerking upright and squealing in relief.

I knelt beside her. "Hang on. This is going to hurt." I braced her neck with one hand, then ripped the tape off before either of us could think twice about it.

She gasped for breath. "Nic!" she cried, and the elated terror in her voice was all the thanks I needed.

"Let's get you out of here." I shifted through the guard's keyring, searching for the key to the cuffs.

She patiently held still. "How did you find me?"

"Jayde's stupid and made himself easy to track." I tried a key and grunted when it didn't fit. "I also feel obliged to admit that your stupid cat helped."

As if on command, the dumb animal made his appearance. He flounced in the door, meowing and flicking his tail like I was an announcer who had just welcomed him on stage. He jumped in Phil's lap and rubbed up against her, purring.

"Tommy!" she shrieked, and sounded like she was about to cry.

I gave her a once-over. Her eyes were bloodshot, and there were scratches on her hands and knees. Most telling, however, was the fact that one side of her face was inflamed.

"Are you okay?" I asked, before realizing that was a stupid question to ask someone who had just been kidnapped. I narrowed the search parameters. "Did he hurt you?"

"H-he hit me," she stuttered, as if she wasn't sure how to quantify her pain. "But I'm fine."

That was a lie if there ever was one. After the fifth attempt, I found the right key, and the cuffs released. I hurled them across the room with a growl. *I never should have set my weapon to stun.*

Finally free, Phil scrambled up, grabbed me around the neck, and burst into tears. She buried her face in my shoulder and sobbed, her whole body shaking. I braced myself against the bedframe and tried to recalibrate. I couldn't decide which was worse: the feel of her cold fingers gripping my shirt, or the sound of her shattered cries in my ear.

I straightened and gingerly pried her arms off my neck. "Look, I know you've had a traumatic experience..." I set her on her feet an acceptable distance away. "But that is not an excuse to sneak a hug in."

I expected her to laugh, but she didn't. She blinked, like she was too shellshocked to process that sarcasm was an acceptable form of communication. "Okay," she mumbled. She wiped her eyes and just stood there, apparently having no idea what to do next.

I didn't either. I wished I could take it back, but that would involve me *initiating* a hug. And that was a line neither of us were ready to cross.

I decided to exit the stage by leading the way towards the door. "Well, come meet our new friends."

She scooped up the cat and stumbled after me. "Friends?" She said the word with the same amount of skepticism I usually used for the concept.

I glanced back at her. "I found Jael."

18: PHILADELPHIA

John and Dowe were the last people I was expecting to find waiting outside, but I was nonetheless thrilled to see them.

"Philli!" they shrieked in their accidental unison. They both rushed at me and crushed me in a group hug from both sides. Tommy howled and squirmed out of my arms. I was so grateful for the physical reassurance that I almost started crying again.

Dowe soon got bored and let go, but John seemed to sense my need for comfort and stayed. He held me gently, standing firm and tall like my father used to, while I sniffled into his shoulder. "It's okay, Philli," he whispered, voice deep and clear. "You're safe now."

"Not yet she isn't," Nic barked. "We need to get out of here."

I tensed as the feeling of cold dread returned. *If Jayde catches me again…*

Dowe interrupted before my thoughts could reach their dark conclusion. "Yeah, those chickens won't distract them forever," he agreed.

I pulled away from John. "Chickens?"

He looked downright ashamed. "Don't ask—let's go!"

We ran to a place where the courtyard wall was broken down. I saw Lanzhou on the other side, waving at us. "This way!"

Dowe gave me a boost, and Lanzhou helped me down the other side. Tommy followed on his own, clearing the wall in one leap. Bowen and a young man I didn't recognize met us in the alley. Without a word, we headed west, Tommy trailing on Nic's ankles.

I kept glancing behind us as we ran. Lanzhou touched my shoulder. "Don't worry about Jayde. He won't try anything in public."

I struggled to believe him and stayed close to Nic.

We slowed when we reached the populated part of the neighborhood. We collected the motorbikes from an elderly gentleman who gave me a sideways glance but tactfully said nothing. Both John and Dowe tried to convince me to ride with them, but Nic overruled them with a stoney glare. I let John carry Tommy in his jacket as a compromise.

As soon as we got back to the house, the family took over. I was showered, fed, and checked over by a cousin who claimed to be a doctor. He declared me fine except for some scratches, gave me a handful of pills, and told me to rest.

While my aching joints longed to obey him, I realized as soon as I got upstairs that sleeping would be easier said than done. I pushed open the door to my bedroom and was instantly assaulted with a wave of cruel memories. The room felt dark and claustrophobic, even though it was blindingly lit with the noonday sun. I shut and latched all the windows and dragged the stool in front of the door to the hall, but I couldn't shake the feeling of being watched.

"It's fine," I coached myself aloud, suddenly afraid of the silence. "It's the middle of the day, and there's a dozen people in the house."

There were a dozen people in the house last night, too. I backed up and hit the bedframe. The feel of the pole between my shoulder blades reminded me of a dozen other painful senses: the sharp cuffs bruising my wrists, the sticky tape suffocating my cries for help, Jayde's hand hitting—

Something rustled behind me. I shrieked and whipped around, then let out my breath. It was just my cat lying in the middle of the bed. He meowed and rolled over, stretching out his belly as if tempting me to join him.

I forced myself to sit down next to him. "Are you trying to help?" Sinking back on the pile of pillows, I gathered him into my arms and was somewhat surprised when he didn't complain. I pressed his furry body to my chin and closed my eyes, focusing on the steady rumble of his contented purr.

"I need You," I whispered aloud. I wasn't talking to the cat.

I don't remember falling asleep, but I must have, because the next thing I knew, it was late afternoon. The darkness shattered, flinging me mercilessly back into reality. I jerked upright with a gasp. I frantically scanned the room and tried to figure out who or what had woken me, but there was nothing there except for my cat, who was quietly cleaning himself on the end of the bed.

I groaned and stood up. I wasn't about to try going back to sleep. If anything, I felt worse than before. My head was throbbing, and my wrists were red and sore. But most disconcerting was the fact that my face was still tender. I stared at my cheek in the wardrobe mirror and tried to decide if it looked swollen. Wincing, I laid my hand on my face and desperately prayed that it wouldn't bruise.

I changed back into my t-shirt and ripped jeans, which Mrs. Tang had washed. Shrugging on my leather jacket, I grabbed my backpack and made sure Nic's phone and the tablet the Tangs had loaned me were inside. I slid on a pair of house shoes out of respect for the family but grabbed my walking boots, intending to put them on as soon as I got downstairs. I had to get out of this house.

Tommy darted past me as I opened the bedroom door and disappeared down the stairs. I ran to follow him and nearly tripped over Nic. He sat on the top step, elbows propped on his knees, watching the stairwell in silence.

He looked up at me and frowned. "You're up already?"

I shrugged. "How long have you been sitting there?"

"Not long enough," he returned. "The doctor said he gave you some sleep medication—you should have slept at least six hours."

I rubbed my temple. At least that explained why my head hurt and the world was fuzzy around the edges.

Nic stood up as if to block the stairs. "You need to go lie back down."

I cringed; I wasn't nearly medicated enough to want to go back in that room. "I'm not tired," I lied.

He glared at me, but I shot him a look that begged him not to push it. He relented and stepped aside. "Then we may as well get this over with. Jael is ready to see you."

Lanzhou and Bowen met us downstairs. We took a short motorbike ride back to the factory, where they led us up to a conference room on the second level. The room looked like it belonged in a different century than the rest of the building. A wall of one-way mirrored windows flooded the room with brilliant afternoon sunlight, while a glowing digital whiteboard covered the opposing wall. Behind the head of the conference table, a terminal in the ceiling projected a 3D rendering of meeting notes like a hologram.

I would have been fascinated by it had the bright lights not worsened the pounding in my head. I turned away from the windows and scanned the faces in the room. A dozen people were gathered around the sleek metal table, at the head of which resided Jael.

At least, I presumed it was Jael by the way she commanded the room. Her pull on the crowd was magnetic, as if she had redistributed gravity around her. She wasn't particularly tall, but she didn't need to be: Her giant turban and bright green heels added eight inches. She wore a sharp black skirt set that was contrasted with layers of colorful jewelry. She sat with one leg crossed smartly over the other as she listened with an air of motherly benevolence to the talk around the table.

Everyone silenced when we entered. Jael rose and beckoned to me. "Philadelphia." Her accent embellished the name into a title that sounded far too regal for me. "What an honor to finally meet you."

I took the invitation and walked up to her. After a moment of internal debate, I offered my hand.

She glanced at it and clicked her tongue. "No offense but… you haven't had your chip removed, have you?"

I flushed and shook my head.

She smiled reassuringly. "May I?"

I held my right hand out. She gently grabbed it and flipped it over, careful not to touch my palm. She pulled a small device out of her skirt pocket. It was slender like an old phone, its screen cluttered with unreadable code. She slowly passed it over my palm, murmuring with interest.

"This is going to make me sound like a geek…" She chuckled and put the device back in her pocket. "But that's some fascinating programming. A genius device, really."

I managed a smile. That sounded like something my brother would say.

She let go of my hand to gesture at the empty chairs next to hers. "We'll make arrangements to get that removed as soon as we're done here. But please, have a seat. We have much to discuss."

I took the seat to her right. John and Dowe waved at me from across the table, mouthing "hi" like we were mischievous schoolkids. Nic quickly claimed the spot next to me. Lanzhou sat on his other side and dropped the key to his motorbike on the table.

Jael settled back on her throne and fixed Nic with a reprimanding glare. "Q, were weapons necessary for this meeting?"

I threw a glance at Nic. *How did she…?*

Nic grunted and unzipped his jacket. He yanked his gun from its holster, switched it off, and threw it on the table in front of him. Several people murmured around the room.

I stared at the weapon as the light faded from the buttons. He'd had the weapon warmed up and ready to fire. He still didn't trust Jael—and after what happened last night, I didn't blame him.

"Thank you. Before we begin, Philadelphia…" Jael drew my attention back to her. "Please accept my sincere apologies, and those of the Tangs, for last night's incident. They assure me that the guard responsible and his associates have been dealt with."

I glanced down at Lanzhou, who dipped his head in an apologetic bow.

I swallowed. If only an apology could wipe the feeling of being violated from my nerves. "And what about Jayde?" I dared to ask.

"That depends on how quickly he returns my calls," she replied, the threat unveiled in her tone. "But rest assured that I'm keeping a very close eye on his internet activity. If he—or anyone I don't trust—checks in anywhere nearby, my people will get there first." She leaned across the table and laid her hand gently over mine. "I promise, he will not hurt you."

I stared down at her brightly colored nails, not sure I believed her. No one else had been able to protect me from Jayde; what made her think she could?

She withdrew her hand. "We'll see how Jayde responds, but I'm aiming to keep this debacle between us. I have a feeling he'll be more cooperative once he finds out I'm involved."

"And how are you involved in this?" Nic demanded.

"And who are you exactly?" I added, which seemed the more important question.

She grinned at us both. "I'm what you would call a tech mogul. I own one of the largest internet service providers in the world—which is also, incidentally, how I'm involved in this."

She stroked her fingers across the tablet inlaid in the conference table. The projection behind her chair went blank, then snapped back into focus. There, in full color, was an eerily 3D rendering of a video I wished I could forget: the security footage from Rott.

I flinched. I was already struggling to keep the memories of last night at bay; I didn't need to be assaulted with more horrors from my past. Thankfully, the sound on the video was muted. I deliberately turned away, focusing instead on the flashing bangles on Jael's wrists. They clacked together as she narrated with her hands.

"We were aware that the government was developing something on Rott, so I sent my agents to investigate."

"She means us!" John and Dowe squealed, and then gave each other a high-five.

I winced as the sharp sound made my ears ring. "You guys are... spies?"

Dowe folded his arms and dropped his voice an octave. "The name's Dowe. John Dowe."

"Please don't *ever* do that again," Nic groaned.

"I just... would have never guessed you guys were spies," I managed. *Or were employed at all.*

"Exactly," Jael beamed. "They're some of my best."

"So glad she assigned the pick of the litter to our case," Nic muttered, quietly enough that probably only I heard. I would have found it funny if my head wasn't spinning. I was in no frame of mind to process information this outlandish. Maybe Nic was right; maybe I should have gone back to bed.

Jael swiveled her chair to face the projection. "We discovered that the United was planning to mass produce a weapon, but they hadn't secured the formula yet. When they sent Ambrose to retrieve Dr. Nic, I knew we had to get him out of there."

I turned to Nic, who looked equally surprised by this revelation. "You were going to rescue me?" he scoffed, incredulous and ungrateful.

"We *tried* to rescue you, bro," Dowe insisted.

"You were supposed to order pizza!" John thumped his hands on the table.

Nic copied the gesture, making my headache even worse. "I didn't know! That coupon didn't exactly come with redemption instructions."

John cocked his head to the side. "Yeah, it did. It's in the fine print on the back."

"Enough," Jael mercifully interrupted. "What's done is done. Unfortunately, the United got the formula before I could intervene, and Thames sent you two back to Rott. And then this happened."

I saw a flash of colors out of the corner of my eye and instinctively turned to look at the projection. It was the moment everything changed: the moment I came on screen and identified myself to the world.

Jael grinned and spread her hands. "Our Blue Fire was born."

Something about her choice of words sent a weight dropping into my stomach, like someone had cut the line on an elevator. "I don't... I don't understand."

She rotated her chair back to face me. "I was watching the whole time. As soon as I saw this clip, I knew I'd found my thunderbird."

Her statement slammed into my heart, shattering my reality on impact. Nic's words came rushing back to me like a gust of cold air.

God didn't choose you for anything, Phil.

"To be fair," Jael typed on the tablet as she continued to explain, "the 'Blue Fire' imagery was Jayde's idea. He leaked the video before I was ready, but no harm done. The association served us well."

"No harm done?" Nic screeched. "You and I must have very different definitions of that word."

Jael misinterpreted his comment. "I had been planning to release the video myself, but I was hoping to extract you two first. I sent Tower the order to have you deported to the mainland, where my team was going to intercept you."

"My uncle knew?" I asked, even though I couldn't remember formulating the question. My voice sounded faint and echoey to my own ears, like it belonged to someone else. Like *I* belonged to someone else.

Jael nodded. "Unfortunately, after you arrived on the mainland, Thames got to you first. We didn't know Nolan was involved at the time, so I had no way of tracking where he'd taken you. While we were searching for you, Jayde leaked your first video. So I seized the opportunity and made it trend."

Her statement cycled around and around in my head like a warning siren. "You're the reason I trended," I whispered, afraid that if I spoke louder, it would make it true.

Jael grinned, revealing a row of perfect teeth. "I made you, Blue Fire."

I sank back in the chair and grabbed the seat—first with one hand, then the other. I gripped the plastic, desperate for something solid as everything I thought I knew crumbled away.

Nic was right. God hadn't chosen me. Jael had.

"How'd you manage that without getting arrested?" Nic demanded. He furrowed his brow, like this whole situation was a math problem to be solved. "Surely the government can review the analytics and figure out it was you who let it slip through the algorithm."

Jael's eyes sparkled, as if she'd been waiting all day for someone to ask. "As an internet service provider, I control the algorithm in my region. One of my biggest markets is Africa, which the West still considers to be 'third world.'"

She tapped the tablet, and a complicated pie chart appeared on the projector. "Being labeled as 'underdeveloped' has its perks. With the exception of a few population centers, the United doesn't care what most of the two billion people on my continent are doing. They're too busy negotiating for cobalt to keep their precious electric cars on the road. Besides, Africa has always been behind the world average in internet accessibility—who's going to know if I don't report a couple thousand users here and there?"

She smirked coyly, as if she'd just unlocked the key to the universe. I looked at Nic to see if this was making any sense to him. He was studying the chart on the screen, eyes flicking as he scanned the text.

"For the first forty-eight hours, I released the video in select markets, focusing on areas with big populations and minimal government oversight," Jael continued to explain. "I let the keywords trend briefly in different regions, always changing the parameters so it would look like I was doing my job."

The diamond on her finger danced as she rapidly swiped through menus. The image on the projector cycled through analytics and graphs and statistics that must have meant something to her. All I could think was that each number, equation, and data point was breaking down my identity, reducing Blue Fire to a search term a single woman could control.

Blue Fire wasn't a miracle. She was a lie.

"We did the same thing in Russia, South America, rural China— anywhere United control isn't as strict. By the time we released the video to the wider market, the movement was already too big to contain. The internet did the rest—with some help from my friends in social media, of course," Jael finished with a grand sweep of her hands.

Nic let out his breath, low and threatening. "You have no idea what you've done."

"I created a freedom movement," she snapped. "*We* created a freedom movement. Philadelphia was the perfect candidate. An unscripted act of rebellion from the person you'd least expect, plus an explosive story about a secret government weapon—it was the ideal combination to drive views. I couldn't have created a better story myself."

"But you did create me," I said, my doubt forming into words. "This is all scripted."

Jael's giant earrings bounced as she tipped her head to the side and smiled at me. "Nothing about your defiance is scripted, honey. That's why you're the perfect thunderbird."

No, I wasn't. I wasn't the thunderbird—I wasn't anything. This was all an illusion. Everything about the Blue Fire movement had been manufactured by a human. I was nothing more than a product of the algorithm and creative editing, all curated for one woman's gain.

I choked as the realization filled my lungs like water. Jael was using me; she'd been using me this whole time. Everything that had happened to me over the last few months, all the lucky circumstances I thought were miracles, had been orchestrated by her or Asia. I had merely been a pawn in their game as they'd used my image to fight for power.

And I was so naïve that I believed *God* had called me. God didn't choose me; He didn't have anything to do with this. He didn't speak to me. I made it all up in my head. I let Jayde or the Devil or *someone* lie to me about how important I was, and in my pride, I thought I could save the world. I'd fed into the machine, and now hundreds of thousands of people were prepared to fight and die in a war I'd created.

Nic was right. I was not a hero.

And I was not going to let anyone use me ever again.

19: NIC

Well, that explains a lot.

I stared at the graph on the projection as my brain adopted this information into the equation. I found it strangely comforting to know that all the terrible and annoying things that had happened to us over the past few months weren't freak accidents. Even John and Dowe—I was relieved to learn that they had a function on this planet other than building my character.

Jael was a problem, however. She had almost as much intel on us as Asia did, and I doubted she would be happy when I announced Phil's retirement. She created Blue Fire; she wouldn't let her go without a fight. And given how much influence this woman had over the algorithm, I wasn't sure I wanted her to know about our new files, anyway.

Before I could rationalize that problem, however, Phil presented me with a bigger one. She gripped the edge of the table and shoved her chair back. "I am not your thunderbird," she snapped.

There were whispers around the table. I seconded her statement, but now was a terrible time to announce it. "Phil…" I warned.

Bowen tried to help. "Blue Fire—" he said, rising.

"I am not Blue Fire!" she screamed. She slammed her fist on the table, causing the tablet to rock and the projection to glitch.

Jael just arched an eyebrow. "Philadelphia. You need to calm down."

"Don't tell me to calm down!" She turned on her. "You've been using me! You're no better than Asia."

Jael, to her credit, didn't deny it. "It was necessary."

Poor choice of words.

Phil took a step back. "Funny," she retorted in a voice devoid of feeling, "that's exactly what Thames said to me."

Jael studied her, calculating. "You chose this, Philadelphia. You didn't have to record more videos. You know how important this is."

"Yeah, well, I was wrong." Phil's voice cracked, and for a flicker of a moment, she was a scared little girl again.

And then that girl died.

Phil took a deep breath through her nose and straightened. Her eyes glinted, the pain vanishing from her expression like a lake freezing over. She lifted her chin and declared to the entire room, "I'm not going to do it."

Lanzhou scraped his chair back. "Please, let's talk about this."

"Yes, let's. *In private*," I added, reaching for her shoulder.

She shrugged me off. "There's nothing to discuss. I'm done. Nic and I are getting new files and going back to Mars."

If only it were that easy, but I could tell by the shift in the room that it wouldn't be. Bowen and Lanzhou shared a nervous glance. The guard near the door reached for his taser, even though he was too far away to have a clean shot. No one spoke.

Jael shifted in her chair. She had one final moment to regain control of the situation, one final opportunity to win back Phil's trust.

She didn't take it. She beckoned at the guard. "I'm afraid that won't be possible, Philadelphia."

Wrong answer.

Phil reacted before the guard could. She lunged and grabbed my gun off the table. Flicking it on, she planted her feet apart and aimed it at Jael.

"Then make it possible," Phil spat.

Someone gasped. It took a second to realize it was me.

"Drop your weapon!" someone behind me yelled.

Jael lifted a finger to stop him, and wisely so. I could tell by the stance of Phil's body that she was prepared to shoot—and she would not miss.

"Let us go," Phil demanded, "or I'll shoot."

Jael barely flinched. "I see we're still upset over the events of the past few days," she said, putting her feet on the floor and slowly raising her hands. "Perhaps we should have this conversation later—"

Phil apparently agreed whole-heartedly, because she shot her. It was a clean shot, too—straight to the heart. Jael slumped over instantly, her immaculate suit marred with a smoking scorch mark.

The room erupted in shouts. I stumbled back, tripping over my chair. "Philadelphia!"

"Don't worry, it was set on stun." She whipped around to face Lanzhou and aimed the gun at his face. "Keys," she demanded.

The guard in the corner of the room leveled his rifle, but I put my hand out. "You might reconsider. Jayde's the one who taught her how to shoot."

Lanzhou factored that into his calculations. "Stand down," he ordered after a breathless minute.

No one obeyed him. "I said stand down!" he shouted again.

The guard lowered his rifle. Everyone else gingerly eased back into their seats. Lanzhou waited until they had stopped moving before turning to Phil. "Consider what you're doing."

"I know exactly what I'm doing," she snapped, and I believed her. "Keys."

Lanzhou hesitated a moment more, then grabbed his motorbike key off the table and tossed it at me.

"We're leaving," Phil announced, as if there was any doubt. "And don't even think about following us. If you give me any trouble, I swear I will go online and tell the government exactly where to look."

The silence rang in the room. I stared at her as she filled me with an emotion she had never before inspired.

Fear.

Satisfied no one was going to make a move, Phil lowered the gun slightly but kept her finger on the trigger. "Let's go," she said to me.

"I don't think we have much of a choice at this point." I ran out into the hall, keeping a wary eye on the guard.

Phil backed out after me. She made one last threatening sweep with her weapon, then punched the button to close the door. "This way!" She held the gun out of sight underneath her jacket and took off running.

I struggled to keep up. She ran to the stairwell, wisely bypassing the elevator. We pounded down the stairs to the docks. She took the steps two at a time and managed to keep ahead of me.

Thankfully for all involved, there was no one in the employee lot where the bikes were parked. Phil ran up to Lanzhou's bike. "Drive," she ordered.

"Gun first," I returned, then realized that was a foolish way to talk to someone with a loaded weapon.

Mercifully, I was still on her whitelist. She powered off the weapon and tossed it at me. I holstered it and jumped on the bike. Phil climbed on behind me. I tensed as her sharp fingernails gripped my jacket.

I started the bike and peeled out of the parking lot. Thankfully, the gates were open for shift change, so I blew past security, scattering a few disgruntled workers. I turned onto a side street and revved the engine as much as it would go—which unfortunately wasn't much. I didn't trust the guards to heed Phil's warning, so I wanted to get us as far away from the factory as possible before Jael came to. Then we would hide out until everyone calmed down. I could only hope Phil would be more reasonable after the sleep medication fully wore off.

She, however, had her own plans. "Head for the bus station!"

"Why?" I shouted back over the grind of the engine.

"We need to get to the subway!"

"It's almost rush hour. There will be a huge wait for the bus."

"Then we'll walk. Turn here!" She leaned forward and pointed with her arm.

I decided I'd better not argue with her while we were both balanced on a bike I only sort of knew how to drive. I followed her haphazard directions as we wove through the neighborhood, twisting and turning across alleys to avoid the increasing traffic. Soon the roads grew too clogged, and Phil ordered me to brake and abandon the bike behind a dumpster.

She jumped off and ran almost before I came to a complete stop. I parked the vehicle and hid the key in the basket on the back, muttering an apology to Lanzhou. Then I took off after Phil.

"Wait!" I shouted.

"Keep up!" she unhelpfully yelled back.

She was too far away for me to physically stop her. I pushed myself to catch up as she darted down the street. She shoved through the afternoon crowd, ignoring the protests and shouts in Mandarin. I almost lost sight of her as she sprinted across the street without looking. A car screeched to a stop, barely missing her.

Thankfully, I could see where she was headed; the subway station was in the square across the street. I waited until the crosswalk was clear, then ran after her. "Phil! Philadelphia!"

She didn't turn. I broke past the last crowd and fairly screamed at her. "Phil, stop, please!"

It took her three more yards to slow down, like she was a speeding train trying to brake. "Don't yell my name in public places."

"That's the least of our concerns right now. Slow down."

"The subway entrance is just ahead," she returned, her back to me.

I finally caught up to her. "I'm aware, and it'll still be there if we catch our breath for a minute." I collapsed on a bench and hoped she would take the hint.

She relented, yanking her backpack off and tossing it on the bench next to me. She stomped a few paces ahead and stopped under a tree, glaring up at the leaves like they held all the answers.

After making sure she was distracted, I pulled her backpack closer and silently undid the zipper. As I'd hoped, the tablet she'd borrowed from the Tangs was in there. I turned it on and made sure it was online.

Phil didn't notice. "Are you ready to go?"

I zipped the backpack shut. "That depends on where we're going. You seem to have a plan—care to enlighten me?"

"Same thing we were always going to do: Get out of the city and call Ephesus. I thought that was your great idea all along."

I could tell fatigue was catching up to her, and her attempt at being bratty just came out sounding pathetic. I knew this was my window to get through to her.

I took a breath to filter the sarcasm from my voice. "Philadelphia, we need to talk."

"What's there to talk about?"

"The fact that you just shot someone and stole a bike, for starters. Please, sit down."

She didn't. "Don't you get it? You were right all along."

As much as I loved to be right, something about her tone told me that, maybe this time, I would rather be wrong.

"You were right about everything," she continued. She wrapped her arms around her chest, like that could keep the dark emotions inside. "God didn't choose me. He had nothing to do with this. I let my fame go to my head, and I made this whole thing up. I am not a hero."

I stared at her. I had, in fact, said that.

She roared and yanked on her short hair. "I am such an idiot! I can't believe I went through all of this for nothing."

"What do you mean?" I said slowly, realizing she was balancing on the precipice of something very dangerous.

She flicked her hand broadly, as if her life story were mere scribbles to be wiped off a whiteboard. "My dad, Rott, this *stupid* operation… I literally just got drugged and locked in a dark room for twelve hours, and for *what*?"

Her voice reached a pitch and shattered, drawing glances from passersby. I stared at the red welt on her cheek as the events of recent months flashed through my mind. This fragile teenage girl had been through immeasurable trauma, and she hadn't gotten a moment's rest. She hadn't received any therapy, and she'd been forced to make terrible decisions no child should ever have to consider. All the adults in her life had failed her.

Including me.

She laughed, a sinister, unhinged sound. "Do you know why I did it?"

I swallowed, but she didn't wait for me to gather my wits. "I did it because I thought God wanted me to. I really thought He'd called me. I really thought I'd heard from Him."

Her voice stretched into a plead, as if she was begging someone, anyone to believe her. I knew she was telling the truth. I knew that's exactly why she did it, and that was the only thing that had kept her from having a mental breakdown before now. Her faith in God was the only thread that had prevented her from becoming the villain of her own story.

And I'd broken that thread.

"I really thought this was the 'right thing to do.'" She mocked her own existence with air quotes. "But it wasn't."

Yes, it was, that voice in my head reminded me. And, for the first time in a long time, I agreed with Him.

"Phil—" I started.

She wasn't listening. "They all lied to me!" She yanked the jade bangle off her wrist and hurled it at the ground. I flinched—but thankfully, she missed. The bracelet clipped the edge of the sidewalk and bounced harmlessly into the dirt.

Phil gave an annoyed gurgle, as if she was frustrated with her inability to complete this simple task. "Come on," she snapped. She grabbed her backpack and strode towards the subway entrance.

I scooped up the bangle and jogged after her. We passed the defunct ticket scanners and started down the stairs to the platform. It was the beginning of rush hour, and the queue snaked halfway up the stairwell already. We joined the back of the line. Phil stared straight ahead, her back to me.

I looked down at the bangle in my hand. She'd chipped it on the concrete. I fingered the rough edge, remembering all the coffee cups, beakers, and soup bowls I'd sacrificed to my anger. I remembered the moment I'd hurled the contents of an entire table onto the floor, reeling from Asia's betrayal. That was the moment I'd determined to finish Red Rain. That was the moment I'd told the voice in my head to shut up and decided to do things my way.

And I realized, if I didn't pull Philadelphia back from the brink, she was going to end up exactly like me.

"Phil," I said, nudging her arm.

"What?" she snapped without looking back.

I glanced around. The old man in front of us was so ancient that he probably couldn't hear even if we shouted, and the teens who had joined the line behind us all had headphones. I took a deep breath and turned to face Philadelphia.

"They didn't lie to you."

"What do you mean?" Her voice was short, almost like she didn't care about the answer.

"They didn't lie to you," I repeated, making sure I was heard. "I did."

For the first time since we'd left the warehouse, she turned and looked up at me.

I met her gaze. "I lied to you. He does want you to do this." I omitted proper names in case there were any eavesdroppers.

She snorted. "You're just saying that to make me feel better." She looked away again.

"No, I'm not." I grabbed her shoulder and tried to turn her back towards me. "I've seen it. The Nolans, the party invite, everything—He wants you here."

She furrowed her brow. "What do you mean you *saw* it?"

I hesitated. My inclination was my best kept secret, but if she was going to believe me, she had to have the whole truth.

"I mean I *saw* it. The night before last, when you claimed you were never supposed to be a Nolan—I saw it all. You, in Beijing, as a Nolan, on even playing ground with Asia. He showed me."

She frowned at me like I was insane—which was how most normal people reacted when I told them I had an open vision. "You don't really believe that."

The line surged forward as a train pulled into the station, relieving the platform of a couple hundred people. Phil shrugged out of my grasp and ran down the steps.

I caught up with her. "You think I'd make something like *that* up? Trust me, I've tried to return this gift to sender several times."

"Stop patronizing me, Nic," she groaned. "I know what you really believe."

What do I really believe?

The line shuffled forward again. Phil squeezed a step ahead, putting the old man between us.

I knew I was losing her. She was no fool, and I'd spent too many days breaking down this bridge to lie my way across it. There was no amount of charismatic speaking that could convince her to go through with this if my heart wasn't in it. I had to decide right here, right now, what I believed, or I was taking her to hell with me.

I traded places with the old man, apologizing in Mandarin as I shoved him up a step. I stood next to Phil and spoke just loud enough for her to hear.

"I believe in God."

I took a deep breath as those words erased a thousand sins.

Phil was less forgiving. "That's great," she mocked. "Even the demons believe, and at least it makes *them* tremble."

"Yeah, and why do you think I ran the other way?" We shuffled forward a few more steps, and I leaned over and tried to get in her line of vision. "You want to talk about faith by actions—why do you think I've been trying to get us to go back to Mars? Because I know what you're supposed to do, and I know that if you stay in Beijing… then that means I have to stay too."

She jerked, as if my words had finally pierced through her armor. I saw the anger in her expression crack, and when she spoke again, I heard her: the old Philadelphia. "You—you mean that? But you said—"

"I know what I said," I cut her off, but gently. "Phil, I said those things because I didn't want to go back. I don't want to stay here and play politics. Don't you think I've seen this all before?"

Unbidden, the memories of my idealistic younger self reared their foolish head, and I remembered all the reasons why I'd lied to her in the first place. I twisted the bangle in my fingers and sighed. "You're in the exact same position I was when I met Asia. I had money, influence, and political connections. I could have done something. But after what she did to my parents..."

I didn't have to finish the sentence. As the words left my mouth, I finally understood why God had chosen Philadelphia.

It wasn't because she was anyone special. It wasn't because she had done anything particularly amazing. It wasn't even because she was in the right place at the right time.

He had chosen her because she had said *yes*—when I had said *no*.

I remembered the moment I'd taken my life back into my own hands. I'd walked to the whiteboard, the one covered with the incomplete formula for Red Rain, and told God I was going to do it myself. The way I saw it, doing things God's way had cost me my parents' lives. If that was how the game was played, I might as well do it my way and save myself in the process.

I am no better than they are.

I'd said no to God that day—and then time and time again, I'd refused His counteroffers. I could have taken responsibility for my crimes instead of using Smyrna as my scapegoat, forcing him to complete the formula. I could have helped Philadelphia destroy the factory instead of trying to salvage Red Rain, nearly killing her in the process. I could have helped her find her father instead of letting her go back to Earth alone. I could have helped her be the leader she was called to be—instead of letting her fight a war by herself and then yelling at her when she made stupid choices.

I'd said no to God's call on my life. But now, standing next to me— looking up at me with vulnerable, bloodshot eyes—was one final offer.

We reached the platform. I glanced up and realized there was only a short line between us and the subway. If we squeezed, we could make it on the next train. It was now or never—and if I thought about it too hard, *never* still looked very tempting.

I took a breath and turned to face her. "Look, I still don't want to stay here, and I don't expect that to change any time soon. But I know what I saw. I know what you're supposed to do, and I know you need my help. So, I'm making the decision to do what you've always done." I held the bangle out to her.

She took it very slowly. "And that is?"

“Do it anyway.”

I scanned the platform and spotted a gap in the crowd that led to the exit—back to Beijing, Jael, the revolution. I turned to look at Philadelphia where she stood behind me on my left. She watched me, waiting.

I smiled and held out my left hand.

20: PHILADELPHIA

What have I done?

I stared at the bangle in my hand. The feel of the cold jade brought reality crashing back down on me, and I wasn't sure I liked what I remembered.

Did I really shoot someone? What if she's hurt? Oh God, please let her be okay! What was I thinking, running away? I can't believe I stole Lanzhou's bike! How am I going to fix this? I can't go back there and face them! They'll never forgive me! Oh Jesus, who have I become?

But even as the shame and grief swirled around in my head like a dust storm, several other truths solidified out of the noise.

I knew I didn't make this up! I knew I heard from God. I know what God's voice sounds like.

I had the Holy Spirit. If I'd had any doubts about what God was saying, I should have tried the spirits and found the answer for myself. But instead, I'd let a bunch of humans—Nic, Jayde, Jael—reframe my truth. I'd let their words *and* my own fears convince me that God was lying to me.

And all the while, God had been showing Nic the same things, confirming His Word to both of us.

I stared at the back of Nic's head as he scanned the crowd. Had he really seen all that, about me? Why would God show him my future? What did any of this have to do with Nic?

Nic's last words echoed back to me. *"I know what you're supposed to do, and I know you need my help."*

I clenched my fist around the bangle as the last piece of the puzzle, the checkmate in the game of chess we'd been playing for the last nine months, snapped into place. This was why God had sent my family to Mars in the first place, why He'd allowed me to get tangled up in Wing 74 and Red Rain. It was because He knew I needed Dr. Nic Von Nieuwenhuyse.

If there was anyone who could help me fight Beijing politics and confront Asia, it was Nic.

Motion in my peripheral distracted me. I looked up to see Nic turning to me with the rarest of expressions: a smile.

And then he held out his left hand.

I stared at it, knowing full well it was an invitation to a life I didn't fully understand yet. But it was the life God called me to have—the life He called us *both* to have.

Nic arched an eyebrow and wiggled his fingers. "If you leave me hanging for too long, I will take it back. You know how I hate physical affection."

I grinned, a sliver of joy finding its way into my soul. Sliding the bangle back on my wrist, I reached out and grabbed Nic's hand with my right.

Our palms contacted—and I felt a shock. I must have built up static electricity in the stairwell.

Nic felt it too. He dropped my hand and jerked back, as if it had caused him a lot of pain. "What the—"

He never finished. He hesitated, for a split second looking panicked, and then he collapsed.

"Nic!" I screamed as his head hit the tile with a crack.

The displaced crowd grumbled and stumbled around us, and I feared he might be trampled. I shoved someone aside and dropped down next to his head. I shook his shoulder with both hands. "Nic! Get up!"

He didn't respond. And that's when I realized he wasn't breathing.

"Nic!" My terror turned the name into a bloodcurdling wail.

Oh God, oh God, help!

The murmur in the crowd changed pitch. "He's not breathing!" I yelled. "Someone help!"

Several people shouted. A man shoved his way through the crowd and knelt next to Nic. He held his fingers to Nic's neck, then immediately planted his hands on his chest and started pumping.

I watched in fascinated horror as he alternated between compressions and deep breaths into Nic's mouth and nose. He repeated the maneuver with relentless efficiency, pausing only to call to someone in the crowd. Time seemed to freeze over as the stranger tried desperately to pump life back into Nic's body.

Jesus, save him!

Nothing changed. I wasn't sure if ten seconds or ten minutes had passed, but I could tell the man was getting frustrated. He paused to check Nic's pulse again, then grunted and resumed compressions.

No, God, no!

A subway employee darted up to us and dropped an orange box on the floor. The other man unzipped Nic's jacket. There were some gasps over Nic's holstered gun, but the man ignored it and ripped Nic's shirt open. He pulled two wired patches off the box and arranged them on Nic's chest. Then he punched a button on the keypad.

The device beeped. Nic's body twitched, but his heart did not respond. The man tried again. Still no movement. I watched as Nic's face and neck began to turn purple.

No, God, don't do this! I need him!

A young woman pushed her way up to the subway employee. She held out her phone and asked a question. He shouted something in Mandarin into the receiver.

Someone behind me translated. "He said it's sudden cardiac arrest."

As soon as he said it, I knew what had happened. The chip in my palm.

I looked down at my right hand.

Nic was dying. And I killed him.

VON

RED RAIN #7.5

AUGUST 2067

1

Having a doctorate in astronomy came with a lot of privileges. At the moment, it gave me a plausible excuse for why I was walking around on the roof of the college library in the middle of the night.

It was early August, and the campus was a graveyard. A few lights flickered in one of the halls across the lawn as the janitors worked to prepare the building for the fall semester. A security guard strolled lazily along the fence, the bounce of his flashlight the only movement in the abandoned parking lot. Even the omnipresent hum of downtown Boston seemed muted, as if the sultry summer heat had blanketed the city in silence.

Leaning against the railing, I inhaled a deep breath of the humid air. Most of the other professors were still on summer vacation, but I never left—mainly because I wasn't allowed to. "Unassimilated" staff did not get employee benefits like paid leave, a fact they reminded me of every May.

I didn't care. I would rather work than sit at home and wonder what the world was coming to. Besides, being on campus during the summer gave me freedom from prying eyes. And since my business was the stars, nobody questioned why I was up on the roof after dark with a box of suspicious electronics.

I reached down and adjusted the radio I had balanced on the ledge, triple-checking to make sure it was tuned to the right channel. She would be calling any minute.

I looked back up at the sky. It was almost midnight, and the constellation Pisces had swum above the horizon, dragging Mars in its wake. Even with the light pollution of the inner city, the red planet was clearly visible, its orange glow like a speck of fire amongst the sea of blue-white stars. I stared at the unflickering disc, imagining the alien landscape I loved so well. I pictured the gorged valleys, the untapped wilderness, the merciless dust storms—and my son, who was no doubt standing in his office on his science station, watching the distant sun rise above the hazy horizon.

I closed my eyes. *Be safe, Nic.*

Static on the radio interrupted my prayer. There was clipped chatter, and then a young woman's voice came through, clear and sparkling. "This is Caesar. Von, do you copy? Over."

I grinned. At least one of my children was still on this planet.

I picked up the handset and pressed down on the button. "This is Von, I copy. How's my girl? Over."

"Bored," she moaned in that pitch only teenagers can master. She dragged the "o" out for a full three seconds.

I chuckled. That was what she usually said. Boarding school, with its rigid schedule and cookie cutter curriculum, was not a stimulating environment for my fiery daughter. "And how was school? Over."

There was a pause before she replied. "It was... rough."

I tensed. "Which class was giving you trouble?"

The line went silent. I waited patiently for her to gather her words. She knew I wasn't really asking about schoolwork. Even though I would have loved to hear about every detail of her day, radio wasn't private. Someone was always listening. But seeing as regulations only permitted me to visit Cea for thirty minutes twice a week, and all her phone calls and text messages were monitored by an antagonistic social worker, a smuggled radio was the only way I could stay involved with my daughter's life. To compensate, we'd invented our own code, so she could keep me apprised without either of us ending up in jail.

"Well," she said finally, filling the dead air with that elongated word. "I had detention."

I gripped the handset a little too hard, accidentally smashing a button and causing my device to squeal. "Detention" meant she'd gotten in trouble with the authorities. "I see," I replied, struggling to keep the emotion out of my voice. "Was it your fault? Over."

The answer was almost always "no." "No" meant she'd been punished for something she couldn't deny—like praying or reading her Bible, all things the government had arbitrarily decided were illegal. And while my every instinct was to protect her, to shield her so she'd never get hurt, I wouldn't ask her to deny her identity.

I would have preferred if "detention" happened a little less often—this was the second time this week—but I really couldn't expect any less. She was my child, after all. And unlike her brother, this apple hadn't yet fallen from the tree.

I realized she hadn't answered my question. "Caesar? Do you copy?"

Static clogged the line. "Yeah, uh... it was kind of my fault."

"Kind of?" I prompted.

More dead air. "I was... out after hours."

I frowned, although my stern expression was wasted on the abandoned rooftop. The boarding school had a strict curfew, and students were forbidden from leaving the grounds—not unlike prison, really. And while I wasn't opposed to my daughter sneaking out, our rule was that she was only allowed to leave when she was meeting up with me or someone I trusted. And I didn't remember approving any outings last night.

"Caesar," I threatened, "what were you doing?"

There was a burst of static, then a new voice joined the conversation. "This is Andes. It's okay, Von, she was with me."

I bristled. Andes was, admittedly, someone I trusted; he'd help me forge files, alter fingerprints, and cover my tracks more than once. But that didn't mean I approved of my fourteen-year-old daughter meeting him after dark.

Andes kept talking before I could express my concern. "She was with me the whole time, and I made sure she got home safely," he explained in his careless Scottish accent. "They just caught her out in the yard after curfew— nothing to worry about."

No, that gave me *plenty* to worry about. I wasn't sure which bothered me more—the fact that my daughter had met with Andes without my permission, or the fact that he'd let her get caught.

Andes didn't wait for me to get it together. "How's that ink healing, Caesar? Over."

"What ink?" I snapped, cutting in before she could respond.

The line abruptly went silent, which told me everything I needed to know.

There were several legitimate reasons why Cea may have gone to see Andes—downloading a copy of the Bible, hacking around the spyware on a device—but a tattoo was not one of them.

"Caesar," I growled, wishing for all the world I could use her full name, "what did you do?"

"It's nothing, Da—Von," she whined. Her voice faded in and out, like she was fidgeting with her handset. "It's just the thunderbird symbol."

"*Just* the thunderbird symbol?" I lost control of my tone of voice as my anger was replaced by genuine fear. The thunderbird was the icon for Operation Blue Fire, the most infamous transmitting network in the nation. I'd gone to jail more than once for displaying that same symbol, and now my daughter had it permanently emblazoned who-knows-where on her body. If her teachers found out, she would go to juvenile—and I'd lose what few visiting rights I had.

"Caesar." I took a deep breath to quell my emotions. "Do you understand what that symbol means?"

"You said I could join the network!" she complained.

"I said we would talk about it!" We had discussed it. I'd been involved with the network for over a decade, sharing Bibles and other censored media through my databases. Cea wanted to transmit from school so she could reach other teens in the system. I was going to help her get started—but I'd said *nothing* about a tattoo. Her mother was going to murder me.

Andes broke in. "I'm sorry, Von, I thought you knew. She had a signed permission slip."

"I did not—" I ran the math and deduced there were more important questions I should be asking. "Caesar, did you forge my authorization?"

The telltale silence gave me my answer, but I had to hear it from her. That was our rule: There was no problem we could not solve, no sin that could not be forgiven, if she told me the truth.

"Caesar," I repeated, and that was all I had to say.

"I… yes, I did." Her voice warbled, and I would have given anything to be standing in front of her so I could look her in the eye. "I'm sorry. Don't be mad."

I was furious—but that wasn't the side of me she needed to see. I sank down on the ledge and gave myself three beats to find my center. "I am upset," I admitted, careful to keep my voice calm. "Do you understand why?"

"Because I should have asked you first," she mumbled, barely loud enough for me to hear over the static.

"So, why didn't you?"

Andes respectfully stayed silent while my daughter made her confession. "Because I was afraid you'd say no."

"I would have said 'no' only because getting a tattoo is a very serious decision that requires careful thought—just like transmitting. And the fact that you didn't ask for my permission tells me that maybe you're not ready for either."

I let off the button as pain gripped my chest. I knew the words were cutting her just as deeply as they were cutting me, but they had to be said. I wanted my daughter to break the rules. I wanted her to be different, to question society, to rebel against the government—but only if she was doing it for the right reasons.

That was the mistake I'd made with her brother. I'd encouraged his rebellion, praising his civil disobedience even when it landed him in detention or worse. I was so focused on resisting the system that I'd failed to realize my son was rebelling against more than just the government.

"I'm sorry," Cea whimpered, obviously crying. It was almost enough to make me drive across town and jump the boarding school fence—regulations or no regulations.

"I forgive you," I assured her, and I did. "But we will have to talk about this the next time I see you."

She sniffed loudly, causing the line to fuzz. "Yessir."

"I'm sorry, Von, it's my fault," Andes inserted.

It wasn't really, but he certainly should have known better. "You should have called me. Why would you think I'd approve of such a thing?"

"I know, I know—but the permission slip looked legitimate, I swear. It had your ID and everything."

I paused and gave that statement the respect it deserved. In this digital age, forging a permission slip wasn't as easy as copying my signature on a piece of paper. To authorize the procedure, I would have had to fill out a form on Andes's site and then prove my identity to put my electronic stamp on the document. Cea must have either hacked into one of my accounts or convinced the computer that it was me—a feat that was doable, but certainly not easy for a teenager with no coding experience.

"Care to explain, Caesar?" I prodded.

"I, uh, used a filter to trick facial recognition," she confessed, still sniffling. "And I made a scan of your fingerprint when you visited me last. It was on the jewelry box you gave me, remember?"

Of course, I remembered. I'm sure my grubby prints were all over the cheap plastic case. I just never expected my daughter to be dusting my gifts for fingerprints.

Andes whistled into the line. "Looks like we underestimated our little initiate, Von," he chuckled.

Apparently so, I thought to myself, and smiled. If Cea was capable of forging my ID, maybe she *was* ready to learn how to transmit without getting caught.

Cea started to respond, but an urgent voice cut in. "Break, break," someone shouted over the line. "Emergency."

I stiffened when I recognized the voice. *Catalyst.*

Catalyst was a callsign I knew well, although we'd never met in the flesh. He had been involved with the Boston underground even longer than I had. Operation Blue Fire had been his original idea, and I'd helped get it off the ground. We'd worked together to spread the network to China and Mars and beyond. For many years, he'd been my closest partner in crime.

That was until the officials busted my server on Mars—and traced the data to several of our most important associates.

We lost a lot of good people that day. Catalyst quit the operation soon after, claiming he had to take care of his family. He took his servers offline and wiped his data before any of us could talk him out of it.

The rash response had crippled the network. Andes and I had been working for years to restore it, but without Catalyst's contacts, the operation would never be what it was.

I'd tried several times to make amends and convince Catalyst to come back. The situation had been an accident, a childish mistake by my then sixteen-year-old son. I took full responsibility, but if Catalyst had forgiven me, he certainly wasn't acting like it.

Catalyst repeated his call several times until the line silenced. Andes took control of the situation. "This is Andes. We hear you loud and clear, Catalyst. Go ahead, over."

Catalyst almost didn't wait for him to finish the sentence. "Any agents in Allston? Please respond."

I snapped out of my reverie. Allston was my neighborhood. "This is Von. I'm in Allston. What's the situation? Over."

There was silence. I gripped the handset. He was always like this, signing off as soon as I joined the line. *Let it go!*

He finally responded. "Police just called for all units, Coolidge and Arden."

My anger evaporated. That was the intersection my house was on—and my wife was home alone.

Andes knew it too. "Von? Do you have a visual?" he prodded, the fear evident in his voice.

"I'm on my way." I stood and started shoveling my gear back into the box. I struggled to keep a level head even as the blood pounded in my ears. It wouldn't be the first time the police had shown up at my house in the middle of the night; I wasn't an unassimilated citizen with thirty-two felonies for no reason. It was probably just the usual pomp and circumstance.

Except, they didn't normally call for backup.

Jesus, protect my wife!

"Dad?" Cea squeaked, forgetting her manners. "What's going on?"

I didn't correct her. "Caesar, you know the drill. Wipe your feet and put your clothes away. Don't leave the grounds until I contact you."

We had rehearsed this. If I was ever caught, she had a protocol for hiding her gear and erasing the history on her phone so it would look like we barely talked. She was still my daughter, but at least I could make it look like she wasn't involved.

"But I—"

"No," I ordered, and waited until the line silenced before continuing. "This is serious. Now is not the time to break the rules. I will contact you— same time, same channel—when it's safe. Do you understand?"

I clenched my fist, waiting for her to respond. *Trust me, Cea.*

"Yessir," she finally acknowledged. "Over and out."

"Thank you. I love you." I hesitated, realizing there was more I wanted to say—but there wasn't time. There was never time. "Over and out."

Then I turned off the radio and ran.

2

"All units" may have been a bit of an exaggeration, but there were certainly more cop cars at my house than I was comfortable with.

They'd blocked off the entire street. At least six vehicles were camped along the curb, their blaring red-blue lights turning the neighborhood into a grotesque circus. Several of our neighbors whispered on their porches, unashamedly gawking in their pajamas, as if they hadn't seen this play a dozen times before.

Police raids were a semimonthly occurrence at my house. What concerned me, however, was the "crime scene" tape. They'd haphazardly staked it around our tiny lawn, making our house look like the set of a horror movie.

I thought of all the impromptu executions, the frequent "police misconduct" episodes that were getting swept so easily under the rug, and wondered if I was too late.

Roseanne!

I abandoned my car at the end of the block. I ran past the barricade, ignoring a shout in a megaphone.

The guard on the porch let me through. I burst into the entryway and was greatly relieved to see my wife, alive and well and vehemently arguing with an officer.

"I'm not doing anything until you show me the signed court order, in triplicate!" she screeched. They'd clearly dragged her out of bed; she was barefoot in a bathrobe, and her smashed curls were flying about as she used her whole body to punctuate her sentence. "Who's your commander?"

"I am the commander," the officer intoned, and he had enough badges on his uniform to back up that claim. I didn't recognize him, which was saying something. My run-ins with the law were frequent enough that I knew most of the force by name.

Roseanne folded her arms. "Then surely you have a signed form 301-C to show me."

He squinted at her as if she'd just asked for the moon. "I don't need to show you anything."

"Actually, yes, you do." I put myself between them. "Unless my wife invited you in—"

"I didn't."

"—then this is considered forced entry, which at a minimum requires a form 301-C that's been signed by a judge."

"Form 2054-A would also be acceptable," Roseanne added helpfully. She discreetly slid her hand in mine.

I glanced back at her. "Don't you need a search warrant in addition to that, though?" I rubbed her ring finger in a signal only she would understand. *Are you hurt?*

"The new regulation doesn't take effect until the 15th." She pinched my thumb. *No.*

The commander huffed, a disgusting gurgle of a laugh that made his fat belly shake. "You're unassimilated. I don't need a warrant."

"That's incorrect, and I find it a little concerning that you don't know that." Holding onto Roseanne with one hand, I extended the other to the officer. "Hi, you must be new to the district. Dr. Paul Von Nieuwenhuyse."

The commander didn't accept my handshake. "Ambrose," he muttered with a raised eyebrow.

Roseanne dug her fingernails into my palm. *I don't like him.*

I resisted the urge to chuckle. "Commander Ambrose, pleasure to meet you. I know it's a lot of paperwork to keep up with, so let me help you. According to Version 27-D of the Reassimilation Assistance Act, a record of all incidents involving law enforcement and unassimilated citizens must be simultaneously submitted to the police department, social services, and the reassimilation division."

"That's why you need form 301-C in triplicate," Roseanne chirped.

Ambrose stiffened to his full height, although the effect was mediocre. "I don't—"

"It's to make sure all procedures are being followed in a way that best promotes reassimilation into society," I cut him off. "To prevent recidivism, you understand."

It was clear from the scrunched-nose look he was giving me that he did not.

I plastered on a charming smile. "If you need some time to get the paperwork together, we'll wait."

He hesitated. The awkward silence stretched between us, as if he were giving me a chance to change my mind.

I gladly let the silence hang.

Ambrose turned to glare at one of the other officers standing in the hall. "Are they serious?"

The comrade, a veteran named Callahan who was just trying to make it to retirement, grunted. "Usually." He leaned against the wall and helped himself to one of the caramels Roseanne always left out for him in a bowl on the credenza.

The young recruit guarding the door stepped forward. "Yeah, I forgot to warn you, boss." He nodded at me. "Hey Paul. Sorry it's so late."

I shrugged. "Surprised to see you on the graveyard shift, McClaine. I thought you worked mids."

"Eh, I picked up some extra hours."

"Enough!" Ambrose yelled. He flung both arms out, as if that would regain control of the situation. "Is this a joke to you?"

"It's apparently a joke to *you*," my wife taunted. "You don't even have your paperwork in order."

He regarded her with a perverted look that made me want to punch him in the face. "You belong in an institution."

"Arguably," she agreed, "but I can assure you, that requires *way* more paperwork."

Ambrose growled and reached for his electric pistol. "I don't have time for this."

I pushed Roseanne behind me. "Maybe you don't, but I do. If you're going to barge into my house in the middle of the night and harass my wife, you're going to do it legally. Show me your paperwork, or get out."

He drew the weapon.

"I wouldn't fire that if I were you," Callahan warned without raising his voice.

Ambrose cursed under his breath. "And why not?"

Callahan chomped on his candy. "Because then you'll have to fill out an incident report."

"In triplicate," McClaine added.

Ambrose gestured drunkenly with his weapon. "Are you on their side?"

"No, I just don't want to answer to the district warden." Callahan glanced at his watch.

"But they have no rights!" Ambrose pointed at me like I was a museum exhibit.

That time, I laughed. "That's not what your 543 pages of reassimilation protocols say."

"546," my wife corrected. "They amended Section 209 last week."

"546," I echoed. I locked eyes with Ambrose and lowered my voice. "Trust me, I know your laws better than you do, and I'm going to make sure you follow every single one of them. If you miss even dotting an 'i,' I'll take you to court."

"He will, too," McClaine agreed. "That's why Starling's not on the force anymore."

I indulged in a smile. "So, Commander Ambrose, why don't you tell me why you're here, and I'll help you figure out where you went wrong in your paperwork. We'll get this all sorted, and you can be home in an hour."

Ambrose glowered at me, his finger still on the trigger. Then he considered his options and, like everyone else on the force, reached the smart conclusion that things would go a lot faster if he did them properly.

"Fine, since you're such an expert on the law, let's see what the law says, shall we?" He snapped his gun back in its holster and pulled out his phone. He held it at arm's length and began to read in an obnoxiously loud voice.

"'Due to your refusal to properly assimilate, it has been determined that you are a danger to yourself and others.'"

"I get that a lot," I muttered.

His lips twitched. "'For your safety and the protection of the community, the court has ordered that you be detained and transferred to a reassimilation facility, where you will receive proper care.'"

"So, we're going to jail? Did you really drag me out of bed just for that?" Roseanne let go of my hand to plant hers dramatically on her hips.

I seconded the emotion and rubbed my temples. "This couldn't wait until morning? Fine, you're going to need a form 2054-B, a form 1096—version C or D—and, ideally, a search warrant, although that's a bit of a gray area."

Ambrose grinned, revealing tobacco-stained teeth. "Oh, but that's beauty of it, doctor. I don't need a search warrant."

I started to respond, but he spoke over me. "Search warrants are designed to protect United citizens—which you aren't, as of 3:02 this afternoon."

I heard Roseanne take a sharp breath. I glanced back at McClaine.

He shook his head.

And that's when I began to worry.

Ambrose continued to orate. "I am very pleased to inform you that, thanks to a nearly unanimous vote by the Council, 'unassimilated' individuals are no longer considered legal citizens. You are an alien and a criminal. That means those '546 pages' of reassimilation code no longer apply to you."

My blood ran cold when I processed what he was saying.

"You have no right to trial or representation, no right to speak for yourself, and no right to appeal." Ambrose looked up from his screen and met my gaze. "So tell me, Dr. Von Nieuwenhuyse, what form do I need in triplicate?"

I stared. There was no paperwork for that.

Roseanne snapped out of her shock. She lunged forward, her motions even more animated than before. "Who proposed this?"

Ambrose didn't even look at her, his eyes still on me. "Councilman Thames Nolan, the newly appointed chairman of the Reassimilation Division. He was just nominated last week and promises *sweeping* reforms." He winked.

I didn't respond as prayers pounded behind my ears like blood. *Holy Spirit, what do I do? Protect us!*

"Of course," Ambrose cooed, milking the words, "Section 103, Subset A of the Reassimilation Assistance Act does require that I tell you that your sentence will be suspended if you begin the assimilation process."

He tapped his screen with his thumb, then began to recite a speech I wish I didn't have memorized.

"'In the event that a currently unassimilated individual voluntarily chooses to initiate the assimilation process, they shall demonstrate their intent by signing File 1.'"

He turned his device to face me. On the screen was a form I knew all too well: The file that granted me full citizenship in the United. In exchange for the protection and provision of the government, I gave them unilateral control over my life and property and agreed to obey their ever-evolving library of regulations.

Including the teeny, tiny, insidious line prohibiting the practice of any and all religions.

"'File 1 must be completed in the presence of at least one authorized government agent. Upon submission of a valid File 1, the citizen shall immediately be placed in the Reassimilation Assistance Program and will be entitled to all the benefits and protections of the same. All outstanding charges and warrants against the citizen shall be temporarily suspended and submitted for reevaluation by a judge.'"

Roseanne muttered a prayer under her breath. I clenched my fists and wondered how much easier this would be if I didn't know she was about to get hurt.

Ambrose slid towards me, our old floorboards creaking under his weight. "If you sign the file, not only will all 546 pages of the Reassimilation Act apply to you, but you can also take advantage of the *thousands* of laws protecting assimilated citizens."

He held his phone out to me. The trackpad at the bottom of the device glowed green, begging for my thumbprint.

"So, what do you say, doctor?" He smiled, wicked and cruel. "Would you like to fill out some paperwork?"

I held my tongue.

"That's what I thought." He pocketed his phone. "Pack your bags. Maximum two suitcases per person, and absolutely no electronics. You have fifteen minutes. Anything you do not take with you becomes property of the state."

Roseanne grabbed my hand again. "You can't—"

Ambrose didn't give her a chance. He grabbed his pistol, flicking it on and aiming it at my chest in one practiced motion. "Pack your bags," he repeated, "or I'll have to fill out an incident form."

Roseanne pinched my wrist. *Should we resist?*

I turned to Callahan. He pushed himself away from the wall. "Sorry, Paul, this came straight from Beijing. No filibustering this time."

Closing my eyes, I took a deep breath and prayed. Then I obeyed the unction—even though it went against every fiber of my being.

I let go of Roseanne's hand. "Get your things."

She stared at me with one wild, terrified look. I nodded.

Without a word, she took off towards our bedroom. Ambrose watched her pass, sneering.

I killed his grin with a glare of my own. "Whatever you're doing, it won't work. I'll find your loophole. I will tear your new law to shreds and make you regret every single word of it."

So help me God.

Ambrose holstered his weapon. "I'll expect your report on my desk by Friday."

3

They didn't take us to jail. At least, it wasn't like any jail I'd ever been in.

The facility was on the outskirts of town, built atop the grave of an old megachurch complex the government had repossessed and demolished. I'd driven by the construction site a few times over the past year. Based on the massive wall and guard tower, we all assumed it was a military base.

We were wrong.

It was a concentration camp. An Americanized one, but a concentration camp nonetheless. Tiny concrete homes were stacked end-to-end along the bare blacktop road. A two-story-high wall fenced in the property, and there was a sniper tower on each corner. As if that wasn't enough security, the cameras mounted on every roof and installed in every house ensured that everything—*everything*—was recorded for Big Brother's analysis.

They didn't call the facility a concentration camp, of course. The guards who escorted us to our assigned house forced us to watch a gimmicky infomercial in which this Thames Nolan—a British do-gooder with too much government funding at his disposal—tried to convince us that this new arrangement would allow us to continue to be productive members of society.

He wasn't fooling anyone. I knew what had happened: The United had won the war for culture. We unassimilated no longer had the protection of public favor, which meant the government didn't have to play nice anymore. Those who refused to assimilate would be removed.

And since imprisonment required far less paperwork than execution— and also generated free labor—a containment camp was certainly the efficient choice.

The camp was mostly vacant when we arrived. There were a dozen other inmates, most of whom I knew from Operation Blue Fire or underground church meetings. All of us were problem children with over twenty felonies a piece. It was clear the camps were a test. If they succeeded, the rest of the unassimilated were soon to follow.

Which meant it was my job to ensure this "experiment" failed.

After the injustice of dragging me from my home in the middle of the night, they had the audacity to insist that I go back to work the next day—unpaid, of course. No one else wanted to grade student papers from the summer semester, apparently.

I didn't complain. For me to do my job, they had to grant me remote access to the college's databases—which, thanks to the political science department, included full transcripts of all the new regulations coming out of the Council. In between creating lesson plans, I scoured the law.

Somewhat to my surprise, Ambrose wasn't exaggerating. The Council had voted almost unanimously to change the requirements for citizenship within the United. Anyone who refused to sign File 1 was now considered a "resident alien"—a sterilized term for someone with no legal rights. And since the United officially or unofficially controlled over 80% of the globe, they'd essentially given themselves the power to decide who could exist and who could not.

I spent three days looking for a loophole. I examined every subset and cross-referenced every regulation, searching for an error, an inconsistency, a contradiction that might give me a way out.

There were none. The problem with loopholes is that they only work if you're under the law. Thanks to my new status, the law didn't apply to me. The United had either been smart or lazy by making us non-citizens; they could now bypass all their own regulations. There was no need to file form 301-C in triplicate if the offender was a foreigner with no legal rights.

Ambrose was right: Paperwork wouldn't save me anymore.

There was, however, one fault in their plan: The fact that this "experiment" was classified. It didn't take me long to deduce that the containment camp wasn't being reported on the news, and the government had redacted our files and made it look like we'd simply been sent to jail for the second time this month. I knew they were testing the ice, relocating us in small batches to see if they could get away with it. If I could expose them to the public, there just might be enough backlash to kill the program.

Of course, they were smart enough not to give us internet access, and all my activity for work went through a censor before it was posted. Exposing them on social media wasn't an option, so I had to turn to more guerrilla methods.

It was easier than it should have been. With a little investigation, I found a ventilation window in the storage barrack that wasn't bolted down properly. That allowed me to get into their cleaning supplies.

And if there was one thing the government needed to learn, it was that you should never, ever let a rebel with a doctorate in chemistry near cleaning supplies.

The commotion drew enough nosy passersby with phone cameras that, try as they might, the censors couldn't keep the video from leaking onto the internet. As soon as Andes and the underground figured out it was me, they spread the video like a virus, and my colleagues in the planetary sciences did the rest.

Despite my felonies, I was still a popular fellow. One does not put the first humans on Mars without generating a fan club. I was a household name in the academic world, and my fame was the government's downfall.

The outrage over my unjust imprisonment was glorious. The United backpedaled, suspending the containment camp program and sending the inmates home with minor felonies. Mr. Thames Nolan himself issued a statement claiming the camps were a "well-intentioned therapy based on flawed science."

As I feared, the government didn't rescind the order that made us non-citizens. They were, however, forced to enact several dozen regulations that moderated how they treated us, which had essentially the same effect.

They would try again. I knew that. They'd traded two steps back for one step forward, and they would use the legal ground they'd gained to rewrite the law, just like they'd been doing for the last thirty years.

But until then, Ambrose would have to file form 301-C in triplicate if he wanted to enter my home.

We were detained in the camp for nearly a week, and then in the county jail for two more days while they cleaned up my mess. After that, it took over eighteen hours of paperwork and harassment before we finally got our electronics back from the censors.

As soon as I turned my phone on, I sent Cea a text telling her we were safe and we'd "talk soon." She would know what that meant; hopefully, her social worker wouldn't.

By God's grace, we hadn't been detained long enough for the government to do any serious damage to our property. Our home was trashed; every single drawer, cabinet, and shelf had been overturned as they ransacked the house looking for contraband. But the only thing missing was the contraband I meant for them to find.

Decades of resistance had taught me that government agents were, like most people, overworked and underpaid. They just wanted to check the box and go home. If they found a few illegal items, most censors would assume they'd found it all and stop searching. So, I'd stashed a few disposables—a broken gun, some old burner phones—in places I knew they'd find, hoping they wouldn't think to look further.

I could only pray that trick had worked again.

Leaving Roseanne fussing in the kitchen, I cautiously climbed the stairs to our second floor. Muddy footprints were tracked all over the carpet in the hallway, and the contents of the linen closet had been dumped on the ground. They'd knocked one of the pictures off the wall, cracking the glass. I checked behind the other frames to make sure the government hadn't installed any cameras. Everything seemed secure.

Taking one last glance around the hall, I slipped into the bedroom on the left and shut the door behind me.

The room was bare, as it had been since Nic left for college. The unused sheets were tucked stiffly around the mattress, and a layer of dust coated the desk and drafting board that had once contained my son's creativity. A few school awards lined the shelf above the bed—mere trinkets compared to the accolades he had now. The three narrow bookcases along the wall were empty.

The only other object in the room was a telescope, sitting under the window. The police had carelessly knocked it over and ripped the cover off. Muttering under my breath, I set it upright and straightened the optical tube. Thankfully, they hadn't broken it.

I ran my hand over the cool metal. It was an advanced model, worth several grand. Roseanne would tell me to sell it—and had, on multiple occasions. But I couldn't, even though it just sat up here collecting dust.

Probably because I still clung to the belief that my son would one day come home.

I shook off the thought and replaced the cover, then turned my attention to the bookcases. They didn't look like they'd been touched. The dust on the shelves was undisturbed except for one streaked handprint, like someone had steadied themselves.

I let out my breath. *Thank you, Father.*

I grabbed the middle case and rocked it forward. It pulled away from the wall, revealing a hidden compartment in the floor.

I knelt and pried the lid open. The loose carpet square detached with a groan and a rip. Tucked in the crevice underneath was the last of my resistance: several guns, a few unregistered cellphones, a laptop with a Bible on it, and a radio.

I pulled the radio out and brushed the cobwebs off the dented case. It wasn't the most reliable device; Andes had ripped it from an old truck and jerry-rigged a laptop battery to it. It was a wonder the thing didn't catch fire when I turned it on.

I didn't like to use the radio from home if I could avoid it. The signal wasn't great, and I knew the police were more likely to be scanning my house than the college. If they picked up the transmission, I'd have nowhere to hide.

But tonight, it was worth the risk. I had to talk to my daughter.

I sat down on the bed and tuned the radio to our channel: 32. After waiting to make sure no one was using the line, I spoke into the handset. "This is Von. Caesar, are you receiving? Over."

Silence.

I waited a moment, then tried again. "Caesar, do you copy? Over."

Static.

I glanced at my watch. It was almost midnight, the usual time we talked. If she'd gotten my message, she should be listening.

I pulled my phone out of my pocket. She hadn't responded to my text.

I tried to swallow an irrational burst of panic. Maybe she'd already gone to bed for the night, or maybe the radio signal wasn't getting through. The boarding school was on the edge of receiving range from my house.

I double-checked the radio's settings. "This is Von. Is anyone receiving?"

Someone finally answered—but it wasn't Cea. "Von!" Andes's large voice clogged the line. "You're alive!"

"I'm fine," I dismissed. "Have you heard from Caesar?"

There was a beat—a horrible, nightmarish beat. "No, not in a week. She called me after the… incident to see what I knew, but I haven't heard from her since."

Not even after the news went viral? I thought but daren't ask over radio. Surely, Cea would have seen the video.

I unlocked my phone and called her.

It went straight to voicemail.

"Roseanne!" I shouted, loud enough to be heard through the door.

"What!" she shrieked back. She was up the stairs in a moment.

"I can't get ahold of Cea," I explained as soon as she opened the door. "Did she reach out to you?"

Roseanne yanked her phone out of the back pocket of her jeans. She scowled at the screen, which told me everything I needed to know.

The radio crackled. "Von? Are you still receiving?"

"10-6, Andes," I snapped, watching my wife.

She dialed a number and put the phone on speaker, holding it out so we both could hear. The line picked up; it was the boarding school. But, of course, it was after hours, so the answering machine just looped through a menu of useless options.

Roseanne hung up and started typing furiously with her thumbs.

Andes tried again. "Do you want me to send someone over there tomorrow?"

Roseanne spoke before I could answer him. "Nic Joseph Von Nieuwenhuyse!" she shrieked.

"What did he do?" I demanded.

But I knew. We'd played this whole scene out before.

"What do you think?" my wife snarled. She threw her phone at me.

I caught it. She started pacing the room, muttering. I couldn't tell whether she was cursing or praying or both.

I looked at the screen. She'd hacked into our daughter's personnel file, something she did frequently.

Cea's file had been eerily silent for the past two days; there hadn't been a new entry in over thirty-six hours. Before that, there was a location ping checking her into transit Flight 737, bound for Mars.

My chest tightened when I realized what that meant.

My daughter was no longer on this planet.

4

It took a week for them to deliver the paperwork.

The boarding school finally returned our call the next morning and confirmed what we already knew: Cea was on her way to Mars. Nic had requested that she be granted a leave of absence to visit him, and social services had happily obliged. After all, her brother was an assimilated citizen in good standing with the government—everything her parents weren't.

Cea would be offline as long as she was in flight. I called Nic—and it went straight to voicemail.

I tried again, and again. I called him no less than twenty times over the next seventy-two hours. He never answered.

That's when I realized something was very wrong. Nic always returned my calls. Sometimes it took him two-to-four business days depending on how busy he was pretending to be, but he always called me back. No matter how much we disagreed. No matter how much we disapproved of each other's lifestyles. No matter how bitterly we argued—my son always, always returned my calls.

There was only other one time I could remember Nic ignoring my messages: When he had appealed to social services and sent Cea to boarding school.

The situation had been eerily similar. We'd been caught attending church. Roseanne and I had been fined and spent a night in solitary, the usual slap on the wrist. It was such a minor incident that it was hardly worth reporting. But it was our third time in jail in so many months, and apparently that was one time too many for Nic.

He'd filed a complaint and claimed Cea was "unsafe" at home. The government couldn't agree more; they'd stripped us of our parental rights, sent Cea to boarding school, and restricted our visiting privileges, all without a trial or warning.

Nic had ignored my calls for several days, claiming I needed to "cool off." I finally cornered him at work.

That was the day I lost both of my children. That was the day I discovered what my son was really developing in his lab. That was the day I realized the only way to keep Nic from killing himself—and millions of others—was to turn him over to the police.

His wealthy investors bailed him out soon after, but the government confiscated his lab and wiped his research. His project was over, the only mercy I got out of the nightmare.

A few weeks later, he accepted a commission to oversee a science station on Mars and left without saying goodbye. He left my texts unread for a month, and I feared he'd never call me back.

Then, out of the blue, he did. He called to ask about work and invited me to contribute to a research project as if nothing had happened. Since then, he'd answered my texts promptly, remembered his mother's birthday, and even came back to Earth for a visit. He never said it in so many words, but he acted like he'd forgiven me.

Clearly, he hadn't. As the days stretched on and there was still no word from Cea—and my calls continued to go to voicemail and my texts sat unread—I finally admitted what I should have known all along.

My children weren't coming home.

Roseanne accepted fate much more quickly than I did. It took less than twelve hours for her mood to go from seething to sullen, like someone had plunged a burning coal under water. We didn't talk about it—mostly because I was still foolishly insisting that there must be another explanation. But I knew our son as well as she did.

I just stubbornly thought better of him.

A week later, Ambrose finally delivered the paperwork. We opened our door to find him standing on the step, a tablet in one hand and an envelope in the other.

"You've lost custody of your daughter," he informed us unceremoniously.

Roseanne held out her hand, and he surrendered the envelope. I stared at the mundane manilla color; they'd invested in real paper, which was somehow even more insulting.

Roseanne tore the seal and flipped through the sheets. "I take it they gave Nic full custody?" she asked without looking up.

"Yes."

She snorted. She didn't sound surprised, which was just as well. Had the news been a shock, she probably would have punched Ambrose in the nose and put us both back in jail.

I was too disappointed to be angry. Not disappointed that they'd taken our daughter—disappointed that our had son betrayed us. Again.

God, where did I go wrong with him?

Ambrose extended the tablet towards us. "I need your thumbprint to acknowledge that you've received the notice."

Roseanne obliged. She pressed her finger to the trackpad until the device chirped and flashed green. Then, without another word, she drew back into the house and slammed the door in his face.

I stood there, staring out the window while Ambrose got in his squad car and left. I turned to find my wife riffling through the paperwork.

"It's all here," she muttered, "surprisingly."

Of course it was. Of course, this would be the one time Ambrose had his paperwork in order.

I pulled my phone out of my pocket and sent Nic another text—even though the last ten were still unread.

WE GOT THE PAPERS. ARE YOU READY TO TALK?

Roseanne interrupted me before I could hit send. "What the—"

I looked up to find her glaring at one of the papers. She clenched her fists, crumpling it. "Nic Joseph Von Nieuwenhuyse, what has gotten into you?"

"What now?" I asked, even as I wondered what more he could possibly do to hurt us.

She shoved the paper at me. "Please tell me that doesn't say what I think it says."

I smoothed the sheet out and skimmed the legalese. It was a court order—a *restraining* order.

Suddenly, the room blurred. I struggled to pick the facts out of the endless fine print. As best as I could translate, neither Roseanne nor I was supposed to contact Cea for six months—and we were forbidden from discussing the court case with anyone.

Nic hadn't just taken custody of Cea. He'd cut us out of her life.

"Son," I murmured, all my grief and disappointment coming out in one syllable, "what have you done?"

My wife echoed the sentiment at a much louder decibel. "What is he thinking?"

I knew exactly what he was thinking; he'd seen the video of the containment camp. He knew full well what I would do once I found out he'd kidnapped his sister: Blow the story up until the entire Eastern seaboard knew what had happened. He didn't want to deal with the bad press, so he'd taken out insurance.

Unfortunately, he'd forgotten that I had absolutely no qualms about disobeying the law.

Roseanne started to pace, even though the entryway was so narrow that she only got about three steps before turning around. "Who does he think we are?"

He thought we were criminals. He thought we were bad parents. He thought we couldn't take care of Cea.

He was right about one of those things.

My wife hissed like a cat ready to scratch. "We won't stand for this."

"No," I repeated, folding the paper in tidy thirds. "We won't."

5

We tried for three weeks to reach Cea. Nic had blocked our number on Cea's phone, of course, but that didn't stop my wife and her PhD in computer engineering.

She tried calling from another number. She tried disguising her IP with an evolving proxy chain. She tried registering her device to a fake file. She even tried using an unregistered device—an attempt which got the cops called on our house due to "suspicious activity" in the algorithm.

Nothing worked. We got a few text messages through—enough to know that Cea was safe and just as enraged as we were—but each time, Nic caught us. He would block the number or change the settings on Cea's device, silencing us.

My wife decided that meant war. She tried hacking into Nic's accounts next. She targeted his email, his social media, even his personal website. Every time, Nic noticed the breach within hours and patched it.

He finally grew tired of the game and told the police we were violating the restraining order. The first time, Ambrose delivered a verbal warning. The second time, we spent a night in solitary, and the judge extended the restraining order by another four months. The third time, they decided we'd racked up enough offenses to justify trying the containment camp stunt again.

That only lasted thirty-six hours. They were smart enough to secure the cleaning supplies, but they forgot that my wife's other PhD was in electrical engineering. And since there were no less than seven cameras and fifteen Wi-Fi-connected devices in our tiny concrete house, she had plenty of avenues to vent her frustrations.

The video didn't go viral this time, mainly because a transformer blew, taking out the power for the entire block and preventing anyone from getting good footage. However, the officials wisely decided not to tempt fate and sent us home with another warning. Ambrose, who at this point was mostly just tried of filing incident reports, assured me that if I was caught violating the restraining order again, he'd make sure we went to prison and stayed there.

I wasn't deterred, but Roseanne was running out of options. Nic had the base's cybersecurity on lockdown, which surprised me. My son didn't love computers and was infamously lazy when it came to digital infrastructure; he was the type to reuse passwords and default administrator credentials. Roseanne had never had a problem hacking into his accounts before. The fact that he'd done his homework this time concerned me for reasons I couldn't explain—and not just because he was keeping us from our daughter.

As a final insult, the boarding school packed up Cea's belongings and shipped them to our doorstep. Roseanne wanted to burn it all. I stubbornly put everything away in Cea's room. I framed the rock posters, even though they were bands I didn't approve of, and hung the cheerleading costume in the closet, even though the skirt was too short. All of it was evidence that my daughter was turning into a person I didn't know—that boarding school had changed her, just like I feared—but I didn't care. We could talk about music and modesty when she came home.

Pretending that she was coming home was the only way I could keep my faith as Nic continued to ignore my texts day after day.

Our routine became quiet and boring. I passive-aggressively went back to work while my wife passive-aggressively cleaned the entire house. The only police visit we had was from McClaine, who came off-duty to check on us once a week.

Finally, towards the end of September, the monotony was broken when the doorbell rang.

Roseanne barely looked up from her tablet. "I'm not answering that."

I didn't blame her. None of our visitors had brought good news lately.

It rang again. I obliged and got up to answer it. I opened the door to find Arnold Sardis grinning at me through the glass.

"Hi, Mr. Von," he said in a voice that was as big and friendly as he was.

I managed a smile. Arnold was the same age as Nic, which meant he was more than old enough to call me by my first name. But Arnold still acted like he was a third grader coming over to do homework with my son, and I liked him for it.

I held the door open. "You're a sight for sore eyes. Come in, please."

He obeyed. "I'm sorry it's been so long. But with the press…" He glanced behind him, as if expecting there to be paparazzi on our lawn.

He didn't need to justify himself. "I'm glad you came," I assured him. "Have you heard from Nic lately?"

Nic and Arnold had been classmates in school and roommates in college, and they'd continued to partner professionally since then. They weren't chummy, but it was the closest thing to a friend that Nic had ever allowed himself to have. Even if Nic refused to talk to me, maybe he was still staying in touch with Sardis.

Arnold pulled his baseball cap off. "Yeah, that's why I'm here—"

Roseanne bustled into the entryway, interrupting him. "Arnold!"

He smiled and gave her one of his generous hugs. "Hi, Mom," he said, which was what Roseanne had been insisting he call her for decades.

She squeezed him. "It's so good to see you. Please tell me you're staying for dinner."

I could tell she desperately wanted him to say yes, but he pulled away and shook his head. "No, I need to finish packing."

"Packing?" both Roseanne and I echoed at the same time.

He scratched his neck. "Yeah, I'm, um, moving to Mars. I leave Friday."

"Mars," Roseanne stated, the name laced with suspicion.

He twisted his hat in his hands. "Nic offered me a job. The base needs a horticulturalist."

If it had been under any other circumstances, I would have been pleased. "Didn't you just get the job at the conservatory?" Arnold had been bidding for that position since college; I'd even written a letter of recommendation for him.

Roseanne folded her arms. "Don't tell me Nic is paying you better." Even I couldn't tell by her tone of voice whether she meant that as a joke or not.

Arnold avoided my gaze. "No, but it's a good opportunity. And after what happened to y'all..."

I autofilled what he was too afraid to say. I wasn't sure if Arnold had signed the file or not, but I knew he was a Christian; he often came to the same underground church as we did. It was only a matter of time before the government incriminated him for something. Nic, for all his faults, would offer him privacy.

At least for now.

I gripped his shoulder and smiled. "You'll love it up there. Martian agriculture is fascinating."

He looked up and returned the smile. "Thanks for all your help. Anything you want me to pass on to Cea?"

I started to respond, but my wife was quicker. "Yes, actually."

She turned and strode over to her computer in the living room. She yanked a flash drive out of the port, walked back, and dropped it in Arnold's hand. "Give this to her and tell her to run the program."

I frowned. Whatever "program" was on that drive, my wife hadn't told me.

Arnold fingered the device. "And if Nic asks what it is?" he said, the nuance not lost in his voice.

I glanced at my wife.

She shrugged. "Tell him the truth: It's just a game."

6

The next seven days were the longest week of my life—our internment in the concentration camp excluded.

Two days for Arnold to pack and leave for Mars. Four days for the transit flight. And another day and a half for him to discretely install my wife's program on Cea's phone.

It wasn't a game, of course—but it sure looked like one, if you were observing the device's data remotely. The program masked text messages and calls to make it look like the user was playing a popular multiplayer online game. There were ways to decode the data, but if you didn't know what you were looking for, it would slide right past the algorithm. Unless Nic was reading over Cea's shoulder—something I was sure she wouldn't tolerate—he would have no idea we were talking.

It was almost 2am when she called. I was still awake, as I had been almost every night for the past month. I was pacing the living room, trying not to wake Roseanne as I prayed into the darkness.

My silenced device buzzed against the coffee table. The screen brightened, and I leaned over to see a welcome username:

CAESAR

I let out my breath. "Thank you, Father." I grabbed my phone and swiped to answer it. "Laodicea!"

"Dad!" Her camera focused, and my beautiful daughter appeared, her unruly golden curls filling the frame.

I counted the freckles on her nose, just to reassure myself they were all still there. "Baby girl, I'm so glad to see you. Are you in a safe place?"

"Yeah, I found a crevice in the wall. No one can hear me." She tipped the camera back so I could see. It looked like she was in a service crawlspace of some kind; there were access panels and electrical boxes along the wall. It was the opposite time of day on Mars, and I could see the familiar butterscotch sky through the glass ceiling above her head.

I realized my playback looked terrifying, with the glow of my screen the only light in the room. I reached over and yanked on the lamp. "How's my girl?"

"Fine, I guess," she replied in that drawl I knew all too well.

I adopted a playful attitude for her benefit. "Don't tell me you're *bored* on Mars."

She leaned against the wall and gave me a small smile. "No, no—the base is pretty cool. Nic won't let me into the labs, though."

I chuckled. "That's probably for the best. Having been on a space station, I can tell you that radiation exposure is a legitimate concern."

Our bedroom door opened. My wife stumbled in the living room, shrugging on her robe. She leaned over my shoulder so she could see the screen. "Hey, sweetie."

"Mom!" Cea scrambled upright. "Are you okay? Mr. Sardis said you electrocuted the whole block!"

I inwardly groaned. Leave it to Arnold to dramatize everything.

"I'm fine," Roseanne said in a tone that could calm a storm, "and no one got electrocuted. I just miss you, sweetheart. I'm sorry you had to go through that."

"Ugh, I know." Cea's teenager whine returned with a vengeance. "Nic is the worst!"

Roseanne deferred to me with a raised eyebrow.

I picked my words carefully. I didn't want to sow hate between Cea and her brother—especially when he was the only family she had up there—but I also wasn't going to lie. "What he did was dishonest and hurtful," I said, "and we will be talking to him about it. But I believe he did it because he wanted you to be safe."

I still believed that, in spite of all the evidence to the contrary. Nic was misguided and lost under a web of false pretensions, but he'd gotten on the wrong path because he wanted to be the hero.

He could have been the hero, once. But he forfeited that role when he walked away from Christ.

"Then why am I not allowed to talk to you?" Cea complained. "Why does he hate you so much?"

"He doesn't hate us," Roseanne inserted, and to my relief, it sounded like she also still believed it. "He's worried that if you talk to us, the government will punish you too."

Cea flushed red with righteous indignation. "I don't care! I want—"

"I know you don't," I interrupted, "and nothing makes us more proud."

Roseanne smiled at the camera to corroborate my statement.

"What Nic is doing is wrong. That's why your mother and I have made the decision not to obey the restraining order." I stared at the screen until Cea gave me her full attention. "We will always be there for you, Laodicea, no matter what the law says."

She hesitated. "So, are you… coming to get me?"

Roseanne looked up at me.

My chest tightened. "I can't—"

I caught myself. There were a million reasons why I couldn't go get my daughter, not the least of which being the fact that I was grounded. The government had restricted my right to travel off-planet years ago as punishment for my continued noncompliance.

But no matter how high the odds were stacked against me, I would never say "I can't." I'd learned that lesson the hard way with Nic; there was always a choice. There might not be a good choice. There might be serious consequences for that choice. But there was always, always a choice—and if I didn't make that clear to my daughter, I would lose her, just like I'd lost my son.

I closed my eyes and inhaled. *Holy Spirit, give me the right words.*

Roseanne pinched my arm.

I looked back down at the screen. "No, not yet. Your mother and I discussed it—we want you to stay with your brother, for now," I said, careful not to make any promises about the future.

"But why?" she cried, all the fear and heartbreak shattering her voice.

I deflected it with humor. "Well, for starters, I haven't found anyone willing to hijack a transit for me. Space pirates are hard to come by." I scratched my mustache, as if this were a real problem I had to solve.

Roseanne played along. "Paul!" she chided, slapping me on the arm.

"Dad," Cea grunted, but she almost smiled.

I put my hand up. "I'll keep looking, but in the meantime, I need you to stay where I know you'll be safe."

Cea fell silent.

I sat down in the chair. Roseanne joined me and perched on the arm. I held the tablet out so we were both in frame. "Did Nic tell you what happened to your mother and me?"

"Kinda." Cea fidgeted with a curl. "He said you went to jail again."

"It wasn't a jail," Roseanne corrected. "It was a concentration camp."

"Really?" Cea paled, making her freckles stand out like a skin disease.

"Itty bitty concrete homes, big wall." I gestured with my fingers. "You would have been very bored."

She glared at me sideways. "How's that different from jail?"

"It's different because the law is changing. The Council voted to take away a lot of our rights, which means we can't rely on the law to protect us anymore." It had been decades since the law truly protected people like us, but that was a conversation for a different time. "They can change the rules whenever they want, and we don't have any right to appeal, ask for a lawyer, anything. I can't protect you in an environment like that."

My intelligent daughter immediately saw the loophole. "But you said you wouldn't always be able to protect me."

"You're right." I paused and measured my next words out with intention. "But I also won't put you in danger if I can avoid it."

Cea stared at the camera and waited.

"I don't know what's going to happen to us," I admitted, keeping the fear out of my voice. "They will probably try to move us into the camp again. Things are changing—and until we know what the government is going to do, your mother and I believe it would be better for you if you stayed on Mars."

Cea looked away, which told me I'd made my point—she just didn't like it. "But Nic—"

"Won't hurt you," Roseanne filled in, "and he won't let anyone else hurt you. He can be rude and selfish, but he does care about you. We want you to stay with him for now, and mind what he says."

"Within reason," I clarified. "If you have any questions, or you ever feel unsafe, call us immediately."

There was a beat, and then Cea acquiesced with a mumble. "Okay."

"Laodicea." I waited until she looked at the camera again. "This is not forever. I promise."

She stared at me. Slowly, she smiled. "I love you, Dad."

Relief brought the air back into my lungs. At least I wouldn't lose my daughter. "I love you, too."

Her device beeped. She squinted at the screen, as if reading a notification in the background. "Ugh, I gotta go."

Roseanne stiffened. "Everything all right?"

"Yeah, I just need to finish my homework."

"Homework?" Roseanne and I shared a glance.

Cea rolled her eyes. "Nic's making me finish my summer classes online."

I laughed. "Well, on that point, he and I are in complete agreement."

I could tell by the pout she sent in my direction that she was hoping for a different answer.

I raised my eyebrow. "Do your best. And if you have any questions, send me screenshots of your homework and I'll help."

She smiled. "Okay. I'll text you tonight." The camera swung wildly as she stood.

"Please do," my wife called. "Love you, sweetheart."

Cea returned the affection, then hung up.

I stared at the dark screen, drowning in the feeling that everything was so right and yet so wrong. If it had been under any other circumstances, I would have been relieved that my daughter was safe on Mars. If only we had made this decision together as a family.

If only her brother was a different person.

My wife yanked her tablet off its charger on the end table. "Well, I'm glad that worked."

I turned my attention back to her. "Did you design that program?"

She shook her head as she pawed through menus. "Andes gave it to me."

I nodded. That seemed like the kind of thing Andes—or one of his dozens of associates—would have his hand in.

"The virus was mine, though."

I frowned. "Excuse me?"

"When Cea installed the 'game,' it also ran a subprogram that gave me remote access to her device," my wife explained without looking up.

"Why?"

She sighed and stopped typing. "I don't trust our son. This isn't like him. Not about Cea—I knew that was coming."

If only I'd seen it coming, maybe I could have prevented it.

"But all this secrecy—the fact that he actually remembered to change his password." She gestured in the air with her device. "He's not usually this careful."

I took a deep breath as the premonition returned to my chest. "No, he's not."

Roseanne resumed swiping on her screen. "I'm sure Nic didn't give Cea very high security clearance, but I should at least be able to see what else is on the network she's connected to—and that gives me an open door."

I propped my elbow on the arm of the chair and watched her work. An open door was all my wife needed. If Nic was up to something, Roseanne would find out what.

I could only pray it wasn't what I thought it was.

7

I let my wife work undisturbed for the next few days. Attempting to stay out of her way, I made myself useful by praying and helping our daughter with her homework. Finally, on Saturday afternoon, Roseanne called me into the kitchen.

"That's everything I found," she said, shouting to be heard over whatever was sizzling on the stove. She gestured with her sloppy spoon. "I couldn't open most of the files, but I could at least see what was on the server."

My laptop—the illegal offline one I used to store Bibles—was in the middle of the island, nearly buried under the remnants of my wife's day at work. I brushed aside her papers and tabbed through the gallery that was on the screen. It was screenshots of all the databases and cloud drives my wife could access through Cea's phone.

Roseanne opened the cabinet and pawed through the spices. "Looks like mundane science stuff to me."

"It's the science I'm worried about," I returned.

She glanced over her shoulder as she shook a generous amount of seasoning into the pan.

I leaned on my elbows and squinted at the screen. She was right—at first glance, it did look like mundane science. I'd spent enough time on space stations to know what I was looking at just by the file extensions. Terraforming, agriculture, low-gravity life support—all the usual experiments they tested on Mars.

I relaxed. Maybe we were overreacting. Maybe Nic really had just taken a commission on Mars to conduct extraterrestrial science.

I scrolled to the last image—and then I saw exactly what I didn't want to see.

Detonation reports. Fallout predictions. Books on the history of chemical warfare.

And a dozen studies on the world's most caustic acids.

I braced myself on the counter as it all came back to me. The warped piles of metal and plastic in the testing chamber. The lengthy chemical equation scrawled across the whiteboard in bloodred. The press photo of my son receiving an award from General Secretary Jiang himself.

Nic had developed a blend of plastic that was resistant to almost every acidic compound imaginable—a scientific breakthrough. It had seemed so innocuous at the time. I'd been proud of him, even.

Until I put it all together and realized my son was trying to end the world.

"Paul?" Roseanne was beside me.

"He didn't stop." The guilt and dread took all the strength out of my voice.

"What?"

I gestured at the computer. "He's still trying to build his weapon."

She gripped my shoulder and murmured a prayer.

She knew what I meant. When I'd cornered Nic in his lab a year ago and discovered what he was working on, I'd explained the science to her as best I could.

It was a chemical superweapon. Nic was attempting to develop an acidic compound that could corrode almost all materials—metal, plastic, concrete, even brick and stone. If he succeeded, it would be the weapon to end all wars. He would have the power to cripple infrastructure, decimate cities, and kill hundreds of millions of people.

He would crush the United—and then start the cycle all over again, this time with himself as dictator.

He claimed he had no intention of committing genocide, but I knew that was the only way this story ended. I tried to reason with him, but it was too late for logic—ten years too late.

I should have stopped him when he put the school bully in the hospital in third grade. I should have stopped him when he nearly scalded a friend to death with acid over an argument about religion. I should have stopped him when he started skipping church services, hanging out with politicians, and accepting funding from people I knew were dangerous. I should have been harsher, stricter, something—anything.

But I wasn't, and now my passionate son thought violence was the only answer. So, my only solution was to surrender him to the one agency powerful enough to stop him.

That day, his mother and I made the heartbreaking decision to turn him over to the police. I thought that was the end of it. I thought the United had wiped his data and stopped his research. I was wrong.

You're a fool.

"Min," my wife muttered, clearly tracking the same thoughts.

I could only nod. Shi Min Tai Mong was a chairwoman on the Council and one of Nic's many wealthy benefactors. She was also his girlfriend.

Well, I assumed they were dating only because, before Nic left for Mars, they met for dinner every Tuesday. Nic never referred to her with any affection—but, then again, he never referred to anyone with any affection.

Min had sponsored many of Nic's projects and was the one who bailed him out of jail. I thought she did it because they were dating. Now I saw what I should have seen a year ago.

The government didn't stop Nic's project. They were funding it.

Roseanne folded her arms, probably to prevent herself from punching something. "Do you think it was her idea?"

I shook my head. It was Nic's science, I was sure of it. But what did Min expect to gain? How many other Council members were involved? Did Nic even realize what was going on?

Did it matter? It didn't, not really. It didn't matter who owned the weapon. Whether the Council or my son pulled the trigger, the world would burn.

Roseanne paced in a tight circle. "We have to tell—"

"Tell whom?" I snapped, louder than intended. "The police won't do anything—the government owns this project. If we turn him in, he'll just pack up and build a lab somewhere else."

And take Cea with him.

The realization hit me like a kick to the ribs. If I turned Nic in, our relationship would be over—and I'd never see either of my children again.

Roseanne said nothing. The kitchen felt cramped as the silence stretched between us. It was over. Our son was lost. There was nothing we could do, nothing we could say, to stop him from—

A pop broke the silence. I looked up. The pan Roseanne had left on the stove was burning. The contents bubbled, splattering food onto the stovetop. The mess sizzled and smoked.

Roseanne scowled at the pan from across the island, as if she were annoyed by its existence. She didn't move to turn the burner off.

I didn't either. Why did it matter? We were criminals. We couldn't read the Bible without getting fined a thousand dollars. The government wanted to put us in a containment camp. My daughter was gone, and my son wanted to light the world on fire. Who cared about some burnt food? None of it mattered—

I stopped.

No, it matters.

I walked over and turned the stove off. The world was changing. The best thing I could do—for my wife, my daughter, and *especially* my son—was be normal.

I grabbed the spoon and started scraping the burned bits off the bottom of the pan. "What are we doing with this sauce?"

"What?" Roseanne grunted.

"I think it's salvageable. What am I supposed to do now?" I squinted at the recipe she had pulled up on a tablet, but it was all Greek to me. I had doctorates in several subjects, but cooking wasn't one of them.

"Paul," she sighed, "is that all you can think about?"

"Yes, because it's nearly 6 o'clock, and I'm hungry." I turned to face her. "Roseanne, I promise we'll figure this out. But burning the kitchen down won't save him."

She looked into my eyes and waited.

I erased the emotion from my voice and made my words calm and steady. "We're going to eat dinner. We're going to church in the morning. Then I volunteered to teach a class at the library at three—and don't you have a coffee date with Miranda?"

"Yes—"

"You're going," I said, and it wasn't a suggestion. "We're going to do what we'd promised we'd do. And then, after we've both had time to sleep on it, we'll talk."

She studied me for a long moment. Then she took a deep and nodded. "Okay."

✳

Late Sunday night, I sat in the darkened living room with the laptop balanced on my knees, praying for a miracle.

I'd gone to bed on time, mostly to encourage Roseanne to do the same. As soon as she'd dropped off, I'd grabbed my devices and retreated to the couch, where I could continue my conversation with the Lord out loud.

"What do I do about Nic?"

I tabbed through the screenshots. I had to stop him before he did irreversible damage, but how? Alerting the authorities wouldn't work. Leaking the story on social media wouldn't work. It might cause a scandal, but the government controlled the algorithm. They would censor the story, and I wasn't keen to create mass hysteria by telling the entire internet about my son's doomsday device.

There had to be another way. Nic was my son. There had to be something else I could say, something else I could do to save him.

Was it too late to talk him down? Talking hadn't worked last time, but maybe that had been as much my fault as his.

"Don't lie to me!"

I closed my eyes and replayed the argument—the argument we'd had when I'd confronted him in his lab. For the first time, I wondered if I'd made a mistake by alerting the authorities.

"Son, what have you done?"

If I hadn't involved the police, Nic wouldn't be a hundred million miles away on Mars shielded by government funding. I should have known he'd have friends and avoided showing my hand. I should have taken a step back, let him calm down for a few days, and then approached him with terms he could understand. I should have met him on his level—treated him like the genius he was—not accused him of genocide.

"You're right, son. I don't have to agree with you. But I do have to protect you—even from yourself."

I knew my son. I knew this was not the person God wanted him to be— and it wasn't the person he wanted to be, either. He didn't want to be the villain. He was violent and deceptive and manipulative because those were the only tools he had, but he still believed he was the hero in his story. Maybe, if I hadn't treated him like a criminal, he would have listened.

He might still listen—if he would return my calls.

The beep of my text tone interrupted my thoughts. I glanced at my phone where it lay on the end table; it was a text from Cea.

Managing a smile, I picked up my device and swiped to read the notification.

HEY CAN YOU HELP ME WITH MY HOMEWORK?

I opened the app. Several more messages came through in short succession: screenshots of a science quiz.

I typed back.

OF COURSE. WHAT'S THE QUESTION?

The typing dots flickered at the bottom of the screen.

NONE OF IT MAKES SENSE

I waited for her to clarify. When she didn't, I ventured:

ARE YOU ASKING ME TO HELP YOU, OR ARE YOU ASKING ME TO DO YOUR HOMEWORK FOR YOU?

She didn't respond, and I had my answer. I chuckled into the darkness and texted back.

DOWNLOAD THE WHOLE LESSON AND SEND IT TO ME. CALL ME WHEN YOU'RE IN A SAFE PLACE, AND WE'LL GO OVER IT TOGETHER.

She replied with a thumbs up and a grinning emoji.

I switched over to my texts and scanned my chat history with Nic. He still had not read my messages.

I refreshed the screen, as if that would magically produce a different answer. It had been almost two months since the incident, and as far as he knew, Roseanne and I were obeying the restraining order. He'd had plenty of time to cool off and see reason. What could I say that would get him to respond?

A file transfer from Cea came through. I clicked on it and skimmed the contents. It was a basic high school lesson about chemical reactions—

I stopped with my finger over the graphic of the periodic table as the solution hit me.

Maybe I *couldn't* prevent Nic from completing his weapon. But maybe I didn't have to.

Dropping my phone on the couch, I grabbed my laptop and scrolled rapidly through the images. If Nic was creating an acid, maybe there was a way to neutralize it. Perhaps I could come up with a compound that would destabilize the formula and prevent it from being deployed. If that didn't work, maybe I could invent a countermeasure, or a material that was resistant to the acid—something, anything to give Earth a fighting chance.

It could be done. If Nic could make death, then I could unmake it. But I needed his research.

I knew vaguely what he was developing. I'd seen enough of his proposal to have a general idea of the chemical compound. But if I was going to create the antidote, I needed all of his data.

Cea texted me again, saying she was ready to call when I was. I stared at her username as the thoughts began to tick faster. Cea could do it—she could copy Nic's data and send it to me. Surely, she could get into a lab or a server room where Nic had his work stored. She'd forged my ID once; she could forge Nic's. Roseanne could help her. If Cea could get access to a computer, she could steal his research for me.

I snatched my phone and started to call her, then caught myself. It would never work while Nic was on base. He'd caught every single one of our hacking attempts within hours; he'd notice immediately if Cea broke into a lab. I wanted to believe that Nic wouldn't hurt his sister, but that was a risk I couldn't take.

I tipped my head back and stared at the ceiling, waiting for peace in the Spirit. We could do this—this could work. If I couldn't save my son, I could at least save some of his victims.

But we had to get Nic off that station.

8

My chance came a month later.

I arrived home from college to find Roseanne vacuuming the living room. "Nic's coming to visit next Monday," she announced.

I could barely hear her over the vacuum as she continued to clean. "What?"

"He's speaking at a convention." She gestured at her desktop monitor.

I sidestepped to avoid the vacuum and walked over to the desk. On the screen was an announcement for an interplanetary climate change symposium, hosted by a college across town. Nic was a keynote speaker; he'd be less than twenty minutes from home.

"Min invited him," my wife offered.

"How do you know?" I asked, although I never doubted my wife's assessments.

"One of her companies is sponsoring the event."

I scrolled down the screen and confirmed her statement. "Did he tell you he's coming to see us?"

"No, but I can do math." She paused to shake out the throw rug. "The symposium is over by four. Assuming he and Min keep their usual schedule, they won't eat until at least six. That gives him plenty of time to stop by."

She was right. That was more than enough time for a quick visit—and under any other circumstances, I'm sure he would have taken the opportunity. Nic always visited when he was in town, no matter what was going on in his life or what was going on between us. He and I could have a knockout, drag-down argument the night before, and he'd still show up the next day for dinner. It had happened multiple times.

But a lot had changed since he was last on Earth.

Roseanne wasn't worried. "If you can keep him occupied for an hour, I can get what we need and get Cea out of there before he notices."

I struggled to catch up with the plan. "Why not do it while he's offline during the transit flight?"

Roseanne wagged her head. "I need to use his credentials—and it will look incredibly suspicious if he accesses the database while he's supposedly offline." She stopped vacuuming long enough to move the plug to another outlet. "I can route Cea's IP and make it look like Nic accessed his own servers remotely. Hopefully, he's not cross-referencing his own activity log."

She was right; it was our best option. My wife knew how to cover her tracks, but it would be impossible for her to fully erase the digital trail. Nic would no doubt work remotely during his trip, so the activity shouldn't raise any red flags in the base's algorithm. Even if he did notice the timestamp, he would have no reason to suspect it was Cea.

The vacuum roared to life again. "Just get him out of the house, and Cea and I will do the rest," Roseanne called over her shoulder as she continued to sweep out of the room and down the hall.

My wife spent the next week preparing her plan of attack. Her browser history made it look like she was planning a bank heist. With Cea's help, she copied a map of the base and sketched out the route our daughter would take, making a note of every door and computer terminal she had to access. She organized Cea's itinerary down to the keystroke so that our little hacker could leave as few digital footprints as possible.

It was my job to prepare our daughter for what she was about to do. The risk was low, we hoped. Roseanne would mask Cea's IP so it would look like Nic accessed his data from our router in Boston. If Nic noticed the abnormality, hopefully he would blame us. But we had no way of knowing what security measures he had in place—or what he would do if he realized his sister betrayed him.

Cea accepted the risks. If anything, she was a little *too* thrilled about the opportunity to undermine her older brother. I did my best to redirect her attitude, all the while praying this would be the last time I had to pit the siblings against each other.

Monday arrived, and there was still no word from Nic or any indication that he was planning to visit. Roseanne stalked the location pings on his file as he arrived on Earth, checked into his hotel, and got his third coffee for the day. I refreshed my texts, but they still sat unread.

The symposium ended promptly at four. Nic went back to his hotel—and stayed there. Six o'clock came and went. By then, even Roseanne assumed the worst.

I locked myself in our bedroom and laid face-first on the floor. There were no words—only terrified silence as I waited for God to move heaven and hell for my son.

Finally, at 6:42, the doorbell rang.

"He's here," Roseanne called from the front room.

I pushed myself to my knees and finally put a period on my prayer. *Thank you, Father.* "Coming!" I shouted back as I struggled to rise.

I hurried to grab my jacket and car keys. Nic's voice echoed from the foyer as his mother lectured him about taking so long to get here. I heard his cold, disinterested tone—that untouchable façade he worked so hard to maintain—and instantly remembered there were a dozen things I wanted to say to him.

I'm appalled at your behavior.

I'm shocked you'd be so foolish as to trust Min.

I'm extremely disappointed in the man you've become.

I gripped the dresser as the words—all the conversations we should have had years ago—rolled over me. No, this wasn't about me. I had one chance, one opportunity to talk to my son, and I wasn't going to waste it on hurt feelings. He needed his father, not a judge and executioner.

I stared at my reflection in the dresser mirror and gave myself one minute to vent all the hurt, anger, and disappointment to the Holy Spirit. Then I shrugged on my jacket and strode into the hall.

Nic stood on the step; Roseanne hadn't even invited him inside. Our son, for his part, looked like he already regretted his decision to visit us. He was leaning so far back he was in danger of falling off the porch.

I deliberately avoided eye contact. "You, car," I ordered with a finger jab in his direction.

"Excuse me?"

"Car. Let's go. We'll be late," I repeated. I gave Roseanne a quick kiss on the cheek. She met my eyes and nodded.

Nic still hadn't moved. "Late for what?"

"You know they close early on Mondays. Come on, we only have an hour." I strode towards the detached garage without looking back, trusting him to follow.

After a minute, he did.

I stole a sideways glance at him as we buckled in. He was a carbon copy of me in every detail down to the angle of his chin, except he was still shaving his mustache. It was a shame, really; the naked lip was doing him no favors.

I stayed silent as I pulled onto the main road, and he gladly followed suit. He kept one hand on the door, as if he were prepared to open it and hurl himself onto the asphalt. I knew from experience that it was impossible to calm my son down once he'd wound himself up, so I opted for the next best thing: catching him off guard.

I asked him about work. I asked him about Sardis. I asked him about his science station. I brought up every subject except the one he expected.

His eyebrows twisted themselves into a knot as he tried and failed to reconcile my behavior. Finally, he got so frustrated that he risked eye contact. "Why does it matter to you what kind of filter I use in the air purifier? Are you earning affiliate commission?"

I braked at a yellow light and returned his stare. "Was the restraining order against me or you?"

"What?"

"Unless I misread the paper, there was nothing in the court order that prevented us from talking about work. So you're under no obligation to be rude about it." I faced the road and let the rebuke hang.

He accepted it. "My apologies, I thought you didn't care."

I snorted. "It's my base. I built it. Of course I care."

And that scares you, doesn't it?

He hesitated—then let go of the door handle.

We talked science for the rest of the drive, letting the comfortable language of chemistry and physics put us both at ease. I could have driven circles around the block and kept the conversation going forever; he had no idea how much I missed this. In another life, I would have made Nic my business partner—a dream I still hoped was possible one day, if I could keep him from unleashing the apocalypse.

But as much as I wanted to simply enjoy my son's company, I knew we didn't have that luxury tonight. There was another conversation we needed to have.

He tensed again when we pulled into the parking lot of the observatory. "Why are we here?"

You know why, I thought but didn't say. It was the same reason I'd bought a telescope and showed him how to find Mars at the age of five: Because if I could teach my son to find the center of his universe, he could always make his way home.

I could only pray that trick would work one last time.

Nic lagged several steps behind me as we climbed to the observation dome on the top floor. I stroked the panel next to the door. The domed ceiling parted, flooding the room with starlight. The massive telescope rested at an angle, her mirrors glittering, ready to discover new worlds.

I walked over to the viewscreen. I had funded the original installation, and my astronomy fellows had built on my investment. The newly upgraded control panel now rivaled the bridge on a spaceship.

I flicked the monitor on. "Show me the base."

"You haven't seen it?" Nic scoffed from where he hovered by the door.

Of course I've seen it. "I want to see how big it's gotten." I gestured at the control panel.

He didn't fall for it. "If you want to see the new additions, there's livecams on the promotional website that are much better."

As if I didn't watch those every day, hoping for a glimpse of my children. "You know, you'd save yourself a lot of energy if you didn't insist on being such a jerk all the time," I snapped, letting some of the annoyance into my voice.

He groaned. "What's this really about, Dad? I know you didn't drag me out here just to stargaze."

"Maybe I did. Not everything I do is rocket science." I keyed the coordinates into the trackpad. The room shuddered as the telescope scanned the skies. A second later, the viewscreen flickered on, and a stunning image of Mars filled the monitor.

I studied the raw gorges and valleys I had once called home. "Maybe I'm just an old man wanting to look up at the stars with his son one last time. Maybe… I just want to know where my children are."

Where are you, Nic?

He stood there, the unspoken question simmering in the silence. Then he walked over and unplugged the handheld touchpad from the panel. "You drive," he said, holding it out to me.

I smiled and took it.

I followed his directions as he navigated across the surface of the planet like he'd been born there. The intelligent machine obeyed us, and we were able to capture a stunning view of the basin. The smudge representing the base stood out like the *X* on a treasure map.

I fingered the trackpad, scanning the camera around the surrounding mountains. "Do you like living there?"

"Better than Earth," he mumbled, a statement which could have equally applied to a black hole.

"And what about Cea?" I said slowly, bracing myself for the wound to reopen. "Does she like it?"

He took a sharp breath through his nose. "I don't think she's decided yet."

I wasn't worried. "If she's anything like you, she'll take to it like a fish to water."

He hesitated, glaring at some random point on the wall, before he spun around to face me. "Are you mad I took custody of Cea?"

I was furious, but that wasn't the side of me he needed to see. I shook my head. "They were going to take her anyway."

"What?"

It was my turn to look away. "It was only a matter of time. I think the only reason they hadn't done it yet was they knew I'd raise a storm in the media, and they needed a good story to cover it."

That was, of course, why he'd taken out a restraining order. But the bad press was never the issue, and we both knew that. I sighed and ripped the bandage off. "No, what bothers me is that I don't think she's any safer with you than she is with them."

"I'm sorry?" he spat, his cruel and ugly attitude returning. "You'd rather she be in the hands of a psychotic government than with her own *brother*?"

I crossed my arms. "I wish you would have left her in that boarding school."

"Oh, you mean 'indoctrination camp full of people who hate her religion'?" he mocked, which was, in fact, what I'd called it.

"Last I checked, so do you," I returned, and how I wished those words weren't true.

He frowned at me like I was a petulant toddler. "I don't know what that word means to you, but I don't 'hate' your religion."

I stared at him and tried to reconcile the arrogant man in front of me with the zealous boy I used to know—the one who would brazenly argue with his professors over evolution and atheism and not care what his classmates thought. "It used to be your religion, too."

I was right, which meant the discussion was over for him. He slid back, putting his hands up. "I'm not having this conversation with you."

"Then don't."

As always, my honesty unnerved him. His eyebrows twitched.

I shrugged. "You can leave. No one's making you stand here and talk to your old man. You're the one that came to visit me."

"A gesture that was apparently wasted," he muttered with a glance at the door.

"Then why'd you come?"

He stared at me, and I knew he was asking himself the same question. "You know my opinions haven't changed," I prodded.

The frown returned to his lips. "I'm well aware. But if you're going to insist on preaching this sermon, I'd rather you do it to me than Cea."

There he was—the antihero, trying to control everyone's lives because he thought he knew better. "If you think a restraining order is going to stop me from parenting my own child, then those PhDs are wasted on you," I scoffed. "I will never stop trying to train my daughter."

My voice rose—then I caught myself. *No, this isn't about Cea.* This was about the child standing right in front of me. I took a deep breath and filtered the anger out of my tone. "Just like I'll never give up on my son."

He silenced.

I struggled to find the next words. There was so much I needed to tell him, and yet I knew none of it would breach the chasm between us.

Father, what do You want me to say?

The Holy Spirit answered. I obeyed the unction, even though I knew I was taking an incredible risk. "I know what you're doing, Nic," I whispered. "I know what you're building on that base."

"Dad," he hissed with a wary glance around the room.

I lifted my hands in surrender. "Don't worry, you won't get any trouble from me. I learned my lesson—I know I can't stop you." It was a lie—somewhat—and I prayed he couldn't tell. "I just wonder if there's room for me and your mother up there."

The anger melted from his face. "All you have to do is say the word, Dad, and I can have you on the next transit. I know the people."

My chest swelled as decades of prayers were suddenly answered. He was alive; Nic was alive. I heard it in his voice—the courage, the empathy, the maddening desire to protect his family—all the clues that told me my son, *my son*, was still trapped in there. My son who loved the Lord and would sacrifice himself to save the world.

If only I could show him that *he* was the one who needed to be saved.

"That's not what I meant," I said, even though I would have given anything to live together as a family on Mars. "I meant, is there room for me in your perfectly balanced ideology?"

"I don't know what you think my 'ideology' is…" His sarcasm returned, then vanished as quickly as it had come. "But there's always room for you in my life."

I didn't bother to stop the tears. "I love you too, son."

He didn't reply. He didn't need to.

I took a deep breath, wishing for all the world that I didn't have to crucify this moment. "But you know that's not true."

The camaraderie shattered. "So I'm a liar now?" he barked.

I wished I could deny it. "Let's say I come with you. Am I allowed to disagree with how you run things?"

"I feel obliged to tell you that this is a completely ineffective use of the rhetorical question," he groused with an eye roll, "but yes. I'm not afraid of your opinions."

I snorted. "Neither is the government. I can have an opinion. I just can't act on it."

"I'm pleased to inform you that there will be plenty of room in my… on my base for people to experiment with whatever they wish," he recited, the pretentious tone of his voice hurting more than words ever could. "Which you would know if you'd listen to me."

I forced myself to match his petty attitude. "Perhaps, until it interferes with one of your experiments. What happens if I don't like what you're doing? What if I try to stop it? What are you going to do—lock me in my room?"

"I'm thinking about it," he muttered.

I shook my head. "No, Nic, you and I both know that there's only room in your universe for people who agree with you. As soon as someone threatens your power, you won't hesitate to toss them aside to protect yourself. Then you'll be no better than the United is—willing to kill anything or anyone who threatens your control."

I braced myself for his rage, but it never came. Instead, I saw the one emotion I feared most: rejection.

"Is that what you think of me?" he whispered, and for a blink of an eye, he was a little boy again, an innocent child desperate for the approval of his father. "I'm not a killer."

I fought back more tears as I gave him the truth neither of us wanted to hear: "You will be if you complete your experiment."

He didn't argue. He just closed his eyes and shut me out of his life once more.

"Nic—son," I begged, scrambling for the magic words that would get him to open the door. "You're a kind, caring young man."

"You don't really believe that," he mumbled without looking up. If only he knew how much I *did* believe that.

I pressed on and told him what I should have said the last time we argued. "And you're brilliant. You're gifted, Nic—and I don't mean with a science degree. I know you can see things, comprehend a reality others can't."

Suddenly, in a flash of cold clarity, I realized where I'd gone wrong with raising my son. It wasn't about his rebellion, his cruelty, his lies. I'd wasted all those years trying to redirect Nic's violence, but his anger was never the problem. It was his dreams, his innate ability to see one step ahead, that had driven him mad. He'd seen a future that terrified him, and he'd tried to change it.

If only I'd seen it sooner, if only I'd taught him that prophecy wasn't about controlling fate. It was about mercy, about encouragement, about seeing the heart of God for the people right in front of you. If Nic had married his gift with compassion, he would have been unstoppable.

It's not too late.

He still hadn't opened his eyes, so I reached out with my words, struggling to show him the future I saw. "I've known since you were born that you were destined to change the world. That's how you got this far—you wouldn't be doing what you're doing if you didn't think the world could be saved."

He unclenched his fists, and I knew he was finally hearing me. My son still believed he was the hero, just like I feared. How could I make him see that he wasn't without turning him into the villain?

"But we both know how this ends." I winced as the harsh truth cut my own soul. "This doesn't end with freedom. This ends with war, bloodshed, and more tyranny. This won't change the world, Nic. The world will end up right back where it started. The only difference is who's on top: You."

His whole body tightened. I forged ahead before he could retaliate. "But you can do so much more. None of this is an accident. Your giftings, the base, even the friends you're making in Beijing—it's all for such a time as this."

I believed it, I really did. None of this—Mars, his scientific breakthroughs, even Min—was an accident. God was giving him power for a reason. But my son was destined to save Beijing, not light it on fire. I knew he would see that—if he would just open his eyes.

There was a beat, and then he did. He turned to look at me. "What do you mean?"

"You're being put in place to change the world." I gestured at the stars, calling all of heaven to witness my statement. "But you can't do it without Him."

"Him who?" he asked, but I could tell by his annoyed frown that he knew exactly Who I was talking about.

"I know He talks to you," I prodded with a smile.

The creak of the door interrupted us. "Doctor?" The ticket clerk poked her head in. "We're closing soon."

I sighed. There was so much more I wanted to say, but there wasn't time. There was never time.

"Yes, of course, thank you. We'll be right down." I walked to the control panel and turned off the instruments. The telescope groaned as it shifted back into its neutral position.

I glanced at Nic. He was glaring at the crack of sky in the dome, and I could tell by the tension in his jaw and the terror in his eyes that his world was ending. The story he had told himself had gotten knocked off its axis, and if he allowed himself to feel that cold emptiness, he would find the truth again.

How I wanted to push him the rest of the way, to reason with him and help him uproot the lie at the center of his existence.

But he was the only person who could do that.

I zipped up my jacket and turned towards the door. "When can I call Cea?"

"What? That's it?" he exclaimed.

I arched an eyebrow. "Is what it? And I asked you a question."

"In June," he grunted, "and I mean—that's it? That's all you have to say?"

I glanced over my shoulder. "Do *you* have something you want to say?"

He cringed, cornered.

"You know you can talk to your old man any time, right?" I swiped my fingers across the panel to close the dome. "Any time you want to talk, feel free to call. I'm happy to help—but I can't help you if you don't talk to me."

I opened the door. He didn't follow.

I smiled and gave him one final invitation. "And neither can He."

Then I stepped out into the hall and let the door drift shut behind me.

9

It was several minutes before Nic joined me in the lobby. He came back to the house, gave his mother the obligatory hug, and then went on his date with Min. He was on Earth for a few more days, doing his usual tour of sponsors and colleges, before returning to Mars. He did not say goodbye.

This time, I didn't initiate. I kept my ringer on loud but let our chat sit silent, waiting.

I prayed he would listen to my words. But if he didn't—there was another way.

My wife and daughter were successful. They copied several of Nic's databases, which I transferred to the offline laptop and organized. I spent the next several days studying my son's manufactured apocalypse—and then I went to work calculating how to prevent it.

The weapon wasn't complete, much to my relief. Nic had invented several horrifically caustic compounds, but none were capable of the widespread destruction he needed to win a war. The few formulas that came close were, as I'd hoped, highly unstable and impossible to weaponize.

I knew it wouldn't be long before he perfected the equation—and in a cruel irony, I couldn't perfect the antidote until he did. Until I knew the exact chemical makeup of his acid, I couldn't create a formula to counteract it. So, instead of trying to predict the equation, I worked backwards.

I knew what chemical properties the finished compound would have; Nic had done extensive research on the acidity needed to melt most known materials. That meant I either needed to invent a new resistant material, or I needed to develop a countermeasure that would destabilize the formula and render it ineffective.

Material resistance would only go so far in a large-scale war, so I focused on the countermeasure. The biggest challenge was predicting how my son would weaponize the acid. He had a dozen insidious theories, the most popular of which seemed to be crop dusting. If he could stabilize the formula so that it wouldn't evaporate, he could disperse it with drones and literally rain fire and brimstone on Earth. Drones, of course, could be shot down—but only if people knew they were coming.

I shoved aside the gruesome thought. If my son planned to disperse the weapon from the sky, then the best countermeasure might be manufactured smog or another airborne chemical, something that would react with the acid and render it inert—or at least a little less caustic. Smog had its own environmental challenges, and the acid rain would no doubt still do incredible damage, but it was a working theory.

My other theory was sabotage. The difficulty with a weapon that could melt most materials was that it was nearly impossible to store. My son had invented a special kind of plastic—the same blend he'd won an award for—that was resistant to almost every acidic compound on the spectrum. But the math was incredibly delicate. If the acidity of the compound changed by even a fraction of a pH unit, the weapon would eat through its own container.

Destabilizing the formula shouldn't, in theory, be difficult. But sabotage required having an ally on the inside, a luxury we might not have when the time came. If my son completed his weapon, we needed more than one option. So, I started compiling as much research as my laptop could hold and organized my theories into functional proposals.

Unfortunately, if I was going to move past computer simulations, I needed more data. I had to monitor Nic's research. Until he told me otherwise, I had to assume he was still working on the project, which meant I needed to know about any progress immediately. And that meant I had to put my daughter in the line of fire.

All the evidence suggested Nic hadn't detected our hacking. There were no angry phone calls, no warnings from Ambrose; Cea claimed her brother hadn't given her a second glance. That meant he wasn't monitoring his own activity log, and the loophole just might work again.

It was easy enough. Roseanne had remote access to Cea's device and had already set up the proxy chain to disguise her location. All we had to do was find a computer terminal that Cea could consistently access without being seen.

My daughter took to the challenge like a born criminal. She crawled all over the walls and corridors of the base until she found a terminal in an abandoned office out of sight of any security cameras. She simply plugged her phone in, and I could see Nic's lab reports in real time.

Cea loved it. I hated it. But until Roseanne developed a better workaround, it was my only option. I could either spare my daughter, or I could train her and have her help me fight for justice.

I knew what choice I would want her to make, if the roles were reversed.

It had been about two weeks since Nic had visited, and I was in his room with my contraband electronics spread out on the bed, waiting for Cea to call. It was late evening in Boston, which meant it was early morning on the station—the best time for Cea to access the database without being noticed. Nic was already at work generating activity, but she wasn't expected to be logged into her virtual school yet.

I drummed my fingers on the back of my phone. Her avatar flashed green, right on schedule.

I'M HERE

I copied and pasted the message I had prepared.

GOOD. I NEED YOU TO LOOK FOR SOMETHING SPECIFIC TODAY.

YEAH?

LOOK FOR FILES WITH THIS EXTENSION. THEY'RE THE SENSOR READOUTS FROM THE TESTING CHAMBERS IN THE LABS.

I sent her screenshots of an example, along with the directory where the logs were most likely synced. She sent back a spy emoji, which I ignored. *Teenagers.*

I switched to my laptop and kept working while I waited. If I ran the testing logs through a program, I could generate a chart of the most common chemical elements Nic was using in his tests. That would give me a baseline for what elements to use in the countermeasure. If I could narrow the parameters—

My thoughts were interrupted by my text tone. I picked up my device, expecting a message from Cea.

It wasn't. It was a friend request from a new user—a fake one, judging by the random string of letters and numbers that formed the username.

I swiped to block them, ignoring the pinch of panic in my chest. No one but Cea was supposed to know my username, but it was probably just a bot.

Another request from a randomized username popped up. I blocked that one as well, then navigated to my settings to see if I could disable all incoming requests. Before I found the button, a third request appeared—immediately followed by a text message.

COME NOW, DON'T BE RUDE. AT LEAST SAY HELLO.

I froze. The user took advantage of my silence.

I KNOW YOU CAN SEE THIS MESSAGE. PLEASED TO FINALLY MAKE YOUR ACQUAINTANCE, "VON."

The panic imploded as I reached the worst possible conclusion. We'd been found out—and my daughter was in incredible danger.

Cea!

I switched to her chat, but she texted before I could.

FOUND THE LOGS, BUT THERE'S LIKE A HUNDRED. DO YOU WANT THEM ALL?

My heart was beating so fast I could barely type the words.

GET OUT OF THERE!

WHAT?

THEY FOUND US. WIPE YOUR DEVICE AND GET OUT OF THERE NOW!

The typing dots appeared. I reached for the button to call her, but the other user spoke first.

OH CALM YOURSELF. I WON'T HURT HER.

I ran the math. *Can they—?*

They answered my unspoken question.

YES, I CAN SEE EVERY WORD YOU SEND ON THIS APP. I'VE BEEN WATCHING THE WHOLE TIME.

Who are you? It couldn't be Nic; Nic would just pull the plug and report me to Ambrose. It had to be someone else, someone with access to the base's servers.

Suddenly, the disjointed facts snapped together, and I realized what I should have seen all along.

Nic *didn't* have control over the base's cybersecurity. He wasn't the one who caught our hacking attempts—someone else was watching.

Min?

Cea finally found her words.

DAD? IS EVERYTHING OKAY?

I hovered over the call button, then changed my mind. I accepted the stranger's friend request.

WHAT DO YOU WANT?

NOTHING. I MERELY WANTED TO GIVE YOU A CHANCE TO SAY YOUR GOODBYES. THE POLICE HAVE AN ETA OF 9:52.

I glanced at the clock as reality collapsed on me.

It's over.

Another message came through, cruel and mocking.

YOU HAVE FIFTEEN MINUTES. DON'T SAY I WASN'T A GOOD SPORT.

Cea texted again, but suddenly, I didn't know what to say. There was nothing I could do to protect her. They already knew she was involved, and they had transcripts of all our text messages. They knew she'd been sending me data—

The research!

I grabbed my laptop and stood up. I had to hide my research. If the police found it, they would destroy it—and then there would be nothing and no one to stop my son from setting the world on fire.

But hiding the laptop wouldn't be enough. Whatever was about to happen, I wouldn't be coming home soon—if ever. I needed to get the data into someone's hands, someone who could finish the work if I couldn't.

But who? I couldn't text Cea; this madman would see the message. I had to tell someone else where to look, and now.

Andes!

Kneeling on the floor, I dredged the radio out of the compartment and threw it on the bed. My phone chimed, but I ignored it as I scrambled with the dial. Andes was the only member of the underground who knew where I lived. If I could tell him where to look, he could retrieve the laptop and get it to someone who could finish the work.

The radio came to life with a burst of static. I snatched the handset. "Break, break! This is Von. Andes, do you copy? Over."

I let go of the button. The channel was silent.

I spoke again, struggling to make my words clear and precise. "This is Von. Andes, do you copy? It's an emergency! Over!"

A door banged somewhere in the house. "Paul?" my wife's shout echoed up the stairs. "What's going on?"

My phone dinged again. I glanced at the screen to see a missed call from Cea and a new message from the stranger.

TICK TOCK, PAUL. ANY LAST WORDS FOR YOUR DAUGHTER?

The line was still silent. I raised my voice. "Emergency, emergency! Does anyone copy?"

There was a fizzle of static—and then a voice I recognized came through.

"This is Catalyst. I copy."

I nearly choked on a sigh of relief. Catalyst knew Andes, or at least knew how to reach him. If he could pass along a message, Andes could retrieve the laptop. "Catalyst, thank God. I need your help. I need to make a drop, tonight."

There was interference muddled with static. Then a clipped, "No, I'm not meeting up with you."

My heart plummeted to my stomach as all my fears regenerated—he still didn't trust me. "No, you don't understand. I just need you to get a message to Andes. Please respond."

He did, but even around the static I could tell that he'd already made up his mind. "I'm sorry, I can't help you."

I shouted an unholy word into the mic. "Get over yourself! Now is not the time! The police will be here any minute!"

I said too much. There was a muttered oath on the radio, like Catalyst didn't realize his mic was on. "No—I'm not getting involved. I won't—"

I yelled over him. "No, please, you don't understand! This is important! If I don't get this research out of the house, millions will die!"

Apparently, the math meant nothing to him. I let go of the button just in time to hear his muffled, "Over and out."

Terror replaced my anger. "Catalyst? Catalyst, please, you have to listen to me! Do you copy?"

Static.

"Does anyone else copy? Anyone!"

Silence.

I roared and threw the handset on the ground. Catalyst was my only hope—and now I'd shown my hand. If the police were listening, they knew my research was in the house. I had to create a decoy, or they'd burn the whole house down looking for it.

I dug my hand into the compartment, feeling in the darkness. *Where is it? I know I had it—there!* I yanked out a dusty flash drive.

Footsteps pounded up the stairs. I jammed the drive into the laptop just as Roseanne threw the door open. "Paul? What in the world—"

"There's no time," I interrupted her. "I need you to take this flash drive and hide it downstairs." I quickly dragged a couple of incriminating files onto the drive.

"What's wrong?" she demanded, but I could tell by the tremor in her voice that she knew the answer.

I met her eyes. "The police will be here in less than five minutes."

I didn't have time to explain—but I didn't need to. She blinked once, took one sharp breath through her nose, then said, "What do I do?"

"Take this drive and put it in the hidden drawer in my desk." I yanked the device out of the port and threw it at her.

She caught it.

I powered off the laptop. "Take both of our computers and bash in the hard drives. Break your tablet in half—anything to make it look like you were trying to destroy evidence."

"Got it." She was out the door almost before I finished the sentence.

I knelt and started shoveling my electronics back into the compartment. A drawer slammed downstairs, followed by a crash.

I jammed the lid back on the compartment. My phone trilled repeatedly, but it was drowned out by a siren igniting on the street.

"Paul!" my wife shrieked. Another crash.

Red-blue lights bled through the curtains. I scrambled up and shoved the bookcase back into position. It thudded against the wall.

I gripped the shelf. "Lord, hide it." Then I snatched my phone and ran out of the room, slamming the door behind me.

There were shouts outside. I glanced at my device. Cea had called twice more. Suddenly, there was so much I wanted to say to her, but there wasn't time. There was never time.

A heavy hand banged on our front door. "Paul!" Roseanne screamed again.

I unlocked my phone and sent three quick words.

WE LOVE YOU

Then I powered off my device and ran down the stairs.

I made it to the foyer just in time to see my front door get kicked down. McClaine filed in, followed by two more officers. Ambrose barged past them and rudely shoved my wife out of his way.

She muttered something rather unchristian. "Get out!"

He cast a dull glance at her before turning his gaze on me.

I collected my wits and approached him. "Let's get this over with."

"You're under arrest," he stated blandly, as if even he were bored with the proceedings.

"And I'm resisting it." I shifted my stance and folded my arms. "So, what now?"

I braced myself for the exhausted litany of threats, but they never came. Ambrose just tipped his head to the side and regarded me. "Don't do this. Not this time."

"No, we're doing this. If you're going to arrest me, then I'm going to make you check every single box. Go ahead," I flicked my hand at the phone he had holstered on his belt, "read me my rights. Tell me how this all goes away if I sign your putrid little file."

He was already shaking his head. "A clean file won't save you this time. I have orders from Chairwoman Mong herself."

I stopped breathing. *It was Min. It was Min the whole time.*

Ambrose gestured. The other two officers held my wife back while McClaine approached me.

"I'm sorry, Paul." He unclipped a pair of handcuffs from his belt.

"No, I am." I sidestepped and swiped a flower vase off the credenza. It hit the floor and shattered, spraying water and broken glass across the tile. McClaine slipped and crashed into the stairs.

I turned to run, but I wasn't fast enough. I heard the crackle of electricity a second before the stun shot hit me in the back of the leg. Roseanne shrieked. I crumpled and landed face-first in the puddle.

"It's over," Ambrose said from somewhere above me.

I spat out water and struggled to rise, but McClaine was on top of me, pinning me down with his knee. "Please don't make me hurt you," he whispered.

I hesitated, long enough for him to grab my hands and cuff them behind my back. He hauled me to my feet, and I turned to see the other two officers doing the same to my wife.

"Unhand me!" she snarled, and my blood boiled.

With a heavy sigh, Ambrose turned to lead the way out the door. "Make this easy on yourselves for once."

"We won't." I jerked against McClaine as he shoved me towards the porch. "We're never going to stop fighting. This may be over for you, but it's never over for us. Put us in a containment camp or whatever you want, but the game will never be over."

Ambrose stopped. "That's just it, doctor. You're not going to jail this time."

He glanced over his shoulder and, for the first time that night, smiled. "You're going to the hospital."

10

That was the first—and last—time I saw my wife cry.

Roseanne wasn't a crier. She'd sooner punch a hole in the drywall than shed a tear. She hadn't cried when they'd taken Cea away. She hadn't cried when we made the cruel decision to turn Nic over to the police. She hadn't cried when we found out what he was developing on Mars—that our son was planning to end the world.

She never cried. Probably because she knew I had already shed enough tears, pounding the floor in prayer and begging God to save my children.

But that night, as McClaine dragged me down the sidewalk to a waiting ambulance, something in her snapped. For the first time in years, there was no anger in her eyes. There was only fear—pure, blinding terror.

She screamed my name. I couldn't even answer as one of the paramedics jabbed a syringe in my neck and tranquilized me. It wasn't strong enough to knock me unconscious, but it was enough to render me useless as they strapped me onto a stretcher. I couldn't move as they lifted me into the ambulance, shouting orders at each other.

The last thing I heard was Roseanne sobbing, shrieking as she begged Ambrose to let me go, before the ambulance doors slammed.

They rushed me to the hospital, sirens blaring. I watched through blurred vision as they transferred me to a room and hooked me up to a matrix of machines. I couldn't feel the needles as they threaded me with IVs and patched wires to my chest. I could only watch as the tangle of wires and tubes grew, spreading out from my body like a spider was weaving me into her web.

The medication was just starting to wear off when a visitor arrived. I rolled my head to find a young man staring at me. He was standing perfectly still in the gap between the curtains that circled my hospital bed. I wondered how long he had been posed there, watching me like a creepy mannequin in a store window.

"Who are you?" I growled, and was annoyed to find that my voice was still slurred.

He took the invitation to step closer. He couldn't have been older than twenty, with gelled dark hair and broad shoulders. He seemed vaguely familiar, like we'd met once or twice. Was he with the police?

He still hadn't said anything, so I tried again. "Have we met?"

"We're meeting now," he replied. He had a chipper voice with a British accent so precise that it sounded fake. He definitely wasn't with the force—and he didn't look like a doctor, either. He wore an immaculate suit that probably cost more than my car. He had no badge or ID, and all he carried was a disposable coffee cup from the cafeteria. The cheap foam, with its brightly-colored pattern that probably hadn't changed since the 1990s, seemed out of place in his hand when everything else about him exuded wealth and power.

Where have I seen him before?

I frowned and struggled to sit up, but my arms were strapped to the mattress. "What do you want?"

"Well, we weren't able to have a proper conversation earlier, so I thought I'd come say hello before they put you under." He took a sip from his cup.

I put two and two together. "It was you. The messages."

He smiled, a terrifying closed-lip gesture, and twiddled his fingers in greeting.

I lurched when my groggy consciousness remembered who else was in danger. "What have you done with my daughter?"

He rolled his eyes. "I said I wouldn't hurt her. Don't you trust me, Paul?"

The answer to that should have been obvious. He put a hand to his chest like he was genuinely mortified. "I'll have you know I didn't even tell the police she was involved. As far as the bobbies are concerned, your wife did all the hacking. You're welcome."

I clenched my fists. "Where is Roseanne?"

"In the room next over." He pointed.

I jerked on the straps, causing the whole bed to rock. "What are you doing to her?"

"The same thing I'm about to do to you. Mercy, don't get all in a tizzy. You're going to get your blood pressure up."

One of the machines next to my bed screeched, confirming his statement. "Let her go," I snarled, even though I knew it was a wasted gesture. "It's me you want."

He clucked his tongue. "Come now, don't be so patriarchal. We both know she's just as dangerous as you are. Do you know how many man hours we wasted trying to keep her out of the system?"

I studied him, struggling to see the facts through the rage and fear. "So, you *were* watching the whole time. You're the one in charge of the base's cybersecurity."

"Well, not me specifically. That's what I have people for." He slid a phone out of his pocket and glanced at it, as if reinforcing the point. "But yes, it didn't take Carnegie long to crack the code on your daughter's 'game.' Clever app, that."

"Carnegie?"

"Nic's assistant," the young man clarified, even though I remembered. "Or rather, Min's assistant."

My chest tightened when I realized I'd been right all along. Min didn't love my son; she was using him.

And I'd gotten in the way.

"I take it Nic doesn't know?" I prompted, careful to keep the emotion out of my voice.

He took the bait. "No, of course not. Where would the fun in that be? He thinks they're equal partners. He's so naïve it's *adorable.*" The revolting inflection he put on the word suggested that he did, in fact, find it amusing.

I didn't respond. Nic *was* naïve. He was an idiot—and as soon as Min was done with him, she'd kill him, too.

No matter what my son had done, the last thing I wanted was for him to die a fool.

The stranger continued babbling. "It's so funny to watch him bow down to her. She's got that boy on a leash, and I think he just might marry her. But do you know what the best part is?"

He leered over my bed, his face inches from mine. His breath was strangely sweet, like he'd just flossed. He shielded his lips with his hand as if we were sharing a great secret. "I dare say she's *actually* in love with him."

I leaned away. The stranger took that as consent. "Isn't it mad?" he crowed like we were teenage girls sharing gossip. "I've never seen her so smitten. I couldn't have written a better soap opera myself. I do hope this ruins everything."

His odd choice of words sent a shudder down my spine. "Ruin… what?"

"Oh, I mean what's about to happen to you." He stepped back and gestured at me with his cup. "I really hope it causes a scandal."

I finally asked the question I didn't want an answer to. "You're going to kill us, aren't you?"

The cruel smile slid across his face again. "Oh, my dear Paul, you have *no* imagination."

He set his cup down on the bedside table and turned to one of the monitors. "Execution would be so much cleaner, I admit. If Min had her way, you'd be dead already. She hates an unnecessary mess—of which you've caused several."

He tapped a button, and the screen beeped at him. I felt a sickeningly cool sensation in my arm as one of the IVs started pumping an unknown substance into my vein.

I yanked my wrist, but the straps were too tight—I couldn't reach the needle. *Jesus, help me!*

"But if you want my opinion," the stranger chirped, "I think life is much more exciting when you're willing to make a mess."

Wild colors splashed across my vision, but I forced myself to focus. I may have only minutes. "What did you do?"

"I convinced the judge to reduce your sentence." He continued to swipe through menus. "He was open to reason. You're a valuable scientist, after all—and Min wasn't paying him nearly enough."

I lost feeling in my arm. I gripped the sheets to ground myself.

"The judge agreed that reconditioning is a far more suitable punishment for you. They're supposed to cut the revolutionary out of your brain and spare the scientist—but it is such a horribly unpredictable procedure." He punched another button and turned around.

A wave of nausea drowned me. "What… pro…cedure?"

"Neurosurgery, Paul," he cooed.

Neurosurgery. It was utter pseudoscience, better suited as a torture device than a correctional one. The theory was that nanobots could be used to selectively rewrite a person's brain circuitry, removing memories and opinions the government found problematic. It rarely worked. Most patients suffered total memory loss and severe disabilities—if they survived at all.

There was more, but suddenly, I couldn't remember the details. I couldn't remember anything. The room seemed dark and claustrophobic as my head began to throb.

Jesus!

The stranger perched on the edge of the bed. "The official court order says they're supposed to erase the noncompliance and let you keep your memories and science degrees. But that just won't do. You see, Paul, it's not the revolutionary that concerns me. It's the scientist."

I tried to speak, but my gut hurled again.

He fingered an IV tube. "I know what you're trying to do. Min thinks you were going to alert the police again, but I know you're not so short-sighted." He frowned at me.

My research. I couldn't have formulated the words had I wanted to. The room was spinning.

"I need that weapon, Paul," he spat, his voice suddenly rigid with hate. For a terrifying second, he sounded completely sane. "I can't have you ruining it."

The clarity vanished as he sprung off the bed and grabbed his cup. "No matter. Turns out your surgeon is also grossly underpaid, so he's going to take care of this little problem for me. By the time you wake up, there won't be anything left of the great Dr. Paul Von Nieuwenhuyse."

Fear screamed in my ear as I lost feeling in my other arm. *My wife... Cea... Nic!* I wouldn't remember them; I wouldn't remember anything. I'd be as good as dead.

Except, I wouldn't be. I'd be a shell of a man, a stranger in my own house, a burden to my children as they cared for an aging father who didn't even know them.

And that's exactly what this madman wanted.

He seemed to read my thoughts. "Don't worry, I'll make sure your son knows exactly who did it. Min thinks she has everything classified. Wouldn't it be a shame if she 'missed' a signature?"

I struggled to make sense of his rambling as the throbbing in my head grew louder. *What is wrong with this man?*

"Oh, how I wish I could be there when he finds out." The stranger drummed his fingers on his cup. "Can you imagine it? The drama, the betrayal—his own *girlfriend* condemned his parents to death. It'll be such a scandal. I really hope he breaks up with her. She needs to be humbled."

I opened my mouth—then realized I was bargaining with the wrong person. Nic could see things; Nic would see right through this. *Show him the truth, God!*

"Of course, I can't make it too easy on him," the stranger mused. "There will just be one or two clues that were accidentally unclassified. He's going to have to work for it. But I have faith in him, don't you?"

I did. Faith that Nic wouldn't fall for their schemes, faith that he could still hear the Lord, faith that he would see the trap and turn their deception back on them. Nic was smarter than Min, than Carnegie, than this madman. This wouldn't work. Not on my son.

I sucked in air and forced the words out, even though I had to form each one separately. "You... won't... get away... with this."

The stranger arched an eyebrow. "I'm not intending to."

What?

"I fully expect everything to come to light one day. If someone doesn't figure it out first, I'll tell them myself. After all, what's the fun in winning if you can't take credit for it?"

He took a sip from his cup and gagged. He pried the plastic lid off and squinted at the contents. "You Bostonians haven't made a good cup of tea since 1773, have you?" He turned and chucked the cup into the nearest trash can.

I tried to respond, but no sound came out. I couldn't move anything, not even my head. The room faded, and this time, I couldn't get it to focus again.

I pushed one last prayer past the gathering darkness. *Save my son.*

"Goodbye, Paul." The stranger's voice echoed in my ears as I lost consciousness. "We will meet again."

OCTOBER 2075

EIGHT YEARS LATER

11

I woke to the sound of my doorbell ringing.

I jerked and nearly fell out of the chair. I looked around and tried to remember where I was. I was in a living room—whose house was this? Was this my house? Yes, those were my loafers on the floor, and my phone on the coffee table—this must be my house. Why was I sleeping in the living room? What time was it?

The TV was blaring. Had I fallen asleep watching TV? I squinted at the screen. What show was this? None of the characters looked familiar.

The doorbell rang again. "Honey, will you get it?" a woman yelled from the other room.

I jumped. *Who is in my...* Then I recognized the voice, and I laughed at myself. It was my wife, of course. What other woman would be in my house?

"Coming," I shouted back. I turned off the TV and stood up, grunting when my back popped. "Are you expecting someone?"

Dishes clattered in the kitchen. "I'm never expecting anyone," she shouted over the commotion.

I chuckled. That was fair—I wasn't expecting anyone either. We never got visitors.

I made it to the door just as it rang for the third time. I opened it to find a pretty young woman standing on the step, dragging a small suitcase behind her.

I pushed open the storm door. "Hi there, young lady. Can I help you?"

"It's Cea," she blurted. "Remember?"

I wished I did. She looked vaguely familiar—I'd seen her face before, somewhere—but I couldn't place her. "Sorry, no," I admitted. "When did we meet last?"

I tried to think of the last couple of events I'd been to, to see if I could remember where I might have seen her... *Wait, I haven't been to any events recently.* I couldn't even remember the last time I left the house.

The girl apparently couldn't remember, either. She stood there awkwardly, twisting the handle of her suitcase in her hands. "It's... been awhile since I visited," she offered.

I glanced at her carryon and put two and two together. "Oh, did you come to see us?"

What a silly question, Paul! I chided myself. Of course, she came to visit us—she was standing on our doorstep with a suitcase! I stepped back and gestured for her to come in. "That's so nice of you! Come in, come in."

"Thanks, Da—" She stopped with one foot in the door. "Is it okay if I call you Dad?"

I grinned. It was a bit forward, but I liked the sound of it. "Of course."

To her credit, she looked like she could be our kid, if we'd had any. She had golden curls and a heart-shaped face that reminded me of my wife. Maybe that's why she looked familiar.

I shut the storm door and led the way down the hall. "You'll have to forgive me—remind me how we know each other?"

She flinched. Was that a rude question? It didn't seem like a rude question.

"I'm your..." She stopped in the middle of the hall and struggled for words. "I used to live here."

I frowned at her. It had always just been Roseanne and me in the house—I would have remembered if we had a roommate!

"I have a key, see." The girl dug in her pocket and held up a small metal object.

I remembered. "The back door!" I exclaimed.

"Yes!" she agreed, matching my enthusiasm.

I remembered—I really did. A man had installed a manual lock on our back door. He said it was so that we could come and go without leaving an electronic log.

Why would we care about leaving an electronic log? Wouldn't it just be easier to use the garage door? And what was his name?

I couldn't remember. And why couldn't I remember this girl staying here? Clearly, she had at one point—she had a key! It must have been a long time ago.

I shook off the thought; it was giving me a headache. "It has been a long time, hasn't it?" I offered, and kept walking.

She sighed. "Yeah. It has."

"Well, you're here now!" My excitement returned—I couldn't remember the last time we'd had someone over for dinner! My wife would be thrilled. "Make yourself at home. Roseanne! We have company!"

We rounded the corner to the kitchen. My wife was rooting around in the cabinets. She opened and slammed two more doors before turning to face us. "Paul, where is the—" She stopped. "Who are you?" she snapped, jabbing her finger at our guest.

"Roseanne! That's no way to greet company!" I scolded. "You know her. This is…" I froze when I suddenly realized I couldn't remember her name. *She just told me…*

"Cea," she helped me out.

"Yes, Cea! She used to live here, remember?"

My wife folded her arms. "No, I don't."

Cea bit her lip.

"It's been a while," I said dismissively. "She came back to visit us. Isn't that nice?"

Roseanne was still scowling. "I wasn't expecting you."

I shot her a glare. In her defense, I wasn't expecting Cea either, but that was no reason to be rude. We never got company.

"I called…" Cea mumbled, and pointed at the calendar.

"I don't remember…" Roseanne trailed off when she turned around and realized that the calendar on the fridge did, in fact, have "Cea visiting" marked on it. It was written on today's date—today was Friday, right?

I laughed. "So you did. Sorry, I guess we forgot."

"It's fine," Cea said, but she didn't *look* like it was fine.

I felt awful. How could we forget we had company coming over?

Roseanne continued to glower at the calendar. "Well, I don't know where she's going to sleep."

"There's a spare room upstairs," Cea said.

"There is?" I exclaimed. I tried to picture our second floor and couldn't. When was the last time I went up there?

"I'll set my stuff down and come help with dinner." Cea grabbed her suitcase.

I reached for the handle. "Let me carry that for you."

She didn't let go. "It's okay, I got it."

"No, it's the least I can do after I forgot you were coming." I gave her what I hoped was a charming smile. *She must think we're terrible people.*

She gave me a small smile in return, then let go of the suitcase.

I led her to the stairs. "I'm sorry, I'm sure it's a mess up here." Seeing as I couldn't remember the last time I'd been upstairs, it had probably been a while since Roseanne had cleaned.

"It's okay," she said as she followed me up.

I reached the landing and discovered she was right—there was a spare room. Two, in fact. Why didn't we have guests more often? We had plenty of space!

"Well, guess you get your pick of rooms! Which one do you want?" I gestured.

She squeezed past me and went to the door on the right. "This one is fine."

"Do we need to put sheets on the bed, or..." I trailed off when she opened the door. We didn't need to put sheets on the bed; the room was fully furnished *and* decorated. It was definitely a girl's room—there were rock band posters and tie-dye pink sheets and a whole dresser full of makeup. How long had this stuff been up here? Who did it belong to?

I dropped the suitcase and picked up a stuffed bear that was sitting on the desk. "Was this Roseanne's?" I asked, but as soon as I said it, I knew that wasn't right. Why did none of this stuff look familiar?

Cea tossed her suitcase on the bed. "No, it's mine. I used to live here, remember?"

Apparently, she did. "Why didn't you take your stuff with you when you moved out?"

She stared at the mirror on the dresser, her back to me. "I don't... I thought I'd be coming back."

I shrugged; that made sense. "Well, you should probably take it with you this time. It's just collecting dust here."

She didn't answer.

I glanced at the room across the hall. What did that bedroom look like? Was it full of stuff, too?

I walked to the door and pushed it open. I was somewhat disappointed to find that the room was mostly empty—clearly, no one had lived here for a long time. There was a bed, three empty bookcases, a desk, and a weird table that kind of looked like a desk, except the top was at an angle. What was that used for?

There was also something by the window. It was a lumpy object hidden under a sheet. I walked over and pulled the cover off.

I had no idea what I was looking at. It was a strange apparatus. A fat metal tube was propped on thin legs. There was a glass lens on each end and several dials and keypads, like the whole thing was adjustable. What in the world was this for, and why did I have one in my house?

The door creaked. I whipped around—there wasn't supposed to be anyone in the house... *Oh, it's Cea.* That was her name, right? I'd forgotten she was here.

"What is this?" I pointed at the equipment.

She hesitated; maybe she didn't know what it was, either. "It's a telescope," she said finally.

That word—I knew that word. Hadn't someone used a telescope in the TV show we watched the other day?

It came to me: Images of people adjusting the fat metal tube so they could study the stars. "For stargazing!" I exclaimed.

She nodded. "Yes, Dad, for stars."

I chuckled; it was so cute how she called me "dad." *Such a sweet girl.* "I didn't know I had a telescope." Why did I have a telescope? These things were expensive, weren't they? When did I buy a telescope?

I ran my hand down the barrel. The metal felt cold under my fingers—and suddenly, I remembered.

I used to use this telescope; I used to use it all the time. I would set it up in the backyard with… someone. I could picture him, but I couldn't quite find his name. A little boy. We would spend hours stargazing in the backyard, looking for… what were we looking for? I taught him how to find it. I know I did.

I whipped the curtain back, but it was the middle of the afternoon. No stars were visible.

I blinked in the bright sunlight. Maybe I was misremembering. I didn't know any little boys. Or if I did, they didn't come to visit me anymore.

I shrugged and closed the curtains.

"Let's go, Dad," Cea whispered from the doorway.

I turned around and studied the bookcases. There were three of them against the wall, all empty. They were nice bookcases, too. They were being wasted up here in a bedroom we never used.

I grabbed one and rocked it, testing the weight. They weren't that heavy; I could move one easily.

"Dad…?" Cea stepped forward.

"Will you help me with these? I bet we can carry them together." I gripped a shelf and dragged the first bookcase away from the wall. "I want to put them in the living room."

QUEEN SACRIFICE

RED RAIN #8

JULY 2076

1: PHILADELPHIA

Nic was dead.

I admitted it as soon as the strangers in the subway stopped administering CPR. Two men had been taking turns trying desperately to pump life back into Nic's chest. The first gave three more compressions—then stopped. He held his fingers against Nic's purple neck. Then he sat back on his haunches with an exhausted sigh.

The other man gestured at Nic's body, as if offering to take over. The first shook his head.

That's when I realized Nic hadn't been breathing for at least twenty minutes, maybe more. Where was the ambulance? I could only imagine it was stuck in Beijing's rush hour, trapped in a sea of cars while a man died.

It was too late now. Even if they could bring him back, there would be nothing left. He would be worse off than my dad.

He was gone.

The rest of the world seemed to reboot around that fact. A subway employee peeled the defibrillator pads off Nic's bluish-white chest and wrapped the cords back up in the orange box. One of the men who had administered CPR stood and pulled out his phone to make a call. Vaguely, I registered the screech of a train arriving at the station, and the crowd shifted as hundreds of evening commuters tried to cram themselves on the cars. All around me, people chattered in a language I couldn't understand as rush hour continued unabated.

I couldn't move. I felt stuck in a time loop, only able to repeat the same thought over and over like a glitched electronic as my brain tried and failed, tried and failed to accept what was going on.

He's dead he's dead he's dead.

I stared at Nic's body, sprawled on the dirty platform tile. Even in death, his face had flatlined into that familiar disinterested frown. A few months ago, I had feared that frown. When we'd met, Dr. Nic Von Nieuwenhuyse had been an enemy, a heartless criminal, a creator of superweapons. Now, all I could think was that I wouldn't be alive without him. He had come back to

Earth from Mars to stop me from making the biggest mistake of my life. He'd saved me.

And now I was the reason he was dead.

I looked down at my right hand. I'd killed Nic. The chip in my palm had given him an electromagnetic shock and sent him into cardiac arrest when I'd grabbed his hand. The chip had been designed as an assassination weapon, intended for General Secretary Mong, the leader of the United. The weapon should have killed my greatest enemy. Instead, it killed the closest thing I had to family, at least on this planet.

My brain suddenly restarted as a torrent of guilt knocked loose a whirlwind of unanswered questions. *How, how did this happen?* My chip should have been coded for the General Secretary's DNA. Did it malfunction? It hadn't shocked anyone else, and I'd had it in my hand for a week. Why now? Why Nic? *Why is this happening—*

I involuntarily shrieked when someone touched my arm. I looked up to see a paramedic gently pushing me aside. I saw her uniform and bag of supplies and instantly grabbed onto a false sense of hope. I gripped Nic's shoulder. "Please, you have to help him!" I screamed. "Surely there's something—"

One of the men who had administered CPR spoke over me in Mandarin, pointing at Nic's body and then at the defibrillator. The paramedic knelt next to Nic and checked for a pulse in three different places, then pulled a stethoscope out of her bag and listened to his heart. Lastly, she pulled out a light, pried one of Nic's eyes open, and tested his unblinking pupils.

All of this happened in the space of less than a minute, but for me, it felt like an eternity. Each thing she checked was like a nail in Nic's coffin, each failed test another screaming reminder that he wasn't coming back. This was really happening. Nic was really dead. Nic was dead, and I was alone, and I had nowhere to go, and it was all my fault...

The paramedic closed Nic's eye, then turned to her partner and dictated something. He nodded and typed on his tablet.

I knew even without being able to speak the language what they were saying, but some unhelpful stranger behind me translated. "They're declaring him dead on the scene."

"No," I whimpered, desperate for this all to be a cruel nightmare, but no one even heard me. *God, why why why? What did I do wrong?*

The male paramedic bent over and grabbed Nic's limp hand. He pressed Nic's thumb to his tablet. Instantly, the device screeched and flashed red. I saw a glimpse of the warning on the screen, written in both Mandarin and English:

NATIONAL SECURITY RISK. DETAIN AT ALL COSTS.

I laughed, a deranged howl that quickly melted into a wail of anguish. Even dead, Nic was still a wanted criminal. And it was all because of me.

I wanted to throw myself on his body and beg and plead for forgiveness—from him, God, anyone. I wanted to recant every choice I'd made for the last six weeks and undo all my actions. All the mistakes, all the times I'd refused to take Nic's advice, all the failures that had brought us to this point, to Nic lying dead on the floor of a Beijing subway station. I would do anything, say anything, take any punishment—if it would just bring Nic back.

"God, I'm sorry!" I shrieked aloud, not caring who heard me. "Please don't do this! I need him!" I shook Nic's shoulder violently, causing his head to roll.

I heard the squeak of wheels on tile and saw them push a stretcher up to us. The female paramedic turned to me. Murmuring something that was probably "excuse me," she gently grasped my arms and pried my hands off Nic's body.

As soon as my fingers left his shoulder, it hit me.

This isn't right.

I snapped back to attention as that revelation filled me with pulsing anger. This *wasn't* right. Nic shouldn't be dead. Less than a half hour ago, he'd told me that he'd seen a vision about my future. He knew we were supposed to be in Beijing—us, together—because I was supposed to lead the revolution and he was supposed to help me. That was the whole reason we were here. That was the whole reason God had brought us together. God had called us. Not just me—*us.*

And God doesn't lie.

"This isn't right," I whispered. I sat up on my knees. "This isn't right!" I repeated, louder, for myself and all the spirits that were listening. "You can't have him!"

The paramedic tried to pull me back, but I shoved her aside. I leaned over Nic and planted my palms flat on his heart. I looked straight into his face and declared loudly and clearly as if he could hear me: "You aren't supposed to die. You're supposed to help me. You're supposed to be here, in Beijing. This is what you're called to do. This is your purpose. God chose you!"

A murmur rippled up the crowd, although whether it was because I'd yelled the name of an illegal religious figure or because I was making a scene on a dead man's chest, I'll never know. I stared at Nic's closed eyes as the Holy Spirit welled up in my throat with an indescribable pressure. There were a million thoughts swirling around in my soul, but there was only one thing I knew for sure. I screamed it out and hoped all the powers of hell heard me:

"This isn't right, and in the name of Jesus, you are going to live!"

I shoved down on Nic's chest with all my weight—and he yelled.

He jerked upright, knocking me backwards. He whipped around, arms flinging like a ragdoll, as he scanned the crowd with rabid eyes. The bystanders shrieked and pulled back; even the paramedics leaned away like they were afraid to touch him. He panted and started sweating profusely as his head jerked back and forth.

And then he spotted me.

Suddenly, he seemed to repossess his body. He blinked, and his vision focused on me, gaze clear. "Philadelphia?"

I burst into relieved tears. "Nic! Oh God, thank you! You brought him back!"

My words gave Nic pause. He looked down at his ripped shirt, then at over at the defibrillator box, then up at the paramedics. "What just happened?"

He added a couple of extra words—one of which I knew I shouldn't repeat—and that's when I knew he'd be all right.

"My—my chip." I struggled to explain as all the leftover adrenaline made my voice shaky. "It—I—killed you. You were dead. You weren't breathing for like twenty minutes."

He looked down at my right hand, then back up at my face. "Then why am I still here?"

I met his gaze. "I-I prayed for you. God brought you back from the dead."

We stared at each other, and in that flicker of understanding, I knew he realized exactly what had happened. He knew what God had done for him—for me.

Nic opened his mouth, but just then, the paramedics decided to come back to work. The female grabbed his arm and tried to lay him back down. The male leaned over and asked him a question. Nic ignored it, instead staring at the tablet in the man's hand.

The red warning was still displayed on the screen. And that's when I remembered: Nic's file was marked with the highest security warning there was. As soon as he checked into the hospital, they would arrest him. And then Asia, his ex-girlfriend and a top United official, would do whatever she wanted with him.

And I doubted it would be pleasant.

I scrambled up, adjusting my backpack. "We need to go!"

Nic struggled to copy me, but he barely made it to his feet. He stumbled, nearly crashing into the paramedic, and grabbed the back of his head. I could see his blond hair was soiled with blood from where he'd cracked his head on the tile.

Both paramedics grabbed his arms. "Please, sir," the male one clipped in poor English, "you need to go to the hospital."

Nic weakly brushed them off. "I'm fine, I'm fine," he insisted.

One of the civilians who had administered CPR joined the chase. "Sir, you really need to get checked out."

I grabbed Nic's sleeve and tried to pull him away. "He'll be fine, I promise." I turned and scanned the clogged platform, looking for a way out. Maybe if we could make a break for it, we could lose them in the crowd.

The paramedics were having none of it. The male one tried to shove Nic onto the stretcher, even though he was barely half Nic's height. Nic jerked back from him and almost lost his balance. The subway employee whipped out his radio and shouted into it, and whatever he said did not sound encouraging. I knew we had to get out of here *right now*, or we'd cause a bigger scene.

I pinched Nic's elbow. "Nic!" I hissed. "Your gun!"

He lifted his jacket and reached for his holstered weapon, then hesitated. The entire crowd sucked in its breath. The paramedics froze, as if waiting to see what he'd do. Nic scanned the throng of civilians around us—then grabbed his gun and threw it on the floor.

The crowd scattered away from it, shouting. "Nic!" I screeched.

He whipped to face me. "Run. Get out of here!"

I forgot to breathe as I struggled to process what he was telling me. "But Nic, I—"

"I'm not getting out of this," he said, words rapid but calm. "I can't run in this condition. Get out of here, go back to the Tangs."

"I'm not leaving you!" I cried. *Not after you just died!*

"Phil, listen to me." He grabbed my shoulders. "It's not me Asia wants—it's you."

"But why—"

He spoke over me. "No matter what happens to me, no matter what you hear, I need you to promise that you won't come for me. Do you understand?"

I didn't, not at all. "Nic, I—"

He shook my shoulders so hard my neck hurt. "Promise me!"

I didn't have a chance to respond. I heard the shriek of a whistle and shouts of "*Jingcha!* Police!" I saw commotion in my peripheral; the crowd rippled like a predator was breaking through the waves on a lake.

Nic saw it too. His eyes scanned the crowd for an escape—and just then the horn of an approaching train echoed down the tunnel. I felt the swell in the crowd and saw several subway employees trying to shepherd gawking bystanders away as the queue flowed towards the edge of the platform.

Nic looked back into my face. His gray eyes were stern but unafraid as he repeated, "Don't *ever* come back."

And then he grasped my shoulders and pushed me away from him.

I stumbled backwards with a yell—just as the train arrived in the station. The crowd surged forward with one accord, crushing me from all sides. I grabbed the arm of the person nearest to me, knowing that if I fell, I'd be trampled. He grunted something and shrugged me off.

I crashed into the person behind us, who elbowed me forward. I struggled to stay on my feet as I twisted around, looking for Nic, but I couldn't see him or the paramedics anywhere. All I could see was a tightly packed mob of jackets and backpacks as a sea of unfamiliar faces funneled me towards the subway.

"No, please, I don't want to get on! Excuse me! Please!" I shoved the person nearest to me aside, but as soon as I created a gap, three more people crammed in to fill the space. No one was listening to me as a garbled announcement blared over the intercom.

I felt myself being carried along like a stick in a river as the congested crowd crammed onto the car. The throng seemed to pack itself tighter and tighter, as if someone was sucking all the air out of the station. Bodies pressed in around me like a noose cinching until I couldn't even move my arms.

No, God, this can't be happening! Get me out of here! Nic!

No one budged. Elbows and knees prodded me forward, while white-gloved subway employees literally shoved people onto the car. I tripped over the gap from the platform to the train and almost knocked the person in front of me over. The queue continued to carry me into the center of the car; I couldn't even see out the windows around the sea of commuters. I blindly groped for the handlebar and managed to grab it just as the train lurched away from the station.

The motion sent my heart plummeting to my stomach. It was too late. Even if I could get off, Nic would be long gone. They'd take him to the hospital, and then Asia would send him to prison—or worse. It was over.

I was alone.

2: PHILADELPHIA

I rode the train to the end of the line.

I didn't have much of a choice; the rush-hour crowd was so thick that I probably couldn't have gotten off had I wanted to. I stood in the middle of the car, gripping the handlebar with both hands. It was the only thing holding me up. My system was still reeling from the sleep medication I'd taken earlier in the day; that, combined with the throb of unspent emotions, was making the world spin erratically like a washing machine that had gotten knocked off balance. The jerking motion of the train didn't help. I clenched my jaw and took shallow breaths through my nose, afraid that if I opened my mouth, I might scream or vomit or worse.

Eventually, the ebb and flow of commuters began to wane. As soon as a seat on the wall freed up, I sank into it. I leaned my head against the window and watched the lights in the tunnel flicker in and out of focus as the train passed an endless number of platforms. Stop and go, in and out, dark and light flashing back and forth, until finally the darkness won.

I jerked awake when a well-meaning passenger shook my shoulder. I sat upright with a gasp, startling her and everyone else in the car. I looked around at their confused faces and tried to remember where I was. How long had I been out? *That stupid medication must have finally gotten the better of me.*

The woman leaned over me and spoke kindly in Mandarin.

"I'm fine," I said, hoping my inflection would overcome the language barrier. I faked a smile and stood up, shouldering my backpack. She didn't look convinced, but she nodded and backed away.

Holding onto the handlebar, I inched over to the door. As soon as the train stopped at the next station, I shoved through the dwindling crowd and ran for the stairs.

I emerged into the warm night. Rush hour traffic had died off, but Beijing's nightlife was more than picking up the slack. Every storefront was lit with a blinding array of spotlights and red neon characters. Lanterns were strung across the road, casting an artificial red-orange glow on everything and making the whole block look like it was on fire. The dinner crowd clogged the street as families crammed around sidewalk tables and college students formed laughing queues in front of order counters. The air thrummed with chatter and the sizzle of woks.

The vendor nearest to the subway entrance—a kindly-looking grandpa manning a cart—called out to me, but I ducked my head and kept walking. I had to find someplace out of sight. I hurried down the block, dodging pedestrians, and ducked into an alley. I emerged onto the next street and found myself on the edge of the river.

Breathing a sigh of relief, I crossed the walking bridge to the other side and ran along the bank until I found an empty dock. The building behind it was either abandoned or closed for the night, and no one was in sight. Further downstream, I heard families gathering on their waterfront verandas, but the night had grown dark enough that I doubted they could see me.

Shrugging off my backpack, I sank onto the mossy brick. I took deep breaths through my nose and willed my heart to slow. Leaning back against the building behind me, I closed my eyes and waited for my thoughts to settle.

They didn't. If anything, they churned faster in the silence. *What am I going to do?*

Nic wasn't coming back—I knew that. As soon as he got out of the hospital, Asia would put him in jail, and then what? I knew she still had eyes for him, but he'd rather die than give her the time of day after all she'd done to us, never mind to his parents. Besides, Nic claimed it wasn't him Asia wanted; it was me.

What did she want with me? I replayed our interactions over the past week and easily came up with the answer: She wanted me to kill her father.

Asia was General Secretary Mong's daughter, and evidently, she had her sights set on his throne. According to Nic, she'd known about the chip in my palm. She'd been aware of the assassination plot and done everything in her power to make sure it succeeded. She'd pretended to be my friend, adopted me into her inner circle, and groomed me until I looked like a porcelain doll. She'd spared no expense to turn me into a polite high society girl, all so that when the time came for me to meet her father at that dreadful state dinner, he'd want to shake my hand.

It had almost worked. The General Secretary had been delighted to meet me and offered me his friendship—but at the last minute, I'd listened to the Holy Spirit and refused. I'd bowed instead of shaking the General's hand. He'd taken it as a show of humility and been none the wiser. He'd even accepted my invitation to host him for dinner.

Asia, however, had been less thrilled by the turn of events. She'd ambushed Nic and me outside of the party and tried to blackmail Nic into turning himself in. He had not obliged, and we'd spent the last few days running across Beijing, struggling to stay off the grid while looking for a way back to Mars. It had been an exhausting game of cat and mouse.

And now Asia had won.

I slapped my hands over my face as a few hot tears escaped. What would she do to Nic? If it was me she wanted, then she wouldn't be kind to him. Would she torture him? Make him stand trial for his crimes? He was guilty of many—and there was no such thing as a fair trial in the United.

I tried to formulate a prayer, but it jammed in my throat. What was I even supposed to pray for? Asia had the first move. I knew she wouldn't kill Nic—at least not right away—not if she wanted to coerce me into coming home. He wasn't safe, but he had time. Until then, I had no choice but to wait and see what Asia would do.

But where was I supposed to go in the meantime? I had to stay off the grid. I had multiple identities, and all of them were dangerous. Philadelphia Smyrna, my birth name, was wanted for being "Blue Fire," the figurehead of a revolution. Andromeda Nolan, my adopted name, was clean as far as the government was concerned, but I knew Asia was watching my file closely. If I made any electronic activity under either name, Asia would know exactly where I was—if the police didn't get to me first.

I had to hide. Nic had said to go back to the Tangs, but I couldn't go back there, not after what I did to them.

I winced as the events of earlier today rolled through me. The Tangs were old friends of the Vons and leaders in the Chinese underground. They'd taken Nic and me in and introduced us to Jael, a powerful tech mogul with the ability to get us off the grid.

The only problem was that we'd found out she'd been controlling our lives for the past several months. When we'd met with her earlier this afternoon, she'd informed us that she was responsible for creating "Blue Fire." She was the one who had made my videos trend, manipulating the algorithm to build a freedom movement around my name.

All this time, I'd believed God was responsible for creating Blue Fire. I thought it—I—was a miracle. Turns out, one woman had been pulling the strings and using my image to start a war—and she'd never even bothered to introduce herself.

I'd felt so enraged and betrayed that I'd *shot* her. I'd grabbed Nic's gun off the table and hit her straight in the chest. The weapon had been set on stun—hopefully—but I'd also threatened to turn the Tangs' underground church over to the government and stolen a motorbike. I'd been reeling from an overdose of sleep medication, sure, but that only accounted for some of my actions. The real reason I'd snapped was that I was sick and tired of being everyone's puppet and was determined not to let anyone use me ever again.

I couldn't go back to the Tangs after that. What was I going to do, waltz into their house and say, *"My bad, I will be your Blue Fire"*? They'd never believe me about Nic's vision, and even if they did, they wouldn't trust me after what I'd done. *I* wouldn't trust me. I'd proven I was an emotionally unstable teenager who shattered under pressure, and that was the truth.

I pulled my legs in and pressed my face to my knees. I couldn't go back to the Tangs, but I also couldn't stay out here. I couldn't go online; if I bought food or made any purchase, Asia would trace the activity. And I had other enemies in Beijing. Jayde, my former ally, was no doubt still in the city. *If he catches me...*

I shuddered and tried to block out the nightmares of Jayde's cruelty. *What do I do, God?* I mentally screamed, struggling to push a prayer past the whirlwind of fear and hopelessness. *I need Your wisdom. Where do I go?*

For an answer, something furry brushed my arm.

I shrieked and scrambled back. I looked down to see a scrawny gray cat rubbing around my legs.

"Tommy?" I gasped in disbelief.

He mewed and climbed in my lap. I scooped him up and pressed him to my chest, squeezing him to make sure he was real. I never thought I'd see my cat again. Calling him "mine" was perhaps being overly optimistic; Tommy was a stray that Nic and I had picked up a few days ago, but he'd seemed content to follow us. I'd left him at the Tangs' earlier this afternoon, and I thought that would be the last I'd hear of him.

I held him up and stared into his yellow eyes. "How did you get here?"

As if on cue, footsteps pounded down the alley, and someone yelled my name. "Philli!"

I jumped up, gripping Tommy in my arms. I turned to see my friends John and Dowe racing towards me, the beam from their flashlight bouncing on the brick.

"It's her!" John shouted, as if Dowe weren't right behind him. "Good dog, Tommy!"

"He's not a dog." Dowe smacked his partner upside the head. "Dogs go *woof*, and Tommy goes... not that."

"Yeah, well, he can track like a dog, so he gets good boy treats."

"I can respect that."

They reached me and crashed to a stop. I took a step back. John and Dowe had been in the room when I shot Jael; they knew what I'd done.

If John sensed my hesitation, he wasn't deterred by it—not that either of them made a habit of paying attention to social cues. He stepped forward and opened his arms. "Philadelphia, we were so worried."

I took the invitation. I set Tommy down and threw myself into John's arms. He caught me and wrapped me in a fatherly embrace. The affection broke down the dam of guilt and shame inside of me, and I gripped his shirt and burst into tears. "I'm so sorry," I squeaked out in between sobs. "I'm so sorry!"

He shushed me. "We know you are. We know when our girl isn't acting like herself."

Dowe rubbed my shoulder. "Yeah, just next time you get lost, remember the rule: Sit down and wait for help to arrive. We've been tracking you for *two hours*, waiting for you to stop moving."

"Wait." I pulled away from John. "How did you find me?" My phone wasn't turned on; they should have had no way to track me.

Dowe pointed at my backpack. "Your tablet. It's online."

I grabbed my backpack off the ground and unzipped it. They were right; the tablet I'd borrowed from the Tangs was turned on. But how? I'd powered it off last time I used it.

I gripped my bag as realization rolled through me. Nic must have turned it on. He must have grabbed my backpack before we went in the subway station and brought the device online when I wasn't looking. The tablet wasn't registered to me, so Asia couldn't track it, but the Tangs could.

I pushed tears away with the heel of my hand. Yet again, Nic had protected me. He'd been thinking ahead and made sure help would be able to find me, even while I was having a mental breakdown and brandishing a loaded gun.

"Let's go," John urged. He scooped my cat up, and Tommy willingly settled on his shoulder. "If we hurry, there might be some dinner left. Where's Nic?"

A sob ripped out of me involuntarily, which probably told them everything they needed to know.

"Oh no," Dowe murmured. "Philli, what happened?"

"My chip, it... he was..." I winced and skipped to the relevant information. "They arrested him."

There was silence, but only for a fraction of a second. "Well, no time to waste, then. We all know how terrible Nic looks in prison orange." Dowe gestured and started walking. "Jael will know what to do."

They turned and led the way down the dock. I didn't follow. "John, Dowe, I... I can't go back there. Jael won't help me."

Dowe glanced back and used every muscle in his face to make an incredulous look. "Why not?" he exclaimed, as if that was the stupidest thing I'd ever said.

"You were there!" I threw my hands up. "I... I shot her."

John shrugged. "Yeah? And it was a real good shot, too."

I gaped at him.

Dowe grinned. "I promise, it's not the first time our boss has been shot."

"And if it's the last, she's doing something wrong," John added. "Come on, let's go!" They took off down the alley, taking my cat with them.

I relented, throwing my backpack on my shoulders and racing to keep up. I doubted Jael would be as nonchalant about the ordeal as John and Dowe, but I knew providence when I saw it. I'd asked God where He wanted me to go, and He'd sent John and Dowe—it couldn't get more obvious than that.

I followed them around the corner, where their motorbikes were parked. Tommy seemed content to stay with John, so I rode with Dowe. We followed the river south to the Tangs' neighborhood. I watched as the glare and neon of the commercial district faded away to reveal the stained white stone of the traditional two-story homes that crammed along the canal. I saw factory smokestacks piercing the horizon, faintly backlit by the light pollution of the inner city, and knew we were close.

John and Dowe slowed as we entered an affluent district of courtyard homes. We drove under a small stone arch into a brick pavilion, and there was the Tangs' house. The family was all gathered on the wooden veranda that overlooked the river, sitting around the long table that contained the remnants of dinner. There were shouts and exclamations as we rode into the courtyard, and Lanzhou and his cousin Bowen ran towards us.

I swallowed a flash of shame as I climbed off the motorbike. I knew custom would have me address Lanzhou's father, the senior Tang, first, but Lanzhou was the one I had wronged the most. It was his bike I stole, after all.

I met him on the edge of the veranda and bowed as low as I could. "I'm so sorry," I declared, struggling to keep the tears out of my voice. "Please forgive me. I think I know where your bike is, and if not, I'll replace it."

He gripped my shoulder. "I'm not worried about the bike. I'm worried about you."

I looked up into his gentle smile. "I promise, it won't happen again. I just..." I struggled to explain my behavior, but there was no explanation for it. So, I settled for the truth. "I panicked."

"I know," he reassured me, "and I'm sorry for putting you in that situation. Will you forgive me?"

I frowned at him. He was apologizing to *me*? He'd done nothing wrong.

He kneaded my shoulder. "I didn't realize the doctor had given you sleep medication. If I had, I would have insisted you stay home and rest. I never should have let you go to that meeting."

"But it was my choice," I argued. Even Nic had tried to get me to go back to bed, but I'd refused.

"I know, and what you did was incredibly foolish," Lanzhou admitted. "But I'm the adult *and* your host. It would be dishonor on me if I didn't recognize that I'd set you up to fail. Will you forgive me and my family?"

I stared at him. I was so used to taking all the blame—to everyone always telling me that everything was my fault—that I didn't know what to do when someone else accepted responsibility. The relief and forgiveness welled up inside my chest so much it hurt. I had no idea what to say, so I hugged him instead. I grabbed him around the waist and resumed sobbing uncontrollably.

He hesitated, then gingerly reached down and patted my shoulder. "You're forgiven, Philadelphia. And you'll always be a part of this family."

Bowen tapped my arm. "Come, sit down, eat something."

I released Lanzhou and allowed Bowen to guide me to a seat at the table. No sooner had I sat down than Mrs. Tang placed a steaming bowl of rice and sauteed vegetables in front of me. I inhaled several lungfuls of the spicy aroma, letting the zest of ginger and garlic ground my nerves.

John and Dowe took up places at the opposite end of the table. John set Tommy on the floor and immediately began feeding him table scraps. *No wonder they're friends*, I thought with a small smile.

Bowen sat down across from me and leaned on the table. "Tell us what happened," he urged. "Nic...?"

I winced. "He's... he's..." I struggled to find the facts under the clutter of emotions.

Lanzhou tried to help. "There's a death pronouncement on his file," he said, sliding onto the bench next to me, "immediately followed by a location ping checking him into a hospital, where he's apparently very much alive. What's going on?"

"It was my chip." I took a deep breath and held my hand out. "I grabbed his hand, and it sent him into cardiac arrest. He stopped breathing, and they spent at least twenty minutes trying to revive him before they finally gave up."

A murmur rippled around the table. "So, he really was dead," Bowen whispered, as if he was afraid to admit it.

I shuddered, remembering how Nic's face and neck had turned purple. "The paramedics pronounced him dead when they arrived."

The words brought all the grief and terror crashing back down on me. *He was really dead*, I repeated to myself. *Nic died.*

"But?" Lanzhou prodded.

"But…" I stretched the word out, struggling to wrap my mind around the miracle I'd seen with my own two eyes. "God brought him back."

"What do you mean?" Bowen exclaimed.

"God brought him back." I sat up straight and raised my voice. I knew what I saw; Nic's resurrection was a miracle, and I was not going to be shy about it. "I knew it wasn't right—I knew he wasn't supposed to die. So, I prayed, and… he came back to life. Just like that. He sat up and started talking like nothing had happened."

I glanced around the table at the others, desperate for them to believe me. Thankfully, they did.

"Amen!" John and Dowe shouted. Several other family members echoed them in Mandarin. Lanzhou pinched his eyes shut and muttered in tongues, and the senior Mr. Tang raised both his hands.

I wanted to join them, but suddenly, I couldn't breathe. My mind was spinning, but not from fear. I'd seen a dead man brought back to life. I knew God was capable of it; I'd read about it in the Bible, even heard a few stories of it happening to other people. But now I'd *seen* it. God had brought Nic back to life.

Because *I'd* prayed.

Lanzhou's voice yanked me out of my thoughts. "But they still admitted him to the hospital?"

I slumped back in my seat as the rest of the day's events caught up to me. "They'd already called the police. Nic made me leave without him. He told me to come find you."

"And I'm glad you did," Mr. Tang said from his place at the head of the table. "We'll meet with Jael in the morning. She'll know what to do."

I wished I could share his enthusiasm. "I don't think there's anything she can do."

"It's not the first time she's broken someone out of jail," Lanzhou consoled me.

I shook my head. "It's not like that. Asia—Councilwoman Mong—is the one who flagged his file. She'll have him locked down under the highest security."

Bowen and Lanzhou shared a glance. "How do you know the councilwoman?" Lanzhou asked hesitantly.

"She's been hunting us this entire time." I looked up at him and admitted the disgusting truth. "She knew about my chip. She wanted me to kill her father."

"Well, that piece of information would have been good to know sooner," Bowen muttered.

I flushed. I'd never intended to involve the Tangs in the failed assassination plot or my feud with Asia, but it was too late for that now.

"We'll figure it out," Lanzhou insisted, but it sounded like a platitude. "In the meantime, we need to get your chip removed before anyone else gets hurt."

"We know a gal!" John and Dowe crowed in their creepy unison. "She's a wizard with all kinds of implants. She's got a great track record—she's been tuning us up for years."

Lanzhou arched an eyebrow. "I don't know if that constitutes as a great track record..."

I had to admit he was right. John and Dowe looked and acted like a failed cloning experiment; if they'd had any work done, it wasn't functioning within normal parameters. Nevertheless, I would trust a friend of John and Dowe's over some stranger from the underground.

"How soon can she get me in?" I asked.

"If I say 'please,' she'll fit you in tomorrow. I'll make the call." John grinned at me and got up from the table.

"Until then..." Lanzhou tapped my elbow. "Maybe don't hug anybody else. We don't want your chip to malfunction again."

I winced and nodded. I looked down at my palm and once again wondered: *Why now?* I'd touched hundreds of people since getting my chip implanted. I'd met dozens of Asia's friends and shaken hands with countless elites at the party. I'd had contact with clerks and strangers in the subway. And when I'd visited the Tangs' church yesterday, everyone had wanted to shake my hand. Not a single one of them had gotten hurt.

So why now? Why had my chip chosen that very moment to malfunction? What had I done differently?

I pinched my hand as the implication hit me, cold and bitter. Maybe my chip *didn't* malfunction.

Maybe someone was trying to kill Nic.

3: PHILADELPHIA

I kept my theory to myself as I quickly ate the food Mrs. Tang put in front of me. If I was correct, that meant Nic—and I—had more enemies than I realized. It meant there were several people in the Boston underground I couldn't trust, and my friends back home could be in grave danger. Those were steep accusations, and I needed more evidence.

Thankfully, I knew exactly who could help me find the truth.

"May I keep this? There's someone I need to call." I pulled the tablet out of my backpack and showed it to Lanzhou. I figured after I'd stolen a bike, I should at least ask before using their electronics.

"Of course," he said as he started gathering empty dishes off the table. "All your things are still in your room upstairs."

I shuddered as the memory of last night's horrors washed over me. I couldn't sleep in that room; I'd been *kidnapped* from that room. I knew the Tangs were taking precautions, and Jael was keeping a close eye on Jayde. If he checked in anywhere near the Tangs' house, her men would get there first. But those facts weren't enough to override the thick sense of dread that soaked my nerves like lighter fluid. All I could think about was the terror of being held down by strong arms and the pain of being stabbed with a loaded syringe.

I couldn't go back in that room. That was how this whole mess had started; I'd refused to lie down and rest earlier today because I didn't want to be alone up there.

"I don't want to make things difficult, but…" I looked up into Lanzhou's face and searched for understanding. "I can't stay in that room."

He smiled, but the gesture was too sad to bring me any comfort. "How about the room at the end of the hall?"

That was the room Nic had been staying in, which would either help or make me feel more alone. But I would much rather be at the end of the hallway. I nodded.

"And until we get this sorted out, my wife and I will sleep in the room at the top of the stairs. Will that help?" Lanzhou offered.

I wanted to tell him that he didn't have to do that, but it would have been a lie. "Thank you," I said.

He squeezed my shoulder reassuringly.

As soon as I finished my dinner, I grabbed my backpack and hurried upstairs. Tommy followed, mewing as he ran. I rushed past the first bedroom, refusing to look inside, and darted to the room at the end of the hall. I shut and locked the door behind me, then double- and triple-checked to make sure the windows were latched. I knew I was being paranoid, but I wasn't taking any chances.

Turning on the bedside lamp, I gasped when I saw Nic's backpack sitting on the floor. I'd made us leave in such a hurry earlier this afternoon that he hadn't taken it with him. I knew there was nothing of value in there—just a laptop I couldn't bring online and the leftover survival supplies from our race across Beijing—but I was still glad to have something of his.

I kicked off my borrowed house shoes and sank onto the wooden shelf bed. Tommy leapt up beside me, the silk comforter rustling under his paws, and settled by my pillow. I scratched him behind the ears, managing a small smile. He wasn't much of a guard dog, but his furry presence still helped.

Pulling the tablet out of my backpack, I opened the messaging app and was assaulted with a tsunami of notifications. I winced. I knew without looking who the sender was: Stanyard, my boyfriend from back home in Boston. Clearly, he had realized something was wrong; every time I did something stupid, he spammed me with worried messages until I responded.

I opened the chat and reached for the call button, then caught myself. As much as I wanted to see my boyfriend's face, I owed it to someone else to call them first.

I switched to another tab and dialed my brother.

The call rang out the first time. I tried again and prayed his device wasn't on silent. I had no idea what the time conversion between Beijing and the science station on Mars was; would he even be awake?

Mercifully, the call picked up on the third ring. "Philli!"

I hesitated; the voice was feminine and not the one I was expecting. "Cea?" I guessed.

"That's me," she intoned. Her video connected, revealing her face. Cea was Nic's sister, and she was in every way a sprightlier version of him. She had wild blonde curls and freckled cheeks, and she was quick on the draw with both her words and her gun. It was as if God had taken all of Nic's personality and crammed it into a shorter frame.

"It's so good to see you," I said, and realized it was true. It had been over a month since Cea had gone back to Mars, and I'd been so busy starting a revolution and attempting to assassinate a man that we'd barely talked.

"I was just about to say the same thing." She tipped her head to the side and studied me. "I thought you were never going to call—was beginning to think you were mad at me."

I snorted. "For what?"

She arched an eyebrow and held up her left hand, which was adorned with a sparkly wedding ring.

"Oh," I mumbled as the requisite emotions came rushing back. "You mean the part where you and my brother got married *without telling me*?"

Cea and my brother had eloped on a whim a few days ago. Not only had they not told me they were thinking of getting married, but I also had to hear the news from Nic, which was the ultimate insult.

Cea deferred with a bow of her head. "I know, I know, it was a little impulsive. In my defense, I wasn't expecting him to propose right then."

My brother's voice echoed from off-screen. "Yeah, but you're the one who suggested we get married *immediately*. Don't forget that crucial detail."

I caught myself smiling as my older brother came into view. He sat down next to his wife and leaned over so they were both in the frame. I searched his familiar brown eyes and instantly felt safer. "Ephesus," I sighed.

"Philli," he returned warmly, voice full of relief. "I was so worried about you. And… I'm sorry you got left out of the proceedings. But it really is all Cea's fault."

"What?" she squawked and jerked away.

He wrapped one arm around her and pulled her back in. "Don't let this woman lie to you. She's the real instigator."

"You're the one who said yes," I challenged.

His eyes sparkled with delight. "I'm not one to waste an opportunity." He looked down at Cea, and they shared a smile that told me neither of them regretted anything.

"I guess I can forgive you," I said with a dramatic huff. It was hard to stay mad when they were both clearly so happy. Besides, I wasn't one to talk; I hadn't involved Ephesus in any of my plans, and none of them had happy endings.

Cea was the first to return to business. "But what about you, Phil? You gave us all a heart attack."

I cringed; it was a cruelly ironic choice of words. "I know, I'm sorry," I said, but the confession felt cheap even to my ears.

"I'm just glad Nic got there in time," Ephesus said. He forced a smile, but I could clearly read the expression in his eyes: pain, worry, disappointment.

Cea squeezed his knee and started to rise. "I'll let you two talk."

"No, stay, please," I urged. "There's something I need to tell you, and you both need to hear it."

I took a deep breath and walked them through the events of the past twenty-four hours: about Jayde, the meeting with Jael, my breakdown, and Nic's death and arrest. Cea, ever in control, managed to keep it together better than Ephesus did; he interrupted me several times with exclamations and demands for more details. Twice he got up and walked off-camera to vent his emotions.

"I never should have let you stay on Earth," he muttered for perhaps the fifth time after I'd finally finished the story. He raked both hands through his hair and paced behind Cea's seat.

She glanced back at him, then turned to face me. "You're sure Nic is fine?" It was the first question she'd asked since I'd started talking, and I could hear in her inflection the familial love she and Nic were so good at hiding.

"I promise," I insisted. "He remembered everything, and he was talking clearly in whole sentences. He even swore."

She managed a chuckle, but the laugh didn't make it to her eyes. "And you're sure he stopped breathing? He should have at least had some brain damage after that."

I met her gaze. "They gave up administering CPR, Cea. He was dead."

Her eyes wandered. "I guess I just don't understand how that's possible."

I chewed my lip. How was I supposed to explain it? There was nothing to explain. It was God.

Cea changed the subject before I could start preaching. "Why do you think your chip malfunctioned? You haven't had any other issues with it, have you?"

"No, and… that's actually the main reason I'm calling." I sat up straight. "I don't think it was a malfunction."

"Unfortunately, I think you're right." Ephesus came back into frame and returned to his chair. He touched Cea's knee. "Remember when we looked up the logs and saw that someone had accessed Nic's DNA?"

She sucked in her breath and washed white.

"What?" I exclaimed.

He looked at the camera. "We thought someone had broken into Nic's office, so we pulled up the logs. According to the timestamps, someone accessed and modified his DNA file a little over a week ago."

The timing checked out, and it made perfect sense. The doors on the science station were controlled by an experimental system that read DNA through the user's fingertips, which meant the code for Nic's DNA was on file on the servers. What's more, almost everyone who had been associated with me would know that. Jayde even had remote access to the door lock software; he and Stanyard had used it to help me escape when Nic and I had been trapped in Wing 74. Jayde could have easily logged into the station's server and downloaded the code for Nic's DNA.

I skipped my next breath when I realized I was right. Someone wanted Nic dead.

And I knew exactly who that person was.

"Jayde," I snarled, all my anger and distrust coming out in one corrupted syllable. Jayde was the leader of the Boston underground, and he had been the mastermind behind the assassination plot. The entire operation had been his idea. Surely, he was the one who had plotted Nic's death.

Ephesus wasn't so easily convinced. "But why would he want Nic dead?"

I didn't have an answer for that. Jayde and Nic barely knew each other. But Jayde was violent and impulsive; he needed very little incentive for murder.

"And why would he use you?" Cea pressed. "You and Nic weren't even on the same planet. Jayde had no idea Nic would come back to Earth."

To be fair, she had a point. I recalled that fateful party where Nic had waltzed in and stopped Jayde from throwing me off a balcony. Judging by the fact that he'd panicked, Jayde had been just as surprised as I was to see Nic again.

No, Ephesus and Cea were probably right. If Jayde had a master plan to murder Nic, he certainly wasn't acting like it. But if it wasn't Jayde, then there was only one other person who could be responsible.

"Data," I murmured, then quickly clarified. "He's the one who programmed my chip."

More accurately, "Data" was his callsign; I had no idea what his real name was. I'd met him only briefly when he'd delivered the finished hardware. He was an active member of the Boston underground and a friend of Jayde's, and that was all I knew about him. He could have a dozen reasons for wanting Nic dead.

My blood ran cold when I remembered what other projects Data had been working on recently.

"I gotta go," I announced. "I need to call Stanyard. Dad could be in trouble."

"Whoa, don't hang up!" Ephesus lunged towards the camera, as if that could stop me from ending the call. "What's wrong with Dad?"

I breathed through my nose and tried to get my heart to slow down enough so I could explain. "Data's been helping with Dad's therapy. Stanyard told me that Data installed some kind of brain chip to help with Dad's speech, and he's been progressing really fast—*too* fast."

Our father, Dr. Smyrna, had also been recently raised from the dead, but his resurrection was a lot less miraculous than Nic's. Our father had been cryogenically frozen, and over the last month we'd been undergoing the arduous process of thawing him out. Physically, he had survived the procedure well. Mentally, however, there was nothing left of the man I'd once known as "Daddy." All his memories were gone—or at least they were inaccessible to him.

He'd also lost most of his speech and social skills. But when I'd called Stanyard yesterday, he'd informed me that Data and several others had been overseeing Dad's therapy. They'd installed something in Dad's brain to supplement his vocabulary, and he'd been making herculean progress. At the time, I'd praised it as an answer to prayer. Now, I wondered if I should have shared Stanyard's suspicion.

If Data was willing to kill Nic, there was no telling what he'd do to my dad.

"I need to call Stanyard," I repeated. "I need to make sure Dad's safe."

"Okay but," Ephesus inserted before I could make a move, "make sure Stanyard is alone when you talk to him, and tell him to keep it quiet until we can prove it."

I hushed and waited for him to explain.

"If you're right..." Ephesus shared a wary glance with Cea before continuing, "then we're dealing with an accomplished killer. That's not someone you want to anger before you've got a plan. And second, speaking as a programmer, he might not have had anything to do with Nic's death."

"What do you mean?" I questioned.

"We have no idea who all was involved in programming that chip. Dozens of people could have had access to that code. What's more, he might have bought the DNA from someone else. Maybe they gave him the wrong code intentionally."

"It could even be—dare I say it—a really unfortunate programming error," Cea suggested.

"But you don't think so," I pointed out, reading between the lines.

Cea looked up at Ephesus. He shrugged. "I just don't want to accuse a guy of murder before I look at his source code."

He was right. I had to be careful—especially since Data had his hands in Dad's brain. "Can you figure out who downloaded Nic's DNA? Trace the IP or whatever?" I asked.

"I'll see what I can find out," Ephesus said. "As soon as you get your chip removed, send the code to me—that will tell us a lot. Stanyard should also search the servers on base. See if he can find any emails, source code, anything."

"Okay."

"And Phil..." Ephesus sighed, and the emotion bled back into his eyes. "Keep me updated this time. Please."

Cea took that as her cue to leave. "I'll go find Sydney," she said gracefully. "Have him start searching the logs. We'll talk later, Phil." She stood up and gave Ephesus a peck on the forehead, then waved at me before stepping out of frame.

Ephesus waited until the door had shut behind her before speaking again. "Why didn't you call me sooner?"

There was no accusation in his voice, but my guilt more than made up for it. When this all started, I *couldn't* have called him; he was on a transit to Mars, which put him offline for nearly four days. And for several days after that, I'd been held hostage by Jayde with no way to call for help.

But that wasn't a watertight excuse, and I knew it. I'd been able to get online several times since then, and I hadn't even sent my brother a text. The truth was that I hadn't called my brother because the thought hadn't even crossed my mind. Not once had I considered involving Ephesus.

Probably because he hadn't been involved in my life for the last two years.

Ephesus seemed to be tracking the same thoughts. "Look, I know I've been MIA a lot lately, but I'm still your big brother. And no amount of warmongering will ever change that."

He cracked a smile, which I knew was an invitation to let him in. I struggled to return the gesture as I recalled the past few months and tried to figure out when I'd made the conscious decision to shut my brother out of my life. We'd been separated several times over the past two years; had I simply gotten used to him not being there?

"Philli," Ephesus prodded when I didn't give him the answer he wanted. "You can trust me. You know that, right?"

"Of course," I answered reflexively. "I've always trusted you, Ephesus."

"Then please, keep me involved this time. Call me immediately if there's any change, and talk to me before you go anywhere. Promise me you'll stay with the Tangs until we figure out what's going on."

I met his gaze. "I promise."

I tried to put as much intention into my words as I could, but it didn't land. He stared, lips pinched in a small frown like he didn't believe me.

I didn't blame him.

He finally relented with a sigh. "I'll keep my phone with me and my ringer on. I'll answer any time of day or night."

"I'll text you after I call Stanyard and let you know what he says," I offered. "And I'll call you after I meet with Jael tomorrow."

"Thank you." He looked into my eyes again. "I love you, Philadelphia."

"I love you, too," I said, and then ended the call.

I flopped back on the pillows. Tommy mewed and got up, coming over to rub against my side. I stroked him absentmindedly as I fought the unfounded urge to cry.

What was wrong with me? I'd spent the last month of my life leading a revolution, and I hadn't even involved my own brother. I hadn't involved anyone. I hadn't involved Cea, I hadn't involved Stanyard, and I certainly hadn't involved Nic.

Sure, for part of that time, I'd been physically unable to contact anyone. But it wasn't like that anymore. Ephesus was there for me; Stanyard was there for me; the Tangs and their entire church congregation were there for me. Even Jael was probably still on my side, and she was a powerful woman with massive resources. I had hundreds of people willing to help me.

So why did I feel so alone?

4: NIC

Getting raised from the dead is not all it's cracked up to be.

My mind didn't miss a beat. If anything, the hard reset of being knocked unconscious gave it *more* energy and focus, and now it refused to shut down. I probably could have solved world hunger had someone given me a pen and paper.

The rest of my body, however, was complaining very loudly about the fact that it had been deprived of oxygen for nearly half an hour. Every muscle ached in a way that shouldn't have been possible, and all my organs were laboring like they forgot how to do their jobs. Sneezing hurt, breathing hurt, *blinking* hurt, and I could feel every single beat of my heart like a sharp slap on the inside of my ribs.

But at least my heart *was* beating.

I looked at the monitor next to my bed and watched the jagged green line jerk across the screen. I was alive, and by all accounts, I shouldn't be. Every single doctor, lab tech, and cleaning lady in this hospital had come by my room to gawk at me and reinforce that fact. The nurses were getting downright annoyed. Every time they came to check on me, they seemed frustrated that there was nothing for them to do, as if they wished I would just keel over so the order could be restored to their universe.

In their defense, I almost agreed with them. I was bitterly aware that this turn of events obliterated every logical and illogical excuse I had not to jump on the Jesus train. It worked in perpetuity, too; fifty years from now, if I even thought about going my own way, all He'd have to do is remind me that I shouldn't be breathing, and I'd be left with no argument to stand on. He'd been smart and written Himself a blank check, and my life was the dividend.

I grunted and sank back on the stiff pillow. It was one thing to stand there and tell Phil that God had a call on her life. It was an entirely different matter to realize that God had pulled a Lazarus because He was so stupendously serious about the call He had on *mine.*

"I guess I can't change my mind now, can I?" I muttered to the empty room.

The answer was immediate. *You're going to want Me anyway.*

As if reinforcing the point, voices in Mandarin echoed in the hall, followed by the all-too-familiar clack of stilettos on linoleum. I groaned and rubbed my temples as a headache preemptively started thrumming behind my ears. "No rest for the wicked," I grumbled, even though I was aware that, as of a few hours ago, I no longer fit that criterion.

Without a warning knock, the door blew open, and my ex-girlfriend breezed into the room. "Nic! I was so worried!"

"Let me guess," I droned, "you came as soon as you heard—after you did your hair and makeup and got a manicure."

Asia had dressed for the occasion, as she always did. She looked like she'd walked right off the senate floor with her designer skirt set, patent heels, and signature bloodred lipstick. The outfit choice a power move, no doubt—and considering the fact that I was barely clothed in a hospital gown, it was working.

She reached up and patted the pearls she had pinned in her dark updo. "I always get dressed up for you, sweetheart."

I rolled my eyes. "I'm going to need you to at least put on a *pretense* of authenticity. You never called me 'sweetheart' even when we were dating."

She smirked and clacked over to the bedside. The stench of her perfume followed her like a wave of mustard gas. I gagged as my eyes watered; at least if I suffocated from the smell, the nurses would have something to do.

Asia perched on the edge of the bed and studied me. I sat up as best I could and plastered on a bored expression. Being bedridden in front of my ex was not a power balance I was comfortable with, but I was not going to give her the satisfaction of watching me squirm.

You know you can ask for My help, right? the Voice in my head inserted.

Asia spoke again before I could take Him up on His generous offer. "I came to tell you the good news, but I can see the staff has spoiled my fun." She flicked her acrylic fingernail against the handcuff that tethered my left wrist to the bed.

"Ah yes." I rattled the chain. "I was hoping you'd put in a good word to the warden for me."

She arched a waxed eyebrow.

"If they could assign me a number shorter than '120518,' that'd be great. You know how I hate long names."

A wicked grin spread across her face, revealing perfect teeth. "I'll slip a few hundred yuan to the clerk. But I haven't decided where I'm sending you yet—I'm still picking out which celebrities I want on the jury."

I stifled a groan. Unlike jail time, the fake trial was a cruel and unusual punishment I was *not* looking forward to. "Far be it from me to deny the public of their pomp and circumstance. Should I tell them about our tragic love story? That will really bring in the views."

"What love story?" she chirped with practiced innocence.

I sighed to acknowledge my defeat. While her list of accomplishments was not nearly as illustrious as mine, Asia was guilty of plenty of crimes—or, more accurately, she was guilty of *funding* plenty of crimes. Notably, she was the one who had given me the science station on Mars so I could develop Red Rain, my world-ending chemical superweapon. That alone would get her sent straight to the gallows—except I couldn't prove it. Asia had always been thorough about covering her tracks; even if I could get online, I wouldn't be able to find any digital evidence proving she'd been involved. It would be my word against hers.

And we both knew who her "celebrity jury" would believe.

"Face it, darling," she crooned, dragging a sharp fingernail along my tethered arm, "I'm over you."

I let all the air in my lungs out in a dramatic *whew*. "Took you long enough. You really should have seen a therapist about eight years ago."

She shrugged and stood up. "I still think you're cute, though, so if you get bored..." She winked and strode towards the door. "Besides, I'm hoping we can avoid a trial. It's always so much cleaner to settle out of court, and you know how I feel about an unnecessary mess."

My blood ran cold when I remembered what this was really about. Asia didn't care whether I lived or died, but she would hang me out to dry if it would blackmail Phil into blowing her cover.

"It won't work," I called after her.

She paused in the doorway and glanced back.

"As much as I'd love to see you go through this whole song and dance for nothing, I feel obliged to inform you that this evil scheme of yours will not work."

"Whatever do you mean?" she taunted.

"Phil," I said, and hoped none of the nurses were listening. "She won't come for me."

Asia cackled. "Have you no faith, doctor?"

Until earlier this afternoon, no, not really. "We've been practicing the whole 'obey your parents' thing. And even if she doesn't," I forced myself to admit that very real possibility, "she's smart enough to get her chip removed. You're not going to get what you want out of this."

I desperately hoped—prayed, even—that Phil would heed my warning and stay away. But even if she didn't, I knew she was in no danger of killing the General, accidentally or otherwise. Phil had made a lot of mistakes, but that was one I was confident she would not repeat.

Surely, Asia knew that. She was, regrettably for all involved, not an idiot. She had to realize that the game was up. If she wanted her father dead, she was going to have to do it herself.

Unless, of course, she wanted Philadelphia for something else.

Asia smirked, confirming my fears. "Nic, you surprise me. For someone with three PhDs, you're so narrow-minded."

I swallowed my next comeback. The game was not up; it had just started.

She relished my discomfort. "But then again, you always did underestimate me, didn't you?"

I lifted one finger. "Underestimated? No. Naively thought the best of you? Guilty as charged."

She smiled benevolently, as if she found my failure adorable. "I guess that's why I'm going to win."

I opened my mouth, but she didn't give me a chance to detangle that threat. She opened the door to the hall. "I'll come see you off when they discharge you. Get some sleep, sweetheart—you've had a long week."

And then she blew me a kiss and disappeared.

5: PHILADELPHIA

I lay on the bed, staring at the ceiling and struggling to pray, for so long that exhaustion almost claimed me. Thankfully, my tablet pinged with a notification, jerking me awake. I picked up the device and found a new message from Stanyard:

I CAN SEE YOU'VE READ MY MESSAGES. WHY HAVEN'T YOU CALLED ME?

I cringed and sat up. *Why do I always forget about that setting?*

Stanyard started typing again, but I hit the call button before he could finish. He answered on the first ring.

"Phil!" he gasped, the connection crackling as the call struggled to bridge the ocean between us. "Where are you? What's going on? Didn't you see my messages?"

"Yes, yes, I did." I raised my voice to be heard. "I'm sorry, I called Ephesus first."

He paused, long enough for his video to connect. The screen brightened, revealing my best friend in his natural habitat: in front of a computer. The dual monitors behind him were cluttered with a dizzying number of windows, and the backlit screens framed his unkempt dark hair in a blue glow as he pushed his headphones back. He spun his desk chair around and held his phone away from him so he could frown at the camera.

"I'm glad you talked to Ephesus," he conceded, "but you were supposed to call me twelve hours ago."

I flinched when I remembered I'd promised to call him when I got up this morning. I hadn't, since I'd been busy getting kidnapped, but I also hadn't checked in with him since then. I hadn't even sent him a text, and I'd had plenty of opportunities to. I'd just forged ahead, never once considering his feelings. I'd made a life-changing decision and put myself at risk, all without involving the people who cared about me the most—just like I always did.

"I know, I'm fine now, I promise. Stanyard, I'm so sorry," I insisted. But as soon as the words left my mouth, I realized we'd been through this whole song and dance before: I would apologize, he would forgive me, and then nothing would change. *I* wouldn't change.

He was slow to respond. I could tell by the tension in his jaw that he was very angry and struggling not to be. "What happened?" he said, skipping the preamble.

I took a deep breath. "There's not going to be an easy way to tell you this…"

"Please, Phil," he sighed. "Just tell me."

I swallowed a prayer. "Jayde… he…"

Stanyard jerked upright as every muscle in his body went rigid. "What did he do?" He was so furious that his words slurred.

"He… broke into the house…" The kilter of my voice pitched like a ship lost at sea as I struggled to put words to the trauma. "…drugged me and kidnapped me. He was going to make me record more videos."

Stanyard threw his device down and slammed his fist on the desk. I flinched as the camera shuddered. There was a flicker of silence, and then I heard him muttering. It took me a minute to realize he wasn't using English.

"Stanyard…" I called hesitantly.

"I knew this would happen," he snapped, but his voice wasn't angry anymore. It was broken, shattered like a dozen pieces of mirror, reflecting a jagged array of emotions.

"Stanyard," I repeated, "come back, please."

He picked up his phone. "I knew he would try something like this. I should have—"

"Should have what?" I cut him off. I knew exactly where this conversation was going. "There was nothing you could have done. You're not even on the same continent."

"I could be."

The statement was spoken softly, almost wondrously, as if the thought had just occurred to him. I looked down to see him frowning in concentration. "You're not really thinking of flying over here, are you?" I challenged.

"I am now."

"Stanyard, you can't," I objected. "Asia—"

"Could have killed me a month ago if she was so inclined." It was his turn to interrupt. "Frankly, it's not her I'm worried about. It's Jayde."

I almost agreed with him. Even though Asia was far more powerful than Jayde, she was at least a lot more civil.

"I know, but I promise, they're taking precautions. Jael…" I paused when I remembered Stanyard would have no idea who what was. *Add it to the list of information I unintentionally withheld from him.* "I've got a friend here with access to the algorithm. She's watching Jayde's file. She'll protect me."

"And what if Jayde's smart and starts using a temp file?" Stanyard countered, presenting a hideous possibility I hadn't even considered. "Or he's got other friends? Phil, this has gotten so big that I don't think anyone can protect you."

I stared at the blinking light of my camera as I realized he was right.

"But that's not going to stop me from trying."

I focused on his face again. I could see the red seeping into the corners of his eyes—the stress accumulated from hours of sleepless worry and frantic prayers.

"Philadelphia," he sighed, dragging out my full name to give us both time to gather our thoughts. "We can't keep doing this."

His statement dropped an unfamiliar weight on my chest. "What-what do you mean?"

"I mean I can't keep watching from the other side of the camera while you throw yourself into the path of speeding trains. I know you've got a reason for being in Beijing..." The statement came out condescending, and he caught himself. He worked his jaw and tried again. "I know you've got a call on your life, and I know what you're doing as Blue Fire is important. I still support you. Please don't take any of this to mean that I don't."

I nodded and tucked his statement away in my heart, knowing I would need it later.

"But I can't keep watching you die on live TV and then getting the synopsis via text twenty-four hours later. I'm not just a viewer on your videos, Phil. I'm your friend." There was a breath, and then he found the words he really wanted to say. "And I'll be a lot more than that if you let me."

"Yes," I breathed, the word coming out like a gasp as the air caught in my throat.

"Then you have to let me help you," he insisted, voice growing firm. "You have to let me protect you. It's my job."

His words sent warmth radiating down my arms, but I knew I couldn't let him jump on a plane to China just because he was worried about me. "I know, Stanyard, but there's nothing you can do—"

"You need to let me be the judge of that," he snapped. He groaned and ran a hand through his hair. "See, Phil, this is what I'm talking about. You can't keep making all the decisions and then just hand out information to me when you think it's important. If this is going to work between us, then we need to be partners."

I swallowed as an entirely new breed of fear wrapped its cold fingers around my neck. He'd said "if."

He shifted, as if aware of the burden he'd created. "Do you trust me, Phil?"

"Yes," I declared, and then realized, in a flash of cruel clarity, that wasn't the problem. "But can you trust me?"

His silence told me all I needed to know. I pinched my eyes shut as tears flooded the corners of my vision. *Oh God, where did I go wrong?*

"I know a lot has happened that neither of us could have controlled. I'm not blaming you *or* myself for that." Stanyard's voice reached out to me, gentle and forgiving. "And I know you did what you thought was right at the time."

He sounded confident of my character, but suddenly, I wasn't so sure.

"But I have no reason to believe that, as soon as we hang up, you won't run off and start another war—and I won't hear about it until it's too late."

His voice was so heavy with unfiltered pain that it took the wind out of my lungs. He truly *didn't* trust me—and I'd given him no reason to.

Ephesus was right. I should have called somebody—anybody—sooner.

I blinked, even though it did nothing to clear my vision. "What can I do to fix it?"

"Let me in." He leaned forward, like getting three inches closer could span the distance between us. "You have to start involving me. You say you trust me—so, start trusting me with things."

He made it sound simple, but as I replayed my actions over the past few days, I struggled to pinpoint what I would have done differently. Sure, I should have talked to him sooner, but what would that have changed? He couldn't have prevented what happened with Asia or Jayde. Maybe if I'd talked to Stanyard, I wouldn't have had a breakdown and shot somebody, but eventually I would have touched Nic and activated my chip. In a sick way, I wasn't sure *any* of what happened was avoidable—and if Stanyard had been here, he would have just gotten hurt in the crossfire.

And that was exactly why I couldn't let him come to Beijing now. Besides, I needed him on the ground in Boston.

"Well," I said, and tried to make my voice approachable, "there's something else I need to tell you."

He sensed my shift in tone and sat up straight. "What's wrong?"

I slowly walked him through the events of the day. He almost lost his cool again when he learned Nic was no longer with me, but I managed to keep the conversation on track.

"I don't think it was an accident," I finished. "I think someone is trying to kill Nic."

I paused and waited for him to turn back to the camera; his gaze was taking a lap around the room like it always did when he was struggling to process. When he finally looked at me again, I saw that his eyes were even more bloodshot than before. "You're probably right," he admitted, "which means you're in danger."

I didn't necessarily agree; just because someone wanted Nic dead didn't mean they would hurt me. But it definitely meant they weren't my friend. "That's why I need you to look at the servers on base. See if you can find any evidence that someone planned this."

"On it." He swiveled his chair around to face his desktop. The backlight from the monitors washed out his face as he propped up his phone and started typing.

"I'm getting my chip removed tomorrow and sending the code to Ephesus. I'll send it to you too."

He nodded, his eyes flickering as he focused on his screen. "If Jayde hasn't changed his password, I might still be able to hack into the door lock software and see if it was him who downloaded Nic's DNA."

The more I thought about it, the more I agreed with Ephesus; Jayde probably had nothing to do with Nic's death. But it was worth a look. "There's one other thing I need you to do," I added.

"Yeah?" he said, the word nearly drowned out by his aggressive typing.

"I need you to keep an eye on my dad."

He stopped and faced the camera.

I let out my breath and tried not to release all my anxiety with it. "Data's the one who coded my chip. And you said he's been working on my dad."

I could tell by the way Stanyard's expression darkened that my fears were not unfounded.

"Ephesus said it might not be him," I added, mostly for posterity. "Other people could have worked on that code."

"Possibly," he grunted without consent. "But if it was Data, I'll find out."

It was a threat—and in some strange way, that made me feel safer.

"How was Dad today?" I asked.

Stanyard's eyes cleared as he blinked away the anger. "Better. I think he's coming to terms with his new life. He's been more patient when we try to teach him new information. You can tell it means nothing to him—it's all just random facts—but he's more willing to listen."

I managed a smile and thought about asking to see him—then realized, with a stab of guilt, that I didn't want to. I couldn't manage a third broken relationship tonight.

"What are you going to do now?" Stanyard's question cut through my daze.

"What do you mean?" I returned, even though I immediately knew where this road would lead.

"Are you staying in China?"

"I have to find out what they're going to do with Nic," I said, which wasn't an answer and definitely not the one Stanyard was looking for.

"And then what?"

I didn't have a response, because untangling that question involved speculating about the morbid details of Nic's fate. And while I ultimately had no idea what Asia would do next, I knew in my heart that Nic would not be getting out of prison anytime soon—if ever.

And I wasn't ready to live in a world without him.

No, God, please—there has to be another way! I thought, for the first time since the accident finding the words to pray. *This can't be how it ends.*

All of that emotion must have made it onto my face, because Stanyard dropped the subject. "We'll figure it out, Phil, I promise."

There was no point in acknowledging that. "I need to go," I said, knowing that if I didn't concoct an excuse to end the conversation, Stanyard would never hang up. "I promised to text Ephesus after I talked to you."

He accepted that and leaned away from the camera. "I love you, Philadelphia. And I'll always be here for you."

"I know," I mumbled, and was surprised when my voice shattered. I quickly hung up before he could see the first tear fall.

6: PHILADELPHIA

John and Dowe woke me before my alarm did.

"Phil. Philli!" one or both of them hissed through my door. "Are you awake?"

Not by choice, I thought to myself as I groaned and pushed the blanket aside. Tommy contorted his body in a terrific stretch, then jumped off the bed and pranced to the door. He mewed and scratched at the frame.

"Tommy's awake!" John crowed, losing all concept of an inside voice. "Go get your mom out of bed, kitty."

"I'm up, I'm up," I mumbled. I groped for my house shoes in the near darkness; judging by the lack of light bleeding through the shutters, it was barely sunrise. What were they doing here so early? "What do you need?" I groused, fully aware I was being saltier than necessary.

"Uh, come outside, and then we can talk," one of them returned, which wasn't ominous at all.

I sighed and opened the door—and almost screamed when I came face to face with their identical grins. They were both standing unacceptably close to the door, crammed shoulder to shoulder in the narrow hall, like they were a jack-in-the-box that could spring out at any moment.

"Wow, hi," I managed, leaning back. "What are you doing?"

"We know it's early," John said in a voice still too loud for the time of day. They were both fully dressed and looked like they'd been up for hours, not that I'd ever seen either of them act tired.

"That's why we brought a peace offering." Dowe held out a mug of coffee with both hands. With slow, dramatic movements, he bowed and set it on the floor at my feet. Then both he and John folded their hands and backed away slowly, like they'd just made a sacrifice at a shrine. They looked so ridiculous, with their hips scraping the wood paneling as they stumbled over each other, that I couldn't help but laugh.

"Ceasefire accepted," I said, and bent to pick up the mug.

Dowe grinned and elbowed his partner. "Told you! It works on Nic, too."

I smiled sadly at the steaming liquid as the memories invaded my groggy brain. Picking up Nic's coffee habits had been an accident, but, just like our unexcepted relationship, it was something I didn't regret adopting.

I took a slow sip. "What are we doing up so early?"

"We called our mechanic, did some sweet-talking," Dowe said.

"*I* did some sweet-talking," John interrupted. "She hung up on you!"

"It was a bad connection!" Dowe argued, then looked back at me. "Anyway, we got an appointment to get your chip removed—but it's all the way across town, so Lanzhou wants to head out before rush hour hits."

"Which, on a weekday, is about 5am." Lanzhou stumbled out of his bedroom at the top of the stairs. He shrugged on a jacket and offered me a sleepy smile. "Better take that coffee to go—we've got some walking to do."

After spending five minutes convincing John to leave Tommy at home, we started the long trek across the sprawling city. Even though the crowds hadn't fully woken up yet, it still took us over an hour of transferring between buses and subways to reach our destination. Lanzhou was armed, and I kept my hood up and my head down, but I wasn't really worried. Most of the Chinese populace didn't know I was here—yet.

The commercial district we found ourselves in was on the bleeding edge of downtown. The high rises were so tall that they blocked out the rising sun, making the street seem dark and chilly like a cave. A glinting array of neon and automated vending machines struggled to modernize the concrete buildings and backlit signs that had clearly been there since the last century. The narrow storefronts competed for attention with a circus of flapping banners, while lanterns and flags strung across the road added to the noise. The whole place was loud, cluttered, and colorful, but after being in Beijing for a week, I was surprised at how comforting the chaos was beginning to feel.

John and Dowe led us to a phone repair shop at the end of a long alley. The only part of the store's banner that was in English were the words "KIMCHI MOBILE," but the intent was made clear by the fact that every inch of the windows was plastered over with posters advertising the latest devices for suspiciously low prices. I felt a bit guilty thinking it, but it definitely looked like the kind of place where someone would try to scam you into buying a knockoff watch.

The door buzzed as we entered. I took one look at the place and almost walked back out. To say the shop was a disaster would have been putting it kindly; it looked like a shipping container of electronics had gotten upended in the store. The smudged glass display cases were crammed with refurbished phones, while stacks of laptops balanced precariously on the shelves. Every flat surface was strewn with hard drives and broken keyboards, as if a serial killer had gutted a dozen computers and left the corpses to rot.

I was suddenly feeling much less confident about letting this woman dig into my hand to remove a very delicate bomb. *Oh Jesus, I hope this is the right choice.*

The young clerk behind the counter put his own phone down long enough to wave at us. "Ahh! You here for the latest phone? We've got the 87S, very new—70% off, just for you!" He turned his grin on me, as if correctly assuming that I was the one with the most disposable income.

Dowe planted his hands on the counter. "No, no, we're here to pick up a *custom order…* if you know what I mean."

John folded his arms and jerked his head in a way that was probably supposed to look cool but came off as anything but. "It's under the name John Dowe."

The clerk glanced at his monitor and clicked a button, then crooned in understanding. "You have an appointment?"

"I have a lifetime subscription," Dowe intoned.

"Very good… this way." The clerk lifted the gate and waved us behind the counter. John and Dowe went first. I had to suck in my breath to keep from knocking over a pyramid of computer towers as I squeezed through the narrow hallway to the back of the store.

We followed the clerk into the storeroom. He kicked aside a box, revealing a trap door. The secret entrance had clearly been retrofitted; the shiny metal panel was at least fifty years newer than the building, with a massive latch and a blinking keypad. It looked like something out of a space station, which somehow made me even more uneasy.

The clerk pressed his thumb to the keypad, and it chirped welcomingly. The lock released with a hiss, and he threw the panel back, revealing dimly lit concrete stairs. He gestured at John and Dowe to lead the way, which they did eagerly.

I hesitated at the top of the stairs. "I'm right behind you," Lanzhou whispered in my ear, but even I could tell he wasn't thrilled by the prospect.

I muttered a prayer and started down the steps. The clerk stared at us until we had cleared the entrance, then slammed the door. I heard the lock slide shut with a loud click. Shivering, I ran the rest of the way to the bottom.

Beneath the store was a massive workshop. It was a huge space—at least four times the size of the sales floor above—but there was barely room to walk around all the mechanical paraphernalia. The owner of the workshop was clearly a jack of all trades and a master of none; a glance around revealed at least a dozen abandoned projects. There was a vintage car with its engine gutted on one side of the room and a wingless helicopter on the other, and the skeleton of a robot dangled from the ceiling by thick wires. The stuffy air reeked of grease and freshly fabricated plastic, and an abundance of fluorescents lit the room as bright as noonday, making the place buzz like a hornets' nest.

Dowe stepped forward and rapped his knuckles on a worktable. "Seoul? You in here, beautiful?"

A screeching voice echoed from somewhere across the room. "Don't you *dare* try and flatter me!"

Something crashed into the wall behind Dowe's head and clattered to the floor. I looked down to see a rusty wrench skid across the stained concrete. *Did she just throw something at him?*

Dowe sidestepped so he was partially hidden behind a stack of boxes. "I take it you missed me?"

She was not appeased. "Some nerve you have coming in here after you didn't pay me!"

"I paid you!" he protested.

"Not enough!" she shrieked back. I saw movement from behind the broken helicopter and turned to see a young woman emerge. She was in her twenties, but she was at least half a foot shorter than me and looked like she couldn't have weighed more than a sack of rice. Her boyish hair was dyed an electric shade of blue, which contrasted sharply with the orange tracksuit she wore. She had goggles strapped to her forehead and two utility belts hanging off her thin waist. She was distinctly Asian, but I could tell by her accent that she wasn't from around here.

She aggressively wiped her fingers with a rag, then threw the cloth on the floor. "I told you, I'm not doing any more work for you until you repay me with interest—oh, hi John."

She broke off mid-sentence to smile at him. He wiggled his fingers. "Hi, Seoul."

Dowe gaped at his partner. "Is there something I should know?"

"What's there to know? He tips." Seoul skipped over to John and stood on her tiptoes to plant a kiss on his cheek. He reddened and beamed like she'd just scratched his favorite spot behind the ears.

Dowe huffed. "I don't even know you."

Seoul ignored him and turned to me. "Now who's this?"

I started to offer my hand, then remembered why we were here. I settled for a polite bow of my head. "Blue Fire."

She whistled. "You boys are working for Blue Fire now? How'd you lie your way into that job?"

John shrugged. "She needed a distraction."

"As a matter of fact," Dowe inserted, "we were her first partners—"

Seoul cut him off with a flick of her hand. "Still not talking to you." She focused her attention on me again. "I heard a rumor that you were in the city but didn't realize you were working with these saints. What brings you to my shop?"

I held out my right palm. "I need an implant removed. Careful—it's reactive to touch."

She grunted and pulled her goggles down over her eyes. She snapped her finger against the side of the eyepiece, and the device whirred to life, a maze of blue code reflecting on the lenses. She leaned over and scanned my hand. "And what exactly was the purpose of this contraption?"

"It's an assassination weapon." I winced; it felt uncouth to talk about it so forthrightly, but if she was going to remove the chip, then she needed to know what she was dealing with.

"Who were you trying to assassinate? Godzilla?" she mocked. "This thing is juiced. I could probably power Jimin with this battery."

"Jimin?" John questioned.

She gestured at the robot hanging from the ceiling.

"Well, you're welcome to keep the battery if you can get it out," I said. "All I need is the code off the programming chip."

She pushed her goggles back on her forehead. "Add 10,000 yuan, and you've got yourself a deal."

I glanced at Lanzhou. Thanks to my inheritance as a Nolan, ten grand— in any currency—wasn't a sum even worth mentioning, but until we could figure out a way to launder my money without Asia knowing, the Tangs would have to front the bill.

Lanzhou nodded. "Get it done."

"We're going to need mood music for this." Seoul clapped her hands, and K-pop music started blaring from one of the computer terminals at a volume too loud for comfort. The anti-government lyrics were an angsty mix of English and Korean and were somehow strangely appropriate for the illegal activity going on in the shop.

Seoul gestured at a rusted metal chair next to a workstation. "You, sit. The rest of you, make yourselves at home—but don't you dare touch my car." The threat was directed with a glare at Dowe.

He opened his mouth to object, but Lanzhou shepherded them over to the other side of the room. I sat down in the chair and tucked my backpack underneath, then obediently laid my arm on the cold metal table.

Seoul turned on a spot lamp and shone it over my palm. After glancing to make sure the others were out of earshot, she leaned over and whispered, "Look, I'm sure you get this a lot, but it's an honor to meet you."

I had, in fact, been getting that a lot lately. "Thanks for your help," I deferred.

She went in for a handshake, then reconsidered. She settled for a sloppy salute instead. "Name's Seoul, in case you missed it."

"Like the city?" I guessed, finally putting two and two together with her accent. Although, "former city" would have been a more accurate term for the crater that represented the defeated South Korean capital.

"It was my parents' subtle way of protesting the North Korean takeover. Never mind that happened twenty years before I was born." She grinned, and the sharp lighting from the lamp made the gesture look mildly terrifying.

I shifted back in the chair to restore some personal space. "We all do our part."

She mercifully took the hint and turned to open a tackle box that was sitting on the table. "Now that we've gotten acquainted, I'd better be at the top of your contact list. Anything you need, you just call me. Don't bother with those other guys down the street."

"Thanks, I won't," I repeated, not that I had any idea who the "other guys" were.

"If it has a wire, I'm your girl. Phones, laptops, cars, implants..." She rooted through the tools in the box, tossing what she didn't need aside.

I watched her carelessly hurl implements on the floor and remembered what John and Dowe had said about getting work done. I glanced across the workshop, where they had gathered a pile of tools and screws and invented some impromptu board game. Lanzhou sat between them, looking utterly confused and more than a little bit unnerved.

"So..." I ventured, making sure my voice was low enough not to carry across the room, "how do you know John and Dowe?"

"Doesn't everybody know a John Dowe?" she quipped, then laughed at the exhausted joke. "They came asking for my help after the government botched their neurosurgery."

I stiffened at the mention of the all-too-familiar punishment. "They've been through neurosurgery?"

"Trust me, the government has tried *everything* to get those two to shut up." Seoul glanced at me. "They didn't tell you?"

I shook my head. John and Dowe hadn't been forthcoming with their personal history. Although, in their defense, I'd never actually *asked* about their past.

"They probably forgot." Seoul pressed a button on a mini power tool, and it whirred violently. "To be honest, I'm surprised they lived to tell about it."

As was I. I knew two other people who had been through neurosurgery: Nic's parents, Mr. and Mrs. Von Nieuwenhuyse. According to Nic, they'd both been brilliant scientists prior to the procedure; Mr. Von was almost single-handedly responsible for putting humans on Mars. But all of that had been erased when Asia had them convicted for religious noncompliance and put under the needle. She'd done it to try to convince Nic to complete Red Rain. She succeeded, but Nic found out who authorized the procedure and broke up with her.

The Vons had survived the surgery physically, but their minds were shattered. I'd lived with them for a month when I was last in Boston, and the only way they could function was by developing precise patterns. If there was even the slightest deviation from the status quo—like me coming home five minutes late—they had a nervous breakdown.

John and Dowe were hardly neurotypical, but compared to the Vons, they were doing brilliantly. They at least remembered people and events from the past six months; the Vons couldn't even remember their own children.

I looked down at Seoul. "But how… how can they remember stuff?"

She bowed and spread her hands dramatically. "One of my finer projects."

"I don't—I don't understand," I said.

She grabbed a rag off the table and splashed some rubbing alcohol on it. "I installed experimental brain implants that helped restore some of their memories. I say 'some' because they got aftermarket prototypes—cheapskates."

I struggled to process what I was hearing. A hundred undead hopes resurrected and created a hurricane in my chest. If John and Dowe were functioning on Chinese knockoff versions of this device, then what was the original implant capable of? Was it possible that the Vons could be brought back from the dead?

"How does this implant work?" I asked.

"The logic is fairly simple, honestly." She picked up a tool and started sanitizing it with the rubbing alcohol—although seeing as the cloth was stained with grease, I wasn't sure the device was getting any cleaner. "Neurosurgery doesn't erase memories. It just rewrites the neural pathways so people aren't triggered by things the government deems problematic."

I knew that was true; I'd read as much in a medical journal while studying the Vons' condition. Instead of brainwashing the victim and starting with a clean slate, neurosurgery was supposed to "cut out" the noncompliant parts of a person's psyche. The theory was that you could delete the Christian or the revolutionary but keep the doctor or teacher. The problem was that it almost never worked.

"Think of it like snipping the wire to a light bulb." Seoul demonstrated with a clack of the tiny shears she had in her hand. "The light bulb's still there—there's just no power going to it."

I was beginning to catch on. "So, if you can reconnect the power…"

She grinned. "Exactly. Unfortunately, repairing the neural pathways themselves is an art we haven't quite mastered yet. But a synaptic device doesn't need any fancy neurons to access those memories."

I frowned and waited for her to explain.

"It's a combination of two very basic technologies: synaptic reading and augmented reality." She shifted through the junk on the table until she found two pieces of circuit board, then turned to face me. "The synaptic device reads the stored memories," she held out one piece of circuitry in her right hand, "and the reality augmenter projects it to the mind." She held out the other piece of circuitry in her left hand, then smashed the two together.

"You can bypass the damaged neurons entirely," I murmured.

Seoul muttered a proud *mmhmm* and tossed the circuit boards back on the table. Taking the same alcohol-soaked cloth, she grabbed my arm and started sanitizing my hand.

I numbly let her work. My heart was pulsing as I remembered who else had a damaged brain.

My father.

I looked down into Seoul's eyes, begging her to tell me this was all true. "You can bring someone back. You can restore who they once were."

She contorted her face in a disheartening gesture. "Sort of. It's not flawless, and it takes a lot of programming before the device really starts working. You have to 'teach' it what memories you want it to pull for certain words."

"What do you mean?" I asked, struggling to swallow my heart as my hopes plunged back down again.

"Think of it like a search engine. If you say 'daughter,' it's going to scan the memory banks and pull up *all* images associated with that word. It's really overwhelming at first, and there's no order to the results. You have to train the algorithm, and even then, sometimes it gets it completely wrong."

I looked over at John and Dowe, who were bickering over what number their makeshift die had landed on. "Is that why they're…?"

"They're what?" Seoul prodded.

I struggled to come up with a polite way to say it, but there was no polite way to describe the mental state of John and Dowe. "Well, most people, when you tell them you need a distraction, would reach for a flare gun, not a can of whipped cream."

Seoul laughed. "Oh no, Dowe's always been creative like that. And John... well, it's not really his fault. He's the second."

"Second of what?" I demanded.

The question apparently wasn't important enough to answer, because she kept blathering on. "No, their problem is they bought fake implants off a scammer. Their chips can only hold about a dozen terabytes of information. As soon as you learn something new, *poof...*" She fluttered her fingers like a fleeing bird. "There goes something else important. Like how much you owe your mechanic."

She paused to stare at them, but I could tell by the tweak in the corner of her lips that she wasn't really mad. "Thankfully, the technology has come a long way in the last few years, or so I've heard."

That was all I needed to hear. "I need three of these devices."

She dropped whatever she was holding. "What?"

"I need three of these implants," I repeated, "as soon as possible."

"Okay, first of all." She took a step back and punctuated with both of her hands. "There is no 'as soon as possible' on the black market. You get what you can when you can get it. And second of all—"

"I thought you said you were 'my girl' when it came to anything with a wire." I arched my eyebrow in a gesture Nic would have been proud of.

She halted with her mouth open. "Okay, erase that list and start over. New first of all: That's rude."

I shrugged.

She growled and tensed her muscles in a pose that would have been threatening had she been more than five feet tall. "Fine. Then let me put it this way: These devices are extremely illegal and use extremely rare components. That means they're extremely expensive."

"Money is no object," I replied, and it really wasn't. "Besides, if that's the case, then it seems a job like this would warrant a pretty hefty finder's fee, wouldn't it?"

She blinked as every muscle in her body relaxed, and I knew we had a deal.

"And if adding an extra zero doesn't provide the necessary incentive..." I traced my finger through the grime on the worktable. "You can tell them Blue Fire sent you."

"That... might actually work," she admitted. She let out a puff of breath, causing a stray chunk of her blue hair to flop into her eyes. "All right, fine, I'll do it. I make no promises that I can get three of them—but I'll start making calls."

"That's all I ask." My voice was calm, but my mind was anything but as my soul whirled out of control. Would this work? Could we bring the Vons and my father back from the dead? Would I finally be able to put my family back together? Seoul claimed the devices weren't perfect, but any memories would be better than none. I would spend the entire Nolan fortune if it would bring even a piece of my father back.

The Holy Spirit pressed down on my chest, and I took a deep breath. As much as I wanted to drop everything and save my father, I knew I had to trust Seoul to do her job. I wouldn't know who to call about one of these devices even if I could safely get online. There was nothing I could do but wait—and pray.

I closed my eyes and started doing just that, and hard.

"Well," Seoul chirped, ending the subject like one closes a book, "let's get you disarmed before you blow up a rhino with this thing."

I looked up just in time to see her snap a magnetic clamp over my wrist, pinning it to the table. She tugged on a pair of gloves, then yanked her goggles over her eyes. Grabbing the tiny shears, she reached for my finger, then hesitated.

"Oh, I should probably warn you." She glanced at me, her expression unreadable behind the code flickering across her lenses. "This is going to hurt a lot."

7: PHILADELPHIA

In a cruel irony, removing the implant took twice as long and hurt three times as much as installing it.

The procedure was excruciating. I blacked out once and almost vomited multiple times. John and Dowe did their best to try to entertain me, but even they weren't distracting enough to keep me from crying in pain. The whole ordeal took over four hours and involved more than a little blood.

To make matters worse, Seoul wasn't even able to remove the whole device. She claimed extracting the wiring would be too dangerous, and after seeing the state of her workshop, I didn't want to push my luck and lose my whole hand. Instead, she removed the programming chip and the battery, then cut into each of my fingers and snipped the wires in multiple places.

I was disheartened by the fact that I would still be carrying the fragments of a bomb in my body, but Seoul assured me that it would be impossible for anyone to reconstruct the device. If someone wanted to turn me into a weapon again, they would have to install brand new wiring.

Seoul finally released the clamp that held me down. I lifted my hand slowly, afraid to look. With a prayer, I rallied the courage to open my eyes—and was surprised to find that my palm looked unscathed. The newly regenerated skin was flawless, each incision fully healed. I flexed my fingers and felt all my nerves respond; they weren't even numb.

"Thank you," I said with more than a little admiration.

Seoul winked. "I told you I was your girl." She walked over to one of the computer terminals and yanked a flash drive out of the port. "Here's the code."

I shakily stood up and reached to take the drive. I slid it in an inner pocket of my backpack and zipped it shut. *Hopefully, this will give us some answers.*

"And here's the chip."

I looked up. Seoul rooted around on the table until she found a small plastic case of nails. Dumping the nails out on the table, she dropped the chip in the container, snapped it shut, and held it out to me.

I almost didn't take it. Why would I want to keep the bullet that had killed Nic? It took everything in me not to throw the chip on the floor and stomp on it. But I knew I should keep it until we figured out what was going on; Stanyard or Ephesus might need more code from it.

I forced a smile and accepted the container, dropping it in my backpack. "Thanks," I mumbled.

"Anything for Blue Fire," she said, and grinned.

Lanzhou paid her, and then we eagerly climbed the stairs and left the store. I stumbled out onto the sidewalk, breathing deeply. The air in downtown Beijing wasn't much cleaner than the air in the shop, but I was grateful to see the sun again.

"We need to hurry back." Lanzhou gestured and led the way towards the bus stop. "Jael is waiting to see you."

I flinched when I remembered I still had one more apology to make. "What did you tell her?"

"She knows about Nic and your chip." Lanzhou glanced back at me. "I figured I'd leave the rest to you."

I rubbed my arm. I had no idea how merciful Jael was, but I knew *I* wouldn't be lenient if a crazy teenager shot me in the chest at pointblank range. Thankfully, it was going to take us an hour to get back to the factory—and that gave me an hour to find my own forgiveness.

Holy Spirit, please help me make this right.

It was well into the afternoon by the time we returned to the factory. The Tangs owned a business on the river downstream from their home. Over a decade ago, Mr. Von had granted Mr. Tang an exclusive contract to produce a specialized part for space stations, and the Tangs had profited handsomely. In exchange, Mr. Tang agreed to let an underground church meet in his building. That venture had also been extremely successful, judging by the crowd I'd seen at the service two days ago.

First shift was grinding to a close as we arrived. The dock gates were open as a trickle of office workers fled the scene, eager to beat rush hour. Bowen met us in the lobby and led us past the noisy locker rooms and up an elevator to the third floor.

Jael was waiting in the same conference room we'd met in the day before. She presided in the same chair at the head of the table, one leg crossed over her knee in the same regal pose, as if she'd been waiting all day for my arrival. If it weren't for the fact that she'd changed her skirt set and rotated her heavy ensemble of jewelry, I would have thought she hadn't moved at all.

She rose when I entered. "Philadelphia, you've returned." Her Hausa accent made her words so thick that I couldn't detangle the emotion behind them.

I halted just inside the door, suddenly wishing I could be anywhere else. It didn't help that I'd forgotten how imposing Jael was, with her tall heels and crown-like turban.

She flicked her hand. "Come here."

I somehow found the will to obey, walking to the end of the conference table and stopping a few feet in front of her. Lanzhou and Bowen followed at a safe distance.

Jael waited. When I didn't initiate, she arched an eyebrow. "Is there something you want to tell me?"

"Jael, I..." I sighed. All my prepared speeches evaporated, replaced by a meek and simple: "I'm sorry."

"You are forgiven," she announced. "Now, why did you do it?"

I jerked back. "What?" I hadn't expected to reconcile that quickly—or to have to produce an explanation for my actions.

"You shot me, child." She stared at me with an expression that was neither angry nor amused. "For the safety of all involved, I think it's important that we both understand why you did it, so it doesn't happen again."

I struggled to put my insanity into words—and that's when the Holy Spirit answered my hours of prayer. "I did it because... I felt used. You took my image and built a war around it, and you never asked my permission. We hadn't even met."

She accepted the accusation with a slight shrug. "And?"

"And what?" I returned. That seemed like reason enough to shoot someone—or at least it had, in the moment.

"If you were only upset about being made into the thunderbird, then you would have shot Jayde a long time ago." A hint of a smile made it onto her face. "No, Philadelphia, you've made peace with Blue Fire. She isn't the problem. So, I ask you again: What is?"

I searched my soul and found the answer I had been too afraid to share with anyone but Nic. "I broke down because... I thought I'd made a mistake. All this time, I thought God was the one who had created Blue Fire and made my videos trend. I thought it was a miracle."

I scrolled back through the inconceivable events that had transpired over the last six months and tried to find the same sense of wonder I'd had before. I shook my head. "And then I find out it was just you controlling the search engine the entire time. I felt like a fool and wondered if I'd gone through all that pain for nothing."

Bowen moved in my peripheral. "Of course, it wasn't for nothing. You—"

Jael lifted a finger to stop him, her eyes still on me. "And how do you know God wasn't also speaking to me?"

I looked up and met her gaze.

"Philadelphia, no one's denying that this has been hard on you. Lanzhou and I both agree: Our meeting should have been handled differently. But this revolution isn't about you. It's about freedom. And if you want to have a part in saving the world, then you're going to have to accept that you're but one piece of the puzzle. Things are going to happen that are outside of your control. People are going to make decisions without you—including me."

Her bright heels clicked on the floor as she closed the gap between us. She laid her hand gently on my shoulder. "I'm asking you to join a war, not lead it. Can you follow? Can you learn to take orders from me?"

I swallowed as apprehension made my throat go dry. "What do you mean?"

"Blue Fire works for me, not the other way around," she announced without ceremony. "I'm the one leading this operation, which means I give the orders. If I tell you to record a video, you smile for the camera. If I give you a script, you read it. If I tell you to stop and wait for directions, then you don't move until I tell you to."

I searched her face and tried to grasp what she was asking me to do. She was asking me to surrender, to put my identity in her hands and let her write the script. The way she saw it, this was her revolution, and I was just another soldier in her army. Blue Fire was hers to control—and I had to trust that she was using my image for good and not evil.

Was that what God wanted? Was that why He had brought us together?

"Because if you can't do that, you can go home."

"What?" I gasped more than spoke as I jerked out of my thoughts.

Her expression was devoid of emotion. "You're seventeen—eighteen if you ask Andromeda. I won't make you sacrifice your life for this if you don't want to. If you can't handle taking orders, I can get you off the grid and send you back to Boston."

"No!" I shouted, more loudly than I intended. I couldn't leave Nic, and I knew giving up was not what God wanted. Nic literally had a vision about me being in Beijing, as a Nolan, fighting Asia. I may have messed up God's original plan by trying to kill the General and getting Nic arrested, but I still had a purpose. I was still Andromeda Nolan for a reason. If Jael hadn't given up on me, then I wouldn't give up on her.

"No," I repeated, more resolutely this time. "I want to help. Tell me what I need to do."

A genuine smile finally broke Jael's expression. "That's what I needed to hear, soldier. I want you to record a video today, just a short one. Your followers need to know you're alive and well, and that you want them to await further instructions."

She turned and strode back to the table. I stumbled after her, suddenly dizzy. *That's it, then?* After days of running and questioning God, it was disorienting to suddenly find myself back where I started, recording videos as if the last week never happened. It was like someone had reset the game and dumped me at the beginning of the level.

"I've written a few remarks for you to cover—you can embellish them how you see fit." Jael picked a tablet up off the table. "But first, there's something you need to see."

She swiped on the screen, and the projector in the back of the room brightened to life. The elaborate device projected a 3D rendering of the contents of Jael's tablet against the blank wall. I gripped the back of the nearest chair as a larger-than-life picture of Nic consumed the screen.

It was a bland, washed-out shot in front of a white wall: an intake photo. Nic glared stoically at the camera as his uncombed hair cast defiant shadows on his face. The orange collar of his prison jumpsuit stuck up on one side, as if he couldn't be bothered to fold it down.

I bent over the chair as all the guilt and regret threatened to push themselves back up my throat. I knew Nic would get sent to prison, but it still hurt to see it emblazoned on the screen in ugly, undeniable orange.

Nic, I'm so sorry. I did this.

"His trial is scheduled for next week," Jael said softly.

"Next week?" Bowen sputtered. "You can't even get a parking permit that fast. Mong must really have a grudge."

She does, I thought, shuddering. *Against me.*

"What are they charging him with?" Bowen asked.

Jael shook her head, her gigantic earrings drifting listlessly. "Classified."

"Can you do anything?" Lanzhou ventured. The question was directed at Jael, but there was no hope in his voice.

"I haven't been able to find out where she's holding him." There was a pause, and I could tell by the pinch in her expression that Jael was just as despondent as the rest of us. "But I promise, my people are on it." She shifted her gaze to me, watching for my reaction.

I pushed myself upright, then hesitated when I noticed some highlighted text in the corner of the projection. I pointed. "What does that say?"

Jael turned her head to follow my finger. "They've set bail."

"Bail?" I gasped as my world doubled over again. "You mean we could—"

"That's not bail, that's extortion," Lanzhou interrupted. "That's an astronomical amount."

I stepped closer to the screen and squinted at the numbers. There was an excessive number of zeros at the end of the sum, enough that it felt like a made-up figure.

Bowen slammed his fist on the table. "That's insane. No one could pay that."

"I could."

It was only when everyone stopped to stare at me that I realized I'd spoken aloud. I straightened as hope ram-rodded my heart. "I can afford that—Andromeda can. I can bail him out of jail. We need to—"

"Absolutely not." Jael's command was cold, callous. "You will not be bailing him out."

"But we have to! I can't let Asia—"

"*Asia* is the one who's watching your bank accounts. If you show up to post bail, she'll be right there to catch you."

Jael had a point, but surely there was a way around that. "Then help me launder the money. Someone else can post it—I just need you to help me transfer it. You control the algorithm. Surely, you can hide a transfer."

Her hesitation told me that she probably could, but she shook her head. "It won't solve anything. Even if he gets out on bail, he'll still have to show up for trial—and I can guarantee you that Asia will be tracking him very closely. If you bail him out, she'll follow him straight to you."

I braced myself on the table as helplessness washed over me. "But I can fix this," I murmured, mostly to myself.

"It would be a waste of money," she said, tone only one degree warmer than heartless. "This is not the first time I've fought Asia, so I know her tricks. She's baiting you, Philadelphia, and you cannot afford to fall for it."

She was right, of course, but that just made the situation even more agonizing. Asia was doing all of this because of me. The trial, the outrageous bail—this was personal. She was manipulating the chess board to ensure that the only way to save Nic would be for me to turn myself in.

And it was only going to get worse.

"No matter what happens to me, no matter what you hear, I need you to promise that you won't come for me. Do you understand?"

"If you want to help him," Lanzhou touched my arm, "the best thing you can do is record a video."

I looked up. Bowen nodded at me from across the table. "Do your part. Let Jael manage the rest. She'll figure out where he's being held—just buy us time."

I turned back to face her. She lifted one eyebrow. "Can you handle this, Philadelphia?"

I sucked in a breath through my nose. If fighting for Nic meant becoming Blue Fire again, then that's exactly who I would be. "Yes," I declared, and hoped my voice came off more confident than it sounded to my own ears. "Put me on air."

"Excellent." Jael clapped her hands like a judge banging a gavel, ending the discussion. "Everyone, back to work. Internet usage is going to peak in a little over an hour, so if we're going to hit that window, we need to move. Philadelphia, go get dressed."

"Get dressed?" I repeated. I glanced down at my ripped jeans and nondescript t-shirt; what was wrong with what I was wearing?

She flicked a bejeweled finger at my bleached blonde hair. "You can't go on camera looking like a Nolan."

She had a point. If I was going to record videos again, then I had to bring Philadelphia Smyrna back from the dead. But that would be easier said than done when I didn't have any makeup or supplies; I didn't even have a change of clothes, except what I'd borrowed from the Tang daughters. Nic and I had fled into Beijing with nothing but some water bottles and a blanket.

"I may be able to help with that."

I turned to see Bowen approach. He held out a black duffle. "Narissa sends her regards."

I took the bag hesitantly. "But how did you…"

"Nic mentioned her. I figured if you were going to be staying while, you'd need a wardrobe change, so I put in a special order." Bowen grinned.

I caught myself returning the smile. Narissa was my stylist; she'd designed the gown I'd worn at the state dinner. She'd also helped us get a head start on Asia by letting us out a back way and distracting the guards. I trusted her, and she certainly did know how to make me look good.

"Follow me." Bowen gestured and led the way out of the conference room.

I shouldered the duffle and followed him down a floor to a private bathroom. After thanking him, I locked the door and set the bag on the counter.

For the first time since yesterday, I paused to really look at myself in the mirror. Andromeda Nolan stared back. A bleach job, blue contacts, and three ear piercings attempted to transform me from an unassimilated criminal into a societal elite—and so far, it had worked.

I squinted at my face. My right cheek was faintly red. I gingerly touched it—and remembered.

Jayde had slapped me on the face yesterday. I'd prayed that it wouldn't bruise, and it hadn't. It wasn't even tender anymore.

I murmured a prayer of thanks, but somehow, I wasn't surprised. The whole situation seemed almost mundane. After all, I'd seen a man raised from the *dead*; a bruise was inconsequential.

I stared at my fingers as that thought disrupted something in my soul. Then I shook off the feelings and turned my focus back to the task at hand. I unzipped the duffle and discovered Narissa had crammed an entire dressing room into the bag. There were several outfits, two pairs of shoes, and a pouch of makeup. I chuckled; since I couldn't get to her studio, Narissa would send the studio to me.

I unfolded the top outfit. It was a pair of army green cargo pants and a matching jacket. It was paired with a black mock-neck tank top and fingerless utility gloves. I fingered the sturdy linen fabric of the pants and fought down a wave of trepidation. The outfit looked like something a military officer would wear—which was, I suppose, exactly the look we were going for.

I quickly changed before I could second guess myself. I turned to the mirror and realized that the tank top proudly showed off the thunderbird tattoo I had on my right shoulder. The thunderbird symbol—a silhouette of a black hawk with a bolt of blue lightning clutched in its talons—was the icon of the revolution and the brand that permanently marked me as "Blue Fire." Narissa, as always, had thought of everything.

Something had to be done about my hair, however; most of the internet still thought Philadelphia had a long dark brown mane. I rooted around in the bag until my hand closed around a soft package: a wig.

Inside was a handwritten note:

I CAN'T FIX THAT ABYSMAL BLEACH JOB, BUT AT LEAST I CAN COVER IT. —N

P.S. SORRY ABOUT Q. LET HIM TAKE CARE OF HIMSELF. YOU'RE DOING THE RIGHT THING.

I blinked back a stray tear and desperately hoped she was right about the last part.

I pulled the wig out of its plastic packaging. The long, fake hairs were a chocolate brown color and done up in a twisted bun that was somehow both elegant and demure at the same time. A single curled strand was left to hang loose against the left side of my face.

After pinning my short hair back, I slid the wig on. The look was convincing—no one on the street would be able to tell that it wasn't my natural hair—and I was surprised at how much the refined style aged me. With a little bit of eyeliner, I could pass for twenty-five. I looked bold, confident, mature.

Everything I wanted the internet to see.

I reached for the makeup pouch, then noticed there was something else tucked in the corner of the bag: a jewelry box. I opened it and found a hairpin made with a real feather. The barbs were black and flashed iridescent blue in the light, like a raven.

The symbolism was not lost on me. This was a thunderbird feather.

I pinned the accessory against the base of my bun. Closing my eyes, I took a deep breath and prepared to face my old self in the mirror.

But when I looked up, it wasn't Philadelphia Smyrna who was staring back at me.

It was Blue Fire.

8: NIC

They kept me in the hospital for "observation" for another twenty-four hours, probably so that they could add an extra zero to the bill. By then, I was so inhumanely bored that they were at risk of needing to readmit me to the psychiatric ward.

Turns out, the high-security jail cell Asia had prepared for me was almost the same thing.

The space was so narrow that I could touch the opposite walls at the same time. The door was eight inches thick, and beyond that was a gate that dropped down like the airlock on a space station, blocking out the light from the hall. There were no windows, because criminal geniuses can't be trusted with such things—not that there would have been much of a view. Judging by the long elevator ride down, the cell was several floors underground. They probably designed it that way so that if I should somehow figure out how to drill through the solid steel walls, I'd hit only bedrock.

But just in case the earth's crust was not strong enough to contain me, they added an ankle bracelet. Asia came to watch them fit it, grinning gleefully like we were trying on wedding outfits.

Her smile vanished when I told her this was the only "ring" I'd ever wear for her.

The cell was painted solid white, which in itself was a form of torture. As if that wasn't mind-numbing enough, there was also a TV tuned to the United's usual fare of fake news and censored sitcoms.

I kept the device off for the first three days. I preferred to go insane the old-fashioned way: by talking to myself in the mirror. Besides, Asia provided more than enough entertainment. She visited me at least twice a day, giving me updates on my court case like she was planning our honeymoon.

"I'm legally obliged to tell you that they've set bail," she informed me after I settled in. "Not that you can afford it."

"This is why you always paid for dinner," I replied with a shrug. But I knew who could afford to post bail: Andromeda Nolan.

It was a cheap shot, but I couldn't blame Asia for trying the bloodless option first. I prayed that Philadelphia wouldn't take the bait, and for the first time in a decade, my prayers were answered. The week blurred into the weekend, and there was no word from Andromeda.

By then, even Asia's conversation was starting to sound intellectually stimulating, so I knew I had to resort to drastic measures before my mind cracked.

I turned on the TV.

I scrolled through the stations, changing the channel whenever the programming became too stupid to bear. That worked for about forty-eight hours, but the tide of insanity was gaining momentum. I scrolled faster, my finger punching the button like a woodpecker, desperate to see the image shift, the colors flash, for there to be any change in my environment whatsoever.

And that's when I saw her.

Philadelphia.

I almost scrolled past her, but her voice pulled me back. She was broadcasting on some obscure local channel, a gimmicky shopping network the censors probably forgot about. Jael must have hijacked the signal.

Phil sat in a chair in the center of the frame. She was in a nondescript office, with a map adorning the wall behind her, like she was a stateswoman issuing a speech. Through some fashion wizardry, they'd brought her brown hair back. A layer of makeup concealed the circles under her eyes, and smokey eyeshadow added eight years.

She looked halfway to thirty, and I hated it.

"The rumors are true," she narrated, clearly reading prepared remarks. "My position was compromised."

"That's an understatement," I grunted at the TV.

"But I can assure you that I'm safe—and I have no intention of giving up this fight. Operation Blue Fire is still on, and we need your help more than ever."

She leaned forward, and I saw the same glimmer in her eyes that she'd had when she'd spoken in church a week ago. It was that moment of possession when Philadelphia left and Blue Fire took over.

"They're calling this a 'petty demonstration'—but we know that's not true. Operation Blue Fire is not another riot. This is not some march around the capital where we hold signs and scream at politicians who will never hear us. We don't need the government to wake up—we need *the people* to wake up."

She's getting closer, the Voice in my head commented, abruptly reminding me of His presence.

Closer to what?

But she needs you to get there, He said, which didn't even remotely answer the question.

Phil's recording spoke over both of us. "This is about saving a generation. If we don't do this, then our children will just repeat the cycle—and there will be no end to the United."

She looked down, picking at the remnants of polish on her fingernails. "But we can end it. We can stop the cycle. We just have to be brave enough to be uncomfortable."

The sparkle faded from her eyes as she faced the camera again, her voice becoming rote. "Operation Blue Fire continues as scheduled. Await further instructions, and please forward this video. Thank you."

She fell silent, and for a second, I thought the playback had paused. But then she shifted, and I could tell by the change in her tone that she was going off-script.

"Q." Her voice halted, like she hated saying the nickname as much as I hated hearing it. "I don't know if you're seeing this, but…"

I involuntarily stood up and stepped closer to the screen.

She brushed a strand of hair behind her ear and looked straight into the camera. "But if you do… I'm sorry."

And then the video looped, cutting back to the beginning of her speech and starting over.

I threw the remote across the room. When it didn't break, I picked it up and hurled it into the wall—again and again until chips of plastic started flying off. The image on the TV glitched and changed channels before finally going dark.

"It's not supposed to be this way!" I yelled, my voice tinging irritatingly off the metal walls. "She needs me—You even said so Yourself!"

He had, in fact, said that—a mere five minutes ago.

"Yeah, well, you know what I'm doing right now? *Not* helping. In fact, I'm no expert, but based on circumstantial evidence, this is just making things worse."

It was. As much as I hated to admit it, I was playing right into Asia's hand. Even if Phil was smart enough not to fall for Asia's trap, she was no doubt watching the proceedings. She'd witness my trial unfold on TV and blame herself for the whole debacle. And if there was one thing I knew about Philadelphia, it was that she would let guilt grind her into the dirt until there was nothing left of her soul.

And that's when Asia would win—thanks to my help.

"You can't let that happen! Are You just going to let Asia use me like this, after You went to all the trouble of bringing me back to life? Because that seems like a waste of a good resurrection."

I looked up at the ceiling and spun in a circle, half-expecting Him to pop out of a corner. "I have to get out there and help her! That's the whole reason You dragged me back to this stupid planet!"

I didn't use the word "stupid"—and that's when I realized that yelling at the King of Creation was probably not the most effective way to get an answer.

I sighed and pinched the bridge of my nose. "Look... I need You."

The words tasted disgusting—although that was probably on account of the sacrilegious tone I'd used to say them. I spat in the sink and tried again.

"I can't do this by myself. I'm sorry it's taken being locked behind eighteen inches of steel and a mile of bedrock for me to admit that, but here we are. If You want me to help her, then You're going to have to get me out of here."

As if in response, the gate outside the door groaned open.

I whipped around. "That... wasn't the answer I was expecting, but I'll take it."

There was beeping as someone typed on the door's keypad. The door squeaked open, and I was more than a little disappointed to see Asia standing in the hall.

And I thought we were having a real moment there.

She tossed a stack of clothes at me. "Get dressed, and don't make me wait."

I caught the clothes and shook them out to find a halfway decent suit and button-up. "What's this for? Is it Tuesday?"

"It's actually Monday," she intoned, missing the joke, "and you need to look nice for the judge."

My good mood faltered when I realized the worst of my punishment was about to begin. I started unbuttoning the shirt. "I hear they'll give you a lighter sentence if you wear fake glasses."

"I'll see what I can conjure up. In the meantime, wash your face, and *please*," she coated the word with enough drama to win an Oscar, "shave that hideous mustache."

I grabbed the door handle. "You'll have to convict me first." And then I slammed the door in her face.

After I took as long as humanly possible to tidy up—which is harder than it sounds when you're a guy—Asia cuffed me and loaded me into the back of a police van. We drove across town and parked in an underground garage. As soon as we got off the elevator, I recognized where we were: the Supreme

Court Building in Beijing. Clearly, Asia had pulled out the red carpet for this event.

She herded me to the lobby. Even though I couldn't see past the line of guards, I could hear the thrum of a commotion outside. Half a dozen police stood with their backs braced to the front door, as if they were afraid someone was going to break in.

Suddenly, I knew what was going on. And for the first time since my arrest, I felt the tiniest bit afraid.

Asia's deadly fingernails scraped my forehead as she tried to straighten my hair for the third time. "Remember, keep your chin up, eyes forward. Smile for the camera."

"Why should I?" I snapped.

She sneered. "Because your daughter is watching."

Then, at the flick of her finger, the guards dragged the double doors open, releasing the onslaught of cameras and press.

The flash from a hundred bulbs was so blinding that it lit the foyer like a lightning strike. I instinctively shielded my face as my vision washed white, then black.

"You'll ruin the shot!" Asia protested, yanking my arms back down.

Someone shoved me forward onto the step. A gaggle of reporters clogged the stoop, shouting their inane questions over each other.

"Dr. Von Nieuwenhuyse!"

"Over here!"

"Please, sir, a statement!"

I stared out at the throbbing mob as the whisper of fear grew louder. I looked inward and struggled to hear the Voice in my head over the noise.

So, you know that miracle we were just discussing?

He finally responded. *Yeah?*

I'm going to need it now.

"Dr. Nic!"

I made the mistake of turning in his direction. The intrepid reporter took that as an invitation to elbow several people out of the way and come stand in front of me. "Sir, are you aware of the charges laid against you?" he demanded.

I actually wasn't; that was a minor detail Asia had left out of her incessant gabbing. "I'm going to need you to rephrase the question," I grunted, unwilling to admit my ignorance on live TV. "My teleprompter is broken."

The chatter of the crowd finally stilled, as if everyone was waiting to hear the reporter's reply. He held his microphone close to his lips as he shared my darkest secret with the world.

"The environmental weapon, sir. They're saying you invented Red Rain."

9: PHILADELPHIA

I didn't sleep for a week.

There was no word on Nic. His file was never updated; all it said was that he had been arrested and the initial hearing set for Monday. Jael searched every device connected to her company's network, looking for information on his location or the charges laid against him, but found only rumors. It wasn't like the information was classified; Jael might have been able to hack into it. It was like the information was never recorded. Whatever Asia was planning, she had been very careful not to leave a digital trail.

I knew why. Asia hated an unnecessary mess. If she had her way, she'd bargain with me quietly, and Nic's arrest would never make it onto the news. His court date was the ticking time bomb between us: I had until Monday to turn myself in before she made him suffer.

But I couldn't fall for it. Stanyard and Ephesus both repeated the sentiment when they heard the news; even Cea called and, in her own grief-stricken way, gave me permission to essentially abandon her brother. Every time I asked Jael if there was any new information, she closed the conversation with a platitude like, *"You're making the right decision,"* as if she correctly assumed I was drowning in doubts.

I let silence be my response. I couldn't agree; to make a conscious decision to walk away from Nic, to verbally admit I was leaving him behind, felt like signing his death warrant. So, for five long days, I did nothing.

I couldn't even sleep. No matter how much I prayed, no matter how much I paced the room and tried to make myself tired, darkness never came until it was too late. I would snatch a few broken hours before sunrise, and then the restless cycle would begin all over again as soon as daylight peered through the shutters.

I didn't know what was wrong with me. Why wasn't prayer working? Talking to the Lord had always brought me peace in the past, but not now. I tried listening to worship music, I tried reading the Bible, I even tried crying and pounding the floor. Nothing worked. It was like all my thoughts and emotions were locked in a glass coffin. No matter how much I screamed and banged on the walls to get out, nothing changed.

I didn't tell anyone. I was afraid that if I told the Tangs I wasn't sleeping, their doctor would try to give me more sleeping pills, and I didn't trust myself on medication. So, I lied my way through breakfast every morning and used concealer and extra coffee to cover up what was really going on.

It was a cruel mercy when Monday finally rolled around. I arrived in the conference room at the factory to find everyone gathered in front of the projector.

Jael turned to me as I entered. "Bad news."

"What? What's wrong?" I threw my backpack on the table and shoved past the others to stand next to her.

"Asia brought friends." Jael stepped aside and pointed at the screen.

Live footage of the Supreme Court Building was rolling. A mob of reporters clogged the lawn, vying for position in front of the steps, while the alarming words "Breaking News" scrolled across the ticker in English and Mandarin. The anchormen in the studio gossiped about who or what could have the government in such an uproar.

"Every station is playing this," Jael explained. "She stopped all the regular programming."

I bent over the back of a chair as a wave of seasickness crashed into me. Our time was up. As soon as Nic walked out those doors, his life would be over.

Just then, the courthouse doors opened. The crowd erupted like a pot boiling over. At first, there was such a jostle of bodies and microphones and drone-guided cameras that I couldn't even see him. But then a guard shoved him onto the top step, and the footage focused on his face.

He stood there, blinking as the flash of a dozen bulbs drowned him in harsh light. He squinted at the crowd, like he couldn't figure out where he was or why he was here. He looked lost, confused.

My heart went to my throat. I'd seen Nic display a lot of emotions, but confusion was never one of them. He always put on a façade of being in control, even when he wasn't. But in that moment, as he involuntarily stared at the camera, I could tell that he was just as afraid as I was.

Suddenly, I understood how Stanyard felt. Watching from the other side of the screen while someone I cared about was raked across the coals was the worst kind of agony—especially when I knew it was my fault.

There was motion in the background. Asia walked out of the courthouse, looking immaculate as always. She took up station in the shadows next to the door and scanned the crowd, feasting on the chaos.

I clenched my fists.

The reporters continued to shout unintelligibly over one another. I couldn't make out a single word as their questions muddled into an aggressive mess. Finally, the reporter from the station we were watching managed to elbow his way through the crowd to the foot of the steps.

"Dr. Nic! Are you aware of the charges laid against you?"

Nic turned towards him. The crowd took that as their cue to quiet as everyone waited for his answer.

"I'm going to need you to rephrase the question. My teleprompter is broken," he muttered, the sarcasm a weak attempt at self-defense.

The reporter gestured for his camera to come closer. Nic's face filled the screen in high definition as the reporter gave him his sentence.

"The environmental weapon, sir. They're saying you invented Red Rain."

Someone gasped, but it wasn't me. For one breathless minute, nobody moved, not even Nic. It was like the video had frozen. Then, perhaps involuntarily, he glanced back at Asia.

She smiled.

"No! Stop!" I screamed as everything restarted in a rush. I lunged forward, believing for a wild moment that I could reach her. I tripped and landed in the middle of the projection. The colors flashed around me as the mob ignited again, their frantic shouts shrieking in my ear like a hurricane.

"You can't do this," I sobbed, even though I knew she could, and she had. The only reason Asia had kept Red Rain a secret for so long was because Nic was useful to her.

But he wasn't useful anymore.

Someone pulled me to my feet and hauled me back. I let them guide me to a chair as Jael barked orders and people began to move in all directions.

Nic struggled to face the camera. "I don't know what you're talking about," he returned, answer stiff and practiced.

The reporter was prepared. "Then it's not true that you've been using your science station on Mars as a cover for your operations?" he challenged.

Nic's stunned silence told him all he needed to know.

I gagged. I slapped my hands over my mouth as the world spun out of focus. *Oh God, no. Not the base.*

Even though the truth was plainly written on Nic's pale face, the reporter was persistent. "What do you have to say to these accusations, doctor?" he demanded. His voice was so calm, like he had no appreciation for the destruction he was wrecking with his words.

Nic stiffened. The clarity returned to his expression as he set his jaw. He looked above the reporter's head, straight into the camera lens—as if he knew I was watching from the other side.

"Warn Klez," he ordered. "Tell him Code 2319. Tell him to—"

Someone shouted an objection. The police reacted; I saw guards lunging towards Nic while press people scrambled, and then suddenly the image went dark.

I scrambled up. There was a flicker of static, and then the broadcast cut to the anchormen in the studio as they hastily apologized about "technical difficulties."

Murmurs ignited around the room. "Who's Klez?" Bowen asked me.

"My brother." Klez was my brother's callsign. I sucked in my breath when I realized what Nic was trying to tell me. "We have to warn them!"

The commotion in the room increased. "Warn who? Philadelphia, what's going on?" Lanzhou demanded.

I ignored them all. I grabbed my backpack off the table and fumbled with the zipper. *Oh God, please don't let it be too late!*

Jael stepped closer and watched me.

I yanked my tablet out of my bag. I almost dropped it as I scrambled to dial Ephesus. It rang once, twice, three times.

"Please pick up!" I shouted, shaking the device.

He did. He was sitting at a desk, typing casually on the computer. "Hey sis," he greeted, only one eye on the camera. "Everything okay?"

"No!" I shrieked. "You need to get out of there. They're coming for the base!"

Jael turned and started issuing orders.

Ephesus set his mug down and gave me his full attention. "Whoa, who's coming? What happened?"

I took a deep breath and slowed my words. "Nic's trial—they've implicated the station. Asia told them about Wing 74."

He blinked while he ran that information through his internal processors—then he shoved his chair back. The camera jerked as he took off running. "Cea! Cea! Laodicea!"

"What?" she screeched from off-screen. I heard the *whoosh* of a door, and her voice came through more clearly. "What's gotten into you?"

"Asia told the court about Red Rain and Wing 74," I explained, loud enough for them both to hear me. "The government's coming—they're going to investigate. Nic told me to warn you."

She stepped into the frame. "When did this happen?"

"Just a few minutes ago."

"Then we've got a few hours." Ephesus kept his voice steady. "The nearest settlement is at least three hours away."

"No, that means we have thirty minutes," Cea snapped. "We need to be out of here and far enough away that they'll have difficulty tracking the vehicles."

Ephesus's stalwart expression wavered. "But where—"

"Nic has a friend who owns a mining operation on the other side of the quadrant. It's extremely remote—no one will find us there. It will take a few days' drive, and we'll have to navigate the old-fashioned way. No GPS, or they'll be able to track us." She laid a hand on his arm. "Nic planned for this."

"Nic also said to tell you 'Code 2319,'" I inserted.

Cea gasped.

Ephesus looked down at her for an explanation. She went pale as she relayed, "That's the emergency code to wipe all the servers—even Wing 74. You'll essentially factory reset the entire base."

I failed to breathe as I registered what that meant. It wouldn't be just Nic's illegal projects that would be lost. My brother's work, the Bibles Nic had in his media archive, all the scientific experiments that had been conducted on the base since its construction—over a decade of work, erased like a chalk drawing.

Ephesus inhaled and found his courage. "There will be some physical evidence in Wing 74 that I won't have time to destroy, but it will keep a couple of people's files clean." He grabbed Cea's shoulder. "Make an emergency broadcast to the entire base. They have thirty minutes to be in the docking bay, or I can't guarantee their safety. Tell them to bring only what will fit in a backpack—it's going to be tight. I'll handle the servers."

Cea nodded and disappeared.

The camera bounced as Ephesus took off running again. "As soon as we hang up, you need to delete me as a contact and wipe your call history," he ordered, voice jagged as he pounded down the hall. "I don't know how thorough this system reset is, but you don't want any record that you ever talked to anyone on this base."

"I will," I promised, even though my voice was shaking.

"Call Stanyard and tell him to do the same with the servers in Boston— and then they need to make themselves scarce." Ephesus looked down at the camera, as if making sure I was paying attention. "If Asia is willing to sacrifice this station, then the base in Boston is probably next."

I gasped as the insidious possibility seized my soul. I glanced across the table at Jael; she was already swiping furiously on her tablet.

I heard a door open and a sharp crack as Ephesus threw his device on a desk. I could just barely see him moving on the edge of the frame as he bent over a computer terminal.

"Ephesus, I'm so sorry," I called. "This is all my fault. What are you going to—"

He wasn't listening. The computer screeched at him, and he growled. "You're going to have to authorize this. My security clearance isn't high enough."

"What?"

"The emergency wipe requires Level 2 security access or higher—you're going to have to do it." He picked up the device and flipped the camera so I could see the computer screen. A bright red warning confirmed his statement.

"I have security access?" I wasn't aware I had any clearance on the base at all.

"Nic gave you Level 2," Ephesus said, his voice sounding distant from off-camera.

I stared at the text on the screen as this admission warped my reality. That meant the only person with a higher security clearance than me was Nic. He'd entrusted the entire station to me.

And now I was going to use that power to destroy it.

"We don't have much time." Ephesus punched the button to run the program.

"*Voice authorization required. Please state your name,*" the computer intoned.

"Andromeda Nolan," I answered reflexively.

The computer chirped and flashed a cruel, ironic green. It prompted Ephesus to specify a time limit, and he typed in thirty minutes. The screen locked, displaying only a ticking time bomb as it counted backwards. I whimpered when I realized what I'd just done.

Ephesus paused, as if he, too, abruptly realized there was no going back. Then he flipped the camera back around so I could see him. "I'm going to be offline for a few days until we get there," he explained.

All the grief dropped to my stomach as I realized this situation was bitterly familiar. *No, not this again.*

"Stay off the grid and don't go anywhere until I can call you again," he continued to dictate. "Keep a low profile and don't let anyone know where you are."

"But Ephesus, I—"

He was already on the move. "Keep your head down," he repeated, and hung up.

10: NIC

The base was gone.

Asia forced them to run the story on the news for several days, playing the clip over and over until even the liberal anchormen were tired of talking about it. The raid wasn't even exciting, thanks to Ephesus's quick action. By the time federal agents got to the base, it was deserted, all the servers wiped clean. As a final insult, Ephesus had shut off the generator, taking the environmental controls offline. It took the government two whole days to restore the pressure so they could get in the building, and then all they found was damaged equipment, frozen experiments, and dead plants.

Base #9.6.11 was ruined.

I told myself I shouldn't cry over spilled milk. After all, Asia was the one who had given me control of the station; it was only a matter of time before she took it away. But as the clip of federal agents breaking down the door of *my* house played over and over, I realized logic couldn't cauterize this wound.

That base represented my entire life's work. In between my various attempts to take over the world, I'd accomplished some glorious science; my office was plastered with awards and commendations for experiments I'd overseen. "Governor" had been my identity for a decade, and now I had nothing to show for it.

What aggravated me most was the senselessness of it all. Destroying the station was a waste. Since Red Rain had been deleted, nothing sinister had gone on up there; the most illegal thing on the premises was Ephesus himself.

But Asia didn't need him or the data from my servers; she had more than enough evidence on her own cell phone to convict me. No, she had done this simply to be cruel. It was a last-ditch effort to get either Philadelphia or me to break.

After staring at the white walls of my cell for another five days, I was forced to admit that she almost succeeded on the latter.

Even though my guilt was undeniable, she still made me suffer through the spectacle of a trial. For three days I sat under the scrutiny of cameras as she paraded my sins before the court. Sensor logs proving I had been in

Thames's office, security footage from Rott, data she'd salvaged from old servers—every piece of evidence she could present without incriminating herself was thrown at me like rocks at a stoning. By the time she rested her case, the entire world knew just how evil "Dr. Nic" was.

I considered trying to implicate her. I knew it wouldn't work, but I would have done it just to give her more paperwork to slog through. But, in a rare moment of foresight, the government was smart enough not to let me speak for myself. I'd proven I couldn't be trusted with a microphone at the press conference. Instead, they kept me behind a plexiglass booth for the entire trial, staging me like a museum exhibit while Asia and her hired witnesses dragged my reputation through the mud.

When Asia was finally done burning me at the stake, they tossed me back in my cell to await my sentence. The typical punishment for my crimes was death, but I knew Asia had other plans.

She finally came to visit me. I heard the door open but refused to turn around.

"Your sentence has been issued," she said when I did not initiate. "Seventeen consecutive life sentences, if I counted correctly."

"How many judges did you have to bribe to get that light of a punishment? I was expecting at least twenty-five. I'll have to modify my will."

She grunted. "Thanks to your little 'phone a friend' stunt, there wasn't enough evidence, so I had to drop some of the charges."

"Don't lie to me!" I yelled as my anger overruled my defenses. "You and I both know you didn't need evidence to convict me."

"No, but it would have saved me a lot of paperwork," she snarled.

I raked a hand through my hair. "Why? Why did you do it?" I didn't want a real answer, but I had to say something. Someone had to acknowledge how revolting this whole situation was. "You didn't have to involve them."

"I didn't have to involve your parents, either." She delivered the wound effortlessly, like a papercut.

I slammed my fist into the wall. "Phil wasn't even on the station!" I knew I was giving Asia exactly what she wanted, flailing my emotions about like some stupid circus animal, but "caring" hadn't made it onto my to-do list for the day.

"I'm just eliminating possibilities." She sighed, sounding exhausted.

I glanced over my shoulder and realized she looked terrible—for her, anyway. Other women would have killed to be her even in this state, but by her standards, she looked positively undone. Her unwashed hair had been plastered into a prude bun, and her makeup was beginning to peel. But most telling was the fact that she'd traded her murderous stilettos for demure pumps. The heel was so short that even Phil probably could have walked in them.

Mortality wasn't a weakness Asia displayed often, so the fact that she was willing to look human in front of me could only mean one thing: She'd failed.

Phil hadn't come for me. That meant she was still safe, and Asia had gone through this whole song and dance for nothing. She'd invested time, money, and extortion into this ridiculous court case—and now she would have to clean up her own mess.

The thought gave me so much joy that my soul returned to my body. I straightened and clapped my hands. "Well, it's been terrible seeing you, but I've got work to do."

"What?" she screeched, jerking out of her own pity party.

"I don't know what your plans for the weekend are, but I've got seventeen life sentences to fulfill. Which, if I've done my math right…" I counted on my fingers, "…is about five hundred and ten years. So, if it's all the same to you, I'd like to get started."

✳

It took us over twenty-four hours by high-speed train to reach my new prison, which gave me some concern. Once I escaped, it would take me a month to hitchhike back to Phil.

But the walk was only one of the many logistical problems I had to solve. The other issue was the altitude.

The prison sat atop a snow-covered mountain. From the train platform at the base of the range, I could just barely see the blackened steel structure clinging to the side of the peak like a leech. It looked like the building had washed up there during Noah's flood, and the enterprising communists had just taken advantage of it.

The terrain was so impassable that they hadn't even attempted to build a road. Instead, we followed a tunnel into the center of the rock and boarded an elevator. The elevator was a solid steel box with airtight doors like a submarine, and as soon as we started to ascend, I understood why. Had the elevator not been pressurized, all the vessels in my brain probably would have burst as we shot to twenty thousand feet above sea level.

As it was, the first thing I did when I stumbled off the elevator was vomit. Judging by the state of the vestibule, it was something of a tradition for new arrivals.

They herded me into a receiving area, where they forced me to change into an orange jumpsuit (not sure what was wrong with the one I had on) and took a thumbprint scan and a DNA sample. I then had the unique pleasure of throwing my ankle bracelet in the incinerator.

"I like you guys better already," I commented to the guard, to which he actually smiled.

The camaraderie expired when the secretary approached me with a gun. Without ceremony, she grabbed my right arm, pressed the barrel to my wrist, and fired. I yelped as something cold and sharp bit my skin like a staple.

"Nice to meet you too," I muttered, as a substitute for the choice words that came to mind.

She let go of me and frowned at the tip of the gun. "Oh, I forgot to sanitize that. I hope the last guy I used it on wasn't sick."

"Don't worry, I've had all my shots." I rubbed my wrist and felt a tiny metal capsule shift beneath my skin. "Let me guess: If I leave the premises, this device will explode."

She snorted and walked back to her desk. "No, it will just give them a beacon to find your body in the snow."

I sighed. "Glad to know they don't litter around here."

She used two pointy artificial nails to key a command into her computer terminal. "0118 999 881 999 119 725," she announced.

"What are those, your digits?" I snarked, even though I had a sinking feeling in my stomach.

"No, they're yours."

I facepalmed aggressively. "I would expect nothing less."

"Oh sorry, I read that wrong. It's 0118 999 881 999 119 725..." she squinted, "3."

"Have you *no* mercy?" I shouted at the ceiling.

The secretary lurched. "Excuse me?"

I wagged my head. "Not you. I'm talking to the Voice in my head."

Personally, I think it's hysterical, He replied.

"Well, come on then, let's get to work." One of the guards shoved me out the door. He prodded me down the hall and through another airlock into the main area of the prison. I stumbled onto the walkway, stopped, and stared.

"Keep moving," the guard yelled.

"Hang on." I put up both hands. "I have to appreciate this view."

The prison was an engineering marvel. It was built like a silo, with rings of rooms circling a hollow center. The structure was so tall that I could see neither the top nor the bottom; there must have been at least a hundred floors. But what was truly impressive was that they'd retrofitted the entire structure into a factory. Each floor housed a different enterprise as materials were ferried up and down the center of the silo by a network of elevators. It was like someone had taken an assembly line and made it vertical. The cavernous space throbbed like the inside of an organ as workers flowed in and out and the elevator chains danced.

"I could get used to a view like this," I murmured, then checked myself. "Yup, I'm used to it. God, I want a factory. Preferably one that isn't also a prison."

I can arrange that.

Wait, are You serious?

Are you?

"Glad to know you like the accommodations," the guard interrupted. "Now come on."

His tone of voice had changed into a threat, so I decided to obey. We got on an elevator and ascended another umpteen floors. My stomach protested the additional two hundred feet of altitude, but I managed to keep the contents inside.

We stepped off the elevator just in time to watch a guy get murdered.

I heard the infernal screeching even before the doors opened and thought it was the elevator in need of grease. The doors parted to reveal a stocky female officer exacting vengeance on a prisoner. She had him backed up against the railing as she lectured him with both her words and her firsts.

"How many times do I have to tell you, keep the plasma at a precise 563.28 kelvin!" The officer's Russian accent made her screams sound utterly barbaric.

The hapless prisoner was dumb enough to open his mouth. "I-it's at 563.27, miss..."

"I can read the dial," she snapped, "and that one hundredth of a kelvin could ruin the entire machine! Do you know how much this equipment is worth?"

"N-no," he chattered.

She grunted. "More than you."

And then in one karate-like move, she picked him up and hurled him over the railing.

We all stood still and waited for his screams to stop. I'm not sure they ever did; I think he just fell out of hearing range.

Wow, who threw off her groove?

"Now, why did I do that?" the officer groaned. She turned to the nearest guard. "When I got up this morning, I told myself I wouldn't kill anyone today—and now look. It's not even noon."

"I'll put it on your tasks for tomorrow, ma'am," the guard replied demurely.

"Thank you, you're such a gentleman." The officer looked up and spotted us. "What do you want?"

My escort shoved me forward. "This is the one Mong sent over. You asked to see him when he arrived."

Oh great, my reputation precedes me.

The officer sized me up. "What did you do? Dump her?"

I saw no point in denying it. "Actually, yes."

She cackled. "I would have too. I'm the warden here. You can call me warden, or if you're trying to get on my good side, Warden Ivanova."

"Thanks for the tip, Warden Ivanova," I returned with a salute.

She smirked. "You look like a smart boy with good survival instincts. How would you like a job?" Without waiting for an answer, she turned and gestured to the spot at the machine that had just been vacated. "Can you figure out how to run an interdimensional plasma fabricator, or do I need to show you the tutorial?"

"I prefer to learn by doing." The truth was that I could probably *build* an interdimensional plasma fabricator, given enough time and super glue, but I decided not to burden her with that information.

"I like your attitude," she praised. "What's your designation?"

I cringed. "I haven't memorized it yet."

"Then make one up." When I hesitated, she shrugged. "Don't waste too many brain cells on it. I won't remember it."

I groaned and took the obvious bait. "Q."

She hummed. "Short, a little mysterious—I like it." She turned to go, and the guards fell in line behind her. "Welcome to Russia, Q. Don't cause trouble, and we won't have to talk to each other ever again. Sound good?"

She didn't expect an answer; the door on the elevator closed almost before she finished her sentence.

Not talking to the woman ever again sounded like a fabulous idea, but I doubted I would be so lucky. As much as I would have loved to settle down and enjoy a quiet life in prison, I knew that wasn't an option for me. I had to get home to Phil.

And that would involve causing a little trouble.

After adjusting the machine back to 563.28 kelvin (the autoregulator was off), I scanned my surroundings until I found a window. A narrow pane next to the elevator afforded a beautiful view of the scenery—not that there was anything to see. The world outside was a blur of white and gray; it was impossible to tell where the cloudy sky ended and the snow-covered rocks began. The wind moaned as it tirelessly beat into the side of the building, like it was trying to bury us alive in a snowdrift.

I stared at the ice gathering in the corner of the window and calculated the odds. My last prison had been surrounded by the frigid north Atlantic, but swimming across the ocean would be a picnic compared to trekking down this mountain. I'd have better luck hacking into the elevator and riding down. But even if I could get to the bottom, what then? I'd have to hike back to civilization and beg for a ride to Beijing. All without going online, spending money, or revealing the fact that I was an escaped convict.

"All right, Jesus." I slapped my hand on the cold glass. "This is going to be exciting."

I thought you wanted a factory?

"Not a prison one," I reminded Him aloud. He went silent, so I closed the tab and brought my engineer's brain online.

Walking up to the railing, I surveyed the dazzling building and let my mind do its work. I began to see schematics, charts, and equations as my brain analyzed the laws of physics that made the enterprise run. It was a complicated machine—which meant there were a million ways to break it.

I grinned as I realized Asia had made her first fatal error. She never should have sent me to a place like this; the factory truly was a thing of beauty.

It would be such a pleasure to watch it burn.

11: PHILADELPHIA

The red *Record* button mocked me.

I glared at the sheet of remarks Jael had prepared. I was supposed to be making a statement about Nic. The publicity of his trial ensured that everybody—*everybody*—knew he was the anonymous "governor" I'd referred to in my videos, and my followers were demanding answers. But no matter how many times I paused the recording and tried again, I couldn't get the words out. It sounded like I was reading a eulogy—and in a way, I was.

Nic was gone. I knew he wasn't dead; Asia would have made a spectacle out of his execution. Instead, he'd been convicted with an absurd number of life sentences and sent to prison amidst the jeering of the media.

Of course, the location of his prison had been carefully omitted from the records. Jael, as always, claimed her people were on it, but so far, they had found nothing on or off the record indicating what had happened to him.

Jael finally told me I had to move on. Her team would keep searching, but in the meantime, I had a rebellion to lead—and my radio silence was causing rumors. So, she'd shut me in the recording studio with a list of soulless bullet points and ordered me to tell the world that I'd been orphaned for a second time.

Of course, I had to carefully omit the fact that it was all my fault.

No wonder it wasn't going well. It didn't help that they'd left me alone to stare at the merciless camera. I was in an office at the factory that had been converted into a recording studio, and the unnatural silence of the soundproofed space was claustrophobic. All I could hear was the rattling of my own grief as it beat into my chest like a whip. My breath was hot and shallow, and I ruined several takes by bursting into tears as I struggled to get the truth out.

I rubbed my eyes with the heels of my hands, ignoring the smear of mascara, and punched the button to restart the recording. Jael wouldn't let me out of this room until I recorded something usable.

Please, God, just help me get through this.

"Yes, Nic was an ally of mine," I droned. Maybe if I kept the emotion out of my voice, it would keep the feelings from crushing my lungs. "And his loss is my biggest regret. He shouldn't even have been on Earth, but he was trying to protect me—and now he's paid the ultimate price."

I shoved my notes aside with a grunt. I sounded just as bad as the liberal anchormen, blathering about platitudes that meant nothing. The truth was that Nic was in jail because I'd fought Asia and lost.

"I know you did this just to get back at me," I muttered at the camera. I probably shouldn't engage her, but I knew she was watching my streams. It was no secret what was going on between us.

"You did this because I didn't complete the mission, didn't you?" I gritted my teeth. "You thought I would give you your war, but I failed to perform, didn't I? I wasn't the gullible, obedient little daughter you needed me to be."

Suddenly, I could see her face, her narrow eyes glinting as she told me I was smart and beautiful and deserved to be a Nolan. She'd been grooming me, using flattery and makeup and gifts to cover up the evil in her heart. She had been luring me close—so she could murder what was most important to me.

And she succeeded.

A familiar heat ignited in my chest like flash paper. I lunged towards the camera, my voice rising to a shriek as I yelled at the one person who had caused all my pain.

"You monster! All this time, you claimed that you 'cared' about me, that you just wanted me to come home, that you wanted to be my friend. Well, those were all *lies!*"

I gripped the edge of the desk, afraid that if I didn't, I'd punch something. "You're a wicked, despicable woman, and people like you are the reason I hate the United. How do you sleep at night? You already took my dad away— wasn't that enough for you?"

I felt a burning behind my eyes and braced myself for the tears, but they never came. There was no more grief in my heart. All I could sense was a black, blinding rage.

"You took everything from me! You—"

I choked and slapped my hands over my mouth when I abruptly realized I was about to call her something much worse.

I stumbled back into the desk chair. *Oh God, I'm sorry, please forgive me.*

I dared to look at myself in the playback monitor. My face was so flushed and angry that it looked like I was about to murder someone with my bare hands. What had come over me? Had I really almost cussed someone out *on air?*

I couldn't do this anymore. I stabbed the button to stop the recording. At least we weren't live.

I stormed out of the studio and walked a few doors down to the conference room, where the others were meeting. Lanzhou, Bowen, and John and Dowe were all gathered around the head of the table with Jael, discussing whatever important memo was displayed on the projector. Well, Lanzhou and Bowen were getting work done; John and Dowe looked like they were doodling on a tablet.

Jael glanced up when the door whooshed open to announce my arrival. "Done for the day?"

"You're not going to be able to use the recording," I declared. I trudged up to the table and took the chair next to John and Dowe, but only because they made a big show of pointing it out to me.

Jael raised an eyebrow. I sighed and twisted my hands in my lap. "I got upset and yelled at Asia. We probably shouldn't put that on air."

Jael shrugged. "Sounds like a video I'd watch."

I frowned at her. In her defense, I would probably watch that video too—and I wasn't sure that was a good thing.

"I don't know that we should engage the councilwoman head-on," Lanzhou cut in. "We don't want to antagonize her."

Jael's earrings flashed in the light as she propped her chin on her hand. "Everything Philadelphia says antagonizes Asia. That's why we have her on air."

The last thing I wanted was to be used as a cattle prod to provoke Asia, but I could tell that this conversation didn't involve me anymore.

"She's still the most powerful woman in China and arguably the United," Lanzhou insisted. "We already know this whole sham of a trial was to get revenge on Philadelphia. Don't you think that's enough collateral damage?"

Bowen shook his head and bounced his knee agitatedly. "No, I agree with Jael. I think we need to tell the whole world exactly who did it and why. Why are we not having Phil go on air and reveal everything she knows about Mong?"

I longed to tell the world who Asia really was, but Jael had forbidden it. I didn't have any evidence; I only knew what Nic had told me. To make matters worse, if I explained how I had met Asia, I would have to admit that my legal identity was Andromeda Nolan. And forfeiting Andromeda's clean file—and her money—was a sacrifice I knew Nic wouldn't want me to make.

"I need you to promise that you won't come for me. Promise me!"

"As much as I'd *love* to air that story," Jael said with gesture close to a smirk, "we need to focus on the operation. Asia isn't the real enemy—the United is."

"Respectfully, I disagree." Bowen stabbed the table with his finger. "This kind of behavior is precisely what makes the United evil. People need the truth, and if that means going to war against Mong, I say we do it."

"Except the person you're sending into battle is a teenage girl." Lanzhou at least had the decency to look in my direction as he talked about me like I wasn't in the room. "I don't like it. Philadelphia's suffered enough."

I opened my mouth, but Bowen was quicker to speak. "She's going to have to deal with her grief whether we air the story or not. She may as well use it to her advantage."

I glared at him. They were treating me like a paid actor, like my life's story was disposable propaganda for the rebellion. Did I not get a say in this?

"You make a good point," Jael agreed without the slightest bit of remorse. "Engagement goes up when she's vulnerable. It's part of why her videos trended in the first place—her pain is relatable."

I slapped my palms on the table. "My emotions are not clickbait!"

Everyone stopped and looked at me, and I flushed red.

Dowe jumped up to my defense. "That's right, they're not! Wait, what are we arguing about?"

"Dowe, please sit down," I groaned tiredly. He obeyed me with a shrug, but I felt a pinch in my chest. John and Dowe's antics had never bothered me before. What was wrong with me?

Jael frowned. "Do you need a break, Philadelphia?"

Probably, I thought but didn't say. What I needed was for this endless nightmare to be over.

"Because you look exhausted," she declared. If she was trying to be compassionate, she was failing to land the delivery.

Lanzhou leaned towards me. "Are you sleeping all right? We can get you medication for that."

I cringed at the thought. "I'm sleeping fine. I just cried a lot today." At least only half of that statement was a lie.

Jael studied me. "If you need a break, all you have to do is say something. If this is too much for you, I can send you back to Boston." The words were harsh, but her voice was too kind for it to be a threat. "We can do this remotely. I'll send John and Dowe with you."

"Road trip!" John cheered and went in for a high-five.

Dowe left him hanging. "Pretty sure we're going to have to fly."

I took a deep breath and tried to screw a lid back on my emotions. "No, I'm sorry, it's fine. I just—"

"No, I think that's a good idea," Lanzhou cut me off. He rose and faced Jael. "I really think she should go home. It's not safe here."

"Boston isn't exactly safe, either," Bowen argued. "And Mars is, regrettably, no longer an option."

I grimaced. He was right—there was no place for me on Mars anymore. My brother, Cea, and the rest of the residents had made it safely to the mining outpost, but it was so remote that Ephesus had difficulty getting a call through. It was only a temporary solution until we could figure out where to send them, and in the meantime, I couldn't even consult my brother for advice.

So much for keeping him involved.

Meanwhile, my friends in Boston weren't much better off. Stanyard had taken Ephesus's advice and convinced everyone to abandon the base. He'd sent his parents, his sister Mira, and my father to stay with friends, while he and a few others set up operations in another office building. Stanyard wouldn't tell me exactly where they were—just in case someone was listening to my calls.

"At least Boston is farther away from Councilwoman Mong." Lanzhou frowned at his cousin, a twinge of annoyance making it into his voice. "Look, we know the councilwoman did all of this to bait Philadelphia. Keeping her here is just tempting Mong to do something worse—and in the meantime, the entire Chinese surveillance state is helping track Philadelphia down. We'll have an advantage if we keep them apart and at least make the government work for it."

I swallowed as uncertainty gripped my chest. Everything Lanzhou was saying made sense—except it flew in the face of what God had promised me.

"I saw it all. You, in Beijing, as a Nolan, on even playing ground with Asia."

Bowen saw the same thing. "I disagree. Operation Blue Fire has twice as many followers here than it does in America, and this is where we need her most. If we can shake the government here, it will trickle down to other regions."

Jael drummed her acrylic nails on the table. "I tend to agree, as do the analytics on her videos."

"The analytics have nothing to do with where she records from," Lanzhou grunted. "I'd personally feel a lot better if she went home."

"Well, I wouldn't!" I raised my voice to be heard, desperate not to be left out of the conversation again. "I can't leave."

"Why not?" Lanzhou demanded, before checking the tone of his voice. He leaned on the table, eyes pleading with me. "Philadelphia, I promise you'll be just as effective from Boston as you would from—"

"Don't lie to her," Bowen snapped. "People will know if she leaves. It will weaken everything we've built here. Do you want to be responsible for that?"

Lanzhou folded his arms. "I don't want to be *responsible* for sacrificing a child."

"I'm not a child!" I protested, then realized I definitely sounded like one. I took a deep breath and tried to find the words that would make them understand. "Look, I won't leave until we find Nic."

"Philadelphia," Jael inserted, voice as smooth as unforgiving glass. "We've been over this. Nic is gone."

I felt the rage climb back up my throat. Why did everyone keep saying that? Nic was alive—I knew he was. Why was everyone else so quick to leave him for dead? Did he mean nothing to them?

Jael reached for my hand. "You need to let him go."

I jerked my wrist out of her grasp and shoved my chair back. "Well, I *can't!*"

It was only after the silence returned that I realized I was shouting again.

I winced. Since when had I become so angry? *This isn't like you.*

Jael shifted in her chair. "Philadelphia." It was a warning. "Are we going to have another incident?"

Shame flashed across my cheeks. "I'm sorry, I just..." I tried to lower my voice, but that just made me sound more pathetic, even to my ears. "I can't leave him, okay? He's like family, and besides, it's my fault he's in prison."

"No, Philadelphia, it isn't." Lanzhou's voice reached out to me, begging me to see his side. "You need to stop blaming yourself."

"Yes, it is! Do you know how many times he tried to get me to go back to Mars? He only came down here to save me, and he only got caught because of my *stupid chip.*"

No one denied it. I braced myself on the table and took a deep breath, trying and failing to find some clarity under the garbled emotions. "You're right," I admitted. "Asia is doing this because of me. And even now, I know that if I pick up the phone and call her, she'll tell me where he is. I could save him—I know I could. But he sacrificed himself for me, and now I have to just walk away and leave him for dead."

Tears stung my eyes. I tipped my head back and stared at the harsh fluorescents in the ceiling, hoping gravity would help me keep it together. "You have no idea what that feels like."

"Yes, I do."

I started and turned to Jael.

She wasn't looking at me. She picked up her tablet and swiped her fingers across the screen. The image on the projector changed to a cluttered dashboard of data and readouts.

"As an internet service provider, I control the algorithm on my network." Jael continued to narrate as she tabbed through submenus. "Every day, I get a new order from the government telling me what to censor and what to promote. I have to push the United's corrupted agenda—and suppress people and ideas I know are right."

She clicked a button, and a lengthy list of search terms appeared on the screen. She highlighted one and enlarged it so we could read it:

JEWISH GENOCIDE

I thought of Lev, the Russian teenager who worked for me back in Boston. He'd been orphaned by the government's attempt to purge America of race and religion. According to the statistics on Jael's screen, Brookline wasn't the only community the United had erased off the map.

I shivered and gripped my arms as a cold reminder prickled my skin. *This isn't about you.*

"I could fix this." Jael swiveled her chair to stare at the projection. "With one click, I could push this content to the front page and tell a third of the known world about the United's atrocities. I could end ignorance overnight. But I only get one chance before the government catches me and takes my job away." She tapped the tablet, and the projection went dark.

I stared at the bland wall where the image had been. She was right; she did understand how I felt. It would be maddening to know that I had the power to change everything but couldn't—and in the meantime, I was the primary weapon the United was using to enforce their rule.

"That's why I chose you."

I jerked out of my daze as she turned back to face me. She folded her hands on the table and leaned over to get in my line of vision. "I know exactly how you're feeling, and I can't promise that it will get any better. You're going to have to live with the weight of your decisions, and every day you're going to wake up, look in the mirror, and wonder who you've become. That's why you have to center your gravity on what you know is right, not on your feelings."

I let the tears fall. I already had that center. Even Nic knew what I had to do.

"Don't ever come back."

Jael found my hand. "So, I'll ask you again, Blue Fire: Can you handle this?"

12: PHILADELPHIA

It was almost five o'clock by the time we left the conference room.

"Who's ready for church? Besides me!" John cheered. He jumped up and slapped the doorframe with an agility that was terrifying for his age.

Dowe jostled my shoulder. "Race you to the cafeteria." He took off without waiting for an answer. John hollered and bolted after him, waving both arms above his head like an inflatable.

Bowen chuckled. "Yes, you should come with us." He encouraged me with a smile and started walking towards the elevator at a much calmer pace.

I forced myself to return the smile as I followed him. Being crammed in a room with hundreds of people—most of whom thought I was a war hero—sounded closer to hell than heaven, but I knew church was the best place for me.

Lanzhou picked up the rear as we descended into the basement of the factory. The Tangs hosted nightly services in the company cafeteria, where shift change concealed the flow of people in and out of the building. Several off-duty workers greeted me by name as we walked past the lockers and down the back hallway that led to the podium.

The thrum of chatter and prayer vibrated in the corridor, like a giant engine was rumbling in the walls. I peered around the corner and saw that the cafeteria was packed. You could barely see the stained plastic tables amongst the throng of excited worshippers. Had there been that many people the last time I visited?

Bowen unwittingly answered my question. "Attendance has nearly doubled since you started coming," he explained with a grin.

I felt a pressure form in my chest and tried to decide if it was joy or anxiety. "Won't that raise suspicion?" The Tangs had been hosting this church for over ten years without incident, but surely the government would notice if an extra thousand people started visiting the factory every night.

Lanzhou didn't seem concerned. "I might have to slip a little extra to my contact at the police station, but I'm not going to turn away hungry souls."

"Besides, people feel safe when you're here." Bowen grabbed a microphone off a stand and checked the battery.

I stared at him. "They do?"

Instead of answering, he handed me the microphone. "Will you come on stage with us?"

All my panic lodged in my throat as the weight of the microphone settled in my hands like a dead body. I was the last person who should be on stage. I was emotional and sleep-deprived, and I hadn't heard from God in what felt like years. But I didn't want to admit that in so many words, so instead I stuttered, "I-I don't know what to say."

"Then don't say anything." Bowen pressed his thumb to a locked cabinet door. It beeped and popped open, revealing a stack of contraband Bibles. "Just worship. That's what people really need to see."

He made it sound so simple, but I wasn't sure I had the soul to put on a show tonight. All I wanted to do was curl up on the floor at the altar and beg God for mercy. I needed the worship to carry *me*—how could I carry someone else?

"What do I do?" I asked the question aloud, but I wasn't really talking to any of them.

Bowen's expression softened, and I could see that the revolutionary had been replaced by the pastor. "What is the Spirit asking you to do?"

Nothing. I searched my soul, but there was only dark, cavernous silence. Just like there had been for weeks.

Bowen laid his hand on my shoulder. "Remember, worship isn't about feelings—it's about obedience. If you don't hear anything, do what you know you should do, and the rest will catch up."

Lanzhou joined the conversation. "Your mind, will, and emotions are yours to control. So, tell them what to do." He reached into a closet and pulled out a suit jacket. "'Why, my soul, are you downcast?'"

"You want a list?" I muttered, and too late realized I'd used real words.

Lanzhou winked as he shrugged on the jacket. "David also had a lot to complain about—but he wrote a whole psalm telling himself what to do."

"'Praise the Lord, my soul, and forget not all his benefits'!" Bowen echoed, his voice tripping on the edge of song. He guided me gently towards the stairs that led to the podium. "You don't have to use the microphone if you don't want to. Just help me show the people what kind of God we serve."

I instinctively followed him onto the stage, even though I couldn't remember making a conscious decision to move. I felt the shift in the crowd— the excited murmurs as the center of attention tipped to one side—as soon as I walked onto the platform. I forced a pretty smile, the same one I put on for the camera, and avoided looking anyone in the eye.

Bowen took center stage and greeted the crowd in Mandarin. He was repaid with cheers and shouts, the only word of which I understood was "Amen." Lanzhou then took over, pacing back and forth as he read from his Bible. I listened politely to the foreign words and fidgeted with the jade bangle around my wrist. The jewelry had been given to me by this very congregation as a reminder that they were interceding for my protection. I'd barely taken it off since, and I could only hope they were still praying for me.

Because at the moment, I didn't even know how to pray for myself.

Another leader I didn't recognize struck up an a cappella song. Almost everyone was singing in Mandarin, so I turned my microphone off and did just what Bowen suggested: I went through the motions. I sang along in tongues, I bowed when everyone else bowed, and I raised my hands when anyone took the stage to pray. I did everything I knew how to do and threw my whole body into it, desperate to feel anything besides confusion and fear.

I never did. I slipped into the rhythm of the service and participated along with everybody else, but all my actions felt empty. I'm sure I looked holy and passionate to an observer, but I knew I wasn't there, no matter how much I wanted to be. It was like my body wasn't even mine anymore.

I knew what it felt like to lose control to the Holy Spirit. This wasn't it.

This was death.

✳

It was 3am, and I was nowhere near sleeping.

Even Tommy had given up on me. Annoyed by my constant tossing and turning, he'd vacated the bed and claimed a spot on the windowsill. With the shutters closed, the ledge was incredibly narrow; half his legs dangled off, and he looked like he could end up on the floor at any moment. But apparently that was still preferable to lying next to me.

I didn't blame him. Every few minutes, I flipped over, contorting this way and that, searching for the center of gravity that would make it all go away. But as soon as I laid still, as soon as I stopped rustling on the sheets, the silence came back, and with it the keen knowledge that my heart was racing. I could practically hear my thoughts echoing in the room as they whipped around and around without purpose.

I finally gave up and turned the bedside lamp on. If I was going to lie awake, I might as well read. At least then my mind would be filled with something other than unanswered questions.

I grabbed my backpack and pulled out the paper Bible Stanyard had given me. It was a vintage black leather-bound volume, one of the most beautiful—and illegal—things I owned.

I fingered the slight water damage on the corner. I hadn't spent much time reading the Bible lately—maybe that was my problem.

Propping myself on the pillows, I opened the book to a random page. I flipped through my favorite passages, searching for inspiration. Eventually, I landed on the chapter with my name on it, as I often did.

"See, I have placed before you an open door that no one can shut."

I sighed and tapped the page. *I sure don't feel like any doors are opening for me right now, God.*

Before I could wait for an answer, my tablet pinged. I knew without looking who it was: Stanyard.

It had been incredibly hard to hide my insomnia from him, if only because the time difference meant I was awake when he was online and working. I knew I should tell him what was going on; he'd want to know. But I was so afraid that if anyone found out I wasn't sleeping, the Tangs would put me back on medication, and then I wouldn't have control over my life—or my actions—anymore. So, I'd kept my mouth shut and avoided reading Stanyard's messages late at night so he wouldn't know I was awake.

He'd been busy today; this was probably the fifth time he'd messaged me. I set my Bible on the bedspread and took my tablet off its charger. I couldn't open the app, or he would know I'd read his messages. I also couldn't turn off that feature; I knew I'd get a lecture about it. Instead, I swiped through the previews on my home screen.

FINALLY FINISHED DECRYPTING THE CODE ON YOUR CHIP. YOU WERE RIGHT—THERE'S TWO SETS OF DNA ON HERE.

I chewed my lip. In some weird way, I was relieved to know that my chip *had* been coded to kill the General Secretary. At least I didn't go through all the pain and terror of resisting Jayde for nothing.

But that also meant I was right about everything else: Someone was trying to kill Nic.

But who? A flip through the rest of Stanyard's messages confirmed we weren't any closer to answering that question.

IF IT WAS DATA, HE CLEARLY DIDN'T TELL JAYDE. I CAN FIND ABSOLUTELY NO EVIDENCE ON THE SERVER THAT JAYDE HAD ANY IDEA WHAT WAS GOING ON. IN FACT, I DON'T THINK ANYONE ON BASE KNEW ABOUT IT.

THE ONLY TIME NIC IS MENTIONED IN THE LAST MONTH IS WHEN I CALLED HIM.

I remembered. Jayde and I had been deep in planning the assassination. It was a blackout mission, so I couldn't even talk to Stanyard. I'd spent all my time in the shooting range, training to kill. Stanyard saw I was on a downward spiral and alerted Nic.

THERE'S A RECORD OF THE CALL BECAUSE I MADE IT FROM BASE, AND JAYDE MUST HAVE SEEN IT. HE TEXTED DATA AND A FEW OTHERS.

The message was followed by a screenshot. The text in the thumbnail was too small to read, but I knew what had happened. Jayde had realized that Stanyard was trying to talk me out of the mission. He knew Stanyard was a threat; that's why he used him as blackmail. No wonder he'd been watching the security cameras in the range the next day and saw when Stanyard and I kissed.

I pinched my tablet until the screen flashed up a warning. *We should have been more careful.*

I forced my fingers to relax and scrolled to Stanyard's last message.

I'LL KEEP DIGGING. THIS DOESN'T COMPLETELY RULE OUT THAT DATA IS INVOLVED—BUT IT'S NOT LOOKING LIKELY. EVERYTHING I'VE FOUND FROM DATA SUGGESTS HE SUPPORTS YOU. HE EVEN BLACKLISTED JAYDE AND REVOKED HIS ACCESS CODES AFTER JAYDE KIDNAPPED YOU.

I read the last sentence a second time. The fact that Data hated Jayde didn't necessarily mean he could be trusted—but it was certainly a point in his favor.

I tossed the tablet on the bed and buried my chin in a pillow. Some of my anxiety drifted away, leaving confusion in its place. Stanyard was right; just because there was no activity on the base's server didn't mean anything. Data—or even Jayde—could have been smart and avoided talking about it while they were on base. But seeing as there was a bunch of other sensitive information on the server—including, apparently, the fact that Jayde had been planning to hold Stanyard hostage—that didn't seem likely. Since neither Data nor Jayde had an obvious motive for killing Nic, I was beginning to favor the simple solution: It wasn't anyone on base.

But if Jayde and Data didn't want Nic dead, then who did?

Another message came through. I tapped the screen and read the notification.

CALL ME WHEN YOU GET UP. THERE'S SOMEONE WHO WANTS TO TALK TO YOU.

He followed it with a smiling emoji, which I found mildly horrifying. Stanyard *never* used emojis. How was I supposed to interpret that? Was that a good sign or a bad sign?

Curiosity overcame my resolve. I wasn't in any danger of sleeping anyway.

After putting on a sweater and smoothing my hair, I opened the app and dialed Stanyard.

He answered immediately. "Phil! What are you doing up? My texts didn't wake you, did they?"

"No," I begrudgingly admitted. "I couldn't sleep."

His video connected. He squinted at the camera, but my face was half in shadow thanks to the soft light of the bedside lamp. Hopefully that meant he couldn't see how bloodshot my eyes were.

"How long has this been going on?" he prompted.

I shrugged dismissively. "It's no big deal—"

"Phil," he cut me off, but not unkindly. "You promised."

I flinched. He was right—I did promise. And if I couldn't trust him with something as simple as this, how could I trust him with anything else?

"You say you trust me. So, start trusting me with things."

"About two weeks," I confessed.

"Why didn't you tell me sooner?"

I avoided his eyes. "Because I was afraid that if I told anyone, the Tangs would try to put me back on medication. I can't take any more pills." I swallowed the shame and forced the truth out. "I don't trust myself on medication—not after what happened."

I braced myself for the disappointment, but it never came. "Thank you for telling me how you feel," he said gently. "I'll talk to Mrs. Nolan. Surely there's something else you can do besides medication."

According to the government, Mrs. Nolan was Andromeda's mother. We'd never been family, but I did trust her—and she was a nurse. If anyone would know what to do, it was her.

I looked back into the camera. "Thank you." I took a breath and was surprised to find that my chest didn't feel as tight.

You can trust him.

Stanyard sealed the deal with a warm smile. "Since you're awake… are you up to talking to someone?"

"Yeah, that's why I called. What's with the emoji? Are you feeling okay?"

He chuckled and stood up. "You'll see. It's good news, I promise."

The camera swung to a view of the ceiling as he started walking. I watched the fluorescent lights flash by and tried to match his anticipation. Who would want to talk to me, and why didn't they just call me themselves?

A door opened. "Hey," Stanyard greeted someone off-screen. "She's actually awake, so if you're up to talking now…"

The other person must have nodded an affirmative, because the camera jerked again as the device was handed off. The stranger waited until Stanyard had left and shut the door, then lifted the camera to his face. I sucked in my breath.

Dad.

13: PHILADELPHIA

My father looked exactly as he had on the day we'd been separated. You couldn't tell he'd been frozen and revived—if anything, he looked *too* young, the freshly-regenerated skin replacing the wrinkles that should have been there. But his hair was still feathered with a tired gray, and his eyes were still framed with crow's feet that weren't quite happy as he gazed at me with an unreadable expression.

I stared back, unable to formulate words. It had been over two months since I'd spoken to my dad, and suddenly, I was afraid to. There was so much I needed to say, but all the words felt trapped underneath the apology it was too late to give, like water at the bottom of a freezing lake.

To my surprise, he initiated. "Philadelphia?"

I gasped. "You-you know who I am? But how—"

He raised a hand, as if to pause my racing heart. "Stanyard has been telling me all about you—about us."

"He has?" My breath caught in my throat again, but this time, it wasn't a painful feeling.

My dad nodded. "He's visited me every day and told me stories, showed me pictures... He repeats everything multiple times and makes me recite it back to him. It's like being in, ah..." He hesitated, like the chip in his brain was struggling to find the word. "...School."

I could picture the scene—and realized, perhaps for the first time, just how much Stanyard loved me.

"I wish I could say I remembered it for myself." My dad sighed, and doubt flickered across his expression like lightning behind a cloud. "But from what he's described, you sound like an..." he searched for the words, "...intelligent, courageous young woman, and I should be proud to have you as a daughter."

I blinked away warm tears. "He may have embellished my resume slightly. Did he... tell you about what's going on between us?"

Dad squinted at the camera. "What about you two?"

Heat crawled across my cheeks, and I could see in the playback monitor that I had turned bright red. Why was it so embarrassing to say it out loud? Literally everybody else knew about it.

"Is there something I should know?"

My father arched one eyebrow—and I burst out laughing. The gesture was too cute to be stern, and I abruptly realized just how much I had missed this.

"Stanyard and I are dating," I managed after I swallowed my giggles. "And, I guess after all that's happened, I never expected to be talking to my dad about boys."

"That does explain a lot," my father admitted with something close to a smile. "I'm afraid I don't know enough about either of you yet to give an opinion, but from what I've seen of him, he seems like a good man."

"He is." I sank back against the pillows, letting the silence of the quiet night return. I wanted to float away on this feeling—this sense that, for the first time in a long time, something was right in the world. Asia had taken a lot from me this week, but I hadn't lost everything.

Thank you, Jesus.

Dad seemed uncomfortable with the lull in conversation, so I sat back up. "How are you feeling?"

"I've only got a couple weeks' experience to compare it to," he grunted with a morbid attempt at humor, "but better."

"And your... mind?" I wasn't sure what I was asking, but I wanted to know everything.

"I'd be lying if I said it wasn't frustrating that everyone expects me to have fifty years of life experience when I can only remember the last three weeks," he snapped.

I cringed. "I'm sorry, we don't have to talk about it."

"No, I'm sorry. I'm just tired." He rubbed his head self-consciously. "I know everyone's trying to help, and they tell me it's working."

I swallowed when I remembered who "they" were. "I heard Data helped you with your speech," I said, parsing my words slowly to keep the suspicion out of them.

My dad nodded. "It was dis... disorienting at first—to go from not being able to find the words for anything to suddenly knowing a dictionary. But it really did help."

I picked at the bedspread. "Has he been taking good care of you?"

"He's nice. I haven't seen him much this week," Dad commented, unbothered. "It's been... the big guy with the tattoos?"

I helped him out. "Andes." Andes was a Scotsman who, like Seoul, was willing to perform all kinds of procedures outside the law. He'd done my tattoo and implanted the wiring for my chip, and he'd overseen my dad's revival.

"Yeah, him. They said they're going to try and help me recover my science degrees next. If a chip can expand my vocabulary, maybe it can teach me chemistry, too." He flicked his finger against his temple like one might kick a delinquent vending machine.

I stiffened. *If Seoul can get me one of those memory devices, I can bring all of you back.*

"It won't be the same as if I learned it from scratch, but maybe if I start doing it, muscle memory will kick in. I don't know." He groaned, and for a second, I could see all of the hopelessness and pain clouding his expression. "I just wish I could remember some of this for myself."

I pinched my eyes shut. How I wanted to tell him that it might be possible, that we might be able to recover what he lost. But I knew I shouldn't get his hopes up until I had the device in my hand. The last I'd heard from Seoul was that she had a lead, but she still didn't have a timeline—or a price.

Please, God. Grant me favor.

"Just like I wish I could remember you."

I looked back down at the screen. My father's face had softened as he studied me. I realized, in his mind, he was seeing his daughter for the first time. I brushed my bleached hair behind my ears and wished I could be the girl he'd left behind.

"I want… I want to talk with you more." His voice tripped as he struggled to overcome the barrier between us. "I want to get to know you again. If I can."

"Of course, Dad," I whispered, fighting tears. "I'll call as often as you want."

He frowned. "Are you not coming back to Boston?"

I stiffened. "Did someone say I was?"

"No, I just assumed you were." He visibly leaned way from the screen. "Your family is here, after all."

"I'm sorry, I didn't mean it like that." I tried to shove past the doubts that cluttered my mind like books upended off a case. "But I can't leave Nic behind."

"Who?"

"Nic, my…" *My other parent.* "The man who came over to China with me."

"Oh, him." My father's eyes darkened. "I don't think you should wait for him. He's not your responsibility." He said it flippantly, callously—just like everyone else I'd talked to today.

"I have to! It's my fault, okay?" I shouted, and then caught myself too late.

My father flinched and looked confused, like a dog that had been kicked for no reason. I glanced away as shame burned behind my ears. I was probably the first person to yell at him since he woke up.

"I'm sorry, I shouldn't have shouted," I whispered. "It's just... everyone keeps telling me I should leave him behind. But I *can't*."

"Why not?" This time, the question was gentle.

Because it's not supposed to be this way. This wasn't right—I knew it wasn't. God didn't bring Nic back to life just to kill him again, and He didn't drag both of us to China without a reason. We had a purpose for being here. I couldn't give up on that—I *wouldn't* give up on that. I was supposed to be in Beijing, even if no one else but Nic could see that.

But I couldn't explain all that to my father. He was confused enough already; listening to me rant about an open vision some strange man had about me would push him over the edge. So instead, I told him the other half of the truth: "I can't leave him behind because he didn't leave me behind."

My father seemed to accept that answer. He nursed the silence for a minute before responding. "Look, I don't know this man, and from what little I've heard, I'm not sure I like him."

I chuckled as the air came back into the room. I'd feel the same way if I'd only gotten the synopsis of Nic's life. "There's another half to the story. I'll tell you, when you're ready."

My dad acknowledged the offer with a half-smile. "But I've heard a *lot* about you, and if everything they're saying is true, then I know you won't give up."

I focused on his face again. He shifted in his chair and leaned towards the camera, closing the gap he'd created. "To hear Stanyard tell it, you don't give up on anything or anyone. You keep fighting even when you know you'll lose. That's why they picked you to be... what is it again? 'Blue Fire'?"

I gripped the tablet as my father's words muddled with Jael's in my mind.

"I only get one chance. That's why I chose you."

"I won't pretend that I understand anything that's going on," my dad admitted, "but if this man means that much to you, then you should fight for him. Just like you fought for me."

He offered a sad smile. I returned it, not bothering to stop the tears this time. "Thanks, Dad. I love you."

"Give me some time," he murmured, choking on his own tears, "and I think I'll be able to say the same thing about you."

The light in the room behind him shifted as a door opened off-screen. "Thomas, are you—oh, sorry, didn't know you were on a call."

"Tower!" I called, recognizing my uncle's voice.

My dad looked up at his brother-in-law as he walked into frame. "'Tower'?" he questioned.

"Old codename. You used to be Catalyst." Tower clapped my father on the shoulder and greeted me with a nod. "Good to see you, Phil. I won't interrupt."

My father started to rise. "No, that's okay."

I could tell he was exhausted from the conversation, so I gave him an out. "I actually want to talk to Tower—I mean, Uncle Bart, if that's okay."

Dad nodded gratefully and handed the tablet over to Tower. My uncle waited until my father had walked away and the door had shut behind him before claiming the vacant chair. "'Uncle Bart,' eh? Sounds weird coming from you," he chided.

I had to agree. Tower had been estranged for most of my life, and it wasn't until several months after I met him that he decided to admit we were related. Mom's death—a tragedy my dad was partly responsible for—had made everything more complicated than it should have been. "We can stick with Tower. You two seem to be getting along, though," I noted with a twinge of happiness.

"I think he likes me better now that he can't remember me." My uncle smiled, but I could tell the gesture didn't make it to his sunken eyes.

"Thanks for taking care of him," I offered.

"We'll always be family, Phil," he deferred. "But that's not what we need to talk about it, is it?"

I sighed. "No, it's not."

He mercifully took the lead. "Heard you met Jael."

"Yeah. When were you going to tell me?" I accused, even as I wondered how many times I'd have to open conversations with my uncle like this. Tower had met Jael several months ago. They'd both known about the assassination plot, and they'd mutually agreed to send me to Beijing with Jayde. John and Dowe, Jael's agents, were supposed to intercept me before I got to the General.

That plan had failed miserably, but I didn't blame Jael or Tower for John and Dowe's mistakes. What I wanted to know was why my uncle had seen fit to send me on a suicide run without telling me.

Tower shook his head listlessly, as if he didn't know the answer to that question either. "I didn't trust Jayde. I had no idea how many allies he had, and I didn't want you to get hurt."

That wasn't the first time I'd heard that excuse, but it didn't hold water. "You literally drove me home the night before we left. If you were worried about my safety, you could have gotten me out of town."

Of course, it wouldn't have been the first time my uncle had the power to get me to safety—but didn't.

He stared at me long and hard from somewhere under his mop of disobedient hair. "If you want the boring answer, I was just following orders. Jael wanted you in Beijing. She knew you would be more effective there than in Boston."

I sighed. My uncle wasn't telling me anything I didn't already know—I was here because Jael was in control.

"And I agreed with her."

I looked back down at the screen. "Then you think I should be here?"

"Still do," he consented without emotion.

I tapped my fingers on the back of my tablet nervously. "Everyone else thinks I should come home. They say it's not safe here."

"'Everyone else' doesn't know how to fight a war," he returned. "And no, it's not safe. I didn't send you to Beijing because I thought it was safe. I sent you to Beijing because I knew you could win."

I swallowed as my heart started thrumming in the back of my throat. Maybe Nic wasn't the only person who saw the truth.

Tower leaned towards the camera, his posture conveying the urgency his drawling voice did not. "This is war, Phil. I'm not your uncle—I'm your ally. And if you're going to survive out there, you need to start thinking of the world in those terms."

I had to admit that this whole ordeal would have been a lot easier had I not expected Tower to act like family. Maybe that was why he never wanted to tell me we were related.

"You need to pick your battles and fight to win," he continued sternly. "There are people—like your boyfriend—who aren't going to agree with your decisions. But you're not a civilian anymore, and you can't afford to think like one."

I glanced at the bedside table, where I'd abandoned my wig and hair clip earlier in the evening. The feather glowed a dull blue in the diffused light of the lamp. Was that what I was now—a soldier?

"So yes, I think you should stay in Beijing." Tower settled back in the chair, as if he'd done his duty and was clocking out. "But I'm not your commanding officer. Jael is."

With a familiar check in my spirit, I remembered that she wasn't my only "commanding officer." I answered to Someone Else—and He had made it explicitly clear that He wanted me in China.

"So, what are your orders, Blue Fire?" my uncle prodded.

"'Wake the people up,'" I recited. That's what Jael was always saying, but I realized, as soon as the words left my mouth, that she wasn't the only one speaking it over me.

Wake My people up.

I dropped the tablet in my lap and gripped the bedspread with both hands. Suddenly, I knew what God was saying. I couldn't explain how I knew. I hadn't heard a voice, but the knowledge was so overwhelming that it was like a concrete object I could hold. I felt the pressure in my chest and the motion in the Spirit that told me it was the Lord.

I glanced at my open Bible. With my finger, I traced back a few verses to the letter to the church in Sardis:

"Wake up! Strengthen what remains and is about to die, for I have found your deeds unfinished in the sight of my God. Remember, therefore, what you have received and heard; hold it fast, and repent. But if you do not wake up, I will come like a thief, and you will not know at what time I will come to you."

I pressed my palm flat on the book. *This* was my purpose. This was why I was here. This was why Blue Fire existed.

Because it was time to wake up.

"There she is," my uncle chuckled, and for the first time, some joy made it into his voice. "I can see it in your eyes—you figured it out."

I blinked as the room came back into focus. "Yeah, I guess so."

"Glad to be of assistance. Now, how can I help you succeed, lieutenant?"

He said it with a wink, but I knew he was serious. Only trouble was, I had no idea how to answer him. How *could* he help? How could anyone help? Of course, he could promote my videos, but everyone did that. There had to be something more that he could do—there had to be something more that *I* could do.

Tommy finally decided to join me on the bed. He jumped up in my lap and flicked his tail against my chin, demanding attention. I absentmindedly stroked him as I let the thoughts churn over in my mind.

If this was my calling, then I wanted to do more. Spamming the internet with propaganda videos would only go so far, and Operation Blue Fire was a little over a month away. We needed more people and more support. I couldn't just sit back in my glitzy recording studio and hope everything turned out all right. There had to be more to Blue Fire than looking pretty in front of a camera.

I stiffened as Bowen's words came rolling back to me.

"Attendance has nearly doubled since you started coming. People feel safe when you're here."

"What is it?" Tower prodded.

I pushed Tommy aside and picked up the tablet. "I have an idea."

14: NIC

"Q, I thought we had an agreement never to speak to each other again," Warden Ivanova cooed as she perched on the edge of her desk.

I gestured with cuffed hands. "In my defense, if my plan had worked, we *wouldn't* be talking."

Regrettably, Warden Ivanova and I had gotten thoroughly acquainted over the past week. My attempts to escape had ensured that we'd talked almost daily.

The first few infractions were minor; I was mainly gathering data on the effectiveness of their security systems. But yesterday I'd tried to hack the controls on the elevator that led out of the complex. When that failed, I'd attempted to break into the maintenance shaft and hitch a ride down. That had also failed, and after they'd dredged me out of the bottom of the maintenance shaft (I don't want to talk about it), they hauled me straight to the warden's office.

"As much as I'm enjoying our chats, I really don't have time to entertain your repeated stupidity." She sighed and contemplated the contents of her mug.

"Neither do I, frankly." I drummed my fingers on my knees and wondered what deterrent she'd try this time. The fact that they'd dragged me to her office made me hopeful that I wouldn't be thrown over the railing, at least.

"Unfortunately," she slammed her mug down on the desk, "you don't seem to be motivated by pain, and I'm under strict orders from Mong not to kill you intentionally."

I filled in the blanks. "But accidents do happen."

"Frequently," she admitted. "But you've only been here, what, a week? That's a bit early for me to be losing my patience. I don't think she'll buy that story."

"Regrettably for both of us, you're probably right." I had no doubts Asia was keeping me alive like an ace in her back pocket, and that, weirdly, would be my saving grace. "So, same time tomorrow?"

"I'll clear my afternoon." Warden Ivanova jumped off the desk. "But factor this into your calculations, Q: Whatever Mong wants you for, it has an expiration. As soon as she's done with you, if you haven't fallen in line, I'll be collecting my vengeance with interest."

"Noted. Moving on, what are you feeling like today?" I hoped whatever torture she picked was short; I had to get back to my cell and plan for tomorrow.

"Honestly, Q, I've had a bad day," she whined, like we were friends commiserating over coffee. She walked over to the wall and surveyed the weapons she had hanging there. "Production is down, and the big boss docked my pay."

"That does sound terrible," I admitted. "Do you need to talk about it?"

"I think a nice, old-fashioned beating would relieve the stress, if you're offering." She yanked a baton off its hook and turned to me.

"Happy to be of service," I grunted, and braced myself.

✳

The beating did wonders, and by the time Warden Ivanova was finished with me, her mood had turned completely around. She was so grateful for my help that she told me to take the rest of the week off.

I spent the first forty-eight hours of my vacation in the infirmary, getting my bones put back together, and the remaining seventy-two locked in solitary confinement. The privacy was welcome; I needed to rework my escape plans.

There was only one problem: My plans didn't need to be reworked.

The more I ran the simulations in my mind, the more I realized there was nothing wrong with my theories. My calculations were flawless, as they always were. I had spent every waking hour cataloging how this prison was run. I had memorized the guards' rotations, the prisoners' shifts, and the timing of deliveries. I knew exactly where everyone was supposed to be at any given moment, and I could tamper with every machine in a dozen ways. There was absolutely no logical reason one or more of my attempts shouldn't have succeeded.

And yet, all of my plans had failed for the most inane reasons. The first time, my wrench broke. The second time, the guard who was supposed to be on shift overslept. The third time—when I'd tried to break into the elevator shaft—we had the warmest temperatures on record (which is saying something when you're 20,000 feet in the air). That threw off the pressure in the shaft and caused the maintenance hatch to stick.

As a scientist, I was always prepared for unexpected variables. But this was too ridiculous to be coincidental. The fact that they'd recorded a double-digit temperature for the first time in a hundred years made me wonder if something—or Someone—didn't want me to escape.

"Look," I said, breaking the silence in my cold cell, "I could use Your help with this."

There was no response. He hadn't said much for the past week. And even though I got way more done when I was the only one talking, I was smart enough to know that silence in the Spirit was rarely a good sign.

"Let me rephrase." I took a deep breath to filter the frustration out of my tone. "I *need* Your help with this. I can't do this without You."

That must have been one of His favorite phrases, because He responded immediately.

You didn't ask Me if I wanted you to leave.

I shot a glare at the corner of the room next to the door, because that's where I'd decided, arbitrarily, that He was standing. "I thought it was implied. In case You forgot, the teenager *You* told me to take care of is stranded by herself *in China*, and she's trying to lead a revolution. And, unless there was a typo in that vision You sent me, You wanted me to help her."

I don't do typos.

"Exactly. So, I think our highest priority should be getting me out of jail."

It's certainly your highest priority.

I heard the pause—that breath of air that told me God was about to leave the chat and let me simmer in my own thoughts—and realized what He was implying.

"What? You really want me to stay here and freeze while she's out there alone?"

He would have arched an eyebrow had He had one. I stood up and gestured broadly at the corner.

"That's Your endgame? Leave me to rot in prison while she fights and dies in a war she doesn't understand?"

And what if it is?

"Then we have a problem."

There was silence—one opportunity for me to repent.

Then He took the cue and left, leaving the room colder than before.

I shivered in solitary for another twelve hours, and then they finally decided I could play with the other kids again. I sulked down to mess hall to get my first hot meal in five days.

I walked into the cafeteria and was alarmed to find that the place was packed. A rough calculation told me there were 37% more workers crammed in the greasy room than usual, which could only mean one thing: They'd served two shifts at the same time. That never happened.

I tried to swallow the rock that spawned in my stomach. *What are You up to?*

I was a little surprised when He responded. *I thought you were hungry.*

I was actually considering starting a forty-day fast. I already have a three-day head start.

I didn't ask you to fast. Get in there.

The inmate behind me in line encouraged me with his elbows, so I obeyed begrudgingly. I grabbed my rations and then wandered around the room for ten minutes, looking for an empty table. There wasn't one, so I chose the lesser of two evils and picked a table with only two people at it.

I realized I'd made a mistake when one of them saw me approach and started waving.

"*Hola*, Q!"

I halted a safe distance away. "Do I know you?"

"No, but everyone heard about your stunt in the maintenance shaft. Is it true they had to use old cooking grease to get you loose?" The little man propped his elbows on the table and waited eagerly for my answer.

"It was clean oil," I mumbled. "And the pressure in the shaft was off."

The other man at the table spoke up. "That's because the insulation in that corridor is not up to code." His heavy German accent made the words so thick they dragged on the floor. "They should be using insulation with an R-value of at least 80, but I'm pretty sure that shaft has R-60, at best."

"It looked like R-55 to me," I started, then caught myself. "Wait, who are you, again?"

"Oh, my apologies. I'm Vance." He nodded his head.

"Ryan!" the other guy volunteered. "You going to sit down or what?"

I did so hesitantly, studying them from across the table. The two were so proportionately imbalanced that it was a wonder the bench didn't tip over. Vance was so big and hulking that if he claimed to be three full-size men in a trench coat, I would have believed him. Every square inch of him was packed with dense muscles, and cruel scars decorated his face and hands like battle trophies. His dirty blond hair shadowed his stonewalled face as he hunched over the table, like he was a giant who condescended to live with us mere mortals.

Ryan, on the other hand, had to stretch every vertebra in his spine to be seen over the edge of the table. He was a compact man who acted like a windup toy whose gear and been cranked one too many times. All his motions were broad and dramatic, like he constantly overshot how far he had to move his limbs. He was investing way too much energy into everything, including breathing; I was getting exhausted just watching him, and I had only been blessed by his presence for sixty seconds.

"Whatcha in for, Q?" he chirped. His voice was about seventeen pitches too high for my comfort, and his perky Hispanic accent wasn't helping.

"Breaking my girlfriend's heart," I deadpanned, which wasn't entirely inaccurate. "You?"

"Domestic terrorism," he replied around a mouthful of food. "Apparently I organized an incredibly successful riot in Shanghai."

I knew better than to ask, but I was a glutton for punishment. "'Apparently'?" I prodded.

He scratched the back of his neck like an anxious dog. "Yeah, so, I was *trying* to organize a demonstration in San Antonio. But I outsourced the distribution of the pamphlets to this Chinese factory, and apparently there was a miscommunication, because the papers got printed in Mandarin instead of Spanish…"

"That's what you get for not supporting American jobs," Vance grunted.

Ryan shrugged and made a drawn-out "aye" sound, punctuated with a flap of his hands. "So, I'm not exactly sure what I organized, but it was very successful—enough that they extradited me here."

A random prisoner walking by our table must have overheard the comment, because he stopped and declared, "Best riot ever!" He offered Ryan a high-five, which he returned, although he practically had to stand on the bench to reach it.

I guess Philadelphia isn't the only one guilty of accidental terrorism, I thought, and then paused when the memory made me unduly sad.

Ryan sat back down and turned to me with a grin. "People keep telling me I should organize another one. I don't know if you'd be interested in something like that—you reckon you'd be interested?"

"No, but I know someone I can pass your information along to," I returned. I leaned back on the bench so I could look up at Vance. "And what's your story?" I figured I might as well get all the annoying pleasantries out of the way now, so if we were unfortunate enough to meet again, we could spare ourselves the misery of small talk.

He laid his fork down and cleared his throat. "It's quite complicated…"

"Sorry I asked," I muttered.

He kept going. "In fact, had I reported the numbers differently, what I did would not have been considered a crime in most jurisdictions. But in the United's Consolidated Tax Code, there's a subset of ordinance 1023(c)4 that states—"

"You lost me at 'subset,'" I cut him off. "In stupid people's terms, please?"

He hesitated for a long moment, like he had to mentally edit down his speech. "I committed what you Americans would call tax fraud."

I stared at him. That was a way less exciting explanation than I was hoping for, and suddenly, I was having painful flashbacks to my last time in prison. "You guys don't happen to know a John Dowe, do you?"

"John Dowe? Isn't that the guy they just brought into the morgue?" Ryan asked.

Vance slapped a hand on the table. "No, that's Tony. I keep telling them, but they won't believe me. If they pull the dental records, they'll see I'm telling the truth."

I leaned my elbows on the table and pinched my temples. "What are the odds?" I moaned.

"Odds of what?" Vance asked.

I stopped rubbing my head long enough to glare at him. "Huh?"

"You said 'what are the odds.' I can't calculate the odds unless I have all the data points. What probability are you trying to estimate?"

The statement was delivered without even the tiniest hint of sarcasm, and I abruptly realized that Vance and I would not get along well.

I swung my legs over the bench and stood up.

"Hey, you didn't eat!" Ryan protested.

"I'm late for my shift," I lied, and strode towards the door.

I was almost to the hall when the Lord stopped me. *You turn around and head right back to that table, young man.*

"Why should I?" I snapped.

It hit me like a lightning strike. I stumbled against the door frame as my mind briefly left this plane of existence. The images flashed by too rapidly for me to discern all the details, but I saw enough to know that the vision was about Vance and Ryan—and the Lord had big things planned.

God waited until I repossessed my body before speaking again. *Don't ask questions you don't want the answers to.*

"All right then, I won't," I returned, and went to take another step.

He slapped me with it again. I could make out more of the details this time. It had something to do with this factory—and I was right there with them.

I shouted a choice word I probably shouldn't have used in the presence of the Lord. "Really?" I yelled, throwing my hands up to the ceiling. "Is this really what You want?"

Several guards looked my way, but they quickly decided that me shouting like a deranged idiot at empty space wasn't enough of a threat, and their attention drifted.

I realized I'd better make my conversation internal before someone else tried to join it. *I thought we went over this yesterday—I need to get back to Phil.*

Stop using her as an excuse.

I froze as all my arguments shriveled up and died.

He took advantage of my rare state of speechlessness. *I meant what I said. But you can't even obey Me long enough to sit at a table and have lunch with two friendly guys. Why should I trust you to take care of Philadelphia?*

I grimaced as the conviction rolled over me. He was right—Philadelphia *didn't* need me, not in this state. She didn't need another father who was selfish, reckless, and stubborn.

She already had one of those.

The silence in the heavens was patient and forgiving. I closed my eyes, took a deep breath—and gave up.

All right. If there's something You want me to do in this prison, show me.

I just did.

I tugged on my mustache. *Do I really have to bring* them *along for the ride?*

For an answer, a fragment of the vision flashed through my mind again—and it was definitely Vance and Ryan standing there.

"Will You stop that!" I protested aloud.

I told you not to ask questions you didn't want the answers to.

I groaned. Clearly, I wouldn't make any progress towards my goal until I helped Vance and Ryan achieve theirs. "Fine! I'm going!" I conceded. "But I'm pretty sure this qualifies as blackmail."

He didn't deny it. I spun on my heel, ignoring the amused stares from the guards, and strode back to the table.

Ryan saw me approach and waved wildly, as if I was in danger of walking past them. I marched up and leaned my knuckles on the table. "All right! We can be friends," I announced.

"Yay!" Ryan cheered.

"Who said anything about being friends?" Vance grunted.

I lifted my hand. "On one condition."

"Anything," Ryan swore.

"Not you." I turned to Vance. "There's one thing I need to make perfectly clear, sir."

He arched a bushy eyebrow.

"About 95% of the questions I ask are rhetorical and should *not* be answered. Understood?" I stabbed my finger in his face for emphasis.

His eyebrow relaxed as his face flatlined again. "I make no promises."

15: PHILADELPHIA

I hid in the shadows in the hallway, once again preparing to go out on stage and speak to the congregation. Only this time, it wasn't the Tangs' church. This time, I would be ministering to a congregation in the neighboring city of Tianjin.

I'd attended five churches in as many days. Most of the pastors had been friends of Bowen, but this church had sought me out. They'd sent a messenger to the factory with a gift, begging me to come speak.

Lanzhou had been hesitant; we didn't know these people. But Jael had been delighted and agreed immediately. After all, this meant my plan was working.

I'd presented my idea to Bowen first: Let me go on tour and speak to churches and other unassimilated groups throughout the city. If people trusted me, then letting them see my face was the best way to repair the damage Jayde and Asia had done. I could rally the troops and demonstrate that I was on the ground, fighting alongside them. I would show the world that Asia had not intimidated me—and the more people felt emboldened by my presence, the more our numbers would grow.

Bowen had been enthusiastic about the idea, as I suspected, and Jael took surprisingly little convincing. It was Lanzhou who insisted on being the voice of reason. I was still the most wanted woman in the United, and the more I went out in public, the greater the risk that Asia would find me. His fears weren't unfounded, but I didn't care. After all, I didn't stay in China because it was safe.

He'd been pacified when Jael promised to send security. The black-suited, heavily armed bodyguards seemed to calm Lanzhou, but they had the opposite effect on me. Having security made me feel pretentious, like I was above all these civilians who risked their lives every day to go to church. Even now, my guards stood on either side of the door that led to the meeting room, their expressions masked by dark shades as they frowned in my direction.

I shivered and turned away to face the window, trying to focus my thoughts back on my mission. *This isn't about you—it's about the people behind that door.*

I closed my eyes and tried to picture the faces I'd seen when I'd met with the pastor before service. This congregation was different than the ones I'd spoken to before. This church was comprised entirely of businesspeople—most of whom were highly successful and very influential, according to Bowen. Everyone I'd met so far had been dressed immaculately and carried an air of money. Even their secret meeting place was opulent: They met on the top floor of a glittering high-rise—a floor that didn't exist, based on the buttons in the elevator. The one-way windows in the hall afforded a dizzying view of the city, with the bustling harbor out one side and a glittering Ferris wheel out the other.

Thankfully, Narissa made sure I was dressed for the occasion. She'd sent over a sharp skirt set and black patent shoes with just enough heel to make me look like an adult. As the finishing touch, she'd included the pearl necklace Asia had given me—a classy act of defiance.

I fingered the smooth beads and tried to swallow the feeling of inadequacy I always got right before I took the stage. Normally, if I took a moment to speak in tongues and make room for the Holy Spirit, the feeling faded, but not this time. I never had problems speaking to the churches in the slums; it was easy to give hope to people who had none. But these people were rich; they didn't worry about the same things. They had different problems, which meant they needed different solutions.

What do they need to hear?

I looked up and caught my reflection in the window. If it weren't for my brown hair and brown eyes, I would have passed as Andromeda Nolan. And that's when I remembered—I *was* one of them. Andromeda was rich. Andromeda had influence. Andromeda had power and family name that could move mountains—but she still needed to hear from God.

The nervousness faded when I realized I had my answer. *What is God saying to me?*

Just then, Bowen came out of the door and gestured at me. I straightened my skirt, found a smile, and followed him into the conference room.

The open hall was crowded with black suits and navy dresses. All hands were in the air as men in ties and women with three-inch heels worshipped with just as much enthusiasm as the factory workers. The moan of prayer in a language I didn't understand filled the room like incense.

I took a deep breath of it and strode up the stairs to the podium. The crowd silenced unbidden as someone introduced me. Walking to the edge of the stage, I held out my hand and gave them exactly what the Lord had given me.

"You're in this position for a reason."

Lanzhou stood beside me and translated into Mandarin, the intensity of his voice matching mine.

"You are not a mistake. Your success is not an accident. Every single thing that brought you to this place was of the Lord. Don't waste it."

I flinched when the words hit the inside of my ribs like a stab of pain. *Please, God, help me not waste this. I know You put me here for a reason. Show me what You want me to do.*

In response, the words came faster. "He gives seed to the sower and talents to those who are faithful—so be faithful! All your money, all your influence, all your political connections—those aren't for you. Those are for the Kingdom of God. The Lord put you here because you have an assignment, and now is the time to do it!"

I paused to let Lanzhou catch up. All eyes were on me as the silence returned. "God invested in you," I whispered, speaking as much to myself as to them. "And like any good businessman, He's expecting a return. Now is the time to give Him what He's due."

Commotion swept across the room as several people dropped to their knees and started praying. I raised my hand and my voice with it. "'Look, I am coming soon! My reward is with Me, and I will give to each person according to what they have done.' So, I ask you—what have you done?"

I needn't have said any more. The Holy Spirit took control as conviction washed over the crowd. Almost everyone responded, breaking out in prayer or weeping. I set the microphone down and sank to my knees, shuddering as the fear of God dropped on my shoulders.

God had chosen me to be Blue Fire. I knew beyond a shadow of a doubt that was true, and I wanted nothing more than to please Him. And I knew this—worshipping in church and encouraging His people—gave Him joy.

Then why did I feel like I was still falling short?

It was three hours later by the time we left the building. Service had gone on for a while, and then the congregation hosted us for dinner. I barely got a bite in between all the handshaking as Lanzhou struggled to translate the constant stream of thanks.

As with the other churches I'd spoken at, everyone seemed to have brought a gift. I'd been informed that it was considered polite in China to refuse a gift once or twice before accepting, which was convenient, because my genuine reaction was to tell people to stop. It seemed wrong to accept gifts from the church, but everyone gave with such joy that I didn't know how to refuse them. So, I let Bowen collect the growing pile of flowers and jewelry and resisted the urge to cry.

I was grateful when Lanzhou finally led me away. We had almost made it to the elevator when I heard someone running after us, shouting in Mandarin. I turned—but not as fast as my guards. They instinctively stepped in front of me as a breathless businessman approached.

He stopped a respectful distance away and bowed. "*Lei niao*," he greeted.

I dipped my head in acknowledgement. It meant "thunderbird" and was one of the few Mandarin phrases I'd managed to pick up, despite having been in the country for nearly a month.

The man smiled and rattled off a question in Mandarin. I looked to Lanzhou for a translation.

"He says he organizes a prayer group that meets tonight," Lanzhou explained. "He's asking if you would give him the honor of attending."

I smiled and opened my mouth to reply, but Bowen spoke first. "She can't tonight. I've already made another appointment."

Lanzhou apologized to the businessman, who nodded graciously and left.

"Where are we going?" I asked, and hoped I didn't sound as exhausted as I felt.

Instead of answering, Bowen held my black duffle out to me. "You'll want to change."

I did as I was told, ditching my heels and switching back to the military jacket and cargo pants Narissa had designed. My guards escorted me down to the parking garage, where Lanzhou and Bowen were waiting. A giant black SUV with the United seal on the side was idling in front of the door.

I froze as an instinctive wave of fear washed over me. Bowen touched my elbow. "It's okay, they're friends, I promise."

I couldn't read the characters on the side of the vehicle, but Lanzhou must have recognized the logo. He glared at Bowen and barked a question in Mandarin.

"It's fine, they know we're coming," Bowen answered in English. He guided me towards the car. "She deserves to see it for herself."

"See what for myself?" I demanded.

Bowen grinned at me. "You don't just have churches supporting you."

Everything about this situation made me uneasy, but I climbed into the backseat of the vehicle when one of my guards opened the door. Two of them slid in beside me as Bowen took shotgun next to the driver. I sat up straight and tried not to fidget as we drove out of town.

Within an hour, the bustling highways and manicured green spaces gave way to the austere concrete ocean of factories and shipping yards.

Towers of rusted shipping containers blocked out the setting sun as we passed the docks that were the lifeblood of Tianjin's industry.

Abruptly, the road ended in a concrete wall. The top of the barricade was lined with barbed wire, and the United flag flew from every corner. Sniper towers stood watch over the complex, the tips of their rifles seeming to follow us as we rolled up to the electrified metal gate. I leaned forward and caught a glimpse of a parked tank in the yard—and suddenly, I knew where we were.

A military base.

"Bowen…" I started, panic closing my throat.

"I told you, they're friends. You need to see this." He nodded at the driver, who began to pull forward slowly. The base evidently *did* know we were coming; the guards at the gate took one look at the license plate on our vehicle and let us in. Our driver didn't even roll his window down.

The gate groaned like the yawning jaws of a tiger as it pulled back into the wall. We drove into the yard and circled around to the office at the back of the complex. All across the lawn, troops were training in groups of a hundred. The rhythmic stamping of feet and the shouting of orders created a sinister symphony as we were dropped off at the main building and hustled inside.

Half a dozen ranking officers were waiting to meet us, their black uniforms dripping with medals. Someone gave an announcement in Mandarin, and all six saluted me. *"Lei niao!"* they shouted in practiced unison.

One of the officers stepped forward and bowed. "Blue Fire, this is Jin *Shao jiang*—Major General Jin," Bowen introduced. "His entire regiment has vowed to defect to you on operation day."

My ears rang as his words thundered in the cavity in my chest. "What?" I croaked.

General Jin gestured. "Come and see."

He led us up a floor to a balcony that overlooked the yard. He guided me to the railing, then pulled a whistle from his jacket. The sharp sound split the air, immediately silencing the activity in the yard. All the personnel turned to look up at the balcony, their faces anonymous in the long shadows of the setting sun.

General Jin flashed a signal with his hands, then called to his troop, his voice carrying across the entire yard. The regiment responded in unison. Like one being, every single soldier spun on his heel to face me. They threw salutes, their arms moving in rhythm like cogs on a machine, and shouted a military chant. The only word I understood was *"lei niao,"* but I knew what the chant meant.

This army answered to me.

The yard grew eerily still as all the soldiers lowered their arms and stood at attention. General Jin trilled another command on his whistle. The regiment immediately fell into formation, the clusters of soldiers rearranging themselves into precise lines as if guided by an unseen magnet. A commander at the head of the crowd shouted, and all the soldiers echoed back. On cue, they began to march across the yard, parading in front of us. As each row passed under the balcony, they saluted by moving the tip of their rifles from their left shoulders to their right. The sound of their boots stamping the concrete filled the air like thunder.

I gripped the railing, desperate not to fall over as the world spun. *God, what is going on?*

"Five thousand soldiers report directly to me," General Jin narrated from somewhere in my peripheral. "We are armed with fifty tanks, ten anti-aircraft guns, two intercontinental ballistic missiles..."

His voice blurred as he continued to catalog his artillery. I pinched my eyes shut, my vision flashing black and blue. What was I supposed to do with five thousand armed soldiers and a storehouse of heavy machinery?

"Does Jael know about this?" I managed.

"Of course," Bowen responded. "She's been coordinating the efforts across the country."

"We have spies in a dozen other regiments, sowing propaganda," General Jin added. "Our hope is that several more troops will pledge allegiance to you before operation day."

I felt Bowen step up beside me. "If enough of the army defects, the government won't be able to retaliate."

He was right. If enough of the army fell to our cause, the government wouldn't be able to strike back.

But we would.

I forced my eyes back open. I watched as row after row of upheld rifles passed beneath me, the polished tips gleaming like shark's teeth. "And what will all of these troops do on operation day?" I whispered, afraid of the answer.

General Jin smiled. "Whatever you command, Blue Fire."

16: PHILADELPHIA

Later that night, I sat on my bed and rewatched my newest video.

Thanks to Jael, I now had a team of professionals editing my content. My videos were no longer just me staring at a camera and narrating; they were fast-paced, trendy productions that made it look like we had the world on our side. Clips from my rallies were interspersed with moving graphics, compromising footage of government officials, and anonymous testimonies from civilians who had joined the cause. All of it was overlaid with fiery audio as I screamed into the microphone under the power of the Holy Spirit and urged people to wake up and see what was right in front of them.

This latest video was particularly scathing. It began with me listing the United's ethical atrocities, my voice catching as I recited the gruesome statistics of oppression and genocide. As I narrated, a whirlwind of classified photos flashed across the screen, including several showing the depravity inside the religious containment camps I had once called home. Then my voice changed pitch as the images melded into clips of my acts of rebellion. Suddenly, those same oppressed people were joining me as we broke my old neighbors out of camp and gathered as a praising mob in church, lifting our hands and falling on our faces without fear of the government.

The video culminated in a call to action, carefully scripted by Jael: *"You can end the United. You can save the world."* The last image before the screen went dark was a clip from my visit to the military base. I stood on the balcony, the setting sun flaring behind me, as a hundred armed soldiers saluted. The footage had been carefully cropped so you couldn't pinpoint the location, and the only face in focus was mine. But the message was clear: This was war, and I had an army behind me.

I paused the video. Is that what Operation Blue Fire had become: a call for war? I'd always known that resistance would bring some bloodshed. The United would retaliate, and they would not be kind. But their sins were on their own hands, and I didn't have to play by their rules. I'd never thought of my acts of rebellion as war; I just wanted to be brave enough to say "no."

Did I still believe that? Would the scattered resistance of a hundred thousand civilians be enough to end the system? Or were Bowen and my uncle right—had I been put in this place to do more?

"You're not a civilian anymore, and you can't afford to think like one."

My chest tightened. It didn't hurt, but it was that off-kilter feeling that told me I wasn't seeing the whole picture. It was like I was about to complete a puzzle, but one piece was missing.

I flopped back on the pillows and stared at the carved clouds that circled the top of the bed frame. "Is this what You want, God?" I asked into the soft darkness. "Is this why I'm Blue Fire?"

I closed my eyes and listened, but all I could hear was the rustling of the river and the distant grind of traffic.

I sighed. I knew silence meant "keep asking," but still I wondered, not for the first time, how much easier this would be if God would just *show* me things like He showed Nic.

What would it be like to see visions? God had spoken to me before, but never like that. What would it be like to hear the voice of God all the time, clear as day, like He was a friend sitting across the table? How would it feel to be trusted with snippets of the future like Isaiah and Jeremiah? If someone like Nic could prophesy, was it possible that I could learn to do it, too?

Sadly, I would never get to ask Nic about his experiences. I flinched when the repressed grief hit the back of my throat. *I miss him, God. I need him right now.*

My tablet pinged. I picked it up, expecting a message from Stanyard—but it wasn't. It was a friend request from a username I'd never seen before, and the content of their text made my heart freeze.

HEY, IT'S DATA. CAN WE TALK?

I jerked upright. Why was Data texting me? Surely, it wouldn't have been that hard for him to find out my username, but he and I hadn't talked since I left Boston. And even before that, I'm not sure we'd ever had what would constitute a full conversation. The fact that he wanted to call now could only mean one thing.

I opened the app and considered blocking the message, but I felt that breath in the Spirit that told me everything was going to be okay. After muttering a prayer, I accepted his friend request. I hit dial before I could second guess myself, but I disabled my video.

He had no such reservations. He answered immediately, and his video connected to reveal him sitting in a cluttered office. He looked a lot like Stanyard, with his headphones hanging around his neck and the backlit glare of his screens highlighting his face in blue. The only difference was that Data had at least three times the number of monitors; the whole side wall of his office was paneled with them, making the room look like the bridge on a spaceship.

"Hey," he initiated, his eyes roaming the screen as if expecting me to appear out of a corner. "Thanks for answering."

I decided I didn't have the patience for the preamble. "What do you want?"

"Look, I think we both know what this is about."

"Do we?" I challenged, and hoped he could read the threat in my tone of voice.

"Phil," he sighed, sounding almost bored, "I have access to every single byte of information on the base's server. As soon as Stanyard started running searches for my name, I found out about it."

I swallowed a wave of trepidation and waited.

He leaned forward. "Is there something you want to ask me?"

I gritted my teeth. "Did you try to kill Nic?"

"No," he answered, voice calm and unashamed. "I bought the code for the DNA off the black market. I had no idea it was programmed for more than one person."

I chewed on my lip. In some weird way, I almost wished he had said yes. At least then, I would have reason to believe him.

He seemed to read the meaning behind my silence. "If you want me to prove it, I will. I'll give Stanyard access to anything he wants. This is the laptop I used to code your chip." He held the device up. "I'll give it to him tomorrow and he can scan the whole thing. He'll find the change log for the code, all the text messages I had with Jayde, and the email I got from my source. He can even search my phone if he wants to cross-reference it."

I sighed. The fact that Data was going out of his way to prove his innocence reinforced what I already suspected: It wasn't him. But this was all still hearsay, and even I was smart enough to realize that it was too soon to trust him. If Data really wanted to cover his tracks, he would edit the device before he gave it to Stanyard. The only way to definitively prove that he didn't do it would be to find out who did.

And we weren't any closer to answering that question.

"What do you want me to say?" I groaned finally.

"Nothing. I don't expect you to trust me." He put his hands up dismissively.

"Then why did you call?"

"Because there's something else you should know." He grunted and glanced away, as if he were afraid to admit what was coming next. "I figured out how they got the code for Nic's DNA."

I gripped the bedspread. "How?"

He looked back at the camera. "They used your credentials."

My heart stopped, then restarted in a panic like someone was holding a gun to my chest. "But I didn't—"

"I know *you* didn't do it," he snorted, as if that was the most ludicrous idea he'd ever heard. "Unless you're really good at setting up a proxy chain."

I wagged my head, not that he could see it. I didn't even know what a proxy chain was.

"You suggested to Stanyard that they might have gotten the DNA off the door lock software from the base on Mars, and you were right." Data leaned forward and typed on a keyboard as he explained. "I used Jayde's old login to access the software before Ephesus wiped the server, and according to the logs, someone used your credentials to access the database and download the code. You had the clearance."

I remembered what Ephesus had said about Nic granting me Level 2 security clearance. Not only had I used my privileges to destroy the base, but apparently, I'd also given someone the keys to kill Nic.

This really *was* all my fault.

I gripped my stomach and tried not to be sick. "But how did they get my credentials?"

Data shrugged. "Depends on how they accessed the system. They could have hacked into a device registered to Andromeda and used it as a proxy. Or if they were on Mars, they might have just used a voice clip or DNA sample to access a terminal. Realistically, anyone with full security access on Jayde's team could have done it, if they were smart enough."

Including you, I thought but didn't bother to say. I knew Data wouldn't spell his plan out to me if he was guilty.

"I can send you the screenshots," he offered.

"Please," I said, even though I believed him.

He clicked his mouse several times, and my tablet pinged. "I'm trying to trace the IP, but like I said, either our criminal is working from Jupiter, or they set up a wickedly good proxy chain." He leaned back in his chair. "I'll keep digging. My best guess is that our killer downloaded the DNA and bribed my source in the black market to add it to his code, but I haven't been able to prove it. I'll let you know if I find anything concrete."

"Thanks," I mumbled. I had no reason to be optimistic.

Data let me nurse the silence for a moment, then dragged his chair closer to the desk. "Look, there's another reason I called."

"What?" I sighed, exhausted.

"It's about your videos. I think it's time to go wide."

I frowned at the screen. "Go wide?"

He spun his chair to face one of the monitors on the side wall. "I've been working for the last month to expand our broadcasting capabilities. If we're going to win this thing, your videos need to be seen by more people."

He dragged his mouse to expand a window, filling the screen with a ream of code. He pointed at it like he expected the technical gibberish to mean something to me. "Thanks to an in at the local news station, I've coded a backdoor into the program the United uses for compulsory announcements. With a couple of clicks, I can use that program to push your videos onto every single registered device on the planet—and boost the live feed on all the social networks."

The words sounded so fantastical that I was sure I hadn't heard right. "I'm sorry, what?"

"You've seen a compulsory announcement, right?"

It was an inane question; that was the whole nature of compulsory announcements. They were always prefaced with a hideous beep like a tornado siren, and then the video would autoplay on every registered device like a virus. The government used them for "important" announcements, like new regulations and public executions.

"There's a fancy program they use to populate those videos. Every registered device has it installed. Now that I'm in the system, all I have to do is plug one of your videos into the program, and suddenly Blue Fire is mandatory viewing."

I sucked in my breath so hard my ribs hurt. Jael had hijacked a few obscure channels in Beijing, but that was nothing compared to what Data was promising. If he was telling the truth, we could bypass the algorithm and force the entire world to watch. We could use the United's own technology against them and bring the entire system crashing down in minutes.

All without firing a single shot.

"We need to test it," Data stressed, his voice cautious. Flickering code reflected in his eyes as he typed a command on his keyboard. "As soon as we broadcast something, they'll be working around the clock to patch my backdoor. I want to run a couple of tests in localized areas—say, Boston—so I can see how they react and create some workarounds for their fixes. It's going to take a couple of weeks, and I'll need Jael's help."

He turned back to the camera. "Again, I'm not asking you to trust me," he said, as if anticipating my objections. "Just give my contact information to Jael. I will give her all my access codes and let her do it herself if she wants. And if she doesn't take it—well, at least I tried."

"Why are you doing this?" I blurted. If Data was being honest, then he was willing to sacrifice his entire livelihood for the cause. He was willing to hand me the keys to his digital empire free of charge—and I didn't even know his real name.

He smiled, his eyes glinting in the glare from his screens. "I'm in this for you, Blue Fire. I know you can do this. So, let me help you win this war."

17: NIC

The third week of my incarceration was mind-numbingly uneventful.

Ryan, who was apparently something of a supervisor, convinced the warden to transfer me to his shift by promising he would keep an eye on me. This he did religiously. He rearranged the schedule so I was always working within three yards of him, and he insisted we take every break together. He even pulled some strings and got my bunk assignment moved to the same cell as him and Vance, much to my dismay.

He needn't have bothered. I was under strict orders from the Lord not to cause trouble for either of them. So, I shut up and did as I was told—much to the surprise of management. Warden Ivanova was so suspicious of my sudden compliance that she sent guards to check on me for the first few days, just to make sure I hadn't escaped.

I told her that if the Lord ever gave me permission to run again, she'd be the first to know.

Eventually, everyone got over the spectacle, and Vance, Ryan, and I settled into a boring rhythm. And I mean *boring* literally; taking laps around Rott had been more intellectually stimulating than this. My job on the assembly line was so pedestrian that a ten-year-old could have done it. In fact, had they rearranged the line a little bit, I could have done my job, Vance's, *and* Ryan's all at the same time—and met a higher quota.

I wasn't about to volunteer myself for more work, but a reformation would have saved them a lot of money. I remembered what Warden Ivanova had said about production being down, and I wasn't surprised the higher ups had docked her pay. I would have fired her, personally. It was a crime how poorly this factory was being run. The assembly line was gloriously inefficient, the guards' and workers' schedules were a hot mess, and the resource waste was scandalous. The only part of the operation Warden Ivanova had down to a science was the discipline.

The Lord consistently pointed out all the ways the factory could be improved, as if me and my three doctorates couldn't clearly see it for ourselves. In fact, that was all He wanted to talk about. I would have preferred to talk about His vision for Vance and Ryan; the sooner I could figure out His end game, the sooner I could get this show on the road and earn my way out of here. But He insisted on dissecting the entire operation until I could have written a master thesis on the subject.

I wasn't sure why I needed this information. I couldn't do anything about it; my job was simply to show up and let Ryan boss me around. And even if I could make some changes, I wouldn't want to. Why would I want to improve my own prison? If these communists wanted to bankrupt themselves with a failed business venture, let them.

This went on for several days, with the Lord pointing out inefficiencies and me pretending not to care. In an effort to avoid conversation with anybody, I practiced memorizing the digits of pi. At least *that* was information I would probably use later.

It had been a particularly monotonous shift, and I had just recited to the 3,587th digit when the Lord rudely interrupted.

You know you can fix this, right? You could save this factory.

I groaned. "Are You still on about that?"

"Ay yi, talking to yourself again, Q?" Ryan peeked out from behind the machine. "Tell Him I said hi!"

I looked up at the ceiling. "Ryan says hi."

"Vance says hi too!"

Vance leaned out from around the other side of the machine. "I said no such thing."

"I'm just putting in a good word for you, buddy."

I squatted down and pretended to fiddle with a control panel so I wouldn't have to look at either of them. "Yes, I'm fully aware I have the *ability* to reform this entire operation," I hissed, keeping my voice down. "What I fail to recognize is why I should care."

I didn't ask you to care. I asked you to obey.

I growled and hurled my wrench on the floor with a terrific clang.

"Oy, sounds like Q lost the argument again," Ryan whispered, as if I couldn't hear him.

"I don't believe it's theologically possible to win an argument with the Lord," Vance whispered back.

"What do you call that deal where Abraham was like, 'What if I find one righteous dude?'"

"First of all, that wasn't an argument. Second of all, that passage illustrates a very important theological point about intercession—"

"Enough!" I shouted, loud enough for them *and* the entire floor to hear me. "I can't take it anymore." I turned and stomped off.

"Wait! Don't do it, Q!" Ryan scampered after me. "Don't jump!"

"I'm not going to jump." I reached the elevator and punched the button. "I'm going to fix their efficiency output."

He skidded to a stop. "Their what now?"

I didn't bother to answer him. I stepped onto the elevator and called Level 57. If Warden Ivanova was on schedule today, she should be supervising the unloading of supplies on Dock 12.

She was running a few minutes behind, but I caught her as she strode around the corner to the docking bay, her usual entourage of guards in tow.

She paused to give me a sniveling look down her nose. "What are you doing here?"

"Talking to you. You're late—did your Monday conference call go over?"

"How did you—never mind." She shook her head and brushed past me. "I thought we'd mutually decided not to talk to each other again, Q. And you were doing so well. Get him back to his station."

The latter comment was directed at the guards, but I sidestepped them and ran after her. "I know, but if I don't get this off my chest, I won't be able to live with myself."

Or, more accurately, I won't be able to live with the Holy Spirit.

She halted. "Please tell me you're not about to propose."

"You're a... fascinating woman, but no. Remember how you said production was down, and they'd docked your pay?"

"Thanks for announcing that in front of literally everybody." She glared at her guards, who conveniently looked elsewhere like they hadn't heard.

"Well, I'm here to tell you I can fix it."

The elevator opened, and Vance and Ryan ran towards us.

Warden Ivanova snorted. "Sounds like a scam."

"I'm serious. I've been analyzing this factory for three weeks now, and I've identified twenty-one ways you can increase production today. None of them will cost you anything except the time it takes to implement them—and we might need to do some maintenance in Shaft 5 to fix the load distribution issue."

My coworkers reached us. "Sorry, ma'am," Ryan panted, extremely out of breath. "We tried to stop him, but he's got really long legs."

The warden put up a hand to silence him. "And why should I believe you?" she challenged, eyes on me.

I hesitated. *"Because the Lord spoke to me"* would have been the correct answer, but probably not the one she wanted to hear.

Vance spared me the misery. "He's right, ma'am," he said, stepping up. "This factory is operating at roughly 57% efficiency. You're easily losing twenty grand in revenue a month, and that's a conservative estimate. I've run the calculations myself."

I gawked at him. "And you didn't say anything before now? You've been here, what, a decade? If I find out the Lord sent me here just because you were too lazy to say something, I *will* kick you."

He shrugged. "I don't publish my findings until they've been reviewed by expert peers."

One of the guards jabbed his thumb at me. "What about him? He's got three PhDs."

Vance squinted, as if weighing my competency. "Is one of them in biomechanical engineering?"

"Um, lemme look." The guard pulled out his device and started scrolling through it.

Before I could object to details of my personnel file being shared without my consent, Warden Ivanova mercifully intervened. "Enough! Look, since you're the 'doctor' here, I'm going to ask you." She locked eyes with me. "Is this true?"

I straightened. "Yes. If you give me a computer, I can have a full report and a model simulation on your desk by Friday."

She arched an eyebrow. "And what do I get out of it?"

"Besides increased profits and a raise?" I held her gaze. "If you don't believe me, then let's do a bet. If you want to test my theories for a month, I'll put my life up as collateral. Implement my model, and if your productivity hasn't increased by at least 20% in thirty days, you can take it out on me."

The words slipped out before I could properly ingest them. That's when I registered—far too late to back out—that it wasn't me speaking.

Now look what You've gotten us into!

I've got your back, He coolly replied.

"Aww man," Ryan whined, "I was just getting used to having more than one friend."

Warden Ivanova's face cracked in a wicked grin. "I love a good wager. Fine, you've got yourself a deal, Q. One month, and you don't touch anything until you've run the plans by me, understood?"

I offered her my hand. "Done."

She shook it violently. "I can't *wait* to see how this goes."

18: PHILADELPHIA

Early on a Tuesday morning, I sat in the recording studio and prepared to hijack one of China's most popular networks.

It was going to be our first live test. Jael, Data, and their team of moles in the media had been working around the clock to bulletproof our control over the system. We started by running several innocuous tests; Data commandeered the signal during off-peak hours and broadcasted a graphic that said "technical difficulties." The hope was that if anyone caught it, they would assume it was a system error instead of a hacker.

The ruse worked. Data watched to see how quickly the network responded and what steps they took to restore service, then adapted his program to compensate. Stanyard pulled overtime helping him rewrite the code; even Ephesus pitched in, traveling to a nearby base so he could come online and assist the team for a few days. After a week of testing, Data was able to take control of a channel and keep broadcasting the graphic for over fifteen minutes before the network finally took themselves offline.

After that, we started sinking our teeth into more popular networks. At first, we would interrupt the broadcast only for a second, flashing up the thunderbird symbol and then immediately restoring the regular programming. Sometimes, it was so fast that the anchormen didn't even notice they'd been hijacked, but we knew the people were seeing it.

Then we started streaming video clips. They were short at first; most of them were just my face in a nearly dark room as I hauntedly repeated, *"Can anyone hear me? It's Blue Fire. I need your help,"* over and over.

That got the government's attention. They reacted swiftly; my next broadcast was shut down in seconds. Data adapted his code, and it took the government three minutes to stop my next stream. Then five, then ten.

We started broadcasting whole videos then. All my old streams were republished, aired on a random network at a random time so that the government wouldn't know where to look. We let the videos loop over and over, filling the screens of millions of devices until the censors finally found us and took the networks offline.

We knew we were making progress when gossip about the hijackings began to escape the algorithm and circulate on social media. Civilians who had never heard of "Operation Blue Fire" were now talking about me as I repeatedly usurped their favorite programming. Meanwhile, studio executives began to complain about the government's lack of response, which was almost as damaging to United morale as my videos themselves. The internet was starting to do my job for me—and that's when we knew it was time to go live.

I stared at my reflection in the curved camera lens and tried to appreciate the magnitude of what was about to happen. In less than two minutes, I would be commandeering one of mainland China's most-watched morning talk shows. Over a hundred and fifty million people were about to get snapped out of their complacency as their daily routine was disrupted by my desperate call for help.

This would be our biggest broadcast yet. Jael had warned me that I would likely get shut down quickly, but Data was confident he could have us back up and running within twenty-four hours. If this worked—if we were able to keep me live on China's largest network for even a few minutes—then that was a sign we were almost ready to go wide. Once Data fully perfected his code, we would pull the trigger, and my broadcast would simultaneously hijack every registered device between here and Mars. Every connected citizen in the United would see me.

After that, even the government wouldn't be able to stop Operation Blue Fire.

I looked up to see Jael moving behind the plexiglass window of the control booth. The giant digital clock behind her counted down, the seconds seeming to fly by faster than time itself.

Twenty-nine, twenty-eight...

"Remember," Jael coached over the speaker, "you may only have a minute. So, open strong and talk fast."

Fifteen, sixteen...

I inhaled through my nose and nodded.

Ten, nine...

I pinched my eyes shut and squeezed out a final prayer. *Holy Spirit, speak through me.*

Three... two... one.

I opened my eyes and stared straight at the camera.

"My name is Philadelphia Smyrna, and I'm here to tell you that the United's days are numbered."

*

I stumbled out of the recording studio in a drunk daze. The broadcast had been an exhilarating success. Data had managed to keep my stream up for a heroic eight minutes and fifty two seconds—long enough that I ran out of prepared remarks and had to go off-script. For nearly nine minutes, I held the captive attention of the nation as I told the world about Operation Blue Fire. I spelled out the government's doom as I told China exactly what the revolution—civilian and military alike—would do on operation day.

At precisely 9am on Thursday, September 17th—a date that had been significant for freedom and peace more than once—the revolution would start. Bureaucrats would quit their government jobs. Clerks would burn paperwork and delete files. Teachers would tell their students the truth about why the United was created. Policemen and containment camp guards would lay down their weapons. Civilians everywhere would stand up and say no.

At precisely 9am on Thursday, September 17th, 2076, the world would end, and the new one would begin.

John and Dowe met me outside the recording studio with loud cheers and crushing hugs. Bowen was next in line; he pumped my hand in both of his and grinned. "Now *that's* a revolution."

I shakily returned the smile, bumping into the door frame as I struggled to regain control of my nerves.

Lanzhou touched my shoulder. "You okay?" he said gently.

I wasn't; I hadn't been for a week. I couldn't keep up with all this. The revolution had ignited the world like a forest fire; it was growing so fast and so hot that I couldn't even wrap my mind around what it—what Blue Fire— had become. Even now, the world was spinning so hard that I didn't feel like I possessed my body anymore. But it was a small price to pay for victory.

"Yeah, just dizzy," I fudged.

He frowned. "Come sit down."

He guided me towards the conference room, where Jael and several others were waiting. The network I'd just hijacked was playing on the projector. Service had been restored, but instead of the scheduled talk show, they were running an emergency broadcast. I watched as an ugly picture of me flashed up on the screen, superimposed with the demeaning words "WANTED." A pre-recorded clip of Asia looped in the corner as she prattled about the reward the government was offering in exchange for information about my whereabouts.

I cackled at the irony as I sank into a chair. Clearly, I'd struck a nerve. Blue Fire was turning the tide of war—and Asia knew it.

"Check," I muttered to the screen.

Jael's heels clacked on the floor as she approached me. "Excellent work. Your engagement has increased tenfold. Activity around your name is surging, especially in demographics we haven't reached before."

She held out her tablet. A bouncing pictograph filled the screen as the algorithm struggled to catalog my popularity.

"A hundred million gossiping housewives will take it from here," Bowen snarked. He winked at me in a way that suggested he had experience with such things.

I started to laugh but realized I didn't have the energy to finish. Lanzhou set a glass of water on the table next to me, and I gratefully took it.

"Hey, I know it's been a big day." Bowen sat down next to me and softened his voice. "But do you feel up to making a visit?"

I glanced at him out of the corner of my eye and contemplated refusing.

Lanzhou did it for me. "Are you sure that's wise? 'A hundred million housewives' just saw her face—the entire country is going to be on high alert. I don't think she should be seen in public at all right now."

He had a point, and that gave even Bowen a slight pause. "We're not bringing cameras to this visit. And… it's a request from a friend."

He reached across the table and grabbed a large white shirt box. He slid it towards me. A note was taped to the top:

THERE'S SOME OLD FRIENDS OF MINE I WOULD LIKE YOU TO VISIT. CALL IT A FAVOR FOR ME—IT WOULD MEAN A LOT. – N

P.S. WEAR THIS

I pulled the note off and handed it to Jael, then lifted the lid of the box. Inside, on a bed of white tissue paper, was my old outfit.

Well, the clothes were new; I could tell the fabric had been freshly minted on Narissa's fabricator. But the garments were modeled exactly after the industrial outfit I used to wear when I lived in the containment camp: a gray jacket and leggings layered with a linen skirt. She'd updated the design a little bit; the fit was more flattering, and the skirt fabric was light and flowy. But the resemblance was unmistakable.

I fingered the tight stitching on the hem. Philadelphia Smyrna was truly back from the dead.

"Of course, I'll go," I murmured. "Anything for Narissa."

"I knew you'd say that. We'll leave in an hour." Bowen grinned and started to rise.

I moved to follow, but Lanzhou gripped the back of my chair and stopped me. "Are you sure about this?" The question was directed at Jael.

She set the note in my lap. "No cameras, and I absolutely do not want her seen from the street. You go in a back way and leave by a different one, and they better keep the shades drawn. Understood?" She arched an eyebrow at Bowen.

He nodded. "I'll make the arrangements."

19: PHILADELPHIA

Narissa's friends lived in an apartment across town. The residential subdistrict was a few miles from downtown and had been developed rapidly to contain the overflow of people from the suffocating inner city. The streets were less crowded and the buildings less imposing; most of the apartment complexes were only a modest fifteen stories tall. It was the perfect place for some rebels to hide in plain sight.

Our driver took us around to the back of the apartment building at the end of the block. We were riding in an unmarked delivery van with forged license plates; the windowless load area afforded some privacy, and the vehicle was unassuming enough. Jael had sent six security guards with me, which seemed like an excess, but I knew better than to argue. They'd dressed down for the occasion, switching their black suits for generic work uniforms and leaving the sunglasses behind. Personally, I preferred the new look.

The apartment's loading dock was open to receive us. A laundry delivery truck idled in the alley, blocking the way. My driver honked twice before the other driver finally looked up from his device. With an impatient glare, he begrudgingly pulled forward so we could back up to the dock.

Bowen jumped out and opened the hatch. The laundry ladies pushed their carts out of my way as the disguised guards hustled me up the service elevator to the third floor.

As soon as the elevator door opened, I realized this wasn't a typical apartment. The sterile scent of bleach fought to overpower the stench of illness and death. It smelled like a hospital, and it sounded like one, too. I heard the beeping of monitors, the murmuring of hushed voices, and the squeak of wheelchair wheels on linoleum. Carts of medical equipment crowded the hall, along with an ominously empty stretcher.

"What is this place?" I dared to ask.

Bowen led the way down the hall. "Think of it as a group home. These are all people who have been rejected from the healthcare system—or rescued from it, depending on who you ask."

I followed him hesitantly, the guards trailing on my heels. The first few doors we passed were shut, but the fourth was cracked open. I heard the blare of a TV from inside.

Bowen rapped on the doorframe with his knuckles and shouted something in Mandarin. He was answered enthusiastically. The door banged open, and a man with no legs appeared.

I jerked back involuntarily. From the waist up, he looked perfectly normal, but his legs were gone. It didn't even look like they'd been amputated; it looked like he'd never had them in the first place.

I realized too late that I was staring. He chuckled disarmingly. "I have that effect on women."

I flushed and offered my hand. "Blue Fire—I mean, Philadelphia."

He grabbed the door frame and used his arms to swing himself out into the hall. "Oh, I know who you are—we all saw your stint on the news." He gestured with his shoulder at his TV while he pumped my hand. "Call me Huan."

I smiled. "Pleased to meet you."

"Now, I know what you're going to ask." He rocked back and put both hands up. "First question I usually get: It's called *amelia*, and it's a rare birth disorder. Second question I usually get: Yes, I'm single." He winked.

Bowen swatted him on the shoulder. "This is why I can't take you anywhere."

"No, the reason you can't take me anywhere is because the government wants to kill me." Huan rolled his eyes. "But Blue Fire would know all about that, wouldn't she?"

I frowned and looked to Bowen for an explanation.

He squeezed Huan's shoulder. "Everyone in this building is on the government's 'do not resuscitate' list. Some, like Huan here, were born with disabilities or deformities."

Huan reached up and patted Bowen's hand. "I'm lucky—I was born in a small village under a midwife, so my parents were able to hide me. For a while, at least."

I thought about Narissa's blind eyes—a deformity that had been corrected by robotic implants—and abruptly realized how she knew these people.

I felt a weight drop to my stomach as the Holy Spirit pressed on my ribs. "I'm sorry," I managed.

Huan shook his head. "Don't be. I have it good here. I'm working an online job under false credentials, and the apartment manager lies about who she's renting to. But if you succeed…" He looked up and met my eyes. "Maybe

I can put my name on the mailbox without worrying they're going to take me away."

Narissa's haunting words came floating back to me.

"The government doesn't like imperfect people any more than it likes religious brats."

Bowen gave Huan's shoulder one last squeeze and bid him goodbye in Mandarin, then turned and continued down the hall. "This whole apartment is a sham. All the residents here have been condemned to die for one reason or another. Some have conditions the government deems untreatable."

My eyes scanned the disorganized racks of second-hand medical equipment as I followed him around the corner.

"Others were abandoned as children because they came from parents who weren't supposed to have kids—or from minorities the government thinks we have a 'surplus' of."

He paused and pointed towards an open door. I glanced inside and saw the room was crammed with mismatched cribs. A frazzled nurse bustled about, tending to at least half a dozen squalling babies.

Bowen stepped up behind her and spoke softly. She whipped around, almost smacking him in the face, then relaxed when she saw who it was. Bowen pointed at one of the cribs. The nurse nodded, picked up a child—and walked out into the hall and handed it to me.

I almost dropped it—her, judging by the color of her onesie. I couldn't remember the last time I'd held a baby. I hadn't grown up around children; I was the youngest in my family, and most of the people in camp had stopped having kids.

Suddenly, I wondered if that choice hadn't been voluntary.

Bowen reached up and brushed the baby's dark peach-fuzz hair. "Most children like her aren't even making it out of the womb."

I tightened my grip around the child, causing her to fuss and stir.

"This is what true evil looks like, Phil." Sudden tears clogged Bowen's voice. "I know we've got problems with taxes and fraud and religious oppression—but *this*, murdering innocent children, is what grieves the Savior's heart."

I choked on my next breath. He was right, and America was no better. We'd been killing our own for a century.

Maybe that was why we were in this mess in the first place.

I shoved the baby back at the nurse. "Please, I can't."

She nodded and took the child. Bowen kept walking. "This is why I joined the operation. Yes, I think the government is evil, and yes, I think the world needs to change. But that's not what bothers me. That's not what gets me down on my knees, night after night, begging God to have mercy on my nation. It's these people."

He stopped in the middle of the hall and spread his hands. "When Jesus came to earth, He fought for the diseased, the widows, the Samaritans. He loved the people society rejected. If I don't fight for their right to exist, how can I claim to love the world like He did?"

The room blurred out of focus as my eyes stung with tears. "Bowen, I—"

A heavy *thump* against the wall interrupted me.

I jumped and looked for the source. It was coming from the room a few doors down. I heard it again, and again—a dull beating on the wall, repeated but erratic.

I swallowed. "What's that?"

Bowen smiled sadly. "That's Sienna. Come meet her."

He walked over to the door and opened it softly. I stepped up next to him and looked over his shoulder.

The room was practically bare, completely stripped of breakables and hard edges, and I immediately saw why. In the far corner, a girl only a year or two younger than myself was beating her head into the wall. She had a foam helmet strapped under her chin, but that didn't stop her from incessantly trying to injure herself. The plaster was dented throughout the room, and several holes had been hastily patched with plywood. The window was braced with a board to keep her from banging into the glass.

"Severe autism," Bowen answered my unspoken question.

"But why is she doing that?" I managed, even though I was afraid of the answer.

Bowen rubbed his chin. "Think of it like being chronically overstimulated. There are a lot of things in this world—sounds, bright lights—that her body simply can't process. What's normal to us might be excruciating for her, and repetitive pain is the only way she can distract herself."

I remembered all the times I had slammed my fist into concrete floors, desperate to feel anything but confusion and fear, and thought I might understand, in a sad and incomplete way.

"She'll require lifelong care, which isn't something the government is eager to fund. I'm told they smuggled her out of a hospital where she was going to be euthanized," Bowen explained softly.

I braced myself against the doorframe as the world washed out.

"Come on, there's more I'd like you to meet." Bowen touched my elbow and tried to pull me away.

I couldn't move. I was rooted to the floor as despair drained the blood from my face like water. Blue Fire couldn't help these people. Sure, I could fight for a society that wouldn't kill them, but that wouldn't *save* them. There was no amount of money or power or prestige that could save people like Sienna. I could reform the world, birth a brand-new government, and bring freedom for all—and Sienna would still be stuck in a corner somewhere, banging her head into a wall as the disease of this fallen world stripped her of the woman she was created to be.

A revolution couldn't save her.

I couldn't save her.

"Phil?" Bowen's voice tried to reach me through the waves of fear. "Are you all right?"

Before I could answer him, a gunshot ripped the air.

We all whipped around. Several more shots followed. I heard glass shattering and a door banging, and a muffled scream echoed from a few floors down.

"*Jingcha!* Police!" someone shouted.

My guards drew their weapons. Bowen ran to the nearest window and threw the curtain back. I saw red-and-blue lights flashing off the windows of the building across the street and knew what was happening before he said it.

"They've got the building surrounded! They know you're here."

But how? The question didn't even make it out of my lips. We'd barely been here fifteen minutes, and I'd only talked to three people. Who would have called the police?

Then I remembered Huan's blaring TV and his comment that "everybody" had seen the news. I thought about the whispering laundry workers in the alley—and suddenly, I knew who had turned me in.

Bowen rushed back to me. "We need to get you to the truck, now."

One of my guards stuck out his arm to stop him. "They'll have thought of that. We need another way out of this building."

"There is no other way out!" Bowen shouted. "What, you think we can just walk out the front door?"

Several doors banged open as the apartment's residents poured into the hall. Children cried and nurses shouted for help, and several people called my name. I tried to tune them out as my heart jammed itself up my throat.

Oh God, I can't protect all these people! What have I done?

Bowen continued to bicker with my guards. "We can have another vehicle here in five," one of them insisted, voice calm.

Another gunshot echoed from below. "She won't live that long if we don't get her out of this building!" Bowen screamed.

I pinched my eyes shut and tried to think around the noise. *Holy Spirt, Holy Spirit!* I shrieked over and over, too panicked to get a full prayer out.

Sienna, agitated by the commotion, roared and threw her weight into the wall. I turned to look at her—and saw her boarded-up window.

The idea rammed into me like a brick. "The fire escape!"

It took my guards only a second to catch up. The leader pointed and started barking orders. "You two, with her. Get her to the alley and head to the end of the block—the car will meet you there. If anyone comes into the alley, you shoot first."

Oh Lord, I moaned.

"The rest of you, with me. We're going to stall them in the lobby." The leader flipped the setting on his gun, but I couldn't see what he changed it to. I prayed it was set on stun.

Bowen gripped my arm. "Come on!"

I held back. "Wait!" I grabbed the elbow of the leader. "Please, what about the rest of these people? We have to help them!"

He hesitated for a fraction of a second, his stonewalled eyes scanning me. Then he jerked his head at one of his comrades. "You, evacuate these people out the fire escape—but keep Blue Fire's path clear! The rest of you, with me!"

He pounded towards the elevator, two of his men falling into line behind him. The third turned and shouted at the confused residents, shepherding them down the hall in the opposite direction.

Bowen hauled me into the room. "Let's go!"

I stumbled after him. The two remaining guards followed, slamming and locking the door behind us. Sienna continued to moan, almost as if she was unaware of our presence.

The guards grabbed the board across the window. With a coordinated yank, the nails ripped from the soft plaster. They threw the board aside, opened the window, and punched the screen out.

One guard climbed out onto the balcony first. He scanned the street below with his gun, then gestured at us. Bowen climbed out after him. He turned and held his hand out to me. "Phil, now!"

The gunshots were getting closer. I heard a scream and the distinct sound of a body hitting the floor and realized the government was taking no prisoners.

"Sienna!" I ran to her and grabbed her arm with both hands. She resisted me, but I begged the Holy Spirit to make me stronger as I dragged her towards the window.

The guard took over. He scooped Sienna up and handed her out the window to his partner. Then he turned and gave me a boost. I hiked up my skirt and slid over the sill, where Bowen caught me.

The wailing of sirens filled the alley, but no one was in sight. The guard tossed Sienna over his shoulder and led the way down the rickety metal stairs. I followed, Bowen and the other guard a step behind me.

We had just reached the ground floor when someone shouted after us. I saw the shadow of a figure entering the alley at the far end. The guard behind me did what he was told: He shot first. I quickly turned away.

Jesus, please! I begged, even though I had no idea what I was asking for.

Commotion filled the alley as the other residents climbed out their windows onto the fire escape. There was no time to look back as the guards hustled us around the corner and down to the end of the block. It seemed like an eternity before we reached the main street. It was like we were running in slow motion, while all around there were screams and gunshots as my guards sacrificed more lives to keep me safe.

Lord, have mercy!

We raced around the last building onto the main road—right into a barricade. Two cop cars blocked the street. I stumbled as the blaring lights blinded me while an officer shouted at us to *"Drop your weapons!"*

The guard in front didn't even hesitate. He shot the nearest officer square in the chest.

Bowen yanked me back around the building as the other officers opened fire. There were six more shots and two screams. A car window shattered. My second guard shielded Sienna with his body as glass rained across the sidewalk.

Finally, the gunshots stopped. Tires squealed and metal crunched. An SUV screeched up to the curb, rear-ending one of the police cars. "Come on!" the first guard yelled at us. He clutched his bleeding shoulder.

I couldn't bring myself to look at the carnage on the street as Bowen hauled me to the car. One guard all but threw Sienna into the backseat, then hoisted me up next to her. He and Bowen crammed in beside us, while the other guard took shotgun and shouted directions to the driver. We peeled away from the curb and raced through a red light, narrowly avoiding a collision.

I struggled to maintain a sense of direction as our driver whipped through side streets. For a horrific moment, I was afraid the motion would never stop, like we were caught in a whirlpool with no way to escape.

But then, finally, our driver slowed, and the world stopped rocking, and the car grew eerily silent. We'd escaped.

I collapsed against the seat, all the adrenaline making my limbs shake as it cycled around in my body with nowhere to go. *What just happened?*

"It's okay, it's okay," Bowen repeated, more to himself than to me. He muttered in tongues. "This is why you have security."

I have security so they can kill people before they kill me. I pinched my eyes shut and willed myself not to be sick. Was this who Blue Fire had become?

Sienna moaned and rammed her head against the window. I pulled her away from the door and wrapped my arms around her. Ignoring her fists pounding into my skin, I closed my eyes and tried to find my center of gravity as my thoughts continued to spiral out of control.

It's not supposed to be this way.

20: PHILADELPHIA

A few hours later, I huddled in a chair at the conference table and trembled while the adults yet again had a heated conversation without me.

We'd made it safely back to the factory, only to find it in an uproar. The United had wasted no time in doctoring and airing the video of the raid. Gruesome footage of bloodied glass and sobbing children was interspersed with sinister shots of medical equipment and dirty linens, making the home look like the set of a horror movie. The anchormen called it inhumane and concocted a story about how the underground was imprisoning sick people and denying them medical care.

But even more damaging was the clip of one of my guards shooting a police officer. The soldier assured me that his weapon had been set on stun, but the United omitted that fact from their reporting. Again and again, they replayed the shot of the officer collapsing, his bodycam glitching as he hit the concrete with a groan. Meanwhile, I ran down the alley in the opposite direction without a single glance back.

That five-second clip was all it took to turn Blue Fire into a violent murderer. Social media exploded with vicious speculation about the real nature of the operation, and the algorithm let it through. Suddenly, the hundred and fifty million people who saw my stream this morning thought I was a dangerous terrorist.

And, in a way, they were right.

My loyal followers immediately responded with the truth, broadcasting their support for me and condemning the government's violent raid. But the damage had been done. It would take weeks of PR to restore the confidence of the Chinese people, let alone the rest of the world.

But that wasn't what worried me. What worried me was all the people I'd just killed. Three of my guards didn't make it back. Several police officers were down. Jael didn't know how many of the home's residents had escaped, but I doubted the numbers were good. Someone like Huan couldn't run and would have a difficult time hiding—never mind the helpless infants who had probably been abandoned in their cribs.

I sobbed and slapped my hands over my face. *God, why is this happening?* This wasn't what He promised me. If God was with me, then this shouldn't be happening. People shouldn't be dying.

Unless God wasn't with me anymore.

"This can't happen again!" Lanzhou shouted for at least the third time. He paced back and forth in front of the projection, his face flashing in and out of color as he walked under the sensors.

"And it won't!" Bowen insisted, trying to match his pace. "Look, I take full responsibility. This trip was my idea. I saw the laundry attendants—I should have turned around."

"Yes, you should have," Jael chided from her usual throne at the head of the table. "You're lucky you had security with you."

Everyone else is not so lucky, I thought with a whimper.

"I know, I'm sorry," Bowen pleaded, the confession directed at me. "But please, take this out on me, not her. We need her in the field." He grabbed Lanzhou's sleeve.

Lanzhou shrugged him off. "No, we don't, and I'm done having this conversation with you." He spun to face Jael. "You have to pull her from the operation and send her home."

"No!" I screeched, lurching upright. "I can't leave!"

"Philadelphia," Lanzhou sighed, the patience in his voice as thin as paper. "You can't do this anymore. You can't go out in public—and frankly, I'm not even comfortable with you staying at our house."

The statement was made with shame and regret, and he looked away as he continued. "The neighbors know we've had a houseguest for the past month. Sooner or later, someone's going to do the math, or they'll realize 'Blue Fire' doesn't always wear a brown wig."

I shivered at the thought of the Tangs' house getting burned to the ground by the police. I couldn't put Mr. Tang and his family in danger like that, not after all they'd done to help me. "I understand," I admitted. "So, I'll go somewhere else."

Lanzhou shook his head. "There isn't 'somewhere else,' Philadelphia. Not on this continent."

"I'm afraid he's right," Jael spoke up before I could object. "There are too many people in this country who know your face—and the further we expand your reach, the worse it will get. You can't be seen in public."

"Fine, take me off the PR visits, whatever," I muttered as if it didn't matter, when it definitely did. "But I can't leave Beijing."

"You have to," Lanzhou insisted. "The state is too powerful here. You need to be somewhere less populated, somewhere we haven't promoted your videos yet."

None of that mattered—why couldn't they see that? This wasn't about playing it safe; this was about doing what God told me to do. God told me I was supposed to be in Beijing, and I wasn't about to let Asia bully me out of my destiny. "But I need to be here!" I repeated. "I have to stay in China."

"I'll decide where you need to be," Jael cut in with a warning glare. "We've been over this. You can record videos remotely."

I stood up, as if adding a few inches to my height could make her understand. "This isn't about the videos!"

"Then what is it about, Philadelphia?" She groaned and leaned back in her chair, as if this whole debacle was beneath her.

I hesitated, twisting my skirt in my fingers. I hadn't told anyone about Nic's vision, not even Stanyard—probably because I knew they wouldn't believe me.

"Philadelphia," Jael threatened. "What are you not telling me?"

I took a deep breath and forced the truth out. "God told me He wanted me in Beijing."

There was a moment of utter silence. Then Jael arched her eyebrow.

"What do you mean, 'God told you'?" Bowen asked, voice laced with suspicion.

My soul cracked. Of all people, I thought Bowen would believe me. "I mean He *told* me!" I insisted, raising my voice as if that could make it sound true even to my ears. "He gave Nic a vision—"

"What about Nic?" Lanzhou interrupted.

Jael didn't give me a chance to explain. "Philadelphia, for the last time, you need to let him go."

"I can't let him go! He had a dream about me!" Even I realized how that sounded, but I pressed on. "Before we got separated, he told me God had given him a vision about me. He said he saw me in Beijing, fighting Asia."

Bowen and Lanzhou shared an uneasy glance. Lanzhou looked like he might believe me, but neither of them spoke in my defense.

"Don't you see?" I begged, reaching out with both hands. "I'm supposed to stay in China. That's the whole reason all of this happened—Red Rain, the Nolans, everything. God wants me to be here!"

"Look, I don't know what Nic saw or didn't see," Jael said in a tone that suggested she had her own opinions, "but I know you're here because I brought you here, and I can see now that was a mistake. I was wrong—you can't handle this." She stood up and strode towards the door.

I ran after her. "No, it wasn't a mistake! This is what I'm called to do!"

She didn't even look back at me. "I should have sent you to the doctor weeks ago. You're clearly not coping."

I froze, a weight dropping to my stomach. Did she really think I was sick?

Jael paused in front of the door and pointed one neon-colored fingernail at Lanzhou. "Call your physician and have them refill her prescription. She needs to sleep tonight."

The thought of being drugged filled me with dread. I couldn't lose control again, not now. "I'm not going back on medication!"

"I promise, it will make you feel better." Jael made no effort to soften her voice as she pulled out her phone and started typing.

I stared at her, my throat suddenly dry. "I just told you I heard from God," I squeaked. "Are you even listening to me?"

"I'm listening," she snapped, "and what I'm hearing is a traumatized teenager who hasn't slept in weeks and probably has undiagnosed depression." She finally spared me a glance. "Philadelphia, I know you think you had a vision, but it's just your brain trying to cope. This isn't healthy, and I'm not going to let you hurt yourself."

Tears welled up in my eyes as my friendship with Jael evaporated like smoke. She really thought I was crazy. She thought I was sick and diseased and making the whole thing up.

But I *wasn't* making it up. Nic had seen a vision that prophesied I was supposed to be in Beijing. He wouldn't lie to me—God wouldn't lie to me.

And if God wanted me to do this, then I didn't care if anyone else believed me. I would do what I had to do, even if I had to do it alone.

"Fine." I wiped my eyes as resolve dried my tears. "If that's what you think, then I'm leaving."

The room went silent, as if my words had stopped time. It took Jael several seconds to react. "What?"

"I'm leaving." I measured out each syllable to make sure I was understood. "I don't care if you don't believe me. I know what I heard, and I'm going to do what the Lord told me to do. So, if you won't help me, I'll find someone who will."

"Phil," Bowen warned, moving towards me.

Jael put up a hand to stop him. She locked eyes with me. "Is that what you really want to do? Because that sounds like insubordination."

I returned her gaze. "If you can't listen to the Lord, then I can't follow you."

She let my words hang there, forming a glass wall between us. Then she sighed. For a brief second, her cold expression wavered, and she looked genuinely upset. "Then you're not my Blue Fire."

"What?" I exclaimed.

Her voice hardened again as she returned to her phone. "I created Blue Fire. She can be replaced."

My heart restarted as a new emotion pumped through my veins. "You can't replace me!"

"I can, and I will if it will save this revolution." She swiped a command into her screen. "You're going back to Boston, and you're going off the grid for a week while I clean up this mess. Then I'll decide if you're recording any more videos."

I lost all words as my respect for her shattered. She'd become just like every other adult in my life—refusing to hear me and resorting to threats when I failed fit her mold.

She resumed dictating before I could find my voice. "Find a room for her to stay in," she ordered Bowen. "She does not leave this building until we're ready to fly out. Lock the door if you have to."

"But—" he protested.

"If I find she's set even one foot outside this factory, it's on your head," she snapped without mercy. She turned to Lanzhou. "I'm ordering some sleep medication—make sure she takes it."

"Did you just threaten to drug me and lock me in my room?" I screeched.

"You made your choice, Philadelphia." She put her back to me. "Now you can either make this easy on yourself, or you can force me to do what I must to protect my people." Then she opened the door and breezed into the hall, ending the conversation.

"But you can't—" I started, lurching forward.

Lanzhou gripped my shoulders. "Philadelphia, please."

I turned to look up at his face. He was heartbroken.

"Let me talk to Jael," Bowen insisted.

"No," Lanzhou cut him off. "You've done enough. I'll handle this. Come on, Philadelphia." He scooped my duffle and backpack off the table, then nudged me towards the door.

I was too stunned to resist. Lanzhou took advantage of my silence and gently pushed me out into the hall. I numbly let him guide me to the elevator, my feet tripping over each other as my thoughts started and stopped like an engine that was struggling to ignite.

Lanzhou led me to an abandoned office on the second floor. It was a tiny room with a tiny window and no furniture except a dusty desk.

"I'll have a cot and some dinner sent up," he said as he shoved me the rest of the way inside. He set my duffle and backpack next to the door.

I whipped around to face him. "Lanzhou, please, listen to me. You believe me, don't you? About Nic?"

He didn't answer. He stared at me, all the joy stripped from his expression. Then his eyes shifted to the keypad on the door.

I reached for the handle. "Don't, please—"

"I'm sorry," he whispered, then slammed and locked the door.

The sinister beep of the keypad sent my heart to my throat. This couldn't be happening—I *wouldn't* let it happen. I couldn't become a prisoner again, trapped behind a locked door while someone else decided my future.

I had to get out of here. I wasn't about to get drugged and thrown on a plane back to Boston. I had to get as far away from this factory as possible before Jael realized I was gone.

I spun around and scanned the room. *The window!* I ran to it and cranked the blinds open. In a stroke of luck, the office faced the back of the factory where the docks were. If I waited until nightfall, the alley would be abandoned.

Except I couldn't afford to wait. Lanzhou would return any minute with sleep medication, and he would force me to take it. I had to run *now*.

I shoved the window open, the ungreased hinges protesting. The office was two stories up, a decent drop—but there were several open dumpsters in the alley. If I could aim my fall just right...

I grabbed the sill, swung my leg up—and stopped.

What are you doing?

I wasn't sure if it was my subconscious or the Lord speaking, but He probably would have used the same tone of voice.

I jerked back from the sill as if it had burned me. I held up my hands and realized they were shaking. *Everything* was shaking. My heart was hammering and my ears were rattling as I sucked in breaths over and over without getting any air. The room pitched to one side as my vision faded in and out, like a light that was short-circuiting.

I slapped my hands to my face, but I couldn't feel them. Had I really almost just jumped out a window? What was wrong with me? I tried to answer that question, but all I found was confusion and fear and rage.

This wasn't right. None of this was right. This wasn't what God had promised—why couldn't anyone see that? Why was everything going wrong when I was doing what the Lord told me to do? Had Nic lied to me? I didn't believe that. Did he misinterpret what the vision meant? I didn't believe that either. So, what was I doing wrong? Where was God?

And why won't He answer me?

I collapsed to the floor on my knees. I'd never felt so alone in my life. I'd gone through periods of missing the Lord's voice in the chaos before, but nothing like this. He'd only spoken to me once in the past month: *"Wake My people up."* Sure, I'd preached to people at church, but that was just repeating what I already knew. I'd only received one word from the Lord for myself, and I thought I was doing what He wanted. But since then, it had been radio silence, and now everything was crumbling, and people were dead because of me, and everybody thought I was lying about Nic's vision, and absolutely nothing was happening like God said it would.

And I couldn't help but wonder if it was my fault.

Did I sin? Was this because of what happened with the General and my chip? Or was it because I almost killed Nic? Did I mess up so badly that God had chosen someone else?

I would have. I would have chosen anyone but me.

I pounded my fist into the floor and relished the shudder of pain in my arm. Maybe I *should* go home. Maybe I should give up, stop recording videos, and let someone else be Blue Fire. If God wasn't with me, then I certainly shouldn't be leading the revolution, let alone a church service.

But what would Nic say? He'd sacrificed everything—his reputation, his freedom, Mars—to get me here. What would he think if he found out I gave up and walked away? I would have given anything to talk to him, but I couldn't. I couldn't talk to Nic, I couldn't talk to my brother, I couldn't talk to my dad, and I couldn't…

I stopped when I remembered there was one person I could call. Suddenly, through the blinding hurricane of doubt and terror, I knew what I needed to do.

I dragged my backpack towards me and scraped at the zipper. I yanked my tablet out and called Stanyard.

It rang once, twice, three times. "Please pick up!" I wailed, starting to cry. I knew in my heart that if he didn't answer the first time, I'd lose my nerve.

By the grace of God, he picked up on the fifth ring.

"Hey, Phil," he mumbled groggily. His video connected, but there was nothing to see. The room was completely dark except for the backlight of his screen faintly illuminating his face. Clearly, I'd woken him up, but I didn't care.

"Stanyard," I begged, "I need you."

"Whoa, what's wrong?" The camera jerked as he struggled to detangle himself from the sheets.

"I almost jumped out a window!" I declared, then burst into tears when all the confusion and fear came rushing back.

"What?" There was a crash and a yelp, and then a lamp flicked on. He came back into frame. "You did what?"

I realized how that sounded. "No, no, not like that, I mean I almost ran away."

He tried desperately to rub the sleep from his eyes. "But why? What's going on?"

I struggled to figure out where it had all gone wrong. "They busted the group home, and we almost got caught, and a bunch of people got shot, and now Jael wants to send me back to Boston—"

"Philadelphia," Stanyard interrupted. "Slower."

I took a deep breath, even though it sounded like I swallowed water. "I visited a group home today, and someone must have given the police a tip, because they found us. I got away," I added quickly when I saw him start to react, "but they arrested several others. A couple of people got shot."

I flinched. It sounded so callous, so informative, like I was just relaying the weather. Several people *died* today—and it was because I was there.

"Phil," Stanyard breathed. I could hear the anguish in his voice, but I pushed on before he could say anything more.

"And now the government is promoting the video and making it look like I'm a murderer. Jael thinks I can't do this anymore—it's too dangerous for me to go out in public. But I *know* I'm supposed to be here."

The world shook like an earthquake when I realized I wasn't sure I believed that anymore. I repeated it again, desperate for something to make sense. "But I know that's what God wants, and I tried to tell her, but she thinks I'm insane. She really thinks I'm sick, Stanyard. She threatened to put me on medication."

I searched Stanyard's eyes, begging him to believe me. Surely, someone had to agree that this wasn't right.

He did. His eyes narrowed. "Where are you now?"

"At the factory. Lanzhou locked me in an office. Jael wants to send me back to Boston, but I know this isn't right. I wanted to run away, but I know that's not right either, and I just…" My voice shattered as my emotions came out in a garbled torrent. "I'm scared and confused and I don't want to take any pills, but she's not listening to me and I don't know what to do… so I called you."

I broke off in a sob, that last statement putting a period on my pathetic existence.

Jael was right. I couldn't handle this.

Stanyard was silent for a long moment, long enough that I began to worry I'd scared him off. I swallowed and forced myself to look down at the screen.

He was smiling, the gesture completely dissonant from the cold darkness in my heart.

"What?" I prodded.

"Did you hear what you just said? You called me *before* you made a decision." The joy was so thick in his voice that he sounded like he was two steps away from crying himself. "I'm so proud of you, Phil."

A tiny sliver of warmth crawled into my soul when I realized he wasn't the only one. I felt the shift in the Spirit and tried to grasp the feeling before it slipped away.

Please don't go. I need You.

Stanyard sat cross-legged on his bed and held the camera out in front of him. "Now, talk to me. Why do you think you shouldn't come back to Boston?"

I struggled to gather the thoughts that were scattered on the floor of my mind like pieces of shredded paper.

"Is it because of Nic?" Stanyard prompted when I didn't speak for a minute.

The Holy Spirit gave me the answer to that question. "No," I admitted to myself and the Lord. "At least... not for the reason everyone thinks."

Stanyard waited.

I flinched. "This is going to sound crazy, but... you have to believe me. Please."

"Phil," he said, his gentle voice reaching across the airwaves like a hug, "I'll always believe you. I can't promise that I'll always agree with your decisions, but I'll always believe you."

I stared into his eyes as mine welled up again.

"Do you trust me, Phil?"

"Okay." I took a long breath and waited until my heart stopped thrumming in my ears before speaking again. Then I walked him through everything as best I could—about Nic's vision, my conversation with Tower, the command the Lord had given me. I laid it all out in the open—for Stanyard and myself—and explained why I knew in my heart of hearts that I was supposed to be in Beijing.

"I know that sounds insane, but..." I stopped when I realized there was no second half to that sentence. I sighed and braced myself for his reaction.

He let his breath out through his nose. "I'll admit, this completely reframes the way I think about Nic." The statement was too genuine to be sarcastic. "But, coming from you, it doesn't really surprise me. To be honest, I suspected it had to be something like that."

I scrunched my brow. "What do you mean?" An open vision was the last thing I would have suspected.

"Phil, don't take this the wrong way, but..." Stanyard almost smiled as he confessed, "You're kind of emotional. It's really not that hard to convince you to change your mind, especially if there's hurting people involved."

I flushed when I realized he was right.

He put up his hand. "Don't overthink it. All I'm saying is, the only time you dig in your heels is when you believe you're doing what's right. The fact that you've been so adamant about staying in Beijing when it's really dangerous tells me that God's involved somewhere."

"Then you believe me," I stated, relief finally putting the breath back in my lungs.

"Of course," he said without hesitation. "I absolutely believe God called you to be Blue Fire. I've never doubted that."

He paused, and I filled in the blanks. "But…?"

"But I think you're going about this the wrong way. Just because God said you're supposed to be in Beijing doesn't mean you're supposed to be there *right now*. And what if you've already accomplished what He wanted you to do? He could have…"

Stanyard trailed off, as if he realized he was using too many words. He glanced away and drummed his fingers on his knee. I held my tongue, even though every nerve in my body wanted to argue.

Stanyard finally condensed his thoughts and turned back to the camera. "Remember Abraham and Issac?"

"Yeah?"

"God told him he was going to have a son—but it didn't happen for, like, twenty-five years."

I stiffened. For the first time in the last hour, my head stopped ringing as Stanyard's words reset my reality.

"And what about Joseph? God told him he was going to rule the world, but then he got sold into slavery and sentenced to jail for something he didn't do. And David—he could have killed Saul in that cave."

I knew exactly what passage he was talking about. I grabbed my backpack and pulled out my Bible. I flipped through the pages until I found what I was looking for:

"The men said, 'This is the day the Lord spoke of when he said to you, "I will give your enemy into your hands for you to deal with as you wish."' Then David crept up unnoticed and cut off a corner of Saul's robe.

"Afterward, David was conscience-stricken for having cut off a corner of his robe. He said to his men, 'The Lord forbid that I should do such a thing to my master, the Lord's anointed, or lay my hand on him; for he is the anointed of the Lord.' With these words David sharply rebuked his men and did not allow them to attack Saul."

"David could have made himself king," Stanyard spoke into the silence as the Scripture sank its teeth into my soul. "But he didn't, because he knew God would fulfill His promise in His time."

I closed my eyes.

"Phil, you said yourself, you didn't create Blue Fire. Jael did."

I nodded as several tears slid down my face.

"If you didn't create her, then you don't have to protect her. You don't have to make this happen. If God wants you to do something in China, then He'll open the door. Maybe it's today, maybe it's next week. Maybe it's not for a few years. I don't know—and you don't either."

And that's okay, the Holy Spirit echoed him.

I opened my eyes. I knew what I had to do.

"I gotta go," I announced.

"Wait," Stanyard called. "Look, take it from someone who's done this before: It will be scary. You're going to feel like you're breaking apart and losing pieces of yourself. But I promise—you're not losing anything you want to keep."

I focused on the screen. He was smiling softly, and I found myself returning the gesture. "I'll text in half an hour," I promised, and hung up.

Tossing the tablet aside, I jumped up and closed the window and the blinds, then turned off the lights. This was between me and the Lord.

I returned to the floor and pulled my knees to my chest. I rocked in silence for a minute, almost wishing the Holy Spirit would initiate. But I knew I had to be the one to move.

"God, I'm sorry," I started—then stopped again. How was I supposed to do this?

Just tell Him the truth, I coached myself.

I closed my eyes again and rocked harder. "God, I'm sorry. I don't want to do this anymore—I mean, I don't want to do this by myself anymore. I'm tired of being alone and confused and trying to figure it out. I want to hear You again."

I shivered as that feeling of being lost at sea swept over me. "I miss You," I whispered. "I miss You, and I miss Nic, and I feel like no one else understands. I'm scared, and I don't understand why this is happening. You brought me to Beijing, but now Nic is gone and people are dying and I don't... I don't know what to do. I don't know where I went wrong."

There it was—that sharp, icy pain in my soul. That deep-rooted fear that this was all my fault, that I'd sinned and ruined my future, that God had left me and was never coming back. And underneath it all was the maddening desperation that if I just tried a little harder, held on a little tighter, I could fix this. I could prove myself. I could avoid all this pain and darkness and loneliness if I just worked harder and behaved better.

I lay down flat on the floor, but the world continued to shake. Stanyard was right—I was breaking apart. I felt like a cracked porcelain doll; if I didn't hold myself together, I would shatter into a million unrecoverable pieces. There was darkness everywhere—inside, outside, blurring my vision—like a wave capsizing a boat. If I fell in, I would drown.

I wept. I had no idea what else to do. I was trembling so hard I couldn't feel my face or my hands, and I had no idea if it was the Holy Spirit or terror that was rolling over me like a windstorm. The room seemed both too quiet and too loud at the same time. I couldn't breathe, I couldn't swallow, and I knew, no matter what, that I wasn't getting up off this floor alive.

You have to let go.

I couldn't stand it any longer. "I give up, God," I hacked, the words barely making it past the anxiety in my throat. "I surrender."

Nothing changed. The world was still dark, and the fear still screamed in my ear. Everything I knew I needed was hanging just out of reach—locked on the other side of that glass coffin I'd been trapped in for so many weeks.

I jerked upright and screamed into the empty room. "I give up!" I shouted again, desperate for whoever was on the outside of the box to hear me. "I don't have to be Blue Fire, I don't have to stay in Beijing, and I don't have to lead the revolution. If You want me to go back to Boston, I will. If You don't want me to record any more videos, I won't. If I never do anything important in my life ever again, then fine! Do what You want to do, God. I just need *You* back!"

The glass shattered. Like a breaking dam, all the emotions that had been trapped inside of me spilled onto the floor. Suddenly, I could feel myself again—I could feel *Him* again. There was peace and uncertainty and regret and forgiveness all at once, and I accepted it all. I went limp and let it wash over me, soaking up the weight of His presence until He was the only thing I was breathing.

Eventually—I had no idea how much time had passed—the waves of emotion subsided, as if the storm had blown over. I felt almost empty, but not in a frightening way. It was as if I had room to breathe again.

And into that newly created silence, the Spirit spoke.

I love you.

"I love You, too," I whispered back.

My tablet pinged. I pushed myself up and looked at the screen; it was Stanyard.

YOU OKAY?

I glanced at the clock and realized it had been a lot longer than a half hour. I quickly opened the device and texted back.

YEAH, SORRY

AND?

That one word was an invitation. And this time, I took it.

I'M COMING HOME

21: NIC

"I have to admit, I'm very disappointed, Q."

"What part of 'your profit margin has increased by 26.52%' is disappointing?"

I squinted at the graph displayed on the projector and tried to figure out what part hadn't made it past translation. Vance, Ryan, and I were gathered in Warden Ivanova's office to review production reports. It hadn't even been two weeks, and I'd already won the bet. The factory was operating at an impressive 92% efficiency. Profits had doubled, and that didn't even account for all the money they were saving on conserved resources. If the higher ups didn't recognize her achievement, the warden could just creatively "allocate" some of the surplus funds and give herself a raise.

She, however, did not seem to recognize the significance of this achievement. *Maybe I shouldn't have used a pie chart.*

She cackled. "I was really looking forward to feeding you to the lions if you lost."

"You can't win every round," I intoned.

She stood up and offered me her hand. "Then remind me to never bet against you again. Good job, Q."

Ryan whooped and jumped three feet off the ground so he could slap me on the back. Vance clapped politely and cracked something close to a smile.

I deferred the praise with a small bow. "However, if you want this to last, there's one more change you need to make."

"What's that?" she asked.

I shoved Ryan forward. "You need to make him your floor supervisor."

"Hold up! What are you volunteering me for?" Ryan struggled to get away, but I held him by the collar.

The warden sneered down her nose at him. "This guy? He can't even see over the railing."

"Then get him a stepstool. Look, I can engineer your assembly line to death, but it will fail without productive workers. If you want your prisoners to be compliant *and* happy, you need to put Ryan in charge."

I looked down at him as I revealed what the Lord had shown me, piece by piece, over the past few nights. "This guy is so good with people that he organized the most successful demonstration in a decade—and he wasn't even on the same continent."

Ryan stopped squirming. "Huh, never thought about it that way."

"Fair enough," Warden Ivanova said with a careless shrug. "Anything else I should do?"

"Yeah. You need him to do your books." I grabbed Vance's sleeve and tried to pull him forward, then gave up when I realized it would be like dragging a boulder.

Warden Ivanova frowned. "I've already got an accountant."

"Not a good one," I argued. "If you want to make sure all these increased profits are reinvested properly—and have some left over for yourself—then you need a wizard with numbers. Besides, I heard he's really good at tax fraud, and that's something you're going to need if you don't want the feds snooping into your sudden productivity boom." I punched Vance's muscular shoulder and immediately regretted it.

He folded his arms. "I told you, what I did is not considered fraud in most jurisdictions..."

I glared up at him. "Don't help me."

"Well, I can't believe I'm saying this, but I trust your judgment, Q." Warden Ivanova turned and barked at the guards standing by the door. "Get these men an office and anything else they need. I want this implemented tonight."

The guards saluted and turned to go. Ryan scampered after them, mouthing something about *"We'll talk at dinner."*

Vance followed at his own pace. When he got to the door, he stopped, glanced over his shoulder at me, and winked.

I smiled back.

"Well, seems you worked yourself out of a job, Q."

I turned to the warden. She leaned against her desk. "You've completely turned this factory around *and* given me a new management team. I don't suppose I need you anymore."

"No, not really," I admitted. "So, can I go home?"

She smirked. "Nice try. I have another job for you."

She gestured for me to follow. We walked to the elevator and descended to one of the subbasements—one of the few floors of the factory I hadn't been on. The warden pressed the button to open the doors, then stepped back to let me see.

The entire floor was a giant open lab. A glittering array of workstations and fabricators ran the perimeter of the room, and in the center was a massive testing chamber manned by two robotic arms. The space thrummed with activity as half a dozen scientists bustled around the plexiglass cube, murmuring and taking notes.

I gaped. "What else do you have hiding in your basement?"

She walked up beside me. "We don't just produce the products here—we develop them. And these Einsteins are in desperate need of leadership."

I glanced at her. She smiled and gestured broadly at the lab. "Welcome to management. I figure this is a more *profitable* use of your three PhDs."

I managed to mumble an affirmative as the Voice invaded my consciousness.

I told you I would give you this factory.

"Oh, you'll need a different uniform." Warden Ivanova walked over to a supply cabinet and opened it. She yanked a lab coat off its hanger and tossed it at me.

I caught it. "But I look so good in orange."

"You don't." She strode back to the elevator. "Make yourself comfortable. Work starts at 0900 tomorrow, Q—or should I say, Dr. Nic?"

I looked up just in time to catch her wink before the elevator doors closed.

I fingered the starched cotton as I surveyed the lab again. All the familiar sounds and smells enveloped me and put me right at home: the sterile scent of acetone and latex, the clatter of flasks on a metal table, the squeak of oxfords on the linoleum floor. The facility was a lot smaller than my station on Mars, but it was state of the art and beautiful nonetheless.

And now it was mine.

"Thank you," I said aloud.

He smiled. *Well done.*

The arrival of the elevator interrupted our bonding moment. I turned to see a breathless guard approach.

"I'm sorry, Q, I mean, Dr. Von Niewen—"

"Just Nic is fine. What's wrong?"

"Someone's here to see you."

I stared at him for a solid ten seconds before gathering my wits and following him back to the elevator. Who would be coming to visit me?

I was in such a good mood that I flirted with irrationality. *Could it be her? Did the underground find me?*

Disappointment didn't even begin to describe my reaction when I opened the visiting room door and saw Asia standing there.

"You seem surprised to see me," she cooed after we'd finished gawking at each other.

"I was just hoping it was… well, literally anyone but you."

She flicked her finger. "Come here."

"That's a nope." I pulled back into the hall and prepared to slam the door.

"It's about Philadelphia," she called, barely raising her voice.

I hesitated.

"That's what I thought. I'll ask you again: Come here."

I stepped into the room and closed the door to prevent eavesdroppers, then folded my arms and leaned against the wall.

She rolled her eyes. "How would you like a full pardon, doctor?"

I snorted. "At what price? If it involves kissing you, then no thank you. I'll take my chances in here."

She shook her head, her deathly gorgeous smile returning. "I thought we discussed this: I'm over you. All I ask is that you tell me where Philadelphia is staying, and you'll both be pardoned."

"You still haven't found her?" I guffawed. I was so elated that I doubled over and laughed maniacally. "I was already having a great day, but that's just icing on the cake. It was so nice of you to fly all the way out here to tell me the good news."

There was a pause before she retaliated, which told me all I needed to know. "I almost caught her," she growled.

"'Almost' doesn't win wars, sweetheart. Just admit it: You were bested by a homeschooled teenager. Join the club. We'll get t-shirts made."

She took a minute to collect her evil serenity before continuing. "Maybe I haven't set the stage properly. I had that building surrounded. I could have burned it down on top of her."

I wasn't fond of that mental image, but I kept a straight face. "And you didn't because…?"

"Her security shot first." Asia shrugged, as if the failure didn't bother her—and I genuinely believed that it didn't. "The rest of the people in that building were not so lucky."

I swallowed my next comeback.

Confident she'd regained control of the conversation, Asia took a menacing step forward. "They won't be able to hide her forever. Everyone knows she's in Beijing, and the entire province is in an uproar."

I'd always known that was a risk; that was why I hadn't wanted us to stay in China in the first place. But I knew Phil had a calling—and I knew Who had called her. For the first time in a long time, Asia was not in control.

She wrinkled her nose, as if my silence was disappointing. "I *will* find her," she announced, raising her voice to compensate for my lack of theatrics. "And if the police catch her first, they will burn her at the stake. Do you really want to see her go through that? The trial, the humiliation?"

"What do you want, Asia?" I barked. "Get to the point before you suck all the oxygen out of the room."

She tipped her chin back. "I'm here to make a deal. Tell me where she is, and I'll make this all go away. You know I don't want to hurt her. I'll get her to safety, and all her friends can go free."

Terrifyingly, I knew she was telling the truth. She would do as she promised—and that was precisely why I couldn't agree.

"If the government finds her, they will kill her. But *you* can still save her, Nic." Asia stretched her hand towards me, her fingernails sharpened to a point like knives. "Let me help you save her. If you care about her—"

I pushed away from the wall. "You know what, Asia? You're right."

She stopped.

I threw up my hands in surrender. "You have me completely figured out. I do care about Phil. I care about her more than anyone I've ever cared about before—including you."

She *tched*, but the sound fell short.

"But do you know what that means?"

I closed the gap between us. She straightened and stared me down. I leaned over until my face was inches from hers, enunciating each syllable slowly as I drew my line in the sand.

"I won't let you have her. I'll serve every single minute of my seventeen life sentences before I let you touch her. So, either shoot me now or get back in your helicopter and fly away, because I'd rather die than tell you where she is."

There was a pause as she contemplated me. Then she huffed and stepped aside. "Funny, that's what the rebels I tortured earlier today said."

"What?"

She reached into the pocket of her suitcoat and pulled out her phone. "I've been playing nice so far, but I've got a deadline approaching, so we're going to speed this up." She tapped the screen. "As of today, the price on her life is doubled. Anyone who even calls in a tip will be handsomely rewarded. On the contrary, anyone who is suspected of harboring her will be considered an enemy of the state."

She looked up and met my eyes one last time. "Mark my words: I will turn this entire city against her."

"That will work great," I snapped, filtering out my emotions, "until she leaves the country."

Asia blinked, as if she hadn't considered that before. Then, slowly, her lips parted in a sneer. I saw a flash of her white teeth as she ran her tongue over them. "What a brilliant idea, doctor." She moved to walk past me.

"Wait, what do you mean? Asia!"

I reached for her arm—and my hand went straight through. The hologram glitched as my fingers disturbed the particles.

She cackled. "I mean, you didn't think I'd really come and see you, did you? This place is disgusting."

She stepped through me, her image briefly phasing in and out of existence. "Enjoy your retirement, doctor. But while you're counting off your five hundred and ten years of incarceration, remember this." She paused and glanced over her shoulder. "You could have prevented what's about to happen."

And then she walked out of frame and disappeared.

22: PHILADELPHIA

The next morning found me standing alone outside the conference room.

The sun had just peaked above the skyline and was warming the shadowy hall with yellow light. I'd spoken to Lanzhou the night before and asked him to arrange a meeting with Jael. Somewhat to my surprise, she'd consented to meet with me early, before the others arrived. The off-duty factory was eerily quiet, with the only sound being the distant beep of a truck as it backed up to the delivery dock.

I fidgeted with the strap of my bag. I had used the black duffle Narissa sent as a suitcase and organized my tiny stash of worldly belongings into it. I was sure I'd have a chance to go by the Tangs' house and pick up the rest of my clothes—and my cat—but I wanted to be ready when I met with Jael.

Partially because if I wasn't packed to leave, I knew there was a risk I would change my mind.

I closed my eyes and fought back a wave of uncertainty. Everything still felt dark and scary and watery, like I'd cut the anchor and was drifting listlessly out to sea. Surrendering to the Lord didn't answer all my questions; if anything, I had *more* questions as my vision of my future broke apart like a wrecked lifeboat.

But despite the anxiety that still squeezed my soul, there was one emotion I wasn't feeling anymore: anger. I could tell in my jaw and down my back; I wasn't tense. And that gentle sense of quiet spoke louder than all the doubts and promised me I was doing the right thing.

Not my will, I preached to myself, then pressed the doorbell on the conference room.

Jael answered immediately. "Come in, Philadelphia."

I swallowed my nerves and opened the door.

She was alone, as I'd requested. She was in her usual place at the head of the table, one leg crossed over the other as she worked on a laptop. The projector behind her was playing the morning news, the sound muted.

Suddenly, the conference table seemed a mile long, like the final walk on death row. I hesitated, long enough that the door began to shut again. I quickly caught it with my arm and forced myself to put one foot in front of the other.

Jael did not look up until I arrived in front of her. "Yes?" she prompted, the word devoid of opinion.

I tossed my duffle and my backpack on the table. "I'm going back to Boston."

She glanced at my bags. "You don't have a choice."

"I always have a choice," I returned. "But I'm choosing to obey you."

She shifted her eyes back to my face. "Why?"

"Because you're in charge," I said simply, and that was that.

She arched a plucked eyebrow. "Did you call me in here at the crack of dawn just to tell me something I already knew?"

"No." I stood up straight. "I called you in because I wanted to apologize."

She leaned back in her seat and waited.

"I want to apologize for my behavior yesterday. What I said was very insensitive, and it was immature of me to threaten to run away. I disrespected you in front of the others, and I'm sorry."

If she was impressed by this confession, she didn't show it. I took a deep breath and pressed on. "I hope I can still be part of the operation. I want to stream from Boston, if you'll let me."

"And what if I say no?" she challenged.

I tried to read her tone for a cue but couldn't find one. I resisted the urge to cry as I gave up my last piece of control. "Then I understand. If you tell me I'm done, I'm done. You have my word that I will not go behind your back, and I will not try to undermine you. I trust your judgment, so whatever you tell me to do, I'll do it."

She let my words hang there for a moment. "Is that all?"

"Yes, ma'am." I folded my hands and awaited my sentence.

"Then that's all I needed to hear." The light came back into her eyes as she smiled and set her laptop aside.

Every muscle in my body relaxed as forgiveness washed over me. I let out the breath I'd been unintentionally holding.

Jael chuckled and stood up. "At ease, soldier." And then she did the unthinkable: She opened her arms for a hug.

I hesitated, but only for a second. I grasped her and soaked up the physical affection I had been needing for so many weeks.

She rubbed my shoulders. "You'll always be my Blue Fire," she whispered in my ear.

And Mine, I felt the Holy Spirit say. I didn't bother to blink away the tears.

She gave me another pat and let go. I pulled back—just in time to see myself come on TV.

It was a clip from yesterday's raid. The footage was grainy, pulled from the security camera on the building across the street and enlarged. Some helpful editor had drawn a yellow circle around my blurry face as I slipped away down the alley and disappeared.

The video paused, and the anchorwoman took over. She read from her script as Mandarin characters flashed across the screen. "What does it say?" I asked Jael.

She frowned and stroked her fingers across a tablet lying on the conference table. The sound came on, but I couldn't understand any of the foreign language. Jael hit another button, and a rote, slightly inhuman voice replaced the anchorwoman's and began to speak in English.

"In response to the continued violence of this terrorist group, United leadership has increased the reward for any information regarding the whereabouts of Philadelphia Smyrna." The AI voice lagged a few seconds behind the anchorwoman's lip movements as it translated. "Beijing officials are asking for help identifying several of Smyrna's associates who were photographed at last night's riot."

The security footage zoomed out to reveal several other figures fleeing down the fire escape, their faces highlighted in an ethereal white. My heart caught in my throat when I recognized one of them as Bowen. Thankfully, he was facing away from the camera, so only his side profile was caught on tape. *Had he turned around...*

I closed my eyes and prayed, hard.

"Investigators have already used face-recognition and location services to detain several of the terrorists," the anchorwoman droned, as if this information were about as interesting as a traffic report. "Following positive confessions regarding their involvement with so-called 'Operation Blue Fire,' the terrorists have been convicted and their executions scheduled for this afternoon."

My eyes flew open. "What?"

She needn't have repeated herself. The screen flashed to a livestream of a sports stadium. Civilians were trickling in, shaded with irreverently colored umbrellas as they claimed the best seats. I could tell by the row of armed soldiers lining the perimeter of the field that they were not setting up for a game.

The ugly truth sank into me like fangs. That was why some of my guards hadn't made it back; they'd been captured and sentenced to death, along with all the other innocent nurses and sick residents who hadn't made it out of the building. The government was going to slaughter them all.

A sound I don't remember summoning ripped out of me. *They can't do this!* But I knew they would; the Chinese government had been executing people like cattle for a century. The sentencing of a few unassimilated criminals was hardly worth reporting.

Except they were associated with me.

I whipped to face Jael. "Please, is there anything we can do? I know you've gotten people off death row before."

She squinted at the projector, jaw set like a rock. Before she could answer, Asia appeared on the screen.

Her cruel face filled the monitor as she radioed in. "It is with a heavy heart that I signed off on these executions this morning," she said, the AI translating from Mandarin. "These 'rebels' were regular citizens until Smyrna poisoned them with a false promise of wealth and power."

They flashed up a clip from one of my recent videos—the one where a troop of soldiers saluted me, their guns pointed towards the sky. The clip that made me look like a deadly insurrectionist.

I buckled over and gripped my chest. *Oh God, what have I done?* That wasn't who Blue Fire was at all. But Asia would twist and corrupt and edit my photos until the entire world thought of me as a dictator—and thanks to my recent rallies, I had given her plenty of material.

The screen split between the anchorwoman and Asia as the broadcast returned to the studio. "Clearly, this 'operation' has become a front for glorified gang violence," the anchorwoman prompted.

Asia bobbed her head. "Indeed. And I fear for our young people. The rebels' propaganda is blatantly targeting our most vulnerable..."

Jael spoke over her. "You're going on air."

I stumbled back from the projection. "What?"

She whipped around and opened her laptop. "I'm patching you in. I can hijack this broadcast with Data's program."

"But why?" I gasped, then quickly changed the question. "What do you want me to say?"

"Just keep Asia talking." Jael's nails clacked rapidly on the keys like gunfire. "You're buying me time. As long as you're on air, her people will be scrambling to figure out where you're broadcasting from. If I can send them on a rabbit trail for even an hour, that gives me a window to stop these executions."

I reacted and grabbed my duffle. I popped my blue contacts out and threw them on the table, then slid the wig on and stuffed my blonde hair underneath. It was sloppy, but it would have to do. I stripped my jacket, exposing my thunderbird tattoo, and turned to Jael.

She spun the laptop around to face me. "She will be able to see you."

I sank into the chair in front of the computer, my knees suddenly wobbly. *Oh God, help me! Give me the words!*

Jael brushed my shoulder. "I'll help you. Just follow my lead." She stepped back and grabbed the tablet, muting the projection. "You're on in three, two…"

Before she even got to "one," the image on the newscast glitched, and I was there. My crackly stream replaced the anchorwoman's, so it looked like Asia and I were sitting side by side.

Jael gestured frantically at her lips. I swallowed my trepidation and spoke loudly to cover my own fears. "This is Blue Fire. Can you hear me?"

Apparently, they could. There was a sharp beep, and my stream flickered, replaced with the irritated words "technical difficulties." I looked to Jael in a panic. Had they finally patched Data's backdoor?

"Wait!" Asia shouted in English, lunging forward. "Let her through."

There was a pause, and then my stream faded in again. The camera autofocused until I was coming through clearly.

"That's better." Asia settled back in her chair. "Philadelphia, what a surprise. I see you've finally decided to show your face."

Jael made a rolling motion, so I blurted the first thing that came to mind. "You must not have social media," I snarked, trying to sound bored like Nic, "because I show my face all the time. So much so that I heard your algorithm has a censorship filter for it."

I glanced at Jael for approval. She winked encouragingly and continued to swipe commands into her tablet.

Asia snorted. "How unbecoming. Philadelphia, what *are* you doing?"

Jael took up station on the other side of the table and faced her tablet towards me. On the screen she'd typed in large letters: *"Turn the question back on her."*

"What are *you* doing, Asia?" I returned, mimicking her tone. "I know you're trying to bait me with all these theatrics. These trials and executions—is that what this has come to?"

Asia shook her head. "You can't blame me for your problems, child. You brought this on yourself. That blood is on your hands."

Jael held up another prompt: *"Remind them who the real enemy is."*

"No, it's on yours." I sat up straight as righteous anger filled me with resolve. "That wasn't a 'rebel hideout' you busted yesterday—it was a *hospital.* There were helpless *babies* in that apartment. What did you do with those children, Asia?"

She ignored the last question. "You call that a hospital? Those children were living in squalid conditions and being denied medical care. And when I send in social workers to try to rescue them, you open fire."

My palms began to sweat. "They were just trying to protect me. *Your* government is the one who came in and shot a dozen unarmed people—and now they're going to execute the rest of them."

The words hitched in my throat as I remembered what was at stake. Jael smiled.

Asia held up her hand, as if forestalling someone off-screen. "That sounds like exactly the kind of thing a divisive terrorist would say. You've become just like the rest of them—using race and religion to cover up your thirst for power. I know the real you, Philadelphia, and all you want is war."

"No, I don't," I insisted. "*You* do."

Asia hesitated for a second, long enough for Jael to swipe to the next screen: *"Tell her you're leaving town."*

I met her eyes, searching for confirmation. She nodded.

I focused back on the camera. "But I won't give it to you. If this is the game you want, then I'm not going to play. I'm leaving town, and you won't be able to find me. I'll be gone by nightfall."

The silence dragged on, so long that I wondered if she hadn't heard me. But then, slowly, she grinned.

"Oh, Philadelphia," she crooned, "don't you know it's too late to go home?"

My heart froze.

She turned and gestured at someone off-camera. "Roll the clip."

The newscast rearranged. Our streams were shoved to the corner to make room for a full screen feed of a downtown street. A dozen wailing police cars circled an old stone office building as a regiment of soldiers swarmed the sidewalk. A commander supervised the chaos, barking orders into a megaphone.

At first, I couldn't see any landmarks, but the slant of the light suggested the sun was setting, putting the scene on the opposite side of the world. And then I caught sight of a street sign: The office was on the corner of Bolyston and Washington. I knew that intersection; it was in downtown Boston.

I choked when I realized what was about to happen. *No!*

Asia confirmed my fears. "I'm very pleased to report that, thanks to an anonymous tip, we've located Smyrna's American headquarters," she announced.

"Who told you?" I screeched.

She ignored me. "This building was the main hub of operations for 'Blue Fire,'" she explained, voice clearly not directed at me anymore. "Police have recovered multiple servers of valuable information, and several of her co-conspirators have been detained."

As if on cue, the front door of the building banged open, and a pair of guards hauled someone onto the sidewalk.

"Stanyard!" I screamed, forgetting I was on air.

I barely caught a glimpse as they shoved him, cuffed and struggling, into the back of a van. Right behind him, two more guards were arresting Lev. His tennis shoes scraped on the concrete as they literally dragged him by his collar. I saw a distinct smear of blood on his pale cheek before they threw him into the van.

I scrambled for my backpack, not caring that I was no longer in frame. *Oh God, no no no.* I snatched my tablet and dialed Stanyard. *This can't be happening, this can't be happening, this can't be happening.*

It rang out.

Jael threw her tablet on the table. She whipped around and began whispering harshly into her phone.

I numbly sank back into the chair. I hyperventilated, the air scraping my throat like gravel, as my thoughts started and stopped, started and stopped. *He's dead. Stanyard is dead, Lev is dead, they're all going to die!*

"I have an announcement for all United citizens." Asia raised her voice to be heard over the shouting as the footage continued to roll. "As of today, the reward for information regarding the whereabouts of Philadelphia Smyrna has doubled."

The guards dragged someone else out of the building: my uncle. Two soldiers held him down while they took a thumbprint scan and cuffed his hands behind his back.

The soldier frowned at his tablet and handed it to their commander. The commander took one look and hurled the device on the sidewalk. He lunged at Tower, shoving his shoulders and cussing him out.

That's when I remembered my uncle was military. That meant he was worse than a rebel; he was a traitor.

"All citizens are authorized to detain her and any of her associates by any means necessary." Asia couldn't keep the smile off her face as she narrated. "On the other hand, be advised that associating with or harboring Smyrna will be considered an act of terrorism."

The commander spit in Tower's face, then took a step back. The other soldiers forced my uncle to his knees on the sidewalk.

I saw the commander reach for his holster and knew what was coming a second before it happened.

"Stop, Asia, please!" I shrieked. "Don't do this!"

She spoke as if she didn't hear me. "And the punishment for terrorism..."

I screamed, but the explosion from the commander's gun drowned me out.

"…is death."

Someone yelled in the background, and then the footage went oddly silent. The soldiers gracelessly dropped Tower's body on the curb. The camera continued to roll, the gruesome scene letting the entire world know my uncle was dead.

And it was all because of me.

Tears streamed down my face. I was breathing so hard you could hear it on the TV as I gripped the table and struggled not to black out. *God, what is happening?*

Asia's cackle jerked me back to the cruel present. "I only have one thing to say to you, Philadelphia."

I instinctively turned to face her.

She held me in her wicked glare. "Checkmate," she sneered, and then the screen went dark.

GREEN DRAGON

RED RAIN #8.5

Thu, Jan 9 at 6:13am

WT****

please tell me this is a joke

where are you?

answer your phone!

Thu, Jan 9 at 7:02am

STANYARD
this isn't cool

Mark and Julia said they didn't see
you leave last night

what is going on??

pick up your phone!!!

Thu, Jan 9 at 8:38am

STANYARD
why aren't you answering?

if you don't want to talk to the
Carvers, I can meet you somewhere

Thu, Jan 9 at 10:47am

STANYARD
look, I just want to know what's
going on

what do you mean, you met
someone?

Thu, Jan 9 at 3:22pm

STANYARD
at least tell me you're safe

Thu, Jan 9 at 7:49pm

please, just let me know you're alive

Fri, Jan 10 at 1:26am

I can't believe you would do this to
me

after all we've been through

we went with the Carvers because I
thought that's what YOU wanted

I did all this for YOU and now you
can't even tell me goodbye to my
face!!

Fri, Jan 10 at 7:45am

sorry about last night

I'm just worried

if you don't want to meet me, that's
okay

just please, answer the phone

Fri, Jan 10 at 2:47pm

can you at least send me a text?

Fri, Jan 10 at 6:25pm

was it something I did?

Fri, Jan 10 at 11:19pm

if so, I'm sorry

Sat, Jan 11 at 2:21am

please, just tell me you're alive

that's all I ask

if you want me to leave you alone, I
will

I just need to know you're okay

Thu, Jan 16 at 7:09am

it's been a week

can we talk now?

Mon, Jan 20 at 4:45pm

I got your email

why won't you answer my texts?

Wed, Jan 22 at 8:13pm

at least respond to my email

Fri, Feb 7 at 9:51pm

I talked to Jayde

I know you're lying about marrying
a soldier

what happened?

Sun, Feb 9 at 1:12am

what did I do wrong?

Mon, Feb 17 at 3:47am

I thought we were in this together

AUGUST 2076

1

The shriek of my text tone woke me up.

I groaned and groped for my phone. Leaving my ringer on loud had not been conducive to restful sleep, but I couldn't risk missing a message from her.

I yanked my device off the charger. The screen flickered on at full brightness, making my vision flash. I muttered to myself as I fumbled for the dimmer and swiped through the notifications.

The culprit was an email—spam, judging by the subject line. There were no new texts from Philadelphia.

I glared at the clock. I'd slept for six, nearly seven hours—an Olympic record for me. Why hadn't she texted? It was daytime where she was, halfway around the world in Beijing. I knew she was going to speak at a church today, but service should have been over hours ago.

I opened the chat and initiated—just like I always did.

HOW WAS CHURCH?

Somewhat to my surprise, she typed back immediately.

CHURCH WAS GREAT. SORRY, WE HAD ANOTHER VISIT TO MAKE

Of course, you did. There was always an excuse with her.

I sighed and covered my face as conviction nipped me. This was her job. As weird and uncomfortable as it was to think, my girlfriend was a celebrity—or a public enemy, depending on who you asked. She was "Blue Fire," the face of the revolution. She was currently stationed in Beijing and was touring underground outposts across the city, rallying the people to join the resistance and stand up against the United. It was literally her job to "make visits"—and I knew she was not in control of her calendar. Jael, the true mastermind behind the operation, was the one who gave the orders.

Still, I wished Phil would tell me when plans changed—instead of leaving me unread and making me worry that something had gone terribly wrong. Again.

I pushed the thoughts aside and texted back.

HOW WAS IT?

There was a pause, and I feared she'd closed her device without saying goodbye—something she did quite frequently. After a minute, typing dots appeared. They vanished and reappeared twice before she finally sent a message.

I DON'T KNOW

I frowned and sat up.

IS EVERYTHING OKAY? ARE YOU SAFE?

I'M FINE. I'M JUST NOT SURE WHAT TO THINK RIGHT NOW

I didn't either. Phil was normally enthusiastic about her rallies, especially when she spoke at a church. She was always gushing about how many people were there, and how supportive everyone was, and how God had given her this word or touched that person. She saw the Holy Spirit in everything, and so did I.

In fact, based on the stories she told me, I was beginning to wonder if God was stirring something much more important than political revolution.

This would be the first time a visit *hadn't* gone well, and that gave me plenty of cause for concern.

I phrased my next text carefully.

CAN WE TALK ABOUT IT?

She was silent. I gripped my device. *Please don't leave me hanging.*
She finally replied.

I CAN'T TALK RIGHT NOW. WE'RE STILL HERE. CAN I CALL YOU WHEN WE GET BACK?

I begrudgingly texted an affirmative, and her avatar went dark. I fruitlessly refreshed the screen. Something wasn't right, but as usual, I wouldn't find out until it was all over.

And by then, there would be nothing I could do about it.

I growled and threw my device on the bed. I hated this. My girlfriend was out there risking her life to save the known universe while I hid behind a computer monitor. Phil said she was fine, but I knew she wasn't. She'd been kidnapped, held at gunpoint, and almost killed multiple times. She was stranded in a foreign country without any friends while Asia, the most powerful woman in the government, hunted her down. It was only going to get more dangerous the closer we got to operation day—and there was nothing I could do to help her.

Well, I thought as the Holy Spirit prodded my conscience, *there is one thing I can do.*

Throwing the covers aside, I got out of bed, knelt on the floor, and prayed.

By the time I was done, it was past seven, so I figured I may as well go to work. I spent most of my time at the underground base across town, programming for Jael and helping Data and Tower organize the resistance in Boston. Up until recently, I had been living on base, but ever since Asia had busted our allies and forced us to relocate, Tower insisted we take shifts. Associating with "Blue Fire" was a crime in more ways than one, and there was always the fear that someone would turn us in for the ludicrous reward the United was offering. At least, if we took shifts, the government wouldn't catch all of us.

Yesterday was my night off. I would have preferred to accept the risk and sleep on base, but Tower had lectured me last time I'd tried to pick up someone else's shift. He couldn't stop me from coming in early, though.

I hastily threw on some clean clothes, stuffed my laptop and phone in a backpack, and slipped out into the hall. Our apartment was dark except for the weak morning light peering through the broken mini blinds. I avoided the creaky spots in the floor as I navigated to the kitchen. Maybe, if I hurried, I could get out the door before the rest of the family woke up.

No such luck. My father stood by the sink, measuring coffee into a filter.

I halted and tried not to look surprised. "Morning," I managed.

"Good morning," he repeated. He gave me an awkward smile, followed by an even more awkward, "Stanyard." It was like he'd forgotten how to say my name.

I turned away and opened the refrigerator. "Where's Mira?"

He hesitated, which told me everything I needed to know. "She went out last night. She's not back yet."

I gripped the fridge door. My sister was always "going out." She never said where she was going—and every night, I feared she'd never come back.

Just like last time.

"Here. I made you cereal."

I looked up to see my father holding a stained plastic bowl filled with bran flakes. I almost rolled my eyes and barely caught myself. You don't "make" cereal, and I hated cereal. I never ate it.

Which he would have known, if he'd paid any attention to the first seventeen years of my life.

"Thanks," I mumbled, and grabbed the milk.

He went back to making coffee. I sat at the table and rallied the courage to eat my breakfast. For several minutes, the only sounds were water pouring into the carafe and me crunching on the unsweetened cardboard.

"What are you doing today?" my dad finally ventured.

"I gotta go to work."

"What are you working on?"

"I can't talk about it."

That wasn't a lie. Data had asked me to help him code a program that would hijack the United's mandatory announcement channel so we could push Phil's videos to every registered device on the planet. It was extremely top secret; we hadn't even told Phil yet.

Dad hit the *brew* button and turned to face me. "Can I come with you to base? Maybe I can help…"

I shoved my cereal under the milk with my spoon. "No, Dad, it's not safe."

That also wasn't a lie. The fewer people who knew about our new headquarters, the fewer who could compromise it. Even Mira hadn't been on base yet. The location was on a strict need-to-know basis, and my dad didn't need to know.

He didn't give up. "Well, then, when will you be home for dinner?"

We haven't eaten dinner together as a family in years. "I don't know."

He frowned. "I was hoping you could help me around the house. There's several things that need repair."

The apartment was falling apart at the seams, but it didn't matter. "We're not going to be here that long." Our dingy living arrangements were hopefully temporary. I certainly didn't plan to stay here long.

"Maybe, but I still want to make it nice for your mother." He shook powdered creamer into his mug. "I'm going to fix the leak under the sink today, and then I want to remove the wallpaper that's peeling…"

He droned on with his handyman list. I clenched my spoon. This—with the coffee dribbling into the carafe, and my cereal getting soggy, and my father acting like nothing was wrong—was so *normal.* So unbearably normal.

I would never live a normal life. I had five warrants out for my arrest. I was working for (and dating) the most wanted woman on the planet. I was a hacker, a rebel, a felon. Things could never go back to the way they were.

And I didn't want them to.

"So, can you help me tonight after dinner?" my father finished.

I opened my mouth—but my phone rang, sparing me the misery.

I snatched it out of my backpack, hoping it was a call from Philadelphia. It wasn't. It was Data.

I swiped to answer it. "Yeah?"

"You need to get down here."

He didn't have to tell me twice. "On my way." I shoved my chair back and shouldered my backpack.

"What's wrong?" my father asked.

I waved him off and darted out the front door. I waited until I was in the stairwell before speaking again. "What's going on?"

Data sighed so hard I could hear it on the other end. "Jayde's back."

Thu, Jul 16 at 1:09am

UNKNOWN NUMBER
Don't ask how I got your number.

I'm a friend, I promise.

There's something you need to
know.

The interrogations were only the
start.

They're going to deport your entire
containment camp to China.

I can send you the proof.

GREEN DRAGON
hey

it's good to see you again

2

That's what the activity log said. I stared at the timestamp on the screen as the hated callsign filled me with dread and rage.

Jayde was a lot of things, but a friend was not one of them. He was the former leader of the resistance in Boston—a position he forfeited when he betrayed Phil.

"When did this happen?" Tower leaned his knuckles on the desk and squinted at the monitor. Tower, Lev, and I had gathered in Data's office on base to review the evidence.

"About an hour ago," Data answered. He used both hands to enlarge the window on his touchscreen monitor. "My security system caught it. I have the base's algorithm set to alert me any time there's activity on his accounts. He logged into the server remotely and downloaded a bunch of info before I locked him out."

"Where is he now?" Lev asked. His thick Russian accent made the words sound brash and tough, but the expression on his face was the exact opposite.

His fear wasn't unfounded. If Jayde was back from Beijing, Lev was in more danger than any of us. The kid was barely fourteen, and he'd grown up in Jayde's shadow after Jayde had rescued him from being executed with the rest of Boston's Jewish community. Jayde was the only "family" Lev had left, but Lev had turned on him to protect Phil—and save my life.

I was sure Jayde would show him no mercy if he ever caught him.

"If the location ping is to be believed, he was using the hotspot at the mall across town." Data pointed to the address at the end of the activity log. "Of course, as soon as I blocked him, he turned his device off."

That meant Jayde was close, very close. Lev tensed, jaw rigid.

I clasped his shoulder reassuringly. Even though I shared his apprehension, I couldn't help but feel relieved that Jayde was back on this continent. At least if he was here, he wasn't in China threatening Phil.

"What I want to know is how he was able to log in in the first place. I thought you already blocked all his accounts." Tower stood back from the desk and frowned at Data.

Data slouched in his chair with a sigh. "I tried. But this is his network, not mine."

It was a regrettable truth. When Jayde went rouge, Data had immediately retaliated by blacklisting him and revoking his access to the base's servers. But even though we'd since relocated our headquarters, much of the software was still the same. Jayde had built this network from the ground up, and it was almost impossible to lock a creator out of their own universe.

"How'd he get in?" I asked.

"That's the dumb part," Data admitted. "He used a cellphone I didn't know about. It was signed into an old account that had admin privileges."

That was stupid—stupidly easy.

Data clicked his mouse aggressively. "I blocked the IP and revoked the permissions for that account, but..."

"But there's no telling how many accounts he has," I finished for him.

He grunted an affirmative.

"Forgive me if I'm old and out of touch with technology," Tower interrupted, scratching his graying hair for emphasis, "but can't you just reset the permissions for the entire base?"

"For our internal server here, sure, already did that." Data leaned forward and used his finger to drag a window to the center of the monitor. "But this isn't a department store. We're a network of extremely disorganized rebels. I don't have a tidy list of employees and who needs access to what. Just because I locked him out of my database doesn't mean he can't get into Andes's—or Phil's, for that matter." He glanced back at me.

I grimaced. He was right—Jayde probably had several of Phil's logins. He knew all about her multiple identities and had intimate access to her credentials as "Andromeda Nolan." Not to mention, he had literally *held her hostage* for a week; he'd probably made a dozen accounts for himself while he had control of her devices.

Tower gestured with his hand. "Okay, so we tell our contacts to change their passwords, and then...?"

"Nothing," Data muttered. "There's no way for us fully lock him out— and I'm not of a mind to factory reset everything when operation day is a month away."

Operation Blue Fire was exactly a month away, on Thursday, September 17th. Civilians across the globe had pledged to stand up to the United and revolt against the government's control. Last I'd heard, there were over one hundred demonstrations planned in Boston alone. Tens of thousands of people were involved; trying to restructure our network of communication would be a nightmare.

Especially when we had no idea who in the city was still loyal to Jayde.

Tower folded his arms across his chest. "So, what you're saying is, we should just give him his old office back."

"Wouldn't hurt to change the locks," Data deadpanned, "but frankly, it's not the databases I'm worried about. There's not a lot of information on there that he doesn't already know."

How I wished that wasn't true.

"So, what does he want?" Lev complained. "Why now?"

"Hard to say—the info he downloaded was very scattershot." Data scrolled down the activity log. "But my guess? He's looking for the new base."

He gave Lev a look, long and slow, and then arched an eyebrow at me.

I autofilled what he'd been too kind to say.

Jayde is coming for you.

"Well, let's not leave the lights on for him," Tower grunted. He pushed up the sleeves of his army uniform, and the drill sergeant came to attention. "I want this place on lockdown. Absolutely no one steps foot in this building without being cleared by one of us."

He pointed at Data and me. We both nodded.

"You," he swiveled his finger to Lev, "don't leave this building without a partner. And I'm driving you home tonight."

The last sentence was directed at me. "Maybe I should just stay on base," I offered.

He ignored that. "I want all our contacts on high alert. If anyone sees or hears anything from Jayde, I want to know. Notify me if there's any activity on any of his accounts. If the algorithm even hiccups, you call me." He gripped the back of Data's chair.

"I'll increase the sensitivity." Data turned back to his monitor and started pounding on the keyboard.

My programmer's brain finally kicked into gear. "Let me analyze the data he downloaded. Maybe there's a pattern—"

"*You* won't do anything," Tower interrupted. He stepped between us, blocking my view of the screen. "I need you to stay focused. We need that broadcast program up and running by next Tuesday."

"I can multitask," I grunted.

"I don't care. Let me handle this."

I had several follow-up arguments, but the stance of his muscular body told me I'd better not try my luck.

"Fine. Come on, Lev." I strode out of the office.

Lev scampered after me. "What are we doing?"

"I need your help setting up a new workstation in the computer lab." I didn't actually need his help—I could build a computer with my eyes closed—but I'd spent enough time with Lev to know that he needed a job. Preferably one that was in the same room as other people. "Can you get some aux cables from the storeroom? I'll meet you in the lab."

"Yes, boss." He saluted and darted off.

I hurried to the computer lab on the third floor. After checking to make sure the room was empty, I logged into a terminal and pulled up the server change log.

There he was—over a dozen entries from Green Dragon. What was he doing? And why now? If he'd had this phone the whole time, he could have logged in weeks ago. Why didn't he try to reset his permissions as soon as Data locked him out?

And why did he use an account registered to his name?

I tapped the screen and whispered the question I'd been hesitant to voice in front of the others. Like Data said, Jayde probably had the credentials for dozens of his former employees. He might even still have access to Phil's login. If he had used someone else's account, he probably could have gotten by undetected. Jayde wasn't subtle, but he wasn't sloppy, either. He should have known we'd be watching for him and revoke his access.

Unless... he wanted us to know it was him.

I stiffened as Data's cold suggestion echoed back to me.

Jayde is coming for you.

I clenched my fists. Let him come. If he wanted a fight, I'd be ready—and this time, I wouldn't hide behind a monitor and wait for him to make the first move. Whatever Jayde was planning, the answer was in the code, and I would find it.

The Green Dragon had threatened this operation—and my girlfriend—for the last time.

Slapping on a pair of headphones, I sat down and started typing.

UNKNOWN NUMBER
I heard the news. I'm so sorry.

I was only trying to help. I didn't think she would turn it into a demonstration.

I can't believe she would do that.

This was supposed to be about rescuing your families, and she made it about her.

None of this would have happened if it weren't for her.

GREEN DRAGON

look, I know I was a jerk

let me make it up to you

dinner tonight?

Sat, Jul 18 at 8:42am

GREEN DRAGON

look, I know I was a jerk

let me make it up to you

dinner tonight?

3

Well, if Jayde's coming for me, he's being extremely lazy about it.

It had been three days, and there was no sign of the Green Dragon. There was no activity on any of his accounts or any suspicious behavior on the server. His file was cold; the most recent entry was from several weeks ago, when he landed in Beijing. He didn't make contact with anyone, and there was no movement at his apartment. Even his family hadn't seen him. There was absolutely no evidence that Jayde was in Boston.

The easy explanation was that he had masked his IP. But routing his connection through Copley Place seemed like an oddly specific choice. If he didn't want us to know where he was, he could have used an IP from Venus for all it mattered. Making it look like he'd accessed a public hotspot in downtown Boston seemed like a herculean effort.

That left two other options. Either he actually was in town and was waiting to show his hand—or he wanted us to *think* he was in Boston.

But why? What did he gain by sending us on a witch hunt? If he wanted the advantage, he shouldn't have told us he was coming.

Unfortunately, the code wasn't as helpful as I would have liked. Data was right: "Scattershot" was an accurate description of the information Jayde had accessed.

It was my "day off," so I shut myself in my room with my laptop and reviewed the activity log for the hundredth time. Jayde had been logged into the server for about fifteen minutes before Data locked him out. During that time, he hadn't opened the plans for Operation Blue Fire or any of the other incriminating files that were stored on the server. Instead, he'd logged into the program that encrypted the base's outgoing communication—an app he no doubt had installed on his phone—and used it to read every text message I'd ever sent Philadelphia.

I tried and failed not to let that information irritate me. I knew all the communication I sent from base was permanently recorded—a fact I'd found out the hard way when Jayde had spied on my call history and used the information to blackmail Phil into going to Beijing.

Unfortunately, I wasn't the only one whose privacy had been violated. According to the logs, Jayde had read every text message and email that had been exchanged with Phil's devices. Even conversations that didn't involve her—like an email string where Data and I had discussed one of her videos— had been accessed. In fact, it looked like Jayde had run a search for her name and callsign and downloaded the results—including messages that were several weeks old, from before we relocated the base.

What did he want? While I didn't appreciate his eavesdropping, I knew my chat history with Phil was harmless, relatively speaking. I hadn't told Phil the location of the new base for this exact reason. I'd also been very careful not to let her text me any specifics about her whereabouts or her rallies, just in case our communication was intercepted. The only juicy information Jayde would glean from our conversations was that I was planning a romantic date night as soon as she returned.

That is, *if* she ever came back from Beijing.

I ignored the thought and scrolled to the top of the activity log. There had to be another explanation for the data, some other common denominator that would tell me what Jayde was after. He knew he had a limited amount of time to access the server, and he'd chosen to pull Phil's text history. Why?

I opened the oldest entry and started reading. All the messages seemed benign—until I came to a phone number I had memorized.

GREEN DRAGON
I need you to talk to your brother

he's trying to talk Blue Fire out of
the operation

MIRA
I'm not doing your dirty work for
you.

Why would she be talking to him? I grabbed my phone and searched my contacts to make sure I wasn't hallucinating. No—that was definitely Mira's number.

I quickly read the rest of their chat.

GREEN DRAGON
but he'll listen to you!

MIRA
Yeah right.

> Look, I just came back to save my parents.
>
> Don't drag me into this.

GREEN DRAGON
this is your war too

Unsurprisingly, Mira had not responded. The next message was several hours later, from Jayde.

GREEN DRAGON
when are you coming over tonight?

I clenched my phone. *This can't be happening.* Not only had Jayde been talking to my sister without my knowledge, but they'd also been *seeing* each other?

I knew they'd had a brief—and very painful—relationship earlier this year. Jayde was the reason Mira had run away from our foster family and dropped off the grid. She refused to discuss it with me, and I thought that meant their relationship was over.

Apparently not.

I hurled my phone on the bed. Switching to my laptop, I pulled up the server's encryption program and ran a search for Mira's number. A dozen more messages between her and Jayde appeared.

GREEN DRAGON
look, if your brother is bothering
you, I can get you out of town

I know some safe places

he doesn't have to know

MIRA
Thanks.

I'll think about it.

Think about what? About abandoning me again?
I scrolled faster.

GREEN DRAGON
we've got a problem

Aurelius called Q last night, and
then Q called Blue Fire like 10 times

I don't know what he said to her,
but she's mad

       MIRA

       And how is this my problem?

GREEN DRAGON

it'll be your problem if she quits the
operation

       MIRA

       If you're so worried, tell her you'll
       kill Aurelius if she doesn't do it.

My vision flashed back. Mira hadn't even hesitated; there was barely a ten-second delay between the messages.

GREEN DRAGON

you serious?

       MIRA

       It's not rocket science.

       She'll do anything for him.

Their chat went silent, but I remembered what had happened next. Jayde had taken Mira's advice and blackmailed Phil into going to Beijing on a suicidal assassination mission. Either she killed the General Secretary, or Jayde would kill me.

Lev was the one who was supposed to pull the trigger. He didn't, and Nic had gotten Phil to safety before Jayde could retaliate. But that didn't change the fact that *my own sister* had offered me up for ransom.

And I thought we were in this together.

I slammed my laptop shut. Grabbing my phone, I stormed out into the hall. The door to Mira's room was closed.

I heard her talking on the phone, the muffled words echoing through the thin plaster. I banged the door open without knocking.

She was lying on the bed, legs dangling off the edge. She jerked upright and swore. "Stan!" she objected.

"Who are you talking to?" I demanded.

She muttered an apology into her phone and ended the call. "None of your business. Get out of my room."

I moved closer. "It's Jayde, isn't it? Did he make contact with you?"

"What? No, why would he?" She hastily stuffed her phone in her pocket.

I folded my arms. "I don't know, why don't you tell me? I know you two are back together."

"We are *not* dating." She huffed and tossed her hair.

I abruptly remembered how much I *hated* her new hairstyle. She'd shaved half of it off and dyed the rest a stupid combination of pink and black. It was unnatural and ugly and nothing like the shoulder-length strawberry blonde hair she used to have.

Just like the nose piercing, and the ear piercings, and the stud in her eyebrow, and the revealing clothes, and the gangster dragon tattoo that circled her arm—all the details that spelled out in big, neon letters that my sister was not the person I thought she was.

My sister would never leave me. My sister would never block my number and refuse to return my calls. My sister would never date a jerk like Jayde.

And my sister would never, ever put my life in danger.

Not after all I'd done for her.

"Oh really?" I threatened. "Then why did you spend the night at his house?"

She scooted back on the bed. "What? I didn't—"

"Stop lying to me! I saw the text messages!"

She frowned. "The... text messages?"

I sighed tiredly. "Whatever you send from base is recorded. I know everything."

"Everything?" She avoided my eyes, making me wonder if there was more I didn't know.

"Well, for starters, I know it was your idea to use me as blackmail to make Phil go to Beijing," I snapped.

She just stared.

"Mira." My voice broke, and all the anger and rejection rolled over me in competing waves. "How could you?"

She flinched. "I didn't think he would do it..."

"That's what you were betting on? Have you met Jayde? What if Phil hadn't gone through with it? What if he'd actually shot me? Did you ever think of that?"

She didn't respond, and in the screaming silence I collided with the answer I had spent eight long months running from.

Any other explanation was justifiable. I could have rebuilt our relationship around any other truth—that she really was in love with Jayde, or that she hated Phil, or even that she was on the wrong side of the war. She could have betrayed anyone, killed anyone, or committed any number of gross sins, and I could have dealt with it. I could have accepted any reality but this one.

But this was the reality we were living in. This was the reality she'd created when she'd run away from the Carvers and left me behind.

The reality where my sister didn't care about me.

"How could you?" I whispered again, even though I realized there was no possible answer she could give that would explain her actions. "I thought we were in this together."

She refused to look at me. "Stan, you don't understand—"

Rage flashed through me like a forest fire, overtaking my grief. "You're right—I *don't* understand. Everything I did was for you! I wouldn't have even left camp if it weren't for you!"

"What is going on here?"

I whirled. Our dad loomed in the doorway.

I stared at him. His heavy-set frame blocked the light from the hall—the same imposing silhouette that had filled my bedroom doorway so many times.

I think I knew then what was about to happen. Survival instinct gave me one chance to save myself.

Run.

Mira spoke first. "This doesn't involve you, Dad."

"Yes, it does." He stepped into the room, cutting off any escape. He folded his arms and glared at Mira. "Is it true? Was it your idea to leave camp?"

She cowered. "N-no, Stan suggested it."

That wasn't true at all, but I couldn't formulate the words over muscle memory screaming in my ear.

Run!

He turned to loom over me. "I'm very disappointed in you, Stanyard."

Just six cruel words, and suddenly all the anger and guilt and shame in the room was heaped on my shoulders.

Just like it had been so many times growing up. It was always my fault. The commander's aggression, Mira's failing grades, my mother's depression, my father's financial struggles. Somehow, it all came back to me.

My dad took a step closer. "Do you have any idea how much it hurt your mother?"

I took a step back and put up the only defense I had: rage. "I didn't have a choice! Mira wanted—"

"Don't bring your sister into this! You're the oldest. I expect more from you."

There it was: the expectations. The mystical set of rules that I somehow never obeyed. The unwritten code that made me responsible for everything that ever happened to our family.

Not this time.

"What were you thinking, going with complete strangers?" my father challenged. "How could you abandon your family like that?"

I straightened to my full height. "It was either that or let the commander shoot me. Is that what you wanted?"

Of course it was. That's what he'd always wanted.

"We're your family!" he shouted, as if that justified all sins. "Everything I did was to protect you!"

"Protect me?" I cackled. "You never protected me. The only person you cared about was yourself."

His face darkened. "You have no idea what you're talking about."

I saw it—the tightening of his posture, the clenching of his fists—all the signals that said I'd gone too far. I had seconds to surrender before this ended the same way our arguments always did. "Dad, I didn't—"

I wasn't fast enough. "Don't talk back to me!" he roared, and backhanded me across the face.

I stumbled into the doorframe. My cheek burned and my vision flashed, and everything came back in a rush like I'd been plunged underwater.

A hundred unexplained bruises. Two broken bones. Several dozen absences from school.

And a thousand sleepless nights asking myself what I did wrong.

Mira gasped. My father staggered back. He held his hands up and stared at them, dumbly, as if for the first time in ten years he realized what he'd done.

"Stanyard," he murmured. "I'm so sorry." He reached for me.

I jerked away. "Don't." I let the full force of my anger put a period on the word. "Touch me."

He hesitated, his arms awkwardly raised like a disjointed mannequin. He looked hurt, confused. Like he was the victim.

Mira sat, fists tight in her lap, and said nothing.

Just like she always did.

My father sucked in his breath. "Stanyard, please—"

I didn't wait to hear the rest of the sentence. I stumbled across the hall, slammed the front door open, and ran out of the house.

Just like I always did.

UNKNOWN NUMBER

You're next.

You know the government won't stop at Mars. They're coming for Boston. It's only a matter of time before they find you.

This isn't going to stop. They will hunt us all down—and you know she won't turn herself in. She'll let us die.

We're on our own. You have to save yourself. Get your parents to safety.

I can help.

GREEN DRAGON

thanks for yesterday ;)

you doing anything tonight?

4

It was drizzling outside, and the late evening chill made the water cold and miserable. I pulled the hood of my sweatshirt over my head and started weaving through the alleys, trying to stay out of sight of the main roads. I knew I shouldn't be out at night; if the police stopped me, I was done for.

But at the exact moment, I didn't care. All I cared about was putting distance between me and the apartment, as if a couple of blocks could keep the past in the grave.

The abuse started when I was eight, with "discipline" that went a step too far. I thought it was normal at the time. After all, we were Christians; we were always the kids with strict parents and rules that no one else had to follow.

It was only after they forced us into camp, and privacy became a thing of the past, that I realized what my dad was doing wasn't normal.

It didn't happen often. Why use your fists when your words will do? But as conditions in the camp got worse—and my dad got angrier and angrier— the outbursts became more frequent.

It wasn't hard to hide the unexplained bruises. Everyone assumed Commander Ambrose did it. Even my mom, who got home from work much later than my dad, believed that lie a few times.

The only person who knew the truth was Mira.

The rain increased to a downpour. I picked up my speed to match, my tennis shoes splashing in the greasy puddles that quickly formed.

I thought we were past this. I thought me leaving camp—and then coming back to save him from getting deported to China—was enough to reset our relationship. I thought the tearful hugs, the repeated apologies, the heartfelt *"I'm so glad you're back I missed you"* actually meant something.

I was wrong.

A police siren wailed in the distance. I turned off behind an empty building and sought shelter next to a dumpster. Sinking down on a dry patch of concrete, I threw my sopping hood back and raked my hands through my hair.

Why?

The question echoed in the darkness. *Why, why, why?* It was the same question I'd been asking for ten years, afraid to answer, because every possible answer led to a reality that was more painful and unforgiving.

Because my dad hates me.

Because I'm a bad person.

Because God doesn't care, and Christianity is fake, and everything my parents told me is a lie.

I knew now that none of those statements were true. But truth is hard to find when you're standing in the principal's office, lying about why your lip is split and your eye is swollen.

I closed my eyes and leaned against the dumpster. I could feel it, even now. The doubt, the shame, the fear. All the things I'd spent the last three months trying to scrub from my life. All of it resurfaced in an instant, like all the hours I'd spent praying and pounding the floor and worshipping in church didn't matter. Like my relationship with Philadelphia didn't matter. Like my job and identity and crimes and accomplishments didn't matter.

Like one strike of my dad's hand was all it took to shatter everything.

I slammed my fist in a puddle. I couldn't go back. I *wouldn't* go back.

"Stanyard?"

I scrambled up. My dad stood at the end of the alley.

I backed away. "How did—"

"I asked Tower to track your phone."

I groaned at my own stupidity. Now I would get a lecture from Tower about going out alone.

My dad coughed. "You shouldn't be out here. It's cold." He carried a stupid little umbrella with a broken rib. He shook it for emphasis.

"I'm fine. I'll be home later," I said, even though one if not both of those statements was a lie. "I just need some space."

He wasn't listening, as usual. "Stanyard. We need to talk."

It was ten years too late to talk. I glanced behind me, but it was a dead-end alley. There was nowhere to run.

Just like there hadn't been anywhere to run when he'd thrown me into the living room wall so hard a picture frame had fallen and cracked.

"Stanyard," he said again, as if my name was the only thing we could agree on. He sighed. "I'm sorry."

I clenched my fists. I didn't want to have this conversation. Because I knew what I'd have to say—the same thing I said the last half a dozen times he apologized.

And right now, I wasn't sure I could say it and mean it.

He took a step forward, splashing in a puddle. "I'm sorry. There's no excuse for what I did."

I closed my eyes. *And yet, here you are, about to make another one.*

What would it be this time? That he was doing it for my own good? That he didn't mean to hurt me? That this wouldn't happen if I was a better student, a better Christian, a better son?

"I wish I could take back all those years, but I can't. All I can do is tell you that I'm genuinely sorry for what I did to you."

That's what you said a week ago.

"I'm sorry I hit you. I'm sorry I shouted at you. I'm sorry I threatened you and forced you to lie to your mother."

If you're so sorry, then why'd you hit me again?

My dad hesitated, and the pounding rain struggled to fill the silence between us. "I know I hurt you physically and emotionally. I know I blamed you for things and made you carry a responsibility that wasn't yours. What happened to our family wasn't your fault. It was mine."

I opened my eyes.

He stared at me—for the first time really, truly looking at me. "You were right. I'm your father. I should have protected you. Instead, I made you take the blame for my mistakes, and then I let the commander abuse you. I should have defended you, not made a martyr out of you."

For the first time in days, I felt the Holy Spirit moving in my chest. My father had never before taken responsibility for what happened with the commander.

My dad sighed. "I know it's too late to say it, but I am very, very sorry, Stanyard."

"I know you are," I said, and this time, I believed it.

He gripped the umbrella with both hands. "I'm not asking you to trust me. I know it's going to take time. If you need space, then… I'll respect that. All I'm asking for is a chance to change."

I remembered when I had asked Philadelphia for the very same grace, and I knew what I had to do.

"I forgive you, Dad," I said, and then began listing what that meant to me. "You don't owe me anything. You don't have to make it up to me. I won't hold it against you, and I won't remind you every time you make a mistake."

With each word, I felt the breath come back into my lungs, until my heart was no longer pounding. Maybe my dad wasn't the only one who had lied his way through the last six apologies.

Tears were running down his already-wet face. "Thank you. I'll do what it takes, I promise. I just…" His voice cracked, and with it all the anger and scorn that had terrified me for so long. "I can't lose my son again."

"You won't," I promised. *I'm done running.*

He smiled, and so did I.

For a minute, no one said anything. Then my father took a long breath and collected himself. "Let's go home."

I shook my head. "No, I need some time alone. I'm going to work."

"But it's your day off."

"It's fine." Tower would lecture me, but I needed to be busy.

My father frowned. "I'm not sure I like you spending all this time on base."

I stiffened. "It's my job, Dad."

"But it's dangerous."

"I don't care. Philadelphia needs me."

"She's not your responsibility."

She kind of is. Or she would be, if she'd give me the chance.

"She's the one who…" My dad seemed to realize he was treading on thin ice and backpedaled. "Look. I'm worried about you. The closer we get to operation day—"

"Dad, don't say that out here," I hissed, and then glared at the shadows.

He checked behind him before continuing. "It's just, after what happened to Mars, I'm worried you'll be next. I can't lose you, not like that."

The fear was thick in his voice, so I tried to soften my tone and meet him in the middle. "I promise we're being careful, Dad. But someone has to do it."

"That someone doesn't have to be you. Please, Stanyard, I want you to consider quitting."

He suggested it so casually, as if I were merely flipping burgers for minimum wage. As if I could just walk away from Philadelphia, the unassimilated, the revolution.

My dad kept talking before I could argue. "We need to get out of Boston. Your sister knows a safehouse, in some country town out in the Midwest, where we can drop off the grid."

Since when has Mira been looking for safehouses? And how long have you been planning this?

"Your mother and I are thinking of moving out there. Come with us. We'll drop off the grid, wait until this all blows over. We can be a family again. Work on putting our lives back together." He took a step forward, like that was all it took to seal the deal.

I slid back and widened the gap. "Dad, are you crazy? I can't just quit. This isn't going to 'blow over.' We have a real chance of winning this thing. We need to fight back."

Like we should have done five years ago when they put us in a camp.

"Maybe," my dad said in a way that implied he was on the other side of the war. "But my concern is for my children. I need you to be safe."

"I don't want to be safe." If I wanted safe, I would have left Philadelphia in that alley and never looked back.

But I did look back. I made my choice.

"But, Stanyard, please, this isn't your fight. Come with us—"

"No, I'm not doing this." The air between us froze as the wall we had so easily torn down built itself back up again. "You don't understand. This isn't a game to me. I can't just walk away. Maybe you can, but I can't."

He still wasn't listening. "But I need you at home—"

"Things can't go back to the way they were!"

My shout ricocheted off the dumpster, ending the argument.

My dad stood there, breathing heavily, face pinched like I'd stabbed him in the chest. Like he was once again the victim. "I thought you said you'd give me a chance."

"And I will," I snapped, too quickly. "I forgive you, Dad. I really do. But that doesn't mean I'm just going to drop my life and start over. If you need to move to the country, then okay. But I'm staying here."

This is who I am.

He didn't respond. Maybe because he finally realized there was nothing he could say.

I strode to the end of the alley and shouldered past him before he could come up with the words. "I'm going to work," I said, throwing my hood up. "Don't wait up for me."

UNKNOWN NUMBER

Did you see the video she just uploaded?

She's showing her true colors. This was never about freedom. All she wants is war.

War won't save anyone. The only person who will benefit from war is her. She wants power.

We can't trust her.

We have to stop this before more people get hurt.

I know a solution. There is another way.

Call me.

GREEN DRAGON

my place or yours tonight?

5

Tower didn't complain when I came back to base. Probably because he realized that if I was wandering around at night in the rain, I had bigger problems than a lecture from him.

I had an excuse, anyway: We were preparing to launch Data's program. On Tuesday morning Beijing time, we would commandeer a TV network, interrupting one of China's most popular talk shows, and broadcast Phil's livestream to the entire mainland. It would be our biggest test yet, and if we succeeded—if we could keep the signal online for even a few minutes—that meant it was time for Operation Blue Fire to go global.

Of course, there were a million ways for this to go wrong, so I pulled overtime helping Data bulletproof the program. We coded a dozen redundancies, backdoors, and extra layers of authentication that would hopefully keep the government from locking us out. I worked well into the night, then started again bright and early the next morning.

The distraction worked well. Until it didn't.

It was late afternoon, and I was waiting for Data to approve my latest batch of changes. My mouse was still, which meant my mind was empty— and my dad was trying incessantly to fill it.

He'd texted at least once an hour. Most of the messages were repeats of things he'd said last night. When I didn't respond, he broadened the question.

WHEN ARE YOU COMING HOME? WILL YOU HAVE TIME TO WORK ON THE WALLPAPER WITH ME TONIGHT?

I left the message unread. Why didn't he get it? Just because I forgave him didn't mean I was going to quit my day job and move back home. I couldn't go back to a mundane life and pretend the world wasn't on fire. I had work to do—I didn't have time to strip wallpaper and throw baseballs.

But, as always, he wasn't listening to me.

I silenced my device and stuffed it in my pocket, then turned back to my computer. I scrolled through the dozen windows I had open, searching for another problem to solve.

I landed on the security program Data had installed to monitor activity from Jayde. I refreshed the results, but there had been no new entries since the last time I'd checked. The Green Dragon was silent. It was like Jayde had poked around a bit, run into Data's lockouts—and quit.

I leaned back in the chair and frowned at the screen. It wasn't like Jayde to quit. He was stubborn, and he knew his own server like the back of his hand. Surely, there was a backdoor or a forgotten login he could have exploited by now. And if that didn't work, he had friends. There were still people in Boston who were loyal to Jayde, despite everything he'd done. Surely, one of them would be willing to betray the base's location.

No, I had every reason to believe that if Jayde truly wanted to find the base, he would have by now. Which either meant he *did* know where we were and was simply waiting for an opportunity—or that wasn't what he was looking for at all.

I froze when I realized our error. Jayde wasn't looking for the base. My text messages with Phil wouldn't help him find the base; Phil didn't even know where the new base was.

No, Jayde wasn't looking for us. He was looking for Philadelphia.

Rage seized me—then quickly fizzled out when I realized that didn't make sense either. If Jayde was still in Beijing, he had way better resources for finding Phil. He had contacts in China; he even knew where she had been staying last. As much as the thought disgusted me, realistically, I knew Jayde could have just staked out the house where Phil was living and tracked her that way. It would have been a lot easier than scalping my text messages.

I scrolled my mouse rapidly, as if that could conjure another explanation for the data. Nothing about this made sense, especially for Jayde. Phil wasn't stupid, and neither was I. We'd been very careful not to make a permanent record of her location in case our communication was compromised. Which Jayde would know, if he'd read all my conversations with Phil.

Something wasn't adding up—which meant the Green Dragon was still one step ahead.

Before I could rationalize that problem, Philadelphia screamed.

I lurched out of the chair. I waited for an alarm, a shout, anything to validate what I thought I'd just heard. The silence returned as quickly as it had been broken.

I rubbed my temples. I must be overtired, hallucinating after my lack of sleep last night.

Then the sound came again—and it was definitely her.

I raced out of the office. The hallway was empty, but I heard her muffled voice from somewhere ahead.

"Phil!" I shouted. No one answered me.

I raced down the hall, banging open every door. Her voice grew louder, panicked. I whipped around the corner into an open office—and there she was.

Philadelphia's face filled the monitor as one of her streams played on repeat. Mr. Smyrna sat in front of the desk.

I halted in the doorway. Mr. Smyrna was Philadelphia's father—even though he couldn't remember that. He'd been recently revived after being cryogenically frozen, and his memories were gone. He spent most of his time in therapy with Andes and Data. The rest of the time, he stayed on base watching videos, looking at images, and reading old text messages—struggling to resurrect anything of the man he once was.

I tried to help him as much as I could. But there was one video I never meant for him to find.

"Hey Dad. I know what happened with Mama."

It was the second to last stream Philadelphia had recorded from Mars while she was being held hostage by Thames. It was one of the videos that had made her famous—and the one that almost got her killed. She'd figured out that Thames was using her as blackmail to get Red Rain and tried to warn her father before Carnegie cut her off.

That was after she spent several minutes sobbing in front of the camera as she admitted to her dad that she knew what he'd done.

Mr. Smyrna heard me enter and paused the video. "Is it true?" he asked without looking back.

"Which part?" I cringed.

"About my wife." He switched to another window, where he'd pulled up his deceased wife's file. "That I killed her."

The statement was made without any emotion—which was even more terrifying.

I hesitated, too long for his patience. He slammed his fist on the desk. "Is it true?" he snarled.

I flinched. "Yeah. It is."

He stared at the screen, eyes unblinking. "Did it happen like it says in the police report?"

I sighed. Clearly, there was no avoiding this conversation. I grabbed another desk chair and sat down next to him. "No. You were involved in an early version of Operation Blue Fire."

He finally turned to look at me, his face creased in a frown. "I thought Philadelphia was in charge of the operation."

"She is now. But you started it."

He glared at me, the same surly expression he used whenever he was struggling to accept the stories I told him. "What happened?" he said in a tone that suggested he didn't want to know.

I wasn't sure I wanted to tell him. "You were caught. They came to arrest you."

"And?"

The word stretched out between us, long and painful. "And… your wife got shot."

He stared at me, as if making sure I was telling the truth. Then he turned back to the screen.

"They say it was an accident," I offered for no reason at all.

He ignored the comment. "My children didn't know?"

I braced myself. This was why I'd never wanted to have this conversation with him. "No. You lied to everyone, said your wife was convicted for transmitting."

He stabbed the monitor with his finger. "But why did it never get reported?" His voice was loud with desperation—desperation for me to prove it wasn't true.

I couldn't lie to him. "The commander of our camp didn't want to get in trouble for letting a rebellion slide under his radar, so he forged the paperwork. That's also why you were never prosecuted."

All the anger left him, leaving a puddle of a man. He slumped in the chair. "Why didn't you tell me?" he whispered.

It was my turn to look away. "You'd just woken up, and there were so many other things you needed to learn. That didn't seem like the best story to lead with."

That was only half of the truth. The real reason was I didn't want to sow distrust between him and the daughter he'd just met. I wanted to give Philadelphia the best version of her father, not the one who lied and betrayed to bury his grief.

That was the version of Mr. Smyrna who had created Red Rain.

He covered his face with his hand. He stared at the wall through parted fingers and looked, not for the first time, like he wished he'd never woken up.

"I'm sorry," I said, even though I knew the words meant nothing.

"No wonder she doesn't want to come back," he muttered.

"What?"

He slapped the arm of his chair. "Philadelphia. Now I know why she won't come home. She can't live with me."

"That's not true," I argued, even though I'd have been lying if I said the thought hadn't crossed my mind. I'd been wondering if one of the reasons my girlfriend wouldn't come back to Boston—and why she couldn't give me a straight answer when I asked—was because she found it easier to play the role of Blue Fire than Philadelphia Smyrna.

Mr. Smyrna wasn't convinced. "Maybe she is better off with that Nic character."

"That's not true," I said again, even though I didn't believe that either. Nic wasn't my favorite person, but he'd done what her father hadn't—sacrificed himself to save her.

"Really?" he sneered, the bitterness twisting his voice into something evil. "So what, I should ask her to come home and babysit me through therapy for the rest of her adult life?"

I didn't have a comeback for that—partially because I knew it was true.

He took my silence as consent. He snorted. "I can't live knowing she thinks of me as a father while I can barely remember her name. I won't put us through that. She deserves better."

I stiffened. There he was—the old Mr. Smyrna. The lying coward of a man who had endangered his own daughter to save himself from pain. I would *not* let that Mr. Smyrna come back.

"Of course, she deserves better," I snapped. "But you're still her father. She needs you."

He shoved his chair back and stood up, slamming both hands on the desk. "I am not her father!"

His shout echoed around the cramped office, silencing the argument I had ready to follow.

"I am not her father," he repeated, still yelling. "I'm just a collection of facts and photos like some stupid camera roll. Her 'father' is dead and not coming back."

"You don't know that!" I also stood up, which gave me an inch or two height advantage over him. "He could still be in there. Your memories might come back—Andes said so. You have to try to remember, for her."

He tipped his chin up and met my gaze, expression cold and cruel. "Remember what?" he hissed. "Remember how I killed her mother? Remember how I invented Red Rain?"

"Who told you that?" I interrupted. I'd been avoiding the topic of Red Rain with him, for this very reason.

He kept rattling on. "You want me to remember how I lied to her? Remember how I gave her up to—what's his name? Thames?"

He reached down and punched the keyboard, restarting the video. Philadelphia's sobs filled the room as she listed her father's sins.

"You abandoned me, you really did. You left me with those men and just walked away! 'Just go,' you said. Not 'goodbye' or 'I'll come find you' or even 'I'm sorry.' 'Just go.' How could you?"

Her voice cracked, and my heart shattered all over again. I lunged forward and stopped the recording. "Look, it's not like that."

Mr. Smyrna shook his head. His eyes were filled with nothing but rage as he declared, "If that's the kind of man I was, you should have left me frozen."

I opened my mouth to argue—but the Holy Spirit interrupted me.

"You know what?" I said, taking a deep breath. "You're right. You suck."

My choice of words jerked him out of his stupor. He pulled back and scowled at me.

"You're a terrible parent," I continued. "You made some stupid choices, and then you lied to cover them up. You were never there for her when she needed you. You only cared about protecting yourself, and it's almost gotten Philadelphia killed—multiple times."

He tightened his fists but said nothing.

"But." I paused and made every effort to soften my voice. "But that doesn't matter."

"Why not?" he snapped.

I boldly met his gaze. "Because she forgives you."

I fast-forwarded the video a few seconds, then hit play.

"I'm scared," Philadelphia whispered, her voice tiny and weak and brave all at once. *"I'm frightened and I feel alone and I'm questioning everything you did and I don't know if I can trust you. I don't. I really don't."*

Mr. Smyrna opened his mouth, but Philadelphia spoke before he could.

"But I forgive you." She wiped bleeding eyeliner from her cheeks, then looked straight into the camera. *"I forgive you, Dad. I forgive you for lying, and I forgive you for what happened with Mama."*

I spoke over the recording as it continued to roll. "She forgives you. She really does. I've seen her walk it out every single day."

I stared at her beautiful face on the monitor as I recalled her actions over the past few months. Philadelphia had sacrificed everything to bring her father back. She'd been determined and selfless and downright insane—and that was a big reason why I'd fallen in love with her.

"She came back to Earth to look for you even though she had every reason to stay on Mars. She risked her life to meet with Asia and get the code to unlock your tube even though she knew she could be arrested. She spent millions of dollars on your revival even though she knew you might not remember her. And when you..."

I hesitated. A weight filled my lungs as the Holy Spirit rolled back in, this time with conviction. Suddenly, I realized what Philadelphia had done that I hadn't.

I forced myself to finish the sentence. "And when you asked to be let back into her life, she said yes."

I thought of the countless hours Philadelphia had spent over the last week talking to her dad on the phone. Anytime he called, she answered. She would stay up late, patiently repeating herself and teaching her dad all the things he should have known, even when I could tell she was exhausted and stressed and didn't want to talk to anyone, not even me. She was gentle and kind towards him, while he couldn't muster the courage to say *"I love you."*

She'd given him a second chance. Just like she'd given me.

I gripped the edge of the desk as I remembered how I'd gotten down on my knees and literally *begged* her for a second chance. Now my dad was asking for the same mercy, and I wouldn't even answer his texts.

"But... I'm not the man she remembers," Mr. Smyrna said. His voice was quieter now, almost nervous.

"You don't have to be. In fact, maybe you shouldn't," I added emphatically. "You can be a different person. You can make different choices."

He sank back down in the chair, silent.

"Look." I straightened and turned to face him. "It's not going to be pretty. It's going to be painful and uncomfortable and awkward. Things aren't going to be like they used to be."

I winced as my own angry words echoed back to me.

"Things can't go back to the way they were!"

But maybe... they didn't have to.

I glanced at the screen, where the video had finished playing. My relationship with Philadelphia would never be the same as it was before she'd become Blue Fire—but I wouldn't go back even if I could. Six months ago, I'm not sure Philadelphia would have given me the time of day.

And I'm not sure I would have asked.

"Things are going to be different," I continued the thought aloud, as much for myself as for Mr. Smyrna. "But if you work at it... maybe things could be better."

I pulled out my phone and studied the last text message from my father. This wasn't about wallpaper. It wasn't about me quitting my day job or us moving to the country. It had nothing to do with Philadelphia or the revolution.

"I can't lose my son again."

My relationship with my family would never be the same. But maybe, if I made room for the Holy Spirit, He would do for my father what He'd done for Philadelphia and me.

I looked back down at Mr. Smyrna. He was still staring at his daughter's face on the monitor, but his expression was relaxed, curious—making me hope that, perhaps for the first time, he was wondering what could be.

I laid my hand on his shoulder. "You going to be okay? There's something I need to do."

"Yeah," he mumbled, and his calm tone of voice suggested he actually would be.

I gave his shoulder a squeeze, then walked out of the office and shut the door behind me.

Leaning against the wall, I muttered one last prayer and sent my father a text.

I'M GOING TO BE HOME FROM WORK IN AN HOUR. DID YOU STILL WANT TO STRIP THAT WALLPAPER TONIGHT?

His response was almost instantaneous.

THAT'D BE GREAT

UNKNOWN NUMBER
Look at the news.

Her soldiers killed all those innocent children and shot a police officer—and she just walked away.

This is who she is. This is what "Blue Fire" has become.

Is that really what you believe in?

You know what you have to do. You can stop her.

You have my word, he will not be harmed. You and your parents will be taken care of.

She's the only one who has to die.

This is the only way.

GREEN DRAGON
hey

did I leave a phone at your place?

MIRA
Are you on base?

STANYARD
yeah

what's up?

MIRA
Can we talk?

STANYARD
of course

want me to meet you somewhere?

MIRA
No, I'd feel safer talking on base.

It's about Jayde.

STANYARD
ok

I'll call and give you directions

It took so long for Mira to arrive that I began to worry she wasn't coming. It was almost seven o'clock by the time she texted me to page her in. Only Tower, Lev, and a few others were still in the building. Data had taken Mr. Smyrna to Andes's shop for more therapy, and Tower had sent the rest of the crew home for the night.

I led Mira up to the computer lab that was my "office." She settled stiffly into the chair closest to the door. "Sorry it's so late," she mumbled.

I rolled another chair over and sat down across from her. "It's fine, I'm pulling overtime tonight."

It was true. We had a lot of work to do to get ready for Philadelphia's arrival. She and I had talked early this morning, and she had finally agreed to come home to Boston. The reason wasn't a pretty one; someone had betrayed her, and she'd almost gotten arrested. Several people who were with her had been killed. But while I knew she was extremely shaken, I firmly believed this was the right choice, and I couldn't wait to be on the same continent as her again.

For Phil's safety, we weren't telling anyone about her plans, not even her father, so I couldn't give Mira any details.

She didn't ask for them. She just pulled her phone out of her pocket and turned it on.

My chest tightened. We'd played out this scene so many times—where she shut down before the conversation even started. I couldn't let that happen again.

Which meant I had to make the first move—just like I always did.

"Hey." I waited until she glanced up at me before continuing. "We need to talk about what happened the other day."

She shifted and looked away. "I don't want to talk about—"

"No, but I need to." I struggled to keep my voice patient and calm; I had one shot at this before she locked me out. "I'm sorry I yelled at you. I need you to know that I forgive you."

She flinched. "Stan, please—"

I put my hand up. "I'm still really upset. I don't understand why you did it, and I don't understand how you can be with someone like Jayde. But... I want to talk about it, if you're willing."

I paused to see if I was getting through to her. If anything, she looked terrified, eyes wide and panicked like a bird caught in a trap.

I pushed ahead. "I do care about you, Mira. I know I haven't always done the right thing, but you're still my sister."

Her device beeped. She looked down at the screen.

I reached out and grabbed her arm. "I don't want to lose you."

She jerked back. "Don't—"

My phone rang, interrupting her. I glanced at the device where it lay on the desk and saw the caller ID; it was Data.

"I'm sorry," I groaned. "I have to take this." I rolled my chair over and snatched the device, answering it before the call rang out. "What—"

He cut me off. "Are you on base?"

The tone of his voice made me tense. "Yeah? What's wrong?"

"Jayde just checked in."

I spun around and jiggled my mouse. My monitor brightened. An angry red notification from the security program consumed the screen.

Green Dragon was online.

And, according to the location ping, he was in the building.

I tried to rationalize what I was reading. "I don't—"

"I'm seeing the same thing you are," Data grunted. "You need to act fast. There's a security protocol you can run to lock down—"

He kept rambling, but I wasn't listening. Time stopped as I ran the math and saw the truth.

I turned to look at Mira and the scratched device in her hand.

I slowly stood up. "Where did you get that phone?"

She didn't answer. She didn't need to. I thought of all the overnight visits she'd had with Jayde and realized just how easy it would have been for her to steal one of his devices.

"Mira," I exclaimed, and the world bottomed out.

She jumped out of her chair. "I'm sorry! It's the only way."

"For what?" I shouted.

She didn't have time to explain. A shout ripped down the halls. A door slammed, followed by a gunshot and a scream.

"Police! Stand down!"

Everything happened at once. Sirens ignited on the street outside. I heard people running, and Tower barking orders, and Data screaming at me over the phone. Over it all bellowed a voice on a megaphone, the words muffled through the walls.

"We have you surrounded!"

I ran to the window and peered around the curtain. Red-blue lights blinded me. The police had the road barricaded. Half a dozen officers ran towards the front entrance, guns drawn.

I whirled. "What did you do?"

More doors slammed.

"I'm sorry!" Mira repeated. "We have to do this. She promised she wouldn't hurt you."

"She who?" But I knew who was responsible.

Asia.

A hundred panicked thoughts roared in my ear, but none of them were important. "We have to get out of here!" I yelled, even though I knew there was no "we."

There never had been.

Someone shrieked my name. Mira moved to block the door. "No, Stan, listen to me. This is the only way. If we don't stop this, there will be war, and millions of people will die. Just tell Asia where Phil is, and this will all be over."

"What?" I wanted to argue, to reason with her, to convince my sister that she didn't want to do this, but there was no time. Footsteps pounded in the hall.

I turned and ran towards the emergency exit. I had to get to the fire escape. If I could make it to the roof, I might be able to—

"I wouldn't run if I were you."

The cold command cut me off—followed by a gunshot. The electric bullet hit the computer monitor closest to me, igniting a shower of dangerous sparks. I covered my face and hissed as a shard of glass scraped my skin.

I slowly looked over my shoulder. Two police officers stood in the doorway, their weapons aimed at me.

I swallowed and considered my options. *God, help me!*

"I will shoot," one of the officers threatened, as if he hadn't already made that abundantly clear. "Make this easy on yourself."

Mira stepped between us. "Please, Stan," she begged. "Do as he says. I don't want you to get hurt."

I stared at her as the lie took the air from my lungs.

You don't care if I get hurt.

"Let us handle this," the other officer interrupted. He reached into his pocket and withdrew a flash drive. "As agreed. Three clean files and a generous allowance to get you started. There are directions for how to claim the money and alter your prints to match the files. If you follow the instructions, everything will be untraceable."

He held the drive out to Mira.

"What did you…?" I managed.

She took the drive. "It's for Mom and Dad. I'm getting them out of town."

"But—"

"Go," one of the officers ordered, and Mira obeyed. They stepped out of the way, and she darted into the hall.

"I'm sorry, Stanyard," she said again, and then ran without another glance back.

I struggled to breathe as all the questions I should have asked screamed in the silence.

Why did you how could you she betrayed you. Again.

"All right, lover boy, time to go," one of the officers disrupted my thoughts. He unclipped a pair of handcuffs from his belt. "Asia wants to see you."

FALSE FLAG

RED RAIN #9

AUGUST 2076

1: PHILADELPHIA

I killed my uncle.

The world froze while I struggled to swallow that fact. The conference room was utterly silent. Jael, the only other person in the room, stood as still as a mannequin as she stared at the dark projector. There was no ticking of clocks, no whirring of vents; even the factory on the floors beneath us had grown quiet. Outside the windows, the city of Beijing seemed motionless, like it was merely a picture in a frame.

I stared at the laptop on the table in front of me. The livestream had long since shut off, but I could still see the horrid images reflected on the black screen. Police surrounding our outpost in Boston, the blue-red lights glaring off the windows. Stanyard, my boyfriend, being dragged from the building in handcuffs. Guards beating Lev, one of my Jewish followers, and tossing him into the back of a van.

And my uncle, lying dead on the sidewalk.

Time abruptly restarted, off-kilter and out of focus. *Why is this happening?* Reality lay shattered in front of me like a broken mirror. I tried to shift through the pieces, struggling to see any meaning in the tragedy, but the only truth I could find was that this was all my fault.

I forced myself to rehearse the events. I was—*am*—Philadelphia Smyrna, known to the world as Blue Fire, the figurehead of a revolution. My rebellion had been an accident; I'd only wanted to destroy Red Rain, the chemical superweapon my father had created, and keep it out of the hands of the government. With help from my mentor Nic, I'd burned their factory to the ground. A video of my act of defiance had leaked onto the internet, and Jael, a powerful tech mogul with control over the algorithm, had used my name to build a revolution.

I looked up at her where she stood across the table. The bangles on her wrists rattled as she agitatedly tapped her thigh. Jael was the true leader of the resistance. She'd been working anonymously in the background for months, manipulating the algorithm to push my content past the censors. She'd targeted the unassimilated, the oppressed, the discontent—anyone who was tired of submitting to a government that allowed no religion, no national borders, no individuality whatsoever.

And the people had responded.

In mere months, revolution had gone from fiction to impending reality. Millions of people all over the globe had pledged their allegiance to the "thunderbird." In Beijing, I was a household name; even some legions of the Chinese military had vowed to defect. I was both a celebrity and a public enemy, and in a few weeks, Jael and I would use that influence to end the United.

On September 17th, Operation Blue Fire would launch. At my signal, everyone who followed the thunderbird would fight the system. They would walk out of school, quit their government jobs, abandon their military outposts. Guards would destroy weapons, secretaries would burn files, and teenagers would post Bibles and other illegal documents on social media. On September 17th, the people would say *no*—together.

"If we all stand up together, they can't make us all sit down," my former ally Jayde would have said.

It was working. The world was in an uproar, and the government was losing control. Even Asia, my nemesis in the Council, couldn't deter my followers, no matter how high she raised the bounty on my life. All the tides were turning in our favor, to the point where I believed—no, *knew*—that God had to be behind it all.

I'd believed it. Until this morning.

"I have a message for all United citizens..."

I turned towards the back wall of the conference room, where the projector had generated a 3D rendering of the news. On live TV, Asia had raided my headquarters in Boston, where all my important American allies were hiding. I was forced to watch, unable to do anything but scream his name, as they hurled Stanyard into the back of a van. They arrested everyone—except my uncle.

"Be advised that associating with Smyrna will be considered an act of terrorism..."

My uncle was military. That meant he was worse than a rebel; he was a traitor. And the government had no mercy for traitors.

"And the punishment for terrorism..."

My emotions exploded in raw, unprocessed tears. I covered my face and sobbed, the only penance I could give for the uncle I'd barely known. Uncle Bart—or "Tower," as I'd called him—was the only extended family I had left. Now he was gone. Just like Mom, Nic, and my father. Just like everyone else who was dead or in prison or had their memories wiped because of me.

"Oh Philadelphia, don't you know it's too late to go home?"

"Philadelphia..." Jael's steady voice tried and failed to reach me through the waves of panicked thoughts.

"I killed him!" I shouted. Not out of accusation, but as a declaration—hinging on the desperate belief that if I confessed my sins, maybe, just maybe, the pain would go away.

"These things happen in war," she deferred, the answer practiced, thoughtless.

"In the war *I* started!" Jael may be controlling the algorithm, but I was the one who had endangered these people's lives by antagonizing Asia. I thought God had called me to some glorious purpose in China, and I'd tried to make it happen on my own terms, ignoring Nic's and Stanyard's advice time and again. I'd deluded myself into thinking I could save a planet when I should have just shut up and gone home months ago.

"God didn't choose you for anything, Phil."

I rubbed my eyes with the heel of my hand, trying to shove the tears back in. "You were right. I should have gone back to Boston. This is all my fault—"

"Enough!"

I jumped. Jael was shouting—and she sounded very, very upset.

Her heels clicked and her giant earrings swayed as she strode towards me, making her look like twice the woman. "I will not tolerate that attitude from you."

I instinctively scooted my chair back. "What—"

She cut me off with a slash of her finger. "You did nothing to cause this."

Nothing? I did everything. "But I—"

"Don't interrupt me!" she snapped, then sighed. She leaned her knuckles on the table. "Philadelphia." Her voice softened, if only marginally. "You need to stop this. You cannot keep blaming yourself."

Who else is there to blame?

The question must have made it onto my face, because Jael arched her eyebrow. "Did you not just tell me that I'm in charge?"

I nodded. I had, in fact, said that, a mere twenty minutes ago—right before Asia came on the news.

"And did you not say that you trust my judgment?"

That's exactly what I'd said. I recalled the oath of allegiance I'd sworn as I'd submitted to Jael's authority and put "Blue Fire" in her hands.

"If you tell me I'm done, I'm done. You have my word that I will not go behind your back, and I will not try to undermine you. I trust your judgment, so whatever you tell me to do, I'll do it."

I was not in control. After weeks of fighting and trying to protect my reputation, I'd surrendered. God had given Jael authority in my life, and I trusted her. I still did.

Jael let the silence grow pregnant before she continued. "I told you when we met that I wanted you to fight a war, not lead one. You were only following orders. I'm the one who gave those orders, which means the blame is mine."

She stood back from the table. "I'm the one who put you on air. I'm the one who let you visit that group home. I'm the one who didn't set up more safeguards for our friends in Boston." Her eyes glimmered with shame. "I am the leader of this operation. This situation is entirely my responsibility—not yours."

My stomach twisted, but I held back the words and waited.

Jael let out her breath, releasing a thousand regrets with it. "It's okay to grieve. It's okay to have questions. You can be mad at everyone, including me. But you cannot—you *will not*—blame yourself."

It wasn't a suggestion. I looked up into her face as she came to stand beside me and gripped the back of my chair. "Blaming yourself is a childish luxury you don't have anymore. You work for me now, and your only job is to listen and obey. And I'm giving you new orders."

I straightened. She tipped her chin back and announced, gently and deliberately, "Your orders are to trust. Be honest. And do not give place to guilt."

I struggled to repeat the words as they ricocheted around in my chest.

Trust. Be honest. And do not give place to guilt.

Jael almost smiled. "Do you understand, soldier?"

I nodded reflectively, but I didn't understand, not at all. I stared at her, wishing her words would put a period on my anxiety. They didn't put a period on anything. Instead, my pulse raced faster and my guilt screamed louder as it swirled with nothing to land on. *But what's going to happen to Stanyard? What about Lev? They'll kill him when they find out he's Jewish! What am I going to do—*

I stopped when I realized that wasn't the question I should be asking. I had no idea what was going to happen, and I absolutely didn't trust myself. But there was one thing I was confident of.

You are not in charge anymore.

I closed my eyes and inhaled through my nose. Then I looked up at Jael and whispered, "What do you want me to do now?"

She drummed her acrylic nails on the back of my chair. "I don't know," she said slowly, her thick Hausa accent filling the gaps between words. "Right now, my first concern is getting you out of this building. Too many people know you're here."

As if in answer, the conference door whooshed open. Lanzhou Tang rushed in, his cousin Bowen a step behind him. The Tangs owned the factory and were old friends of Nic's parents, the Von Nieuwenhuyses. Mr. Von had granted Lanzhou's father an exclusive contract to produce a patented part for space stations, and the Tangs had profited handsomely. They'd used that wealth to buy security for the underground church that met in their cafeteria—and for me. For the past month, I'd been living in their home and using Bowen's many connections to build the revolution in Beijing.

I shakily stood up as they approached. If anyone was in danger for assisting me, it was the Tangs. Even though I wore a disguise when out in public, using wigs and colored contacts to switch between my multiple identities, thousands of people had seen me at the Tangs' nightly prayer services. *If any one of those people calls the police...*

"Lanzhou," I started, my voice croaking with fear, "I'm so sorry. I—"

He wasn't listening. He bypassed propriety and gave me what I needed most: a hug. He pulled me to himself and gripped my shoulders with his strong hands—just like my father would have, if he were here.

I accepted the mercy and sniffled into his shoulder, feeling love and forgiveness radiating from his posture. It was no wonder he was a pastor.

"We saw the news. What happened?" he asked, directing the question over my head at Jael.

"I put her on air to stall Asia," she said, snatching the blame before I could even think about claiming any of it. "I was hoping to distract them while I found out where they're holding these executions."

I flinched when I remembered the dozens of people who were scheduled to die this afternoon if we didn't intervene. My friends in Boston weren't the only people Asia was holding hostage; she'd also raided one of the underground hospitals I'd visited in Beijing. She'd arrested all the residents— most of whom were disabled or terminally ill—and ordered their public executions.

Their crime? Associating with the thunderbird.

I pulled back from Lanzhou and turned to Jael. "Can you do anything?"

Her face held neither hope nor despair. "I'll do what I can."

"Let me call my contact at the police station, see what he knows," Bowen offered, barely suppressing the shake in his voice.

Jael nodded curtly. "Get on it. Your job," she pointed at Lanzhou, "is to get her out of sight until I can sort this out. I want her off the premises. Too many people have seen her at this factory."

Lanzhou started to answer, but Bowen spoke first. "With all due respect, I think we should put her back on air."

"What?" Lanzhou snapped.

"I think she should go back on air," Bowen repeated, eyes on me, "and expose Asia."

That was the *last* thing I should do. "Didn't you see what just happened?" I pointed at the dark projector. "I'm only making it worse. She just *shot* someone because of me."

"And she's going to do it again if you don't stop her," Bowen whispered.

My throat dried.

Lanzhou put himself between us. "Absolutely not. We are not putting her on air. She's going off the grid until this calms down."

"This isn't going to 'calm down,' and you know that." The tremor left Bowen's voice as he met his cousin's gaze. "Are we going to stay quiet while Mong murders another dozen people? Phil needs to go on there and demand an explanation for these executions."

"Jael will handle it," Lanzhou returned with a confidence I wished I felt. "But I am not putting Philadelphia through that. Not now."

"He's right," Jael cut in. "Asia is expecting us to retaliate. She wants more conflict. I'm not going to give it to her."

"And in the meantime, she's out there burning Phil at the stake. Have you looked at social media?" Bowen spun to face Jael. "The internet is eating her alive. There's rumors that the operation is a hoax, and I've already heard of several people who are bailing. If we don't fix this now, the entire operation will collapse."

I sucked in my breath. That's just what Asia wanted: for the revolution to crumble, and all the blame to fall on Blue Fire.

"We'll do damage control later," Jael said with a sharp glance at me.

"No, we need to strike now, before Asia writes the narrative. We have to fight fire with fire." He turned back to me, as if I had any authority.

Lanzhou blocked his view. "Enough—"

The trill of my tablet cut him off.

I looked at the device where it lay on the table. All three of us stopped and stared as it rang once, twice, three times, then silenced.

Jael moved towards it. "Who...?"

I had no idea. I'd borrowed that tablet from the Tangs, and very few people knew how to contact me on it. Most of those people were now in prison.

I thought of Stanyard's constant messages and winced. Stanyard had always been there for me, texting even when I didn't want to text back and answering the minute I called. Now, for the first time ever, I'd be the one staring at a blank screen as my messages sat unread.

Tears stung my vision, but I blinked them away. *Later*, I coached myself.

I stepped forward and picked up the device. I swiped on the screen and read the notification—and my heart failed.

It was a friend request from a user I'd never seen before, followed by a simple, cruel message:

HELLO SWEETIE. IT'S ASIA. READY TO TALK?

2: PHILADELPHIA

Lanzhou read over my shoulder and muttered a prayer. Jael stepped up beside us and spat something much less holy.

Asia called again. "Do *not* answer that!" Jael ordered.

I let the call ring out. I stared at the vibrating device in my hands as the whole room seemed to twitch and stutter. *She found me. Asia found me!*

My device silenced, and an emptiness settled in my soul. Where there should have been panic and adrenaline, I found only despair.

It's all over.

Bowen picked up the slack. "How did she get that number?" he demanded.

As if she were eavesdropping, Asia sent a text and answered his question.

WHEN WERE YOU GOING TO TELL ME ABOUT YOU AND STANYARD? I'M SO HAPPY FOR YOU. HE'S SUCH A SWEET BOY.

I felt nauseous as the weight of the world shoved its way up my throat. Of course, Asia had Stanyard in custody. All she had to do was take his phone and see who "Aurelius" had been talking to recently.

Jael muttered to herself and grabbed her own device, swiping furious commands onto the screen. Asia sent another message and twisted the knife deeper.

DO YOU WANT TO TALK TO HIM?

I imagined her leering over Stanyard as he struggled, cuffed to a chair in an interrogation room or shoved to the corner in a dark cell. I knew she wasn't actually in the same room as him; she was here in Beijing while her guards did the dirty work in Boston. But that didn't stop the horrid images from flashing across my vision.

Please don't hurt him, I wanted to beg, but the words didn't make it to my lips, much less to my fingers. I dropped my tablet on the table and gripped the edge.

Lanzhou laid a warm hand on my shoulder. "Can she track the device to here?" he asked. His calm voice was the only thing in the room that wasn't wobbling.

Jael swore again. "Is that one of the tablets I gave you?"

"Yes, ma'am."

"Then no," she declared, sliding her phone in her pocket. "I specifically programmed that device to be untraceable for this very reason. It routes all its traffic through an evolving proxy chain. She'll know it's a hacked device registered to a dummy file, but she won't be able to pinpoint an exact location. All she has is Philadelphia's username and chat history with Stanyard." She glared at me. "Did you tell him about the Tangs?"

I shook my head so hard my neck hurt. "Not in a text." Stanyard had been explicit that I not send him any sensitive information over chat.

"Then we're safe," Bowen said, his pitch warbling like he lost his confidence halfway through the sentence.

"*You* are. I've spent a decade making the connectivity of your home and factory as ironclad as possible." Jael adjusted her turban like a queen straightening her crown, and the army general resumed command. "However, I doubt our other associates took such precautions."

I moaned when I realized she was right. I wasn't the only person Stanyard had been talking to. Hundreds of people had accessed the servers on base—servers that contained detailed plans for Operation Blue Fire.

Lanzhou squeezed my shoulder.

Jael pointed at Bowen. "I need you and your men to start making calls. Call all of our partners and find out if any of them have been in contact with Boston." She fired the commands rapidly like an automatic rifle. "I need a list of everyone whose name might be on those servers, and I need it five minutes ago."

Bowen turned and ran out of the room without a word.

My mind started compiling a list of victims. "Data!" I gasped.

Data had become the unofficial leader of the resistance in Boston after Jayde betrayed me. Data knew more about the demonstrations planned for operation day than I did. If his information was compromised, the resistance of the entire eastern seaboard was in danger.

Jael didn't need to be told. "Call him."

Lanzhou stepped back. Grabbing my device, I minimized the chat with Asia and dialed Data. It rang once, twice, and I began to panic—then he picked up.

"Blue Fire," he panted, sounding like he was running. The line crackled with chaotic background noise.

"Where are you?" I demanded, raising my voice to be heard.

"At the exact moment, running to catch the subway."

As if reinforcing his statement, a garbled voice over the intercom announced the arrival of a train.

"We got away—we weren't on base when it happened," Data answered the implied question.

Lanzhou muttered thanks.

"We?" I asked, and dared to hope.

"Your father's with me."

"Oh, praise God," I gasped, and meant it with every fiber of my being. "Dad, are you okay?"

"I'm fine, Philadelphia," my father called in the background. He sounded rattled but unhurt. I knew he must be terrified. My father had recently been revived after being cryogenically frozen, and he only had a month's worth of fresh memories. He had no idea what was going on. Did he even realize his brother-in-law was dead?

Jael stepped up beside me. "What of the others?

"I've made contact with Andes, the Vons..." Data rattled off some other callsigns I knew but didn't have a face for. "I can't get ahold of the Dasses. There was no one at their apartment, and they've gone off the grid."

Stanyard's family. I bit my lip. Stanyard had left his parents and sister Mira behind in Boston. I could only hope their radio silence meant they'd escaped and gone dark—not that they'd been captured.

Please, God, protect them. Save this family.

"We're scattering," Data continued. There was a rush of noise on his end of the line, then silence, as if he'd stepped onto an abandoned subway car. "I've told everyone I can get ahold of to disconnect their servers and relocate."

I started to relax, but Jael did the exact opposite. She drummed her fingers on her arm restlessly. "It may not be enough. What about your program?"

I stiffened. Data had coded a program that allowed us to hijack the government's broadcasting system. With a few clicks, we could commandeer any TV channel—and on operation day, we were going to use it to make my stream mandatory viewing on every registered device on the planet. Without his program, there would *be* no operation.

"All of the code was hosted on my server. I disabled remote access, so they can't get to it from Stanyard's computer. He might have some notes, but nothing they can exploit." There was a pause as Data reconsidered his statement. "I'll do some reconfiguring to be safe."

"And how much information about operation day was on that server?" Jael demanded.

Data hesitated. "I don't know."

Jael was not satisfied with ignorance. "Find out. As soon as you're in a safe place, I want you to search your history and give me as much information as possible. I need to know what demonstration sites are potentially compromised."

Asia grew tired of being left out of the conversation. She sent another message, the notification superimposing over Data's call.

I DON'T WANT TO HURT STANYARD. I KNOW HOW MUCH HE MEANS TO YOU.

I gripped the tablet.

The others continued to chatter. "Do we need to reschedule the operation?" Lanzhou whispered, almost as if he were afraid to suggest it.

"We can't just 'reschedule,'" Data mocked. "We'll never get back this momentum if we stop now."

"But if Mong sends the army to the demonstration sites—"

"Calm down," Jael admonished them both. "These people knew the risks. We'll do our best to warn them..."

BESIDES

Asia let that one word hang for several seconds before she finished her sentence.

WE BOTH KNOW SUCH JUVENILE THREATS DON'T WORK ON YOU. YOU PROVED THAT WHEN YOU ABANDONED NIC.

An involuntary gasp of pain retched out of me before I could stop it. Asia was Nic's ex-girlfriend, and she'd taken great delight in torturing him to blackmail me. She'd arrested him, convicted him for his involvement in Red Rain, and publicly humiliated him with a fake trial. All the while, she'd constantly reminded me that she could make it all go away if I turned myself in.

I didn't—if only because Nic ordered me not to.

"No matter what happens to me, no matter what you hear, I need you to promise that you won't come for me. Do you understand?"

When I didn't show up, Asia had sentenced Nic and shipped him off to a remote prison. I had no idea where he was—and if Asia had her way, I'd never see him again.

Of all the people I'd lost to Asia's cruelty, Nic was the one who hurt the most.

Jael moved in my peripheral. "Philadelphia? What is it?"

Asia texted again before I could answer.

SO LET'S UP THE ANTE, SHALL WE? YOU HAVE UNTIL 3PM TO TURN YOURSELF IN BEFORE I EXECUTE YOUR FRIENDS FROM THE HOSPITAL.

I blindly held the tablet out to Jael as everything heaved—my breath, my stomach, the room around me. I knew that threat was coming. I knew surrender was always an option. I knew I could end the bloodshed at any moment.

But I wouldn't.

"What's wrong?" Data barked into the sudden silence.

"Is my daughter okay?" Dad murmured in the background, and my heart lurched.

Jael ignored both questions and took the tablet. "I've got calls to make. Contact me as soon as you're in a safe place." She punched the button to end the call before anyone could argue.

I vaguely registered the ping of an incoming message through the daze. I looked down at the screen and saw the text beneath Jael's fingers.

THAT'S 38 LIVES, IF I COUNTED CORRECTLY. PERHAPS THAT MATH IS MORE AGREEABLE TO YOU.

"Oh God," I groaned, and could come up with no words to finish the prayer. I pinched my eyes shut and braced myself on the back of a chair.

"Philadelphia," Jael called, sounding like she was on the other side of a glass wall. "You know you can't."

Lanzhou moved beside me. "Don't ask her to make that decision," he grunted, voice husky.

"She's not making that decision. I am."

Jael's fingernails brushed my chin. I forced myself to look at her, even though I was sure that if I opened my eyes, I would throw up.

She held my gaze, all the fear and grief locked behind a shield of authority. "I will handle this. This is not your decision to make. Do you understand?"

I nodded, even though every muscle movement felt like a lie.

"Remember your orders," she commanded, voice as intense as her gaze.

Trust. Be honest. And do not give place to guilt.

I closed my eyes again, unable to keep the room upright. I trusted her, I really did. She was in charge, and this was her decision.

I could only hope *I* had made the right decision by trusting her.

3: PHILADELPHIA

We failed.

Jael was unable to stop the executions. It didn't take long for her to figure out where everyone was being held, but the information did us no good. Asia knew we were coming and increased security, closing all the vulnerabilities Jael could exploit. Jael spent the afternoon frantically making calls, pulling on favors, and offering bribes, but to no avail. Asia had taken every precaution to ensure there was nothing we could do.

Everyone was going to die.

Jael forbade me from watching the demonstration on TV. Instead, I sat in the conference room and stared at the clock as it mercilessly ticked on towards 3pm. The artificial *tick, tock* synced with my labored pulse, filling the empty room with the roar of a hurricane.

2:51

I gripped the table with both hands, afraid that if I didn't hold onto something, I would run. Every nerve in my body screamed at me to *get up*, to find a device and text Asia, to beg Jael to change her mind. The shrieking choir of a thousand accusations rang in my ears, telling me this was wrong, that my life wasn't worth it, that I was the one who deserved to die.

2:52

I didn't know how to answer the voices. The only thing I could do was try to drown them out.

I can't I can't I can't!

I shrieked when Lanzhou touched my shoulder. I hadn't even heard him come in. He stood next to me, watching the clock, silent.

2:53

He closed his eyes and began to speak in Mandarin. I couldn't understand the words, but I could tell by the pitch that he was praying.

I slid down to the floor and did the same. "God, please, save them!"

2:54

"You're the only one who can do this. You're the only one who can stop Asia. Intervene! They're innocent people!"

2:55

I hyperventilated. Every word I thought of felt too stiff, too theological, too unfeeling. My prayers were inadequate. *I* was inadequate.

2:56

I settled for the only plea I had left. "God, don't let this happen. Why is this happening?"

Desperation—no, *rage* seized me. There was no reason this should be happening. I served a God of miracles. I'd seen a dead man raised to life. If that were possible, then why shouldn't this be possible? He could intervene. He could disable guns, scramble communications, take out the power. Something, *anything*.

2:57

"This isn't right! Those people belong to God, and they are protected! You can't have them!"

2:58

Lanzhou's prayer rose to a shout. I broke off and muttered in tongues, pounding the floor with both fists.

2:59

"God, move, *now*!"

3:00

A bell clanged in the factory below, signaling the turn of the hour. I thought I heard a wail from the other room. Then, silence.

Lanzhou opened his phone. The air left him in one long sigh. "It's done."

I wept, collapsed on the floor and screamed into the cold laminate. Not because I wanted to cry, but because I had no idea what else to do. It was over. I had made my choice, and Jael had made hers. Now thirty-eight bodies had been added to my record.

And I wasn't even supposed to feel guilty about them.

"Why, God, why?" I moaned, even though the words had no substance. There was no why. I knew that. There was absolutely no reason for all this horrid, senseless bloodshed.

Senseless bloodshed that could have been prevented.

Why didn't You do anything, God? I winced as pain gripped my chest. The question made me feel cold and isolated, like I'd cut the line on the only thing holding my soul together. Still, it lingered. It floated there, bobbing on my consciousness like pieces of shipwreck in a dark sea.

Why didn't God save them? He'd saved Nic. Nic had *died*, stopped breathing for almost thirty minutes, and he'd come back to life at the touch of a hand, a single prayer. If God could do that, why didn't He prevent this?

Why didn't You answer our prayers?

If the Holy Spirit responded, I couldn't hear Him. All I heard was cavernous silence as I continued to shiver and weep for the mistakes I couldn't undo.

There was rustling as Lanzhou sat on the floor next to me. His hand found my back, and he started to pray again. This time, it was in English.

"Father," he said, the word gentle and intimate. "Bring Your peace. This is Your daughter, and she needs You."

My sobs hitched in my throat. He was praying for *me*? I didn't need prayer; the families of all those people who had just been slaughtered needed prayer. I didn't deserve—

Lanzhou pressed down on me, as if sensing my objections. "She needs Your comfort, and she needs Your compassion. Show her Your mercy. You are the God who weeps with those who weep, and that's the Lord she needs right now."

Let Me help you.

I felt it. That incomprehensible swirling in my soul that told me the Spirit was moving, the loving conviction that warned me I was avoiding what I needed most.

Don't resist Me.

I gave in. I went limp on the floor and wept, letting the Spirit roll over me in heavy waves. Lanzhou continued to pray. His hand held me steady like an anchor as the competing emotions caught me in their whirlpool. I felt anger and disbelief and confidence and hope all at once—and then, nothing.

My tears evaporated. The emotions faded, leaving me weak both inside and out. Grief still filled my throat, and my mind was black and empty, but I sensed through it all a solid feeling that I could only describe as *peace*. It wasn't warm. It wasn't happy. But it was stable, almost like it was a rock I could hold.

"You may not feel any better," Lanzhou warned as I pushed myself up. "But that doesn't mean He's not there—or that you didn't make the right decision."

I wiped my cheeks and looked into his eyes. "Did I make the right decision?"

"By obeying Jael?" he said, avoiding the dozens of other qualifiers that could have muddled the question. "Yes, you did."

I gave the statement time to soak into my broken soul. "Thank you. For everything."

He smiled, the crow's feet winking around his narrow eyes. "You're part of my congregation now. That means I'm going to take care of you." He studied me, and his expression sobered. "Philadelphia. You can't help anyone if you blame yourself."

I flinched. "I know, I—"

He didn't let me finish. "You're a leader now, and you can't save someone else if you don't let God save you first."

I frowned and listened.

"You are just as valuable to the Lord as all those people who lost their lives today. He cares about your hurts and fears, even if you think you brought this on yourself. He wants to help you, and you're not helping anyone if you cut yourself off from His love."

I swallowed. Is that what I'd been doing? Telling God He couldn't love me—that He didn't know *how* to love me?

"Guilt is not just about finding someone to blame. When you feed guilt, you're denying yourself of the forgiveness God wants to give you. You're telling Him that the cross isn't good enough—that you've found a better way to deal with your problems."

My neck and cheeks burned as everything came back into focus. Suddenly, I understood why guilt and shame were so easy, so familiar— almost comfortable, in a way. It was easy to feel guilty because that meant I was still in control. I didn't have to trust anyone else with my problems *or* the solutions. I didn't have to deal with big, scary questions like *"Why didn't God save those people?"* when I could blame everything on myself.

Lanzhou gave me a minute to process before continuing. "Trust isn't about blindly following orders and ignoring your feelings. It's about letting the Holy Spirit help you manage those feelings—and then asking for wisdom about what to do next."

I knew he was right. Even Jael had given me permission to grieve. My emotions were not a problem—but I still had to surrender them, same as everything else.

I closed my eyes and took a deep breath, inhaling the truth with it.

God, I'm scared. I'm confused, and I'm worried that I didn't make the right decision by staying quiet, and... I do feel guilty. I know I'm not supposed to blame myself, but I do.

The air slowly came back into my lungs, like someone had unlatched a window. I sat up straight and tipped my face towards the ceiling.

I'm giving this back to You. This war is in Your hands. Show me what You want me to do.

The door opened. I looked over to see Jael approach. I struggled to stand. Lanzhou jumped up and helped me the rest of the way.

Jael stopped in front of us. "I'm sorry," she declared, although whether she was apologizing to me or to the people we had lost, I couldn't tell.

I just nodded, not trusting my voice.

Jael also seemed to realize there was nothing more to be said and moved on. "I hate to ask you to do this, but I need you to record a video." She tapped my tablet, which she had tucked under her arm. "Bowen is right—the media is propagandizing this, and we cannot let them write the narrative. I need you to go on air and condemn the executions. I'll give you a script."

The thought of going on air made me want to hurl, but I nodded. "Whatever you need me to do."

She indulged in a small smile. "I want you to keep this in case Asia or any of our friends try to contact you." She held my tablet out.

I instinctively took it. "Shouldn't we block Asia and change my username?"

Her dangling earrings thwacked against her neck as she shook her head. "I want to keep that line of communication open. Just… in case."

In case we need to bargain? I unlocked the tablet and opened the messenger.

"I deleted all the texts she's been sending for the last six hours," Jael explained. "You don't need to read those."

I clicked on the chat with Asia and saw it was blank, except for the message she'd sent just a few minutes ago:

YOU KNOW IT DOESN'T HAVE TO BE THIS WAY. I DON'T ENJOY THIS ANY MORE THAN YOU DO. MEET ME AT THE NOLAN ESTATE, AND WE CAN END THIS TONIGHT. I PROMISE NO ONE WILL KNOW WE TALKED.

The Nolan estate? I stared at the screen, imagining the gorgeous mansion on the other side of Beijing—the mansion I owned.

Thames Nolan had been an associate of Asia's and was one of the many people who had used me and my family for political gain. He was also, in a cruel irony, my "adopted" father. He'd created a false identity for me— "Andromeda Nolan"—intending to convert me into the daughter he never had. He didn't live to see it happen, but I'd had no choice but to adopt the forged file. Since my birth identity, "Philadelphia Smyrna," was on the United's most wanted, I'd begrudgingly assumed the name of Nolan—and the massive inheritance that came with it.

When we first met, Asia had wanted nothing more than for me to become a Nolan in word and deed. She'd pampered me, introducing me to all her high society friends, and told me over and over that I "deserved this" and "belonged with them." I knew why, now: She'd wanted me to kill her father.

I flipped my right hand over and studied my palm. You couldn't tell underneath the healed skin, but I knew there was a network of wires woven through my fingertips—the remnants of a bomb. When I'd first come to

Beijing with Jayde, I'd been intending to assassinate General Secretary Mong, the supreme leader of the United. Asia had invited me to a prestigious party and introduced me to her father. Had he shaken my hand, the chip in my palm would have sent him into cardiac arrest and killed him.

I'd reconsidered at the last minute and greeted the General with a bow instead. He'd been amused by my perceived humility and extended his favor, even going so far as to accept my impromptu invitation to dinner. Jayde, on the other hand, had been furious. He'd betrayed me, kidnapped me, and tried to kill me, and I was sure he would finish the job if he ever found me again.

Asia, of course, knew all of that. She'd wanted the assassination to succeed so she could take her father's throne, and when that plan failed, she'd hunted me across the province. Surely, she was smart enough to realize that I'd since gotten my chip removed; the leftover wires in my hand were harmless. I wouldn't kill her father.

That left us with two options. We could continue to trade blows until the only option was war.

Or I could turn myself in, so she could quietly kill me and clean up this mess before it got further out of hand.

I knew which one she would prefer. Asia hated an unnecessary mess.

The tablet pinged again. Clearly, Asia insisted on having the last word.

THINK ABOUT IT. WHEN YOU'RE READY TO TALK, YOU KNOW WHERE TO FIND ME.

I shivered. Such a sinister word: "when."

Jael glanced at the notification but didn't seem perturbed by the contents. "Get changed and meet me in the recording studio. You're on in—"

She was interrupted by the whoosh of the door. Bowen jogged towards us. "I reached out to every contact I have and traced down every name I thought might be on the Boston servers," he panted.

"And?" Jael prodded.

He paused to take a gulp of air. "Some of them have already gone dark."

I sucked in my breath.

Jael glanced at me. "Tell me in my office. We'll meet in thirty minutes after Philadelphia and I are done recording."

Bowen focused on me for the first time, his eyes flickering with a sorrow he daren't express in words. "We need to get you out of here."

Lanzhou joined the conversation. "I agree. We need to get her to a safe place—too many people have seen her here."

"Unfortunately, now that Asia is hunting down all our associates, this factory *is* the safest place. This is one of the few buildings where I can completely control the internet traffic, and there are a lot more places to hide here than at your house." Jael propped one hand on her hip. "However, you're right. There are too many people here. We need to clear the building."

"But…" Bowen objected.

Jael ignored him, fixing her gaze on Lanzhou. "I know you trust your employees, but Asia is offering a sum that would test any man's loyalty."

I swallowed. The Tangs had managed to hide a church in their basement for decades. Would someone betray them now just for the money?

I looked up at Lanzhou as his expression furrowed, calculating. "If there were to be an equipment failure…" He gestured. "I could shut the line down for a few days, send everyone home on paid leave."

Funding everyone's salaries while his enterprise ground to a halt for who-knows-how-long sounded devastatingly expensive. "I'll pay you back," I blurted.

He smiled gently. "We can afford it."

So can I. The Nolans were stupidly wealthy, definitely more so than the Tangs.

"Make it so," Jael ordered before I could argue. "I want the dock gates locked at all times. No one steps foot on these grounds without your or my approval. And cancel the church services."

My gut pinched. Of course, it was the right thing to do. It wasn't safe for anyone to meet here, especially while I was still on the property. But that didn't stop me from feeling a crushing load of shame. For the first time in a decade, people would not be worshipping God in this building tonight—and I was the reason.

I closed my eyes and pushed the thoughts away before they could take root. *Do not give place to guilt.*

Lanzhou took a breath like he was about to say something more, then stopped. There was a beat of awkward silence while he tried and failed to start his sentence twice. Finally, he turned to Jael. "Have you considered canceling Operation Blue Fire?"

I stiffened. *Cancel the operation? We can't give up!*

I could tell by the arch of Jael's eyebrows that the notion wasn't on the table, but Bowen spoke before she could. "No! It would kill the resistance. We've already lost so many people because of what happened today. If we show any weakness now, we're finished. The United wins."

I winced. It terrified me to admit it, but I knew he was right. If Operation Blue Fire failed, the United would crush the unassimilated, and people would be too afraid to try again. The revolution was hanging by a thread as it was. If I—if *we* failed, we wouldn't get another chance. Not for this generation.

And I wasn't willing to give my generation up without a fight. *For such a time as this.*

"We'll be worse off if the government slaughters hundreds of thousands of innocent people because we told them where to look." Lanzhou's voice was even, but his fists were clenched. "We don't know how much information was on that server. Asia may know exactly where most of the demonstrations are planned. If the government stakes them out, the revolution will be over before it starts."

I looked to Jael in a panic, begging her to deny it. "It's a possibility," she admitted without emotion.

"Then we have to prepare for that," Bowen returned. "We can relocate some of the demonstrations, arm the people, send Phil's military to counteract."

He said it so casually—"Phil's military"—like they were chess pieces I played with in my free time. But I did have a military. Several troops of the Chinese army had pledged to defect to me on operation day. General Jin was my primary contact; he alone commanded five thousand soldiers.

Along with lots and lots of heavy artillery.

Lanzhou paused, the silence harsh and sinister. "What are you suggesting, cousin?"

"I'm suggesting that we defend ourselves. We can store weapons here, use this as a command center—"

Lanzhou cut him off with a flick of his arm. "Absolutely not. This is a *factory*, not a military base. We've worked for decades to make this a safe place where people can worship God, and I'm not sacrificing our position with the police to turn this into an armory. I'm not endangering my employees or my congregation like that."

Bowen bristled. "It's my congregation, too. And they're ready to fight—"

"Then you should consider what 'your congregation' needs from their pastor." Lanzhou raised his voice only slightly, but it was enough. "You have a family, a company, *and* a church to lead, Bowen. You need to remember that."

"I know what my role is," Bowen returned, low and cold. "That's why I'm going to do everything I can to protect them *and* this building."

He swiveled to glare at me. "And you should too."

Before anyone could object, he turned and stormed out of the room, leaving his words echoing in the silence.

4: NIC

I knew something was wrong when the dreams started.

Correction: I knew something was wrong when Asia called to threaten me. She hadn't visited since I'd been banished to Russia, a weird act of mercy, so I knew my luck was over when she summoned me to the visiting room. She radioed in with a freaky hologram and tried to sweettalk me into revealing Philadelphia's location, vacillating between "I'll give you a full pardon" and "I'll kill everything you love." When she finally let me get a word in edgewise, I advised her to save the oxygen.

She left in a huff, blathering about how I was going to regret this. Even though I never would have admitted it to her face, I knew she was right. Phil was running out of time, and I was about to have so many regrets.

If Asia was coming to me, that meant she was desperate. And desperate people were deadly, especially when they were oversaturated with wealth and power like Asia was.

Unfortunately, she hadn't given me any details on the next phase of her evil plan, so I was forced to ask around. I asked my bunkmates, Vance and Ryan; I asked the minions who worked under me at the lab; I asked every guard who would give me the time of day. I even bothered Warden Ivanova on her lunch break, falsely assuming she had at least some contact with the outside world.

No one knew anything. Absolutely no one had any recent information about "Blue Fire" or the revolution. Probably because we were all stuck 20,000 feet in the air in a prison factory on a snow-capped mountain in Russia.

I finally asked the omnipresent Voice in my head. In retrospect, I probably should have asked Him first. But we'd only been on speaking terms for about a month, and I was still forming the habit.

"Look, we need to talk," I hissed into the darkness of my cell. I kept my voice down to avoid waking Vance and Ryan; they had an annoying habit of commandeering (or providing theological commentary on) my conversations with the Lord. "It's about Philadelphia."

I've been waiting all day for you to ask, He responded amicably.

"I'm sure You have," I grunted. "She's in danger."

Yes, she is, He admitted without fear.

"I need to help her—no." I backpedaled before He could correct my grammar. "I want to help her."

I know you do.

I rubbed my mustache. "You told me to help her."

Yes, I did.

I remembered the exact moment the Lord had so indelicately reminded me that my life was not my own. I'd been running across Beijing with Phil, intent on going back to Mars and forgetting the rebellion existed, when the Lord made it clear that was unacceptable. He said He wanted Philadelphia to stay in Beijing, embrace her heritage as Andromeda Nolan, and challenge Asia on even playing ground. Phil would finish what I'd failed to do ten years ago—and I was going to help her.

I had no doubts that all this oddly specific information came from the Lord, because He revealed it in the most obtuse, heavy-handed way possible: He gave me an open vision.

I was prepared to ignore it, just like I'd been ignoring my dreams for the last ten years, ever since I dumped Asia and she put my parents under the knife. I was perfectly content to disobey the Lord and accept the consequences—until I saw that Philadelphia was in danger of losing her own faith.

I knew I was going to hell. But I had no intention of bringing a plus one.

I'd tentatively said yes to God—and then everything went to hell anyway. Everything that could go wrong had gone wrong, and now I was stuck in a prison thousands of miles away doing the exact opposite of what the vision said.

I sighed and studied the unidentified stains on the concrete ceiling. I wasn't stupid. I knew there had to be a reason for this Russian detour. But it would be nice to have some clearer instructions. "*How* am I supposed to help her?" I prodded.

You're helping her right now.

I rolled my eyes; it was low-hanging fruit. "Granted, but You were very specific that You wanted her to be a Nolan and fight Asia, and I was supposed to stay in Beijing with her. Last I checked, she's hiding underground, Asia has the upper hand, and I am nowhere near Beijing."

You've only been here a month. Have more patience.

I rubbed my temples. So that's where this prayer was going—the same place my prayers always dead-ended. "Look, I didn't call so we could have a repeat of this conversation."

Then why are we talking?

I grimaced, convicted. He sat in forgiving silence. I waited until I had scraped together some humility before confessing, "We're talking because… I'm worried about Phil."

He listened.

"Asia is running out of patience. If she finally snaps, she'll either kill Phil or kill everyone she loves, and I'm not sure which is worse."

That was a lie. Having been on the receiving end of the latter, I knew which was worse.

He let my dishonesty slide. *What do you want Me to do about it?*

"Bust me out of jail" would have been the most precise answer, but I knew I wouldn't get away with it, so I broadened the parameters. "I know You have plans for Phil, and I know she doesn't see them. She has no idea what she's doing or who to trust. She needs wisdom. I… need wisdom."

What are you asking? He nudged, ever the teacher.

"What is Asia planning? What do You want Phil to do—what do You want *me* to do?" I sat up and stared into the dark room. "Tell me what I need to know."

He didn't answer directly—which was highly unusual for us. But He did send the dreams.

Only one problem: The dreams didn't answer any of my questions.

It wasn't that they were bad dreams. Usually when I lost control of a situation, I had visceral nightmares; my gift of prophecy was twisted into a cruel joke as I imagined a future I could not change.

Not tonight. My dreams were benign; had I been in a better mood, I might have even dared to call them good dreams. Philadelphia was there, doing exactly what my vision had predicted she would: changing the world. I saw her standing in the courtyard of a white-stone mansion, receiving party guests with perfect grace. I saw her presiding over a board meeting, with several faces I knew gathered around the table: Bowen, Warden Ivanova, my father.

And again and again, I saw her speaking to the Council in Beijing, confronting them with prophetic speeches that I forgot as soon as I woke up.

It was exactly as I had envisioned it a month ago, except Philadelphia was perhaps a little older. Her dark brown hair had grown back in, and she had a wedding ring on her finger—no doubt given to her by that brooding Pizza Boy.

I woke up then. I came into cold, musty reality with a groan and a crick in literally every joint of my body—probably because I'd clenched every muscle thinking about Stanyard laying his lips on my daughter.

I sat up and rubbed my face. "You're not helping," I grunted, unsure whether I was talking to myself or the Lord.

He didn't respond, not that He had a chance to. *"¡Buenos dias!"* Ryan crowed at an indecent volume. His head popped over the edge of the bunk like a possessed jack-in-the-box. "Rise and shine! You're going to be late for work!"

"You're not my boss anymore," I mumbled, and contemplated going back to bed. Ryan had been my supervisor in the factory for all of two weeks. I'd since gotten reassigned to the lab, where I was the boss over a motley crew of scientists, but Ryan had been unwilling to let his superiority go.

"Maybe, but I still told the warden I'd keep an eye on you. Up, up, up!" He grabbed my blanket and yanked it from me. The force was too sudden for his barely-five-foot frame, and he tumbled off the ladder with a yelp.

Vance caught him. "The fact that you have been given a position of management does not mean standard working hours do not apply to you," he accused. "In fact, because you are in authority, I imagine Warden Ivanova is expecting a higher level of adherence..."

Thank you for the early morning sermon, I thought but wasn't stupid enough to say. Even though we were, against my will, friends, Vance's hulking frame, scarred knuckles, and penchant for dissecting my every sentence made me think twice about using sarcasm in his presence.

He's right, you know, the Voice in my head joined the conversation.

I slapped the thin mattress. "Of course, he's right. They're always right!"

"Hi God!" Ryan called. He jumped up and waved; I could barely see his hand over the edge of the bedframe.

Tell him I said hi.

I pinched the bridge of my nose. "God says hi back."

Ryan whooped like he'd won a ticket out of jail.

And tell Vance I agree with him.

"I'm not telling Vance anything," I snapped.

"Excuse me?"

I gave you this factory to steward. So, steward it.

I groaned in defeat. God had, in fact, given me this factory; Vance, Ryan, and I were running the place. When I'd first arrived, the prison, while a fascinating piece of ice-crusted architecture, had been in shambles. The assembly line was grossly inefficient, and the place was bleeding resources. The only thing Warden Ivanova had under control was the discipline.

I would have been content to let the place burn, but the Lord had other plans. He told me to use my three PhDs to fix it. Warden Ivanova, much to my surprise, actually took my advice, and within two weeks we'd completely restructured the factory. Production had doubled and profits even more so. The influx of wealth had brought the warden the approval of her superiors, and she'd returned the favor by promoting us. Ryan now supervised the production floor, Vance managed administration, and I'd been given charge of the lab, where we developed the products to be assembled in the factory.

It'd be a very nice arrangement, if I weren't a convicted felon and completely cut off from the one person I cared about on this planet.

You have a job to do, the Voice in my head came like a cattle prod.

"You still haven't answered my question," I shot back.

I answered your question. I told you what you need to know.

"If the Lord has given you a message for me, it's imperative that you relay it," Vance interrupted, crossing his arms over his concrete slab of a chest.

"There's no message," I groaned, and the statement applied to both of us. Apparently, the Lord thought I didn't need any additional information.

I knew what that meant. And I didn't like it.

I swung my legs over the edge of the bunk and jumped down. Satisfied I was awake, the boys had mercy and left the room. I took my time digging through the clothes on the floor to find an unsoiled lab coat. My promotion had earned me the privilege of not wearing prison orange, so I donned a button up and pair of slacks and checked my reflection in the mirror. My goatee was overgrown and my hair was somewhere between "hippie" and "electrocuted," but I couldn't be bothered.

I stumbled down to the cafeteria, soldiered through Vance and Ryan's invigorating table talk, and then took the scenic route to the lab. The lab was in one of the subbasements of the prison, a good ten floors down from the cafeteria, but I decided to walk instead of taking the elevator. I strolled along the railing, giving the coffee time to make it to my bloodstream and admiring the marvel of the factory.

It was a genius, if not ostentatious, design. It was built like a silo with a hollow center. The assembly line was staggered across the circular levels, while supplies and workers were ferried up the middle on a spider web of pullies and elevators. The building had so many floors that you couldn't see the top from the bottom. The place rang with enterprise, the sounds of productivity echoing in the cavernous space like an eerie choir.

I leaned over the railing and admired the ingenuity. It would be a delightful view—if it weren't also a prison.

"Von Nieuwenhuyse!"

I jumped and almost dropped my coffee cup over the edge. "It's too early for that many syllables," I groaned, and turned around.

Warden Ivanova strode towards me, her usual entourage of guards in tow. "You're needed in Storage Bay 5," she barked.

"Why? I just marked all the bins with a label maker yesterday."

She halted and glared up at me. "I don't have time for your emasculated sense of humor, Nic. Get down there."

I tried and failed not to be offended. Normally, Warden Ivanova could match me wit for wit. The fact that she'd lost her sense of humor meant something was very wrong.

I switched gears. "What happened?"

"Another powercell exploded."

"Again?" It was the third time this week.

Of the many products manufactured in the factory, powercells were the most profitable. We produced a whole range of sizes for different applications—from cells as big as oil drums for interstellar transits to miniature batteries designed for electric pistols and household appliances. The assembly line had just finished a special order of the latter. All had gone stupendously well, thanks to my engineering—until the powercells reached the quality testing phase. Then, suddenly, the batteries started exploding like popcorn kernels.

At first, Warden Ivanova automatically assumed it was sabotage and went on an interrogation spree. When she failed to find anything suspicious, she set up additional security on the assembly line. The next explosion was clearly an accident—and that's when she called me in. I ran a diagnostic and found several of the testing chambers were out of alignment. I corrected the issue and deemed it safe to continue production.

Apparently, I was wrong.

"It's not the testing equipment," I assured her, and hoped she wasn't about to exact all her frustration on me.

"I know it's not," she intoned. "This cell exploded by itself. In a storage bin. On the other side of the factory."

She held it out to me—or rather, what was left of it. The only thing that remained was a charred stub, like someone had chewed off the cap to a pen.

I took it and held it up to the light. "Well, that's not normal."

"This batch had passed testing. I saw the report myself. So, either you miscalibrated my testing machines, *or...*"

I looked up. "I take it I'd better supply the 'or' if I don't want to get sent to bed without dinner."

She sighed. "You want my personal opinion? I think it's by design." She pointed at the fragment in my hand. "This is a proprietary model we haven't manufactured before. They claim their patent has passed federal inspection, but I don't trust the government."

"I can get behind that mantra."

She snorted. "I want you to get the lab on it. Figure out why these powercells are going nuclear. I need a full report ASAP. A shipment of these have already left the warehouse, and my buyer is not patient."

"What about the other assignment you gave me that's due tomorrow?" I returned. It was an honest question, not that you could tell by my tone of voice.

Her expression froze over like the ice on the windowsills. "I think this is more important."

I cleared my throat and adopted a more appropriate attitude. "Yes, ma'am." Just because I was management didn't mean I was above the warden's discipline, and I was not in the mood to give her any free stress relief today.

She accepted the penance with a nod, then stormed off, her guards following like a line of ducklings.

I studied the powercell fragment in my hand. I had to admit, it didn't look natural. I'd overloaded a few powercells in my day, but I'd never seen anything like this. Normally, an overloaded powercell would melt, swell, or catch fire, just like any battery. This fragment looked like it had spontaneously exploded. To make matters even stranger, the edges of the inner component were rough and pitted, almost as if it had been eaten away by acid.

I ran my finger over the sharp edge. Powercell casings weren't made of weak material, for obvious reasons. They were specifically designed to contain caustic chemicals. What could have deteriorated it?

My mind began running through the periodic table, searching for possible candidates, when I abruptly realized the Holy Spirit was hovering over my shoulder.

"All right, all right," I consented without looking back. "I'll use one of my three PhDs to fix it."

He smiled, satisfied.

I slid the fragment in the pocket of my lab coat and started down the hall. "I can take a hint," I said. "But there had better be a *very* good reason for this side quest."

5: PHILADELPHIA

"As much as I hate to admit it, Asia did us a favor."

I stared at the graph on the computer in Jael's office and tried to rationalize any other explanation for the analytics, but I couldn't. The numbers didn't lie. In some twisted and sick irony, the executions had saved the revolution.

The first forty-eight hours after the fall of Boston were a nightmare. Jael and her team scrambled to warn everyone who could be traced from Stanyard's computer; I went on air and begged my allies to save themselves. It was a losing battle. Asia mobilized the army, and within twelve hours she had raided a dozen other outposts on the East Coast. Hundreds of my supporters were arrested. Some vanished as Asia locked them away where we couldn't find them, just like she had with Nic. The rest were systematically executed, one right after another.

Everything crumbled like a house of cards. The media slaughtered me and the revolution. The Council, at the encouragement of Asia, voted unanimously to increase the punishment for associating with the thunderbird. Under the guise of restoring order, Asia instituted curfew and flooded the streets of Beijing with soldiers, and the people bought the lie. Views on my videos plummeted while Chinese civilians praised Asia's decisive action. For two terrifying and agonizingly long days, it looked like Asia would win.

And then, suddenly, the tides reversed.

I put out a video condemning the executions, just like Jael had instructed. The script she gave me was unorthodox; I barely talked about Asia and her politics at all. Instead, I spent most of my airtime honoring the victims. I put faces to the statistics as I went into heartbreaking detail about the mothers, fathers, nurses, and disabled children the United had murdered. I let the whole world know who was really suffering in this war.

And the world listened.

The video trended, more so than any of my other content. Within twenty-four hours, that stream and its reposts had amassed more views than all my previous videos combined. It broke past the censors and dominated the home page of every social media site—even on networks Jael *couldn't* control. It defied the algorithm, to the point where even Jael called it a miracle.

Suddenly, I was writing the narrative. Public opinion shifted sharply as the Chinese questioned Asia's ethics. The people were enraged, and my followers seized the opportunity. They joined me online and exposed the United's other sins, reminding everyone who the real enemy was. Jael let the cycle run its course for a few days, then put me on air to call people to rejoin the fight.

They answered. Most of the groups who had committed to Operation Blue Fire publicly pledged to demonstrate as scheduled, no matter the risks. Dozens of new mass demonstrations were planned. Even the military continued to cast their lot in with me as several more regiments joined General Jin in vowing to defect.

The world was ripe for revolution. It was just like when my father had tried to launch the original Operation Blue Fire four years ago, before my mother died. The United had made an error when they instituted the unassimilated containment camps, and the people had been willing to fight. Now, Asia had made the same mistake. She had gone too far and upset the balance, and her retaliation was adding fuel to the fire. The more she threatened, the more people she executed, the more my popularity grew. She was turning her own people against her and sending them running to me.

Jael was right; Asia did us a favor. And that worried me.

"We're going to let it rest for another twelve hours," Jael was saying, having already moved on to another tab. "I want to give your supporters a chance to raise their own voices and second your latest video. Then I'll have you go on, thank them, and give people additional instructions."

I watched her neon-colored nails clack on the keyboard. "Okay," I mumbled, only half-listening.

She stopped typing. "What's wrong?"

I shifted my eyes to her face. "Nothing," I said, and it was the truth. The fact that Asia was losing was a good thing—wasn't it?

She propped her chin on her fingers. "Philadelphia. I thought your orders were to be *honest* with me."

I flinched and looked away. "I don't… know. I'm not sure what's wrong," I admitted, which was at least slightly more accurate.

She reached down and found my hand. "Just try. What are you thinking?"

I stared out the window at the hazy green river flowing past the docks, giving myself a minute to think. "I just… This doesn't make sense. Why would Asia let us gain this much ground? Surely, she realizes what she's doing." I turned back to Jael.

"It may not be her decision." The swiftness of her response told me she'd been considering the same questions. "Just because she's the public face doesn't mean this is her policy."

That was a possibility, but I didn't believe that—and I could tell Jael didn't, either. We all knew Asia was in charge in every way that mattered.

"She may also be desperate. Violent people tend to escalate with more violence when they're losing control," Jael suggested.

I didn't believe that either. Yes, I was sure Asia was furious with me for scorning her blackmail and death threats. But this wouldn't be the first time her plans had been complicated, and she'd always found a way to compensate. She'd proven again and again that she was willing to play the long game to avoid an unnecessary mess. All this chaos and media attention was not her style—which meant she must have another plan.

Nic would know. Nic knew Asia better than even Jael did, and he was a shrewd politician in his own right. If he were here, he'd be able to decipher Asia's actions—and tell me exactly what I needed to do to stop her.

But he's not here. I looked down at the table as pain filled my chest. Now more than ever, I realized Nic was exactly the person I needed in my life. I could only wonder if he missed me half as much as I missed him.

Jael squeezed my hand. "Take a break. We'll record after dinner."

I nodded. I stood up and let myself out of the office, then waited until the door had shut behind me before taking a breath.

The unnatural silence in the hall settled like a layer of dust. The factory was dead; only a few office staff still worked out of the building, just enough to keep up appearances. The eerie quiet wrapped itself around me like a draft and reminded me that I was very much alone.

I hadn't been allowed to leave the factory for a week. All I could do was wander the halls and pray. It was almost like being back on the science station on Mars—except it was nearly impossible to get lost in the factory, and a security team was watching my every move.

I smiled at the guard who stood by the elevator nearest Jael's office. He gave me a respectful nod.

I turned away and continued down the hall. Pulling out my tablet, I opened a streaming service and searched for a repost of my latest video. There were dozens, some of which were nearly twenty-four hours old—a sure sign the censors were failing. I clicked on the top result and watched the views and likes climb in real time.

What was Asia doing? The government never allowed my videos to trend like this. Asia must be letting it happen. That was the only explanation I could accept—because the other possibility was one I was too afraid to consider.

The other explanation was that we really *were* winning. The government was failing. The algorithm was caving in on itself. Asia was losing control, and in her desperation, she was hastening her own demise. The revolution was succeeding—because God wanted it to succeed.

Is this God?

A week ago, I would have said yes, without hesitation. But now, the thought made me sick, like it was food I couldn't swallow. We were winning—why did that make me uneasy?

Was it because we were morbidly profiting off of people's deaths? That wasn't anything new; martyrs had been winning wars for thousands of years. Besides, Jael had been using my life's story as propaganda for months now. If that truly bothered me, I wouldn't continue to be the thunderbird.

And even if I did disagree with Jael's methods, I would still firmly believe that God could turn anything for good. It was in His rulebook to redeem what the enemy meant for evil. For the past six months, my entire life had been a string of redemptions as God had used death and imprisonment and loss to bring hope and freedom and love.

So why was this time any different? For the last six months, I'd looked at my circumstances and sworn it was God. Why couldn't I do that now?

The answer came to me, cold and formless, like a stranger looming just out of sight behind the fog.

Maybe I was scared because the last time I claimed to have heard God, I was wrong.

I stopped in the middle of the hallway as the ugly memories caught up to me. God had given Nic, of all people, a vision about my future, and I thought I knew what it meant. I thought I knew exactly what God wanted me to do and how He wanted me to do it. I'd stubbornly insisted on staying in Beijing, even though everyone who cared about me—including Jael—wanted me to go back to Boston. And now hundreds of people were dead because of that choice.

I couldn't make the same mistake again. I couldn't lead a war thinking it was God if it wasn't.

I looked at the ceiling. "Is that you, God?" I whispered.

I was more than a little terrified when a real voice answered me.

"Nah, don't be silly. It's just me!"

Before I could turn towards the sound, a hand struck out of the shadows in the side hall and grabbed my arm.

6: PHILADELPHIA

I shrieked. The guard at the elevator reacted, drawing his weapon. My assailant shushed me sharply. "Shh! You're going to get us in trouble!"

I relaxed when I recognized the voice. I stopped struggling and squinted at him. "John? Err, Dowe?"

He grinned. "You had it right the first time. It's John."

I took his word for it. It was impossible to tell which one it was with his face creepily half-shrouded in shadow. John and Dowe weren't twins; they weren't even related, according to rumor. But they looked so cannily alike that my best guess as to their origins was "failed cloning experiment." They were ancient but didn't act like it; they were also supposedly Jael's best secret agents, but they didn't act like that either. They were loud and shameless and had a terrifying habit of appearing in places they shouldn't have been, almost as if they had teleported there. But despite the fact that everything about their behavior defied both logic and physics, they were some of the best friends I had.

Except, maybe, when they were leaping out of the shadows like murderers.

"Don't scare me like that," I grunted, pulling my arm from his grasp.

"Sorry, but I need you for a *covert* mission." He leaned around the corner and scanned the hall shiftily.

"Well, if you're going for subtlety, scaring me out of my wits was probably not the best option." I glanced at the guard. He rolled his eyes and holstered his weapon.

John started walking, gesturing for me to follow. "Come on—and keep a low profile. Jael *cannot* find out about this."

I hesitated. Not telling Jael sounded like a terrible idea, even coming from John and Dowe. "Where are we going?" I whispered, not sure why I was playing into the secrecy.

"The conference room," he hissed back. He tiptoed across the hall—to the conference room, which was all of three yards away.

I looked at the guard. He shrugged. "You're on your own with that one."

I indulged in a chuckle and followed John. I supposed there was only so much trouble we could get into in the conference room.

After making a scene of checking both ways—even though the guard was definitely the only other person in the hall—John opened the door and waved me through. I walked in and halted. "What happened in here?"

"Glitter happened!" John crowed, and that was an accurate description. The conference room was a mess—in the most glorious, colorful way possible. The entire table was coated with craft supplies, from construction paper to scalloped scissors to jars of glitter, several of which had already contaminated the room. There was glitter on the chairs, the windows, the whiteboard. The whole room sparkled like it had been blessed by a fairy.

"How'd you manage to get glitter on the windowsill?" I pointed.

John scratched his head nervously. "I, uhh, tried to get Tommy to help me with a collage..."

"What?" I exclaimed, but a petulant meow answered my question. I looked down to see my cat rubbing innocently around my ankles.

Tommy was a yellow-eyed stray Nic and I had picked up while running across Beijing a month ago. Well, *I'd* picked him up; Nic had tried his hardest to get rid of him. In any case, it was, perhaps, a bit selfish to think of the animal as "mine." If anything, he was more attached to John, who was supposed to be keeping him at the Tangs. Lanzhou had expressly forbidden me from bringing my cat to the factory—something about cat hair and delicate equipment.

I picked Tommy up. He was *covered* in glitter; his gray fur sparkled like a disco ball. I held him at arm's length, even though I knew it was too late; I wasn't getting out of this room unscathed. "You're right," I murmured. "Jael probably shouldn't find out about this."

"Don't worry, we'll clean up the evidence," John said.

"You'll probably have to burn the whole room down," I remarked. There was no way that stuff was coming out of the seat cushions.

Tommy mewed and flicked his tail, sending glitter showering through the air.

I laughed and gave up arguing. "So, what is this 'mission,' exactly?"

"The mission is for you to have fun!" someone whisper-shouted. I looked up to see Dowe sitting at the end of the table, waving a marker-stained hand at me. Next to him sat Sienna.

I sucked in my breath. Sienna was one of the residents of the hospital I had visited a few days ago. She'd managed to escape with us; we'd used the fire exit in her room, and my security got her to safety. She'd been staying at the factory since then because, like me, she was a wanted criminal—although her only crime was failing to meet the United's standard of physical and mental perfection.

She was also, I abruptly realized with a stab in my heart, one of the only residents of the group home left alive.

"Hey, what's that face? You're failing the mission already," John chided. "Come on, let's make a paper chain or something."

He guided me towards the table. I followed and took the chair next to Sienna, settling Tommy in my lap. "Hey," I greeted her softly.

She didn't acknowledge me, but I wasn't offended. Sienna was severely autistic and non-verbal. She rarely even looked in my direction. *"The important thing,"* Jael had said, *"is to treat her like you would anyone else— even if you don't get the response you're expecting."*

I leaned over to see what she was working on. She was coloring, gripping the crayon with fierce intent. I couldn't quite tell what the image was supposed to be, but it was elaborate. She had used every color in the box, filling in all the white on the paper with precision.

"It's beautiful," I said, and it was. I watched her work, trying to find something more to say. I couldn't come up with anything—so, I grabbed a clean piece of paper and started coloring with her.

As was usually the case with John and Dowe, their chaotic methods proved weirdly effective, and the "mission" was a success. I did have fun— and Sienna did too. This was the calmest I'd ever seen her, and she repeatedly engaged with Dowe. She laughed and clapped and responded to his questions, using her body to fill in the gaps where words failed her. I watched in silence and let a little joy into my soul. Not everyone from the group home had been lost.

Thank you, Jesus.

"What is the meaning of this?"

I jumped and dropped my glue stick. Jael stood in the open doorway, hands on her hips. "John Dowe!" she screeched.

Dowe scrambled up, overturning his chair. "I can explain, I swear!" He ran towards her, hands clasped in penance.

She sidestepped. "*Don't* touch me. Where in the world did you get all these craft supplies?"

He looked puzzled. "The craft store?"

I snickered before I could stop myself.

She shot me a glare. "Never mind. I'll court martial *all* of you later."

She sounded serious, and Dowe panicked accordingly. John groaned and flopped back in his chair like his mom had just told him to clean his room. "Ugh! I don't wanna go back to jail!"

"At least she can't send us back to Rott," Dowe reasoned.

"Watch me," Jael muttered. She yelped as Tommy wrapped himself around her ankles, rubbing a visible amount of glitter into her pantyhose. She gingerly pushed him away; he pranced right back over and sat on her foot.

She made a heroic effort to plaster a smile on her face and turned to me. "You have a visitor."

Who...?

I stood up as Seoul waltzed into the room. She looked like a video game character come to life with her cocky blue hair and junkyard-rat outfit of overalls and loaded toolbelts. Her omnipresent goggles dangled around her neck as she winked at me. "'Sup, girlfriend," she greeted with a casualness only she could afford. She was the tech who had safely removed the bomb in my hand; I'd let her get away with anything.

"Hey, Seoul," Dowe crooned. He tried and failed to lean nonchalantly on the table. He slipped, crashing to the floor.

She blithely ignored him and looked over at John. "Hey, baby."

John beamed and wiggled his fingers.

Dowe blistered red all the way up to the roots of his hair. "It's like I'm not even here."

I put myself between them. "What are you doing here?"

"Getting paid for a job well done," she smirked.

I stiffened. "Did you...?"

For an answer, she reached into her messenger bag and withdrew a small metal box. She pressed her thumb to the lock, and it released with a beep. She held the case out to me.

I gingerly took it and opened the lid. Tucked on a bed of foam and shielded by a sheet of glass were three miniature computer chips, no bigger than a square centimeter each. A dozen fine wires sprayed from the circuitry like spider legs.

"Three brand-new memory augmenters," Seoul whispered, giving the treasure the reverence it deserved.

I closed the lid and grasped the box to my chest as warm tears splattered my cheeks. These chips were my ticket to bringing my father back from the dead—and maybe, just maybe, saving Nic's parents.

My dad was the victim of cryogenic freezing. Paul and Roseanne Von Nieuwenhuyse were the victims of something arguably worse: neurosurgery. It was a barbaric corrective procedure that involved severing neural pathways to selectively rewrite the criminal's psyche. It was so grossly ineffective that even the United had restricted it.

That was exactly why Asia had subjected Nic's parents to the procedure after he'd failed to give her Red Rain. She'd killed them in every way that mattered, stripping them of their memories, their personalities, and their ability to function as independent adults.

The Vons weren't the only people I knew who had survived neurosurgery. John and Dowe were also recovering victims. When I'd first met Seoul, she'd bragged about the chips she'd implanted in their brains that had given them (some of) their memories back. According to her, John and Dowe were functioning on prototype knockoffs because they were "cheapskates," which was why they could only retain a couple terabytes of information, most of it useless.

The chips I held in my hand were not prototypes. With enough programming and therapy, they could enable my father and the Vons to access their lost memories.

It might not work. My dad's brain could be damaged beyond repair. For the Vons, they'd undergone surgery almost a decade ago; time may have rewritten their neural pathways beyond retrieving.

But for my family, both literal and honorary, I was willing to try—even if it cost the entire Nolan fortune.

I looked up at Seoul. "How much do I owe?"

"A lot," she intoned. "But I'll accept part of my payment in the form of a private flight out of the country and a couple of hulks to help me move my shop gear."

I frowned. Her weary smile didn't make it to her eyes as she said, "No offense, but Beijing is not a safe place for your friends right now."

"Of course." I sighed and turned to Jael.

She nodded. "I can make the arrangements."

Seoul popped her chewing gum. "Well, guess we're even. It was nice doing business with you, Blue Fire. Good luck with the implants—call me if you have any problems."

I gripped the box as an idea raced through my mind. "Since you're already leaving town... How would you like to extend your employment? I need some work done in America. For an additional fee, of course."

She lifted both eyebrows.

I held the box out. "I need someone to install these. And I heard you're something of an expert on these devices."

Her face split in a grin that bordered on maniacal. "You heard correctly. But you do know that the surgery is almost as much as the device."

I shrugged. "You get what you pay for."

She started to reply, but then the eagerness faded from her expression. "Unfortunately, a mechanic is only as good as her tools, and I won't have my full lab in America."

Jael spoke up. "I'm sure I can find—"

I raised my hand. "I know someone with facilities. Find Andes, tell him Blue Fire sent you. He'll give you everything you need. And if he doesn't, call me, and *I'll* tell him to give you everything you need."

Seoul barked a laugh. "I like this plan."

I paused and reconsidered what I'd just told her to do. "I'll warn you, though—don't expect a warm welcome. He's been running the scene in Boston for longer than I've been alive. He probably won't be thrilled that I've outsourced."

I thought of Andes's bulging muscles and tattooed skin and wondered if I'd just sent a petite, blue-haired David to face down a Scottish Goliath.

Seoul fingered the sadistic array of tools she had in her belt, perhaps involuntarily. "Sounds like my kind of challenge."

Jael took over. "Follow me, we'll get the paperwork done."

"We'll miss you!" John crowed from the table. "Right, Sienna?"

She grunted and scribbled on her paper.

I stared at her as the Holy Spirit whispered in my ear.

Seoul blew John a kiss. "I'll miss you, too."

Dowe squinted. "Is that a plural you, or singular...?"

I spoke before Seoul could retort. "Actually, you're both going with her."

"We are?" John and Dowe exclaimed together.

"No way." Seoul put both palms forward. "I'll take John but not Dowe."

"You'll take whoever I tell you to. I'm paying you, not the other way around," I reminded her.

Seoul gaped. Jael propped her chin on her hand and looked mildly impressed.

I turned to face the boys. "John and Dowe, I have a mission for you. I need you to go back to Boston and take care of some business for me."

Dowe scrunched his nose so hard it was in danger of folding back into his face. "That sounds vaguely like a non-job to get us to go away."

"It's not. I need you to take Sienna with you." I watched her as she continued to color. "Find a family that will take care of her and keep her off the grid."

There was sudden silence in the room except for Sienna's scratching on the paper. Abruptly, she stopped, the crayon dangling from her fingers. Then she glanced up at me.

I smiled.

Dowe laid a hand on my arm. "We'd be honored."

Seoul blew a strand of hair out of her face. "Fine, I promise not to kill Dowe on the way."

"Charmed," he grunted.

I looked to Jael for approval. She winked.

"Just one question…" John called.

I glanced back at him.

He folded his hands under his chin and did his best to look cute. "Can I keep your cat?"

7: PHILADELPHIA

One hour and thirty-seven minutes. That was how long it took to walk a lap around each level of the factory, from the third floor to the basement, and that was information I wish I didn't know.

It was a crime that I should be so bored while the world was waging a war in my name. Even though the public saw me as the leader of the resistance, the reality was that "Blue Fire" did very little. Jael handled all the coordination and planning. While I was very grateful that she was managing the difficult decisions, it meant I spent the better part of the day alone. I would record for an hour, and then maybe kill another hour or two in strategy meetings where I mainly listened to everyone else make decisions. For the rest of the day, I would wander the halls, bored and very, very lonely.

The factory had gotten even quieter with John, Dowe, and Sienna gone. I didn't even have my cat to keep me company; I'd made the difficult decision that Tommy would, in fact, be safer with John. The group had returned to Boston and made contact with Andes, but that was the last news I'd received.

Meanwhile, Bowen, the one person who was always happy to involve me in whatever he was doing, was hardly on the property anymore. Lanzhou made an effort to talk to me when we passed, but I knew he was busy keeping his family business from collapsing, so I tried not to harass him. Everyone else in the building had jobs to do.

And, with Stanyard gone, there was no one to talk to online.

My dad called a few times. They were bittersweet conversations as I patiently answered questions he should have known the answer to: *"How old are you? When's your birthday? What do you remember about your mother?"* But I knew he was trying, so we made the most of each moment.

I was finally able to tell him the good news about Seoul and the memory implant. I forced myself to be realistic; the device would take a lot of programing, just like any algorithm, before it would start recalling the correct memories for each word. It could take weeks of visual therapy before the implant would think of me and not the city when someone said "Philadelphia"—and that was if his memories were salvageable at all.

"It will take several months of therapy to start working," I said. "But I'll help you, I promise. Ephesus will too."

My older brother Ephesus was currently hiding in a remote mining base on Mars with his wife Cea—who also happened to be Nic's sister. We hadn't had time to celebrate our complicated family tree. The mine was so deep in the wilderness that it was difficult to get a call through; it took over a week for me to reach him and break the news of our uncle's death. But Ephesus and Cea wouldn't have to hide for much longer.

After operation day, the unassimilated wouldn't have to live in the shadows anymore.

Dad turned to face the camera, and for the first time since he'd woken up, his eyes gleamed with the tiniest sliver of hope. "We'll do it together. As a family."

Even though we both wanted to talk more, Dad could only handle about ten minutes at a time before he got tired of fighting the implants in his brain—and that was on a good day. Andes constantly had him in and out of surgery as they tweaked the wiring and tried to resurrect my father's science degrees. I could tell Dad was overwhelmed at best, so I pretended I had things to do and hung up whenever he grew anxious.

I only wished I weren't lying when I said I was busy.

I was on my third or fourth lap for the day when something finally broke the monotony. I had just stepped off the elevator into the basement cafeteria, where the church services used to be held, when I heard Bowen's voice. I followed the sound to the back hallway and found him and a military officer I didn't recognize unloading crates from the service elevator.

"Phil!" Bowen welcomed me with a grin.

The soldier paused to give me a long, respectful look—which was how strangers usually greeted me—and then threw a salute.

I acknowledged it with a smile. "What are you doing? And I can I help?" I asked, even though I doubted the latter. Even Bowen was struggling under the weight of the crates.

He dropped the last one in the hallway with a grunt. "Well, I need to catalog these, and then some are getting sent to other churches…"

I nodded; Bowen was well-connected and knew at least a dozen other underground pastors in the province. "What are they? Bibles?"

His lips twitched. "Not… exactly."

The soldier keyed a passcode into the crate on top of the stack. "General Jin sends his regards."

Then he threw the lid back, revealing a row of shiny electric pistols.

I gasped.

"One of your wealthy allies provided the funding," the soldier explained, even though I hadn't asked. "General Jin is redistributing them across the city."

"But—what are they for?" I demanded, even though I knew exactly what guns were for.

"Operation day," Bowen answered. He picked one up and slid his hand down the polished barrel.

"Just what kind of demonstration are you planning?" I struggled to hear my own voice through the panic screaming in my ears.

"The demonstration this city needs." Bowen glanced back at me. "Phil. You know it's too late for peaceful negotiations. The government is going to do everything they can to retaliate on operation day—unless the people defend themselves."

I knew he was right—was he? I knew shots would be fired on operation day; it was unavoidable. But that didn't mean I was going to *fund* the violence, sending weapons to innocent civilians.

This isn't right. This isn't what Operation Blue Fire is supposed to be!

I gripped the straps of my backpack, afraid that if I didn't hold on to something, the floor would cave out from beneath me. "Bowen, I—"

"What is going on here?"

I whirled to see Lanzhou storming down the hall, Jael a step behind him. "Bowen!" he shouted. "Put the gun down!"

He obliged. "Cousin, it's not what you think—"

Lanzhou didn't give him a chance to finish. He shoved him aside and glared into the open crate, his face washing white and then red. "No, it's *exactly* what I think. You went behind my back! And who are you?" Lanzhou shifted his glare from Bowen to the officer.

The soldier looked up from his device long enough to point at the name patch on his fatigues. "General Jin's regiment."

"You need to get out of here before someone sees you. Bowen." Lanzhou took a deep breath and made a heroic effort to remain calm, but every muscle in his body was tense. "You need to get these out of here. If someone reports this—"

"Who's going to report it? Everyone in this building is loyal to Blue Fire." Bowen also tried to talk peaceably, with about as much success.

"It doesn't matter! Our bargain with the police explicitly states we won't possess weapons except our own security. If they find out you're storing guns here, we'll lose the church."

"We'll lose the church if the operation fails," Bowen argued. "If the revolution doesn't succeed, a couple of prayer services won't make a difference."

"They'll make all the difference," Lanzhou whispered.

Jael stepped between them. "Enough. Lanzhou's right. I need to keep this building secure, and if that means bribing the police, so be it. Put these back on the truck." She flicked a jeweled finger at the officer.

He pocketed his device. "It's too late."

"Excuse me?" she snarled.

Before he could offer any clarification, my tablet pinged.

I froze. I think, instinctively, I knew who it was and what was about to happen.

The soldier smiled.

My device beeped again. Everyone stared at me as I scrambled with my backpack and pulled out my tablet.

It was Asia.

THERE YOU ARE

The panic returned—and this time, there was nowhere to run.

IT'S OVER, SWEETHEART

"What have you done?" Jael screeched.

"I thought you were with General Jin!" Bowen echoed.

The soldier ignored them both. "If you're going to ask why I did it," he locked eyes with me, "your ransom will pay for my children's retirement."

I stumbled back as Jael's warning flashed through my mind.

"I know you trust your employees, but Asia is offering a sum that would test any man's loyalty."

"You fool!" Jael shrieked, although it was hard to tell who she was yelling at.

The soldier reached for his weapon, but Lanzhou reacted first. He snatched a gun from the crate and flicked it on, planting himself in front of me.

The soldier eyed him. "You don't want to fire that."

Lanzhou aimed the weapon at his face. "Bowen, take the girls and get out of here."

"But—"

The soldier spoke over him. "Don't even try. Asia has two dozen soldiers surrounding the property right now." He looked past Lanzhou to address me. "If you come quietly, she'll let the others go."

Asia sent another text and seconded his statement.

YOU HAVE FIVE MINUTES TO COME OUTSIDE BEFORE I BURN THE PLACE DOWN. DON'T KEEP ME WAITING.

"Don't listen to him, Philadelphia," Lanzhou said. His voice was deceptively steady even though his chest was heaving. "Bowen, now. You know what to do."

Bowen started to back away. "Lanzhou—"

"Now," he ordered. "Keep Philadelphia safe. Don't come back for me."

I whimpered, remembering the last time this scene had played out—and how it ended.

"Don't ever come back."

Bowen lurched into motion. He snatched two more guns, tossing one at Jael, and took off running. "This way, hurry!"

Jael grabbed my arm and hauled me down the corridor. I struggled to shove my tablet in my backpack as I stumbled after her. The soldier seemed unconcerned by our retreat. "It was a pleasure meeting you, Blue Fire."

I cast one last glance back at Lanzhou, but he didn't turn to look at me.

We raced around the corner and across the abandoned cafeteria to the elevator. "Where are we going?" Jael demanded.

"There's another way out—we planned for this." Bowen called the elevator and waved us in ahead of him. Then he reached up and yanked on the fire alarm mounted on the wall. I flinched as a siren blared, thundering in the empty hall.

He stepped in and keyed a code into the panel, punching the buttons for multiple floors like he was dialing a phone. The doors hissed shut and the elevator moaned as it descended. "This leads to a tunnel that runs under the canal." The warning light in the ceiling drowned his face in bloody red as he explained. "We built it in case the church ever got ambushed. It will dump us out six blocks away—should be far enough."

"It better be." Jael held me close to her, her nails digging into my shoulder.

I braced myself against the wall as the elevator lurched. *God, please, protect Lanzhou!* I begged, even though I knew it was a useless prayer. Lanzhou wasn't getting out of this, not unless he was willing to shoot—

As if in answer, a scream ripped from somewhere above us, seeming to vibrate in the metal shaft. I heard several shouts, a large crash—and then an explosion.

This time, Jael screamed. Bowen cursed. The entire elevator shook. I stumbled into the corner, but before I could find my balance, another explosion rocked the air. Then another. Debris pummeled the roof of the elevator. The car groaned and shifted to one side—then plummeted.

I couldn't even scream as the floor dropped out. Air rushed around me like a surging river—and then the elevator hit the bottom, and so did I. We'd only fallen a few feet, but the world still briefly washed black as I slammed into the ground, elbows first. I moaned and hacked, trying to get air.

Jael and Bowen were shouting, but I couldn't make out the words around the ringing in my ears. Dust rained from the dented ceiling. Bowen crawled to the panel and pulled the emergency lever. The doors thudded as the hydraulics released. He dragged himself up, grunting in pain, and shoved the doors open.

Jael kicked off her broken heels and staggered to her feet. She reached down and pulled me upright, murmuring something in my ear. The only part I understood was "Phil." I nodded and followed her out of the elevator.

The tunnel beyond was cold and nearly dark except for a row of dim lights running down the middle of the ceiling. The sound of the river grinding on the concrete was terrifying; it felt like we might be crushed at any moment.

"What happened?" I managed.

Bowen didn't hear me. "This way!" He coughed and stumbled around the corner. A large object covered by a tarp was hidden in the shadows. Bowen yanked the tarp off, revealing an old SUV. The door squeaked as he opened the driver's side and rooted under the seat for the key. "Let's go!"

Jael shoved me towards the car. She helped me into the backseat, then claimed shotgun. Bowen got behind the wheel and turned the key. The engine sputtered, then ignited. He flicked the headlights on and gunned the engine. The tires crunched on gravel and trash as he raced towards the end of the tunnel.

Jael tried to catch her breath. "Did she bomb us?"

"I-I don't know," Bowen stuttered.

"But it hasn't even been five minutes!" I cried. I shrugged my backpack off and struggled to pull out my tablet with sweaty hands. There was no signal.

Blurry light appeared ahead. Bowen slowed as he neared the end. He pulled carefully out of the tunnel and onto a dock behind an abandoned warehouse. There were no police cars in sight.

I scrambled across the seat to look out the window. Several blocks behind us was the factory.

It was gone.

The building was completely collapsed. Chunks of concrete spilled into the canal like a crumbled cookie. Smoke billowed into the sky as flashing lights swarmed the yard.

"Lanzhou!" I screamed, the sound inhuman. I slammed my fist into the window and wailed.

He's gone he's gone he's gone, oh God!

Bowen yelled something in Mandarin and slammed on the brakes.

"Keep driving!" Jael ordered. "We have to get away from here!"

Bowen obeyed, but the car swerved as he struggled to hold onto the wheel. "This is all my fault!"

I sagged against the seat and sobbed. *No, it's mine. It's mine!*

"Drive!"

The engine revved. I became vaguely aware of the sounds of traffic as Bowen drove out of the lot and merged onto the road.

"This way!" Jael pointed. "I know a safe place."

"No, we have to go by the house!" he insisted. "I have to warn the family—they'll be coming for them."

"Under no circumstances! We have to get Phil out of the city!"

He wasn't listening. He took a sudden left, to the complaints of several other drivers. I grabbed the upholstery to keep from being thrown to the floor.

Jael reached for the wheel. "Bowen!"

He gunned it.

I braced myself against her seat as we violently passed the car in front of us. I scanned the road, watching for police, and that's when I saw it—more smoke, this time a few blocks ahead.

"Look—"

I didn't finish. Bowen let out a sound of pure anguish and cranked the wheel. I smashed my shoulder into the window as he raced the last few blocks. We spun around the corner and came within sight of the Tangs' courtyard home.

We were too late.

The place was in flames. The cruel red-orange light illuminated the historic woodwork like some twisted silkscreen show. A police barricade blocked the road as officers herded a family member into the back of a van. I couldn't tell who it was from this distance, but it didn't matter.

Asia had already won.

"Turn off!" Jael shrieked.

Bowen surprisingly obeyed her. He swerved into the alley at the last minute, taking us out of sight. He threw his door open almost before the car was in park and took off down the road.

"Bowen, don't do this!" I begged, pounding the window. "Please!"

"Bowen!" Jael called. "Stop!"

He didn't. He disappeared around the corner, and I heard a shout in a megaphone.

I slapped my hands over my ears. *Please no please no please!*

Jael cursed. She hiked up her skirt and slid across the console, taking the wheel. She slammed the door shut and stepped on the gas. The car pitched over potholes as she navigated around dumpsters and abandoned bikes back to the main road. She slowed long enough to defer attention before pulling out.

I sobbed as the world continued to quiver. Jael swore over and over, slapping the wheel with her bloody hand. I covered my face and tried to block out the shaking, the screaming, the smell of smoke and the sound of concrete falling. *They're gone, they're all gone!*

I'm not sure how long we kept driving. Minutes, maybe hours. It seemed like an eternity before Jael spoke.

"Well." There were a million regrets crammed in the word. "I guess you're coming home with me."

My tablet beeped. I swiped on the screen and squinted at the notification through the tears.

It was, of course, Asia.

OH, WHAT A BIG, UGLY, UNNECESSARY MESS

8: NIC

It took me several days to figure out what was wrong with the powercells, a fact neither I nor Warden Ivanova was happy with.

The issue was, of course, that the design wasn't faulty on paper. If it had been, they would have figured it out during production. As it was, I had to use one and half of my three PhDs to break the design down to the molecular level and find the flaw.

The powercells were composed of four layers: a solid conductive core, a protective inner casing, and a liquid cooling barrier, all housed in a metal shell. A fairly standard design, and none of the components were inherently explosive. I replicated all the elements in the lab and combined them in a dozen ways, but I produced nothing except toxic fumes.

While the lab aired out, I reviewed the logs from the testing stations and tried to calculate the common denominator. As usual, math was forthcoming with the truth: All the powercells that exploded had been subjected to temperatures higher than 250 degrees Fahrenheit.

That explained why only some of the powercells detonated and why the idiot designer may not have caught it. The average consumer wasn't heating their batteries to extreme temperatures. If used in a low-wattage device like a toaster or hair dryer, the powercells would have operated as intended. But when they were exposed to high temperatures for a prolonged amount of time or subjected to repeated bursts of energy, the coolant couldn't keep up, and that's when the magic happened.

After running several tests, I discovered that the elements in the solid core reacted at high heat and melted to form a new, highly corrosive chemical. That chemical could eat through the inner casing, causing the boiling-hot coolant and corroded inner core to mix.

And that combination was *highly* explosive. The hotter the battery, the faster the reaction and the bigger the impact. It was lucky I was running my experiments in a nuclear-grade testing chamber, or we would have lost the entire lab and I would have gone to meet Jesus for the second time in so many months.

I wanted to believe the whole thing was a fantastic accident. If the batteries were being marketed for toasters, government regulations would have only required them to be tested at household levels of energy. It was completely feasible that the original designers had simply been lazy and not subjected their powercells to extreme temperatures.

But I didn't have that much faith in humanity, and neither did Warden Ivanova.

"I hate it when I'm right," she grunted as she glared at the report I'd presented on her desk.

"Me too." I tapped the tablet screen. "How many have already gone out?"

"A couple hundred thousand."

I blinked. "Oh, so only enough to light about a quarter of the world on fire, that's not too bad."

"I notified the buyer and all the requisite governing authorities, but it's up to them to do anything about it."

"Do you know what they purchased the batteries for? If it's electric toothbrushes, that might buy us some time while the government slogs through their paperwork."

She shook her head. "No idea. It was a distribution company. Could be a shell for all I know."

It is a shell, the Voice in my head informed me.

I sighed and looked at the ceiling. "This was not the apocalypse I wanted to be responsible for. There are so many better ways to end the world."

"I stopped the last shipment. Should I be worried about the ones in storage?"

"If they haven't been through high-wattage testing, then no." I thought of the errant powercell that had almost burned Storage Bay 5 to the ground. That particular batch had been tested at energy levels just barely high enough to trigger the chain reaction, hence the delayed explosion. Everything in storage had been there for at least three days at this point, so in theory, we were safe. But I wasn't about to be proven wrong again. "But maybe let's err on the side of caution."

She nodded. "I was thinking of taking them out back, trying to start an avalanche. Wanna come?"

Before I could pull out my calendar to pick a date, a knock came at the door. A guard poked his head in. "There's someone here to see you, warden."

She glanced at her computer screen. "I don't remember giving anyone permission to dock."

"They didn't need permission."

Warden Ivanova swore gloriously and elaborately in Russian. I resisted the urge to echo her; I was trying to break the habit, and it wouldn't have sounded nearly as tenacious in English.

There was only one entity who could barge in unannounced: the government.

"As if this day couldn't get any more pleasant," Warden Ivanova groaned. "Fine. Send them in."

I backed away. "I'll give you your privacy."

But before I could make myself scarce, the door banged open again, and an officer needlessly decorated with the United's insignia crawled in. I could tell by the greenish look on his face that he'd just stepped off the elevator and wasn't handling the sudden altitude well. "Warden… Ivan…ova?" he slurred.

"What do you want?" she barked at a decibel that would have put the fear of God in anyone.

He staggered back and nearly fell on his rear. "I have a… delivery for Dr. Von Nie-when-house."

He nearly vomited after attempting my last name, which was what I usually did when I heard it. "It's Von Nieuwenhuyse, and he's not here right now, would you like to leave a message?"

He took a gulp of air and struggled to contain his stomach. "I'm supposed to tell you, 'Asia sends her warmest regards, and she hopes you like the gift.'"

It was my turn to contemplate throwing up as my day went from bad to hellish.

Warden Ivanova glared at me. "I thought you two broke up?"

"It's complicated. And whatever it is, I don't want it." I shooed the soldier away. "Return to sender, and tell her 'no thank you.'"

He grimaced. "I can't return *him*."

"Him?" the warden snarled.

The guard turned and gestured at someone in the hallway. I had two seconds to calculate the worst possible scenario before that scenario walked through the door.

Bowen.

He jerked. "Nic! You're alive!" He darted towards me, as if he were somehow going to attempt a hug with cuffed hands.

I took a step back. What little serenity I had collapsed like shattered glass as I put two and two together and reached my worst nightmare.

"Phil," I said, and that was all I needed to say.

Bowen hesitated, looking like a kicked dog with his bruised face and guilty eyes. "She escaped. I think."

"I'm going to need a better answer than 'I think,'" I snapped, even though I knew I was directing my rage at an unworthy source. But the most deserving object was several thousand miles away in her cushy Beijing office, and Bowen was, regrettably for more reasons than one, within arm's reach.

"I'm going to need a lot of answers," the warden inserted. "Who are you, and who's Phil?"

Bowen ignored her. "She's with Jael, that's all I know."

"Who's Jael?" the warden asked.

"Great, and where are they?" I demanded.

"They were in the car. I'm assuming they got away."

"Got away from *what*?" I shrieked. The room trembled. It took a minute for me to realize I was the one shaking.

Bowen swallowed. "Asia found the factory."

I braced myself against the warden's desk, but it did nothing to keep the world upright.

"What factory? What's going on? Can they not hear me?" The warden turned to her guard, who shrugged.

"It's all gone." Bowen's whisper barely reached me through the waves of terror. "They arrested the whole family. My aunt, uncle, everyone."

"What about Lanzhou?" I hissed.

He didn't respond, and I had my answer. I forced myself to look up.

Tears blurred his bloodshot eyes. "Lanzhou's dead."

The room went silent. There wasn't a single sound except in my head, where everything was screaming, screaming.

"Nic," the warden called. "What's going on?"

I gripped the edge of the desk. "Leave us."

"Excuse me? You can't—"

I looked up at her. "Please."

She hesitated, her expression cycling between friend and foe.

After a heavy pause, she chose friend. "Ten minutes," she said, and herded the others out the door.

I waited until their voices had faded before sinking into her vacated chair. "From the beginning," I demanded.

Bowen obeyed, explaining everything that had happened since I'd been sent to Russia. The more he talked, the more my fears became reality. Everything I'd prayed wouldn't happen to Philadelphia had happened, and worse. Not only had she gotten caught in a shootout and nearly killed—*twice*—but she'd lost Lanzhou, Stanyard, her uncle, and everyone that mattered. She was stranded in Beijing with a woman I barely knew, leading an army of disillusioned rebels who were prepared to start a war in her name.

And there was no one left to save her.

"I'm sure she and Jael made it out alive," Bowen repeated for the third time, as if that mattered at this point.

I shoved the chair back and stormed to the door.

"Nic?" Bowen called after me. "Nic! Wait!"

I ignored him. I strode out into the hall and nearly collided with the warden, who was, unsurprisingly, waiting around the corner. "Nic! What's going on?"

"Don't talk to me," I snapped, and shoved her out of the way.

The Voice in my head was the next to attempt conversation. *Slow down.*

"I said, don't talk to me!" I shouted. I punched the button to call the elevator and descended to the lowest floor, where the lab was.

The clatter of flasks and the chatter of people assaulted me as soon as the doors opened. Half a dozen scientists busied themselves around the testing equipment, yakking about molecules and boiling points.

One of them spotted me and scampered over. "Doctor! I have the simulation results you asked for." He held out a tablet.

I grabbed it and threw it on the ground, shattering the screen. "Get out."

"But sir—"

"Are you deaf? I said get out! All of you!"

Thankfully, I'd yelled loudly enough for the entire room to hear me, so I didn't have to repeat myself. They rushed to the elevator like a gaggle of scared chickens. I kicked the broken tablet aside and stomped over to a worktable.

The Voice followed me into the room. *What are you doing down here?*

"I don't know, does it matter?" I returned, because it sure didn't to me. I grabbed a random tube and popped the cap, swirling the contents. "Maybe I'll create a world-ending superweapon, I haven't decided yet."

Incidentally, that's what I'd done the last time I was this angry. Because if the world wanted to play with fire, then at least I would have the last laugh.

That's not why you created Red Rain.

He sounded far away, like He was hovering by the door. I glared over my shoulder, half-expecting to see Him there. But of course, the lab was empty.

"Oh no, that's *exactly* why I created Red Rain—because I want this entire stupid planet to burn."

I didn't use the word "stupid," but the word I did choose felt weak, inadequate.

No, you don't. The Voice came from the other side of the room this time.

I whipped around. "You really want to argue about this?" I snapped, as if He weren't in my head anyway. "Well, then let me state it for the record: I hate this planet and everyone on it, and if You hadn't interrupted, I would have gotten some epic revenge. That's all there is to it. I'm sorry if that's not the deep, introspective answer You were hoping for." I replaced the cap and tossed the tube back on the table.

If all you wanted was revenge, He returned coolly from where He was leaning against the whiteboard, *you would have done it ten years ago. As you said, there are so many better ways to end the world.*

He was right, and I hated that. I could have gone to war against Earth any time I wanted; I had more than enough bombs and computer viruses to have a fighting chance. Red Rain was a ludicrous plan, always had been. What's more, I'd realized about two years in that I wasn't smart enough to complete the formula.

And yet, I'd persisted. I'd hired a hundred scientists and wasted all my money constructing Wing 74. I'd even kidnapped Ephesus and forged his death to protect my secret, all in pursuit of a project I knew was science fiction.

You knew it would never work, the Voice prodded.

"Well, forgive me for trying," I spat, and then grimaced at the irony.

You didn't create Red Rain because you wanted revenge, He continued. *And that's not why you're down here now.*

"You're right, I have no idea why I'm down here. But it seemed like a better option than murder." I turned my back to Him and rooted through the implements on the table, just to hear them clatter against the tray.

You shouldn't be alone, He admonished. *Go find Ryan.*

Ryan, with his screeching voice and unfounded optimism, was the last person I wanted to be around. "I'm busy," I snapped, and then proceeded to make a good show of it.

The command repeated, more a premonition than an audible sentence. *Go find Ryan.*

I resorted to ignoring Him. I grabbed two of the nearest test tubes and combined the contents without reading the labels, savoring the brief rush of adrenaline. Much to my disappointment, nothing exciting happened, not even a fizzle.

Stop before you hurt yourself.

Hurting myself sounded like a wonderful idea. I grabbed another flask and contemplated the warning label.

Nic. He was close, too close, sucking the oxygen out of the room.

I clenched my hand around the tube. "Leave me alone!"

Put the glass down, He ordered.

I obeyed, literally. I slammed the flask down and then swiped my arm across the table, sweeping the entire contents onto the floor. The shatter of glass and crash of metal was terrific, and for a very brief moment, it drowned out the hurricane in my head.

I did it again. I walked to the next table and flipped a tray of instruments onto the floor. Then a burner, then a microscope, then a laptop. I stomped on the screen until the glass cracked. That wasn't nearly satisfying enough, so I turned to the storage cabinet and emptied the contents shelf by shelf. Flask after flask hit the floor until the linoleum was covered in a sea of sparkling glass.

I swiped my hand across the shelf and came up empty. There was nothing left in the cabinet. I hesitated, panting, long enough for that hated silence to return.

I had to find something else to fill the void. I spun around and scanned the room. There were plenty of things to destroy—but once I finished ransacking the lab, what then? I would have to find another distraction, and I knew, deep down, that it would never be enough.

And maybe that was the real reason why I had created Red Rain.

He appeared again, right beside me. *Deeper.*

I sank to the floor, glass crunching under my knees. "I created Red Rain... because I couldn't stand the silence."

It was the perfect excuse—the exhausting schedule, the constant deadlines, the endless pursuit of a project that could never be completed. Red Rain left no time for grief—or other people.

Deeper.

I stared at my bloody hands, as if I could find the truth in the wounds. "I created Red Rain... because I wanted to be alone."

There was always a reason to distrust people when you were a criminal. I'd spent years training my sister to fear me and my employees to hate me. Because if everyone hated me, they would never want to know me.

It had worked beautifully. Until Philadelphia.

She was the first person who wasn't scared. She'd brazenly ignored my warning signs, throwing back the curtains and asking the questions I refused to ask. *"Why did you abandon Red Rain? Why don't you go to church anymore? Why don't you visit your parents?"*

Why don't you visit your parents? He echoed.

I shuddered. I could feel it seeping into the room, like floodwaters soaking through the floorboards—the terrifying answer I had avoided for ten long years and could avoid no longer.

The same reason I created Red Rain.

And why is that?

I gripped the edge of the shelf behind me, wondering, briefly, if this is what it felt like to drown.

Tell Me.

It wasn't a suggestion, and I couldn't disobey. *Because I didn't want to feel.*

Feel what?

Everything.

The betrayal, the heartache, the shame at the realization that I'd actually *loved* Asia. The guilt, the self-loathing, the knowledge that I'd brought it all on myself. The disappointment, the anger, the grief over a dozen things that should be but never would—including myself.

And through it all the disgusting, maddening realization that the one time—*the one time!*—I'd let down my guard and allowed an innocent teenage girl into my life, my mistakes had caught up to me and brought us both down to the grave.

I'd let Philadelphia change my mind. And now I was going to lose her.

Just like my father.

Nic. He was closer than a breath. *Why did you create Red Rain?*

I finally answered the question. "I created Red Rain… so I wouldn't have to admit that I missed my dad."

Everything shattered. All the lies, anger, and rebellion I'd used to build my fortress crumbled, stripped of their power. I sagged against the cabinet as all the emotions, guilt, and fear—so much fear—rushed in with nothing to stop them. There was nowhere to run, nowhere to hide.

So, I didn't. I just sat there and let it all crash down on me like brick after brick until everything was broken. By the time the silence returned, there was nothing left to resist it.

And then, for the first time in ten years, I put my face in my hands and allowed myself to grieve.

9: PHILADELPHIA

It took them over thirty-six hours to pronounce Lanzhou dead.

Jael drove me to her apartment across town. It was a modest high-rise on the edge of an industrial park, where the maze of warehouses afforded some privacy from prying neighbors. She claimed she owned the building and everyone in it, so I'd be safe—for now.

She set me up in the guest bedroom of her top-floor penthouse, then left me alone with my grief while she did damage control. Not that there was much she could do; it was the same tragic song and dance. Bowen, Mr. Tang, and the rest of the family were arrested and vanished off the grid while the media vilified the "traitorous oligarchs" who were funding the rebellion at the expense of their impoverished workers. The overblown story couldn't be further from the truth, but it didn't matter. Asia would use any excuse to mock me.

I spent the day pacing the empty apartment and repeatedly refreshing Lanzhou's file. I knew he was gone; there was no way anyone survived those explosions. But I had to see it for myself. So, I held back my grief and kept the tears from falling until they finally excavated enough of the rubble to retrieve his body and make it official.

It was a mercy the Tangs had shut down the line and put most of the staff on leave; the building had been nearly empty, and only half a dozen people lost their lives in the collapse, a relatively small body count for me. The damage also took out most of the evidence that I had ever been on the property, and Jael was able to secure their cloud servers remotely. Asia wouldn't be able to trace the Tangs to any more of our allies. It was, all told, a minor inconvenience for the revolution—and Asia knew it.

"You got lucky this time," she texted the next day. *"Really, it's my own fault. I should have investigated the Tangs sooner. After all, they've been friends with the Vons for years."*

That's when I cried. I thought of a sane Mr. Von, a younger Nic not yet scarred by Asia's cruelty, and a faithful Lanzhou who should have inherited his father's empire—all the people who couldn't be resurrected. I huddled on the couch in Jael's living room and wept into my knees, mourning the man who had been brave enough to help me and kind enough to pastor me.

That's how Jael found me when she came home after dark. The cushion sank as she sat down beside me.

I sniffed and unfolded myself. "It's official."

"I saw."

Wiping my eyes with the back of my hand, I picked up my tablet and stared at the headshot on Lanzhou's file. "What now?" I whispered, afraid of the answer.

She straightened, drawing herself together with a long breath. "We keep fighting. You'll stay here—"

"Until Asia finds me, and we play this scene all over again."

I hadn't meant to cut her off. The exclamation ripped out of me like a knife yanked from a wound, angry and bleeding.

She didn't deny it. "I know the risks."

So did I, and for the first time in several weeks, I was questioning if it was worth the cost.

"Freedom always comes with a price," she declared, reading the tension. "The world falls when people are no longer willing to pay."

I knew that. I knew this was the right thing to do. But that was neither the question nor the answer.

She touched my knee. "What are you thinking?"

I struggled to sift the fear out of the chaos. "What if... what if I'm alone?"

"What do you mean?" she prodded, but slowly, as if she knew where this conversation would end.

I stared out the balcony windows at the black night and finally conjured the words. "What if, when this is all over, I'm the only one left?"

It was a real possibility—so real that, in some morbid way, I'd subconsciously started preparing myself. Nic was gone. Stanyard was gone. My dad would never be the same, memory device or not. Ephesus was so far away that he might as well be gone—and now Lanzhou was dead. Jael was all I had left.

What if I lose her, too?

I knew leading the revolution was the right thing to do. It wasn't a choice, not really. I had to do it, and I would. But with every ally that fell, I lost a piece of the reason I started this war in the first place. I burned down that factory on Rott because I was determined to fight for the people I loved. I would jump off speeding trains, release deadly viruses, and stare down loaded guns, all for a chance to save my family.

What if, when this was all over, my family was the one thing I *didn't* save?

"You might be."

I looked up. Jael sat rigidly, as if posed for a stoic portrait, staring at some unknown point on the blank wall. "You might be alone."

She sighed, then reached up and unclipped her giant earrings. "Have you ever heard of the United Republic of Nasarawa?"

"Um… no," I said, and wondered if I should feel stupid.

She smirked. "I'm not surprised. They did their best to censor us. It's a fancy name for what was left of Nigeria at the end of the 50s. We were independent from the United for almost three years."

I gave that statement the wide-eyed respect it deserved. "No wonder they censored that." The history textbooks they'd used in school had invariably claimed that the entire free world joined the United unanimously and peacefully. Any dissidence came from evil villains who were swiftly arraigned by the government's global justice.

She set her earrings on the coffee table, then started yanking the bangles off her wrists. "They didn't want to engage in nuclear warfare because we controlled the oil fields, and that was a resource too precious to lose. So, they put us under siege and played the long game: Poison."

I swallowed, my throat closing at the word.

Her voice was stiff like a scabbed wound as she relayed the story. "It was a slow genocide. You think you've seen evil; I can't even bring myself to repeat some of the atrocities they committed to try and force us to surrender. They were contaminating water sources, releasing biological weapons, and using chemical warfare that's been outlawed since the first World War."

I shuddered. It didn't take much imagination to picture the pure wickedness.

"I think most of the Western world would have ceded from the United had they found out." Jael twirled a bangle in her hand before stacking it with the others. "The union was still relatively young and fragile. They couldn't afford to tarnish their reputation of perfection. So, their best defense was to silence us."

"What do you mean?"

She slid her phone out of her pocket and stared at the screen contemplatively. "We went for a whole year without electricity and even longer without internet. They released drones that created a dampening field over the entire country. Even our radios didn't work."

I tried to imagine waging a war without any communication; there wouldn't be a "Blue Fire" if it weren't for Jael's control over the algorithm. "How did you fight back?"

"By raising our voice every way we knew how. I forged credentials and snuck across enemy lines to break into an abandoned cell phone tower. I wanted to hack through the dampening field so we could get a signal out."

I studied her as her story pieced together, almost as if she suddenly became a whole person before my eyes. "That's how you got started."

She nodded and smiled at the memory, but the joy quickly faded from her face. "My hope was that if I could release even one video on social media, the United would have to pull back to save face. It might have been enough to turn the war."

She hesitated, and I sensed the guilt in the silence. "It didn't work, did it?"

She didn't answer. Instead, she removed her necklaces one by one, arranging them on the coffee table in a row. She seemed to shrink, like she was shedding a layer of her armor with each piece of jewelry.

"I couldn't get a signal out," she confessed finally, "but I managed to hack into the internal communications for the United army and intercepted their battle plans. They were going to split the front line: Half of their forces would attack our capital, while the other half would bomb the villages on the border. The hope was that our limited defenses would be divided, and we'd lose both fronts."

I gripped the edge of the couch. "What did you do?"

"I had no way to contact anyone. I knew I could make it to our primary military base in time, but they'd have to pick one front or the other. Either we protected the capital, or we saved the villages."

"What did you decide?" I braced myself, knowing, instinctively, that there was no right answer to that question.

"There was no choice." The declaration was bland, final. "All our remaining resources and important personnel were in the capital. If the capital fell, we fell. So, I didn't tell anyone that I knew about the plan to attack the villages." She avoided my eyes. "I didn't want anyone else to have to make that decision."

The silence stretched between us as the weight of her decision took the air out of the room. I felt sick—even as I wondered if I would have made the same choice.

"I'm sorry," I whispered, all the useless condolences dying on my lips.

"They called me a war hero," she said without pride. "We sent all our resources to the capital and caught the United off guard. We held our independence for another six months."

I dreaded the period at the end of this story, but I had to know. "What happened to the villages?"

"Not one survivor. The United razed every single town." She closed her eyes. "Including mine."

The room blurred as everything I thought I knew about Jael came crashing down. All her friends and family were gone—and she let them die.

Oh God, have mercy.

"I won't lie to you, Philadelphia." Tears clogged Jael's voice, tangling with her thick accent and making the words almost unintelligible. "I wish I could say that I'll protect your family, but no one can promise that. When this is all over, you may be alone."

I started to cry, but for who or what, I didn't know.

"But I know you, of all people, have the strength to face that reality."

I sucked in my breath. "What?"

She finally turned to look at me. "When you destroyed that factory on Rott, did you expect to make it out alive?"

I struggled to recall the person I'd been in that moment. I couldn't remember making a conscious decision to die; I couldn't remember thinking about myself at all.

"All you cared about was destroying Red Rain," she finished the thought for me.

I nodded. Anything to keep that vile weapon out of the hands of the government.

"You wouldn't have survived. Even if they didn't execute you, you wouldn't have made it off the island. And the government certainly wouldn't have spared your family. If anything, your crimes would have put them in more danger."

I wanted to deny it, but I couldn't. I knew when I decided to stand up against the United that I was sacrificing myself—and my family.

"You didn't do it for them," Jael insisted. "If your only priority had been to keep your father safe, you would have stayed quiet and let Thames adopt you."

It was true. I'd had so many chances to sit down, shut up, and save myself, just like my father had. But I didn't. I couldn't.

"There was no choice," I repeated her words.

"There wasn't. And that's why I chose you."

I looked up and met her gaze, even though I was terrified of what I would find.

She didn't smile, but her voice betrayed all the admiration her actions did not. "When I saw that video, I knew I'd found someone who would make the right decision even when it cost them everything. Someone who would save the world even if they couldn't save themselves."

Someone like you.

I twisted my fingers in my lap. Was that who I was now? Was that the person God wanted me to be?

She grasped my hands with both of hers. "I'm not asking you to hide your grief, Philadelphia. Your emotions are what makes you human. If you were just a mindless killing machine who only wanted revenge on your enemies, you would be no better than the United."

I held my breath as her words slowly warped and reformed my reality into something clearer, brighter.

"I don't want you to stop crying. I don't want you to stop asking questions. Even when it comes time to put your feelings aside and follow orders, still ask questions. That sensitivity is what makes you the hero and not the villain. Heroes are leaders who give second chances and save life when they can."

Abruptly, I remembered when Stanyard had said the exact same thing.

"You don't kill people, Phil. You save them," he'd declared, gripping my shoulders. "You give them second chances when they don't deserve them—like me."

"This war will change you, Philadelphia. There's no way to prevent that." Jael's voice hitched again. "You will be hurt, and you will be scarred. But no matter how many wounds you carry, don't ever, *ever* let this war steal that compassion from you."

Stanyard's next words echoed back to me loudly, almost as if he were sitting in the chair across from us.

"That—that compassion, that innocence—is why I believe in you. That's why I came back for you. That's why I..."

My chest ached as I relived that terrifying, exhilarating moment. "*Why, Stanyard? Why what?*"

"*That's why I love you.*"

Jael rubbed my knuckles. "I can't promise I'll always be there for you. But as long as I am, I'll do everything I can to help you put the pieces of your life back together and manage your emotions. Remember that."

I took the implied invitation. "I don't feel like I've been managing my emotions very well lately," I admitted, thinking of the frequent panic attacks, violent tears, and constant doubt that followed me around like a shadow.

She paused. "You still aren't sleeping, are you?"

I winced. Was it that obvious? I hadn't slept consistently in weeks, not since Nic and I were separated. Losing Stanyard, my uncle, and then the Tangs had only made it worse. I got maybe a few hours a night in fits and spurts—and that was on a good day.

I was exhausted and almost always had a headache, but I thought I'd done a good job of covering it up. I used pain medication and caffeine to make it through the day, and I watched my words carefully, making sure not to snap at anyone even when I felt like committing murder. I didn't want Jael to—

She beat me to it. "You really need to take medication."

I shrugged out of her grasp; taking more drugs was the last thing I should be doing. "I feel all right," I said, hoping she'd buy that more than the textbook *"I'm fine."* "It's just been a lot lately."

"Using every ounce of willpower to hold it together is not doing 'all right,'" she chastised.

I flinched and glanced at her out of the corner of my eye. She arched an eyebrow. "Yes, I can tell, and no, I'm not mad."

I bit my lip.

"I want you to start taking these."

She stretched across the couch to grab her purse. She unzipped it and withdrew a pill bottle, setting the container in my lap. I took it instinctively, even though I wanted to drop it like a live snake. "But I—"

"Philadelphia. I know you're scared because of what happened last time, but I promise you, that incident was as much my fault as it was yours. I take full responsibility."

I wished it was that easy to wipe away the guilt. Last time I'd taken sleep medication, I'd only slept for an hour. Nic had tried to convince me to go back to bed, but I'd refused. Instead, I'd acted with impaired judgment and had a complete mental break, stealing a motorbike and *shooting* Jael in the chest.

It was a mercy the weapon had been set on stun.

Jael touched my arm. "Please stop punishing yourself. You *need* to sleep. You can't fight a war if you're fatigued."

I can't fight a war if I lose control.

"Take two a night about a half-hour before you go to bed. I promise, if you sleep at least six hours, it will not impair your judgment."

But what if I don't sleep? What if something happens in the middle of the night? What if—

"It will also help with your anxiety."

I jerked. "But I don't have—"

"Philadelphia. Stop lying to yourself. You've been kidnapped, separated from your family, had several near-death experiences, and witnessed multiple violent murders. You are not fine." She squeezed my arm. "Frankly, it's a miracle you don't need something stronger."

That's because it is a miracle.

Jael stood up, and I followed. "Just try it for tonight. It's a low dose. If you don't feel any better after a few days, we can do something different. All right?"

I just nodded, knowing that if I used words, the distrust would come out. She smiled. "Get some sleep."

I hurried to my bedroom and locked the door behind me. Leaning against it, I waited until the lights in the living room shut off and Jael's footsteps faded before letting out a sigh.

I stared at the pill bottle in my hand and rolled her words over in my mind. She was right—it *was* a miracle I didn't need something stronger. I should be scarred beyond repair, but I wasn't, because I had God. The Holy Spirit had put me back together after each and every crisis. He'd healed me before; He would heal me again. I didn't need medication for this.

I *shouldn't* need medication for this.

I gripped the bottle and looked at the ceiling. "I am *healed*," I declared to the empty room.

Then I slammed the bottle down on the nightstand and turned out the light.

10: PHILADELPHIA

It took three hours for me to admit Jael was right.

I wasn't sleeping. And I was very, very anxious.

My chest was so tight that my ribs hurt. My nerves were so agitated that the very air felt thick, like it was oppressively humid inside my room. And every time I closed my eyes, my thoughts whirred louder and louder, growing bigger and scarier until I thought they were going to take form out of the shadows and devour me.

I prayed so hard. I repeated declarations. I recited Scripture out loud. I begged God over and over and over to heal me. Nothing worked. Not even listening to worship music helped, and every failure just made me feel weaker and more alone.

What was wrong with me? I'd seen a *dead man* raised to life because I prayed. Why couldn't I win the battle for a mere six hours of sleep?

What am I doing wrong, God?

If there was an answer, I couldn't hear it around the throbbing in my ears. Everything twitched and buzzed and vibrated, like there were a dozen ghosts vying for space on the bed. I could hear a thousand whispering voices, and none of them were the Holy Spirit. It was loud and dark and hot and *I couldn't take it anymore.*

I sat up and snatched the pill bottle off the nightstand, shaking two capsules into my palm. Jael was right; even being in a drug-induced stupor would be better than this.

I lifted my hand to my mouth, then hesitated. I glanced at the clock; it was after 1am. If I took the pills now, I wouldn't get a full six hours of sleep before my alarm went off. And we all knew what happened when I took medication and didn't sleep.

I sighed and shoved the pills in the pocket of my shorts. It was too late. I'd just have to fake it for another day.

Flopping back on the pillow, I grabbed my tablet and scrolled hopelessly through the empty home screen, searching for any distraction. But of course, there was nothing that hadn't been there five minutes ago.

I swallowed a lump of selfish grief. Stanyard would normally be awake at this time. Up until a week ago, he had always been there for me in the middle of the night, ready to pray or distract me or whatever was needed. He would faithfully send a message every hour, even when I wasn't responding. Sometimes that's all it took—seeing the screen brighten with a notification in the dark room and knowing, without looking, that it was him. The omnipresent feeling of someone praying for me was enough to muffle my anxiety so exhaustion could do its work.

Not anymore. His chat had gone completely silent; even Asia hadn't mentioned him recently. His file, like Nic's, was frozen. All it said was that he was "in custody," the location of his prison carefully redacted.

Where was he now? Did Asia keep him in America, or had she deported him somewhere else? The thought made me feel waterlogged with hopelessness, like driftwood washed up on shore. Tracking him down in America would be hard enough. If she sent him to another continent, we wouldn't find him until it was too late.

Jael had assured me that her people were on it, scouring the internet for any mention of him, but even her power had its limits. Her company had been searching for Nic for over a month without success. Both Nic and Stanyard were as good as dead to us.

I knew they weren't; Asia would have made a spectacle out of their executions. She would keep them alive like cards in her deck until I forced her to show her hand. But if this war didn't go the way she wanted it to—if the rebellion started to win—she might kill them. She might execute Nic and Stanyard and Lev and Bowen and everybody else before we had a chance to liberate them.

By then, it wouldn't matter who won the war.

"You may be alone."

I stifled a sob. Nic and Stanyard had sacrificed everything to help me. Nic wouldn't even have been on Earth if he hadn't come back to save me from Jayde. And Stanyard had been there for me like a rock on the shore, wading through death and unforgiveness and my own insecurities just to be my friend. The thought of leaving their bodies littered in my wake like sheep sacrificed to an unholy cause made me sick.

"I'm so sorry," I whimpered into the empty room.

I knew what Nic would say. Nic would tell me to do what needed to be done and never look back. But what about Stanyard? What was he thinking right now? Did he regret joining the operation? Or was he still worried about me and spending his lonely nights interceding on my behalf?

I knew the answer, and I owed it to him to have the courage to do the same.

I sat up and started a new message to Stanyard. I knew he wouldn't see it, but if—no, *when* he came back online, I wanted him to be able to read through my texts and know that I cared about him just as much as he cared about me.

HEY. I KNOW YOU WON'T SEE THIS FOR AWHILE, BUT I WANT YOU TO KNOW THAT I'M PRAYING FOR YOU.

I hit send and stared at the blinking cursor.

I KNOW GOD IS GOING TO PROTECT YOU.

I put a period on the words, even though I wasn't sure I had enough faith for them.

HE IS YOUR SHIELD. HE IS GOING TO DEFEND YOU, AND HE IS GOING TO DELIVER YOU FROM ASIA. HE'S GOING TO—

As if her ears were burning, Asia chose that moment to send me a text.

HAVING TROUBLE SLEEPING?

I resisted the urge to use a word Nic had taught me and quickly backspaced my message. I'd forgotten Asia had Stanyard's login.

YOU SHOULD BE IN BED, SWEETHEART

So should you. She must have had her notifications on loud, waiting for me to be stupid enough to contact Stanyard or any of our friends.

I KNOW YOU'RE HURTING. I KNOW YOU DON'T WANT TO DO THIS. YOU'RE BEING USED.

By you, I thought about texting back, but didn't.

YOU WERE NEVER MEANT TO BE A SOLDIER. YOU WERE NEVER MEANT TO BE A LEADER. THIS IS NOT WHO YOU ARE.

You have no idea who I am. But I didn't believe it, not really.

LET'S END THIS

Leave me alone! I closed the chat and tossed the tablet towards the end of the bed, but it did no good. She continued to message me, the screen flashing up notification after notification. The irritating *buzz, buzz* of the vibration against the comforter aggravated my headache and set my frayed nerves spinning again.

I growled and threw off the blankets. I couldn't stay in this claustrophobic room a moment longer. It's not like I was in any danger of sleeping anyway.

Yanking on my shoes and a light jacket, I cracked open the door to my bedroom. The penthouse was dark, and there was silence coming from Jael's suite. The moonlight from the bay windows lit the way as I navigated around the artsy furniture to the front door. I pressed my thumb to the security panel to disengage the alarm. It flashed green and beeped, far louder than was necessary.

I flinched and quickly stepped out into the hall, softly shutting the door behind me. I hurried to the elevator and descended to the ground floor. Surely there was a gym or an empty conference room I could take laps in.

I stepped off the elevator—and shrieked as I walked straight into the broadside of a very large man.

"Sorry, sorry." He flapped his hands. "I didn't mean to scare you. I just saw you coming down the elevator and wanted to make sure everything was all right."

I squinted at his shiny badge and deduced he must be a security guard. "It's fine, I just can't sleep." At least that much wasn't a lie. I glanced around the lobby and saw double glass doors leading to a patio of sorts. "I'm going to get some fresh air," I declared, pointing.

He nodded and stepped back. "Do you want one of us to go with you?"

His partner waved at me from behind the security booth, providing the "us" of that statement.

I grimaced. "Do I get in trouble if I say no?"

The first guard chuckled. "No, Jael said you could go out in the garden."

"Thanks." *Glad to know I'm not a total prisoner.*

"There's security all around the perimeter, and I'll be watching the cameras," the guard behind the counter assured me. He pressed a button to page me through. "Just yell if you need anything. We'll be here all night."

I gave him a grateful smile and pushed the door open.

It wasn't much of a garden. The towering apartment cut off the sky on three sides; the fourth side was blocked by a brick wall so high you couldn't see the street—which was, I suppose, the only reason I was allowed outside. The patio was more concrete than greenery, and what few plants there were had clearly been transplanted against their will. It was austere and fake, but at least there was fresh air. I took a deep breath of the still-warm night and started taking laps.

They were short laps—it took maybe two minutes to get all the way around—but any motion was better than none. I focused on putting one foot in front of the other and counting every step. Around and around I went until

I had completed ten laps or more. The repetitive movement drowned out the ringing in my ears, and I thought that maybe, just maybe, I might be tired enough to go back to bed.

That is, until someone disturbed my rhythm.

A noise broke the silence. It sounded like crunching gravel, or like someone had kicked a rock across the patio. I whipped around and scanned the garden, but there was no one there. The yellow lamps cast rippling shadows on the brick as the greenery shook in the hot wind.

"Hello?" I ventured, desperately hoping it was a security guard.

The answer came from behind me.

"Don't move."

I froze, but not because of the admonition. I knew that voice.

Oh God, no.

Very slowly, I turned and looked up. A figure crouched in the shadows on the garden wall. He jumped down onto the patio and stepped forward, bringing his face into the light.

Jayde.

11: PHILADELPHIA

He put both hands up. "Don't scream."

Screaming sounded like a great idea, but I couldn't get enough air as my heart and lungs panicked. *He's going to kill you he's going to—*

He cut off my crazed thoughts. "I'm not going to hurt you."

I wasn't about to fall for that. "How'd you get past security?"

He shrugged. "They'll come to in about twenty minutes."

Jesus, help! I had to alert the guards inside. A quick glance around revealed we were in a corner of the patio out of sight of both the security cameras and the door. I turned to run.

"Wait, please!" Jayde hissed. "I promise I come in peace."

"Prove it," I snapped.

Keeping one hand in the air, he reached towards his holster. Very slowly, he withdrew his electric pistol and held it out, showing me that it was off. Then he stooped, laid it on the ground, and kicked it towards me.

I snatched it and flicked it on. "What are you doing here?"

"I need to talk to you," he said, voice deliberately slow and quiet.

"You have thirty seconds." I braced my feet apart and mentally prepared myself to pull the trigger.

He put both hands back in the air. "It's about the guns that were delivered to the factory."

I hesitated, my grip slacking.

His eyes tracked my movements. "The Tangs weren't the only ones who got a shipment. Crates have been donated to groups all over the province."

"I know that," I snapped, my patience fading. The soldier who betrayed me had said General Jin received a donation and was redistributing the weapons across the city. "What's your point?"

"I know who paid for the guns," he declared, and then paused, as if wanting a reaction.

"Out with it!" *Why are you listening to him? Just shoot him already!*

He obliged. "The General Secretary."

The suggestion was so outlandish that I felt mocked. "What?"

"I can prove it. I've got text messages, money transfers, even a phone conversation." He patted the pocket of his military jacket. "More than enough evidence to prove that the General is funding Operation Blue Fire in Beijing."

"I don't believe that for a second," I huffed. "There is no reason on Earth or Mars that the General would want the rebellion to win. And even if he did suddenly have a come to Jesus moment, he wouldn't be so sloppy as to leave a paper trail that even *you* could find."

"I agree." Jayde lowered his hands. "That's why I think someone framed him and planted the evidence. Someone is forging his signature and using his credentials to pay for the guns."

"But who—" I didn't even finish the sentence. The information snapped together like colliding magnets: The sudden failure of the censors. The government's apparent indifference to my rising popularity. The generous influx of money and weapons being donated to rebel outposts.

And the one person who was guaranteed to have access to the General Secretary's credentials.

"Asia," I breathed, gagging on the realization.

I was right. Our victory *wasn't* God.

Jayde nodded. "That's my guess."

"But how? Why?" I struggled to maintain control of the gun as my thoughts whirled. "Why would she want the operation to succeed?"

"Same reason she wanted you to kill her father," Jayde explained. "She wants power. And the cleanest way for her to seize the throne while maintaining her popularity is for someone else to start the war. If she funds the rebels under her father's name, she can create unrest and scandalize him at the same time."

Operation Blue Fire would give her all that and more. All she had to do was add a little fuel to the fire *I* started.

She's still using you.

It all made wicked, horrifying sense—except for the fact that Jayde had figured it out before anyone else. "How'd you find out about this?"

"I'm military," he returned. "I can access the shipping manifestos for most of the bases in this province. I'm also part of the underground, which means I have plenty of contacts—despite Data's best attempts to excommunicate me."

A taste of bitterness seeped into his voice. I tensed.

He brushed past the transgression. "I also used to work for Thames," he continued. "I have access to a lot of Nolan's systems. And since Asia is using some of his—or should I say, *your* money to fund this venture, all I had to do was pull up your file and cross reference. You literally own the company that distributed the guns."

The thought of Asia using *my* inheritance for her schemes made me boil with rage. But even more disconcerting was the fact that Jayde had been tampering with my accounts.

I shivered. Jayde had worked for Thames and then for me, posing as my bodyguard for several weeks; he'd had intimate access to my devices and credentials as a Nolan. He knew my multiple identities better than I did— making me wonder why he hadn't tracked me down sooner.

"How'd you find me?" I demanded.

"I've been following you this whole time," he declared with absolutely no remorse.

I wished that revelation surprised me more than it did.

"It's not like I didn't know you were with the Tangs. All I had to do was track you from there to here." The condescension in Jayde's voice made me feel like I'd failed a math quiz. "And, if you're wondering how I knew you'd be in the garden, I was watching Stanyard's accounts. When you texted him a half hour ago, I figured you were up late and I might be able to catch you alone. I know you better than you think I do, Phil."

I tightened my grip on the gun. "Well, if I'm so predictable," I snarled, "why didn't you try to talk to me before?"

He snorted. "I'm not stupid. I knew Jael wouldn't let me get close."

"So why are you here now?" Even though he'd managed to get into the garden, he wouldn't have gotten much farther. If I didn't shoot him, I could easily scream and bring security racing to the patio.

"I'm not stupid," he repeated. "If Asia is funding the rebels, that means she knows where all the outposts are."

Lanzhou's morbid warning about Asia retaliating on operation day sent fear shuddering down my spine.

"We'll be worse off if the government slaughters hundreds of thousands of innocent people because we told them where to look."

"The Boston servers," I murmured.

Jayde nodded grimly. "I know what was on those servers—she could have traced the data to dozens, if not hundreds more allies. But she didn't. She just picked off a few big names to make it look like she'd done her due diligence."

"And sent weapons to the rest," I finished for him.

The dread in Jayde's eyes confirmed my fears. "She's orchestrating the whole thing. The entire operation will be a sham."

And a massacre, I thought but didn't have the stomach to say. I knew our sudden success wasn't God; it was Asia, controlling the chess game from a distance, just like she always had. I'd played into her hand yet again, and this time, I'd left the board wide open for her to checkmate.

Oh God, what do I do?

Jayde interrupted my prayer before I could find my courage. "Look, no matter what I think of you," he said, his tone filling in the blanks, "I want Operation Blue Fire to succeed. If we don't stop Asia, she's going to wipe out the entire resistance. We have to warn everyone—and you're the only one who can do that."

I focused on him and realized there was no malice in his expression—only respect.

I straightened. He was right. They wouldn't listen to him; there was no way he or anyone else could warn them in time. But they would listen to me.

I am Blue Fire. And this is my war.

There was, however, one piece of the puzzle still missing. "Why didn't you contact Jael?" I challenged. "I know she reached out to you. If you really 'come in peace,' you should have gone straight to her."

He arched an eyebrow. "Jael wouldn't have set that weapon to stun." He pointed.

I looked down at the weapon and realized he was right. Perhaps instinctively, I'd set it to stun.

I growled and considered changing the setting just to spite him. "You're a coward."

He spread his hands. "I'm your coward."

I *tched* and took my finger off the trigger, but I kept the gun aimed. "Fine. I'll take you to Jael. But I can't promise she won't shoot you on sight."

He indulged in a smile. "You'll make sure that won't happen."

How I wished he wasn't right.

12: PHILADELPHIA

As soon as we got into the lobby, the guards pounced on Jayde—literally. It took all my persuasive speaking skills to convince them not to strangle him. Unsurprisingly, I was the only one who believed him when he said he "came in peace." We finally settled on a compromise: Jayde got a pair of handcuffs while the guards paged Jael.

It took us a few minutes to ride the elevator to her penthouse on the top floor, and she must have used every second to prepare herself. She was staged dramatically right inside the door when we entered, looking as regal as ever, even though I knew we'd woken her up. She took one look at Jayde and then held her hand out to me.

"Gun, please, Philadelphia."

I obliged. She took it, strode up to Jayde—and then backhanded him across the face with the weapon. Jayde cursed and stumbled into the credenza, nearly sending a priceless African vase to the floor.

Jael leered over him. "Give me one good reason why I shouldn't set this to kill and shoot you in the heart," she hissed, barely raising her voice.

Jayde swiped his bleeding cheek on his shoulder and looked to me.

I sighed. "Please, hear him out. He has something to tell you."

"I'm sure he does. His first words better be 'Have mercy on me, for I am a fool.'" Jael put her free hand on her hip and took a step back, if only slightly.

Jayde, to his credit, took the hint. "Yes, I am a fool, but I'm not here to beg for my life. Operation Blue Fire is in jeopardy."

She aimed the gun at his chest. "Do tell."

I kept a wary eye on Jael's trigger finger as Jayde explained everything he'd told me. Jael asked a couple of clarifying questions, then retrieved the flash drive of evidence from his pocket.

"I'm going to cross reference everything. If I find you're lying..." She gestured vaguely.

He looked, for the first time that night, annoyed, if not utterly exhausted. "You think I'd risk turning myself in if this wasn't true? I'm not that dumb."

"No, I suppose not," she consented. She finally turned the gun off and handed it to one of the guards. "Get him out of here. And I shouldn't have to tell you this, but make absolutely sure he doesn't escape. If he tries anything, you know what to do."

"But don't hurt him," I ordered before I could second-guess myself.

The guards hesitated. Jael whirled on me. "Philadelphia, this doesn't concern you."

"Actually, it does." I took a deep breath and tried to find any semblance of autonomy. "He works for the Nolans, which means he answers to me."

Both of Jayde's bright-orange eyebrows shot straight up. The guards exchanged obvious glances. Jael glowered and looked like she was contemplating overruling me, then thought better of it. "Fine. Make sure he's taken care of. But he does *not* have to be comfortable."

I was too tired to argue on that point. The guards obeyed and prodded Jayde out into the hall. He went willingly, giving me one last glance over his shoulder.

I waited until the door had shut behind them before letting out my breath. I turned and looked up into Jael's frown.

"Why didn't you shoot him?" she demanded.

I shrugged. *I wish I knew.*

"He could have hurt you—honestly, the fact that he didn't is the only reason I'm taking his story seriously."

"I know."

She folded her arms. "I guess I'm just a little offended that you'll shoot *me* before you'll shoot him."

I managed a smile. She didn't return it, but she relaxed, her posture loosening. "If he's telling the truth…"

"I don't think he's lying. He's right—he wouldn't risk turning himself in if this wasn't real."

She didn't argue. "Then we have a crisis on our hands."

"Lanzhou was right," I whispered, finally allowing myself to admit it. "Asia is going to slaughter us all."

Grief gripped my throat as I thought of his fatherly smile. *We should have listened to him.*

Jael clucked her tongue. "No, that would be too kind. If she simply wanted to exterminate us, she would have done it before now. If she waits until operation day, everyone will question how she got the information—and why she didn't act sooner."

That made sense, which only made me feel more afraid. "Then what *is* she doing? Why give us weapons?"

Jael drummed her nails on the credenza and stared into space, as if reading invisible meeting notes. "My immediate guess is that she's planning to let us have a false victory. She'll let us gain control of a few population centers and make an advance on the council chambers. The people will question the government's lax response—and that's when she incriminates her father."

I sucked in a breath and felt the air jam inside my lungs. "And then she uses her knowledge of the underground to crush us and restore order."

"She'll be a hero."

"Then we have to warn them," I insisted. "We need to figure out where she sent guns and—"

"It's not that simple." Jael faced me again. "This isn't an organized army; it's a people's resistance. We have no way of tracking down all those guns, let alone the money she donated. And even if we could, the people who received those donations have already started sharing with their neighbors. If Asia does her job right, she'll be able to trace each outpost to a dozen more. There's no telling how many of our allies are potentially compromised."

"Then I'll blow her cover." I pointed at the TV. "Let me go on air and expose her. I'll reveal all of the evidence Jayde gave us, and then the government will take care of her for us."

It was the perfect solution—Asia's own father would murder her if he found out what she was doing—but Jael was already shaking her head, her earrings flopping about hopelessly. "She'll deny it. I'm sure all the evidence Jayde has is forgeable. Text messages can be faked and money can be laundered. If Asia is truly planning on incriminating her father, she'll have prepared a lot more than screenshots. She no doubt has a very intricate plan involving paid witnesses and a strategic reveal to the Council—all of which she'll abandon if she suspects you're onto her."

Jael's despondency weighed the room down, and I struggled not to lose my grip on my courage. "But at least I can warn everyone. They can relocate—"

"Philadelphia. We cannot reorganize the entire operation in less than two weeks," Jael sighed, sounding more exhausted than anything else. "And if you create a scare, we run the risk of losing the entire resistance. If you tell everyone that Asia knows exactly where they are, most of them will abandon ship. There won't be an operation."

I stared at her, begging her to tell me there was another way. "What are you saying?"

She stared back, expression vulnerable. "I don't know."

I gasped for breath as the defeated silence stretched between us. This was it—checkmate. Either I cancelled the operation and ended the resistance for good, or I gave Asia her victory with a failed war.

Either way the United won. The only difference was I might—*might*—save a few lives if I folded.

No. I felt determination shift in the depths of my soul, weak and fluttering like a candle caught in a draft. There wasn't a lot I was confident in right now, but there was one thing I would never deny: God was in control. Asia wasn't the only one playing chess.

Which meant I could not concede the game.

"There has to be another way," I murmured quietly, willing my thoughts to ignite. God had given me miraculous ideas before; He would do it again. I closed my eyes and reached out to the Holy Spirit. *I need Your wisdom!*

Jael was not convinced. "I'm sorry, Philadelphia. If I thought we had enough evidence to convince the government that she's orchestrating this, I'd let you go on air. But we don't..."

Her voice faded as Jayde's chilling words echoed back to me.

"I have access to a lot of Nolan's systems. And since Asia is using some of his—or should I say, your money to fund this venture, all I had to do was pull up your file and cross reference. You literally own the company that distributed the guns."

Asia wasn't the only one involved in this scheme. Thames had been her business partner.

And I was his daughter.

I looked up at Jael. "I know how we can get more evidence."

She stopped mid-sentence.

I took a deep breath. "I need to go back to the Nolan estate."

"What?" she exclaimed, the word barely forming.

"I need to go home," I repeated. "Jayde said Asia is using the Nolans' money to fund this venture. That means my family is involved. If I go home, I can find proof of what she's doing. I may even be able to talk to her and get her to confess—"

"Absolutely not." The bangles on Jael's wrist clacked like a gavel as she swung her arm. "Are you even hearing yourself? You can't just waltz in there and confront her. She'll shoot you on sight."

"But I know there's evidence on my family servers. Jayde said I owned the company that distributed the guns. If I can access my accounts, I can—"

She cut me off again. "Asia won't give you the chance. You'll be dead before you step over the threshold."

I knew that was a risk, but there had to be a way around that. "I know, but just listen to me, please. I know this will work. This has to be why God made me a Nolan. Nic said…"

I didn't finish. I could tell by the way her whole body heaved with a sigh that I was losing her. "Philadelphia. I am not having this conversation again. Enough with this foolishness."

But it's not foolishness! "No, you don't understand. I can—"

"We're done talking. Go back to bed. I'll let you know my decision in the morning." She pulled her phone out of her pocket and turned away.

I reached for her. "But I—"

The Holy Spirit breathed on me. *Stop.*

I pulled back. *No.* I was not taking us down this path again. I would not panic, and I would not argue. Jael and I were partners, which meant I had to treat her with respect—even if I didn't get the same in return.

I waited until my pulse slowed before speaking. "Jael?"

"What?" She continued to swipe on her screen.

"Remember the orders you gave me?"

She glanced up at me over her phone. "Yes, I told you to trust me. And I've decided—"

"You also told me to be honest."

She stopped typing.

I spoke slowly, tempering my tone of voice. "I'm going to be honest with you and tell you what I think. Please hear me out. After I'm done, if you still don't think it's a good idea…" I paused and rallied my courage before continuing, "…then I'll obey."

She turned her screen off and set her device on the credenza, giving me her full attention. "All right. I'm listening."

I took a minute to order my thoughts, determined to use as few superfluous words as possible. "I think we need to expose Asia. You said yourself—we have no idea how much of the underground has been compromised. We have no way of knowing where those weapons were sent or how many demonstration sites she's tracked down. If we continued as scheduled, she'll slaughter everyone—and use the chaos to make herself general secretary."

Jael didn't argue. She just gestured for me to continue.

"It's impossible to warn everyone or reschedule the demonstrations. The only way to prevent this from being a massacre would be to cancel the operation."

I searched her face for consent. She said nothing, only staring intently into my eyes.

I straightened and forced myself to return her gaze. "But if we can expose her, if we can produce enough evidence that she's funding the operation, we can remove her from power. In fact, the Council will do the work for us. They'll execute her and then go on a witch hunt looking for her allies, and it will throw the government into chaos."

I stiffened when I remembered that Jayde had once said those exact same words to me.

"If you take out the General, it will throw the government into chaos. They'll be scrambling to replace him—and that's when we strike. That's when we launch Operation Blue Fire."

A shiver of raw possibility passed down my spine. Perhaps Jayde hadn't been wrong about everything.

I focused on Jael again. "*That's* when we strike. They'll be cannibalizing themselves; they won't be able to retaliate. And if Asia and her allies are gone, there will be no one to pull the trigger. We won't have to warn anyone—the operation can continued as scheduled."

Jael's gaze drifted elsewhere as she ran the calculations. *Please, God, help her see what I see!*

"And how do you propose we prove it?" Jael asked, but gently. Her eyes returned to mine. "I warned you, everything Jayde has can likely be faked. Asia is a wizard at covering her tracks, and she has plenty of powerful friends. If you want to convince her own father that she's a traitor, you'll need ironclad evidence. Even if she is using your money, simply pulling up your bank statements won't be enough."

I closed my eyes and prepared to reveal what I truly believed. *Holy Spirit, give me the right words!*

"That's why I need to go back to the Nolan estate. If I resume my identity as Andromeda Nolan, I'll have full access to my accounts and Thames's network. I can go anywhere Asia goes, talk to her allies, even show up at a company board meeting—all without raising suspicion. I can catch her in the act. Plus," I made myself talk slowly and clearly even though my mind was racing, "you can modify the router at the Nolan estate. You can bug my devices and the entire house. If she drops even a hint, you'll have video evidence."

I stopped and waited for Jael's response. She continued to stare at me, but her eyes were no longer defensive. She looked simply tired. Sad.

And that's when I knew I was right.

"Philadelphia," she sighed, using the name to brace us both. "I understand what you're saying. I want you to know that I respect your idea, I really do. But it's not that simple. If you go home, Asia will kill you. And that's not a sacrifice I'm willing to make."

I opened my mouth, but she put her hand up. "No, it's my turn to be honest with you. I know this is hard for you to accept, but you are far more valuable than you realize. You are the face of this revolution now."

I wrapped my arms around my chest and wished it wasn't true.

I am Blue Fire.

"If you go back to the Nolan estate, Asia will quietly kill you—or worse, expose your double identities."

That was a possibility I hadn't considered, but I doubted it. "I don't think she will," I calmly argued. "There is no direct evidence linking Andromeda Nolan to Philadelphia Smyrna. Philadelphia died on Rott—I haven't made a single mark on my file since then. The only way for Asia to expose Andromeda's real identity is for her to admit her involvement with Thames. She'd have to reveal that she's known about me this whole time—and she can't afford to do that anymore than I can."

Jael gestured her consent. "Perhaps, but it's far more likely she'd simply kill you and bury the evidence. Then your death will be wasted. I will not sacrifice my most important ally on a fool's errand. I'm sorry, Philadelphia, but if you go home, even I won't be able to protect you."

I knew she was right. If I went back to the Nolan estate, I would be facing Asia alone and unarmed. But there had to be another way. There had to be something I could use as insurance, a trap I could set so that she couldn't quietly sweep me under the rug.

Suddenly, it came to me: the rook God had moved to the side of the board for this very moment.

"Unless…" I looked back up at Jael. "I invite her father over for dinner."

She frowned. "What do you mean?"

"At the state gala. I told the General I would love to host him for dinner—and he accepted."

I remembered the moment with all five senses. The Summer Palace, soaked in incense and bathed in the light of a hundred lanterns. The rustle of dresses and suits as Beijing's elite vied for favor. The clack of my heels on the wooden platform as I approached the General Secretary.

I had stared at him, wondering for one final moment if I should kill him. And then I'd lifted my skirts and bowed. My dress had glittered in the flash of a dozen cameras as the press captured the moment forever.

"We—I—would love to have you visit again. It would be my deepest honor to serve you."

The crowd had been appalled. Asia had been mildly impressed. The General had weighed my life in the scales—and found me worthy.

"I would be delighted to receive your invitation."

For the first time in weeks, I felt powerful—the power that came with influence and wealth. This, *this* was why I was a Nolan. This was why I had been allowed to go to the party, why the General had taken a liking to me, why the Holy Spirit had given me such audacious words. This was the plan all along.

For such a time as this.

"If I send the General an invitation, he'll accept—I know he will." I explained with both hands, drawing a battle plan in the air for Jael and I to see. "And if he does, Asia won't be able to just dispose of me. If I mysteriously vanish or drop dead right after inviting the General over for dinner, he'll ask questions. Asia will have to play along, at least for a few days—long enough for us to get the evidence we need."

Jael didn't respond. She stared out the balcony doors at the black night, silent.

I opened my mouth to make another argument, then stopped.

I'd said enough. I'd promised to tell the truth and then wait for her orders, and I meant it. The decision was hers now—and I could trust her to make the right one.

Give her wisdom, Father.

Jael took a breath, long and heavy, through her nose. "I have some calls to make. I need to verify all of Jayde's evidence and make sure everything he says is true." She turned back to me. "It will take some time."

I nodded. "Yes, ma'am."

"We'll talk in the morning," she said, and it was a promise. She tapped her phone and checked the clock. "Go back to bed. I know it's late, but I want you to get at least five more hours of sleep..."

She paused, and I knew what was coming.

She frowned at me. "Why were you even up wandering around in the garden? The medication should have kicked in hours ago."

I looked down, but I didn't deny it. My face would have told the truth anyways.

There was a beat. "Where are they?"

I pulled the two pills from my pocket and held them out.

She walked around the kitchen island and fetched a glass from the cupboard. "Why didn't you take them? We just talked about this."

Her voice was calm, but the patience was brittle. "I know," I mumbled, and didn't defend myself.

"Is it because of what happened a few weeks ago? I told you, nobody holds that against you, not even me." She filled the glass with water from the dispenser on the fridge.

"I mean, yes, but..."

"And I promise, it will not impair your judgment if you follow directions. If you have any negative side effects, we'll stop, no questions asked. Is that what you're worried about?"

"Yes, maybe, but…" I repeated, trailing off again. It was all of those things and none of those things.

She walked back over to me. "Then what is it?"

I stared at the floor, trying to mash the truth into words.

She set the glass on the credenza. "I promise not to be upset. But *you* promised to be honest with me."

I looked up into her face. "I don't know how to explain this, but… I just… I don't understand why prayer's not working."

She arched an eyebrow, and I almost lost my nerve. The rest of the truth gushed out in a puddle. "I mean, I saw Nic raised from the *dead*. I've seen so many miracles—I shouldn't have made it out of Rott alive, or Wing 74, or even that stupid state gala. I shouldn't even be standing here, and now I don't—"

"You don't know what you're doing wrong," she cut me off softly.

I flushed and nodded. At least she understood.

She studied me. "Did you ever consider that the fact you've survived so much is the reason you need medication?"

I frowned and waited for her to explain.

"Philadelphia, you have been through more trauma than any teenage girl should have to bear. All those experiences, miraculous or not, taught your brain that the world is not a safe place. You've been in survival mode for so long that your body doesn't know how to turn it off—that's why you're anxious."

The pinch in my chest told me she was right. Every time I thought I was safe, the people or places I relied on were taken away. What if it happened again? What if I lost Jael next?

She interrupted my thoughts before they could gain any more momentum. "All this medication does is help your body remember what 'normal' is. It's like giving you a blanket so you can get warm."

I looked down at the pills in my palm.

She held the water out to me. "Thank you for being honest and telling me how you feel. But now I need you to trust me when I say this will help you."

I took the glass. "But if I take these now, I'll sleep 'til noon."

"I'll wait. I promise I won't make any decisions without you, and I promise not to murder Jayde in a rage."

She smirked, and I found myself smiling—just a little.

She laid her hand on my arm. "Do you trust me, Philadelphia?"

The Holy Spirit echoed her question.

Do you trust her?

I did, I truly did. I firmly believed God had put Jael in my life.

Then do you trust Me?

I took a deep breath, then swallowed both pills and washed them down. They settled in the pit of my stomach like coal.

Jael squeezed my shoulder. "Get some sleep."

13: NIC

I'm not sure how long I knelt there. Long enough that the chemicals I'd spilled permanently scarred the linoleum, filling the room with the ripe scent of burnt plastic. I stared at the oozing cuts on my palms and wondered why I'd bothered. I felt crusty and drained and pathetic and generally worse than before.

Just then, the door opened. "Nic! Where you been? We got the new guy settled, and—*whoa!*"

I groaned. It was Ryan. And Vance, judging by the heavy set of footsteps that followed.

Great, I muttered, struggling to rise. *As if I didn't already hate myself enough.*

"What happened here?" Ryan squawked.

"Looks like he dropped some beakers," Vance brilliantly deduced.

"More like the whole cabinet," Ryan corrected. "Oh no, wait, he missed one on the top shelf."

"I'll clean it up." I waded through the broken glass to retrieve the spill kit from across the room.

Vance continued to lecture. "Why did you have that many beakers out at one time? You should only take out what you need for your experiment, in case of an accident like this."

Oh, it wasn't an accident. I grabbed the kit off the wall and turned around.

Ryan read my face, and his expression softened like melted butter.

Vance was oblivious. "Did you spill hydrogen peroxide?" He sniffed the air. "If that had combined with any of the iodides on that table..."

"Uh, Vance?" Ryan tapped his arm.

Vance didn't even feel it. "Even an errant splash of vinegar could have created peroxyacetic acid, and we all know how corrosive that is."

Ryan slapped him again. "Yo, *Vance.*"

"Not to mention, you're not even wearing any personal protective gear. Honestly, you're lucky no one got hurt—"

Ryan jumped three feet off the ground to swat Vance in the back of the head. "Vance! Read the room, for crying out loud!"

Vance finally stopped and looked me in the eye. "Oh."

I opened the kit and pulled on a pair of gloves. "Just stay back."

Ryan ignored both interpretations of that order. He tiptoed around the mess and came to stand beside me. "What's wrong, friend?"

"Nothing…" I started, then clarified before either of them could object. "Nothing I can talk about."

The Voice in my head reentered the chat. *That's not true.*

I glared over my shoulder at the corner where He was figuratively standing. "Fine," I said aloud, "nothing I *want* to talk about."

Ryan leaned over to see what I was staring at. "Oh, is God here? Are we interrupting?"

"Yes," I snapped, and then was immediately convicted. "No."

Ryan waved in God's general direction, then looked back up at me. "So, what's going on? I need details."

I wasn't about to explain why I'd ended up sniveling on the floor of the lab surrounded by a thousand dollars' worth of broken glass, but I knew neither them nor the Voice in my head would accept an excuse.

I was quiet long enough that Vance felt the need to fill the silence. "We talked to the warden."

I grimaced. "What did she say?"

"That you're in *big* trouble for kicking her out of her own office and then ignoring her," Ryan quipped. "Bro, are you trying to get yourself sent to solitary?"

Being in solitary sounded like heaven right now. I stared at the bottle of sodium bicarbonate in my hand and contemplated turning myself in.

"Nic." Ryan elbowed me. "Talk to us. We can't help you if you don't tell us what's going on."

I slammed the bottle down on the table, viscerally remembering the time I'd said those exact same words to Philadelphia.

It was before she'd left for China on her suicide mission. She was training to kill and exerting herself to the point of passing out. Stanyard wisely inferred that something was wrong and alerted me.

I'd immediately called Phil and demanded answers. Admittedly, my first reaction was to come at her in a rage; I was so appalled that she'd lied to me, a sin I didn't know she was capable of. But when I saw how terrified she was, I got over myself and begged her to tell me what was going on.

My head throbbed as I recalled the fear, the heartbreak, the maddening knowledge that *I could fix it.* I knew I could help her. I knew I could save her. I knew I could spare her a world of pain—if she would just let me in.

The Holy Spirit hovered by my shoulder, no doubt feeling the exact same way.

I sighed and straightened. "Okay."

Ryan pulled over a desk chair and sat in it backwards. Vance walked across the room and joined us.

I stared at the ceiling and ordered my thoughts, trying to find the shortest path to the truth. "You know Blue Fire—Philadelphia Smyrna?"

"Uh, *yeah*," Ryan huffed. "We're not that sheltered."

"Who is she to you?" Vance asked. If the words hadn't been beleaguered by a coarse German accent, I would have thought it was the Voice in my head speaking.

I looked both of them in the eye and claimed my identity. "She's my daughter."

Vance, somewhat to my disappointment, just nodded, as if that was the answer he'd been expecting all along.

Ryan, at least, had the decency to give that declaration the slack-jawed, wide-eyed shock it deserved. "Wait, *you're* Dr. Smyrna?"

"What? No! My last name is Von Nieuwenhuyse—you know that." I glared down at him.

"Yeah, well, I didn't know if that was a code name or whatever. Why does Blue Fire call you Dr. Smyrna then?"

"I'm *not* Smyrna," I insisted, trying and failing not to be offended by the association. "That's her father."

Ryan squinted at me. "But you just said you were her dad."

I put both hands up to pause the conversation. "I mean, he's her biological father. I'm... adopted."

"Aww, that's great, buddy. Me too." Ryan folded his arms on the back of the chair and grinned. "So, how did you meet Blue Fire?"

"What do you mean, 'how did I meet her'? I'm the governor."

"Governor of what?"

"The base."

"Like a base for the resistance, or...?"

"No, the base on Mars! Have you not seen any of her videos?"

"Only clips," he admitted with a shrug. "And she definitely never mentioned you or Mars."

"She talks about Mars all the time!" I gestured at the empty space next to me, as if she were standing there, corroborating my story. "That's how this whole Shakespearean tragedy started—I summoned her family to Mars."

"Actually," Vance piped up, "Mars and Project 74 are a relatively small part of her story. A prologue, really. Rott was the incident that made her famous, and she's spent considerably more screentime discussing it. You've been featured in only about 13% of her original videos, not accounting for commentaries and reposts."

I whirled on him. "I assure you, I have affected way more than 13% of her life. Also, how would you know?"

He blinked. "I have access to personnel files in accounting. I've known who you are for about three weeks and have been doing some research."

"First of all, that's creepy. Second of all, how long were you going to let us carry on this asinine conversation?" I flicked my hand at Ryan.

He pouted. "Hey, it's not my fault you don't know how to use proper nouns, pal."

Vance shrugged. "I figured it was your story to tell."

I threw up my hands. "I don't need to tell you if you've already researched my whole life!"

"Well, this is all news to me, so I'd like to hear it from the beginning," Ryan inserted, scooting his chair closer.

"Yes, I think that would be very therapeutic," Vance agreed, and claimed his own chair.

I groaned. *Do I really have to do this?* I asked the Voice in my head.

Do I really have to answer that? He replied.

I rubbed my temples. *Please, anybody but them.*

No, exactly them.

Ryan yawned and drummed his fingers on his arm. "Let us know when you're done arguing with the Lord."

With a grunt that was ignored by all three of them, I dragged over another chair and surrendered.

I told them everything—or at least the highlight reel. I told them how I'd met Asia and attempted to create an apocalyptic superweapon. How Smyrna had finished it and Philadelphia had destroyed it. How I'd gone from wanting to kill her to making her my legal dependent—and how we were both stranded on Earth while various groups of people tried to either save or end the world in her name.

Both Vance and Ryan listened with rapt attention. Vance only interrupted when he thought I was omitting important details. Ryan, on the other hand, provided sound effects as he overreacted to every plot twist.

"Well," he declared when I finally reached the end, "that does explain a lot."

"Thank you for sharing," Vance said, and almost smiled.

I would have appreciated the gesture had I not still felt like a shipwreck. Wasn't therapy supposed to make you feel better?

Ryan rocked his chair and glanced around the ruined lab. "We need to get you a better anger management strategy, though. Have you thought about learning karate?"

"I took three years of it in high school," I admitted. "It had the opposite effect."

"What about yoga?" Vance suggested. "I lead a class every Thursday."

"He's a great teacher, too." Ryan put his arms behind his back and contorted in a way that shouldn't have been humanly possible.

"I'll check my calendar. In the meantime..." I brought my PhDs back online and tried to decide which of my insurmountable problems I should agonize over.

"Oh yeah, we gotta fix this Blue Fire thing first." Ryan spun his chair around and sat in it the normal way. "I think Philadelphia needs him more than we do, right, Vance?"

He nodded. "Arguably, we don't need him at all."

"Love you, too," I muttered.

Ryan pounded a fist on the table. "Then we have no choice."

"Agreed," Vance grunted.

Ryan stood and pointed a finger in my face. "We gotta get you out of here."

"You're... busting me out?" I gaped at them and wondered if I'd undervalued our friendship.

"Oh no!" Ryan put his hands up and slid back. "I ain't risking my promotion for you. Have you seen what she does to escapees?"

Several times. I glanced at the regeneration scar on my forearm.

"No, no, we gotta do this legally. You need to talk to the warden," Ryan declared.

"What's she going to do?" I scoffed. I may have earned some privileges by saving her factory, but I was still a prisoner—a fact she'd made abundantly clear.

"I think you underestimate the power of money," Vance inserted.

I turned to face him. His bushy eyebrows narrated as he explained, "Your reengineering of the factory has more than doubled profits. Her personal salary has increased by a factor of ten—and that's without me falsely reallocating resources. If you calculate in the fraud, you're looking at annual net gains in the millions."

I nodded and tried to pretend he hadn't just admitted to a crime.

"That kind of profitability doesn't go unnoticed. I've overheard some of her recent phone conversations. She is soliciting larger contracts, which creates a favorable supply and demand ratio, which under normal market conditions leads to better clients and more consistent profits…" Vance checked off boxes with his fingers.

"He's saying she owes you one," Ryan translated.

I doubted Ivanova had a healthy concept of justice, but maybe Vance was right—maybe the money would speak for me.

"At least try," Ryan pleaded. "What could it hurt?"

"I guess I've already bared my soul twice today," I growled, standing up. "Why not do it again in front of the woman who controls my life? Sounds delightful."

"That's the spirit!" Ryan crowed. "Besides, we kinda told her we'd find you and send you up, so… you have to talk to her anyway."

I shot him a glare. He shrugged. "I just do what I'm told."

Vance rose and laid a weighty hand on my shoulder. "This is the right thing to do. Trust us."

I didn't particularly trust them, but I did trust the One who had very obviously sent them.

And for Philadelphia, anything was worth the risk.

"All right," I consented, "I'll talk to her."

"Great! Let's go." Ryan took a broad step forward—and his boot crunched on glass. "Well… maybe we should clean this up first."

14: PHILADELPHIA

I was right: It was almost noon by the time I woke up.

It took over ten minutes for me to come to full consciousness. The first thing I registered was the warm light pooling at the bottom of the blackout curtains, then the sound of Jael talking softly on the phone in the living room. I rolled over and tapped my tablet, looking at the clock. *11:37.*

I sighed. A whole day wasted.

I sat up and tried to decide if I felt any better. My back ached and my head felt weighed down like a soaked blanket—but maybe that was because this was the first time in over a month that I'd slept for eight hours straight.

At least the medication worked.

I threw the covers back and reached for my tablet—then stopped. My leather-bound Bible sat on the nightstand. Stanyard had bought it off the black market as a gift for me. It was one of the few personal belongings I'd brought to China, and in some sinful irony, I'd barely read it since.

I picked it up and rubbed the water damage on the corner of the pages. I used to *love* the Bible. I wouldn't go anywhere without my reader, and I spent every spare moment scrolling through the digital pages. Now I had a gorgeous, rare paper edition, and it just collected dust on my nightstand. What changed?

The Holy Spirit sent the answer, gentle but firm. *You changed.*

I gripped the book to my chest and let the conviction break down something inside of me. I'd spent all this time running and hiding and surviving that I'd fallen out of the habit. I'd been so concerned about fulfilling the one message God had given Nic that I'd forgotten the Holy Spirit had given me a thousand other messages in this Book.

I sat cross-legged on the bed and spread the book in my lap. I'd already slept until noon—the world could wait another fifteen minutes.

I'd read Phillipians and gotten halfway through Colossians when I heard Jael's heels clacking on the kitchen floor and decided I'd better get up. I showered and washed my hair as quickly as I could, then threw on a clean sundress Jael had loaned me.

She met me in the living room with a cup of fresh coffee. "You slept well."

"Yeah," I admitted, and gratefully accepted the hot mug.

She gestured at the sofa. "How do you feel?"

I settled down and took a sip before replying. "Good, I think." My muscles were still sluggish, but I didn't have a headache.

And the anxiety's gone, I realized abruptly. My chest wasn't tight, and my nerves weren't frayed. I could take a full breath without feeling like I was swallowing water. I felt almost—almost—normal.

I stared at the dark brown liquid in my cup and wondered how much of that was the medication.

Jael sat down on the loveseat across from me. "Excellent. I, on the other hand, did not get any sleep, because as much as it pains me to admit it, you're right."

I jolted out of my thoughts, sloshing my coffee. "I am?"

She nodded, the gesture slow and final. "You're going home."

I gripped my mug as that declaration filled me with elation, then terror.

"I cross-referenced all the information Jayde had on his flash drive, and it appears legitimate. I was able to replicate almost everything." She picked her phone up off the coffee table and tapped the screen. "I also checked the recent activity on Andromeda's file, and he's right—the Nolans have been investing in some suspicious business ventures lately."

I bristled. *That's my money.*

Jael set her device aside. "I have no doubts now that she's the generous 'benefactor' who donated those weapons, which means our best hope of saving the operation is for you to expose her. If there's not enough evidence on Thames's servers, then ideally you can get her to admit her own guilt on tape. Even if you can trick her into sending a text while connected to your router, that might be enough for us to turn the Council against her."

"I can do it," I declared. That was one thing I was confident of: Asia would talk to me whether she realized it or not.

Jael put her own mug down and leaned forward. "I will not lie to you. This is incredibly dangerous. Asia may be desperate enough to kill you and accept the consequences."

She might be—but I didn't believe it. It would be too risky once I involved her father, and Asia would avoid an unnecessary mess until the last possible moment.

"And even if you succeed... I should say, *especially* if you succeed, she may kill you before I can get you out of there."

That I believed. If Asia thought the ship was sinking, she'd take me down with her.

"But by then we will have saved the revolution," I returned.

"I knew you'd say that." Jael smiled, but it was a pained gesture, like she was closing the door after saying a long goodbye.

I fought a wave of trepidation and returned the smile. "I am Blue Fire."

And the captain always goes down with the ship.

"That you are." Jael glanced away, and I saw her shuffle her emotions aside like papers swept off a desk. When she turned back to me, the determination had returned to her eyes. "I know I said I wouldn't make any decisions without you, but I took the liberty of drafting your guest list."

"My what?" My brain tried and failed to shift gears.

"For the dinner party."

I put my mug down. "But I only need to invite the General."

She shook her head and grunted. "No. First of all, that's terrible etiquette. Just because he thinks you're cute doesn't mean someone of your status can invite him over *alone*. He'd never accept, and Asia would correctly assume the worst."

She had a point; it would definitely look suspicious if I attempted to arrange a private meeting with Asia's father. "So, what are you suggesting?"

"If this is going to look legitimate, you need to throw a *party*." She shoved her device across the table towards me.

I picked it up and scrolled down the screen. She'd compiled a list of two dozen names; the only ones I recognized were Asia and General Secretary Mong.

"You'll raise fewer eyebrows if you throw a large dinner party and invite a crowd. We're stretching the bounds of propriety since you're giving them less than a week's notice, but I have a friend whose birthday is this month who will 'just so happen' to be in town—that's excuse enough."

I struggled to hold onto the phone as my palm grew clammy. The thought of entertaining the General was unnerving enough. But playing hostess for two dozen elites who were almost as powerful as he?

Holy Spirit, I need help.

"Honestly, I'm not expecting the General to attend—it's too short notice," Jael admitted. "The invite is a courtesy gesture, really. He will probably send back a 'regret to decline,' which will be enough to make Asia think twice about hurting you."

I tried not to let her logic disappoint me. "Who do you think will come?" I handed the phone back to her.

"Hopefully, almost everyone else will make the effort once they hear Asia is attending. I'm inviting some people I suspect might be her allies. If we're lucky, some *baijiu* will stimulate gossip, and we can pick up incriminating evidence on tape." Jael took a suggestive sip of her own drink.

"There will also be several of your allies there, along with people I'm hoping to sway to your side. If this plan fails and we can't prove Asia's treachery, then we need more friends in high places."

I nodded even as I tried to sweep the despondent thoughts aside. *This is going to work.*

"Of course, I will also be honored to receive your invitation."

I looked up. Jael winked, and my shoulders relaxed. At least I wouldn't have to face this party alone.

"You'll have to pretend that we've never met, but I'm sure we'll hit it off right away. Let me make the introductions, and then just follow my lead. I'll make it clear who you should talk to who you should ignore."

I struggled to catch up as the plan snapped together—too quickly. "Okay, but what evidence should I be looking for on Thames's servers? Should I download company files, or...?"

Jael's diamond rings flashed as she flicked her fingers dismissively. "I'll handle that. Once I've modified your router, I'll have remote access to everything that belongs to Andromeda Nolan. I'll copy what I need and cover my tracks. I don't want Asia to get suspicious because you're suddenly showing an extreme interest in your financial investments."

I sighed. She was right—and that meant I was back to being a pretty face while everyone else did the hard work. "So, what *do* you need me to do?"

"Besides serve as hostess, provide the food and venue, and put together an entire dinner party in less than five days?" Jael smirked wryly. "I need you to do what you do best—make people love you."

I flushed.

"It's a compliment," she assured me. "I don't know if you've noticed, but you have an uncanny talent for making friends—the General himself being a prime example."

But that wasn't me, I silently protested. *That was the Holy Spirit.*

The response came like a breath of air. *So, use Me.*

I caught myself grinning.

"If all goes to plan, half of the people at the party will be your mortal enemies. Don't act like it," Jael ordered. "Treat them as equals. If anyone invites you to a function, accept. Every invitation is a potential alliance. I'll help you organize your calendar later."

I stiffened as Nic's words rattled around in my soul.

"I saw it all. You, in Beijing, as a Nolan, on even playing ground with Asia."

"I'll warn you—Asia *will* know you have ulterior motives. There's absolutely no way we can convince her you've gotten scared and quit the revolution, not after..." Jael stumbled over the silence, "...after all this time."

My heart autofilled what she'd been too polite to say.

Not after I left Nic and Stanyard for dead.

Jael clicked her tongue. "So, we're going to use that against her. I want you to waltz in there and pretend like nothing is wrong. There is no Blue Fire, you don't know anything about the revolution, and you and Asia are the best of friends. If anyone asks where you've been for the past month, tell them you were visiting family in America. I'll edit your file to match."

"Got it," I said, even as I began mentally rehearsing the words.

Jael leaned over to get in my line of vision. "If Asia questions you, play innocent. It will drive her mad—and that's when she'll make a mistake. If we're lucky, she'll confront you, and we'll get it on tape."

I nodded and took a grounding breath. I could do this—I could play chess with Asia.

I am Andromeda Nolan.

Jael reached across the table and found my hand. "Be careful. You're playing her game now, Andromeda."

I stared at the steam fading from our mugs as I remembered the ostentatious house, the costly dresses, the extravagant dinners. All the elites who fawned over me and told me how delighted they were to meet me. And the gracious Holy Spirit words that flowed off my lips as I smiled and bowed and blended into their ranks like I'd been born there.

And this is how I will fight my war.

"No," I said, looking up. "We're playing mine."

15: NIC

It took us most of the rest of the day to reset the lab. I'm not saying I stalled, but I am saying the lab hasn't been that clean in fifty years.

Vance and Ryan finally kicked me out. I ascended the elevator alone—humanly speaking.

I watched the floor number on the panel scroll up like a reverse time bomb. "You know how You said I could always ask for Your help?"

He didn't respond. He didn't need to.

I swallowed the last of my disobedience. "I need You."

He still didn't say anything, but His presence followed me out of the elevator and down the hall.

The door to Warden Ivanova's office was open. I approached the guards standing watch outside. "Is the warden—"

She answered for herself. "Von Nieuwenhuyse!" she bellowed. The shout echoed beautifully around the acoustics of the open factory until I was sure ten floors heard her.

I waited until my ears stopped ringing. "Well, it was nice knowing you," I said to the guards. "Please don't let Vance read the eulogy at my funeral."

One of them nodded. "I'll do my best."

I took a deep breath, smoothed my hair, and walked into the office.

She was posed behind her desk, fingers tented menacingly. "How do you take it?" she demanded.

I held back by the door. "Take what, my punishment? Anything but a freefall over the railing will be fine, thank you."

"No, your coffee." She reached for a carafe.

"Oh… uh, black."

She filled a mug and held it out to me.

I approached the desk and took it. "I feel confused and vaguely threatened."

She leaned back in her chair, crossing one leg over the other. "I figured after all those theatrics that you'd have a *great* story to tell me, so I brought refreshments. Sit."

I obeyed, flopping in a chair in front of the desk.

She picked up her own mug. "Start talking."

I downed half my coffee in one rallying gulp, then started from the beginning. I got through the story much more quickly the second time, mainly because the warden didn't interrupt me—or react at all.

"Is that the whole truth?" she said when I was done.

"Regrettably."

She picked at her teeth. "I'll admit, I thought you were being facetious when you said Asia sent you here because you dumped her."

"No, that's pretty much what happened." I finished the last of my coffee and set the mug on the desk. "So, can I go home now?"

She snorted. "Absolutely not."

What little hope I had came crashing down like a toy castle. I couldn't decide whether to be upset that I was still stuck here or annoyed that I even tried. "But—"

She put her hand up. "Trust me, if there was *any* way to get rid of you, I would have done it already."

"Charmed."

"But I don't know if you've looked at your file lately, but you've been flagged with the highest national security warning there is. The only people who could pardon you are Asia and the General Secretary himself."

I rolled my eyes; Asia always had to go the extra mile. "I'm not asking for a pardon. Just stage an accident and say I died or something cool like that, and I'll slip out the back door."

She was already shaking her head. "Asia's not stupid. Unless I have a body, she won't buy it. And then it will be my head on the chopping block."

The Voice in my head told me not to make a sarcastic comeback, so I didn't.

Warden Ivanova folded her arms on the desk and leaned forward. "Do you know why I'm so strict about discipline?"

"Because you had a bad childhood and your father never told you he loved you?"

"That too. But the main reason is because all the criminals here are security risks. If any of them escape and actually manage to make it down the mountain, I have to answer for it."

"And I take it they don't just slap your wrist and tell you to do better next time."

She nodded grimly. "I like you, but I'm not dying for you."

I groaned. A year ago, I would have gladly jumped ship and not cared who got hurt in my wake. But now I had too much integrity for such behavior, a fact that immensely irritated me.

She echoed the sigh. "I'm sorry, Nic. I mean it. But you're not getting out of here any sooner than I am."

There was a catch in her voice, and I wondered if I wasn't the only ex-friend Asia had earmarked for destruction.

The warden's flicker of humanity was gone as soon as it came. "Take the week off."

I shook my head. "Thanks, but I'd rather work."

"I wasn't making a request."

"Neither was I." I wanted—no, *needed* to work.

She arched an eyebrow. "I saw what you did to that lab."

I cringed. "You can take it out of my allowance?"

"You're lucky. We're rolling in profits, so the damage you caused is hardly a blip on my radar. Otherwise, I can assure you, this conversation would have gone *very* differently." She fingered her holster.

I swallowed. Maybe Vance was right; maybe I should take up yoga.

The warden stood up. "I'm not putting you in solitary because it's at capacity right now. But I don't want to see you anywhere near the lab or any of the equipment on the line—have I made myself clear?"

I could tell by her tone that arguing would be fruitless and potentially very painful. "Yes, ma'am."

She nodded and gestured at the door. I promptly saw myself out.

I hurried down the hall until I was out of sight of any guards. Then I walked up to the railing and braced myself on it.

"Now what?" I prompted the Voice in my head.

There was no response.

I knew what that meant. And it was the one answer I didn't want to hear. *Wait.*

The factory continued to churn around me, unheeding. The concentric levels stretched as far as the eye could see, sparkling with lights and moving equipment. Elevators passed up and down the hollow center as the sounds of enterprise echoed in the open space. The building thrummed with activity, but I couldn't hear any of it.

All I could hear was thunderous, cavernous silence.

16: PHILADELPHIA

I stayed at Jael's apartment for one more night. She wanted to wait until the invites were received and word about the party got around before I made my appearance. We sent the gilded envelopes by private courier that afternoon, and several of my allies enthusiastically RSVP'd by nightfall.

Asia did not respond. She did, however, block me and delete her account on the messaging app, which I took as a favorable sign. I'd caught her off-guard by making the first move, and, for a brief moment, I had the upper hand.

We spent the rest of the afternoon recording. I went live and did exactly what Jael ordered: I pretended nothing was wrong. With a fierce glare and too much eyeliner, I shouted war cries into the camera and challenged people to the fight. Every word broke my heart; if this mission failed, I would be sending people to their deaths. But Jael was right; we had to fool Asia into thinking Operation Blue Fire was still on schedule. She couldn't know that we were on to her.

I then batch-recorded several hours of generic speeches for Jael to reuse while I was gone. As far as the rest of the world was concerned, Philadelphia Smyrna would be hard at work in the trenches for the next week. Only Asia would know that I'd switched identities, and I hoped the knowledge would drive her insane.

By the time we were finished, I was so exhausted that I didn't think twice about taking my medication. I retired early and slept for ten hours straight. Jael had to drag me out of bed in the morning, a fact she was immensely pleased by.

Even I had to admit that I felt better, but no amount of pills could suppress the rising dread as I packed what few belongings I had. As soon as I left this building, I would become Andromeda Nolan again, with nothing but my wits and social influence to protect me.

Jael escorted me to the elevator. "I want you to keep this on you at all times." She held out Nic's old phone.

I took it and rubbed the crack on the screen, fighting painful memories. This was the phone Nic had on him while we were running across Beijing. He'd registered it to Andromeda since my file wasn't flagged. I hadn't turned it on in almost a month, but now that Andromeda was back from "vacation," there was no reason I couldn't use it.

"I installed some advanced recording and location tracking software," Jael explained as she called the ground level. "Do not go anywhere without it, not even in your own house. I want to know exactly where you are and hear everything you hear." She stared at the floor number as it counted down. "Of course, I won't be able to help you if Asia pulls a gun, but if she says anything incriminating, at least I'll have it on tape."

I nodded and slid the device in my pocket. Guns were the least of my worries right now.

The elevator *pinged* and opened. Jael led the way to the front door, eyes on her phone. "When you arrive, you'll find the internet is out. One of my men will be there to 'fix' your router this evening."

I knew what she meant. She'd done the same thing to the Tangs' router, modifying the settings so most of their internet traffic bypassed the algorithm. With a little tweaking, my house would be safe from the surveillance state—relatively speaking.

"My tech is going to tell you that there's an issue with your wiring and he's sending an electrician tomorrow to run a diagnostic," Jael continued. "I want to make sure the house isn't bugged and then install my own surveillance. Until he's finished, don't say anything you don't want Asia to hear."

I shuddered but nodded.

"Now, listen carefully." Jael pocketed her device and glared at me. "If this is going to work, it has to be authentic. As soon as you walk out that door, you're no longer Philadelphia Smyrna—you're Andromeda Nolan."

I checked to make sure the thunderbird tattoo on my right shoulder— the brand that permanently marked me as Blue Fire—was covered by my shirt sleeve. I wore my blue contacts and had spent an hour putting on my makeup this morning. Andromeda Nolan was truly back from vacation.

"That means you act like her, talk like her, even *breathe* like her. I don't want you to think about the operation or worry about finding evidence. You are the lady of the house, and your job is to plan a dinner party, nothing more."

I fixed my posture and stood up straight. "Yes, ma'am," I said, my voice demure and smooth, the same way I spoke to Asia.

If Jael was impressed, she didn't show it. "From here on out, this is a blackout mission. You don't text anybody, call anybody, record any videos, or go online without my permission. The only people you talk to are your household staff."

I nodded, but the motion sent a weight dropping to my stomach. I knew I was walking into the lion's den, but I'd never once considered that I'd be unable to call even Jael. What if something happened?

My objections must have made it onto my face. "I'll be monitoring everything remotely," she assured. "And I'll be able to contact you if I need you."

"What if *I* need to contact you?" I returned.

"Then you'll send a message through him." She looked past me and flicked her finger.

I spun around. Jayde stepped out from a side hallway where he had apparently been waiting the entire time. He was uncuffed, and he'd shaved and put on his dress uniform.

He was also, notably, armed.

I clenched my fists as the sight of him ignited my fight or flight response. "What's he doing here?"

"He's your bodyguard," Jael replied.

Jayde bowed and tapped his heart with his white-gloved hand. "I serve the Nolan family," he agreed, voice devoid of emotion.

I had to admit it was a reasonable ruse. Jayde had been employed by the Nolans under false pretenses for as long as I'd known him. He'd come to Beijing under the guise of being a member of my security team, and presumably, that's what the official paperwork still said.

But that didn't change the fact that the last thing Jayde wanted to do was protect me. He wouldn't let me die; he needed me, at least for now. But he was not my friend, and I definitely didn't trust him to follow me around with a loaded gun.

Not after what he did to me.

My hands and face went numb—but then I remembered that the conversation didn't have to be one-sided. I took a deep breath and faced Jael. "I'm sorry, but I'm not comfortable being around him." I measured my words carefully, pulling the facts from the raw, unprocessed emotions. "I don't trust him."

"Neither do I," she declared. She jerked her head at Jayde. "Show her."

I glanced back at him. He hesitated.

"Show her," Jael repeated, all the politeness stripped from her voice, "or I'll demonstrate how it works." She pulled a shiny object about the size of a car key from her pocket and twirled it in her fingers.

Jayde grunted. With visible reluctance, he reached up and unbuttoned his starched jacket. He pulled down the collar of his shirt, revealing a flashing device implanted in the base of his neck.

"I'll be monitoring his position, heartrate, everything." Jael patted her phone in her pocket. "I can hear everything he can. And if I hear anything I don't like…" She shrugged.

I sucked in my breath.

"All the wiring's removable," she crooned. "Once a dog's been trained, it can walk off leash."

Jayde flushed a ferocious shade of red.

"Until then, you have the clicker." Jael held the slender object out to me. It was a keyring with a single button on it.

I didn't have to ask what the button did. I forced myself to take the device and put it in my backpack.

"Look." Jael put her hand on her hip. "He's not my first choice either. But running errands between us is going to be extremely dangerous. At least if he gets caught, he won't tell Asia anything she doesn't already know."

She had a point. Asia already knew Jayde was involved in the underground, and he didn't have any information that she couldn't scalp from the Boston servers—except for one fatal detail.

"He can tell her you're involved, though," I whispered, and hoped I didn't just give Jayde any sadistic ideas.

"What part of 'I'm wearing a shock collar' did you miss?" Jayde snarled. "I'm not stupid."

"He's not," Jael consented. "And in any case, he can't prove anything. There is absolutely no digital record that you and I have ever talked. You don't even have my phone number, Philadelphia."

I instinctively reached for Nic's phone in my pocket and realized she was right.

"I'm aware of the risks. But I am the one person in this operation most able to protect myself. No one can wipe a digital trail better than me—not even Asia." Jael's eyes glinted as she smirked. "Everything she knows about covering her tracks, she learned from me."

I searched her face and wondered, for the first time, how far back Jael and Asia went.

Jael stepped forward, closing the gap between us. She laid her hand on my arm. "I promise I will be watching. I can't control Asia, but I will know what everyone else is thinking before they do. For once, the algorithm is your friend."

I nodded and reminded myself who was in charge. *You do not have to be in control anymore.*

"Let me do the investigating. I know what we're looking for, and I can do it without leaving a digital trail. I just need you to open the door and buy me time."

We don't have much time. Operation day was in less than two weeks. If I didn't pull this off, it would be all-out war—and Asia would win.

Jael's acrylic nails dug into my arm as she gripped my elbow. "I'll be at the party and will give you further instructions. Until then, your job is to win friends. Every person you meet is a potential ally. I want you to think of nothing else besides impressing these people."

I took a deep breath and inhaled a wave of courage. They would love me—because I had the Holy Spirit.

I am Andromeda Nolan.

"Philadelphia."

I looked up into Jael's eyes.

She smiled. "Remember your orders."

Trust. Be honest. And do not give place to guilt.

I returned the gesture. "Yes, ma'am."

17: PHILADELPHIA

Jael hired a car to drive us across town to the Nolan estate. Jayde respectfully took shotgun next to the driver and religiously avoided looking at me. I sat alone in the backseat and watched out the window as the chaos of the inner city melted into the manicured affluence of Beijing's most elite district. After about fifteen minutes of driving past gated courtyards, we turned a corner and entered the Nolans' neighborhood.

The street was lined with everything from all-glass structures to miniature palaces that looked like temples. But the Nolan estate was by far the most beautiful home on the block, managing to be both elegant and tasteful. It was modeled after a traditional villa, with a square of two-story halls shielding a private courtyard. The glittering white stone walls contrasted with the black tile roof and the imposing iron phoenix statues that guarded the front door.

I stared at the gorgeous structure as we slowed to a stop, trying, yet again, to grasp the fact that I *owned* it. I'd grown comfortable with the label "Andromeda Nolan." I'd come to expect the surprise on people's faces when they heard my last name. I'd even gotten over the shock of looking at my bank account and seeing a mathematically improbable number of zeros. But I still hadn't gotten used to the *house*.

Ominously, the front gate was open. I failed to swallow the fear in my throat as the driver parked at the curb. Maybe Asia had been telling the truth when she said I could come home anytime.

I'm about to find out.

Jayde opened my door as I thanked the driver. I stepped onto the sidewalk and strode towards the house, struggling not to trip over my heels or my insecurities. Jael had loaned me a business skirt set and an assortment of diamond jewelry, so at least I was dressed like I belonged in this neighborhood.

The phoenixes cast their long shadows over me as I approached the front door. "My name is Andromeda Nolan," I whispered, more for the spirits that were listening than for myself. "And God has given me this house."

I pressed my thumb to the keypad—and it chirped and flashed green.

Jayde echoed the sentiment as he held the door open. "Welcome home, Miss Nolan."

I stepped into the foyer and was instantly greeted with a shout and harried footsteps. "Nolan *Xiaojie!* You've returned."

I looked up to see Peng, the Nolans' houseman, approach. He looked exactly like the butler from a classic movie, with his stout frame and pressed uniform, which I supposed was not an inaccurate description of his role in my life.

He bowed low. "It's so good to have you home. How was your trip to America?"

I faked a smile and wondered who had told him. "Pleasant, but it was much too hot." It actually probably wasn't that hot in Boston in early September, but it sounded like something a rich person on holiday would say.

"I wish I could say we're faring much better." He straightened and wiped his brow for effect. "But I've just had the pool serviced, so it's ready for you when you need a reprieve."

"Excellent," I said, even though jumping in the water was the furthest thought from my mind. I gestured at Jayde. "Will you see that the lieutenant is set up in his old quarters?"

"I can find my way," Jayde interrupted. He gave me a hasty bow. "If you need anything, just call." He hurried away before I could respond, apparently as eager to get out of my presence as I was to get out of his. I let out the breath I'd been holding for the last hour and hoped Peng didn't notice.

There was clattering as the driver dropped my luggage—most of which was borrowed from Jael—on the stoop. Peng scurried forward to collect it. "Shall I call the maid? You must be exhausted from your flight."

The last thing I wanted was for a maid to invade my privacy, but I knew that wasn't what Andromeda Nolan would say. *You are the lady of this house now.* "Yes, thank you. Will you tell the staff I'd like to meet with them in an hour? We have a party to plan."

Peng tipped his head to one side. "May I inquire of the occasion?"

"I apologize that it's such short notice," I said with authority, "but I just found out it's my friend's birthday and she happens to be in town this week, so I'm planning to host her and a few friends on Friday night."

More like her and two dozen of the most influential people in the world.

Surprise flashed across Peng's expression before quickly being replaced by joy. "What a delight! It's been so long since we've had an event—it will be an honor to host again."

I kept the plastic smile on my face. If only he had any idea *why* we were having a party.

"I'd be thrilled to help you coordinate the details, if you'd like the assistance," he offered.

"Please," I said, a little too desperately. "If you could also call Narissa and book an appointment for tomorrow, that would be very helpful. Tell her to expect it to take all afternoon." I tugged on my neglected hair self-consciously.

"Of course, ma'am," Peng replied, already pulling out his device.

"Thank you." I strode across the black-and-white tile foyer towards the staircase. I grabbed the curved iron railing and glanced back. "Oh, and Peng? Please tell the chef to set an extra place at the table. I'm expecting Councilwoman Mong for dinner."

*

Asia must have been across town at the council chambers, because she arrived precisely twenty-six minutes after I unlocked the front door. I heard the squeal of tires through my open balcony, followed by the slam of the front door and her screeched, *"Where is she?"*

She was livid. I smirked. *Forgetting our manners already, Asia?*

"Madame Mong!" Peng joined the conversation. "So good to see you again. Miss Nolan is resting in her room."

"I'm going up there." The announcement was unnecessary; the clack of her heels on the tile was so loud that it filled the entire stairwell.

"Ms. Mong, I must protest," Peng panted after her. "Andromeda is recovering from a very long flight. I simply cannot allow her to be disturbed."

Asia ignored him and stormed up to my bedroom door. "Andromeda!" She rattled the handle, but of course, I'd locked it.

"Beg pardon!" Peng exclaimed, sounding like a ruffled chicken. The door handle bounced as he pried her hand off of it. "Andromeda gave strict orders that she be left alone."

"I give the orders," Asia snapped.

"Not in this house."

The comeback was smooth and quiet, almost too quiet to hear. I stifled a laugh.

Asia, for her part, was speechless. I could only imagine the facial expression that went with it.

"Now, Andromeda will be down shortly. In the meantime, won't you join me in the courtyard for a sip of coffee?" Peng's soothing professionalism returned like an afternoon breeze. "I'd love your opinion on the azaleas I just planted on the east wall..."

Their voices faded as he guided her down the stairs. I turned away from the door with a grin, making a mental note to add a bonus to Peng's paycheck.

I had told Peng I would meet with the staff in an hour, and I intended to make Asia wait for every single second. In any case, it took me nearly fifteen minutes to find an appropriate outfit. Thanks to the benevolence of Thames Nolan, my suite contained a massive walk-in closet with more clothes than I could wear in a lifetime. I ruffled through the hundreds of hangers until I found a fashionable but relaxed black jumpsuit and a smart pair of sandals.

I twirled before the mirrored wall and briefly wondered what Mrs. Nolan would think. Cynthia Nolan had strong opinions about what my life as Andromeda Nolan should be—or she did, before her husband Thames's crimes were discovered and he killed himself. I shivered at the visceral memory.

Mrs. Nolan had refused Asia's offer of amnesty and chosen to join the underground instead. She'd accepted the fact that we would never be mother and daughter, but I knew she still thought about it. I could tell by the way she gave me long looks out of the corner of her eye when she thought I wouldn't notice.

I touched my reflection. In some strange irony, throwing this party was the closest I would ever come to fulfilling Mrs. Nolan's fantasy. I wished, not for the first time, that she'd come to Beijing with me; she could teach me how to host like a lady. But she'd chosen to stay behind in Boston and oversee my dad's revival, a sacrifice for which I was deeply grateful. Last I heard, she was hiding off the grid with my dad and Data.

I prayed for her safety, then hurried to the bathroom to put the rest of my costume together. A maid arrived and helped me salvage my hair and makeup. By the time we were done, I looked like a wealthy housewife ready to run errands—which was exactly the persona I wanted to project.

At precisely the turn of the hour, I left my suite and descended the stairs to the foyer. Peng's congenial chatter echoed from the inner courtyard. He was bustling around the planter boxes next to the pool, pointing out this blossom and that blossom with pride. Asia reclined in a chair on the patio. She had one leg crossed over the other and twirled an empty glass in one hand as she watched my houseman like he was a circus act.

I paused in the shadows of the empty living room and collected my courage. Once I walked out that door, there was no turning back. Even if Asia didn't try to kill me, I wouldn't be able to leave until this mission was complete. Either Andromeda Nolan would win this game of chess, or she would die trying.

I took a long breath through my nose. *Go with me, Jesus.*

Then I plastered on a smile and waltzed out into the sunshine to greet my mortal enemy.

"Asia!" I beamed, as if there were no one in the world I'd rather see.

She uncurled from the chair slowly, like a snake woken from a nap. She turned and stared at me, expression cold and suspicious.

She didn't say anything, so I took the lead. I flounced over and hugged her.

Her glass hit the tile and shattered.

"Oh my!" Peng exclaimed. "I'll get it."

I pretended not to notice. I gave Asia's shoulders a defiant squeeze and stepped back.

She leaned as far away as she could without falling out of the chair and gave me the same look Nic usually did when I hugged him.

I grinned. "I missed you."

She rebooted. "I missed you, too." Her voice held no pretense, and the darkness faded from her eyes. She stood up and nudged a shard of glass with her shoe. "I'm so sorry about the glass."

I waved off the transgression. "Don't even worry about it." Almost before I finished the sentence, Peng reappeared with a broom and dustpan and began cleaning it up.

Asia moved out of his way. "How was America?"

The question was casual, as was my reply. "Oh, it was a good visit, but I'm glad to be back. To be honest, I'm thinking of selling the house in Boston."

She arched one thin eyebrow.

I gazed at the pool as it sparkled in the noonday sun. "You were right—I belong here. Besides, there's nothing for me back in Boston… is there?"

I dropped my tone on the end of the sentence ever-so-slightly. Peng didn't notice, but Asia did. I cast her a hard glare out of the corner of my eye. *You hurt me, and I won't forget that.*

She stared back. She wasn't afraid, but there was one beat, two before she responded. "Indeed," she finally said.

Peng straightened with the dustpan in hand. "All better! The staff is ready, if you are, Miss Nolan."

"Oh, yes, perfect timing! Won't you join us, Asia?" I put my perky demeanor back on like a cloak. "I would love your input on the menu."

Peng led the way across the courtyard. Asia followed a few paces behind. "Menu?" she repeated.

"Yes! I'm having a dinner party this Friday. Didn't you get my invitation?"

"Yes—"

"Are you coming?" I spoke over her. "I didn't get your RSVP." I glanced over my shoulder and smiled sweetly.

She frowned, bloodred lips curled in annoyance. "Of course. I wouldn't miss it."

No. You wouldn't dare.

"Wonderful!" I waltzed into the house—and almost tripped on the threshold when I saw how many people were gathered in the kitchen. There were nearly a dozen uniformed employees standing around the island. I swallowed as my inadequacies caught up to me. I knew I had a staff; I didn't realize I had *that big* of a staff.

Asia brushed past me. "Everything all right, Andromeda?"

I roused myself. "Yes, just still dealing with jet lag. Would you make some coffee?" I glanced at my chef—or at least the man I thought I remembered was the chef. I wasn't convinced coffee would actually calm my nerves, but at least holding the mug would give me something natural to do with my hands.

The chef obeyed me. While he clattered around in the pantry, I faced the rest of my staff. "Thank you for taking time out of your busy schedules to have this meeting. I know this party is horribly short notice, but it's for a close friend, and it will mean the world to me if we can show her a good time."

Asia claimed a seat off to the side. My employees simply stared at me expectantly. I twisted my pants in my fingers. What was I supposed to say now? Should I just tell them what to do? What *was* there to do? I'd never planned a party before in my life; there hadn't been a reason to celebrate when I was growing up in the containment camps.

I decided to start with the facts. "I'm expecting about twenty people. It will be an informal dress code for the guests, but I'd like all of us looking our best."

I received a few nods of acknowledgement. I found a breath of confidence—and then lost it when Jayde slid into the kitchen. He glanced at Asia and then took up station in the back corner, his eyes on me. I involuntarily stared back as my next sentence died on my lips.

The front door chimed, buying me a minute to gather my thoughts. "Beg pardon," Peng said, and excused himself to answer it.

The chef held out a mug, which I gratefully accepted. "I want my friend to see the best of China while she's visiting," I continued, making the words up as I went along. I intentionally looked at everyone except Jayde. "I'd love to serve a traditional family-style feast. I'm thinking an assortment of dumplings to start, then perhaps pork ribs for the main—"

I only got halfway through the list before Peng interrupted me. "Miss Nolan!" he called. "You'll want to take this."

Setting my mug on the counter, I apologized to my staff and hurried to the foyer. The annoying clack of Asia's heels followed me.

Peng held the door open. I stepped out onto the porch and was greeted by a soldier in dress uniform. "Miss Andromeda Nolan?" he asked. An SUV with the United seal idled on the road.

I reminded myself that Andromeda was friends with the law and smiled. "Yes, how may I help you?"

The tassels on his uniform fluttered as he bowed and held out a white envelope in one elegant motion. "His Excellency General Secretary Mong sends his regards."

He responded to my invitation! I took the card and slit the seal.

Asia hovered behind me, her strong perfume choking the air.

I deliberately ignored her as I pulled out the familiar embossed RSVP card. I skimmed the text, expecting a "regret to decline."

Instead, a bold checkmark decorated the box next to "honored to attend." In the margin, a note was written with a drippy fountain pen:

THANK YOU FOR THINKING OF ME. I LOOK FORWARD TO SEEING YOU AGAIN. —M

18: PHILADELPHIA

I stood there, staring at the brazen checkmark as that simple stroke of ink changed my life.

He accepted! Jael had been so convinced that the General wouldn't attend the party that I'd started to believe her. Surely, it was too short notice. Surely, I wasn't important enough.

I was wrong. The most powerful man in the world had cleared his calendar on less than a week's notice—for me. Why?

I rubbed my finger over his signature. *What are You doing, Holy Spirit?*

The soldier shifted, politely reminding me of his presence. I looked up and realized he was expecting a response.

"Tell His Excellency that I'm honored," I said, and hoped I didn't sound as shocked as I felt, "and I'm also very much looking forward to seeing him."

That must have been an acceptable reply, because the soldier nodded, bowed again, and returned to his vehicle.

I stumbled inside the house. "What is it?" Asia demanded, then snatched the card from my hand before I could even think about answering.

"Your father is coming to the party," I said, more for myself than for her. My thoughts restarted in a panic when I realized what this meant. *He's coming. The General Secretary is coming! Here! To my house! And I only have three days to get ready!*

Asia glared at the card as if she suspected it was a fake. Then, abruptly, she grinned.

"Oh, this is just wonderful!" she crowed. "I'm so glad you two will have some time together."

She sounded like she meant it. *Does she?*

"Come on, we have a party to plan! Goodness, there's so much to do." Asia grabbed my wrist and hauled me towards the kitchen. I tried not to trip over my own feet as I ran to keep up.

She pulled me around the corner, briefly out of Peng's sight. Before I could react, she spun me around and yanked me towards her. I was too startled to cry out as she gripped my shoulders and leered over me. Her sickly-sweet breath brushed my neck, and for a terrifying moment, I wondered if it was over.

"You want to play games, Philadelphia?" she hissed, her painted lips almost touching my ear. "Then let's play."

She shoved me away from her. I crashed into the wall, rattling a picture frame. Asia regarded the spectacle for a moment, then winked and led the way down the hall.

❋

I spent the rest of the day fighting to keep Asia from taking over my life.

The old Asia—the one who gushed and crooned and suffocated me with compliments—returned in a blink like someone had changed the language settings on a device. She herded me back into the kitchen and seized control of the party planning with the enthusiasm of a drill sergeant. Suddenly, this was the most important event of the year, and she was going to make sure it was *perfect*.

While I secretly appreciated the help—since I had absolutely no idea what I was doing—I did *not* appreciate the fact that she started ordering my servants around and making decisions as if I wasn't there. This was my party—a fact I reminded her of several times with varying degrees of politeness—and I wasn't about to become a bystander in my own house.

Asia wasn't listening, but Peng was. Every time Asia gave an order, Peng would stop the conversation and look to me for approval. He even had the audacity to disagree with Asia's recommendations on several points. It drove her so mad that she finally decided to save time and start asking my opinion first.

The next few hours were a blur. I made so many decisions that I couldn't remember any of them. A menu was planned, musicians were contracted, and an assortment of flowers and lanterns were ordered. Of course, it wasn't just the house that needed to be decorated; I also had to look flawless, and Asia had strong opinions on that subject, as usual. In addition to my appointment with Narissa, Asia also booked three other beauty treatments she insisted I needed. By then, I was so tired of pretending to be an adult that I didn't have the energy to argue.

It was long past dark by the time she finally excused herself. I was beginning to worry that she'd never leave; maybe that was her plan, to haunt me like a shadow until she could safely dispose of me.

Much to my relief, however, she seemed to understand that I wasn't going anywhere. The General Secretary was coming to dinner; neither she nor I could make a move before Friday. Until the party was over, it was stalemate.

"See you tomorrow," she said as she flounced out the door, and it was a threat.

She left without eating dinner, leaving my chef slightly miffed that he'd cooked for two. I, on the other hand, was very grateful for the peace and quiet of the empty dining room—in part because Jayde finally made himself scarce. He'd hovered in my peripheral all day. He never spoke and never came close, but he was always *there*, watching me like a parole officer. Multiple times I thought about telling him off, but I didn't want to make a scene in front of Asia.

It was after eleven when I limped up the stairs to my suite. I kicked my shoes into the corner and flopped out on the bed. The mountain of purple-blue pillows caught me like a cloud, and I thought that maybe, just maybe, I could sleep without medication.

But I knew what Jael would say to that.

I rolled over and grabbed my backpack off the nightstand. I didn't relish the idea of taking medication with Jayde in the house and Asia a few minutes away, but I also knew what would happen if I didn't. I couldn't be anxious at this party; if I made a mistake in front of the General because I was jittery and sleep-deprived, the operation would fail.

I swallowed the pills with a prayer. *Protect me, Jesus.*

I leaned back on the pillows and waited for the pounding in my heart to slow. It would take at least twenty minutes for the medication to kick in, but I knew exactly what to do to pass the time.

I turned off all the lamps so the only light came from the fairy netting above my bed. Grabbing my Bible, I buried myself in the covers and fell asleep reading under the stars.

Eight hours later, I woke to the sound of my cat clawing at the door.

"Tommy, stop it," I groaned into the pillow. I rolled over, groping for my phone—and that's when I realized what I'd said.

I jerked upright. The sound came again; it was definitely an animal pawing at my bedroom door. *The Nolans don't have pets... and Tommy's back in America with John and Dowe. Isn't he?*

Of course, it wouldn't be the first time John and Dowe randomly appeared somewhere they shouldn't have been.

I slid out of bed and shrugged on a robe. The animal heard me coming and responded with whimpering and slobbery panting. *Please don't be John and Dowe.* I braced myself and threw the door open.

A fat, wrinkly pug sat in the hall.

We stared at each other. His tongue hung out of his mouth as he struggled to breathe through his flat nose. His bulbous eyes were nearly lost in the excessive folds of skin. He looked like a stack of pancakes, and he was so chubby that he could barely keep himself upright.

"Where did—" I started.

He took that as an invitation, yipping and jumping up on my leg. I jerked and almost fell backwards. "Off!"

"His name is Frank."

I whirled. A man about my brother's age stood down the hall, holding a steaming teacup. He wore a house robe and slippers and leaned against the railing like he owned the place. "Morning," he chirped.

I stared at him and tried to decide whether to feel scared or confused or question reality altogether. "What?" was the only word I could get out.

"His name is Frank," the man repeated. A light British accent coated his voice like butter on toast. "The dog."

That seemed like completely irrelevant information when there was a man I didn't recognize in my house at seven o'clock in the morning. "And your name is...?"

"Oh, my apologies, Cardiff."

"And you are...?"

"A lot of things. As far as what's relevant to you... I'm your 'older brother.'"

The quotes were audible, and I abruptly remembered what Mrs. Nolan had said when we first met.

"It's just us, only kid is grown, so we have the spare bedroom, all ready for you."

The man nodded at me with his teacup. "Cardiff Nolan," he repeated, in case I hadn't put two and two together.

I took a second look, and this time, I could see Thames written all over him. The broad shoulders, the dark hair, the chiseled face. He carried himself with the same posh confidence, movements slow and precise like he could bend time and space around him. The only difference was that Cardiff's lips were permanently curled, like he was on the verge of bursting into laughter.

Somehow, that was even more disturbing than Thames's cruel benevolence.

"I thought... I thought you were..." I stuttered and tried to come up with a reasonable explanation for why I didn't expect him to be standing in his own house.

"I've been on a science station in deep space for the last three years," he explained, pushing himself away from the railing. "And yes, I'm aware Mother and Father never talked about me."

His voice darkened, and his entire attitude changed like someone had snuffed out a candle. He seemed to grow taller and more intimidating as he scowled at some invisible ghost past my shoulder.

Suddenly, everything made sense and nothing made sense at the same time.

He blinked and almost dropped his teacup, as if he, too, were surprised by his mood. "But never mind that. He's gone and Mother won't answer my calls, so it's really a moot point. Here, I brought you something."

I felt like we should address one if not both of those statements about his parents, but he didn't give me the chance. He set his teacup on its saucer— *who wanders around the house with a teacup and saucer?*—to reach into the pocket of his velvet robe. He withdrew a jewelry box and held it out to me.

I walked over and took it, despite my better judgment. I opened it to find the most beautiful keychain I had ever seen. Nine charms shaped like planets dangled from a silver ring. The largest charm was a clear glass ball with orange-and-white gas suspended inside. It swirled mesmerizingly like the surface of a planet.

"It's real gas and particles harvested from Jupiter's atmosphere," he explained. "There's a magnet in the center that keeps it in motion. I thought you might like it."

I did, very much. I looked up into his face and saw he was grinning. It was a genuine smile, like he'd been waiting for years to give me this gift.

Maybe he had.

"Thank you," I said, closing the box. "Did they… tell you about me?"

"Of course. They've been planning to bring you home for over two years. What, you think they tried to convince me that my cousin had miraculously come back from the dead?"

I didn't know what I thought—but at this point, nothing would have surprised me.

He frowned. "I remember Andromeda. You're *nothing* like her."

I grimaced. It was easy to forget that "Andromeda" was a real person— or, she had been. Thames's brother and sister-in-law had a daughter who would have been about my age. The whole family had died in a car crash years ago. Except, according to the paperwork, Andromeda survived. Thames had modified her file and bribed witnesses to make it seem like his niece never died, all so that he could adopt me and give me a new identity out of her ashes.

"I know who you are." Cardiff swirled his tea. "I know all about Mars, and Red Rain, and Dr. Nic. I know Jayde isn't here just to be your bodyguard. I know you're responsible for this revolution—and doing a mighty fine job of ruffling some feathers, if I do say so myself."

"How did..." I didn't finish the question. I didn't need to. If Cardiff had access to Thames's servers on Mars—let alone my credentials as Andromeda—then he knew everything.

Including, perhaps, the real reason I'd come back to the Nolan estate.

He took a sip and smiled at me over the rim of his cup. "I'm delighted to finally meet you, *Philadelphia*."

I slid back and almost stepped on Frank, who was hovering by my ankle. "*Don't* call me that."

He blew a raspberry. "Oh, pish posh. Don't be that way. Your secret is perfectly safe with me."

"Why should I trust you?" I demanded, and hoped he had a really good answer to that question.

"Because I don't fancy jail?" he replied, which wasn't the worst explanation ever. "Your alibi is my alibi. We're both Nolans. Revealing that I'm related to the United's most wanted criminal would soil the family name—not to mention, put quite a damper on our financial situation."

Regrettably, he was right. Thames was our father, which meant his crimes were our crimes. Cardiff would suffer just as much as I would if he exposed the truth behind my adoption. Until further notice, he and I were in this together.

Which was also, inconveniently, why I couldn't tell him to go back to his space station and leave me alone.

I folded my arms. "Why did you come home now?"

"Besides the fact that my science mission completed its orbit?" He shrugged and set his cup down on its saucer with a *clink*. "Someone has to run this estate now that the old man's gone."

I thought I was running this estate.

"On the subject of our mutual financial interests..." Cardiff pulled a phone out of the pocket of his robe and flicked across the screen. "Since you've been largely absent for the past several months, I took the liberty of having my financial advisor reinvest some of your shares. We can review the reports later, but I'm personally pleased with the returns."

I bristled. Apparently, Asia wasn't the only one who had been tampering with my inheritance. I started to object—but Frank decided he lacked attention. He rudely licked me on the leg. I squealed and almost fell over.

Cardiff applauded the spectacle. "Aww, you two are precious. He's so excited about the party—he can't wait to meet new people."

I not-so-subtly pushed Frank away with my foot. "Who says you're coming to the party?"

"I live here," he chirped. "Besides, I wouldn't miss this for the world. Speaking of... what time is it?" He pocketed his phone, then reached into the apparently bottomless folds of his robe and pulled out a pocket watch, of all things.

Why didn't he just check the time on his phone?

He popped the cover and squinted at the face. "Don't you have a hair appointment in an hour?"

I did have a hair appointment in an hour, but that was really none of his business. "How do you know?"

"Asia mentioned it."

"You already talked to Asia?"

"She's in the living room."

I groaned and hoped she could hear me from across the house.

Cardiff chuckled. "Welcome to the family, darling."

19: PHILADELPHIA

Frank insisted on following me back to my room. He followed me to the closet, around the bed, and then back to the closet again. The stupid dog even followed me into the bathroom. He chased my heel all the way down the stairs, nearly tripping me in the foyer.

Cardiff thought the situation was "positively adorable." I would have been more amicable had the dog's breathing not sounded like a car without a muffler.

Frank finally gave up on me when he spotted Asia lounging the dining room. He yipped and jumped straight in her lap, inducing an ungodly shriek. That made it *all* worth it.

Asia kicked him off and turned her attention to me. She rattled off a dozen updates that made it clear she had been up early modifying my itinerary. I was still disoriented from being dragged out of bed by a slobbering dog and a weird man who claimed to be my brother, which left me with no patience for her scheming. I glared at her and snapped, "Since when were you my secretary?"

I'm not sure who was more appalled by my attitude—me or her. Cardiff laughed so hard he snorted tea back into his cup. Peng salvaged the situation by stepping up and giving me the same information, just in a much more respectful manner.

Asia recovered and started whining about how I'd be late to my appointment with Narissa. I told her Narissa would wait, grabbed my Bible and my breakfast, and flounced out to the courtyard in defiance of them all. I'd be lying if I said I didn't do it partially to annoy her, but I was finally getting back into the habit of reading the Bible before starting my day, and I wasn't going to ruin it for a hair appointment.

Besides, I needed all the grace I could get if I was going to survive another day with Asia.

She insisted on coming with me to my appointment. Jayde appeared out of the woodwork and said he was driving, and then Cardiff decided a "family outing" would be delightful and joined the party. I tried to get one or all three of them to stay home, but they weren't listening to me.

I caught Jayde in the hallway as we were preparing to leave. "You are *not* coming with me," I announced in a tone I hoped was authoritative.

He glanced around. That's when I realized we were alone—too late to stop him from backing me into a corner. I stumbled and rammed into the wall. He blocked the way and leaned over me, face inches from mine.

I fumbled with my backpack, scrambling to find the clicker.

He pretended not to notice. "Jael sends a message," he whispered.

I stopped.

"Seoul called. Your father went through surgery last night. They haven't woken him up yet, but so far he's recovering well."

My breath caught in my throat as a grateful prayer struggled to break free. *Thank you, Jesus!*

"Lieutenant!" Asia screeched from around the corner. "Where is the car? We're late!"

Jayde stood back. "And yes, I'm coming with you. You're not leaving the house without a guard." Then he strode off before I could argue.

The ride to Narissa's studio was twenty-five minutes of pure agony. Asia's prattling was already torturous; Cardiff made it worse. He overreacted to all her comments and prodded her for details, which in turn made Asia even more dramatic. What's worse, I couldn't tell if he was doing it for the reaction, or if he actually enjoyed Asia's company. I wasn't sure Asia knew, either.

The only consolation was that Jayde hated it as much as I did. When we pulled up to Narissa's studio, he politely informed me that he would wait in the car.

He immediately regretted that choice when Cardiff also volunteered to stay behind.

Asia unnecessarily escorted me into the studio. The artsy salon was empty. All the black-and-chrome surfaces were polished to a shine, glinting in the morning sun that streamed through the bay windows. Soft zither music and the tinkle of the waterfall in the back of the room floated through the air, giving the salon the aura of a temple.

Asia shattered it when she banged on the bell at the front desk. "Narissa!"

"I heard the bell."

Narissa slid out from the back, wearing her usual all-black pant set. With her cropped hair and sharp winged eyeliner, she perfectly matched the aesthetic of the studio, almost as if the building had been modeled after her.

She gave me a *hmm* that I knew was the closest I'd get to a hello, then turned her glare on Asia. "Do you have an appointment?"

"She does." Asia flicked her hand at me, as if my presence weren't obvious.

"I didn't ask about her."

"I'll be staying..."

Narissa didn't even let her finish. She just turned and pointed at the sign on the door that said "no walk ins."

Asia bristled, looking like a hissing cat ready to scratch.

"Oh, calm yourself," Narissa droned. She walked over and grabbed a cape off the back of a salon chair. "It's not like you can't review the footage later."

I flinched. Narissa was blind—or she had been, until she'd received robotic eye implants funded by the government. Now, she could do more than just see; she could take measurements, match foundation shades, and communicate with her dress fabricator, all from her mind. The only drawback was that the algorithm heard everything.

Asia huffed her consent. "I'll be picking her up at noon."

"You'll pick her up when I say she's done. You put this child through a war and now I have to piece her back together. Miracles take time." Narissa turned the chair around and gestured for me to sit.

I obeyed. Asia fumed for a moment more, groping for the last word, then stormed out.

Narissa waited until the car had pulled away from the curb before relaxing. "Insufferable."

I grinned.

My smile faded when she violently spun the chair back to face the mirror. She grabbed chunks of my hair with both hands and scowled at it with a look of utter disgust.

"What?" I managed after withering under her scrutiny for a solid minute.

"I still can't believe you bleached your hair without asking me. I absolutely hate this color on you." She tightened her grip on my hair, and for a moment, I feared she might rip it out of my head.

I braced myself. "I'm sorry." It had been necessary, in the moment. Philadelphia Smyrna was known for her long, dark hair; Andromeda had to be the exact opposite. So, before going back to Earth, I'd impulsively chopped my hair to my shoulders and bleached it almost white.

Evidently, Narissa still hadn't forgiven me. "I'm going to have to lift the roots again and..." She raked her fingers along my scalp, then stopped. Her frown changed to one of concentration as she pinched a strand of my hair and squinted at it. I couldn't see the flashing modules behind her contacts, but I knew the implants in her eyes were doing their work, scanning my hair and matching my exact shade.

With a *humph*, she strode over to the color bar and began grabbing bottles of product off the shelf. I daren't ask what she was doing, so I changed the subject. "I never got a chance to say thank you."

She mumbled an affirmative. When Nic and I first arrived in Beijing, Narissa helped us get a head start on Asia by giving us supplies and letting us out a back way. The only reason Asia didn't punish her for it was because Narissa was worth more alive than dead. It was hard to find a stylist who could be controlled remotely.

Narissa squirted a generous glob of brown dye into a mixing bowl. "I'll be over at 7am sharp on Friday to do your makeup and deliver your outfit. You'd best be ready for me."

"I will," I promised, "but I don't need any new clothes. I have a closet full."

"None you're wearing."

I knew better than to argue. Narissa had been my stylist since my very first video, working for Thames and then for Asia. The only reason the "thunderbird" had an image was because of her. She'd designed the dress I wore at the gala, and she'd even secretly sent clothes to the Tangs for me to use on my tour.

She was also the one who had asked me to visit the group home a few weeks ago.

I dug my nails into the leather arm of the salon chair as I remembered the note she'd taped to the white shirt box:

THERE'S SOME OLD FRIENDS OF MINE I WOULD LIKE YOU TO VISIT. CALL IT A FAVOR FOR ME—IT WOULD MEAN A LOT.

Everyone who lived in that home had been her friends. They were people just like her—people with conditions the government considered incurable, unfashionable, or illegal.

And now almost all of them were dead.

I blinked back tears. "Narissa, I..." I struggled to find words for everything I needed to say but couldn't, for fear the algorithm was listening.

She stopped with her back to me.

I sighed. "I'm sorry."

"So am I," she murmured, and that was all that could be said.

There was silence for a moment while she gathered herself. Then she resumed aggressively stirring the dye. "This had better work. I'm not going to have time to redo your hair."

"I'm sure it will be perfect. You always make me look good."

"You certainly don't make it easy," she snapped, which could have been taken any number of ways. She set the bowl on a tray and wheeled it over. "Eventually you'll learn to give me more than *three days'* notice before you need a custom order. You're lucky I was already working on designs."

I found her gaze in the mirror. "You knew I'd come back."

She returned the stare. "You have a job to finish."

I swallowed. *Yes, I do.*

"Then let's finish in style." She snapped on a pair of gloves. "Now hold still while I fix this atrocity."

20: NIC

Five hours and forty-two minutes. That was how long it took to walk a lap around each level of the factory, all eighty-seven of them, and that was information I wish I didn't know.

It had been five days since my little episode, and Warden Ivanova still refused to lift her moratorium on work. I was on my best behavior for the first two days, hoping to prove I was a changed man. On the third day, I went to her office and begged for mercy. She rejected me—and then promptly left the base on a trip. I decided to try my luck and go down to the lab, only to find she'd revoked my access to everything except the cleaning closet.

I'm not sure which was more unnerving: The fact that I was locked out of my own lab, or the realization that she'd outsmarted me.

Bested, I had no choice but to set a timer and calculate how long it took to walk the entire factory. The result was a highly inconvenient number. It wasn't long enough to fill a whole workday, but it was too long for me to get two complete rounds in. I would have settled for one and three-quarters, or one and a half, or even one and a third rounds. But no, the math worked out to something like 1.41 rounds. Which meant that when dinner was called, I was on some random level in the middle, and that made the whole thing feel even more pointless than usual.

I was aware the math was arbitrary. I didn't need anyone to tell me that I was literally going in circles. In fact, part of the reason I walked from one level to another, instead of picking a level and trying to beat my best personal time from Rott, was so that I could avoid anyone commenting on the futility of my existence.

There was one Voice I couldn't avoid, however, no matter how fast I powerwalked.

He didn't say much for three days. I knew what the radio silence meant: I was going nowhere fast, literally and spiritually. I'd opened a door during our heart-to-heart in the lab, and He wasn't going to let me shut it again. So, if I didn't want to keep going in circles until Jesus returned, I'd better start talking.

I did. I honestly gave it my best effort. I interceded for Philadelphia. I complained about Asia. I even, against my every inhibition, told Him how I was *feeling*.

It was a wasted effort. Don't get me wrong—He listened very politely. But nothing changed. There was nothing I could pray that He hadn't heard already, and all His answers were the same as they had been for the past month. It felt like I was jumping through a dozen submenus on an automated answering machine, only to get the response I didn't want to hear.

Wait.

I would have taken any instruction over that one. If He'd told me to stay up all night praying, I would have set my alarm. If He'd told me to fast, I would have gladly skipped dinner. If He'd told me to pull an Ezekiel and lie on my side in the middle of the cafeteria for 390 days, I wouldn't have asked questions. I would have done anything—literally *anything*—as long as it meant I was doing something.

But apparently, He didn't have any use for me. So, I continued to walk the levels, going faster and faster, until I tripped over the reality I was trying so hard to avoid.

Bowen.

He was on the 85th floor. The top levels of the prison were mostly forgotten storage and hence weren't well-lit. He was kneeling by the railing, completely hidden in shadow. I literally tripped over him and almost sent both of us plummeting to our deaths.

"Nic! I'm sorry, I-I wasn't expecting anyone to be up here."

I braced myself on the railing and waited for my life to stop flashing before my eyes. "In your defense, I *shouldn't* be up here."

"Guess we have that in common." He stooped and started gathering something on the floor.

"Why are you—" I stopped when I saw what it was: candles. He'd stolen a box from the storeroom and arranged a trio of them on the concrete floor, one of which I'd gracelessly snuffed out.

"Sorry," I mumbled.

"It's fine," he said, even though I could tell that it definitely wasn't. He'd made an alcove between two stacks of boxes and draped a white banner over the crates—half of a torn bedsheet, it looked like. Packing paper folded into the crude shapes of flowers and coins littered the ground.

And taped to one of the boxes was a picture of Lanzhou.

It was black and white and grainy, like someone had scanned a webpage on an old copier. The ghost of whatever was printed on the back bled through the paper, marring Lanzhou's stoic face.

I didn't have to ask what was going on. I'd been to enough Chinese funerals with my father to know what I was looking at. It was pathetic and homely—and it was the best Lanzhou would ever get.

Bowen picked up the fallen candle and relit it. He twirled it in his fingers, his eyes chasing the flame, before setting it with the others. He sat back on his haunches, stared at his makeshift memorial, and said absolutely nothing.

My stupid self had to fill the silence. "You... holding up okay?"

He mercifully didn't answer my dumb question. "It would have been my job to plan the funeral," he commented, as if that explained everything. "I'm the next oldest, and elders aren't supposed to grieve for the younger. My uncle wouldn't even have been allowed to read the eulogy."

I wondered if the very traditional Mr. Tang was observing that rite, grieving silently in whatever dungeon Asia had stuffed him in.

"I would have had to read it. What would I have even said?" Bowen turned and glared up at me, like he was actually expecting an answer to that question.

I didn't have one. I had absolutely no idea what to say.

Bowen filled in the blanks, his voice sharp and unstable. "That he was right all along? That it's my fault he's dead? That he should be the one running the company?"

I didn't know what to say to that either—because all of those statements were true.

What am I supposed to do with this? I demanded of the Voice in my head.

He was silent.

Bowen cackled, clearly aware he was coming unglued. "Not that there's a company to run."

He was three for three with irrefutable statements. The Tangs were ruined. Their factory was destroyed, and Asia had no doubt frozen their assets and revoked their rights. To add insult to injury, if the Tangs didn't exercise their patent for a year, the government would grant it to someone else. Even if Philadelphia managed to bail the family out of jail, they would have no fortune—and worse, no reputation.

The Tangs had weathered tragedy and financial hardship before. But through all their decades of resistance and civil disobedience, they had always maintained their honor. They were the most influential family in the district. Even the police—the ones who had been bribed to keep the church safe—respected them.

Not anymore.

"What do I do?" Bowen whispered, still begging for an answer from somebody.

Nothing. That was the answer. There was absolutely nothing he could do to fix this. The Tangs could recover their wealth, and they would, if they survived this war. But their honor was irreplaceable.

Bowen touched Lanzhou's picture. "I'm so sorry," he hissed, and then again, louder. "I'm so sorry!"

He blurted a stream of unintelligible Mandarin. Then he dropped to the floor, prostrate like he was making penance, and wept.

I stood there and panicked. I didn't know what to do. I couldn't help him. I couldn't comfort him, I couldn't reassure him, I couldn't even give him any wise advice. Me and my three PhDs were useless in this situation. Bowen's world was ending, and there was nothing I could do.

You don't have to do anything.

The command came like a gust of cold air—unwelcome, unexpected, and absolutely terrifying.

But I need to do something. Why else was I standing here? Why would God put me in this incredibly awkward situation if He didn't want me to fix it? In fact, why was I on Earth at all? Why would He give me visions and prophecies and a *living, breathing teenage daughter* if He didn't want me to do something about it?

I never asked you to do anything.

He knelt next to Bowen, His hand on the sobbing man's shoulder. His gaze pierced me, and I knew I had a choice.

I could walk away. I could maintain control over my life—and spend the next ten years fighting to fill the void.

Or I could obey... and do absolutely nothing.

He waited. I stared into His eyes like fire and decided which death I wanted to survive.

Taking a long breath, I settled on the floor next to Bowen. Then I stilled my hands in my lap and sat—in silence.

21: PHILADELPHIA

"Well, aren't you a doll!" Cardiff declared. He and Asia were crowding the foot of the stairs as I descended, like they were my parents about to see me off for prom.

It was the day of the party, and Narissa had truly worked a miracle. Instead of lifting my roots, she'd formulated a dye that matched my natural shade exactly and feathered it through my hair. When she was finished, it looked like I'd gotten an elaborate balayage, with my natural color on top and bright highlights underneath.

"Now I don't have to constantly fix your roots," she'd announced with pride. But I knew that wasn't the real reason.

Cardiff loved the new look, not that I'd asked for his opinion. Asia was critical, but it didn't have anything to do with the color. She knew what the hairstyle meant: Andromeda's days were numbered. If the revolution won, I wouldn't have to hide behind a false identity anymore. Philadelphia Smyrna could come back from the dead—and then I would most assuredly be growing my hair out.

Of course, Narissa's subtle rebellion didn't stop at hair dye. My dress also sent a clear message. The fitted bodice was modeled after a qipao, with a starched collar and three-quarter sleeves, but the full skirt had a loose fit and a high-low hemline that made it easy to move around in as I served. The black silk fabric was embroidered with the bold form of a phoenix, its flaming tail sweeping across my waist and down the side of the skirt. It would have been a very traditional design had it not been for the color choice: white and silver with flashes of blue woven into the tips of the feathers. It was subtle, but I knew Asia would understand the threat.

"Positively stunning!" Cardiff exclaimed as I reached the foyer.

I held out my skirt to show off the embroidery. "What do you think, Asia?"

She didn't reply.

Cardiff helped me off the last step. He held my hand for a beat too long, then bent forward to kiss the back of it. "Mother would be *so* proud."

I pulled my hand out of his grasp.

"It is missing something, though."

I turned to see Asia holding out an all-too-familiar blue velvet jewelry box.

My breath caught in my throat. *She didn't.*

I forced myself to take it from her. I opened it to find my pearl necklace. Asia had given it to me as a gift when we'd first met, as an invitation to join her in high society. I'd been wearing it defiantly ever since; it had been in my suitcase back at the factory.

Asia answered my unspoken question. "It was recovered from the wreckage."

I looked up into her smile, cold and cruel.

Memories of Lanzhou's kind face flashed before my eyes, but I willed myself not to grieve. *Don't let her get to you.* I brushed dust off the pearls. "How thoughtful, but you won't be able to see it under the collar."

Then I snapped the box shut and held it out to Cardiff, who took it with a wicked grin.

I excused myself before Asia could recover and went to check on the preparations, not that the staff needed my help. Peng had once again proven his worth and put on a fabulous production. The house was so alive with light and color that you could barely recognize it. An explosion of fresh-cut flowers adorned every surface, blanketing the rooms with their scent. The dining table was draped in red and decorated with fans and shafts of bamboo. Everything glittered with gold, while a trio of musicians filled the air with a hybrid of modern and traditional music.

The courtyard, however, was truly the crown jewel of the estate. Glowing lanterns hung from every balcony, bathing the patio in fire. Incense burned in the fire pits and sent smoke drifting into the air, like there were baby dragons curled up underneath the coals. In the center of it all, the pool shimmered in the moonlight as a hundred lilies and candles floated on its surface.

I paused in the doorway and admired the extravagance. Mrs. Nolan truly *would* be proud.

And so would Nic.

I gripped the doorframe. *Would he?* Nic had never once been proud of me, but he'd sacrificed himself so I could fulfill my calling. If we defeated Asia, would he be proud? Would he even find out?

I brushed the thoughts aside and kept walking. None of us would live to see tomorrow if I didn't pull this party off.

I hurried to the kitchen, where my chef was living his best life directing an army of temporary help as they prepared enough food to feed a hundred.

Spice and sweet competed in the air as a dozen dishes were arranged on gold trays to be served. The chef gave me the obligatory taste test, then politely shooed me out of the kitchen with a stack of dessert plates to take to the dining room.

I bustled around the corner—and ran straight into Jayde. I shrieked and dropped all seventeen plates on the floor. The clatter of metal on the tile was terrific.

"Sorry," he grunted after the noise stopped. "Blind corner."

I sighed loudly. "Will you *stop* hovering!"

"Sorry," he repeated, kneeling down to stack the plates. "I've got orders."

"To do what?"

He shot me a sideways glance, and I stiffened. "What don't I know?"

"Jael didn't tell you?"

"Obviously not!"

He brushed aside the hem of his jacket, revealing his holstered pistol. "If Asia tries anything, I'm supposed to shoot first."

I stared at the weapon as this admission completely reframed our relationship. "But that's suicide," I murmured. It wouldn't matter if Asia came at me with a knife and everyone saw it; they'd still execute Jayde for touching the General Secretary's daughter.

He shrugged. "Better me than you." He stood up, balancing the stack of plates, and gestured with his shoulder. "Where are these going?"

I numbly pointed at the dining room, too stunned to respond. What was terrifying was that he sounded like he believed what he'd said.

Jael arrived a few minutes later, accompanied by a businesswoman I didn't recognize. "Oh, forgive me, are we early?" Jael said, glancing pointedly around the empty foyer.

"Not at all. Please, come in."

I waited until they had stepped inside and been relieved of their jackets and accessories before extending a formal greeting. I gave a short bow to Jael, then offered my hand, just as Asia had taught me. "Thank you for honoring my family with your presence."

Jael returned both gestures, then rattled off a gorgeous and lengthy African name I couldn't pronounce. "But I'd be honored if you called me Chidi," she added.

I smiled gratefully. Remembering not to call her Jael would be hard enough. "Since you're early, would you like the tour before the others arrive?" I suggested, and hoped she would pick up on my meaning.

She did. "I'd love to. Oh, Min," she turned to Asia, "have you met my friend Bristol?"

I hoped my eyebrows didn't expose my surprise. Not only had Jael skipped a formal introduction, but she'd also used Asia's given name, a privilege normally reserved for close friends.

Asia pretended not to be annoyed. "No, I don't suppose I have."

"Oh, you simply must hear about the labor riots they've been having in England. It's an absolute scandal." Jael grabbed her friend's arm and all but shoved her in Asia's face.

Bristol had clearly rehearsed for this moment and immediately launched into a tirade about what the ungrateful peasants were doing. Asia had no choice but to smile and nod.

I quickly led the way down the hall, leaving Asia stranded in the foyer. I waited until we were out of earshot before turning to Jael. "How long have you known Asia?"

"Long enough to get away with that." She followed me to the abandoned dining room and stopped inside the door, admiring the decorations. "This is gorgeous. You've done an excellent job."

I could tell she meant it. A little relief fluttered through me. "Have you found any proof?" I asked, dropping my voice to a whisper.

"Proof of what?" she remarked with a glare over her shoulder.

I flinched. I was Andromeda Nolan; I wasn't supposed to know anything about Blue Fire or the revolution. But Jael hadn't said a word since I'd left for the estate, and we were running out of time. The operation was in less than a week; if we didn't get enough evidence tonight, we wouldn't be able to expose Asia before shots were fired.

"Your only job is to throw a party," she reminded me. "Let me worry about the rest. Your router is doing the heavy lifting."

I nodded and checked to make sure my phone was still in my pocket.

She faced me and spoke quickly. "Your primary focus is the General—but don't crowd him. Let him spend time with other people. A good hostess doesn't have anything to prove, and it will confuse Asia."

She glanced past me, as if verifying that our enemy hadn't escaped from the foyer. "She knows you have ulterior motives for throwing this party. She's going to be watching you like you're watching her, waiting for you to slip up. The more you act like this is just a normal meal—that you don't have anything to gain from her or her father—the more you'll distract her."

I fixed my posture and took a slow breath. *Just look pretty, be polite, and make a good impression. I can do this.*

"There are a few 'friends' I want you to meet, though," Jael continued. "I'll do the talking. Keep the General and Asia busy, and I'll send people to you when the time is right."

"How will I know they're friends?"

"If someone says, 'It sure has been hot lately,' reply, 'Then perhaps it's time we had some rain.' That's your cue that someone is an ally."

I fingered the embroidered feathers on my skirt. "And if someone isn't an ally?"

Jael smirked. "Then convert them."

I closed my eyes. *Give me the right words, Holy Spirit.*

There was commotion on the street—the rumble of multiple vehicles and the clamor of a dozen people on the walkway. Peng called excitedly for me from the foyer, and I knew the General had arrived.

I skipped a breath as panic took one last shot at me. This man wanted me dead. He'd outlawed my religion, murdered my friends, and imprisoned my family. He was the most wicked man in the world—second, perhaps, only to his daughter.

And I was about to serve him dumplings and pork ribs.

"It's showtime," Jael murmured. "Remember, for the next three hours, he's not your enemy. He's your friend."

I nodded and cleared room in my heart for a peace that was not mine.

For such a time as this.

I turned and headed for the foyer.

"Oh, Andromeda," Jael called me back.

I glanced over my shoulder.

"Love the dress." She winked.

I grinned.

My top staff had arranged themselves in the foyer like they were prepared for a military inspection. Cardiff observed from the side. He carried Frank in his arms and was stroking the dog's back slowly like the villain in a kid's TV show. I could only hope he'd keep the animal in check; the last thing I needed was for that slobbering dog to ruin my dinner party.

Peng held the door open as Asia fussed on the step. Two armed guards entered, and then suddenly, the General Secretary of the United was standing in my house.

I was once again taken aback by how unassuming the man was. He wasn't tall; even Peng had a few inches on him. His hair was graying, his face was softly wrinkled, and his expression was calm. It wasn't a pretentious calm, either; not like Thames, who had used his cool manner to control and manipulate. No, the General seemed genuinely calm, almost gentle.

He didn't look like the kind of man who ordered genocide and criminalized religion. And, for the next three hours, I had to pretend that he wasn't.

I gave Peng a minute to collect the General's belongings, then presented myself. "Your Excellency," I said softly, "I'm honored." I delicately lifted my skirt and bowed as low as I could.

The General returned the bow and held it, with each second adding prestige to the Nolan name. Then he straightened and extended his hand. "The honor is all mine."

I looked up. He gave me a knowing smile.

"Next time I offer you my hand, don't refuse it."

Asia watched us, eyes narrowed.

I beamed and grasped the General's hand. Our palms contacted. "Thank you for making time on such short notice. I know it was an inconvenience."

"None at all. I'm glad you thought of me." He squeezed my fingers, then stood back. "Trust me, this will be far more enjoyable than anything else I was planning to do with my evening."

A polite chuckle rippled from the bystanders. The General scanned the crowd, and his gaze settled on Cardiff. "Oh, I didn't know you had returned to Earth." If there was any emotion attached to the statement, I couldn't decode it.

"Fresh off the space station. My apologies if I still reek of hyperdrive fumes." Cardiff forewent a bow and offered his hand.

The General accepted it, even though their palms barely touched. Frank squirmed and struggled to get down. The General hummed bemusedly and scratched the dog behind the ears. "I'd love to know how the mission is progressing," he said to Cardiff. "Have they had any success reaching the surface of Jupiter?"

I remembered what Jael had said about not crowding the General and seized the opportunity. "Yes, Cardiff, you should tell him everything. Show him the samples you brought back. There's a sitting room over here where you can rest until dinner is served."

I started to lead the way, but the General laughed. "You can't get rid of me that easily, Andromeda. I didn't come to talk to this old chap—I came to talk to you!"

The bold declaration silenced the room. I had no idea how to respond.

Asia did it for me. "Of course! Andromeda, you should give him the tour. Show him what you've done with the place."

"What a marvelous idea!" Cardiff echoed, not sounding the least bit offended. "You're going to love it. She's outdone herself—the courtyard is positively stunning."

He and Asia collectively herded me towards the hallway. I gathered my wits. "Oh, yes, of course. Cardiff, would you stay and receive the other guests?"

"With pleasure, sister." He winked.

I put my smile back on and gestured for the General to follow. His guards fell into place as I guided them out of the room. Jayde trailed us at a safe distance.

I did as I was told and took the General on a tour—showing him the dining room, the courtyard, the garden—but it was clearly just a front to avoid the other guests for twenty minutes. He didn't want to talk about the house; he wanted to talk about me. He asked about my trip to America, my college plans, and Mrs. Nolan's health. I gave him what he wanted and answered his questions with as much detail as I could fabricate.

That is, until his questions became personal.

"How are you and Cardiff getting along?"

We'd stopped in a secluded corner of the courtyard. I busied my hands plucking a dead leaf off a bush to buy myself time to come up with a plausible response.

"It's been super awkward" would have been the truthful answer. Cardiff was nice—almost too nice, not unlike his mother. He had been helpful with the party preparations and had assumed management of the estate, reviewing investments and conducting employee evaluations and taking care of things I never would have thought of.

I would have been grateful if it weren't for the fact that he made everything weirdly personal. On paper, we were adopted brother and sister, and he wanted to live that fantasy to the fullest. He insisted we eat meals together, had an opinion about everything I did, and was generally up in my business at all hours. He was more annoying than Asia—not to mention, his dumb dog was constantly underfoot.

The whole situation was extremely weird and unpleasant, but the General couldn't know that. As far as the public was concerned, Cardiff and I were family.

"It's been strange having him home after he's been gone so long," I said, settling for a half truth, "but we're making it work."

"That's good." The General seemed genuinely pleased. "I was concerned it might be uncomfortable for you after what happened with your birth parents."

"What do you mean?" I said slowly. Andromeda's birth parents died in a car crash. There was no story behind it—unless, Thames didn't tell me the whole truth.

And if the General knew something I didn't, then my entire identity was about to collapse.

"I don't mean to be offensive." The General waved his hand, as if clearing the air between us. "I just worry about you now that Thames is gone. With

Mrs. Nolan still in America, you're here alone, and… that's a lot for a young woman to handle."

I looked down and pretended to fidget with my skirt. "I do miss him," I said, which was the biggest lie I'd ever told.

"We all do," the General murmured. "Listen, Andromeda. I know all of this has been extremely difficult for you, but I want you to know that you made the right decision by coming home with the Nolans. I know it took courage to leave your birth parents."

Leave my birth parents? Andromeda hadn't "left" her parents; they were dead. I'd always assumed the original Andromeda Nolan was an elite, living a life of luxury until her parents' untimely demise put her in the care of her aunt and uncle.

And yet, looking back at my time in Beijing, I realized that all of the Nolans' friends had acted like they knew I came from a containment camp. Thames and Cynthia had bragged about me for almost two years before bringing me home, and everyone I'd met had crooned about how "lucky" I was to have been "plucked from the trenches." They didn't know I was Philadelphia Smyrna, of course, but they were aware that I came from poverty.

Suddenly, I wondered if Thames hadn't lied about my past at all. What if his brother and sister-in-law were unassimilated? What if the "car crash" that killed them wasn't an accident? What if they died in a containment camp— just like my mother?

I clenched my fists.

The General didn't notice. "I'm worried about you," he said, sounding disgustingly truthful. "No child should have to witness that."

Witness what? I thought, my blood boiling. *My classmates getting shot for refusing to go to school? My father being beaten and confined to solitary every other month? My own mother bleeding out on our doorstep?*

The General sighed and folded his hands behind his back. "You shouldn't have had to grow up in those conditions. It angers me that there are parents who will make their children suffer for their crimes."

It wouldn't be a crime if you hadn't outlawed religion!

I stared at him, and all at once, I remembered why he was the enemy. Why I blew up that factory on Rott, why I agreed to be Blue Fire, why I was risking my life to throw this stupid party.

The United was wicked. They hated choice, they hated freedom, and they hated God. They censored the truth and glorified everything that was vile and ugly in the world. The government was evil, and I would not let this godless man destroy another family without a fight.

I opened my mouth—but movement caught my eye.

Jayde stood across the courtyard, watching. He shook his head.

I snapped my mouth shut as Jael's words flashed across my mind.

"He's not your enemy. He's your friend."

I took a deep breath and closed my eyes. *Holy Spirit, help me. Help me see him like You see him.*

The General mistook my silence. "I'm sorry, I know it's a painful subject. I'm just concerned about you."

I forced a gentle smile and turned to face him. "You don't need to be worried about me. Peng takes great care of me, and Mrs. Nolan will be joining us soon, after she takes care of some affairs in Boston."

"Excellent." He beamed. "So, you're staying, then?"

"Yes," I lied. "Beijing is my home."

"As it should be. If you ever need anything, please don't hesitate to tell me or my daughter. We know how difficult it can be to adjust after having grown up outside of society."

I shook my head. "I don't have to be defined by my past."

And neither do you.

The thought came like a breath on the wind, and for a brief moment, I saw it. An infinite reality beyond this one, all made possible by one choice. One turn in the right direction was all it would take—and it was possible, right here, right now. One word, one Holy Spirit moment in time, and the General could change forever.

Just like Nic.

I stared at the General, for once not seeing him, but what he could be— what this world could be.

The image faded when he turned to admire the pool. "This truly is fabulous." He gestured at the courtyard. "I'm amazed you pulled this off on such short notice. Is this really your first time hosting?"

I blinked as reality settled back into place like a layer of dust. "Yes, it is, but I must confess that Peng did most of the work."

He chuckled. "All effective leaders have good staff underneath them." He glanced over his shoulder at me. "You could be a formidable householder—or a councilwoman, if you put your mind to it."

I tried not to laugh. *I'd make a terrible politician.* "I don't know anything about politics."

He winked. "Come to the council chambers sometime, see for yourself. Tell them I sent you."

I accepted the offer with a smile. "I will."

22: PHILADELPHIA

The rest of the party went off without a hitch. My staff ran like a well-oiled machine and presented a feast fit for royalty. Asia was unusually agreeable and supported my every decision. Even Cardiff made himself useful, dazzling the guests with stories from deep space and keeping Frank out of my way (for the most part). As for me, I spent the evening herding servants, deferring compliments, and spending a copious amount of time discussing the weather.

It was usually obvious which guests had talked to Jael. They would observe me from across the room, judging me and determining their place in this war. As soon as I was relatively alone, they would slide up, glance around to make sure no one was listening, and then whisper the code phrase.

They were all elegantly subtle about it. All of them except Ms. Ivanova, that is.

She told me to call her Sofiya, a name far too delicate for the brash and commandeering woman. She said she was the warden of "the most profitable work camp in Russia," which seemed like a weird thing to announce in polite company, but she was certainly proud of it. I overheard her bragging about the numbers at least five times before the turn of the hour—partially because all her conversations could be heard at least three rooms away.

It was obvious why Jael had invited her, though. She clearly had a history with Asia, and it wasn't pleasant. The two nearly got into a cat fight when Sofiya walked in the door. Asia was appalled and screeched, *"What are you doing here?"* before abruptly remembering her manners. Sofiya decided manners were optional and cooed, *"Oh, and I thought the Nolans had taste."* She then launched into some conceited spiel about how her increased profits had earned her an invitation into high society before Jael gracefully separated them.

What was amusing was how unnerved Asia seemed by Sofiya's presence. She immediately pulled me into the other room and then proceeded to hover for the next hour, much to Jayde's frustration. Anytime Sofiya would get within earshot, Asia would steer me away and force me into a conversation with one of her friends. I was just beginning to worry that I'd have to spend the entire evening at her side when one of her father's aides finally called her away. And that's when Jael struck.

I saw her and Sofiya talking from across the courtyard. Jael leaned in and murmured in her ear. Sofiya jerked her head up in a motion so sharp she probably sprained her neck. She glared at me for a solid minute, making no attempt to be subtle, then stomped across the patio and shoved her way into my circle.

"It sure has been hot lately," she announced, brazenly interrupting my current conversation.

I winced; at least the two people I had been talking with were known allies. "Then perhaps it's time we had some rain." I demonstratively lowered my voice, hoping she would take the hint.

She didn't. "Excellent." She downed the rest of her glass in one gulp, handed it to a very bewildered guest, and grabbed my arm. "Come with me."

She dragged me towards the house. I looked helplessly over my shoulder at Jayde. He frowned and followed.

Sofiya hauled me down the hallway to the room where the General Secretary was reclining. "Introduce me to the man," she demanded, and pushed me through the door ahead of her.

I tripped into the room, halting the conversation. The General looked up. "Andromeda, I was just asking for you," he chuckled, benevolently helping me save face. He patted the spot on the couch next to him, a seat that had been deliberately left empty by the other guests.

I accepted the honor and approached him, Sofiya on my heel.

The General gave her a onceover. "Who's your friend?"

Sofiya stepped around me and introduced herself. "Warden Sofiya Ivanova." She shamelessly offered her hand.

The General took it, barely allowing their fingers to touch. "Your reputation precedes you," he admitted. "I heard your institution has been very efficient this quarter."

She deferred with a slight bow. "It is, in fact, one of your most profitable ventures, Your Excellency."

I arched an eyebrow, noting the change of possessive adjective. Up until a moment ago, it had been "her" factory.

The General pulled his hand back and propped his elbow on the arm of the couch. "I'd be curious to learn more about your methods. Why the sudden increase?"

"Oh, it's a *hilarious* story. You absolutely have to hear this." She snatched a full glass from the tray on the coffee table and flopped down in the chair next to him without being invited.

"Do tell," he intoned, expression less than amused.

I gingerly perched on the edge of the couch and hoped I hadn't made an irreparable social error by introducing them. Jayde took up station in the shadows by the door and watched.

Sofiya took a swig before continuing. "The truth is, Your Excellency, I can't take credit for any of it."

There was a collective murmur from the others in the room. I had to admit that surprised me too, if only because she'd had no problem taking credit for everything five minutes ago.

"I'll admit, we were struggling," Sofiya confessed, voice dripping with drama. "Profits were plummeting, and morale was at an all-time low. I swear there was a prison riot every week. I was considering turning in my resignation, it was so shameful."

I doubted that, and so did the General. He patronized her with a raised eyebrow.

"But then you won't *believe* what happened." She gestured at the entire room with her sloshing glass, as if inviting the bystanders into the story. They obliged and collectively moved closer like a noose cinching.

"One of the inmates approached me, and do you know what he says?" She leaned forward and made eye contact with the crowd. "He tells me he can increase my productivity by fifty percent in thirty days, and it won't cost me a penny."

"Sounds like a scam," a businessman muttered.

Sofiya cackled. "That's what I said, but he was determined. He was so convinced that he could save the factory that he challenged me to a bet: If profits didn't double in thirty days, I could kill him."

It was such a heartless declaration that it rendered the room speechless. Even the General just blinked, as if he didn't know what to do with such gross social ineptitude.

I scrambled for a way to divert the conversation. *Holy Spirit, what do I do?*

One of the other guests finally recovered from the shock. "You didn't accept, did you?" she squeaked.

Sofiya just winked.

The businessman set his glass down with a mortified *clink*. "What happened? Surely it didn't work."

Jael silently slid into the room and joined the back of the crowd.

"Well, I'm enjoying tripled profits, and he's still breathing, so..." Sofiya twinkled her fingers in the air.

"That's insane," the General grunted.

"Utterly," she agreed. "But the numbers don't lie. He reconfigured my assembly line and restructured the workers' schedule, and profits practically doubled overnight. We're operating at over ninety percent efficiency and saving at least ten grand in resources every month." She glanced at me. "You should hire him to oversee your investments, Andromeda, now that you've inherited the estate."

I winced. Thames Nolan's abrupt demise was not a topic I'd planned on bringing up at this party.

The General intercepted for me. "I'm sure Andromeda has an excellent board of advisors."

Jael stepped forward and salvaged the conversation. "I might have a job for this miracle worker. You said he's an inmate? How did he end up in your institution?"

"That's the unfortunate part." Sofiya gazed into her glass. "I pulled his file, and he has absolutely no criminal history. No record of noncompliance. He's been a loyal, productive citizen his entire life—until he was walking home from work one night and got caught up in one of those 'thunderbird' riots."

I gasped, and too late realized I'd pulled the center of attention to myself. Jael shot me a glare.

"That's so sad," I fumbled, and avoided looking at the General.

"It really is," Sofiya agreed. "I have no reason to believe he ever intended to cause trouble—I mean, a real criminal wouldn't care about the government's profit margin, would they? He even turned himself in when officers arrived."

I struggled to keep my feelings in, knowing full well the grief and shame were burning on my face. *I did this. I put that innocent man in jail.*

Sofiya laid the guilt on thick, her eyes cruelly locked with mine. "It was just a matter of being in the wrong place at the wrong time."

I looked down at my lap. *I'm so sorry.*

"Well, now." The General shifted beside me. "That seems like an easy problem to fix."

I lifted my head.

"The whole purpose of the justice system is to help people assimilate back into society," he recited, soliciting a murmur of agreement from the crowd. "After all, people don't have to be defined by their past, do they, Andromeda?" He turned to me.

I sat up straight. "No, sir."

He smiled, crow's feet wrinkled with affection. "Well, what do you think? Should we give this young man a second chance?"

"Yes!" I exclaimed, too quickly.

He chuckled. "Then it's done."

The group whispered. I looked around and realized they were regarding me like I was an adorable puppy performing tricks in exchange for treats.

I blushed, suddenly second guessing my behavior. I glanced at Jael for reassurance.

She grinned.

"You can handle the paperwork, yes?" The General nodded at Sofiya.

"Of course. Thank you, Your Excellency, this makes me so happy," she praised, for the first time that night sounding completely sober.

He waved dismissively. "Have Asia review it. She has my authorizations."

If only you knew, I thought to myself.

"Wonderful. Let's get it taken care of, Andromeda." Sofiya stood up and yanked me off the couch before I could object. "Don't worry, I'll bring her right back," she promised as she hauled me out of the room.

The General winked.

I struggled to stay on my own two feet as Sofiya barreled down the hall. "So, who is this guy, exactly?"

"I can't believe that actually worked," she crowed, completely avoiding the question. She halted in an abandoned vestibule and pulled out her phone. "Good thing I had his pardon pre-drafted."

"Wait, how long have you been planning this?" I demanded.

She ignored me. She swiped a few commands into her phone and then shoved it at me. "Give this to Asia, tell her to sign it. Do *not* tell her it's from me. If she asks what it is, just say the General is donating money to a project of yours."

I stared at the device and reconsidered the entire situation. "I—"

"Andromeda!" Asia screeched from around the corner.

"We never talked," Sofiya hissed, and darted out of sight into the next room.

Asia's heels popped on the tile as she stomped towards me. "What are you doing?"

"I just... I just came from the General." I quickly composed myself and held the phone out to her. "He wants you to sign this."

She took it. "What is it for?" she said with a healthy amount of skepticism.

I put on a sweet smile. "He's donating money to a little project of mine."

She frowned at me, and for a terrifying minute, I was sure she wouldn't believe me.

Then her bloodred lips parted in a murderous sneer. "Oh, isn't that just *wonderful.* How kind of him." She signed the file without reading it, then pressed her thumb to the screen. The device chirped.

She handed the phone back to me. "Is he still in the east wing?"

"Yes. I'll join you there in a minute—I just need to talk to the chef about dessert."

"Excellent." She swept down the hall, the grin still on her face.

Sofiya waited until she was gone before creepily reappearing at my elbow. "I have waited my entire life for that moment."

"Care to tell me what's going on?" I grumbled.

She didn't, apparently. "Well, I'm going to go deliver the good news. Pleasure doing business with you, Philadelphia." She snatched the phone from my hand and waltzed towards the foyer.

I cringed; thankfully, no one but Jayde was within earshot. "But I—"

She wasn't listening. "You can thank me later!" She waved her fingers over her shoulder and then let herself out before Peng could even make it to the door.

"You realized she used you, right?" Jayde muttered from behind me.

I folded my arms. "I'm aware."

He snorted. "You're so gullible."

I ignored him and watched out the window as Sofiya's cab pulled away from the curb. I could only pray I didn't just pardon a criminal mastermind.

23: NIC

I knew I was in trouble when Warden Ivanova came back early from her trip.

I was eating lunch with Ryan, Vance, and Bowen when she found me. "Von Nieuwenhuyse!" she bellowed across the cafeteria.

I glanced at the giant clock that was mounted on the wall. She wasn't supposed to be back until Tuesday, which meant she was a full three days early. And, presuming the train was running on schedule, she'd just disembarked an hour ago. That meant the first thing she'd done after getting off the elevator was yell at me.

That couldn't be a good sign.

"Nieuwenhuyse!" she shouted again. She stood at the railing three floors up, giving her the perfect vantage point to project her voice with maximum efficiency. "My office! Now!"

Her screech ricocheted around the cafeteria. The entire room silenced and looked at me.

Ryan stood up on the bench to survey the crowd. "Wow, the acoustics in here are amazing! We should definitely organize the next riot in here."

Vance grabbed his shirt and pulled him back down. "You, sir, are not allowed to organize any more riots without the express permission of the warden."

"She said she might let me do one in October!"

The warden had even less patience than usual. "Von! Don't make me come down there!"

I swung my legs over the bench and stood up. "Well, gentlemen, I think this is goodbye forever."

"Oh right." Ryan picked up his spoon and resumed shoveling gruel into his mouth. "Can you see if she'll hold off on the execution until 2:30pm? I've got a meeting with my floor managers after this that I can't miss. If you can get her to move it, Vance and I will definitely be there for you."

Vance checked his calendar on his communicator. "I can't do 2:30pm. 3pm would be ideal."

"I could make 3pm work," Ryan consented. "Bowen, you're free all afternoon, right?"

"I-I…" Bowen stuttered. He'd been doing a lot better over the past few days, but he still hadn't assimilated to Vance and Ryan's existence. "You write my schedule."

"Oh, good point." Ryan gestured at me with his spoon. "Make it 3pm, and we'll all be there to support you."

I saw guards moving in my direction and figured I'd better start walking. "I'll do my best, but I don't think she's in a waiting mood today."

I hurried to her office, flanked by an unnecessary entourage of guards. She was standing in front of her desk, tapping her boot impatiently, which I found highly unnerving. She wasn't normally this eager to see me.

I halted inside the door. "I didn't do it."

She stopped tapping. "Do what?"

"The equipment fire. It wasn't me, I swear."

She scowled. "What equipment fire?"

"The one on Level 56. I'll have you know, I was on Level 32 when it happened, so I had absolutely nothing to do with it. However, if you want my opinion, I think the autoregulator on the interdimensional plasma fabricator is off again and needs to be replaced."

She shot a glare at the guard standing next to her. He cleared his throat. "It was on our agenda to discuss, ma'am."

She shook her head. "Never mind. I've got more important things to deal with. You, thumbprint." She thrust a tablet at me.

I stumbled forward and took it. "Since when did you need my consent for anything?"

She snorted. "It's a form stating that you acknowledge your crimes, recognize the justness of the government's ruling, and will not commit a repeat offense."

I held the tablet back out. "Yeah no, I can't sign that in good conscience."

"Well, it's either that, or your pardon is null and void."

I dropped the device. Thankfully, it had a protective case on it. "What?"

She grinned maniacally. "You're going home."

I blinked. When she didn't recant her statement, I ventured, "I thought you couldn't pardon me."

"I didn't. Asia did." She kicked the tablet towards me.

Picking it up, I scrolled down the screen and saw a signature I knew all too well:

MONG SHI MIN TAI

I stared at the document as the Holy Spirit made His presence known. I looked up to see Him standing in the corner, smirking.

Wait and see the salvation of the Lord.

"Thank you," I said to Him after I'd collected enough of my wits to formulate a sentence. I turned to the warden. "I'm assuming there's an epic story behind this."

She folded her arms and leaned against the desk. "Andromeda Nolan sends her regards."

I froze. If Philadelphia had returned to the Nolan estate, that meant something had gone very, very wrong—or very, very right. "Well, that creates more questions than it answers."

The warden shrugged. "All I know is that she's posing as a Nolan. She's working with a woman named Jael, and they put on one killer party. Even the General Secretary came."

I stared into the void as all the dreams and visions I'd had about Philadelphia flashed across my mind in one terrific blur.

"I saw it all. You, in Beijing, as a Nolan, on even playing ground with Asia."

I glanced at the Holy Spirit. He gave me an *I-told-you-so* look. Well, it wasn't so much a look as it was a general conviction that I should have spent a lot less time panicking and a lot more time trusting and praying over the last month.

"I don't know what trickery Phil pulled," the warden continued, oblivious to the conversation going on over her head, "but the General *loves* her. I think he would have given her half the kingdom if she'd asked. All I did was make up some sob story about the poor, falsely accused prisoner who helped save my factory, and he pardoned you just to see her smile."

"I take it you didn't mention my name."

"He didn't ask."

I tried to imagine how that conversation had gone down. I could believe the General was that gullible; men will do immeasurably stupid things to please a woman, speaking from experience. I did not, however, believe Asia was that gullible. "And how'd you convince Asia to sign it? She knows who you are."

The warden cackled. "She didn't even read it. Phil told her that the General was donating money to a project of hers, and Asia signed it without looking."

I studied Asia's ornate signature. It wasn't like her to be this careless, which either meant she had an ulterior motive, or she'd been blinded by the Holy Spirit.

Both, He answered, *both is good.*

"How long's it take you to sign a form?" the warden chided. "The train leaves in two hours. If you're not on it, you'll have to wait three days for the next one. Hurry and pack your things."

I swiped my signature on the tablet and handed it back to her. "The fact that you think I have something to pack is mildly offensive."

"Then go say your goodbyes. You have twenty minutes to be on that elevator." She sat down behind the desk and returned to her computer.

I stared at her, struggling to close the book on one of the most bizarre chapters of my life. "Thank you."

She winked. I turned and headed for the door.

"Oh, and Dr. Nic?"

I glanced back.

She grinned like a crocodile. "Tell Blue Fire: I'm *so* in."

✳

After fielding several congratulations, farewells, and high fives from the guards, I hurried back to the cafeteria. As soon as he saw me, Ryan waved both arms above his head like he was an air marshal signaling my landing.

"Hey, you're still alive! Did you convince her to move it to 3pm?"

I stopped at the table. "No, I… I'm here to say goodbye."

He deflated like a popped balloon. "Aww, buddy, I'm so sorry. What did you do?"

I put my hands up. "No, I mean, I'm being released. I'm going home."

All three of them stopped and stared at me.

Ryan was the first to reboot. "Now I *really* need to know what you did."

There was no way I was going to attempt to explain the warden's story, which I only partially believed myself, so I summarized. "Philadelphia arranged my pardon."

Vance smirked, as if he'd seen this coming all along.

"So, she's safe?" Bowen demanded.

If Phil really had resumed her identity as Andromeda Nolan, she was less safe than ever, but he didn't need to know that. "She's fine. She and Jael are still heading the operation."

He let out his breath, releasing a thousand pounds of guilt with it.

"Go Team Blue Fire!" Ryan whooped. "When do you leave?"

"Now." I glanced at the clock. "I have to make the next train."

Ryan whined and thumped his fist on the table. "But I was almost done planning your going away party! I'm just waiting for the balloons to come in. They were backordered."

I'd spent enough time with him to know that he was being completely serious. "You've been planning a party?"

"I knew God was going to free you sooner or later," Vance explained, "so I advised him to plan ahead."

I stared at him, feeling mortally ashamed that Vance, of all people, had had more faith in my release than I did.

"Well, I guess I'll just reuse the decorations for the warden's birthday party. We're going to miss you, buddy." Ryan climbed up on the table and stepped over our trays to give me an unsolicited hug.

I resisted the urge to pry him off and drop him on the floor; I owed him this one. "I'll miss you, too." It was mostly the truth.

Vance walked over and clapped me on the shoulder. "Don't forget us."

I met his gaze. "I won't," I said, and realized, much to my chagrin, that the statement made me sad.

A guard jogged up to the table. "Dr. Nic! We need to leave."

I separated myself from Ryan and handed him back to Vance. Bowen stood up. "Tell Phil I'm sorry."

We made a brave attempt at a manly slap-on-the-back hug. "She forgives you," I said as I pulled away and restored my personal space. "When this is all over, she'll get you pardoned."

Such an optimistic word: "when." And for the first time in a long time, I believed it.

He smiled, but the gesture was agonizing. "Tell her not to worry about me. But if she can do something for my aunt and uncle…"

"She'll find them," I promised. "She'll bring you all home."

Home to what? I remembered with a punch to the gut. The Tang family was ruined. Their factory was destroyed, their home was burned to ash, and their reputation was tarnished. Even if Phil did bail them out, they'd be homeless and penniless.

Unless…

I remembered the other vision God had sent me—the one about Bowen and Warden Ivanova presiding over a board meeting—and realized this was one problem I *could* fix.

I gestured at the guard. "Call Warden Ivanova."

He squinted but reached for his communicator.

"Ask her if she'd like to manufacture something far more profitable than powercells."

The guard stopped with his finger on the screen. "Pretty sure the answer to that question is yes."

Bowen frowned at me.

I smiled. "Tell her I know someone who holds the patent to an interstellar space station part—and he's looking for a new supplier."

24: PHILADELPHIA

For the sixth day in a row, Frank woke me up.

The rattling at the door ripped into my dreams like a toddler shredding wrapping paper. I moaned and rolled over, fighting to hold on to either consciousness or sleep, but both eluded me. Darkness and light competed like I was caught at the bottom of a whirlpool, unable to pick myself up. The room swam, my joints were swollen, and the only thing I was confident of was that I had a massive headache.

"Go away," I snarled.

He didn't.

I forced myself to sit up—and that's when I realized it was pitch black outside.

The breeze from my open balcony door fluttered the curtains, revealing the moon high overhead. I swiped on my tablet screen and checked the clock: 4:32am.

I groaned. It was way too early for me to be up. Besides the fact that this was an obscene hour of the night, I'd only been asleep for about four hours— and that was bad news considering I'd taken my medication the night before.

The last two days had been a whirlwind, even more exhausting than the party itself. As Jael had predicted, I'd been invited to at least a dozen other functions before the night was out as my guests vied to secure their position in my social circle. Jayde had forwarded all the invitations to Jael, who told me what to accept—starting with breakfast with the owner of a bank the following morning.

So, before the decorations were even cleaned up, I dragged myself out of bed, put on a fresh layer of makeup, and started the game all over again. I had three engagements on Saturday, which led to four more on Sunday. I visited a factory, toured one of the capitol buildings, and ate every meal with someone important. I was grateful Peng was managing my calendar, or I wouldn't have survived past Saturday afternoon.

I knew each visit was forging a link in my network, even though most of the politics happened behind my back. At almost every event, Jael or one of her friends "just so happened" to be there. I would trade handshakes and pleasantries while my allies forged contracts in the shadows. It was weird to think that a war was being waged when all I was doing was smiling and looking pretty, but I trusted Jael. So, I went where she told me, wore what Narissa sent me, and said what the Holy Spirit gave me as I fraternized with the most powerful people in the world.

Asia haunted me as much as she could, following me around and appearing even when she wasn't invited. She tried to commandeer my calendar, insisting I accept her friends' invites over others. She even went so far as to sign me up for a Sunday night dinner without asking. I wanted to tell her off—mainly because I couldn't stand the thought of another social engagement—but Jael encouraged me to go.

I swapped outfits yet again and became the daughter Asia needed me to be—demure and overwhelmed. I pretended to be starstruck by all the wealth as her cohorts swarmed around me like flies, crooning about how "precious" and "adorable" I was. I loathed every minute, but I knew the phone in my pocket was doing the work as it recorded conversations and scalped text messages, compiling evidence against Asia.

Jayde said we were close. What that meant, I didn't know. Operation day was on Thursday. Under Jael's orders, I hadn't been online or looked at the traction on any of my videos, but I knew the movement was reaching a breaking point. Fear gripped Beijing as even assimilated civilians began to realize violence was imminent. Schools and businesses announced closures for Thursday while people boarded up windows and barricaded apartments.

It broke my heart to think that innocent people were afraid of us. Operation Blue Fire was never supposed to be a violent demonstration. But if I didn't expose Asia, it would be.

And I had less than three days to bring her down.

With every hour that passed, I felt the panic closing in like a gathering shadow, but I would not move until Jael ordered me to. So, I let Asia's friends fawn over me like I was some caged parrot and gleefully accepted all their invitations for the following week. I didn't get home until after eleven on Sunday and didn't take my medication until nearly midnight.

That meant I absolutely, positively should not be up before seven. If I didn't get a full night's sleep, I'd be a wreck all day, and I couldn't afford that.

I heard movement in the hall. "Get lost, Frank!" I yelled.

A nervous voice answered me. "Actually, it's Peng, miss."

I struggled to recalibrate. I had no preset for being woken up in the dead of night by my houseman. "What do you need?"

"I'm sorry, miss, but it's important," he stuttered, which didn't at all answer the question.

What could be so important at 4:30 in the morning? I grunted and climbed out of bed—or tried to. My stiff muscles and groggy nerves got the better of me, and I tumbled to the floor. Now I had an aching shoulder on top of being in the worst mood ever.

Snatching my robe off the chair, I limped over to the door and threw it open. "What?" I snapped, cramming all my displeasure into one syllable.

He took a healthy step back. "There's someone here to see you."

I squinted at him and began to wonder if I was still dreaming. "And you let them in? Tell them to go away! What do I pay you for?"

Peng started to respond, but someone else spoke first. "Watch your attitude, young lady," a familiar voice called from downstairs.

The drowsiness evaporated from my mind. *No, it can't be.* I shoved past Peng and ran to the top of the stairs.

Nic stood in the foyer, grinning.

I stared at him, for one terrified minute convinced the medication was playing tricks on me.

Then he arched his eyebrow in that bemused gesture I had missed so much. "He said it was important."

"Nic!" I screeched, all my joy and disbelief and elation colliding.

I hurtled down the steps and practically fell into his arms. "It's you," I gasped. It was a stupid thing to say, but I had to be sure. I had to be sure it was really him, here, alive.

He braced himself on the railing. "The one and only," he replied, the sarcasm in his voice as comforting as a warm blanket.

I grabbed him and gripped his shirt with both fists, trembling as the world crashed and restarted. I knew I'd get scolded for giving him a hug, but I didn't care. I wasn't about to let go.

The reprimand never came. Instead, he did the unthinkable: He hugged me back.

Well, "hug" was a generous term for the amount of physical contact he was giving. But he did wrap one arm around my shoulder and lean over to whisper in my ear. "Phil," was all he said, and that was all he needed to say.

I buried my face in his chest and burst into warm, happy tears. "Oh God, You brought him back!" I cried. "You brought him back!"

Nic tightened his grip and muttered three words I never expected to hear from him. "Thank you, Jesus."

I pulled away. "Wait, are you...?"

"Did I kiss and make up with the Voice in my head?" Nic shed his jacket and held it out to Peng, who stood petrified at the foot of the stairs like a coatrack. "I didn't really have a choice after He spawned me back in."

I wasn't sure which excited me more: the fact that Nic was home, or the fact that He'd come back to God. I didn't know whether to shout for joy, cry from relief, or ask a million questions. Instead, I just got really overwhelmed and sobbed even harder.

"Maybe we should take this one step at a time," Nic suggested. "Got any coffee?"

Peng roused himself. "I'll put a pot on."

"No, I'll get it." I pulled myself together and wiped my eyes. I needed some time alone with Nic before the rest of the house woke up. "This way."

Nic followed me to the kitchen. I listened to the familiar *squeak* of his Oxfords behind me and struggled to push past the muddled emotions. *Nic is here. He's really here!*

I flicked on the light in the kitchen and finally managed to formulate a coherent question. "How did you get here?"

He settled on a stool at the island. "Heard you met Warden Ivanova."

I gasped as everything snapped into place. "*You* were the prisoner she was talking about!"

"What?" he scoffed. "Some crazy Russian lady concocts a story about a mysterious prisoner and you don't automatically assume it's me?"

"She said you were compliant…" "Innocent" and "compliant" were never words I'd use to describe Dr. Nic.

His eyebrow returned to its locked and loaded position. "It's called lying, sweetheart. Have I taught you nothing?"

I folded my arms. "In my defense, I'm not sure you ever actually *lied* to me. You just got really upset when I started opening random doors."

He smiled, as if it were a pleasant memory. In a way, it was.

Neither of us said anything as I hunted in the gigantic pantry for some coffee grounds. The dribble of liquid into the carafe was the only sound in the sleepy house. I filled our mugs, handed one over to him—and stopped.

"What?" he finally broke the silence.

I stared at the liquid rippling in my mug, thinking of all the times I'd refilled Nic's coffee on Mars. Of the time his father gave me my first cup. Of the time my brother laughed at me because I took my coffee the way Nic took his, black as dirt. Of the time I got us coffee while we were running across Beijing, when we sat in the park and stole a moment of peace.

Nic set his mug on the counter. "Phil."

I looked up. "I missed you."

He met my gaze and said exactly what I needed to hear. "I missed you, too."

I blurted the next most important thing. "I'm so sorry."

"It's not your—" He stopped, as if realizing that *wasn't* what I needed to hear. He took a deep breath. "I forgive you."

The tears started all over again as a thousand broken things were made whole. I slammed my mug down and threw myself in his arms.

He caught me with a grunt. "You're going to milk this, aren't you?"

"For the rest of your life," I mumbled into his shoulder.

He patted my head awkwardly. "I guess I did sign up for this."

"You literally volunteered." I squeezed him for good measure, then stepped back. "Oh, I did get my chip removed." I showed him my right hand, not that you could tell it had ever contained a bomb.

"Thank you for establishing that *after* you hugged me—twice."

I blushed.

He picked up his mug. "So, did you figure out who tried to kill me? Was it just a happy accident, or...?"

I pulled up another barstool. "No. The chip contained two sets of DNA— yours and the General's."

Nic's mustache twitched as he considered that.

"It wasn't Data—the guy who programmed my chip," I clarified. "He bought the code off the black market. He tried to track the source, but... something about an evolving proxy chain."

I tried to remember what else Data had told me about the code, but I could barely string a thought together. The adrenaline was wearing off, bringing the effects of the sleep medication crashing back down on me. The world blurred as my head began to throb.

"Are you all right?" Nic asked.

"Still groggy," I mumbled. "You talk—tell me what happened."

He obliged, recounting the wildest story I had ever heard. It sounded like the lead-up to a bad joke—*a Mexican rebel, a German accountant, and a Martian scientist are all sentenced to the same prison*—except there was no punchline. Perhaps the craziest part was that Nic actually *had* saved the factory and doubled profits.

"Is Bowen going to be okay?" I stared at the bottom of my empty mug and tried to decide which of my dozen emotions was most relevant.

"Don't worry—the warden will treat him like royalty once she finds out how much that part is worth. He'll be fine until this is all over. On that subject..." Nic reached for the carafe, then changed his mind. He shoved his mug aside and leaned towards me, folding his arms on his knees. "What are *you* doing here, Andromeda?"

I closed my eyes and tried to gather my thoughts, but it was like trying to chase bats out of a dark attic. My half of the story was even more complicated—and it didn't have a happy ending. "Well..."

A slamming door and approaching footsteps interrupted me. Jayde stumbled into the kitchen, looking barely awake. He scratched his tousled hair as he glared blearily at his device. "What are you doing up so early?" he grunted. "You shouldn't be awake."

"Jayde…" I tried to warn him.

He looked up and spotted Nic. "Oh—"

The word he started to say wasn't nice, but he didn't get to finish it. Faster than anyone could react (least of all me), Nic had Jayde pinned to the floor on his back with his own gun aimed at his face.

It took everyone a full ten seconds to recalibrate. Jayde looked more perplexed than afraid. "How did you—"

Nic jabbed him in the chest with the weapon. "I ask the questions, punk. First question: What are you doing here? Follow-up question: How would you like to die?"

I grabbed Nic's shoulder and tried to haul him back. "Nic, stop, it's okay. He's with me."

Nic whirled on me. "He's *with* you? Oh no, don't tell me… You *forgave* him?"

I put my hands up. "Jael vetted him, it's fine."

"That's a cute way of putting it," Jayde muttered.

Nic used one hand to keep the gun in Jayde's face and the other to shake a finger at me. "I can't believe you just forgave him! Nope, never mind, poor choice of words. I *can* believe it, and I hate that."

"Sorry to disappoint," I sassed, "but a lot has happened. Which I would tell you if you'd put the gun down."

He didn't take the hint. "You can't just keep letting people off the hook like this, Phil."

"Yes, I can. That's kind of how Jesus works. Also, you're one to talk—I forgave you." I put my hands on my hips.

"She has a point," Jayde quipped. "Can I get up now?"

Nic kneed him in the ribs, his eyes still on me. "I think you had best start from the beginning."

I obeyed, explaining about the guns that had been donated to the underground and Asia's plot to undermine the operation and overthrow her father. About halfway through the story, Nic let Jayde up, but he kept the gun. He wandered over to the door and stared at the pool as the sun began to warm the sky. He refused to make eye contact with me until I finished talking.

"What are you thinking?" I prodded when he still didn't react.

"You want the literal answer?" he muttered, then didn't wait for an affirmative. "I'm livid that you had to go through all that without me."

Silence blanketed the kitchen except for the *tick, tick* of the ornamental clock.

"You're here now," I finally said.

He glanced back at me and almost smiled.

Jayde shifted uncomfortably on his barstool. "I hate to break up the moment..."

"Then don't," Nic snapped.

Jayde ignored him, even though I could see he was starting to sweat. "But we need to talk." The statement was directed at me.

Nic took a step forward. "She doesn't *have* to do anything as far as you're concerned."

Jayde held my gaze. "I think you should consider recording a video."

"What?" both Nic and I said at the same time.

"I think you need to go online and address the underground. The operation is in three days—they need a call to action. One that *isn't* prerecorded."

I didn't disagree, but it wasn't my call to make. "I'm not doing anything without Jael."

"Jael still hasn't contacted me." Jayde tapped the screen of his device, as if verifying that was still true. "If we don't have enough evidence to turn the Council against Asia, then we're going to have to do it ourselves. You need to warn the people that the government's coming and tell them to shoot first."

Nic looked ready to lunge, but I put up my hand to stop him. Jayde answered to me. "Jayde, I'm not telling a bunch of schoolkids and factory workers to open fire."

"Then why do we have weapons?" Jayde pointed at the gun Nic still had clenched in his hand. "Phil, it's now or never. We won't get another chance. You started this—you have to finish it."

I opened my mouth, but someone beat me to it. "Personally, I agree with the lad."

I whipped around. Cardiff loomed in the doorway, almost as if he had teleported in. I certainly hadn't heard him approach.

Nic was, of course, the first to react. He flicked the weapon on and aimed it at Cardiff's face. Jayde cursed and dived off the stool to get out of the line of fire.

Cardiff was unbothered. "Dr. Nic," he greeted, taking a sip from his inexplicable teacup. "Pleased to finally make your acquaintance."

"Nolan," Nic snarled, clearly not pleased to make anyone's acquaintance. "I thought you were dead!"

I glanced at Jayde. "Is that what I sound like when people randomly resurrect?"

He brushed himself off. "Yeah, kinda."

"Oh, my apologies, you're clearly confusing me with my father." Cardiff set his cup on its saucer and extended a hand to Nic. "Cardiff, the younger Mr. Nolan."

Nic didn't accept the handshake *or* lower the gun. "Nope, definitely still thought you were dead."

I reached for him. "Nic, put the gun down, please."

"Come now," Cardiff whined, "I think it makes introductions much more exciting."

"What are you doing here?" Nic demanded.

Cardiff shrugged. "I live here."

"Nic, turn the weapon off!"

He continued to ignore me. "Last I checked, Andromeda was the only name on the deed."

Cardiff's expression flatlined. "Trust me, I'm aware. But she's been very kind to let me stay in *my* rooms."

"Well then, take your British self back to bed, because this conversation doesn't involve you."

"On the contrary, as her 'brother,' I'm deeply involved." Cardiff slurped his tea pretentiously. "Certainly more so than you, doctor."

Nic took two whole steps forward and jabbed the weapon at Cardiff's chest. "Don't pull that card on me. She's already got one annoying older brother—I'm not putting up with two. I don't care what the paperwork says—"

I put myself between them. "Will you stop arguing about the paperwork! Nic, seriously, drop the gun."

He just leaned around me to get a clear shot at Cardiff. "And how much do you know about the operation, anyway? Give me one good reason why I—"

"Nic!" I yelled. "Gun! Now!"

He finally looked at me. I gave him the best glare I could conjure. With an incoherent mumble, he reached down to turn the weapon off.

"As we were saying," Cardiff continued seamlessly, "I agree with the lieutenant. The reward clearly outweighs the risk. I recommend you move forward with the operation."

I frowned at him, a little unnerved that he had an opinion on the whole ordeal. Of course, he knew I was Blue Fire; he was more involved with my alternate identity than I cared to admit. But he'd been off planet for years. How much did he really know about the operation? Whose side was he on?

Jayde didn't give me a chance to ask. "Just listen to him, Phil," he pleaded. "I know you respect Jael, but the people don't follow her. They follow you. You need to go online and rally everyone before it's too late."

"Precisely my thoughts," Cardiff concurred with a wave of his teacup.

I took a step back. "I'm not having this conversation with either of you," I insisted, and hoped my tone of voice was understood. "Nobody's doing anything until we talk to Jael. Now if you'll excuse me, Nic and I…"

I turned and realized Nic had gone completely silent. He was staring at the gun in his hand, face rigid.

"Nic…?" I ventured.

He jerked his head up and glared at Jayde. "Where did you get this gun?" he demanded.

Jayde put his hands up. "It was in one of the shipments Asia sent. Why?"

"Is this the powercell that came with it?" Nic tapped the charge bar.

"Of course. Why?" Jayde repeated.

"Were all the guns that were donated from the same manufacturer?"

Jayde glanced at me, as if I had any idea what was going on. "All the shipments I tracked were, yeah. Why's it matter?"

Nic tightened his grip on the weapon. He was shaking.

I stepped closer. "Nic? What's wrong?"

He drew a sharp breath and faced me. "We have a problem."

25: NIC

I stared at the cursed weapon in my hand. The world bled black and red as hopelessness and rage turned my mind into a hailstorm.

Oh yes, there was a very good reason why I had been sent to Russia. But I was too late to do anything about it.

"Nic?" Phil appeared beside me. "What's wrong?"

I took a deep breath and tried to put a cap on the hurricane. "We have a problem."

She stared at me with those wide, watery eyes. How I wished I wasn't about to destroy her world—not after I'd just put it back together.

The Voice in my head stirred. *Let Me help you.*

I faced the group and spoke slowly and clearly. "If you fire these guns, they will explode."

"What?" both Phil and Jayde exclaimed with equal amounts of horror and disbelief.

Cardiff slammed his teacup down on its saucer.

I carefully pried the casing off the side of the gun and showed them the powercell. "This brand of powercell has a faulty design. The conductive core reacts at high heat and melts, causing it to mix with the coolant. The result is extremely explosive."

Phil stood rigid as all the courage drained from her face.

"How do you know this?" Cardiff challenged.

I glanced at him. "We were manufacturing them in Russia. We realized there was a problem when all the batteries that had been subjected to high-voltage testing started detonating."

Jayde gripped the back of a barstool. "And an electric pistol shot…"

"Is the perfect amount of energy to set off the chain reaction," I finished for him. If the weapon was set on stun, it might take two or three shots to reach the needed temperature. If the weapon was set on kill, it would be nearly instantaneous.

A disgusting thought seized me. If I'd shot Jayde—which I'd strongly considered doing at least a dozen times in the last hour—I would have killed us all, including Philadelphia.

Jayde didn't give me time to wallow in that horrific universe. "How big of an explosion are we talking about?"

Phil answered before I could. "Enough to bring down a building."

We all turned to her. She stared at the floor, shivering, not seeming to realize she had spoken. When she finally looked up, her face was running with tears.

"Lanzhou," she whimpered.

Jayde swore.

"What?" I demanded.

"The factory..." Phil struggled to explain, her voice shaking as hard as she was. "There was an explosion, and we thought Asia had bombed us, but... Lanzhou. He-he'd taken one of the guns to defend us. There were shots, and... Oh God, *no.*" She broke off, muttering in tongues, and hid her face in her hands.

I watched her weep as I acknowledged the truth she was too afraid to say: Lanzhou would still be alive, and the factory would still be standing, if he hadn't fired that gun.

Cardiff set his teacup down on the counter. "Do you suppose Asia is aware these guns are defective?"

"She has to be," I insisted. If there was one thing I was confident of, it was my ex-girlfriend's ability to be cunningly evil. "It's a proprietary design, and the source company is a shell. She had them manufactured just for this purpose."

Phil sucked in a breath. "Didn't you say the Nolans owned the company that distributed the guns?" she asked Jayde.

He whipped out his phone and scrolled in a panic. Cardiff walked over, read the screen, and said something incredibly impolite, at least for a British person.

"It's true," Jayde admitted. "You and Cardiff own the majority of the shares—and it's made you a *lot* of money lately."

"You're welcome," I groused, even as I wondered if we'd be in a better situation had I *not* saved the factory and expedited production.

The Holy Spirit didn't move. *Trust Me.*

"There goes the family fortune," Cardiff muttered.

Phil wiped her face on her sleeve. "How many of these guns have we received?" she asked with a sniff.

Jayde hesitated a beat too long. "At least one hundred thousand, that I know about."

"We manufactured around a quarter million powercells," I added, "and that's assuming she doesn't have another supplier."

Phil winced; that wasn't the answer any of us wanted to hear. "Can we replace the powercells in the guns we have?"

"It's not that simple." Jayde pocketed his device. "It's a specialized part for a restricted weapon—you can't just buy them at the corner store. It's also not that easy to replace a powercell. It's a rechargeable battery; it's not meant to be removed. I could do it, because I have military training, but your average civilian isn't going to know what wire to cut."

I glared at him, only because I wished he wasn't right.

Phil closed her eyes. Her lips moved, but no sound came out. About thirty seconds too late, I realized I should join her.

And that's when the Holy Spirit moved, saturating the air until He was the only authority left in the room.

Phil tipped her chin back and squared her shoulders, as if she had to brace herself for what she was about to say. Then she opened her eyes and looked straight at Jayde. "We need to call it off."

"What?" It was Jayde and Cardiff's turn to react with equal measures of shock and anger.

"We need to call it off. We need to cancel Operation Blue Fire." She glanced at me, looking for support.

Jayde didn't give me the chance. "Phil!" he exclaimed, the name ripe with disgust. "You can't just 'cancel' the operation! We'll lose the war!"

"I concur—it's much too late to pull back," Cardiff moaned. "This is a preposterous idea."

"I didn't ask for your opinion." Phil silenced him with a glare before turning back to Jayde. "And we don't have a choice. If the underground uses those guns, we'll lose the war anyway."

"But—"

"Don't you see? Asia's not planning to track us down. She's planning to slaughter us."

No one argued with her, because there was nothing to debate. Anyone who used one of those guns would become a suicide bomber—and would take out everyone around them within a quarter-mile radius. Asia wouldn't even have to deploy the military.

Maybe that was the real reason the government's response had been so lax. Asia had already done the work.

I looked down at the weapon I still had in my hand. I rubbed the manufacturer label on the powercell, finally appreciating just how cruel my ex-girlfriend had been. I would have found out about the guns eventually; word would have gotten around once the weapons started blowing up in people's faces. By then, blood would have been spilled, and I would have rotted in prison with the knowledge that I'd indirectly helped massacre the underground—no doubt killing Philadelphia in the process.

I slammed the gun down on the counter.

Jayde took a deep breath but made no effort to temper his tone. "So, we recall the weapons, swap as many powercells as we can, and warn the people we know got shipments. We can't just call off—"

"And what about the people we don't know about?" Phil didn't raise her voice. She didn't need to. "Jayde, if even a hundred people use these guns—"

"It would be worth it to take Beijing," he snapped.

Almost anyone else would have agreed with him. Anyone but Philadelphia.

She stared at him, fresh tears brimming in her eyes. "If we use these guns, there won't *be* a Beijing."

No one said anything. She picked up the weapon and flipped it over in her hand. "You saw what it did to the factory—and that was just one shot. If there's a thousand explosions—never mind a *hundred* thousand—all across the city on the same day, it will reduce this province to rubble. We'll kill *millions* of innocent people."

I imagined apartment buildings falling, the subway caving in, crowded streets turned to bloodbaths, and realized she was right. If the underground used these weapons on operation day, it would wipe Beijing off the map.

"We might as well have used Red Rain," I murmured.

"Honestly," Cardiff grunted. He picked up his tea and resumed swirling it aggressively.

Jayde clenched his fists and looked ready to do something stupid. "They're not innocent, Phil."

To my surprise, Phil didn't argue. "Enough," she declared, setting the gun back on the counter. "I'm not having this conversation with you. I need to meet with Jael."

"But they're part of the problem! If they're supporting the system, they're the enemy."

He took an insolent step forward. I prepared to knock him down a peg, but Phil beat me to it. "I said enough," she repeated. Her whole body stiffened.

Jayde missed the warning signs. "No, you listen to me! This is war, and we have to do what it takes to win. Now you need to—"

"You are not in charge!"

Her shout silenced the room. Everyone froze. Even Cardiff held his teacup above its saucer, as if he were afraid to put it down and make a noise.

Phil collected herself. "You are not in charge anymore," she repeated. She lowered her voice, which was somehow even more damning. "I am Blue Fire, and I answer only to Jael."

Jayde bristled, and I began to very much regret not killing him thirty minutes ago.

Phil merely frowned. "I have made my decision, and I do not want to hear another word on it until I've talked to Jael. Furthermore, this is my house, and I will not tolerate any more disrespect. So, you can either do your job, or I can send you back to Jael and let you explain yourself to her."

The threat hung in the air like ice. I stared at her and realized that a lot had changed in the month-and-a-half I'd been gone—and some of it was for the better.

Jayde considered his options and wisely chose life. "Yes, ma'am," he mumbled, and pulled back.

"Thank you." Phil sagged, as if the fight had taken everything out of her. She rubbed her temples. "When am I supposed to meet Jael?"

Jayde checked his phone. "You're scheduled to tour one of her facilities this afternoon and then have dinner with her."

"Move it up. I need to speak with her as soon as possible." Phil walked around the island and searched in the cabinets for a glass.

"With all due respect," Jayde said, for once in his life sounding like he actually had some, "I don't think that's wise. If you cancel your other appointments and move up your meeting with Jael, Asia will be suspicious."

Phil scowled, but she didn't argue. "Fine. But contact Jael and tell her what we know—the facts only—so she's prepared." She filled the glass at the sink and gulped it down with a grimace.

Jayde was already typing with his thumbs. "That said, I think you should skip your breakfast appointment."

She glanced up at him.

He met her gaze. "You should go back to bed."

I didn't like the look he was giving her; it said he knew something I didn't.

Although, in his defense, Phil did look awful. If it had been under any other circumstances, I would have regretted waking her up at the bewitching hour of 4:30am.

"But you're supposed to have breakfast with Asia," Cardiff complained.

"All the more reason to cancel it," Jayde argued, and for once, I was in total agreement.

"But she'll be here in less than an hour." Cardiff withdrew a pocket watch from the folds of his house robe, as if he couldn't get any more ostentatiously annoying. "She's going to expect you to be ready."

Now *this* was a problem I could solve. "Oh, you need someone to tell Asia off?" I chirped. "I volunteer as tribute."

Phil didn't share my enthusiasm. "Nic, no, when she finds out you've escaped, she'll—"

"Throw a hissy fit and start hurling empty threats? Yes, I'm quite looking forward to it."

"Nic!" she objected, and then winced, as if her own voice were giving her a headache.

I lowered my volume to help her out. "Stop worrying, Phil, I'll be perfectly safe. She can't do anything as long as Andromeda Nolan is in good standing with the General. Just let me have this one. I feel like I've earned it after spending six weeks in a Russian freezer."

She eyed me, as if debating whether or not I could be trusted with such power. "Okay, but show some discretion. Asia doesn't know we suspect her—she can't even know that you've discovered the fault in the powercells."

I threw a salute. "Don't worry, I know how to keep a secret. I kept your brother 'dead' for two years, remember."

She rolled her eyes, but I saw the tiniest sparkle of a smile in them. She refilled her water and walked towards the door. "Send a maid to wake me up at ten. And I don't care what you have to do, but do *not* let Asia disturb me. And keep Frank away from my room."

The last bit was directed at Cardiff with a glare. "It's not my fault he loves you," he whined.

"Who's Frank?" I demanded. *If she picked up another boyfriend, I will shoot him, exploding powercell or not.*

She either didn't hear me or chose to ignore me. "And Jayde?" she called over her shoulder.

He tensed.

"Get your gun fixed."

He nodded. "Yes, ma'am."

I still didn't love the idea of him having a weapon, but given the circumstances, I suppose at least one of us needed to be carrying.

We all waited until Phil was out of sight before resuming our lives. "Wow, did you see that?" I gestured down the hall where she had gone. "She handled both of you with perfect grace."

Jayde scowled. "I've got calls to make," he grunted, and then stormed out onto the patio.

"As do I," Cardiff added. "It was a pleasure finally meeting you face-to-face, doctor." He gave a curt little bow and waltzed out of the kitchen like some unseen director had told him to clear the stage.

"The feeling's not mutual," I muttered. I didn't like him, although the bar was set really low in that department. In theory, he was no more a threat than Mrs. Nolan was, and he had ample incentive to stay quiet. But he was deadweight, and Phil didn't need any more conflicting voices in her life. I was sure Jayde had provided more than enough unsolicited commentary over the past few weeks.

Peng rapped on the doorframe, interrupting my stewing. "May I show you to your rooms, doctor?"

I decided I'd better stop plotting Jayde's murder and focus on one enemy at a time. "Please. When is Asia supposed to be here?"

He checked his watch. "If she's running on schedule, she'll be here on the hour. Mind if I observe?"

"Please do," I encouraged. "The more people who witness her epic downfall, the better."

He showed me to a suite on the second floor that was, thankfully, only a few doors down from Philadelphia's. I took ten minutes to cull my hair and return my mustache to its former glory. Then I refilled my coffee cup and staged myself dramatically in the foyer. Peng and half of the staff gathered to watch.

Asia didn't arrive until almost fifteen minutes past the hour. She bustled in without knocking. "Andromeda!" she screeched, not looking up from her device. "We're going to be late!"

"And whose fault is that?" I chided.

She screamed—an immensely satisfying shriek of pure terror—and dropped her device. Of course, she was too perfect to put a case on her phone, so it shattered immediately.

Peng gave us ten seconds to savor the moment before he stepped forward. "Allow me to clean that up."

Asia gaped at me, apparently unable to breathe.

I took a slow sip of coffee. "Good morning, sweetheart."

She gripped the door handle. "You... you..." Suddenly, her anger returned like a lightning strike, chasing the panic out of her expression. "What are you doing here?"

"Enjoying my first day of freedom. Why? What's on your calendar?"

"But how—"

"If I had better manners, I would thank you." I let the silence hang just long enough for the sarcasm to ripen. "That was such a nice thing you did for Andromeda. Too little too late, if you ask me, but still, the gesture was appreciated."

She finally caught on that she was the brunt of a joke. "What did you do?" she slurred. She sounded like the demon from a B-rated movie.

"That's the beauty of it, *Min*," I taunted. "I didn't do anything. You're the one who signed the pardon."

"I didn't—"

"You didn't? Well, then you might be the victim of identity theft." I scratched my mustache. "It was your signature and thumbprint on the paperwork."

I watched the blood drain from her face and smiled. I had been waiting nearly ten years for this moment, and it was everything I hoped it would be.

I returned to my coffee and gave her a minute to cycle through all the requisite emotions. She eventually rotated back around to anger, but her voice was more squeaky than threatening. "You tricked me!"

I rolled my eyes. "I wasn't even there. And don't go blaming Andromeda—she was clueless, bless her heart."

She growled and stood on her toes, fluffing herself up like a little frilled lizard. "You won't get away with this!"

I pinched the bridge of my nose. "Seriously, I'm going to need you to stop looking at the bad guy Tumblr for your one-liners. You're a highly educated woman—this is embarrassing."

She didn't take my advice. "I'll have you killed!"

"Go ahead."

She jerked.

I blew on my coffee cup. "Knock yourself out. I can't *wait* to see how you explain yourself when Andromeda goes crying to the General that you killed her favorite person."

"He doesn't care about you," she sneered.

"Of course not. He might wonder who signed my pardon, though."

She choked on her next threat.

"I'd say you should have read the fine print, but that wasn't even the fine print. My name was in big, bold letters at the top."

She tried pitifully several times to form a word, like an engine failing to ignite.

I set my empty coffee cup on the credenza. "Tell you what, I'll make you a deal. I'll stay here and keep my mouth shut so you don't get executed for your laziness, and you go away."

I strode towards her. She stumbled back out onto the front step. "But— Andromeda and I have a breakfast appointment."

"Oh, didn't I tell you? She's cancelling. She wasn't feeling well—on account of me waking her up in the middle of the night and all." I grabbed the door and blocked the way. "I'll have her secretary let you know when she's free."

"But you can't—"

"*She* can. You have no authority here."

It was only after the words left my mouth that I realized they were true in more ways than one.

Asia tipped her chin back and stared at me, for once having the decency to look afraid.

I leered over her. "I just want you to remember one thing, sweetheart."

She glowered.

I smiled. "You could have prevented all of this."

And then I slammed the door in her face.

26: PHILADELPHIA

Jael's Beijing headquarters was a gorgeous and imposing building—not unlike the woman herself. The skyscraper was at least fifty stories tall. Its asymmetrical floors were staggered, making the whole building curve like a human spine. The endless windows flashed in the dying sun, while a giant digital sign cycled through the company name in a dozen different languages.

Jael didn't join us for the tour, which was just as well; I wasn't sure I could have kept the emotion off my face. Nic and I followed an excited staffer around as we visited massive server rooms that glittered like caves of diamonds. But even more impressive was the control panel for the algorithm. It was a behemoth piece of equipment, not unlike the original computers of the pre-2000s.

I stared at the thrumming machine. This program had ruined so many lives, including my own. Now, it might be our only hope of saving millions.

Finally, the staffer led us to the top floor of the building—a floor that didn't exist, according to the elevator. The windowless space was lined with rows of servers, no doubt the ones that held all the incriminating data for my revolution. A guard took our electronics and locked them in a case with a dampening field. Even "Blue Fire" couldn't be too careful in the room that contained the secrets of war.

Jael was waiting in a meeting area off to the side. She rose when we entered. She approached me without greeting and dropped something small and sharp into my hand.

I looked down at it: It was the remnant of a powercell. Only the first letter of the company logo was still legible; the rest of the fragment was charred and pitted.

"So, it's true," I whispered. I'd believed Nic, of course, but some part of my soul had clung to a shred of hope. Maybe there had been a miscommunication; maybe only some of the powercells were defective. Maybe there was still another way out.

She nodded. "I tested it myself."

I pinched my eyes shut. *Then there's only one thing we can do.*

Jael turned to Nic and offered her hand. "Glad to have you back. I only wish you had brought us better news."

He accepted the handshake. "I only wish I had gotten here sooner."

"I'm not sure it would have mattered," Jael said in a tone too bitter to be consoling. She faced me again. "I've spoken with General Jin and Warden Ivanova. I have reason to believe all the guns we received from our mysterious donor are defective."

I swallowed and tried to gather the courage to say what needed to be said.

She kept talking before I found it. "Unfortunately, it gets worse. I reached out to Data and was informed that several outposts in Boston also received munitions. Different company, but... I'm having him run some tests."

I clenched the fragment in my fist. It was one thing to set fire to Beijing, but now Asia was trying to destroy my hometown, too? What if she sent these guns to our allies all across the world?

Nic had the same thought. "Do you suppose any of our other friends have received a 'donation'?"

"I'll make some calls, but my guess is she concentrated her efforts around Beijing and Washington. It will be much easier for her to restructure the United if she destroys both seats of government."

Jael tapped a tablet that was sitting on the coffee table. The screen brightened, and a small hologram projected from the surface. It was a map of the world, speckled with dots—the sites of known demonstrations for operation day. Most of the dots around Beijing and Boston were red, making the world look like it had been stabbed in the chest twice.

It all made wicked sense, and I briefly wondered why Asia *wasn't* using Red Rain. If her plan all along had been to wipe cities off the map, Red Rain would have left no survivors. It had been within her power; she could have scalped the formula from my father's broken brain months ago, and manufacturing the acid would have surely been quicker than planting the defective powercells. The only benefit to using the guns was that the resistance—and, by extension, her father—would be blamed for the destruction.

I suppose that was reason enough.

"General Jin is recalling all the weapons within his regiment." Jael gestured at the projection, as if she could just wipe the red away with her hand. "We're working to track down as many shipments as possible."

"And what about the guns we can't track?" I asked. "You said yourself— even if we could find all the original shipments, people have already distributed the weapons among their friends. Those guns are all over the city." I searched her face, begging her to contradict me, to provide a different explanation, to conjure another solution.

She hesitated, and I had my answer. There was only one choice.

Sliding the powercell fragment in my pocket, I took a deep breath. *Jesus, help me save this city.*

"I'm hopeful we can recall most of the guns," Jael continued without optimism. "We have two days before Operation Blue Fire launches. If we can pull most of the weapons—"

"It won't be enough."

She stopped. I glanced at Nic.

He nodded.

Courage finally flooded me. I straightened and raised my voice. "Recalling the weapons won't be enough. We have to cancel the operation."

She didn't even hesitate, making me wonder if she'd already considered the possibility. "That's out of the question. First of all, launch time is in less than 72 hours. It would be impossible to pull people back."

"Not for me, it isn't," I argued. "You said yourself—they follow me. If I go online and warn everyone, they'll listen."

"They absolutely will—and that's exactly why I can't let you do it." Jael sighed, her voice soaked with condescension. "Philadelphia, this isn't just about Beijing or Washington. This is a global movement. We have managed to galvanize resistance in every sector of the world. If we strike together, the government will not be able to maintain control."

Jayde's voice haunted me. *"If we all stand up together, they can't make us all sit down."*

"We will not be able to organize that level of resistance again," Jael continued. "Even you would not be able to rally the people a second time."

I didn't fully believe that, but that wasn't what I was afraid of. "We won't *have* any people left if we use those guns. You saw what it did to the Tangs' factory—imagine a hundred, a thousand explosions like that across the city."

"I'm fully aware of the situation we are in," Jael returned. "That's why we're going to recall as many guns as possible."

"And then what? Leave those groups defenseless?" I stepped forward and pointed at the red blur on the map that represented Beijing. "They're not going to be able to find enough replacement weapons in two days. If we recall the guns, Asia will simply send the military to slaughter them. She still knows where everyone is."

"She's right," Nic spoke from where he hovered on the sidelines. He leaned against the wall, arms folded, observing. "Either way, you lose Beijing."

"I'm willing to sacrifice Beijing if it means winning the war," Jael returned, the words cool, slicing. "We need the global momentum of operation day to break the system. If we can disrupt the government's network of control, we can form regions of independence and fortify ourselves. We'll take Beijing later by force if need-be."

I didn't like the sound of that, but I struggled not to get lost in a hypothetical reality. "And in the meantime, what about our allies here?" I demanded. I thought of the dozens of churches, safehouses, and underground hospitals I'd visited. All the poor, underprivileged, and oppressed citizens who believed in me. The citizens I'd been telling, in video after video, that I would fight alongside them.

"I'll do my best," Jael promised.

That's what you always say.

"I'll contact my network and warn them to destroy the guns and relocate. I won't be able to reach them all, but I'll save those I can."

"So, we'll abandon the rest?" In my head, the words were angry, but my voice came out heartbroken and frail. No matter how many guns we pulled, there would still be hundreds in the field, enough to collapse half of Beijing. I couldn't abandon a city of thirty million people. I couldn't walk away—not like I had with Nic, and Stanyard, and all the other people Asia had executed.

I could barely hear Jael over the ringing in my ears. "They knew the risks."

I backed up. "No, they didn't." No one had committed to becoming a suicide bomber with a rigged gun, and I couldn't let them die when I had the power to save them.

Jael closed the gap, her clacking heels loud and irritating in the silence. "Philadelphia. I promise I am not making this decision lightly."

"But I told them—"

"You did what you were ordered to do. This is my call to make."

But I can't go along with it.

"I know this is hard for you to understand." Jael gripped my shoulder. "But this is a sacrifice we have to make. And your orders are to trust me."

"You also told me to ask questions." I pulled away and faced her. "You told me heroes save life when they can. What happens when people find out we knew the whole time? Someone else is going to figure out the truth about the guns. What are we going to tell them when they realize I left them to die?"

Jael shook her head. "That's my problem, not yours."

No, it was mine. It was very much my problem.

"I will handle the damage control. I'll give you a script—"

"Covering up what happened isn't damage control," I snapped. "I won't lie to people."

Her face tightened in a gesture I knew all too well. "You'll say whatever I tell you to say."

"No."

The declaration ripped out of me before I could censor it. Jael frowned, her hand poised midair, as if giving me a chance to recant.

I didn't. This was a line I wouldn't cross.

"I can't go online and lie to people," I repeated, slowly, firmly, struggling to keep my emotions under control. "I won't sacrifice an entire city just to win the war. This is wrong."

This time, Jael did hesitate, and the silence was threatening. "Philadelphia, this is not your decision to make. Your job is to trust me."

"I do trust you," I insisted, and believed that, maybe, it was still true. "But I can't do this."

"I didn't ask for your—"

"I *won't* do this!" I shouted, then caught myself. I lowered my voice even though everything was shaking. "Jael, please, just listen to me. If I don't warn them, millions of people will die. If Asia sent these guns to other countries, we could kill *billions* of people."

She sighed, the sound dangerous. "It's a sacrifice we have—"

"No, it's not! Don't you see? If I let those people die, I'll be no better than Asia or Thames or anyone else." The realization hit me with a rush of cold memories. "If I'm willing to sacrifice millions of people just to win, I should have stayed on Mars and let Nic finish Red Rain."

I turned to him. He tugged on his mustache and said nothing.

I kept my eyes on him as I reached for the Holy Spirit. "This is not who we are," I insisted, and I'd never held a statement with more conviction in my life. "The way we win matters. I blew up that factory on Rott because I refuse to fight with their weapons. I will not be the next dictator—that is not what Blue Fire stands for."

"Blue Fire stands for whatever I tell her to."

I whirled. Jael stood at the coffee table with her back to me. "I created Blue Fire, and she works for me. That means she does what she's ordered to do."

The room began to pitch and blur; I knew what was about to happen. "Jael, I—"

She didn't let me finish. "Any disobedience will be treated as insubordination and punished accordingly."

I stared at her as she drew a line between us in bloodred. I had a choice. I could do what I knew was right and fracture the underground by alienating Jael. Or I could obey her orders and allow the deaths of millions of people.

And that was a choice I couldn't make.

My eyes burned. "Jael, please, don't make me do this."

"Enough," she declared, passing judgment with that one cruel word. She tapped the tablet and turned off the projection. "I've made my decision, and now you need to do as you're told."

I can't, I can't!

She glared at me over her shoulder. "Am I understood?"

I couldn't answer. *This isn't right!*

She turned. "Are we going to have a problem, Philadelphia?"

"I've got a problem."

Nic's sudden declaration cut through the noise like a knife. He unfolded himself from the corner, straightening to his full height. "This conversation is not helpful." He frowned at Jael.

She wasn't intimidated. "This conversation doesn't involve you, doctor."

"It does now. Go home, Philadelphia, and Jael and I will discuss this."

Every nerve crackled with panic. I was *not* going to be shut out of the room while other people decided my fate again. "Nic, please, you don't—"

He caught my arm. "Phil."

I looked up into his face. His expression was stern but not unkind. "Let me handle this."

I stared back as a new emotion invaded the chaos.

"Let me help you."

I took a deep breath and stepped back. "Okay."

He let go. I turned to the guard standing by the door, not trusting myself to look at Jael. "Please bring the car around."

27: NIC

The guard moved to obey her without a word, and she followed him out of the room. I waited until they were both safely beyond earshot before turning to Jael. "Let's talk about this."

"We were talking about this. I don't know how you expect this conversation to go any differently." She put her hand on her hip and fixed me with that condescending stare that made me feel like I'd forgotten to shower.

I did my royal best not to return the look in kind. "Well, seeing as I'm not a seventeen-year-old girl, I'd expect this conversation to go very differently. We're adults here."

She wasn't convinced. "If that's the case, then you should know that she's being immature and impulsive."

"And *you* should know that you're being cruel and insensitive." I sighed. "Were all the death threats necessary? You're killing her."

"Better me than someone else. I cannot allow her to entertain such foolish ideas."

"Forgive me," I drawled, "but I'm something of an expert on foolish ideas. And I have to say, turning a quarter million of your most loyal followers into suicide bombers without their consent tops anything I've ever come up with."

"I told you both," she enunciated loudly, like she was overexplaining herself to a toddler, "we'll do our best to minimize the damage. We'll warn those we can—"

"And what about those you can't? Philadelphia made a good point. Several, in fact."

"They knew the risks." Jael picked up the tablet and started scrolling, as if she weren't being rude enough already.

I crossed my arms and scowled, not that she was looking at me. "I don't know what that phrase means to you, but I think the average civilian would disagree. 'We'll give you a defective gun that will blow up in your face' was nowhere in the fine print. I looked."

She continued typing. "These things happen in war."

"Okay, pause for a second." I put both hands up. "The fact that you keep giving me textbook answers is a little insulting. So, I'm going to need you to drop the pretenses and tell me what's really going on."

She arched an eyebrow. "I don't 'have' to do anything."

"No, but if I stand here and harass you long enough, you're going to wish you'd taken the easy way out."

She finally glanced up at me and looked like she couldn't decide whether to laugh or punch me in the face.

I shrugged. "I just spent six weeks dealing with Warden Ivanova. You're easy."

That did the trick. She hurled the tablet on the coffee table with a thud. "You want the truth? Fine." She paused, breathing sharply through her nose, like she had to go digging in the back of her closet for the words. "The truth is, I wasn't expecting to win Beijing in the first place."

I froze. My brain had autofilled several explanations, but that wasn't one of them.

"I never expected to win the front in Beijing," she repeated. "The military presence is too strong here. Resistance is suicide, exploding guns or not."

That statement was more than a little concerning coming from the woman who was supposed to be leading said resistance. "So... what *was* your plan?"

"My plan was to cripple their infrastructure and disrupt their communications, then retreat to strongholds in the countryside. They would have driven us out of the capital, but if we gave them enough internal problems, it would have made it difficult for them to retaliate on other fronts."

It wasn't the worst plan ever, except for one minor detail. "That's not what Phil said in her videos."

She didn't even blink. "Would you join an army if the leader was prophesying failure?"

"As someone who knows a little bit about prophecy, I would prefer the truth."

She scoffed. "This world hasn't operated on truth in at least a century."

"No, but Philadelphia does."

And that's what makes her different than you.

"Look," Jael sighed, and for once, she didn't sound like she hated me, "I'm not saying we wouldn't have tried. If anyone can rally the people to overthrow the Council, it's Philadelphia."

I could tell she believed that statement with every fiber of her being, as did I.

"But when I found out Asia had planted the guns and was tracking the underground, I knew it was a losing battle." Jael looked away, and I could tell by the creases around her lips that she had spent many long nights calculating failure. "Even if Philadelphia could turn the Council against Asia, it wouldn't have saved everyone. Asia's information is on a server somewhere. The government would have just seized her devices and found her map of the underground, and then our allies would be worse off."

She was right. The underground had been exposed, and it was impossible to fully erase that data. "The only way to save them all *would* be to call off the operation," I said, finally understanding what Phil had seen all along.

Jael nodded, the gesture slow and final.

Asia truly had created an inescapable trap—but that still didn't answer one question. "Then why did you let Philadelphia go back to the Nolan estate? If you knew it was a lost cause, why put her at risk like that?"

"Because Asia is still our greatest enemy," Jael confessed. "If I can take her out—and send the government on a witch hunt—then we just might have a chance of winning the war. It was worth the risk to potentially expose Asia."

I didn't agree, but I knew Philadelphia would—if she had been given the truth. "Why didn't you tell Philadelphia?" I asked, and genuinely hoped she had a good answer.

She didn't. "Do you think she would have gone through with the operation if I did?"

My general aversion for this woman returned, thick and slimy. "So, you sacrificed *my daughter* just to get intel on Asia, and you didn't even tell Phil what you were doing?"

"She wouldn't have understood."

"I beg to differ, but she'll never learn if you just yell at her instead of explaining your actions. Why'd you threaten to court martial her?"

"Because I'm not stupid. I know I'm playing with fire. If she'll defy Asia and Thames, she'll certainly defy me."

Under any other circumstances, it would have been a compliment. "So, your solution is to scare her into submission? I believe they call that manipulation, and it's usually what bad guys do. I've tried it a few times. Do not recommend."

"I can't risk it!" She swiped her hand like a murderer slashing a knife. "She has no idea how much damage she'll cause if she goes online and scares everyone off."

"She won't know if you don't explain it to her!" I shouted back, fully aware we were going in circles. I struggled to be the better person and lowered my voice. "Please, just try talking to her. She's more mature than you give her credit for. If you explain it to her, she'll follow you."

For better or for worse.

Jael turned away from me. "No. I can't do that to her."

"Do what? Treat her like an adult?" I mocked. "Yeah, because no teenager ever wants to be treated with respect."

"Enough!" she shouted, as if that word could end all wars. "I will not put her through that!"

"Through what, Jael?" I demanded, and then realized what wasn't the question. "What are you afraid of?"

She flinched, and I knew I'd finally broken past her defenses. She stood with her back to me, silent.

I waited.

Finally, she drew a sharp breath and whispered, "Seventy thousand."

"What?"

She stared at the wall, like she was having a conversation with someone else. "71,632." She turned and looked at me again. "That's the estimated number of people the United killed when they bombed the border of my country. The casualties were mostly the elderly, women, and children—including every single member of my extended family."

"I'm sorry," I said, and then wondered if it would have been better if I'd kept my mouth shut.

She twirled one of the bangles on her wrist. "I had to make that decision. There was no one in the room when I intercepted the transmission, no one I could reach in time. I had to decide between saving the two million people in the capital or saving my family."

I stared at her. I of all people knew that you couldn't judge by appearances—and I had definitely judged this woman too swiftly.

"I am responsible for every single one of those deaths!" she screeched. "Sixteen years old, and I had to decide who lived and who died." She jabbed her finger in the air, as if making a case for an invisible jury.

What verdict she received, I'll never know. She sighed and lowered her arm. "I don't want Philadelphia to have to make the same choice. That's why I demand obedience—because if she's just following orders, she doesn't have to bear the consequences."

The Voice in my head muddied the silence. *That's not true.*

"She's going to bear the guilt whether you sign off on it or not," I murmured.

If Jael forced Philadelphia to go through with this, Philadelphia would live with not only the guilt of causing the deaths of millions of people, but also the knowledge that she violated everything she ever stood for. That after a year of running and fighting and sacrificing everything, including her family, she'd become what she hated most and handed the baton to the next dictator.

I couldn't let that happen—and the only way to stop it was to prevent Jael from taking that role.

I spread my hands. "Jael, listen to me. I think you need to consider what Phil is saying."

"Don't you think I have?" she snarled, her voice still too loud for the room. "Don't you think I've spent every waking hour studying predictions and looking for another solution? Every simulation I've run says that if we save Beijing, we lose the war."

"Then maybe it's a war you need to lose."

"You can't be serious," she scoffed.

I was—and so was the Voice in my head. "I think you're underestimating how dangerous this plan is. Phil is right. If the people find out she knew about the guns, they'll turn on her—and your newly-forged democracy or whatever will crumble."

"Don't you think I've thought of that? I have a whole PR campaign planned—"

"Oh, so you'll cover it up with the media? Sounds like the United."

She had enough character not to deny it. "You have no idea how to lead a war."

"You're absolutely correct."

She froze, which was what people usually did when I admitted they were right. I continued before she could reboot. "I *don't* have any idea. I've spent the better part of the last decade either off-planet or in prison. And if it were up to me, I'd still vote that we set up a colony on Mars and let this place burn." I paused. "The Voice in my head says I'm not allowed to say that."

She backstepped. "The Voice in your…"

"Never mind. The point is, I'm out of my league, and I'm not afraid to admit that."

Actually, you're terrified, the Voice in my head corrected.

I laughed cruelly. "You're right. I have three PhDs, and none of them prepared me for parenting a traumatized teenage girl while also trying to save the world. I have absolutely no idea what I'm doing."

Jael was silent, perhaps because she, too, abruptly realized how underqualified I was for this.

You're going to make me unpack this baggage later, aren't You? I challenged the Voice in my head.

He smiled. *Whenever you're ready.*

I bookmarked the conversation and turned my focus back to Jael. "Listen, I'm not here to stage a mutiny. I refuse to drag Phil into another custody battle. If this is what you decide, then fine. You won't get any trouble from me."

She paused, as if making sure I wasn't going to take it back. "Thank you," she said finally.

"Just promise me one thing."

She tensed.

"Promise me you'll do what I didn't."

"And that is?" she returned, the distrust creeping back into her voice.

"Talk to her."

She frowned. "Meaning?"

"Meaning, if this is your decision, sit her down and explain it to her."

"I thought I just did."

"No, that was called issuing an order like a heartless despot. I mean you need to tell her the truth, no matter how ugly it is. Tell her the real reason you sent her back to the estate. Tell her your plan for the war. She may not agree with you, but at least you'll save your relationship."

She pulled back like an eel into its den. "This is war. I don't have time for feelings—"

"Then make time, because this isn't about you. This is about saving Philadelphia."

She hesitated. I took a deep breath and pulled on the Holy Spirit every way I knew how. "Look, I know you don't see it yet, but she needs you. And not all these military-general-court-martial vibes. She needs *you*, the woman who's survived a war."

The Holy Spirit answered the call, and I saw a fragment of what the woman was inside, beneath the cold attitude, ruthless morals, and heavy jewelry. "You know what it's like to sacrifice everything and be the last woman standing. You know what it's like to have blood on your hands and ghosts in your closet. You are the one person who best understands what Philadelphia is going through, and you're the only one who can help her put her life back together when this is over."

Jael looked away. Perhaps because she realized that she, too, was grossly underprepared for the burden that had been handed to her.

"She needs you," I repeated, "but if you don't tell her the truth, you'll lose her. You'll join a long list of adults who never listened to her, myself included."

My name was on that list a dozen times. I should have encouraged her to stay on Mars instead of letting her make her own decision; I should have helped her find her father instead of leaving her to fend for herself; I should have taught her how to be a leader instead of watching her fail. I'd had so many opportunities over the past six months to make her a friend instead of an enemy, but I'd chosen to stay walled up in my prison because I didn't want to be responsible for her life—or my feelings.

I was a pathetic, inadequate, wholly dysfunctional excuse for a father. But by God's grace, I wouldn't make the same mistake again.

"Jael."

I waited until she looked at me before continuing.

"Please don't do this. Don't force her to choose between your respect and doing what she thinks is right."

"I don't need her respect," she returned, but there was no conviction behind the words.

"Maybe you don't, but she does. She needs your love—and right now, you've told her that she has to blindly obey or lose that love. She's probably on the floor back at the house right now, praying her guts out, begging God for another solution."

Jael winced. There was no denying it; she knew Philadelphia as well as I did.

I took a step forward, desperate to close the gap over the one person we both cared about. "Please don't make her go through that again. Don't force her to choose between your relationship and her conscience."

She didn't respond, breaking eye contact once more.

I opened my mouth, but the Holy Spirit got there first.

Enough.

I obeyed and turned to go. I'd made my case; the power of life and death was in Jael's hands now.

She didn't stop me. I stepped out into the hall, then paused.

"Besides," I called over my shoulder without looking back, "I think we both know what she'll choose."

28: NIC

I was right. When I got back to the house, Phil was on her face in the courtyard, sobbing.

"She's outside," Peng said unnecessarily as he collected my jacket. The information was superfluous; I could hear her crying through the half-open patio door.

Jayde stood watch in the shadows of the living room. He looked up at me as I approached. "Fix this," he hissed, "or the war is over."

"I'll handle it," I snapped, and hoped he could read the threat in my tone of voice.

He obeyed and disappeared. I waited until he was out of sight, then opened the screen door silently. I needn't have bothered; Philadelphia was in no danger of hearing me. She was splayed out on the tile next to the pool like she'd been shot and left for dead. A Bible lay open beside her, its pages crumpled. Her gauzy house robe fanned around her like a prayer shawl as she beat the ground with her fists.

"Jesus, Jesus, *Jesus*," she wailed, as if that name was the only thing keeping her head above water. She scratched at the tile with broken fingernails. "I don't know what to do. I can't let them die! I can't destroy this city!"

I took a step towards her. She jerked upright, the motion inhuman, but she was facing away and didn't see me. "This isn't right! This isn't what You called me to do!" It was almost a question as she stared at the stars, begging for an answer.

She hugged her knees and fell silent, long enough that I almost said something. But then she spoke again—and she said exactly what I didn't want to hear.

"Please don't make me do this," she rasped like there was a hand around her throat. "Not again."

As if realizing words were insufficient for the crisis, she broke off in weeping and tongues. There were more tears than the latter as she curled into a ball and quivered, completely unaware of me.

I stared at her as regret after regret crushed my lungs. I'd had a dozen opportunities over the last six months to prevent this horrific universe, and I'd missed them all. Now the weight of the world was on her shoulders, and I couldn't fix it.

You don't have to fix it.

The Holy Spirit rippled the waters of the pool.

You don't have to do anything.

I walked over and sat down cross-legged on the patio beside her. She didn't hear me. I watched her shake and sob and wondered if I should speak up.

And that's when I realized there was one thing I *should* do.

I knew exactly what she needed. I knew what one simple act would keep her world from collapsing.

And it was the one thing I couldn't give.

I clenched my fists. Everything in me told me that I didn't want to open this door. That if I did, Philadelphia would never let me shut it again—and I would be responsible for her in more ways than one.

Religion was all well and good when it was just me and the Voice in my head.

A breeze gusted across the courtyard. *I didn't give you a gift so you could save yourself.*

I closed my eyes and let the cold air wrap around my shoulders. Then I took a deep breath, looked out across the pool, and prayed.

"God," I started, and then almost didn't go any further—because I abruptly realized I had nothing to say.

Philadelphia started and almost fell into the pool. She hastily wiped her cheeks. "Nic?"

I kept my gaze on the moving water. "Phil needs You. She needs Your wisdom, and she needs Your presence."

Philadelphia fell silent. She gripped her knees and stared at me with those wide, vulnerable eyes.

I had no idea where to go from there, so I just started listing the facts. "You brought her here. You connected her with Jael. You gave her this position of influence and power—and now she needs to know what to do with that power."

I hesitated when I realized Philadelphia wasn't the only one who needed intercession. "Give Jael wisdom. You put her in a place of authority for this very hour—show her why. Show her what You showed me."

I trailed off. There were a dozen other things I could ask for, but I felt like I'd said too much already. It was definitely the lamest, dumbest, and most theologically pedantic prayer I'd ever prayed, and putting an "Amen" on it felt even dumber.

The Holy Spirit did it for me. *Amen*, He breathed, and then smiled.

Philadelphia sniffed. I finally turned to face her. Her breathing had returned to normal as she dried her face on her sleeve. "Thank you," she whispered.

Saying "you're welcome" seemed weird, so I just smiled.

She adjusted her robe and turned to dip her bare feet in the pool. "Did you talk to Jael?"

I leaned back on my hands. "Yeah."

"And?" The word was tiny, fearful.

"She's going to call us in the morning."

Phil hugged herself. "And if she says we're going through with the operation?"

I'd been asking the Holy Spirit and my three PhDs for an answer to that question and hadn't gotten a solution out of any of them. "I think you need to give her a chance to speak for herself before you plan alternatives."

She nodded, but she barely made it all the way through the motion.

"But... if she refuses, *we* will talk."

I put the emphasis on the plural. I couldn't promise a solution, but I could promise that she wouldn't go alone.

She looked up at me. "Thanks, Nic."

Her eyes were watering again, but this time, she wasn't afraid. And in that moment, I realized I had absolutely no regrets.

The breeze danced across the patio again, ruffling the pages of her Bible. I picked it up. "Where did you get this extremely illegal piece of paper?"

Her lips twitched. "Stanyard gave it to me."

How I wished that name inspired anything but utter disgust. The kid deserved better from me, of course; he was in jail because he'd risked his life for Philadelphia. But if I was being honest, I wasn't entirely mad that they'd been on separate continents for the past month. At least I didn't have to worry about him kissing her or hugging her or, heaven forbid, *proposing* to her when he was halfway across the world.

I flipped through the crinkled pages. "Have you heard from him?"

"No." Her voice shuddered. "Asia hasn't mentioned him in several weeks. She won't tell me where he is."

I slammed my fist on the tile. *Can I please kill Asia?* I begged the Voice in my head.

No.

But it would solve so many problems!

I said no.

I grumbled out loud. Phil gave me a look.

"Sorry," I said, "just arguing with the Voice in my head." I closed the Bible and tried to find a clean way to end the conversation. "You should get to bed. It's late." *Wow, taking this "old man" role a little too seriously, are we?*

She sighed. "I guess I should take my pills."

"Pills?" I repeated, and my suspicion made my voice way too loud for the acoustics of the veranda.

She reached into the pocket of her robe and pulled out a prescription bottle. She held it in both hands and stared at it in the moonlight. "I've been taking anxiety medication."

"Jael put you on *medication*?" I tried to figure out why that thought made me so irrationally angry. I would have recommended the same thing, had I been there. But I wasn't there, and now someone had put *my daughter* on medication without asking me.

Phil was oblivious to my parental crisis. "It's supposed to help me sleep, too."

I brushed the feelings aside. "Is it working?"

She shrugged. Her eyes wandered elsewhere, looking anywhere but in my direction.

"What?" I prodded.

"I just..." Her fingers tightened around the bottle. "I don't... I don't understand why Jesus won't heal me."

The anguish in her voice sent my soul to my throat. "What do you mean?"

She finally turned to me. "Nic, He *healed* you. I've seen a dead man raised to life, and now I can't even sleep without taking a dozen pills!" She drew her arm back and looked like she was about to hurl the bottle into the pool, then reconsidered. She dropped her hands back in her lap. "I just... don't know what I'm doing wrong. Why won't He heal me?"

There were a dozen possible answers to that question, none of which she needed to hear. Good theology wouldn't save her, but I knew that if I didn't say something, she'd have a wound that medication couldn't heal.

I turned my thoughts inward and let the Voice in my head speak first.

"Sometimes God fixes our problems," I repeated slowly. "Other times, He gives us the wisdom to fix it ourselves."

Phil stared at the bottle in her hands, reconsidering.

"And, don't take this the wrong way, but... if you stop praying just because you're on medication, that seems like a personal problem."

She jerked, and I knew I'd saved a life.

I stood and led the way to the house. "Let's get some sleep."

She scrambled to follow. "Nic, wait."

I glanced over my shoulder. She fidgeted.

I groaned and held one arm out. "Make it quick," I said, even though I didn't mean it.

She darted over and grabbed me around the waist. "Thank you," she sniffled into my chest.

I squeezed her shoulder. "It's our little secret. If you tell anyone, I'll deny everything."

That worked. She giggled and let me go.

"Now, bedtime. I'm not telling you again." I shoved the Bible at her.

She pushed it back. "I want you to keep it."

"Why? Because I need it more than you do?" I snarked.

You said it, not Me, the Voice in my head commented.

She tried and failed to laugh. "No, I… I just want someone to take care of it."

She avoided my gaze, and I realized what she was implying.

I gripped the spine. "I don't think Pizza Boy will be happy when he finds out you regifted his love offering."

She shrugged.

I decided not to push it. "I'll keep it safe."

She gave me a smile, then ran for the step. I stood on the patio and watched her disappear into the shadows of the house.

I looked down at the Bible in my hands. Phil didn't expect to get out of this alive—and even if she did, she didn't believe she'd ever see Pizza Boy again. And that was a future I couldn't let her live in.

Someone had to save that boy.

29: NIC

I went back into the house and fetched the phone Jael's people had given me. They told me it was fully secure—not that it would matter after I sent this text.

I opened the app and typed in a number I wished I didn't have memorized.

IT'S NIC. CAN WE TALK?

She left me unread for an indecent amount of time. I was quite sure she saw the message immediately, but she didn't respond for almost twenty minutes, just to be petty.

YOU MUST BE DESPERATE IF YOU'RE COMING TO ME

WHAT DID WE SAY ABOUT THE ONE-LINERS? OF COURSE I'M DESPERATE

WHY SHOULD I MEET WITH YOU?

BECAUSE YOU'RE CURIOUS. LET ME BUY YOU A COFFEE. OUR FAVORITE PLACE IS STILL OPEN.

Back in the good old days when Asia and I were dating, we'd both been incredibly busy—me, a decorated scientist and her, a scheming politician—so we'd mapped out several places in Beijing that were open late. There was a coffee shop close to the council chambers with a quaint upper room that Asia would rent out so we'd have our privacy.

The thought of being alone with Asia gave me about as much joy as an aneurysm, but if I was going to save Phil's future husband, I'd have to make a deal with the devil.

Thankfully, the devil was willing to play.

I'LL MEET YOU IN AN HOUR

The coffee shop was in a kitschy shopping district, the kind of neighborhood they showed on the news to make it look like communism was working. Everything was clean and sparkly and perfect. The shops were all gimmicky, with plastic tile roofs and neon signs styled to lure tourists. Even the people seemed fake as they posed for selfies under the archways.

The coffee shop was vacant when I entered. The only person in the room was a soldier guarding the foot of the stairs. He bowed and gestured for me to follow.

Asia sat at our usual table in the balcony. She'd dressed down—relatively speaking—for the event, which I found somewhat threatening. She wore a simple top and slacks and had no lipstick on. On the table in front of her were two mugs of black coffee.

"It was my turn to buy," I groused.

She didn't respond. She picked up a small metal case off the floor and opened it. "Phone, please."

I obliged, turning off my device and tossing it on the dampening field. She added her own phone to the pile as a gesture of goodwill, then latched the case and set it aside.

I sat down across from her. I exchanged eye contact with the soldier standing watch in the corner, then turned my focus on Asia. "Thank you for meeting me," I said, and I actually meant it.

"Curiosity killed the cat." She slid a mug across the table towards me. "Besides, I think we can make an equal exchange."

I took a rallying sip. "Name your price."

She picked at the chipped laminate on the table. "Let's keep it simple tonight. I'll answer your questions, and you answer mine."

"Fair enough. You first—because then if you ask a question I can't answer, I still have time to back out."

She smirked. "What is Philadelphia planning?"

"Besides the overthrow of your government? Narrow the search parameters, please."

She swirled her mug. "Why is she here?"

I stalled by gulping down half my drink. Asia clearly still didn't realize that Phil knew about the guns, and I had to keep it that way. Unfortunately, Asia wasn't stupid, and she knew me better than I cared to admit. She would know if I lied.

So, don't lie, the Voice in my head commented, as if it was that easy.

Maybe it was.

I set my cup aside. "Why do you think? To get close to your father."

She tapped her acrylic nail on the handle of her mug like an irritated typewriter. "She had her chance."

"And she blew it. Jayde almost killed her, I had to swoop in and save her, it was a whole thing."

"You did look good in that suit," she consented. "But why now? She could have come home anytime. I've given her plenty of… incentive."

"Yes, I heard you two did a lot of bonding while I was gone," I hissed, letting a bit of the distaste into my voice.

She liked it. Her tongue frisked the edge of her teeth. "I'll admit, I really thought the stunt with your fake trial would work. I'm still surprised she left you out to dry."

As was I, although I was more proud than anything else. "I guess you misjudged her motivations."

"Apparently so." Asia propped her elbows on the table and tented her fingers. "So, educate me. What's inspired our little princess to come home?"

I hesitated a beat too long. "Don't avoid the question, doctor," Asia cooed. "You promised. Why didn't she just take the shot when she had the chance?"

"She wasn't ready," I mumbled, and as soon as the words left my mouth, I realized they were the complete truth. "The assassination was a childish plan from a very childish man. If she'd gone through with it, she would have handed the world to you on a silver platter—and she knew that."

Asia flicked her fingers in a gesture of vague consent.

"But now she has real power. Your father is obsessed with her. She doesn't need to bargain with you—he'll give her anything she asks for. She's playing with the big boys now, and if she deals her cards right, he'll hand her the keys to the kingdom and never even realized he's been fooled."

Asia arched one eyebrow. "I almost believe you're telling the truth."

"You wish I was," I returned, "because that's what you want to happen, isn't it?"

It is, the Voice in my head whispered.

Asia winked. "Is that the question you want an answer to?"

"Nah, that was just a rhetorical statement for dramatic effect. I have bigger problems than dissecting your evil schemes."

"Very well." She crossed one leg over her knee and leaned back in the chair. "What can I do for you, Dr. Nic?"

Unlike her, I had no reason to be catty, so I came right out with it. "Where's Stanyard?"

She paled, and I lost all courage. "Is he alive?" *Dear God, please don't let me be too late.*

"I… I don't know," Asia fumbled.

"What do you mean, you don't know? Last I checked, he was rotting in *your* prison. Where is he?"

"I don't know," she repeated.

I slammed my hands on the table, and the guard tensed. "I'm going to need a better answer than 'I don't know,'" I hissed. "I answered your questions, and now you'd better keep your end of the bargain. Tell me where he is."

"How many times do I have to say 'I don't know' before you believe me?" She sat up and punctuated with both arms. "He was being held in Boston. They were transporting him here, but we lost contact with the plane. The signal cut off over the middle of the ocean."

I searched her face for any signs of guile, but she seemed just as panicked as I was. "Do they think the plane went down?"

"Maybe," she said in a way that suggested she had her own theories. "But no distress signal was sent out, and they haven't recovered any wreckage."

A flicker of hope flashed across my mind, but Asia promptly snuffed it out. "But if they survived, the plane would have landed somewhere—or surely my pilot would have made contact. Everyone who was onboard has dropped off the grid."

I could tell by the pace of her breathing that she was telling the truth. And for once, I wished she wasn't.

"I'm sorry," Asia whispered, and I realized that was the only genuine apology she'd ever given me. "If I hear anything, I'll tell you."

I gripped my coffee mug with both hands and resisted the urge to throw it across the room. What was I going to tell Philadelphia? That her boyfriend vanished into the Bermuda Triangle and wasn't coming back?

The Voice in my head shifted. *Trust Me.*

"Thanks for not lying," I sighed. "We should have tried this ten years ago. It's surprisingly efficient."

She propped her chin on her hand. "Would things have been different?"

I stiffened. She didn't need to clarify, but she did anyway. "If I'd left your parents alone."

I wanted to say no. I wanted to believe that even if Asia hadn't gone on a killing spree, it still wouldn't have worked between us. That there was no universe in which she and I ended up together.

But that was not, in fact, the truth.

"Maybe next time you should ask these questions before you commit murder." I stood to leave.

She stared at me. I knew that look. It wasn't a conniving stare. It was a gentle, thoughtful, affectionate stare. She used to look at me like that all the time.

And that's when I remembered why I hated her so much. It wasn't the betrayal. It wasn't the lying and the bloodshed and the cruelty. It was because

I could never, after all these years, figure out if she'd truly loved me, or if she'd just been manipulating me the whole time.

I would have preferred the latter. But that was a mercy she would never give me.

I stormed to the stairs.

"I enjoyed this, doctor," she called after me. "I'll miss you when they send you back to jail."

"I would say the feeling is mutual," I cast over my shoulder, "but we've been weirdly honest with each other tonight, so I think I'll continue that trend."

She cackled. "You know I'm over you, Nic. But I don't think you're over me."

She's right, the Voice in my head agreed.

I glared up at the ceiling. *Excuse me?*

If you were over her, you wouldn't be so angry.

He was annoyingly correct. I was *furious*. It was moments like these when I remembered why I wanted to end the world. Why I avoided friendship like the plague. Why I never wanted to be a husband or boyfriend or significant other to anyone ever again.

It was because Asia had stolen the one thing that couldn't be replaced, and now she didn't even have the decency to say *"I never loved you."*

She doesn't need to apologize.

I gripped the railing as I remembered what I'd said to Philadelphia this morning.

"You can't just keep letting people off the hook like this, Phil."

"Yes, I can. That's kind of how Jesus works."

She'd forgiven so many people—her father, the Nolans, Jayde, even Pizza Boy. She'd erased the debts of a dozen sinners, most of whom had never asked.

Including, I realized with some embarrassment, me.

She hadn't waited for permission. And maybe I shouldn't, either.

I inhaled through my nose. "Min?"

Her chair scraped on the floor. "Yes?"

I faced her. "I forgive you."

I descended the stairs before she could respond. And then I walked out the door a free man.

30: PHILADELPHIA

Where is Nic?

It was nearly ten o'clock, well past the time when he should have been up, and I still hadn't heard a word from him. Jael had arrived unannounced before breakfast, much to my alarm. Thankfully, Asia had informed me that she would be busy all day. Cardiff had also left the house early, claiming he would be supervising maintenance on his private transit—because apparently an interstellar spaceship was also something the Nolans owned. I was grateful, especially since he took Frank with him; Cardiff may know about Blue Fire, but he definitely didn't need to overhear this conversation.

I stalled as long as I could, serving breakfast, delegating staff, and fielding Peng's usual morning litany of messages. I knew I was making Jael wait in the sitting room much longer than was proper, but I didn't want to meet with her alone.

She finally pulled me aside. "Philadelphia, sit, please."

I'd run out of excuses, so I was forced to oblige. I took the armchair next to her.

She slid down the couch to be closer to me and leaned over so we were eye to eye. I struggled to hold her gaze.

"We need to talk," she announced.

I clenched my fists in my lap. *Please, God. I can't do this.*

She gently pried my hands apart. "I want to apologize."

My heart restarted.

"I am sorry for how I handled our conversation yesterday. I told you that I never want you to be afraid to ask questions, and I mean that. I always want you to feel like you can come to me with your opinions and concerns." She rubbed my knuckles. "Even if we disagree, I want you to trust me as much as I trust you."

A flicker of hope beat in my chest. "You trust me?" Jael had never asked for my trust; I just followed orders.

She smiled. "Why wouldn't I? I asked you to be honest with me, and you have been. You've handled yourself with maturity, and you've followed orders even when it's hard. I know that when you say you'll do something, you'll do it. This whole time you've been at the estate, completely on your own, and I haven't once worried that you'll endanger the operation." She let go of my hand to gesture at the room.

I straightened as her words patched the cracks in the bridge between us.

"You can't imagine how valuable that loyalty is to me, as a leader. There are not many people I can trust with the amount of power you have."

I frowned. "What power?" I didn't have any power; I wasn't in charge of the operation and never had been. I was just a figurehead.

She arched an eyebrow. "You have immeasurable power, Philadelphia. You could command this army if you wanted to. With one video, you could convince even my top advisors to follow you instead of me."

I squirmed. The thought made me royally uncomfortable—in part because it had never occurred to me.

"But I know you would never do that, even if we disagreed," Jael continued, as if reading my mind. "And I do not want to take that loyalty for granted. Which… is what we need to discuss."

I braced myself.

"You were honest with me yesterday, and for that, I am grateful. However… I was not honest with you."

She shifted on the couch, and the room swayed, like the Earth had gotten knocked off its axis. I closed my eyes and gripped the chair to keep from being thrown overboard. *No, not again. I can't do this again.*

"I told you I was willing to sacrifice the front in Beijing. There's a reason for that." She paused, as if this conversation was just as terrifying for her as it was for me. "I never expected us to take control of Beijing in the first place."

I opened my eyes. "What?"

She bravely met my stare. "The military presence is too strong here. We never would have been able to fully break the government's control. I was planning on them driving us out within the week. It was always a suicide mission—even without the defective guns."

"But…" I thought of all the hours I'd spent on air telling people that we could win if we acted together—reading from scripts Jael had written.

I lied to them… You lied to me.

"My plan was to cripple their infrastructure and break down communications, then retreat. That would have prevented them from retaliating on other fronts, so we could liberate regions of independence and hold them. We don't need to control Beijing to end the United—we just need to break the monopoly."

She was right; it would only take one free country to change the future. "Then why aren't we doing that in the first place? Why not liberate Africa or South America and advance from there?"

"Do you know how many have tried that and failed?" she said gently.

I remembered what she'd told me about her home country—and the war crimes the United had committed to force them to surrender—and winced.

"We need the global momentum to break their system of control. We need Operation Blue Fire—and that's why I needed the thunderbird to promise victory."

I wanted to argue, but there was nothing to debate. Jael had done exactly what any military general would have done: strategize to win the war. But she'd won the same way the United did: by manipulating the truth with propaganda.

And Blue Fire had been her mouthpiece.

"That's also why I sent you back here," Jael continued before I could formulate an objection.

"I don't understand," I said, and wondered if I really wanted the truth.

"Asia is our greatest enemy—and that was before she donated a shipload of bombs. I knew that if you could expose her, the government would turn to cannibalism, making it impossible for them to regroup. It would make them weak—and we just might be able to topple the giant."

"Why didn't you tell me?" I blurted. Everything she was saying made sense—and that made the wound sting all the worse. If she had told me what she was planning, I would have obeyed without question. I would have given her what she wanted. Instead, she'd stolen my loyalty through lies and false promises.

And now I wasn't sure I could continue to follow her.

She didn't hesitate. "Because I didn't want you to have to make the same decision I did."

With a flash of regret I could taste, I remembered the other half her story.

"I didn't tell anyone that I knew about the plan to attack the villages. I didn't want anyone else to have to make that decision."

"I won't sugarcoat it, Philadelphia." Jael looked out the window and tapped her foot, her heel drumming the rhythm to a doomed war. "There is no right answer. Whether we go through with the operation or not, someone loses. Either people risk their lives in a fight we cannot win, or we yield the floor and the government continues to execute your followers one by one."

My vision blurred as the tiny flicker of hope in my chest snuffed out. Either I could sacrifice an entire city to end the government, or I could retreat and condemn the universe to another hundred years of tyranny.

I knew what the right answer was. But either way, Asia won.

Jael touched my knee. "There is no happy ending where we save everyone—and I didn't want you to have to decide who lived and who died."

I tried to blink away the tears and focus on her face.

"I am sorry I yelled at you yesterday," she whispered, her own voice cracking around the edges. "I thought that if you were just following orders, I could spare you the guilt. But I know now that's not true. You still would have been responsible for your decision, because you would have had to decide whether or not to follow me."

I felt the Holy Spirit moving between us. *Obedience is always a choice.*

Jael found my hands again. "And I know that if I'd asked you to obey, you would have."

Would I? I thought of all the times I'd told her I trusted her—the overwhelming conviction that God had placed her in my life—and thought that, maybe, I would have.

"But that's not the kind of relationship I want to have with you." She tugged on my hands, pulling us closer. "Soldiers are a dime a dozen. I have plenty of people who will blindly follow orders. But I want to be more than a commanding officer to you, if you'll let me. I don't want our relationship to end when the war does."

Breath rushed back into my lungs when I realized what she was implying, offering.

The smooth metal rings on her fingers brushed my cheek as she cupped my face with one hand. "You are going to have regrets after this war, Philadelphia. But I don't want trusting me to be one of them. From now on, I promise to be as honest with you as you have been with me. Will you forgive me for lying? Will you help me fight this war—together?"

"Yes," I whispered, and then broke down into gentle tears.

She drew me in and kissed my forehead. "You'll always be my Blue Fire."

I hugged her. *Thank you, Jesus.*

"Hold on, time out."

I jerked back. Nic waltzed into the room, followed by Peng with a breakfast tray.

Nic halted in front of us and pointed at my face. "Are those Jesus tears, or I-need-to-kill-someone tears?"

I started to laugh, but the sound caught on the sob in my throat and came out a garbled mess. I snorted through my nose and shot goopy snot everywhere.

Nic arched an eyebrow. "Better out than in, I guess."

That just made me laugh and snot harder. Peng set his tray on the coffee table and magically produced a handkerchief from his pocket.

I mumbled thanks and mopped my nose. "Yes, they're good tears."

"Excellent. I don't fancy murder before breakfast." Nic pulled up another chair.

"Where have you been, anyway?" I accused.

He poured himself a cup of coffee, then leaned over to refill mine. "I overslept my alarm."

"Seriously?"

"What? I haven't slept that great since before you were born." He grabbed his plate and began devouring his breakfast with enthusiasm.

I eyed him. He seemed… different, not that I could have identified why. He wore the same neutral expression he always did, and he was using an acceptable amount of sarcasm.

"So, what did I miss?" He glanced at Jael.

"Nothing you and I didn't already discuss, doctor." She helped herself to a slice of fruit from the tray.

"You followed my advice?" he exclaimed around a mouthful of food.

"Does this surprise you?"

He paused to finish chewing. "Yes, actually."

She leaned back in the chair and crossed one leg over the other. "Maybe it wouldn't be so shocking if you made a habit of giving people good advice."

I cringed and glanced at Nic, expecting the worst. But he just shrugged and washed down his food with a chug of coffee. "I'll factor that into my calculations."

I stared at him. Suddenly, I knew what was wrong—he was *happy*.

I'd been around Nic long enough to know that his moods usually ranged from disinterested to antagonistic, with disinterested being a good day. I'd never, ever seen him act genuinely joyful. Gloating over the death of his enemies, maybe, but never at peace.

What in the world happened last night?

Jael didn't give me a chance to interrogate him. "Send for Jayde, please." She gestured at Peng, who obliged. "We have something to discuss."

My stomach clenched when I remembered what was at stake. I abandoned my coffee mug on the end table.

Nic did the same and dragged his chair closer to mine.

"My team has been working nonstop to pull the guns from the field," Jael sighed, exhaustion stretching her voice. "So far, we've accounted for about twenty thousand."

I gripped my chest and muttered in tongues. That wasn't even half of the guns Jayde said General Jin had received.

Jael touched my knee. "We'll keep working—we have forty-eight hours. I have all my contacts spreading the message through their networks."

"But it won't be enough," Nic spoke for me. He folded his arms on his knees and leaned forward, his eyes watching me carefully.

"No," Jael admitted. "Beijing will burn."

"And you think we should let it fall," I said before I could stop myself. I recalled what she'd said about the operation being a suicide mission and wondered—briefly.

"No."

I looked up.

"I've consulted with my advisors, and they all agree: You're right." She pinched my knee, but it felt like she was grounding herself more than anything. "We have to warn everyone. You have to go on air and tell them the truth."

I stared at her as all my uncertainty evaporated. *We have to save this city.*

Nic muttered something under his breath that sounded vaguely like a prayer.

"If we use those guns, we'll lose too many of our own people, not to mention the catastrophic loss of civilian life," Jael said, confirming what I already knew. "If Asia shipped guns to our allies in other regions, we could be looking at a death toll in the billions."

"I can't be responsible for that," I declared. But this time, there was no fear in the statement, only conviction.

"No, you cannot," Jael agreed. "The good doctor here reminded me of something very important: Blue Fire is not a killer. You inspire people because you chose to save the world instead of yourself."

She glanced at Nic with a gesture close to a smile. He returned it.

Heavy footsteps sounded down the hall, and Jayde appeared in the doorway. Jael looked at him as she continued. "If you sacrifice Beijing, you'll ruin everything you ever stood for. And that is a sacrifice you cannot make."

Jayde folded his hands behind his back and said nothing.

"If people find out you sent your followers on a suicide mission, they'll lose faith in you—and I can't afford that. If we're going to keep our hard-won independence, I need the thunderbird to continue reigning after the war." Jael beamed at me, expression filled with nothing but pride.

I stared back. I'd never once considered that the thunderbird would be needed after the war. Blue Fire's job was to inspire people to fight for independence. Once we ended the United, the world wouldn't need me anymore—would it?

Jael didn't let me dwell on it. "You need to show the people that you care more about them than bringing down the government. You're going on air and telling them the truth. Tell them about the guns and warn them that Asia knows where they are. Give them a chance to save themselves."

"You're cancelling the operation," Jayde declared. There was no accusation in his voice—just a dejected, sullen sense of finality, like he was slamming the lid on a coffin.

"Not necessarily." Nic sat up straight. "Rebels are creative. When they find out that Philadelphia risked her life to save theirs, I think it will inspire them to do something equally insane."

I took a sharp breath through my nose as the hope returned to my heart. This is who I was—who the thunderbird was. This was who God called me to be.

I am Blue Fire, and this is my war.

"That is the hope," Jael agreed. The cunning sparkle returned to her eyes, but it was short-lived. "However, it's not so simple as recording a video and warning everyone. Unless we can also remove Asia, the people will still be in immediate danger. Asia has no doubt already put her army in place, ready to respond on operation day. As soon as she knows we've exposed her, she may retaliate and kill as many as possible—never mind the dozens of hostages she has in prison."

"Stanyard," I murmured. *Oh God, please protect him.*

Nic rubbed his mustache and frowned.

"We have enough evidence to expose her," Jael said, "but we need the Council to act immediately. If she gets wind of it, she will wipe her data and run."

"Then I'll tell the General," I declared. Adrenaline rushed through my system as everything snapped into place—my identity as a Nolan, the General's adoration of me, all the little miracles God had put in place to save the world. "If I tell the General, he'll act before she can. I'll say I found suspicious activity in my financial investments. He'll believe me—at least enough to investigate. I can call him—"

"That's not going to be easy."

I turned. Jayde pulled his phone out of his pocket. "Asia called an emergency council session that lasts until Friday. Not a single councilmember is allowed to leave the building until the crisis is over, the General included."

He stepped forward and handed the device to me. A news headline emblazoned on the screen confirmed his statement.

Nic read over my shoulder. "She made them sitting ducks."

Jayde nodded.

I pushed aside the gruesome thought. "Then I'll go to him."

Jael shook her head, rattling her earrings. "If it's an emergency session, they'll have the building on lockdown. They won't let anyone in."

"They'll let me in," I whispered. I remembered the General's benevolent offer and realized what I had to do.

"Come to the council chambers sometime, see for yourself. Tell them I sent you."

I closed my eyes and searched for the Holy Spirit. He answered, smothering the fear that burned in my lungs. This—this is why I was a Nolan.

The room had gone still. I looked up to find everyone staring at me.

I spoke slowly and clearly to force the words out around the anxiety in my throat. "I need to go to the council chambers. They will let me in; the General invited me."

No one argued, even though I could tell Nic desperately wanted to.

I kept talking, laying out the pieces of the plan as the Holy Spirit revealed them to me. "I'll expose her in front of the whole Council and warn the underground at the same time. It's the only way to prevent Asia from retaliating and give everyone time to run."

"Philadelphia," Nic prodded, the syllables sharp with grief, "what are you suggesting?"

The room spun. I gripped the arms of the chair and turned to Jael. "There's cameras in the council chambers, right? For when they broadcast sessions on TV?"

"Yes, of course."

"Can you commandeer them?"

She didn't answer. She stared at me, expression pained, as if she knew where this was going.

Nic grunted something I couldn't make out. He lurched out of his chair and began to pace.

I forged ahead. "If you can hijack the signal, we can use Data's program to broadcast it to the entire world. Make it mandatory viewing. We can warn everyone—it's the only way to reach all our allies at once."

Jael started drumming her foot again. I knew what that meant. I was right—I had to be. This was the only way.

Jayde moved beside me. "The resistance won't listen to Andromeda Nolan, though." His voice was barely above a whisper, as if he, too, knew how this ended.

No, they won't.

I pushed up my right sleeve and stared at the thunderbird tattoo on my shoulder—the mark I'd kept carefully hidden for the past week. "They'll listen to Philadelphia Smyrna."

Nic rammed his fist into the wall. He stopped, his back to me. His shoulders were heaving.

"I have to do this," I announced—for him, for me, for everyone. I looked at Jael.

Tears left two bright streaks down her dark face. "Yes. You do."

I closed my eyes and waited for the world to stop shaking.

For such a time as this.

"Philadelphia."

Jael waited until I met her gaze before continuing. "I won't be able to go with you. I'll have to stay behind and run the broadcast."

She was right—I needed her at the computer. This mission would fail if I didn't have someone to keep Data's program online and manage the algorithm.

Of course, that was only half the reason. If she came with me, she'd be incriminated—and then there would be no one to lead the war.

I forced a smile. "This is something I have to do alone."

"I beg to differ." Nic spun around. "I'm coming with you."

I shook my head. I couldn't lose him again—not when he'd already died once for me. "But Nic—"

"They'll probably recant my pardon anyway as soon as you make a scene. Might as well go out in style." The words were indifferent, but the look he was giving me was anything but.

"I'm also coming," Jayde announced.

I frowned at him. I wasn't sure I wanted him on this mission—I knew what he thought of cancelling the operation.

"You're not leaving the house without your bodyguard." He planted his feet apart and folded his arms behind his back, as if daring me to argue.

I didn't.

"Philadelphia," Jael pulled my attention back to her. "You know they won't be able to save you, right?" She laid her hand on my arm, her acrylic fingernails digging into my skin. "The General will arrest you. If they put you in jail, I'll do everything I can, but..."

She didn't need to finish the sentence. I knew what the word "if" meant.

"You don't have to save me," I replied, and let the tears fall. "Just save the world."

She stood up, and I followed. She pulled me into a hug. "That's my thunderbird," she whispered in my ear.

I soaked in the strength of her embrace. I took a long breath—*one, two, three*—then pulled away.

"You'll go tomorrow morning," she announced, wiping her eyes. "I need time to prepare Data's program. Do not leave until I send word."

I nodded and faced Jayde. "Find Peng," I said, drying my own tears. "There will be no food served in this house today. Not a single member of my household will eat until tomorrow."

"Yes, ma'am." He moved to obey.

I turned back to Jael. "Get ahold of any churches you can, ask them to join us."

She nodded.

"I know someone who may be able to help with that." Nic approached us. He laid a hand on my shoulder and looked at Jael. "Can you reach Warden Ivanova? I need to talk to Ryan."

31: PHILADELPHIA

"Hold still."

I sucked in my breath and obeyed, holding my arms perfectly straight as Narissa circled around me. I stood on a stool in my dressing room, facing the trio of giant mirrors that lined one wall. It was Wednesday morning, and Narissa had shown up before first light to outfit Blue Fire with one last dress.

The cut was similar to the gown I'd worn at the party, with a stiff collar and a flowing skirt. The asymmetrical hemline hit my knee on my left side and nearly touched the floor on my right. Unlike the other dresses Narissa had created, however, this one was sleeveless. The thunderbird tattoo on my shoulder stood out against my pale skin like a wound.

This dress was also strangely understated. The entire garment was made of cool, shimmery black silk. The skirt and bodice were covered with embroidery, but the thread was also black, making it almost invisible against the fabric. I studied the complex stitches and wondered what the design meant.

Narissa hadn't given me any details. She gave my hem one last tug, then grunted in satisfaction. "That'll have to do," she mumbled around the pins in her mouth.

She helped me down. "Thank you for working on such short notice," I said. "I'll pay you double."

"Oh, I've had this dress finished for a while. I've known operation day was coming for three months." She plucked the pins out of her mouth and stabbed them in a cushion. "But I'll take the money."

She arched a thin eyebrow. I smiled. I knew Narissa wasn't in it for the money, but Andromeda wouldn't need her family fortune, not after today. It might as well go to someone I cared about.

Of course, after today, Narissa might not be able to use the money, either.

She turned back to the dress bag she'd brought with her. She pulled a black velvet jacket off a hanger and helped me shrug into it. The soft fabric covered my tattoo and made the whole outfit look sophisticated and mature.

Narissa's cold fingers brushed my neck, and I felt something snap in place on the edge of my collar. "Leave the jacket on until you're ready to make a scene," she instructed. "When it's time, yank it off, and let your dress do the talking."

I nodded and struggled to come up with a proper goodbye. What would happen to Narissa after I "made a scene"? Would they punish the stylist who had turned me into a living thunderbird? Would they care?

Narissa must have read the anxiety on my face. She straightened my jacket. "Focus, Blue Fire," she admonished. "It's your time to burn."

The house was somber as we followed our morning routine. The staff tread softly and spoke in whispers, like they were conducting a wake. In a way, they were.

Peng found me while Nic and I were eating breakfast on the veranda. "I cancelled your afternoon appointment." He held a tablet in his arm like a waiter and typed on the screen.

"Very good," I said, once again grateful that I had him. I'd completely forgotten about my other engagements this week. "I asked my accountant to give you a bonus this morning—you should see it in your account already."

He bowed. "That's extremely generous, ma'am. Thank you. What time would you like dinner to be served?"

I frowned. Peng didn't know everything that was going on, but he was aware of my alternate identity. Surely, he realized I wouldn't be home for dinner. "That won't be necessary. And, Peng, if you need to leave…"

His lips twitched. "I need to winterize the east garden today. What time for dinner? 6:30?"

I smiled and tried not to cry; Narissa would commit murder if I smeared my makeup. "6:30 will be fine."

Cardiff and his slobbering dog were weirdly absent all morning, which was just as well; I wouldn't have known what to say to him. Nic and I went through the motions of breakfast without exchanging a word. I had a dozen things I wanted to say, but I didn't want to break the silence. I just wanted to sip my coffee, stare at the pool, and pretend for one last moment that everything was normal.

Jayde met us in the foyer when it was time to leave. "Jael sends a message," he announced as I approached. "She said everything is ready. She'll be watching the stream. Just go with the flow, and she'll flip the switch when it's time."

I nodded. For the first time in months, there would be no script. No one would be there to give direction or cut the feed if things went wrong. It was all on me, and I had one shot to save the world.

I am Blue Fire, and this is my war.

"Everything you need is on here. Text messages, bank statements, all the evidence we have." He held out a small tablet.

I took it and rubbed the dark screen, fully aware that the tiny hard drive contained data capable of destroying a nation. I slid it into the velvet pocketbook Narissa had given me to match my outfit.

I'd only packed two other things. The burnt powercell fragment—a sharp reminder of how many lives were at stake if I didn't pull this off—and the star of David pin Lev, one of my Jewish followers, had given me.

For such a time as this.

"Jael regrets she can't be here," Jayde continued, "but she wanted me to tell you that she's proud of you."

I smiled and forced myself not to attach any emotion to that statement, tucking it away in my heart for later.

"We need to go. The car's waiting." Jayde moved to open the door.

"Jayde," I stopped him, "you don't have to come. You've done your job."

"My job isn't over. I still work for the Nolans. Unless this is your way of firing me." He brushed an imaginary crumb off his sleeve. He wore his dress uniform, a pin with the United seal on his breast pocket. I noticed his omnipresent holster was missing.

"You're not carrying?" I asked, and was surprised at how nervous that made me feel. Not that it mattered; Jayde wouldn't be able to help me, gun or not.

He unbuttoned his jacket, revealing an underarm holster. He'd swapped his electric pistol for an old-fashioned handgun with a clip. "I don't trust Asia's guns," he explained, "even with a new powercell."

"They're not going to let you in the building with that," Nic warned.

Jayde shrugged and redid his buttons.

"Here. There's something I need to give you." I reached into my pocket and pulled out the clicker. I dropped it in Jayde's palm.

He stared at it for a moment. "Guess you don't need this anymore." He held the door open for me.

I gathered my trailing hemline and stepped outside. "I never did."

The main council chambers sat on the edge of Tiananmen Square—a somewhat ironic choice. Several priceless historical buildings had been demolished to make room for the structure; I suppose the meager sacrifice was China's gesture of goodwill towards the new world order.

The building had been constructed in the 2030s to commemorate the founding of the United, and at the time, the design had been avant garde. Now, it looked like someone had asked a badly programmed AI to design a beached spaceship. The building was little more than a giant concrete donut. The side curved upwards, shading the sidewalk in gloomy darkness, and the windows were spaced irregularly like a mouth of broken teeth. The whole place was undecorated except for the boring United emblem.

Police had the square gated off. Jayde presented my credentials, and they flagged us through. The whole street was ghostly quiet, devoid of the usual tourists. Jayde handed the car off to a valet, then led the way to the main entrance.

Half a dozen armed soldiers manned the security booth. "Thumbprint, please," one of them demanded of me.

I obliged, pressing my hand to the screen on the outside of the bulletproof window.

He glanced at his computer. "I'm sorry, Miss Nolan, but they're not allowing visitors today."

"I'm aware," I said politely, "but General Secretary Mong invited me."

It was the truth, but he didn't believe me. The guard glanced back at his partner.

The other soldier was frowning at Nic, who stood behind me. I tensed and wondered if I should have made Nic stay home; if someone recognized him, I'd never get in the building.

The second guard started to say something, but just then a staffer walked up, rattling off a request in Mandarin. She got halfway through her sentence before she spotted me.

"Miss Nolan!" She bowed. "Are you here to see the General?"

I smiled. "Yes, he invited me."

"Oh, he'll be delighted to see you. Come with me." The staffer turned to the guards and chirped something in Mandarin that probably translated to *"Let her in, you idiots."*

The guards obeyed, opening the side door and ushering us through. We bypassed the security scanners and hurried to follow the staffer down the curved hallway.

The interior of the building was just as austere as the outside. The corridor was cavernous and drafty, and our voices echoed like the place was haunted. Plaques and statues were scattered along the wall, leaving huge stretches of undecorated concrete in between. The only color in the whole place was the dark red carpet, which looked like a trail of dried blood running up the hallway.

"It's so great to meet you," the staffer gushed as she led us around the corner. "His Excellency has talked about nothing except your party."

"I'm honored," I said, and I was. "He wanted me to come visit him here, see how things are run. I hope I'm not interrupting?"

"Oh no. I'm sure they'll be going on break soon; he'd love to take lunch with you. Here, this way."

She dropped her volume to a whisper, and we all softened our footsteps. She approached a mahogany door and opened it silently. The chatter of agitated voices flooded the hall. We followed the staffer into the auditorium and stood in the shadows at the back of the room.

"Wait here," she hissed. "As soon as he's free, I'll bring him over."

I thanked her, and she disappeared. I stepped forward and studied the room. I had seen it on TV many times, but it was even more imposing in person. The place was built like a concert hall. The building was at least five stories tall, with several balconies and a domed ceiling painted with a map of the world. The floor sloped downwards, allowing everyone a clear view of the podium in the center of the room. The General Secretary and two other world leaders sat in places of honor on the rostrum, listening to some politician as he strutted across the open floor and ranted about the "violent insurrectionists." The proceedings were projected on screens that hung from the balconies—no doubt the same feed Jael was watching from her office.

I scanned the crowd. The main floor was lined with rows of mahogany desks and plush chairs. Most of the seats were filled, although a few politicians paced the balconies and open aisles, whispering into their devices. Each councilmember had their own desk, ordered alphabetically.

I read the names. *K...L...M... Mong.*

There she was, in a desk only two rows back from the podium. She sat with one leg crossed over the other, picking at her bloodred lipstick with a pointed fingernail. She seemed bored as she watched the proceedings, like she'd scripted the entire scene in her head and was just waiting for it to play out.

Next to her was an empty desk. The surface had been stripped of everything personal except for the metal nameplate bolted to the back of the chair.

NOLAN, THAMES

My breath caught in my throat. "Wait here," I ordered Jayde.

He nodded and pressed himself against the wall, unobtrusive.

I took a step forward. Nic caught my arm.

I looked back at him. He stared at me, expression almost angry. But I knew better.

"I have to do this," I insisted.

He didn't argue. He gave my shoulder a sharp squeeze, then let go, muttering one name under his breath.

"Jesus."

I whispered in tongues and felt the stirring in the Spirit, weak and fluttery under the scream of fear. I filtered the noise until the only thing I could hear was a suffocating, overwhelming sense of conviction.

I am Andromeda Nolan.

I squared my shoulders and shook out my skirt.

And this is how I will fight my war.

Then I walked down the aisle to Thames's desk.

A few politicians whispered and glanced in my direction, but the orator continued to hold the attention of the rest of the room. Asia didn't notice me until I slid into the seat next to her.

She jerked upright and slammed her heels on the floor. "Andromeda!" she hissed. "What are you doing here?"

I smoothed my skirt over my knees. "Isn't this my father's chair?" I spoke coolly, confidently—and just loud enough for everyone around us to hear.

The orator stopped and turned. The noise in the room died off to a shocked gurgle. The General Secretary looked up, and our eyes met.

He stared at me, looking a bit surprised, perhaps somewhat annoyed. I waited. It was fully within his power to throw me out of the courtroom, or worse.

One of the guards standing near the podium pulled his communicator from his belt and held his hand over the button.

The General grinned. "Andromeda! I see you decided to take me up on my offer. Come down here and say hello." He beckoned to me.

"Beg pardon, Your Excellency," the orator stuttered, "I was speaking…"

"You haven't said anything in twenty minutes. We could all use a break."

Several people snickered. The orator scurried back to his seat, thoroughly culled. The guard snapped his communicator back in its holder.

I got up and walked to the center of the room. The General rose and stepped down to meet me, grasping my hand with both of his before I could even offer a bow. "It's so good to see you."

"It's good to see you again as well," I returned with my prettiest smile. "Thank you for inviting me."

Asia stood. "Father, this is very inappropriate—"

He shushed her. "She's fine. I invited her. What do you think of the place, Andromeda?"

"It's gorgeous." I glanced at the screens on the balcony and saw that I was perfectly centered in the camera, my face visible to the world.

The Holy Spirit pressed on my heart. *It's time.*

"Thinking of taking your father's seat?" the General teased, his hands still holding mine. "That district is up for commission next summer." He winked. A few nearby advisors laughed.

I took a breath, but the air stopped in my throat. I spoke around the bubble. "Actually, I… I came to talk to you." I withdrew my hand from his grasp.

I heard Asia's heels clacking behind me. *Don't turn around.*

The General glanced at the crowd. "Is it private?"

"No." I slid back and straightened. "Everyone needs to hear this."

The guards around the podium came to attention. One reached for his holster.

"Andromeda!" Asia screeched, her voice warped like a corrupted recording. "This is unaccept—"

"I am speaking!" the General snapped. "Andromeda, this had better not be a joke." The threat was thick in his voice.

Whispers broke out across the crowd. I saw several people pointing at their phones and knew Jael had flipped the switch. Thanks to Data's program, I was now mandatory viewing on every registered device across the globe. The world was watching.

Be with me, Jesus!

I met the General's stare. "No, sir. It's about Operation Blue Fire."

Asia made a sound like she'd been strangled.

"What about it?" the General returned.

I knew I might only have seconds, so I spoke as fast as I could. "Someone is trying to frame you. They've used your credentials to authorize shipments of weapons to underground outposts all across the city. They're planning to let the rebels take control on operation day and blame you for it."

There were several shouted exclamations in different languages from around the room. The General arched an eyebrow. "Frame me?"

"That's ridiculous!" Asia mocked, her laughter bright and fake. "Andromeda, this is embarrassing."

"I have proof. Text messages, phone calls, money transfers—evidence that someone set up a fake company and used your signature to authorize it." I opened my pocketbook and held out the tablet. My hand shook so hard that I nearly dropped the device. *Oh God, please let him believe me!*

The General gestured. The soldier standing nearest to me grabbed the device and swiped on the screen.

Asia tried to read over his shoulder. "Father, if this is true, then we need to convene immediately and review the files—"

"Silence," he snarled. "Andromeda, I need you to be very clear. Where did you get this information?"

"My servers, sir." I braced myself and sacrificed the privilege I'd been hiding behind for months. "The Nolans own that company."

Someone cursed.

"It's true," the guard declared. He tapped the screen. "If these screenshots are real, then she's telling the truth."

The commotion in the room boiled over.

The General was the only one who remained calm. His stare was still fixed on me, as if he knew the worst was yet to come. "And why would the Nolans be involved?"

Asia yanked her phone out of her pocket and scrabbled at the screen. I knew that if she made even one call, this would all be wasted.

Now.

"It's her!" I yelled, pointing. "Asia and Thames were working together!"

The room iced over. Not even Asia moved, as if she were afraid that she'd seal her own fate if she breathed.

The General was the first to speak. "Min?" he exclaimed, and the heartbreak in his voice shattered time.

Asia lurched back to life like a cursed mannequin. "That's preposterous!" she slurred, her voice waffling between a deranged cackle and a violent shriek. "I don't know anything about this."

"She's been trying to overthrow you this whole time," I insisted. "First it was Red Rain—"

"Red Rain!" the General barked.

"I had nothing to do with that! This is insane. I'm calling my lawyer." Asia typed with both thumbs.

"Don't let her send any messages!" I screamed.

The guards obeyed me. One lunged forward and grabbed Asia's phone.

"This is an outrage! Don't touch me!" She tried to yank the device away and lost her grip, stumbling gracelessly on her tall heels. She struggled to compose herself and looked at the General with a grotesque smile. "Father! This is a disgrace. You'll let a *child* barge into *your* courtroom and accuse a councilwoman?"

"What if the girl is lying?" one of the advisors on the podium echoed.

"It's all true!" I exclaimed. "You can cross-reference everything. I can show you the factory—"

"You're pathetic," Asia cut me off. "I'll have you sued for slander. Now, give me my phone!"

I turned to the General. "Please, sir, don't let her make a call. If you do, dozens of people will die. She has hostages."

"Father!" Asia objected. "You're not going to allow this, are you?"

The guards didn't move. The General studied her, weighing her life with one cold stare. Then he glanced at me.

I bunched my skirt in both fists. This was all for nothing if he believed her over me. *Please, God! Intervene!*

The General straightened. "Lock down the building," he ordered, his voice commanding the room without a microphone. "Absolutely no one comes or goes without my permission. Shut down the livestream and cut off communications. I don't want anyone—"

I reached for him. "No, wait!" If he put the building in blackout, it would cut off Jael's broadcast. "There's more. Everyone who got those guns is in danger."

He stopped mid-motion. "What do you mean?"

"They're rigged with a faulty powercell. If you fire the guns, they will explode."

"*What?*" Asia gasped.

I dug in my pocketbook for the ruined powercell. "It's an intentional design flaw in the power core—we've tested it. It reacts at high voltage and causes the battery to melt, triggering an explosion." I held the fragment up, making sure it was visible on camera.

The General snatched it from my hand.

"She distributed at least a hundred thousand of these guns in Beijing and Washington," I explained, fighting to keep my voice steady as the adrenaline clogged my throat. "If the underground uses these guns tomorrow during operation day, you'll lose the city. She was trying to kill you, the Council, everyone."

"No, I wasn't!" Asia was trembling, barely able to stay upright. Hair flopped out of her bun as she gestured with both hands. "I didn't know about the powercells—"

"It's true!"

I whirled. Nic jogged down the aisle.

"You!" Asia took a drunken step forward. The guard behind her clasped her shoulder in warning.

Two more soldiers moved to block Nic's way. He skidded to a stop and lifted his hands in surrender. "I can vouch for everything," he explained. "I was working in the factory where they produced the powercells. At least a quarter million were shipped out."

A nearby advisor muttered an oath.

"What are *you* doing here?" the General demanded, clearly recognizing Nic. "Arrest him!"

The two guards grabbed Nic's arms. He didn't resist. "It's also true about Red Rain," he declared calmly, his eyes on the General. "She's been funding the project for over a decade. She was the one who gave me the base on Mars."

The sound that came from Asia's throat wasn't human. "Lies!"

"Min, if you take one step, I swear I will shoot you myself!" the General roared.

I took advantage of her terrified silence. "It's true, sir. She and Thames have been working together this whole time. Red Rain, Rott, Blue Fire—it was all her idea. The only reason Thames recorded those videos was to cover his tracks on Rott."

It was only after I finished the sentence that I realized the room had again grown deathly quiet.

The General narrowed his eyes. "How did you know Thames was responsible for the recordings?"

I hesitated. It wasn't too late; I could claim that I'd simply uncovered evidence on Thames's servers. It wouldn't even be a lie. I could escape with my money and my clean file and hope that everyone saw the stream and knew the guns were rigged.

But it wouldn't be enough. The underground didn't listen to Andromeda. They only followed Blue Fire.

And it was time for her to lead.

I looked at Nic. He nodded.

I dropped my pocketbook on the floor and straightened. A glance at the screen showed I was dead center in the frame.

"Andromeda…?" the General said haltingly.

"My name is Philadelphia Smyrna," I announced, my voice ricocheting around the dome. I slid my arms out of my jacket sleeves. "And I am Blue Fire."

Then I yanked my jacket off my shoulders.

Something under my collar snapped, and my dress came to life. With a crackle of electricity that I felt down my spine, the fabric lit up. Suddenly, all the embroidery glowed bright blue. Bolts of lightning jagged across the skirt, exploding in a shower of sparks near the hemline. In the camera, I could see that a thunderbird was stitched across my back, its wings fanned over my shoulders.

Several people screamed. Those standing closest to me drew back like I was a live snake. I ignored them all, spinning so that everyone could see the tattoo emblazoned on my shoulder.

"I am Blue Fire!" I shouted. "And I'm cancelling the operation!"

"Andromeda!" the General yelled again, and this time, it was a threat.

"Andromeda Nolan is dead!" I declared. I popped my blue contacts out and threw them on the floor. "Thames altered her file to protect me."

The General muttered an oath. Asia wailed. I whirled to face the camera so my face filled the screen. "This message is for everyone who follows Blue Fire. The operation is cancelled!"

"Stand down!" someone yelled.

I refused to look back. "You cannot use those guns! If you fire them, you will die, and you will destroy this city."

The commotion in the room escalated. "Don't shoot!" another voice ordered.

I yelled to be heard over the noise. "Think of all the people you'll kill! You will reduce this city to rubble and take thirty million innocent people out with you! That is not who we are!"

There were shouts and orders and motion everywhere, but no one touched me. No one tried to stop me. Perhaps because they, too, realized I was the only one who could prevent this.

"We are not like them." I glared at the screen, my eyes flashing with authority. "We do not fight with their weapons. I refuse to sacrifice an entire city to win the war. Please, hear me: Stand down. Destroy the weapons and run."

"Philadelphia!" Asia screeched like someone getting burned alive. "I will kill you!" She lurched, but the guard held her back.

"You have to run!" I shrieked. "She knows where you are! She's been tracking the guns. If you stay, the government will find you! Get out of the city!"

"Cut the stream!" the General ordered, and then everything happened at once.

Asia roared. She lifted her knee and slammed the guard in the shin with her deadly heel, knocking him back. Nic yelled my name and threw off his guards as several people rushed towards me. Asia grabbed the soldier's gun and whirled.

"Andromeda!" someone shouted, but it was too late.

Nic crashed into me just as Asia fired.

I landed on the floor. Nic screamed. I struggled to rise as my ears rang and the wind escaped my chest. The whole room spun, and all I could see was the blurred mural of the world twirling around me, like I was trapped in a globe rolling downhill.

"Watch out!"

The room slammed back into place, as if we'd crashed at the bottom. I saw Nic kneeling on the floor, blood oozing from his shoulder, and Asia leering over him with the gun, and knew we were not safe.

"Asia, don't!"

Her whole body twitched and stuttered. Her eyes were inhuman as she aimed the gun at me.

A gunshot exploded from above us. Asia lurched to a halt, wobbling on her stilettos. She didn't breathe, didn't scream, didn't move. No one reacted, as if the shot had stopped time. The only thing moving was the blood seeping through Asia's dress.

I scrambled up. Jayde stood on the balcony, his smoking gun in his hands.

He tossed the weapon aside. Our eyes met. *I told you I would shoot first.*

Time restarted. Guards on the balcony lunged for Jayde. Nic staggered to his feet. Politicians scattered like birds, shrieking. There were shouts and a call for an ambulance and the distinct sound of a body hitting the floor. Asia gagged.

I started to turn, but Nic grabbed me. He pulled me to himself with his good arm and pressed my face against his chest. "You've seen so much death," he hissed in my ear. "Let me save you from this one."

I relented. I covered my ears and closed my eyes as the room descended into chaos. I heard a siren blaring and the General barking orders. Doors slammed. Someone was crying.

And underneath it all were the visceral sounds of Asia dying violently.

Suddenly, the silence returned, thick and choking. Nic loosened his hold, and I lifted my head.

The room was in lockdown. Metal shutters covered all the windows while guards blocked the doors. Politicians clumped around the edge of the room, whispering in fearful clusters. Jayde still stood on the balcony, handcuffed between two soldiers, looking entirely unbothered by the situation.

I dared to turn around—just in time to see paramedics wheel a sheet-covered stretcher away.

I struggled to breathe, feeling, for the first time in months, like I could. *She's dead. Asia is dead!*

Nic muttered something under his breath and kept his hand on my shoulder.

The General knelt on the floor. He stared at the stain on the carpet for a moment, then took a deep breath and pushed himself to his feet. His gaze settled on me.

I stared back. He didn't seem angry. If anything, he was disappointed.

"I'm sorry I lied to you," I said, and in a way, I was.

He turned away. "Confiscate everyone's electronics," he ordered. "Absolutely no one leaves this building until approved by me."

Someone shouted an objection in Mandarin from the back of the room.

The General didn't even look in their direction. "If anyone resists, I will assume the worst."

I stiffened. The witch hunt had begun.

The General pointed at a guard. "Lock them up. No one speaks to them without my permission."

The guards on the balcony shoved Jayde towards the door. Two more moved towards us. Nic tightened his grip. I looked up into his scowling face and realized he was contemplating doing something very stupid.

"It's okay." I gently pried his hand off my shoulder. "I'll go."

He jerked out of his stupor. His eyes focused on me, and his expression broke.

I stepped away from him and faced the General. "Please, sir, he's injured."

He glanced at me, then at Nic. "Get this man taken care of, then bring him to my office."

The guards separated us. I followed one willingly to the door. As they ushered me out into the hall, I took one look back.

Nic still stood there, clutching his bleeding shoulder, body tense like he might bolt.

I gave him an encouraging smile, then stepped out into the hall.

It was only after the door shut behind me that I realized I may have missed my chance to say goodbye.

32: NIC

I spent the afternoon in a nearby hospital, getting my shoulder stitched back together. There was nothing I could do but lie extremely still while the regeneration machine did its work, so I decided to use the time wisely. I filled the hours praying silently and not-so-silently. It worked; when the procedure was done, I felt pretty good, all things considered.

I could only hope Philadelphia would still be alive by the time I got out of the hospital.

As soon as the doctor released me, they cuffed me and hauled me back to the council chambers. The building looked like a refugee camp. Police had the entire block cordoned off. Disgruntled politicians shivered in lines as they waited to be interrogated. Several were in handcuffs. Everyone looked like prisoners of war as soldiers screamed orders at them through megaphones.

They patted me down not once, not twice, but *three* times for weapons before letting me into the General Secretary's office. Why they hadn't checked me while I was half-naked in a hospital gown was beyond me. They finally deemed me clear and opened the door.

The General sat behind a behemoth desk. Three staffers were talking to him at once as they fired agitated updates. He silenced them all with a wave of his hand when he spotted me.

"Leave us," he barked in Mandarin.

The staff scattered. Only three guards remained. One of them pushed me inside, then shut and locked the door.

"Any electronics?" the General demanded, still in Mandarin.

"No sir, he's clear," the guard replied, clearly not realizing I could understand them.

"Good." The General flicked his own phone off, then tossed it on a thick mat on the corner of his desk—a dampening field, no doubt. The guards followed suit with their communicators.

The General leaned back in his chair and regarded me silently. I stood as far away from the desk as I could without stepping on a guard's toes and tried to figure out how to greet the man. Despite the fact that I'd dated his daughter for five years, I'd never actually met the General Secretary face-to-face, and I was none too thrilled about breaking that record.

Thankfully, he spared me the misery of proper etiquette. "I know who you are," he declared in English.

It was a pathetic threat; everyone in Beijing knew who I was. My fake trial had been a sensation, and I wasn't putting any effort into hiding my identity. "It's the mustache, isn't it?" I returned. I spoke in his native tongue, hoping that would buy me some points.

"I should have you hanged," he continued, taking me up on my offer and switching back to Mandarin.

This, too, was common knowledge. "Undoubtedly. But that seems like an awful lot of paperwork when you just pardoned me."

"Quite," he agreed. "In any case, I may have another use for you."

I took a whole step back, ramming into a guard's armored chest. "Ooh, I don't like the sound of that. Is going back to jail still an option?"

"We'll discuss it later," he deferred. "In the meantime, you and I both have a more pressing problem. Androme—ahh, Philadelphia."

I sighed. She was, as usual, my most pressing problem. "You're going to kill her, aren't you?"

He hesitated just long enough to be cruel. "I'm signing the execution order this evening."

How generous of you to give me a few hours to prepare myself. "She won't resist you," I said, then grimaced when I realized just how true that statement was.

His silence suggested he was aware of that fact.

"Just do *me* a mercy and make it quick," I pleaded.

He looked away, but not before I saw the truth spelled out in his eyes: He loved her, and he had no idea what to do with that information. I could see it written all over the pinched lines in his face.

I recognized that look, because I'd spent the better part of the last six months making the same expression in the mirror.

Suddenly, I knew why we were having this conversation. *Oh God, help me.*

I raised my voice ever so slightly. "You don't have to do this."

He glanced back at me with a frown.

I stepped towards the desk. "You don't have to kill her. You can save her."

"Don't patronize me," he groaned, even though I was quite sure the inverse was happening. "You know I can't."

"That's grammatically incorrect," I snapped, clenching my fists. "You own this planet. You *can* do whatever you want."

The guards shifted in my peripheral. *Patience,* the Holy Spirit warned me, and I forcibly loosened my grip. "You have the power," I repeated. "Let her live. Please."

He shook his head, eyes avoiding mine. "It's not possible. The Council will rule—"

"Then make it possible." It took every ounce of willpower to keep the anger out of my voice. "The Council will know that this is a suicidal idea. Operation day is tomorrow—if you kill her now, you'll make her a martyr. You'll seal your own fate."

"I will not show weakness towards this insurrection!" He was doing a terrible job of filtering his anger, which told me there was still hope.

"I'm not asking you to pardon her," I argued. "Just stay her execution, wait until the operation blows over. Then you can quietly send her off to prison. I know a good one in Russia."

He didn't get the joke. "That is not an option."

"Then why'd you call me in here? You don't want to do this. You don't want to kill her."

I was right, and that just made him more furious. "Do not mock me!"

"You want a way out. I'm giving it to you. Please, just consider—"

He slapped his hands on the desk and stood up in one livid motion. "I will not risk the stability of the entire nation for one life!" He gestured at the guards. "Get him out of here."

I eluded their grasp. "Why not? That's what she did for you."

Everyone in the room froze, and I winced.

"What did you say?" Mong snarled.

Tell him, the Holy Spirit coached.

I took a deep breath. "Do you want to know the real reason she came to Beijing?"

"What do you mean?" He stood back from the desk.

I looked him straight in the eye. "She was going to kill you."

He was silent.

"The rebellion found out 'Andromeda' had been invited to the state gala and knew that was their opportunity to get close to you. They rigged up a kill switch in her palm. If she had shaken your hand, it would have reacted to your DNA and sent you into cardiac arrest."

"That's ridiculous," he scoffed, and the flicker in his eyes told me that he didn't want to believe it.

"Run a medical scan on her hand. You'll find the wire remnants and subdermal scarring," I insisted.

He glanced at the guards. One of them snatched his communicator off the dampening pad and paged for a doctor.

I kept my eyes on Mong. "That's why she didn't shake your hand at the party. She wasn't being polite—she was saving your life."

He stared at the wall, and I knew he was replaying that moment in his mind, seeing all the red herrings he should have noticed before.

His gaze cleared, and he turned back to me. "Why?" he demanded.

There were a dozen answers to that question, none of which were relevant. "She spared you, and in exchange, she not only put herself at risk but also endangered the entire operation. She could have lost the war because she let you go. She was willing to risk a hundred more years of tyranny just to save *your* life."

I let the words hang between us as the Holy Spirit added His own commentary.

"The Lord is not slow in keeping His promise, as some understand slowness. Instead He is patient with you, not wanting anyone to perish, but everyone to come to repentance."

Suddenly, I saw the whole picture. I understood why God had picked Philadelphia, and it had nothing to do with Red Rain or Rott or the Nolans or Jael.

A few people might be willing to lose the war to save a city of thirty million innocent souls. But there were even fewer who would look the General Secretary of the United in the eye and prophesy life, freedom, and forgiveness.

Philadelphia Smyrna was one of those few.

I looked back up at Mong. "I guess you're lucky she's not more like you."

A knock on the door ended the conversation. "What?" Mong barked.

The door opened, and Cardiff waltzed in.

"Who let you in here?" Mong demanded, sounding as annoyed as I felt.

"I'm a Nolan," he chirped in his pretentious British accent. "Which, up until a few hours ago, actually meant something."

Mong folded his arms across his chest. "What do you want?"

"Unless I'm mistaken, that's *my sister* you've got in a holding cell."

She wasn't really his sister in any meaningful way, but I let him have it. Any votes Phil could get in her favor, the better.

"Yes," Mong hissed, "and that's where she'll stay until I say otherwise."

Cardiff propped his elbow in his hand and twirled his fingers, as if this conversation were beneath him. "Forgive me, but I'm not particularly in the mood to watch another family member die a gruesome death on live TV. Even if she is adopted."

Mong hesitated.

"I've come to offer you a solution," Cardiff declared. "Release her to me, and I'll get her off planet."

"Off planet how?" I demanded.

He spared me a sideways glance. "I literally own a space station."

Mong recovered from the shock. "What's in it for you?" he demanded.

"My sister doesn't die?" Cardiff returned, as if it was a stupid question, which it kind of was.

Mong huffed. "Since when have you cared about Androm—Philadelphia?"

I was tempted to ask the same question, but I wasn't about to argue with someone who was trying to save Philadelphia's life.

"Look," Cardiff sighed, "I'm aware I've made mistakes regarding my family. It's too late to apologize to my aunt and uncle, and it's too late to save my cousin. But it's not too late to do right by Philadelphia."

He attached a lot of emotion to that last sentence—a lot of anguished, humble, genuine emotion—and I somewhat hoped he was just putting on a show for Philadelphia's benefit.

Cardiff stepped forward and gripped the desk with both hands, getting eye level with the General. "Let me save her."

Mong glanced at me. I didn't love the idea of Philadelphia going off planet with her weird adoptive brother, but anything to keep her alive one more day. "You have the power," I reminded the General.

He inhaled through his nose. "What are you proposing?" he asked Cardiff.

Cardiff stepped back from the desk. "I have a transit ready to leave. We can be off the planet in three hours. The station we're going to is extremely remote. She'll be completely off the grid, unable to record any videos."

And unable to contact me, I realized, and almost changed my mind about the whole thing.

"No more Blue Fire, no more propaganda," Cardiff explained. "Best case scenario, her followers will think she's abandoned them, and they'll disband on their own. But even if they do concoct a story, at least you won't have created a martyr."

Jael would most certainly concoct a story, but Cardiff had a point. A public execution would galvanize the resistance; if the government left Phil's fate open to speculation, the media would have room to modify the narrative.

"In the meantime, you freeze her assets, mark her file, make it look like you're doing your due diligence." Cardiff gestured at the General's computer. "And after everything has blown over and you've taken care of this petty insurrection… we'll talk."

It was a good plan. I hated it, but it was a good plan. Cardiff would buy us time—time for Jael and me to figure out how to safely bring Philadelphia home.

Mong was silent. He exchanged a coded stare with one of his soldiers.

I put myself between them. "Please," I begged one last time. "Do it for her."

*

I ran to keep up as we followed a pair of guards through the gloomy halls of the basement to the holding cells. The General was surprisingly agile, especially considering he was at least twenty years older than me. At least he'd had the decency to let me out of the handcuffs.

Mong had made a few calls and then led us out the back way. Unsurprisingly, he had a hidden exit from his office to a private fallout shelter. We slipped through there to an empty stairwell, avoiding prying eyes. I could only assume the guards Mong had with him were undyingly loyal and could keep a secret, but frankly, I didn't care. As soon as Philadelphia was safely off planet, it wouldn't be my problem anymore.

Several armed guards and a man in scrubs waited outside of her cell. Mong waved his hand, and they unlocked the door.

I shoved past the others. "Philadelphia."

She sat calmly on the bench. "Nic!" She darted into the hall and hugged me.

I didn't let her savor it. "We don't have much time. You need to leave."

"What—" She stopped when she saw the General. She pulled back from me.

Mong gestured at the man in scrubs, who passed him a med scanner. Mong stepped forward and held out his hand.

Philadelphia swallowed and slowly extended her right hand, palm up.

Mong didn't touch it. He passed the med scanner over her fingers, squinting at the readout. Then he looked into her face.

They exchanged a wordless stare, and I knew they both understood.

Cardiff interrupted the moment. "My pilot's ready. Let's go."

Phil turned to me. "What's going on?"

"You're getting out of here," I explained. "Cardiff's getting you off the planet while the General looks the other way."

She whirled on him.

He folded his arms. "Stay offline," he warned, the threat uncensored. "If there's even the tiniest blip of activity on your file, I will retaliate."

She nodded. "Yessir. Thank you, sir."

He didn't respond.

Cardiff led the way down the hall. "We need to move!"

Philadelphia started to follow—then hesitated. She glanced back at the General.

I reached for her. "Phil…"

"Be kind to the rebels on operation day," she said. "If you punish them harshly like Asia did, you will lose control. The United will fall."

I could tell by the shift in her tone and the sheen in her eyes that she wasn't speaking her own words—and she was absolutely right.

"Leave," the General ordered. There was no emotion in his voice.

I grabbed her arm. She gathered her skirt and ran.

The soldiers led us down the hall and up a ramp to the parking lot. The police had cleared the area, their vans blocking the view from the road. A helicopter idled in the middle of the asphalt.

Cardiff whispered something to our escorts, then ran for the aircraft. "Come on!" he shouted over his shoulder. "We have ten minutes to be out of restricted airspace!"

Philadelphia pinched my arm. "You're coming with us, right?"

How I wished I was—and I realized, in that moment, it was within my power to say yes.

But there was something I had to take care of first.

"No. There's something I need to do here."

Panic flooded her expression. "But—"

"Phil. It's about Stanyard."

She sucked in her breath.

Cardiff climbed into the helicopter. The pilot cranked the engine, and the blades whirred to life.

I shouted to be heard. "Listen. I talked to Asia a few days ago, and something's wrong. I don't have any details. All I know is that they were transporting him and lost contact with the plane."

Her eyes watered as the wind from the chopper whipped her hair into her face. "Do you think he's…" She couldn't bring herself to say the word.

"No," I declared, and I still believed it. "Maybe he escaped, I don't know. But whatever it is, I need to find him."

"Let me go with you," she begged.

I started to object, but someone beat me to it. "Philadelphia!"

We turned. Dr. Smyrna leaned out of the aircraft.

I stiffened when I recognized something I should have seen all along: Cardiff had been prepared for this.

"Dad!" Phil shrieked.

"Hurry, please!" He beckoned with both hands. "We have to go! Your brother will meet us up there."

She started to pull away, but she still hadn't let go of my arm.

I gripped both of her shoulders and got down on her eye level. "Philadelphia. Listen to me. I need you to go with your father."

"But Stanyard—"

"I will find him. But you have to get off this planet while you still can. The General will kill you if you don't leave."

She started to cry. "But I can't leave you! Not again!"

"I know." She had no idea how much I hated this. "But you have to trust me. Let Jael and I handle this. As soon as I can, I'll come find you."

"But—"

"Philadelphia," I interrupted, and waited until she focused on me before continuing. "I promise I will come find you."

She resisted, her whole body withdrawing—and then she obeyed. "Okay." She swallowed a sob. "I trust you." She hugged me.

I hugged her back. "I promise," I repeated, although she wasn't the one who needed the reassurance.

She gripped my shirt. "I love you."

I froze as the entire universe ground to a halt.

"Philadelphia, please!" her father shouted.

She let go of me and ran for the helicopter. Cardiff offered her a hand, and she climbed in without a glance back.

Her father hesitated in the doorway and cast me a look that wasn't quite kind. But then he remembered his manners and mouthed a *"thank you."*

I didn't respond.

He dragged the cockpit door shut. The propellers kicked into high gear. I braced myself against the wind as the helicopter lifted from the pad. Philadelphia pressed her face against the window and waved one last time.

I stood on the asphalt and watched until they were out of sight. It was only after the helicopter disappeared behind a high rise that I wondered if I'd made a mistake by letting her go.

JOHN DOWE

RED RAIN #9.5

SEPTEMBER 2076

1

Of all my interrogators, I hated Williams the most.

It wasn't that he was the most brutal. Holt was always yelling like he forgot to put his hearing aid in. Blonde liked to use his fists, although he had yet to do anything worse than my dad had done. And Landa—well, Landa was the only one who scared me. He wasn't loud and he wasn't violent, but he was relentless. He would question me for hours, twisting words and spiking lies with the truth until I wasn't sure what was real anymore.

Williams did none of that. If anything, his dull pragmatism was kind of annoying. But he did smoke—a lot, judging by the smell.

Every thirty minutes, he would go on break and come back reeking. And in the cramped interrogation room—with its sterile walls and too-bright lights—the effect was positively torturous.

I held my breath as he slid back into the chair across from me. "You know, this could all be over," he drawled, which was how he opened every session.

I didn't answer, mostly because I was trying not to cough.

He rubbed his lips with a stained finger. "I only have one question."

I clenched my fists.

"Where is Philadelphia?"

I hated how he said her name, all croaked and craggily like she was an old witch. Philadelphia was beautiful and kind and courageous, and I'd die before I turned her—or any of our friends—in.

Which, at this rate, it might come to that.

When I didn't respond for a long moment, Williams shifted in his chair. "You know where she is."

I did know—or, at least, I could give a good description of the family who was sheltering her in Beijing.

"We won't hurt her."

That's exactly what they'd do. The United would make a public example out of her. The government would burn "the thunderbird" at the stake, and then the revolution would be over before it started.

I couldn't—wouldn't—let that happen. Not on account of me.

"I talked to Lev." Williams leaned forward and wheezed, assaulting me with his stale breath.

I pulled back as far as I could with my hands cuffed to the table. Lev had been arrested with me when the government busted our base. I hadn't been allowed to see him since. I could only hope they weren't keeping him locked in a blindingly-lit room and depriving him of sleep.

But at least they'd taken him alive—unlike the other person who had been on base. I flinched at the gruesome memory.

Williams squinted, as if searching for my weakness. "Lev already told me everything he knows."

That was a lie, I was sure of it. Lev was only fourteen, but he wasn't weak. He'd already seen more death and violence than the rest of us put together. And he was fiercely loyal to "Blue Fire"; he'd supported her at the risk of his own life once before. I prayed that hadn't changed.

Besides, Lev didn't know where Phil was, not specifically. I'd intentionally kept the information from him so he wouldn't become a liability.

Unfortunately, that also made him expendable.

"We will find her," Williams grunted, pausing after each word as if I could be threatened by enunciation. "We have other leads."

I doubted it. If they had a lead, they wouldn't have kept me alive. Philadelphia's location was strictly classified. There were only three people in Boston who could give a name and address: Data, Tower, and me.

Data was still at large. Tower was dead. If the government wanted the information, they were going to have to go through me.

I resisted the urge to parrot Williams' words as he finished his exhausted act. "If you make this easy, we'll spare her associates and give you a full pardon."

So many false promises. They'd offered me money, freedom, a chance to see Philadelphia one last time. What was offensive was that they thought it would work.

I'd had a dozen opportunities to save myself. But I'd made my choice, and I'd make it again and again, no matter how many times they asked me. After years of running and failing and being other people's punching bag, I was finally doing something good. I'd done right by Philadelphia, and I would never throw that away, even if it killed me.

I looked Williams straight in the eye and said the one word that had become my lifeline: "No."

He groaned, as if he were just as bored with the proceedings as I was. He slumped back in his chair and pressed a button on the table. "I can't break him," he announced, not that he'd tried all that hard. "Bring her in."

I sat up. "Her?"

The door unlocked, and two more guards entered. One set a glowing tablet on the table in front of me. A hologram flickered to life above the screen, bringing me face to face with the only person I hated more than Williams: Asia.

Her technical title was Councilwoman Mong, but she'd long since lost the privilege of being addressed with any respect. She was the one who put a bounty on my girlfriend's life. She was the one slaughtering my friends and persecuting the unassimilated. She was the reason I'd spent the last week cuffed to a table in an interrogation room answering stupid questions.

Of course, she never would have caught me if my own sister hadn't turned me in.

"Hello, Stanyard," Asia cooed. She was always cooing and purring and curling her fingers in weird motions like a demon-possessed cat.

"Hi," I grunted.

"How are you feeling?"

As if it wasn't obvious with my black eye and split lip. "I was doing better before you showed up."

She smiled, revealing teeth that were so white they had to be fake. "You know it doesn't have to be this way."

"Yes, I'm quite aware there are several worse alternatives."

"We can end this. We can stop all this bloodshed."

"*You* can stop mass-murdering people anytime you like. You don't need me for that."

She continued reciting from her script like she hadn't heard me. "All I need is her. She and I can end this war together. You have my word that I will not hurt her."

"Still don't believe you."

Her perfect smile started to curl downwards. "I don't enjoy this, Stanyard. I don't want to hurt you."

"Coulda fooled me. Landa certainly enjoys his job."

Williams smacked his lips.

She glanced at her diamond-encrusted watch. "And I normally pride myself in having a lot of patience, but I'm coming up on a deadline."

We all were. Operation Day was in two weeks. In two weeks, if Philadelphia was successful, the revolution would start. People all over the world would stand up and say no to the government's control.

After that, none of this would matter. If I could just hold out for two weeks, it would all be over.

Asia, of course, knew that. "So, I'm going to ask you one last time."

"That's what you said yesterday."

She leaned towards the camera. "Where is Philadelphia?"

I pulled my shoulders back, set my jaw, and glared at her.

She let the silence hang for one minute, two. One of the guards coughed. I said nothing.

She finally took the hint and sank back in her chair with a sigh. "I wish it didn't come to this."

I shrugged, even as I braced myself for a new threat.

"But we have ways of making you talk."

"Like what, waterboarding?" I snarked.

She fixed me with the same disapproving frown my high school teacher used to use. "Attitude," she reproved. "But no. This is communist China. We're much more... technologically advanced than that."

I stiffened.

Her coy smile returned. "Have you heard of synaptic reading, Stanyard?"

My throat closed. *No, not that.*

"It's quite a fascinating technology," she continued, purring again. "Assuming you *do* know where Philadelphia is, all I have to do is implant a little chip in your brain, and I can read anything I want to know."

I could barely hear her over the blood pounding in my ears. *You can't!*

She tapped a pointy acrylic fingernail on her chin. "I would just love to get a look at that brilliant mind of yours. You're such a smart boy—I'm sure you're a treasure trove of information."

She was right. I was a walking flash drive of intel—some of which was, arguably, even more dangerous than Philadelphia's location. I knew dozens of names, passcodes, and addresses that weren't stored on any server. Most importantly, I was very familiar with the code for Data's broadcasting program.

Data was the unofficial leader of the Boston underground, and he was a close associate of Philadelphia's. He and I had developed a backdoor that allowed us to highjack the government's mandatory viewing protocol. With a few clicks, we could force any of Blue Fire's videos to autoplay on every registered device on the planet.

It was the key to Operation Day's success. If Asia found out, they'd patch our backdoor and silence us for good.

"I can get what I want," Asia declared. "But it is such a *messy* procedure. All those wires and needles... And I hear it's not really reversible."

It wasn't. Synaptic interfacing was permanent; it was almost impossible to remove all the wiring without causing brain damage. Once the chip was installed, my brain could be read by any synaptic device, anywhere. They could even make it wireless.

Asia relished my silence. "I'll give you a few minutes to think about it. Give me what I want, and I'll let you keep your mind to yourself."

I bit my tongue.

"Bring him to me," she ordered with a flick of her finger over her shoulder. "If he doesn't talk within the hour, I want him on a plane to Beijing."

"What about the Jew?" Williams asked. He slurred the name into an insult.

"Bring him along. I'm sure Philadelphia would love to see him."

I shuddered. Lev was disposable. If Philadelphia—or I—didn't break, they'd kill him. They might kill him anyway.

Asia was grinning now, eyes glittering with pure wickedness. "I look forward to meeting you in person, Stanyard."

She winked, and the hologram went dark.

One of the guards retrieved the tablet. All I could hear in the sudden silence was heavy breathing. It took a minute to realize it was me.

Williams stood up. "You have twenty minutes to make your decision." He left with the other soldiers, and the door thudded and locked behind them.

I put my head in my hands and raked my hair. I had to get out of here. I couldn't let them rip my mind like a hard drive. It would compromise hundreds of people—Data, Jael, Philadelphia—and give the government a map of the underground. They already had the data from my servers, but it was nothing compared to the memories in my own mind.

Worse, once my brain was wired, I'd be a liability to everyone. The government would have the power to eavesdrop on all my thoughts. I could never see Philadelphia, or my parents, or anyone in the underground ever again—the United would immediately know everything.

I had to get out of here before they put me on a plane. But how? I'd been cuffed to a table or locked in a cell for the last I-don't-know-how-many days. I had no idea where I was or what kind of building I was in. I didn't even know what time it was.

I yanked on my chains in frustration. *God, we can't let this happen! I need you!*

This couldn't be how it ended. We had a real chance of winning this thing. We had global support from all levels of society and a broadcast program that could break the government's control in one click. After over forty years of tyranny, we finally had the opportunity to end the United, and I was not going to be the reason we lost the war.

God, I need you! I screamed again, because it was the only thought I could string together. I tipped my head back and shouted at the ceiling, not caring who heard me. "I need a way out!"

There was no answer.

Time ticked by—slowly, the only sound in the cramped room the scrape of the chair on the floor as I fidgeted—until I could have sworn it had been more than twenty minutes. I prayed fiercely and searched my mind for any idea, any inspiration, any peace or burst of courage or anything. There was nothing.

Finally, the lock slid in the door. I braced myself as it swung open, bringing Williams' disgusting scent back into the room. There was fumbling and clattering, like he tripped over the chair.

I refused to look up. He said nothing, his breathing ragged. I let the silence hang until I could stand it no longer.

"I'm not going to do it," I declared, stating the one and only thing I knew to be true. "I won't tell you where Philadelphia is."

"Rude, but we didn't ask."

I jerked upright and would have fallen out of the chair had I not been cuffed to the table. I knew that voice—*voices*—and it wasn't Williams.

Across the table sat John and Dowe.

2

We stared at each other while I tried desperately to convince myself I was hallucinating. It was definitely them: thinning hair, lumbering frames, and creepy copy-paste features that made them look like defective clones. They were both wearing ill-fitting guard uniforms with Williams' name tag.

It was that inexplicable detail that convinced me I was projecting the whole thing. John and Dowe had appeared in unexpected places before, but showing up in a locked cell at the heart of a maximum-security prison *wearing my interrogator's uniform* was just too much. Apparently, I'd finally snapped, and this was my brain's warped idea of a coping mechanism.

"What are you doing here?" I managed, then braced myself for the dumbest possible answer.

I got it. "Talking to you," the one I thought was Dowe quipped. It was always a fifty-fifty guess which one was speaking.

"Sorry it's outside of visiting hours," the other added. He squirmed and shoved his partner with his hip; they were both trying—and failing—to sit in the same chair.

"But... how did you get in here?"

"The door?" John gestured at it.

Dowe must have read the look on my face, because he lifted his finger. "Ohhh, you mean how did we get in the *building*. Yeah, well, we were supposed to be running an errand for Seoul. Andes asked us to pick up some flowers while we were out..."

"...but we brought the wrong screwdriver, so we got caught, and they threw us in here," John finished.

I almost believed that story, except Seoul was supposed to be back in Beijing working for Philadelphia, and Andes was not the type to buy flowers, and I had no idea what screwdrivers had to do with anything.

"But it all worked out, because we got to see you!" John chirped. "I do need to figure out where I put that screwdriver, though."

"But, how...?" I couldn't even formulate a complete question. *This can't be happening.*

"Well, *obviously* we stole a key and these disgusting scrubs," Dowe intoned. He sniffed his uniform and retched.

"Yeah, how else were we supposed to get past security?" John yelped as he slipped off the chair.

"I don't—"

"Spray foam," Dowe interrupted.

"What?"

"Spray foam insulation," he repeated. "Spray foam insulation is a lifesaver in these situations." He blithely slid to the middle of the chair and blocked John when he tried to climb back on. John crossed his arms and fumed.

I watched them struggle. *This isn't real.*

John accepted defeat and turned back to me. "Anyway, Tommy heard you out in the hall, so we figured we'd come say hi."

"Tommy?" I asked.

For an answer, John unbuttoned his jacket. A gray cat leaped out.

Now I *knew* I was tripping.

It flounced across the table and perched on the edge. It stared at me, bright yellow eyes unblinking, like it was judging my soul. I didn't know what to do but stare back.

I must have passed the unspoken test, because the cat abruptly started purring. It crawled into my lap and rubbed against me.

"Aww, he likes you!" John or Dowe crooned.

"I was a little worried," the other admitted. "He's so picky about his friends."

"No, he's not. He hangs out with you!"

"That's because Philli told him he had to listen to me!"

I jumped, and the cat dug its claws into my leg in protest. "Phil? You've talked to her?"

"Of course." John scrunched his nose, like that was a stupid question. "It's her cat. I'm pet-sitting."

Vague recollections of a cat prowling around in the background of video calls with Philadelphia came to me. She'd mentioned the animal maybe once; getting my girlfriend to talk about anything but the war had been an uphill battle.

The thought made me frustrated, and then sad, and then *enraged* when I remembered that nothing made sense, and I desperately needed it to.

Unfortunately, logic was in short supply with John and Dowe. Dowe scraped his chair back and thumped his palms on the table. "Well, we'd better get going. We don't want to keep our ride waiting."

"We're fine. He always runs late on Tuesdays." John turned towards the door, and the cat ran after him.

I lurched forward. "Wait!"

Dowe rolled his eyes. "Don't worry, you can come too."

He reached into his pocket and pulled out a keyring—and at that exact moment, the door banged open.

Williams stumbled in, gun drawn. He was wearing nothing but an undershirt and drooping pants without a belt. That explained where John and Dowe had gotten at least one of the uniforms, and I had even more questions than before.

"What are you doing here?" he raged.

"We're busting a friend out of jail. What are *you* doing here?" John challenged. He reached into his jacket.

"Don't move!" Williams fumbled with his weapon, still struggling to hold his pants up.

"Too slow!" John whipped out a can and sprayed him in the face. Williams dropped the gun as he took a mouthful of white foam. Choking, he stumbled back—and the cat skittered between his legs. Williams crashed to the floor with a grunt and a crack.

Dowe sidestepped. "Yikes, is that foam insulation?"

"No, are you insane? It's whipped cream! I'm not trying to kill the guy!" John rattled the can for emphasis.

"Will you two just shut up and get me out of here?" I yelled.

"Wow, okay, working on it. Chill, dude." Dowe reached over and unlocked my cuffs.

I scrambled up. This was crazy, and I still wasn't convinced I wasn't having a total mental break, but we had a chance. The door was open, and Williams was still hacking on the floor—we could make it.

"Let's go!" I ran into the hall.

They scampered out after me, Tommy on their heels. I slammed and locked the cell door. Williams' muffled curses echoed from the other side.

I scanned the hall. The corridor was lined with more cells, all shut. No one was in sight. Whatever John and Dowe had done to get rid of security, it had worked.

"You said you had a ride?" I asked.

"Sure do. This way!" Dowe took off.

We raced to keep up. He led us to the door at the far end of the hall, then up a winding stairwell.

It was only after we'd passed two floors that I processed which direction we were headed. "Wait, shouldn't we be going down?"

"No, the launch pad is on the roof!" Dowe called back.

I halted. "Launch pad?"

They both kept climbing. "Hurry, you'll miss your flight!"

My flight? My panic returned, and I contemplated doubling back. John and Dowe had never betrayed anyone before, but they were mentally unstable. It wouldn't be the first time they'd botched a mission—and I wasn't about to get caught again because of their incompetence.

I turned—just as a door slammed further down the stairwell. Shouts echoed up the corridor.

I muttered a word I am not proud of and raced after John and Dowe.

A dozen soldiers spilled into the stairwell. Someone yelled at us to stop a second before a gun fired. It missed, slamming into the bottom of the floor above us, but I knew it would only be a minute before they caught up and had a clear shot.

I pushed myself to keep up as John and Dowe took the stairs two at a time. More soldiers joined the chase, but we managed to stay several floors ahead of them. The stairs never seemed to end as we passed landing after landing. My lungs burned and my head spun, and I was sure the only thing keeping me upright was adrenaline.

You can do this! We can make it!

Finally, I saw daylight streaming through a window. We burst through the door onto the roof.

The ferocious wind hit me almost as hard as the light did. I hadn't seen the sun in almost a week, and now all I could see was flashing colors.

Something was grinding loudly—an engine. I pushed past my growing headache and tried to focus. The roof was, in fact, a landing pad. A small military jet idled at the far end, its rear ramp open.

"Come on, they're waiting for us!" Dowe took a step forward, then pivoted on his heel. "Oh, botheration, I am such an idiot!"

I didn't disagree, but that was not an inspiring statement coming from the man who was supposed to be breaking me out of jail.

"What did you do now?" John moaned.

"I forgot Lev!"

We both stared at him, and I wondered if I was dreaming. No, I *needed* this to be a bad dream.

John crossed his arms. "You had one job, Dowe. One job."

"I have to go get him. Don't leave without me!" Dowe threw the door open and ran back into the stairwell.

"They won't hold the plane for you!" John shouted after him.

"Yeah, they will. It's a private jet!" The door slammed behind him, and he was gone.

I struggled to breathe as the world started spinning again. *He's dead, he's totally dead.* The guards would catch him before he made it two floors—and then they'd be coming after us.

I spun to face John. "We have to get out of here!"

"You're right, the sooner we get going, the sooner we'll get there!" He put Tommy on his shoulder and darted towards the plane.

Go where? My vision had finally cleared enough for me to read the writing on the side of the jet: It was the United seal, followed by several Chinese characters.

Suddenly, I realized what was happening. "You led me right to them!"

"Well, how else are we supposed to cross the ocean? We can't walk!"

I stayed where I was and hyperventilated. This was just like the last time, and the time before that. John and Dowe had failed Operation Thunderbird, they'd failed on Rott, and now they'd failed me. They'd put me right back where I'd started—on a plane to China where Asia would rip my brain to shreds—and angered the guards in the process. We'd be lucky if they didn't shoot Lev here and now.

Reality slammed into my chest. I *wasn't* hallucinating.

And how I wished I was.

John was almost to the plane. I scanned the roof. There—the fire escape. I'd be totally exposed, but it was my only chance.

Someone shouted over the roar of the engine. A guard jumped from the plane, his weapon drawn.

I had a split second to make a decision. I could turn myself in and hope that maybe, *maybe* they wouldn't shoot me on sight. Or I could make a break for it and take my chances.

I made my choice and did what I did best: I turned and ran.

It was the wrong decision.

"Wait, buddy, come back!" John yelled after me.

He needn't have bothered. A whistle shrieked, followed by a shout to *"Stop right there!"* Before I could even think about complying, a gunshot ripped the air.

Something hit me in the back, hot and burning. My muscles seized like I'd been tazed, and all I could feel was pain. I think I screamed.

I don't remember hitting the ground. I just remember falling, falling—and then, darkness.

"Come on, Phil, nobody has to know."

I leaned against a workstation and watched as my sister Mira and several of our classmates circled Philadelphia's chair like hawks on roadkill. It was Tuesday, which meant most of us had stayed after school for extended study hall.

Most of the after-school programs weren't open to unassimilated kids, mainly because they needed an armed bus to take us back to camp, and they were short on drivers. But since study hall was considered an academic program, they were legally obliged to include us. That meant every Tuesday and Thursday we could elect to stay on campus until seven o'clock.

I always signed up, even though I had no intention of studying. It was better than being at home.

"Yeah, the teachers won't even know we're gone." Concord propped his elbow on the back of Phil's chair. Concord was an assimilated senior who was in study hall because it was the only thing keeping his GPA above a measly 2.0. He also had no intention of studying—which was evident by the fact that he'd gathered us all together and suggested sneaking off school grounds.

"We're just going to the convenience store and back," Mira argued. "We'll be gone like ten minutes."

We'd already be back if you weren't dragging your feet, I thought. I had no idea why we kept including Phil in things; she never said yes.

Today, clearly, would be no exception. She ducked her head and made a show of scrolling on her reader. "I can't—I have to finish studying."

Mira snorted. "Don't lie. I bet you turned your paper in a week ago."

"Wednesday," I offered, causing them all to look at me. "She turned it in last Wednesday."

Phil panicked like I'd caught her cheating. "How did you—"

"I hacked into the teacher's account and saw the date stamp."

I did not add that I'd used the teacher's permissions to tweak my English grades. Just by a few points, hopefully not enough that he'd notice.

I didn't care about my report card; the Outside was going to reject me whether I had straight As or not. But my English grade had slipped below passing since I'd missed too many days, and I did not want my dad to find out.

"Well, since you worked so far ahead," Concord chirped in a fake posh accent, "I think you definitely deserve a break."

"It'll be totally fine," Mira insisted. "Stan turned off the cameras on the back of the building."

Phil gasped. She turned and gaped up at me like I'd just confessed to murdering someone.

I scowled. That was the other reason I didn't like bringing her along—she was so judgmental. "I just disabled the video feed for an hour. I do it all the time," I lied, then looked away. *Why are you explaining yourself to her?*

Concord winked and gave me a thumbs up. "We'll just slip through the fence, run down to the corner store, and be back before they know we're gone. It'll be fun."

"Come on, Phil," Mira repeated for the tenth time, jostling her shoulder. "Let's go."

Our classmates murmured their encouragement.

Phil avoided their eyes. "I don't have any money."

I sighed. Of course, she didn't; none of us unassimilated kids did. But that wasn't the point, and she knew that. She was always avoiding confrontation by giving stupid excuses.

Concord held out his hand. "I'll buy."

She, as usual, was oblivious to any and all interpretations of his behavior. "I can't," she mumbled, and tried to shrink further back into her chair.

Mira groaned. Even Concord began to look annoyed, probably because his oh-so-obvious affections had been rebuffed. He hastily pocketed his hands. "Seriously, Phil, what's your problem? Why you gotta ruin everything?"

The pitch of the group changed instantly. "Yeah, stop being such a baby!" one of our classmates jeered.

"Aww, is little Philli too scared to cross the street by herself?"

"I'm not scared!" she cried in a tone that said the exact opposite. "I just—"

"I bet she's afraid her daddy will find out," Mira muttered.

I flinched. In Phil's defense, that was the only thing I was afraid of, too.

Concord smiled again, and this time, it wasn't a nice smile. "Daddy's girl."

Phil scraped her chair back. "You're right, I am!" she shouted.

The group silenced, mainly because Phil never raised her voice.

"He wouldn't want me to go, and I care more about him than I care about you." She jabbed her finger at Concord's chest.

I stared at her, feeling something close to admiration. Even I didn't have the courage to tell six-foot-five Concord off to his face.

He, for his part, was speechless.

"I'm not going." She glared around at the circle, eyes settling on me. "And… you shouldn't either."

Her conviction faltered, and the accusation came out sounding weak and pathetic. She quickly looked away, the flush returning to her cheeks. She snatched her backpack and darted out of the library, eyes on the floor.

The others glanced at me. I pushed myself away from the desk. "Let's go."

✼

We didn't get very far. It should have been the perfect plan: The cameras were off, and there was no one watching the back of the building. What we didn't realize was that the fence had a security system of its own. As soon as we started climbing it, it sent off a motion alert, and the school officer came running. We didn't even make it to the sidewalk.

I didn't really care that we'd been caught; I just wanted something to do besides stare at the ceiling in the library. What bothered me was that it was kind of my fault. Had I poked around in the security system a little more while I was messing with the cameras, I probably would have known about the fence. But I'd been lazy, and now we definitely wouldn't be getting away with that again.

We spent a half-hour in the principal's office, where she made Mira and me listen while she called Commander Ambrose, the supervisor of our containment camp. He gleefully assured her that we'd be dutifully reprimanded.

That's when I began to have regrets. If Ambrose detained us in his office when we got back, we'd be late getting home—and then there would be no keeping the truth from my dad.

It would be another hour before our armed escort came, so they deposited us back in the library under the vengeful watch of an underpaid staffer. I sulked in a chair in the corner and tried not to think about the punishment waiting for me at home. If Dad gave me too many bruises, I'd miss school tomorrow—and it was a test day.

Philadelphia stumbled on me when she came to claim an encyclopedia off the shelf. "Oh—you're back."

I could have lied to her, or ignored her. But for reasons I can't remember, I did neither. "We never made it."

She stared, fidgeting with her stack of books. "Are you… in trouble?"

What do you think? "Ambrose will talk to us when we get home."

She flinched at the mention of the hated name. "I'm… sorry."

I shrugged; Ambrose was the least of my worries. "Go ahead. Tell me 'I told you so.'"

Part of me wanted her to do it. Then at least I'd have someone to be mad at besides myself.

She didn't. She just frowned and looked perplexed, as if that thought had never occurred to her.

After a minute of awkward staring, she mumbled another apology and hurried away.

It wasn't until later that I realized I was right: The thought *hadn't* occurred to her. Philadelphia never was the gloating type.

3

I woke with a jolt. I couldn't see anything; all I could hear was a high-pitched whine like air rushing down a tunnel. Everything was grinding—the floor, the wind, my head. I felt like I was falling as gravity seemed to pitch in and out. I couldn't tell which way was up, I couldn't take a full breath, and the only thing I was confident of was that I was in a lot of pain.

A worried voice broke through the chaos. "Boss!"

It was Lev. And that's when I remembered what happened.

I went limp and waited for my senses to come back to me. I became aware of cuffs biting my wrists and a textured metal floor scraping my cheek. My back burned; no doubt the stun shot had given me a nasty welt. The room was vibrating, and the roar of air outside was deafening—like an airplane.

I opened my eyes. That's where we were: the cargo hold of an airplane. It looked like an overgrown fighter jet. Two pilots manned the front, and the center compartment was lined with half a dozen sidewall seats, in which lounged one heavily-armed guard. John, Dowe, Lev, and I had been shoved in the back with the gear.

I shuddered when I realized what that meant: We were on our way to China.

Lev knelt over me and shook my shoulder with cuffed hands. "Boss. Boss!" His thick Russian accent undermined the panic in his voice, making it even harder to translate. "Are you okay?"

"Nope," I groaned. Apparently, they'd just ingloriously dumped me on the floor after tazing and cuffing me, and I was feeling it. I braced my palms on the floor and managed to push myself to a seated position.

Our guard glanced up from his device. "You wouldn't have gotten hurt if you'd just come quietly." He lazily twirled his key fob around his finger.

"I'm well aware," I muttered. I rubbed my temples and tried to rationalize how I'd gotten myself into this situation.

The reason scooted up beside me, shattering my personal space. "Breakfast! Or is it lunch?" John crowed.

"Just go with brunch. Cover all your bases," Dowe suggested. Or was that John? I didn't know; my head was still spinning.

The first one grunted his agreement and laid a cracker snack in my lap. It was one of those silly lunchbox treats with the fake breadsticks and even faker cheese. I hadn't eaten one since grade school, before they put us in a camp and we became too poor for such luxuries.

I stared at it and tried to decide why it made me furious.

Dowe slid in on my other side, turning me into an uncomfortable sandwich. "Wait, you gave him one with the breadsticks? No fair!"

John shushed him. The guard spared us a sideways glance but didn't get up.

Dowe dropped his voice a whisper-shout. "I wanted breadsticks! I'll trade you!" He held his own snack out in cuffed hands. He had one with crackers. It was halfway eaten, of course.

"I've got more!" John protested. "Just ask nicely."

"Where did you get food?" Lev pointed.

"My pockets." John reached into his jacket—or tried to. With handcuffs, the motion was incredibly awkward.

I dug my fingers into my hair. *Just stop.*

John somehow managed to get his hands into his inner pockets. "Whatcha want? I've got crackers, fruit leather, half a banana…"

"But… how did you get it past the guards?" Lev hissed with a wary glance at the same.

"Don't ask," I moaned.

John wrinkled his nose at me and answered the question. "Oh, it was easy. You know what I always say."

Lev, clearly not understanding the idiom, took the bait. "No, I don't know what you always say."

Dowe grinned, showing all teeth in a gesture that was almost evil. "Give them bigger problems."

"I do not understand," Lev said, and it took all my will power not to yell at him to shut up. *Stop encouraging them.*

John pulled a fruit leather from his pocket and tossed it at him. "You don't think about things like checking for contraband when you're choking on a mouthful of whipped cream."

I looked up. "Wait, what?"

He winked. "They were so worried about keeping us from escaping that they didn't think to ask what I had in my pockets. Works every time."

"Except that one time in Berlin," Dowe corrected.

"That's because I wore the wrong kind of pants—"

"No, stop." I put my hands up. "Are you telling me you broke into my cell and jumped Williams just so you could avoid a pat down?"

"Yeah?" John shrugged. "What did you think we were doing?"

I clenched my fists. "I thought you were busting me out of jail!"

He blew air. "Pfft, that would have been a suicide mission. Did you see how much security they had in that prison? Even we're not that good."

I actually hadn't seen anything except the inside of the interrogation room, but that was beside the point. "So, you angered the guards, dragged Lev into it—"

He grunted.

"—and got me tazed in the back, all for some stupid *snacks*?" I grabbed the offending package and shook it.

"Keep it down!" John reached for the breadsticks, but it was too late.

The guard jumped up. "Hey, what's that? Drop it!"

Dowe obliged, spilling his crackers on the floor. I lifted my hands and hoped I wasn't about to get tazed again over artificial cheese.

The guard shoved his key fob in his pocket and stomped over. Lev scooted way, cowering in the shadows.

The guard snatched the package from me. "Where did you get this?"

"Well, you don't have in-flight service, so I brought my own." John stuck his tongue out.

"We'll give you one if you don't say anything." Dowe picked a broken cracker up off the floor and waved it at him.

"Hands in the air," the guard ordered with a frown.

We all obeyed. The guard bent over John and started emptying his numerous pockets. He was carrying a rubber duck, six cans of cat food, several plastic vials that looked like they came from a play chemistry set, and the infamous spray can of foam insulation. There was also enough fruit leather to last a week.

Of course, none of it would have been even remotely useful in an actual escape.

The guard surveyed the growing pile on the floor. "How did you get all this in your pockets?" he exclaimed, which was exactly what I was wondering.

John smirked. "You should be less worried about what's in my pockets and more worried about what's behind you."

The guard folded his arms. "Seriously?"

But John, as usual, was being weirdly honest. I looked up and saw what he meant: Tommy was poised on top of an equipment rack, ready to pounce.

The surprise must have made it onto my face. The guard turned—a second too late. Tommy leapt onto his face with an ear-splitting howl and scratched him in the eye.

The guard roared. Dowe, in a move that should have been impossible based on both his weight and his age, ducked and rolled, knocking the guard's legs out from under him. He crashed into the wall, cracking his neck on a bar. He slumped to the ground with a groan.

His key fob tumbled from his pocket. I snatched it.

The other soldiers reacted, scrambling up and drawing weapons. Tommy sprung off the ground, grasped one of their legs with all claws, and *bit* him. The soldier screamed murder. His partner tried to save him, but they only succeeded in tripping over each other and crashing into the yoke.

The plane pitched perilously sideways, then jerked nose up. I grasped for a handhold, struggling not to drop the key. Lev shrieked as he skidded into the rear wall.

"Hold her steady, Tommy!" John or Dowe advised.

The cat did the exact opposite. He jumped on the dash and waltzed across the console, his paws flicking random buttons. There was a groan, and what sounded like a gun firing, and I swore the engine sputtered.

I scrambled to undo my handcuffs. *I am not going out like this!*

One of the guards made it back to his feet. He cursed and swiped at the animal. Tommy eluded him, and the soldier slammed his hand into the dash.

A warning light on the wall started blinking, joined by a piercing beep that made my head spin even more. The whole plane shuddered, and I felt the floor shift beneath me.

I glanced back. The drop hatch was opening.

The roar of air drowned everything out as a crack appeared in the rear wall. The pressure burst, shattering my eardrums. Everything went dark, and for a second, I feared I'd pass out.

The world came back into focus when Lev screamed. He scrabbled helplessly at the floor with cuffed hands as the hatch yawned open.

I don't remember consciously thinking through my next actions. Before I could second-guess the physics, I let go and slid towards the back of the plane. I couldn't even see where I was going as the sudden onslaught of daylight made my vision flash. I reached out and grabbed a dangling harness at the last minute, then swung my other hand down. Lev grasped it for all he was worth as gravity threatened to suck him out of the plane.

"Don't let go!" I screamed. Outside was a blur of sky and sea, and I couldn't tell where one ended and the other began. I tightened my grip on the harness and tried to pull him back, but just then, the plane swerved, flinging us forward. Lev swung through the air as the hatch dropped out from beneath him.

All his weight yanked on my arm, and I almost lost my grip. He shrieked and dug his fingernails into my wrist as he fought to hold on. He yelled at me, but all I could process was the endless water flashing beneath us as he dangled in midair.

Oh God, oh God, don't let me drop him!

Someone shouted behind me, and a gun fired. A flash of yellow flew by. I managed to focus on it as it fell through the air in slow motion: John's rubber ducky.

Then there was the can of insulation, and an assault rifle, and a *whole body*. One of the guards tumbled from the plane, his shout drowned out by the roar of the engine.

I didn't see him hit the water. *Don't let go don't let go don't let go!*

The other soldier slammed onto the floor next to me. He grasped for any handhold as his boots skidded down the ramp. He managed to grab the tail end of a harness—and it slipped right through his fingers.

He reached for me. "Help—"

I couldn't have even if I'd wanted to. He plummeted off the edge of the ramp, his scream cut short.

I struggled to stay conscious. If I didn't find another handhold, we were next. *Jesus, help me!*

The plane shook again. Lev shrieked and swung on my arm. I yelled as my shoulder tore and my chest burned. I felt like I was suffocating.

"John!" I managed, but the wind snatched the words right out of my throat.

I had to get a better grip. If I could just brace myself on something, I could pull Lev onto the ramp.

"Hold on!" I shouted as I drew my knees back, fighting for every breath.

It was the wrong decision. No sooner had I gotten my feet under me than the ramp shifted, and I lost my balance. I landed hard.

I knew it was coming a second before it happened. I felt Lev's grip loosening, his palm slipping from mine.

I screamed his name. And then he fell.

4

Someone slammed into me, knocking me down. I scrambled up and saw John or Dowe dangling over the side of the ramp. Then, suddenly, arms were dragging me back into the cockpit, and John was hauling Lev over the edge, and the hatch was groaning closed, and before I could register what was happening, we were on solid ground again.

The hatch sealed, plunging the cockpit into abrupt silence. I stared into the darkness until I could see something other than flashing colors and hear something other than my panicked breathing.

We made it. We're alive! I tried to conjure a prayer of gratefulness and just ended up muttering *thank you, thank you* over and over.

I dared to sit up. Lev knelt on his hands and knees, heaving, looking like he was either going to throw up or pass out or both. I scrambled to find the key fob where it had slid under a chair. I freed him and then gripped his shoulders.

"Hey, it's okay, you're okay, just breathe," I said, coaching myself as much as him.

John and Dowe, having somehow gotten out of their own restraints, stood and brushed themselves off like nothing had happened. "Good boy, Tommy!" John bent to scratch the cat behind the ears.

I was finally able to process an emotion besides panic. "'Good boy'?" I snapped. "That animal almost got us killed!"

"It wasn't his fault!" Dowe protested. "They're the ones that freaked out and thought it was a good idea to fire a gun in the cockpit of a moving plane."

"Yeah, who does that?" John echoed.

That's when I abruptly remembered the third guard. I turned and saw his body splayed on the floor where he had fallen. I stooped over him and felt his neck.

There was no pulse.

Tommy meowed. I looked down to find him rubbing around my ankles, purring. I stared at him and tried to rationalize the fact that my girlfriend's cat had just killed three people.

John and Dowe had absolutely no reservations about the whole ordeal. They claimed the vacant seats in the cockpit.

"How's it looking, partner?" Dowe asked as he started flipping switches on the dash with what I hoped was intention.

John rolled up his jacket sleeve to reveal no less than five wristwatches strapped to his arm. "Well, thanks to Tommy's theatrics, we're about eight minutes and forty-two seconds behind schedule... but I think we can make that up."

"Clark always runs late on Tuesdays, remember?"

"Oh, right. We're probably fine then."

I straightened. "Clark?"

"Our ride," one of them answered without looking back.

"Our ri—" I backspaced when I realized that wasn't the most important question. "Are you two going to tell me what's going on?"

"Last I checked," John condescended to match my tone, "we were helping you escape so Asia can't turn you into a walking hard drive."

Dowe continued to flip switches until I could have sworn he'd touched every button on the dash. "We've got a safehouse. As long as we can make up eight minutes and forty-two seconds, we'll rendezvous with our ride and get you off the grid."

That was a completely sane and logical answer, which was somehow even more disturbing. "Wait, you mean you *planned* this?"

"No, actually, finding you in jail was a happy accident. We just know an opportunity when we see one."

"No, I mean, hijacking the plane—you planned *all* of this?"

They finally glanced back at me. "Which part?"

I gestured emphatically at the dead body on the floor.

"Ooohh," Dowe crooned. "Yeah, no, that wasn't supposed to happen. I blame Tommy."

The cat hissed at him.

"Watch your language." John shook his finger at the animal. "You need to learn to wait for the signal. Everyone would still be alive if you'd let me use the foam insulation."

Tommy ignored the reproof and licked his paw.

John turned back to the dash and resumed poking random buttons. "This would have been a lot cleaner if we'd stuck to the original plan. I know we come up with some crazy ideas, but they never involve ejecting people from moving planes."

Dowe lifted a finger. "Ehh..."

"Well, okay," John rolled his eyes, "we never eject people from moving planes *without* a plan to get them safely to the ground."

"Look, I don't care what the original plan was," I snapped, even though I definitely did care, "but now we've got three people dead, including everyone who was qualified to fly this thing, so I really hope you know what you're doing."

"Relax, dude, of course I know how to fly this thing." Dowe flexed his fingers and grabbed the yoke. "Do you think I would have hijacked it if I didn't how know to drive it?"

He turned the yoke. I grabbed a nearby seat to brace myself, but nothing happened. The turn was so smooth that I could barely feel the motion.

Maybe he does know how to fly.

Rational thought tried to worm its way into my addled brain. Had this really been the plan all along? John and Dowe said they wouldn't have been able to get past security in the prison. So instead, they'd concocted a plan to make a ruckus and sneak contraband onboard the plane, intending to take control when there were fewer guards around.

That can't be it. It can't be that simple.

Lev groaned. I turned and saw that he'd managed to stand.

"You all right?" I asked.

He didn't answer, which was just as well. He leaned against the wall and took several long breaths through his nose. Then he looked into my eyes and whispered, "Thank you."

I managed a smile.

We joined John and Dowe in the cockpit. I leaned on the back of Dowe's chair. "So, where are we going?"

"First things first, we need to make sure we're untraceable." Dowe reached above his head and grabbed a lever in the ceiling. It thudded into the "off" position.

"Stealth mode activated!" John crowed.

I pinched my nose. "Please tell me you didn't just say that."

"Please tell me it was not that easy," Lev added.

Dowe returned to steering. "Nah, it's a military jet, it was already in stealth mode."

Lev ducked under the dash and fiddled with something. There was a *thunk*, and he emerged holding a wire. "You probably should turn off the onboard transponder, though."

I frowned at him. "How did you…?"

He shrugged. "Jayde taught me."

I nodded, even as I wondered when Jayde would have had the opportunity to teach Lev how to hijack a plane. Jayde had essentially raised Lev after he'd saved him from getting executed with the rest of the Boston

Jewish community, and he'd taught him everything he knew about waging war and shedding blood.

I was just grateful Lev hadn't picked up on Jayde's more violent habits. If he had, I wouldn't still be alive.

Dowe slapped the dash. "Awesome! So *now* we're in stealth mode."

Lev cringed. "Hopefully."

"I don't like the sound of that," John said.

For once, he and I were in total agreement. "What do you mean?"

Lev leaned over and scrolled on the dashboard screen. "I mean there could be another transponder or a coded tracking beacon. The autopilot is probably also relaying data."

"That's okay, I prefer manual anyway." Keeping his eyes locked with Lev's, Dowe leaned over and punched a button. Instantly, half of the dashboard went dark.

Well, that's it, this is how you die, I thought, and I hoped my face didn't say the same thing. I focused on Lev. "Is there a way to find out if there's another transponder?"

"Not unless you want to open the dashboard and look at all the wiring."

Ripping the walls off and snipping random wires did not sound like a smart idea while the plane was in flight.

"So, what you're saying is," John inserted, "the only way to make us truly untraceable is to blow the plane up?"

The panic returned, fresh and throbbing. "That—that isn't even remotely what he said," I exclaimed.

John fixed Lev with a raised eyebrow.

"I mean, I suppose that would work," he stuttered.

John sighed so hard he coughed at the end. "I was hoping it wouldn't come to this."

"No, wait." I grabbed his shoulder. "Why can't we just crash land somewhere and go on foot?"

"Because that'll give them a place to start! If they can find the plane, they can find our trail. We gotta get you off the grid entirely."

He wasn't wrong, but I was still confused as to how that had escalated into *blowing up the plane*. "No, seriously, stop, there has to be another way."

John looked at the ceiling. "Well, there is, but I don't like it."

Dowe paled. "Oh no."

John put his hands up. "You asked for alternatives. I'm giving them to you."

"You can't be serious!"

"I agree!" I shouted, even though I had no idea what John was implying. All I knew was that I didn't want to know.

"We have to consider all possibilities." John reached into his jacket—which apparently operated on the same physics as Mary Poppin's bag—and pulled out a tiny glass tube.

Dowe snatched it. "This isn't nearly enough!"

"Enough of what?" Lev asked.

John ignored him. "It'll have to do! The rest is floating in the ocean somewhere, thanks to Tommy."

The cat mewed and actually sounded apologetic.

I tried to see what was in the vial. A sparkly liquid sloshed against the glass. It looked like craft glitter suspended in water.

Dowe shook the vial. "You could *maybe* send a toaster with this. I won't allow it."

"'Send'?" I echoed.

They were still ignoring us. "We don't need to go very far," John argued. "Just enough to give us a head start."

Dowe wagged his head. "No, this is where I draw the line. It's not safe."

Now I knew we were in trouble. If *Dowe* thought something was unsafe, it was already too late.

"I have no idea what you're talking about," Lev interrupted, "but how is it any less safe than blowing up the plane?"

John cast him a glance as he maneuvered controls on the dashboard with both hands. "Believe me, kid, there are way worse ways to go than being blown to smithereens. Besides, you weren't going to be *on* the plane when I blew it up—who do you take me for?"

I had no idea. I had no idea who I took them for, not anymore. The only thing I knew was that we were going to die.

John shoved his sleeve up and unclasped one of his wristwatches. He squinted at the face and twisted the dial on the side—then stopped. He glanced at Dowe. "Or... we *could* just send the empty plane."

Dowe tapped his lip in thought. "That would take significantly fewer resources."

"And, if it doesn't work, the plane will just blow up anyway."

Dowe snapped his fingers. "Genius!"

"What? No! Not genius!" I shoved between them and tried to grab the watch.

Dowe put his whole hand on my face and pushed me away. "If you want to be helpful, go put your life jacket on."

I didn't want to be helpful, not with this. "Seriously, John, Dowe, drop the act. This isn't funny."

"No one's laughing, buddy." John popped open the face of his watch. "Lev, get your life jacket on."

"And then buckle up. The drop's gonna be rough." Dowe uncapped the vial and dribbled three drops onto the gears of the watch.

I couldn't breathe again. *This can't be happening, this can't be happening.* "No, please, just listen to me."

"Life jacket, seatbelt, now," Dowe ordered, sounding exactly like my father.

I looked at Lev. He hesitated, glancing between us—then he ran and snatched a life jacket off the wall. He shoved it over his head, grabbed the nearest seat, and scrambled with the harness.

I didn't move. *You're going to die you're going to die you're going to die!*

Dowe cast me a glance over his shoulder. "Last warning."

I clenched my fists. *Please, wake up!*

With a sigh, Dowe shook his head and turned back to the dash. "Brace yourselves!" he shouted. "This is where we make up those eight minutes and forty-two seconds."

He slammed a button. The engine shuddered—and then it stopped.

I'm not sure how to describe what happened next. From my perspective, we went into a freefall. The plane veered downward, and we nose-dived towards the ocean. Everything in the cockpit that wasn't strapped down—including myself—was thrown as we screamed through the air.

The water outside loomed closer and closer—and then, we braked. The plane leveled out, and we violently slowed down like a landing parachute had been deployed. The engines kicked in again. Everything rattled and groaned, then stilled. It seemed like we were hovering as the engines hummed contentedly.

I'm sure that's not an accurate description of what happened, because that would have broken every law of physics known to mankind, but that's what it felt like as I skidded across the floor, screaming.

Dowe stepped over me as he climbed out of the cockpit. "Seatbelts save lives."

I moaned. Lev gripped my arm and helped me stand.

Dowe yanked the emergency lever at the back of the plane. The hatch groaned open, flooding the cockpit with light and the sound of churning water. I found the courage to walk forward and look out.

We *were* hovering. The copter blades on the underbelly of the plane whipped the water into a frenzy as it suspended us a few stories above the waves. There was absolutely nothing but ocean and blinding sunlight in every direction.

"Where are we?" I asked, knowing full well there was no good answer to that question.

"The rendezvous point! Come on, we have to hurry!" John shouted.

I glanced back at him. He was flipping random switches on the dashboard—and I mean *random* literally. As I watched, he flipped the same switch back and forth at least three times.

"Help me with this!" Dowe yelled. He pulled the deflated life raft from its pouch on the wall.

Lev ran to his aid. They unfolded it, then yanked on the cord. It inflated with a squeal.

Dowe shoved it off the edge of the ramp. It landed in the water with a splash, where it floated like a gigantic yellow rubber duck.

I caught up. "Wait, you can't be serious!"

"You don't want to be on this plane in exactly... two hundred and thirty-three seconds, buddy." John knelt and laid his watch on the floor, arranging it so it was perpendicular to the wings of the plane.

Dowe buckled his life jacket. "Let's go!" He walked to the edge of the ramp—then turned and plummeted backwards like he was doing a trust fall. I heard the splash as he hit the water.

Lev backed away from the edge. "I can't—"

John grabbed his shoulder. "You can. It's not a big jump. I promise you'll be okay—just trust me."

"Don't!" I reached for Lev. "This is crazy!"

"Stanyard," John warned, "there's no time—"

His watch started to beep.

I shouted over it. "Don't listen to him! Just stay with me. We'll fly to the nearest land, send out a distress signal, something."

Even I knew how crazy that sounded. But it was better than diving into the middle of the ocean when we had a perfectly functioning plane.

"Stanyard..." John started, then grunted and turned his back on me. He shook Lev's shoulders. "We need to go. Now."

Then, without waiting for either of us, he ran and dove off the ramp headfirst.

Lev looked at me. I held out my hand. "Please, don't do this."

He sucked in his breath—then turned and leapt into the water.

I stared at the empty plane. John's watch ticked louder, faster. All I could think was that I was alone, and the others were going to drown, and I had absolutely no idea how to fly a plane, and to top it all off, Lev somehow trusted John and Dowe more than me.

I jumped when the cat brushed my ankles. He mewed and clawed at my shoe.

John's watch vibrated against the metal floor.

"Stanyard, hurry, please!" one of them shrieked from below.

The cat flounced to the edge of the ramp, then stopped and looked back at me.

The beep increased to a shrill whine.

"Boss!" It was Lev that time.

"Oh God, please," I muttered, and hoped He would infer the rest.

Then before I could second-guess what I was doing, I ran to the edge, grabbed the cat—and jumped.

I hadn't seen my sister in over six months, and now she wouldn't even talk to me.

I told myself she wasn't ignoring me. After all, she was on a mission. She'd come back to base with intel that our old containment camp was being deported to China tomorrow—and that included our parents. We had less than twelve hours to prepare for an emergency extraction, and everyone had a job to do.

Mira's role was to pick up Philadelphia for a "sleepover" so that Phil's host family wouldn't freak out about her being gone after dark. That meant Mira needed a car with untraceable plates, a fake driver's license, and an unregistered phone, among other things. She spent the afternoon getting outfitted and refusing to talk to me. Every time we passed in the hall, she said she had somewhere to be and kept walking.

I told myself it wasn't personal. I told myself she was busy, and we were under a deadline, and this was important. My sister wasn't ignoring me.

I was lying to myself.

I finally cornered her in the armory—which, in retrospect, was probably not a good place to confront anyone. Lev was helping her adjust an underarm holster when I approached. He saw me and scattered, mumbling an apology to Mira as he passed.

She didn't look up. She stood with her back to me, her hand dangerously close to the pistol resting on the table. "What do you want, Stan?"

I decided I'd better keep my distance and waited by the door. "We need to talk."

"About what?"

It was such a stupid question that I didn't know how to answer it.

About the fact that you ran away from our foster family without saying goodbye and then blocked my number?

I took a deep breath. "I've been looking for you."

"I know."

I wondered who had told her. "Why didn't you call?"

She hesitated, her finger idly tracing the barrel of the gun. "I didn't want to talk."

I wasn't sure which infuriated me more: the fact that that was a terrible excuse, or the fact that it was probably the truth. "But I'm your brother."

Now *I* was the one making stupid statements. The fact that we were family hadn't mattered to her six months ago—why would it now?

I closed my eyes. I tried to pray, but all my thoughts seemed stuck inside my chest, like birds in a cage. I had no trouble praying in church. I had no trouble praying for Philadelphia. Why couldn't I do it now?

I tried a different approach. "I missed you."

It almost worked. "I know," she said again, but her voice was softer.

I took a step forward. "I was really worried."

"There's nothing to worry about. I'm safe, I promise." She glanced over her shoulder and smiled.

It was a fake, plastic smile that barely stretched her lips—and oh, how I wished she was lying to me. How I wished she would tell me that she'd been in danger, or stuck in a bad relationship, or on the run from the law—something, anything, to justify why she hadn't even sent me a text.

But I knew it wasn't a lie. She was fine—fine without me, fine without our parents, fine with whatever hotshot soldier she'd hooked up with.

"Well, I hope you two are happy." I meant it as an insult, but it just came out sounding dumb and pathetic.

Her smile vanished. "'You two'?"

"You said you got married," I returned, remembering the callous goodbye note she'd taped to the bathroom mirror, scribbled with so many cruel hearts and fake promises.

She grunted. "It didn't work out."

"Didn't work out? What's that supposed to mean?"

"It just didn't, okay?" She grabbed the clip off the table and jammed it into the gun. "We're not together anymore."

My rage collided with grief. Part of me—the better part of me that missed her and loved her and wanted to start over—was upset that she'd been hurt and rejected. The other part of me—the ugly part that wished she'd never come back, that didn't want to see my parents again, that wanted to run off with Phil and start over—was mad. More mad than when she'd left. More mad than when she'd blocked my number. More mad than when she'd shoved me away in front of literally everybody in the command room, making me look like a fool and a loser.

That part of me was furious. Because if it "hadn't worked out," why didn't she just come home? Why didn't she call me?

"But what happened?" I demanded. I was fully aware we were going in circles, but I needed a better answer, a reason, an excuse other than my own failures.

She held the gun stiffly by her side. "I don't want to talk about it."

"I don't care! I need to know!"

"It's none of your business, Stan!" Her shoulders shook.

"Yes, it is! You ran off and left me, and I deserve—"

"Leave me alone!"

She whipped around, and I registered two things too late: Her finger was on the trigger, and she was crying.

I put my hands up as all the bitterness and rage fled back into the shadows where they belonged. "Mira, I'm sorry, I didn't mean it like—"

She swiped at her eyes. "Look, if you're so desperate for gossip, why don't you go ask Jayde, huh? Ask *him* why we didn't get married."

I froze. Mira kept heaving, her shoulders shaking as she struggled not to cry, but I couldn't breathe. "You... you were with *Jayde?*"

She seemed confused by my anger. "He didn't tell you?"

"No! He said he'd seen you around but had no idea where you were."

He lied to me—you lied to me.

She shrugged. "I didn't tell him where I was going. If it makes you feel any better, I blocked him too."

It didn't make me feel better. It made me feel worse. I was right, right all along. I was worthless, and a failure, and apparently, I'd screwed up so badly that my own sister had left me for *Jayde.* Jayde, a brash know-it-all who'd used me and put Phil in danger, and who also happened to be muscular and handsome and respected and everything I wasn't.

"You left me for Jayde," I said again. It wasn't a question or an accusation.

"I didn't 'leave' you, Stan," she retorted, even though that's exactly what she'd done. She'd left me, and then Jayde had lied to me, and then he'd kept me around like some stupid pet because I was marginally useful to him.

I'm going to kill him, I thought, but I was lying to myself, again. I wouldn't kill him. I wouldn't even confront him about it. I knew that as soon as Mira left the room, everything would go back to the way it was, with me minding my own business and keeping my mouth shut because I was a coward and didn't want to start a fight I couldn't win.

It was the same reason I'd never stood up to my dad. It was the same reason I'd never intervened between Mira and Mrs. Carver. It was the same reason I followed Jayde's orders even though I knew his ideas were stupid and risky.

And it was exactly why I was letting Mira walk away now, her arm barely brushing mine as she pushed past me to the door.

She paused, gripping the handle. "Just let it go, Stan."

There were a million things I needed to say, a thousand things I should have shouted after her. But all that came out was: "Don't call me Stan."

She frowned over her shoulder. "Why not?"

I didn't have an answer for that. "I don't like it."

It wasn't until later that I realized why: The only person who called me Stan was Mira and, sometimes, my father. Philadelphia always used my full name.

5

It wasn't a far fall. But in that split second, as I hurtled towards the water, I processed what was really happening.

I just jumped off a plane. I jumped off a perfectly good, working plane into the open waters of the north Atlantic. I was literally freefalling into the ocean, clutching my girlfriend's cat—who, of all creatures, seemed the least bothered by the situation.

Then I hit the water.

The cat sprang from my grasp as I went under. For one terrifying second, there was nothing but water all around—then I broke through the surface. I coughed and struggled to stay afloat as the waves continually slapped me in the face. *Where is the raft?* I couldn't see anything around the glaring sunlight.

Something roared above me—the plane engine? I turned, and then everything happened at once. The sky lit up with a flash of light, blinding me. I heard a crackle like lightning, followed by an explosion. Well, it didn't sound so much like an explosion as it did like something was breaking the sound barrier. Everything went eerily silent as my ears rang.

A gust of wind slammed into me. I thrashed and managed to keep my head above the surface. I spun around, looking for the raft—but all I could see was a giant wave rolling towards me.

I screamed for help, but I didn't get the word out before the wall of water crashed into me. I went under. I couldn't tell which way was up. The force pushed me deeper, deeper, until there was only darkness, and a burning in my lungs, and the terrifying knowledge that I was about to die.

And then there were hands grabbing me, and wet plastic dragging across my skin, and a burst of air and light, and suddenly I was on the raft coughing up more water than I remembered swallowing.

Lev shook my shoulder. "Boss! Boss! Are you okay?" he screamed.

I put up my hand to silence him while I finished hacking up my insides. I waited until my lungs stopped burning and my vision stopped flashing before I looked up.

I made it; we all made it. John, Dowe, Lev, even the cat—we were all safely on the raft. The cat wasn't even damp, except for the very tip of his tail, which he was currently cleaning.

I watched him aggressively lick himself and tried to decide why that made me furious.

"Dude, don't scare me like that. I thought you were never going to jump." It was John or Dowe; I didn't turn to see which one.

"Next time, put your life jacket on when we tell you to. We almost lost you." The other one tossed an extra jacket at me.

I had several comebacks to that statement—like we wouldn't have needed life jackets if we hadn't jumped out of a plane for seemingly no reason, and where did he get another jacket when I hadn't seen him grab one?—but I thought better of it when I saw the look on Lev's face.

I snapped my mouth shut and pulled the life jacket over my head. He relaxed as soon as I had it buckled on.

Moving slowly to avoid sloshing the raft, I sat up and looked around. It was, thankfully, a nice day, and the sky was clear in every direction. There was no sight of the plane. I scanned the waves for any wreckage but saw nothing beyond the glint of light on water.

I turned to Lev. "What happened to the plane?"

He hugged his chest, shivering a bit. "I think they put it on autopilot and sent it into hyperspeed."

"You think?" I repeated.

He shrugged. The wary look in his eyes said that he didn't believe it, but he didn't have a better explanation.

I didn't have a better explanation either. In theory, it wasn't the absolute worst plan ever. Eventually, the plane would crash, and if Asia tracked it, she'd find a dead end.

Of course, none of this explained why we couldn't have landed on solid ground and *then* put the plane on autopilot.

I glanced at John and Dowe. "So, where's this Clark guy?"

John fiddled with one of his remaining wristwatches. "If he's on schedule, he'll be here in… oh, botheration."

I would have panicked if I'd had any adrenaline left in my body. I was really starting to hate that word.

"Don't tell me," Dowe said without looking up. He was bent over the side of the boat, splashing in the water. "You had your watch set to the wrong year."

John tapped the watch face. "Eyup."

"What?" both Lev and I shrieked.

John twisted the dial to adjust the time. "Assuming I didn't miss a leap year, today is September 8th, which means it's Monday, not Tuesday. Clark won't be here until tomorrow. We'll just have to wait here overnight."

"Are you kidding me?" I yelled.

He glanced at me out of the corner of his eye. "No, why would I joke about that?"

I slapped my hand on the raft, but it just made a weird squeaky sound. "This is just like in Beijing!"

"Which time in Beijing?" both John and Dowe asked in unison.

"The party! You almost got Phil *killed* because you had the date wrong."

Dowe turned red. "Bro, that was an accident."

"Then what do you call this?" I gestured at the merciless ocean around us.

"Well, seeing as I had no control over what day of the week I would find you in jail and have to do an emergency rescue, I call this a minor inconvenience that we'll just have to work through." John once again fixed me with that frown that made him look like my father, or my high school teacher, or any of the other numerous adults who were always disappointed in me.

I groaned and raked my hands through my hair. But since my hair was wet and tangled, the motion was incredibly painful.

"It'll be fun," Dowe chirped. "Just think of it like a guy's camping trip!" He yanked something out of the water and tossed it in the puddle in the middle of the raft.

It was the rubber duck.

The rubber duck, the one John had in his pockets that had fallen out of the plane. That stupid rubber duck, which we should have left behind a hundred miles ago, had somehow survived when three people and a *whole plane* didn't, and that was just so inexplicably wrong.

I grabbed the duck and hurled it into the water.

But, of course, rubber ducks float, so the effect was mediocre. The squeaky toy did a lazy twirl through the air before plopping into the water all of two feet away. It bobbed there, giving me an incredulous side eye with its painted features.

Well, that was pathetic, it seemed to say, and I totally agreed with it, or my subconscious, or whomever was speaking.

"Beg your pardon!" John objected. "What did Sir Walter ever do to you?"

I didn't answer as the plastic toy and I continued to have a pointless staring contest.

"Fetch, Tommy," Dowe ordered.

The cat obeyed—literally. It sprung into the water and paddled out there, grabbing Sir Walter by the neck like a mother cat would carry a kitten. Then he swam back and returned the duck to John like he was some golden retriever.

"Sure, why not?" I announced to literally no one, because a cat that could fetch was definitely not the weirdest thing I'd seen today.

"Boss?" Lev asked, the word drawn out. "You good?"

"No," I snapped without looking at him. "And stop asking me that."

John shook Sir Walter off and then balanced him on top of his head. He went back to fiddling with his watch. "We'll be fine. There's no storms forecasted for tonight, and I've still got some fruit leather—wait, the year is 2059, right?"

"It's 2076," Lev replied.

John squinted at the watch face. "Wow, I was way off. No wonder I missed Philli's birthday."

"Let me guess, Clark won't be here until next week?" I snarked.

"Oh, no, he'll be here in like five minutes."

Before I could process that, Lev scrambled up, rocking the raft. "A ship!"

I turned. There it was—a large black object, slowly gaining shape amongst the waves, and getting closer.

"Wow, he's running early today," Dowe remarked. "I'm glad we made up those eight minutes and forty-two seconds, or we might have missed him."

I stared at the distant ship. Suddenly, everything made sense and nothing made sense at the same time, and I wasn't sure which I would have preferred. *Did they really have this all planned out?*

Lev unzipped the waterproof pouch on the side of the raft and yanked out the flare. He tore it open and waved it above his head, the bright red light drawing circles in the air.

I held my breath. One beat passed, two—and then the ship sounded its horn.

John and Dowe cheered. Lev lowered the flare. "We're going to be okay, boss," he whispered.

I closed my eyes and nodded. Slouching back on the raft, I tried to breathe as an emotion somewhat resembling guilt formed in my stomach.

John and Dowe were telling the truth.

It took almost an hour for the ship to row a rescue boat out and haul us back. As soon as we were on board, we were greeted by the captain, whose name really was Clark. He didn't seem very surprised to see John and Dowe, which reinforced the theory that they did, in fact, have this all planned out.

The captain was, however, very alarmed to find that John and Dowe had brought guests. He immediately called for a steward and ordered him to take care of us. For the first time in over a week, Lev and I were treated like human beings as we got medical care, a shower, and a change of clothes. We were fed and then put up in an empty crew cabin. The room was even smaller than my prison cell back on the mainland, but it was dark, quiet, and private.

Not that I expected my brain would let me take advantage of that fact.

Lev claimed the top bunk and fell asleep within minutes, his breathing rising and falling in tune with the rocking of the boat. I stared at the bottom of his mattress as my thoughts whirred in the darkness.

Where is Mira? Why would she do this to me? Was she telling the truth when she said she was taking Mom and Dad off the grid? Dad must be freaking out. This is exactly why he wanted me to quit! Maybe he'll try to make contact with Phil. Does she know what happened? Asia will probably lie, say I died at sea. I can't let her get away with this!

I rolled over and punched my pillow. I could fix all of this if I could just get online. Normally, I could hack my way out of anything if I had a computer—but this time, getting online wouldn't be so simple as borrowing a device. My file was marked with blood. If I made any activity under my real name, Asia would know immediately where I was.

Even worse, all my aliases had been exposed. Asia had stolen my phone and confiscated the computers on base. That meant all of my accounts were compromised.

I could make new ones, but without my contacts, it would be incredibly difficult to get ahold of anyone who could help us. If my allies were smart, they would have changed their contact information and relocated after the base was busted. All the phone numbers I had memorized were probably useless—and I had to be extremely careful about what I said online. Asia was no doubt hunting for me almost as aggressively as she was for Phil. If the algorithm picked up any mention of my name, Asia would get there before our allies could, and we'd be right back where we started.

I flopped back on the mattress. I could only hope John and Dowe's safehouse was as safe as they claimed. I had to get off the grid entirely—and, maybe, that's where I should stay until this was all over.

But Operation Day is in a week! I need to help Data finish that program. What if some of the code is compromised? But if Asia catches me, everyone will be worse off. Maybe it would be safer if I stayed offline until after Operation Day. But what about Phil? I can't leave her! And I have to get ahold of my dad! He has to know I'm okay—

I jumped when something leapt onto the bed.

I jerked upright, almost hitting my head on the top bunk. Something rustled on the sheets—and then soft fur brushed my hand.

"Tommy?" I hissed into the darkness.

He mewed and shoved his head under my chin.

I pushed his tail away from my nose. "How did you get in here?" The room had been locked and empty when we arrived, and we hadn't left the door open. There was no way he could have gotten in, at least not without me hearing.

I picked the animal up. "Did John let you in?"

"Who are you talking to?" Lev groaned.

Tommy answered before I could, meowing to self-identify.

The bed creaked as Lev rolled over. He peeked over the edge of the top bunk. "Who let the cat in?"

"That's what I'd like to know." I stared into the cat's glassy eyes, half-expecting him to provide an explanation for his actions.

"Maybe he was hiding under the bed?"

"No—it's storage under there." The base of the bed was solid metal, and there wasn't a closet, or a desk, or literally anywhere else to hide in the cramped room—even for a cat.

"Odd," Lev grunted.

"Add it to the list." I sighed and sank back on the pillow. Tommy resumed aggressively demanding affection.

Lev stared at me, his pale features ghostly in the low light. "We're going to be okay, boss."

It sounded like both a statement and a question, and I couldn't tell whether he was asking for reassurance or trying to reassure me. I wasn't sure he knew, either.

I took a deep breath and put on a calm voice, just like I'd done for Phil so many times. "Yeah, we're going to be fine."

It worked. He grasped the bedrail and leaned further over so I could see his whole face. "They said it's an island."

"What is?"

"The safehouse. I heard John and Dowe talking to the captain. We'll be there tomorrow."

I nodded. I supposed that made sense. A remote island was as good a place as any to get off the grid, and that would explain why John and Dowe knew a shipping captain.

The guilt returned to my stomach, heavy and cold. *Was that—was that why John and Dowe decided to hijack the plane instead of breaking me out of prison? They knew they could fly us to their safehouse in the ocean if we took the plane.*

Lev climbed back on the bed. "We're safe," he said again. This time, it was a statement.

I held still while he settled down. His soft snores returned almost immediately.

Tommy batted my hand. I obliged and scratched him behind the ears as my thoughts started whirring again, this time more slowly.

John and Dowe were telling the truth.

They really did have everything all planned out. They'd managed to crash land a plane in the middle of the ocean at the *exact spot* where a shipping liner would be passing by. That couldn't have been an accident.

That still, small voice answered me. *It's not.*

I remembered the desperate prayer I'd screamed into the empty interrogation room. I'd asked God for a way out, and He'd sent one. While I was panicking and begging for answers, John and Dowe were out in the hall tricking a guard and stealing his keys. They'd broken me out of my cell and concocted a plan to get me off the grid—all in about ten minutes and using only spray foam insulation or whatever else they had in their pockets.

I gripped Tommy's fur. Maybe John and Dowe were Jael's best agents for a reason. Maybe—maybe I shouldn't have yelled at them.

I'm sorry.

Tommy pushed my arm aside and climbed on top of my chest. I winced as his paws pressed one of the many tender spots the police had given me. I started to shove the cat off, but then he laid down. He settled in the center of my ribs, his legs tucked under him like a loaf of bread, and started purring.

I hesitated, hands still raised. I didn't really want the cat on top of me, but he was heavy and warm, and kicking him off felt incredibly wrong. You weren't supposed to move cats once they chose you, right?

I laid back and petted his side. His purrs grew louder. I closed my eyes and felt the sound vibrate in my chest.

Maybe it really is going to be all right after all.

✳

The safehouse was an island, and that was really all that could be said about it.

I stood on the deck with the others and watched the land grow closer. It was clearly man-made; there was so little organic matter left on the shore that it looked more like a partially submerged oil rig. Metal buildings crowded for space on the rock, and smoke poured out of giant concrete stacks. Even from this distance, I could smell the rust and burning chemicals.

Dowe leaned on the railing and took a deep breath. "Ahh, it's so good to be home—" He broke off coughing.

John slapped him on the back. "Don't worry, you'll get used to the smell," he said with a grin at me.

I didn't acknowledge that as we pulled ashore. A crumbling concrete dock snaked out into the water to meet us. At the tip of the pier was a guard tower manned by two snipers, which was less than inviting. One of the soldiers leaned out of the window and watched us, his binoculars aimed straight at me.

I involuntarily stared back. *What is this place?*

"Wave!" John insisted, doing just that.

The guard swiveled his gaze to John. He dropped his binoculars and grabbed his radio, shouting something into it.

I swallowed the wave of trepidation that threatened to resurface. *They know John and Dowe—that's a good sign, right?*

The crew scrambled to anchor the ship to the dock as the gangplank lowered. John took off at a run. "Last one to the shore is a rotten egg!"

Lev and I started after him. Dowe shoved us out of the way and got two steps ahead. "Hurry, or you'll miss dinner!"

"Yeah!" John called over his shoulder. "The warden doesn't like to wait!"

I halted. "What—the warden?"

Lev rear-ended me. "Where are we?"

John stopped at the top of the gangplank and turned around, arms flung wide. "Ladies and gentlemen, welcome to Rott!"

"I think we're all gents here," Dowe corrected.

"I didn't want to exclude Susie." John gestured at a female soldier who was standing on the dock. She popped her gum in annoyance.

"Hang on," I said, and then realized there was definitely nothing to hang on to. "You brought us to *Rott*?"

Suddenly, it all looked familiar—the belching factory, the sandless shore, the metal turrets where Tower used to sit guard—I'd seen it all in Philadelphia's videos. This *was* Rott, the factory where the United had been creating Red Rain. The prison where the government sent unwanted criminals to die.

Which was definitely what was about to happen to us now.

All the fear caught back up to me. "*This* is your safehouse?" I screeched.

The only other person who looked alarmed was Lev. John and Dowe were, of course, completely unbothered. "This is the safest safehouse there is!" John insisted. "No one comes back from Rott. The government will never find you here."

"Yeah," Dowe echoed, "we were undercover here so long that even Jael forgot about us."

Before I could detangle even half of that sentence, a booming voice shouted from the shore. "Stay right there!"

I looked up. The warden—presumably, judging by the fact that his uniform was a different color and he had half a dozen guards trailing him— stormed across the dock. He planted himself at the end of the gangplank, hands on hips and feet apart. "You take one step off that boat and I'll shoot you where you stand."

The threat seemed primarily directed at John and Dowe, but I wasn't about to test that theory and stayed right where I was.

Dowe waved. "Hi, Mr. Harrelson! Did you miss us?"

The warden gave him a look that could have shattered glass, then turned his glare on the captain. "Clark, I thought we had a deal."

Clark put his hands up. "They were floating in the middle of the ocean! What was I supposed to do, let them drown?"

"Yes," the warden deadpanned.

"Well, that's just rude," Dowe sassed, folding his arms.

My curiosity got the better of me, and I decided to risk opening my mouth. "Wait, this has happened before?"

"Twice," both the warden and Clark answered in disgruntled unison.

"How do you think we got to Rott the last time?" John added with complete innocence.

The warden pinched the bridge of his nose and inhaled sharply. "Look, I don't care why you're here or what secret mission you're on, but you can't stay."

"But it's a matter of national security!" Dowe protested.

"That's what you said the last time, and I don't care. I'm not cleaning up after another one of your 'demonstrations.' I'm still finding dried frosting in unmentionable places."

John giggled. "Yeah, that was one of our better riots, wasn't it?"

The warden ignored him and pointed over our heads at Clark. "Take them back. I don't care if you throw them overboard or dump them on the next deserted island—just get them out of here. I'll pay you."

What little hope I had left surged through me. If Clark could drop us off somewhere else, we still had a chance of making it on foot. Plus, if he could be bribed, then I knew several people with lots of money—notably, Philadelphia and Jael—who could convince him to take us somewhere that was *actually* safe.

Clark started to respond, but John and Dowe, as always, couldn't leave well enough alone. "But we're criminals! You can't let us go—that's a violation of your civic duty!" Dowe insisted.

"Yeah, you can't imagine all the crimes we've committed since we saw you last!" John added.

"Not my problem." The warden shooed them away with a flick of his hand. The guards on the shore drew their weapons and started advancing up the ramp, herding us back like a bunch of stray cats.

I pinched John's sleeve and tried to haul him back on the boat. "Come on, guys, let's just go."

I shouldn't have spoken. Dowe looked at me, then at John, and they both grinned.

"But what about him?" Dowe grabbed my shoulders and spun me around. "He's on the United's most wanted!"

He shoved me down the ramp. I almost tripped and ended up in the water.

The warden folded his arms and frowned over his nose at me. "Him? Really?"

I stared back and tried to decide why I found that vaguely offensive.

"Yeah! He's working with Blue Fire!" Dowe announced.

"They're *dating*," John crooned.

The warden's eyebrow inched even further up his forehead. I clenched my fists and resisted the urge to corroborate the story. *Why is that so surprising to you?*

Dowe leaned over my shoulder and dropped his voice to a sinister whisper, like he was narrating a ghost story. "Asia's looking for him. If you send him back to the mainland, she'll find him and hook him up to a brain machine. Then she'll know *you're* the one who let him go."

I jerked out of his grasp. "*Why* would you tell them that?"

Even Lev was on my side with that one. "Yeah, why would you tell them that?"

"Just trust us," Dowe hissed in my ear.

I backed away. *I never should have trusted you.*

"Mong?" the warden repeated. He shared a heavy glance with one of his guards, and that's when I knew it was over. The warden would turn us in for the reward money, and then we'd be right back where we started—with me hooked to a computer giving Asia the key to winning the war, and Lev in jail or worse.

And it was all because of John, Dowe, and their stupid ideas.

The warden turned back to me. "Please tell me this isn't true."

I sighed. "Would you even believe me?"

For an answer, he pulled his phone from his pocket, tapped the screen, and held it out.

The thought of running briefly skirted across my mind. But my only other option was diving into the ocean, and I'd done more than enough swimming for a lifetime.

With a groan, I pressed my thumb to the phone's trackpad. It screeched, and the screen glared an angry red.

The warden flipped it around and read the contents. I knew without asking what he was looking at: My file, which was plastered with a million warnings and an absurdly high price for my capture.

"Arrest them," the warden ordered with a tired groan.

The guards advanced. Lev grabbed my arm in a panic, but I avoided his eyes. There was nowhere to run. Thanks to the thumb scan, my file now had a location ping putting me on this island. Asia would be here as soon as she could get a plane dispatched.

A guard laid his hand on Lev's shoulder and gently pushed him down the ramp. They were less ceremonious with John and Dowe, although neither of them was resisting.

The guards waited until the others were several paces ahead before flanking me. I willingly followed them across the dock.

The warden watched me pass. "I'm sorry about this," he whispered.

"So am I," I said without looking back. I glared at John and Dowe as they pranced across the yard. "So am I."

7

I ended up right back where I started: Staring at the blank wall of my cell.

After they registered us on the database, they forced us to change into prison orange and separated us into different cells. It was just like being back on the mainland, with a guard telling me when I could eat and when I could sleep and someone always screaming at me through a megaphone.

The only difference was that no one on Rott seemed interested in cuffing me to a chair and asking me stupid questions. Instead, they put me to work, which I supposed was a marginal improvement.

Rott was, after all, a factory. Philadelphia and Nic had melted the original structure to the ground when they were imprisoned here four months ago. The United, not one to waste a good labor camp, had promptly rebuilt. The vats that had once contained the raw materials for Red Rain were repurposed into water tanks, and giant pumps were drilled into the production floor. The factory was now a water processing plant, I was told; a terraforming company had contracted them to extract chemicals from seawater.

I didn't care what they were doing. I was just grateful I had some menial labor to distract me from my impending execution while I waited for Asia to come collect us.

Which she was taking an inordinately long time to do. I expected her to send a helicopter by morning. But one day passed, and then another, and I began to wonder if she wasn't coming. There was no word from her, and no United officials showed up on the island. Even the warden said nothing. Apparently, Asia didn't need me anymore.

I prayed that didn't mean she'd found Philadelphia.

I might never know. The island was completely off the grid. John and Dowe, unsurprisingly, had a contraband laptop with a broken screen, but there was no signal. Presumably the warden had internet access in his office, but there was no way I could hack into it from the outside. I asked several guards, and none of them had any recent news about Philadelphia or the revolution. The only regular contact anyone had with the outside world was Clark, who delivered supplies once a month.

The days dragged into a week, and I started to accept the fact that we were being left on Rott to do just that. I threw myself into my work. It was a pointless job, but at least if I exceeded quotas, nobody yelled at me. I picked up shifts from other people, worked as much overtime as they would allow, and strictly avoided talking to John and Dowe.

That was no easy feat. They, clearly, still thought we were friends. They waved whenever we passed, invited me to join some dude's book club, and tried to get our supervisor to transfer me to their department so we could work together. He didn't oblige, thankfully. We were assigned to opposite ends of the factory, so I had an excuse to avoid them during the day. As soon as my shift was done, I shut myself in my cell and let the locked door do the talking.

There was one place I couldn't get away from them, however: mess hall.

All the prisoners were fed together, so we had no choice but to be in the same room. Sometimes I avoided them by sitting at a full table. Sometimes I ate my food standing up and left before they could talk to me. Sometimes I skipped meals entirely.

It worked for a couple of days. But then they got smart and ganged up on me—*literally*. They convinced the entire mess hall to conspire with them. I realized this after I tried to sit at six different tables, and they all refused me. I took a whole lap around the room before I deduced there was only one place I was allowed to sit: the table in the corner with John, Dowe, and Lev.

John and Dowe watched me approach, their elbows propped on the table and fingers tented in identical sinister gestures. Tommy perched on John's shoulder, his tail flicking back and forth. The whole effect was positively evil, like they were supervillains from a bad movie.

I almost dumped my food in the trash and left, but Lev turned and gave me that lonely smile I couldn't refuse.

I dropped my tray on the table with a *thunk*. "What?" I snapped at John and Dowe.

"Sit, please, Stanyard," Dowe cooed. He gestured like a mafia boss welcoming me into his office.

I obeyed with a sigh. "What do you want?"

"To eat dinner with my friends?" John shoveled food into his mouth.

I grabbed my fork, although I had no intention of actually eating. *We are not friends*, I thought but thankfully didn't say.

Tommy jumped onto the table and pranced over to me. He rubbed against my arm, purring. I pushed him away.

Dowe watched us. "Is everything okay, Stanyard?"

I was so sick of people asking me that when everything was clearly *not* okay. "Oh, I'm just peachy," I snarked. "Why, how's *your* day been?"

Dowe, of course, was completely impervious to my sarcasm. "Well, let's see... I'm alive, we're having spaghetti for dinner, and, last I checked, Jesus still loves me..."

"Can confirm," John grunted, and slurped a noddle.

"So, yeah, I'd say I'm doing pretty good." Dowe winked at me.

That was the most pedantic, pathetic, Christianese answer I'd ever heard, and I was tired of being treated like a moron. "Really? Don't you guys ever drop the act?"

"What act?" they said in unison.

I gestured at them with my fork. "This hillbilly idiot thing. It's annoying. Give it up."

John turned to Dowe. "Did he just call us..."

"Yeah, he did," Dowe said, all the joy stripped out of his voice. "Which is really insensitive considering all we've done for him."

He might as well have been my father—the condescending tone of voice, the gaslighting, the absolute refusal to see things the way they were. "Done for me?" I scoffed. "You've done *nothing*."

Dowe opened his mouth, but Lev spoke first. "They got us out of jail, boss."

"And where do you think we are right now?" I glared at him. "A jail. Only this one is in the middle of the ocean where nobody will ever find us."

"I thought that was the point," Dowe inserted. His tone was still cool, calm—almost sane. "You needed to get off the grid."

"I *needed* to get ahold of Phil," I corrected. "But now we're lost, and Phil probably thinks I'm dead."

The word clogged in the back of my throat and stayed there.

Tommy pawed me again. I shoved him away, harder this time.

"We won't be here for long," Lev said, but I could tell he had absolutely no faith in that statement. "Someone will come for us."

"Don't you get it?" I yelled. I hated how weak my voice sounded. "Nobody's coming for us. If Asia cared, she'd have been here by now. She doesn't need me anymore—which probably means she found Phil, and Phil's dead, and the war is over."

"That's certainly one interpretation of the events," John mused. "But definitely not the only one."

I snorted. "You don't know Asia like I do. She doesn't just 'give up.' She's doing this on purpose—she's leaving us here to die."

I clenched the fork in my fist. I didn't want to die, not like this, on some forgotten island where a guard would record my death in a ledger and then toss my body into the ocean. I was more than that—or, I had been. For a brief moment, I'd had everything—*everything!* Philadelphia loved me, I'd made up with my dad, and I had a job that mattered. For a few short weeks, I'd meant something to someone.

And now it was all gone. My file would say something stupid like "lost at sea"; my own family wouldn't even know what happened. Meanwhile, the revolution would fail, my girlfriend would be executed on live TV, and I would be stuck here, stripping nitrogen out of seawater so some rich dude could fulfill his fantasy of terraforming his own planet.

And it all meant absolutely nothing.

I drew the fork back and stabbed it into the table.

John squeaked and slapped a hand over his mouth. Tommy hissed and jumped off the table, disappearing. Dowe barely spared me a glance as he returned to his pasta. "Good thing that wasn't mahogany."

"Boss." Lev shifted beside me. "Please, calm down."

He grabbed my shoulder. His fingers pinched that tender spot on my arm—the spot my dad had bruised so many times—and all the pain came rushing back.

"Don't touch me!" I yanked out of his grasp, turned around, and hit him. Swung my arm and backhanded him across the face. I barely clipped him on the ear, but the damage was done.

He glared at me—first with fear, then anger. Then he mumbled an apology, grabbed his tray, and slid down to the end of the table.

I stared at him. No one said anything, but in my head, there was so much noise as my conscience screamed at me.

Who are you?

What had come over me? I'd hit him—I'd hit *Lev!* He hadn't done anything. He didn't know I hated being touched. He was trying to help, and I'd taken my anger out on him. The person who was least deserving. The person I should have been *protecting.*

Just like my dad had always done.

I swallowed. "Lev, I—"

John interrupted me when he screamed—literally. He squealed and jumped out of his chair like he'd seen a mouse.

Dowe did the same. "What is it?"

"Wanda!" John yelled, pointing.

Dowe followed his gaze. "No. Way. But her file…"

John waved his arms above his head like an air traffic controller. "Wanda! Over here! WANDA!"

The entire room turned to look. A female prisoner about John and Dowe's age stood at the food line. She grinned and sprinted over.

John met her halfway, smashed her in a hug, and burst into tears. "Wanda! I thought you were dead!"

She delicately patted his shoulder. "So that's why you never call."

"No, like, we actually thought you were dead," Dowe explained, expression unusually sober. "Your file says you died two months ago."

She jerked back. *"What?"*

"I was going to send you a birthday present," John sniffled, "but when I saw you were deceased, I donated to an animal shelter instead."

"Aww, that's so sweet of you, but *what*?" she screeched again at a pitch that shouldn't have been humanly possible. "I'm *dead*?"

Dowe shrugged. "That's what your file says."

"I'm only serving seventy-two life sentences." She *tched* and threw her hip. "I am *not* dead."

"Well, then someone screwed up your paperwork real bad, because they had the autopsy report and everything."

She rolled her eyes. "Probably the imbeciles at the county jail. They always mess up my paperwork. What did they say I died from?"

"Eh, some stupid virus."

"Are you kidding me?" She embellished with a couple of extra words, none of which were ladylike.

John clucked his tongue. "They'll do anything to make their statistics these days."

She snarled like an angry cougar—at least, had I been faced with an angry cougar, I image that's what it would have looked and sounded like. "Over my dead body!"

"Literally!" Dowe exclaimed, and as soon as he said it, something clicked. *Maybe there's a reason Asia hasn't found us yet.*

Wanda continued her tirade. "I'll sue!"

"Can dead people sue?"

"We're about to find out."

I tuned them out as my thoughts whirled faster and faster. I leaned over and tapped the arm of a prisoner at the table next to us. "Hey, what are you in for?"

He turned to face me, slowly, each motion grinding like he was a machine in need of oil. "Mass murder," he deadpanned.

I swallowed. He was a massive, grizzled man—probably not the person I should have picked on, but too late now. "What's your sentence?"

"They gave me a choice. I could come here, or I could sit in the electric chair." He held my gaze, unblinking.

"Great, perfect, thanks." I spun around and got the attention of the table behind me. "What about you?"

"Same deal. They stayed my execution," one prisoner said around a mouthful of food.

"A computer virus corrupted my paperwork," another offered. "I'm here waiting retrial."

"Death row!"

"I got sick in prison and almost didn't make it. When I got out of the hospital, they sent me here."

"Reassigned from a work camp in China."

"Purgatory!"

The answers continued down the line, but I'd heard enough. "That's it. You're all dead."

I'd announced it a little louder than intended. Several prisoners stopped and looked at me.

"What are you doing?" Lev hissed.

"Don't you get it?" I gestured. "Everyone on this island is dead!"

The entire hall silenced.

"Hey, don't speak that over me!" John sassed with a finger wave.

Dowe folded his arms. "Yeah, just because you're having a bad day doesn't mean you need to go prophesying death all over the place."

There were some scattered *amen's* from the back of the room. I put my hands up. "No, I mean, the paperwork. That's why everyone here is from death row, or their file is altered. The government wants everyone to think you're dead."

Whispers rippled around the tables. I scanned the crowd as everything suddenly made sense. "'Rott' doesn't exist. They're keeping this entire island off the grid."

John and Dowe shared a glance. "That actually does explain a lot."

It explained everything. I remembered what Philadelphia had said about her file. Mr. and Mrs. Nolan, her wealthy benefactors, were the ones who had sentenced her to Rott. The plan had been for "Philadelphia" to die on the island so she could adopt a new identity and return as "Andromeda Nolan."

It hadn't worked, because Phil had blown up the factory, but now I knew why they'd chosen Rott. What better place to build your secret superweapon than a forgotten island in the middle of the ocean staffed by expendable inmates who were already dead?

"So our arrest..." Lev ventured.

"They never reported it." Why would they? We'd washed up out of the ocean. There was no way to track us, and there was no trace of our plane. We were as good as dead—and if they reported us, it might solicit some unwanted questions.

I remembered how edgy the warden had been when I'd mentioned Mong's name and reached the obvious conclusion. "That's why Asia never came to get us—she doesn't know we're here."

Relief flooded me, before I abruptly realized that generated more questions than it answered. Who was running this place? Thames Nolan, the original investor, was dead. Asia had been his business partner, but all evidence suggested she had no idea what was happening on Rott now. If Asia wasn't involved, then who was? Why did a terraforming company need a factory staffed with dead inmates?

These were all important questions, but Lev didn't give me time to contemplate them. "So, you're saying," he growled, "we're serving life sentences on a deserted island in the middle of the ocean, and not even the *government* knows where we are?"

"You're welcome," John and Dowe crowed together. "We said we'd get you off the grid, and we did."

They had—which meant we had a chance of getting out of this alive. Assuming the guards' computers had some internet accessibility, it would be very easy for me to get online and make contact with a friend.

Or it would be, if my accounts weren't compromised. I could make a temp login, but it would be very difficult to get a coded message to someone without access to my contacts. Plus, there was no telling how much of the Boston underground had been compromised. I didn't even know who was still alive. My best bet would be to log into my old accounts, spam all my contacts, and hope someone would get the message.

But Asia would see anything I sent—and if she got here first, we'd be worse off.

Something brushed my leg. I looked down to see Tommy clawing my pants, meowing.

I scooped him up and stroked his back, trying to focus. There had to be a way for me to get online without Asia noticing. If we could distract her...

John and Dowe's words echoed back to me.

Give them bigger problems.

I slapped my hand on the table. "John and Dowe, you're a genius!"

There was an audible pause. "We know that," Dowe said slowly. "We're just surprised *you* know that."

"Don't you see? It's just like you said—give them bigger problems."

"Okay, back up, first things first, what's the small problem?" Dowe asked.

"I need to get online, right?"

He grunted an *uh huh* and folded his arms.

I gestured, as if that would make my garbled thoughts easier to translate. "And I can't give Asia my location."

"That would, in fact, defeat the entire purpose of this adventure, yes," John agreed.

"So, we give her bigger problems."

They both arched opposite eyebrows, like they were one face. "How big of a problem are we talking?"

That was a good question—and the answer came to me with a rush of adrenaline. "What day is it?"

John rolled up his sleeve. The guards had confiscated most of his watches, but he still had a cheap plastic one that looked like it was made for children. "The 16th."

Tomorrow. "Operation Day—Operation Blue Fire is tomorrow!" I exclaimed.

Lev murmured something in Russian. Several prisoners gave me their full attention.

Dowe pursed his lips. "Operation Day is, in fact, a big problem."

"Yeah, if Philli is successful, the government should have a couple *million* extra problems," John added.

"Exactly!" I said. "Asia will have much more important things to deal with. If I can get online while everything's in chaos, I can get a message to one of our friends—and they might be able to get here before Asia can."

It was still a risk. If I used any of my old accounts, Asia might see the message. But once Operation Day launched, there would be no point in tracking me down. Even if she did catch me, there would be nothing I could tell her that she wouldn't already know.

John snapped his fingers. "You're right. We *are* geniuses."

"You know that was the plan all along, right?" Dowe said.

I looked up to find him smirking at me. "What?"

"We had a plan?" John echoed.

Dowe nodded. "That was the plan the whole time. We knew there was no way to get you safely home while Asia was on the hunt. So, we were going to hide off the grid until it was safe to call Jael."

"You planned this?" I exclaimed, then realized I needed to stop asking that question. If I'd learned anything over the past week, it was that John and Dowe, against all evidence to the contrary, always knew what they were doing. "If you had a plan, why didn't you tell me?"

"Or me!" John objected.

"*You* missed the staff meeting," Dowe chided. "And *you* never asked." He pointed at me.

I grimaced when I realized he was right.

"Waiting until Operation Day is a nice touch, though," he consented. "I wish I'd thought of that."

"Well, glad we're all on the same page now," John chirped. "So, how are we getting him online?"

My brain reset. I scratched Tommy behind the ears and tallied all the variables. "The warden has to have some kind of connectivity in his office. If we can break in, I can take care of the rest."

"I can get you in his office," Lev declared.

I didn't question it. "We also need to get the warden out of the building—for as long as possible."

John and Dowe exchanged a coded glance that involved a disturbing amount of eyebrow movement. Slowly, mirrored grins spread across their faces.

"So, what you're saying is..." Dowe started, dragging each syllable out with drama.

"...you need a distraction?" John finished. He turned to me with a look that was somehow both condemning and forgiving at the same time.

I laughed; I deserved it. "Yeah, I guess I am," I said, and smiled.

He smiled back. "Leave it to us."

Please, Phil, I don't want to do this now.

I knew she was about to ask. I could tell by the way she'd gone eerily silent as she stared at me from where she sat across the lab.

She took a sharp breath. "Hey."

I braced myself. "Yeah?"

"While I was on Mars… how much of that was you talking?"

It was the question I'd been avoiding for weeks, ever since I donned the alias "Aurelius" and decided Philadelphia would like me better if she didn't know who I was.

It worked—until she learned the truth, and we ended up right back where we started, with her flinching every time I moved.

I refused to turn around. "Jayde dictated a little. The rest was me."

You're lying again. It was me the whole time.

She looked down at her dad's cryogenics tube, which lay between us like a frozen lake. She traced fidgety circles in the fog on the glass. "Did you do all that hacking yourself?"

I scrolled vainly on my laptop. "It was a team effort. Jayde had access to the programs, but I did a lot of the legwork."

More lies. I did all the work. Jayde had been more interested in starting a rebellion than rescuing Phil. I was the one who stayed up late helping, who lost sleep waiting for her to message. I was the one who saved her—and I hated to think that she gave Jayde any of the credit.

Just tell her!

She found her courage before I found mine. "Did you mean what you said?"

Do we have to do this now? Now was literally the worst time. She still hadn't come down off the adrenaline from yesterday; she'd barely slept, hadn't eaten, and looked like she was two breaths away from having a complete mental break. I needed to hack into her father's machine so we could thaw him before he was gone for good, and I couldn't work while she was staring at me.

I should have told her that; I should have taken charge and insisted we have this conversation later. But instead, I just avoided the issue, like I always did. "Which part?" I blurted.

"Everything," she whispered.

All my desperate text messages echoed around in my head.

I THOUGHT I LOST YOU

JUST PLEASE TALK TO ME

I'M SORRY PHIL. I REALLY AM

How I wished I could go back and have those conversations again without a filter—to tell her what I really thought.

I finally turned to face her. "Everything I said was the truth."

"Except the part about you being Jayde," she returned, the accusation prepared.

I couldn't stand the disappointment in her eyes. I glanced down at her father—not that the look on his petrified face was any more forgiving. "I never actually said I was..."

She sighed. "Why didn't you just tell me?"

A dozen excuses leapt to my mind.

Because you wouldn't have believed me.

Because it was too dangerous.

Because it wasn't the right time.

That's what I'd said the last time, and the time before that, always telling myself there would be a better moment to break the truth—until there wasn't, and I almost didn't get a second chance.

I wouldn't make the same mistake again.

I slammed my laptop shut. "I was scared, okay? I was afraid that if I told you it was me, you'd block me—or give me the look you're giving me now."

She looked like she was afraid of me. She looked like she didn't trust me. She looked like she hated me.

"All I wanted was the truth," she squeaked, and then burst into tears.

But that is the truth. I watched her sob and wondered, briefly, if it was even worth trying.

You can't fix this.

Yes, I can. I stood and walked over to her. "Phil," I whispered, and reached for her shoulder.

"Don't touch me!" she shrieked—and then she hit me. Swung her hand and slapped my arm away.

I jerked back. She gasped, staring at her hands like they didn't belong to her. Then she hid her face and cried harder.

She gushed apologies, but I couldn't hear her. I couldn't hear anything over the ringing in my ears, the memory of a hundred rejections. My arm burned while my muscles screamed at me.

Run.

I couldn't do this—I *wouldn't*. Phil was being unreasonable and taking her anger out on me, and I wasn't going to put up with that. I couldn't deal with another relationship where someone screamed at me, blamed me for everything, abused me.

Not like my dad.

I glanced at the door. I should leave. I should walk away, find someone else to do the hacking. My file was still clean; I could be gone tonight. There was nothing keeping me here.

Except... there was.

I stared at Philadelphia as she continued to sob and realized, for the first time in a decade, I didn't *want* to run. I wanted to fix this. I wanted to be the better person, turn the other cheek, let the past go—because I knew that if I did, things would be different.

Jesus, help me.

I knelt in front of her. "Philadelphia."

It was a minute before her tears slowed, like a storm blowing over. She wiped her face and looked at her lap.

I leaned forward until she was forced to look at me. "Philadelphia, I'm sorry. I'm sorry I lied to you. I'm sorry I left you behind. I almost got you killed, and I've never regretted anything more in my life."

She just stared, and I wondered if she didn't believe me. How could I make her see I was telling the truth?

The answer came with a rush of the Holy Spirit. "Will you forgive me?"

She opened her mouth, but I raised my hand before she could say anything. I had one chance to do this right. I'd apologized to Philadelphia before, and nothing had changed. I wasn't going to continue the cycle, with us trading Christian pleasantries while we nursed wounds that would never heal.

I couldn't do that with Philadelphia. Not like I'd done with my dad.

I met her gaze. "I don't want you to say it just because we're Christians and that's what we're supposed to say."

She frowned. "How do you want me to say it, then?"

I glanced at the icy machine beside us. "I want you to say it like you said it to your dad."

I remembered watching the livestream, where she'd sobbed in front of the camera and confessed that she knew about her dad's secret sins. She told him she was afraid of him. She told him she didn't trust him. She told him she was mad at him.

And then she forgave him.

She'd forgiven him—and then she'd walked it out, day after day. She'd sacrificed herself to stop Thames, even though it was her dad's fault she was in danger. She'd come back to earth to find her father, even though she would have been much safer on Mars. And even now she was staying with him when she had every reason to run.

That was when I learned what real forgiveness looked like. That was when I began to hope that she might forgive me, too.

And I wasn't leaving this room until I had an answer.

"I don't... I don't know if I trust you like that," she stammered.

"You weren't sure if you trusted your dad, either," I returned.

She stared at his body, twisting her hands in her lap.

"I know I need to earn your trust back," I said. "That could take months, years—I don't care."

I didn't care. I didn't care how long it took or what hoops I had to jump through. I would do whatever she needed—all she had to do was ask.

She turned back to face me. "Then what do you want from me?"

"I want you to give me a chance."

That's all I wanted—a chance. A chance to prove myself. A chance to be a different person.

She didn't say anything, so I kept going. "I know it will take time. But if you're going to say you forgive me, I need you to mean it. I need to know that you're wiping that from my account and letting it go. I need to know that when I try, you're not going to remind me of all my past sins—that every time I hold out my hand, you're not thinking of the time I left you behind."

"I don't know if I can do that," she stuttered, each word like a nail in a coffin. "Because right now, that's all I see."

I looked away. That's all I saw too, but I knew I could change that—if she'd just give me the opportunity. *Please, Phil, I promise I'm not the same guy.*

Her voice rose. "I know you tried to make it up to me on Mars, but our whole relationship was based on a lie. And now every time I look at you, I have to ask myself if you're still lying."

But I'm not lying! I'd never lied to her, not really. I didn't tell her it was me, but everything else I'd said was the truth. I was sorry. I did want to help her. I couldn't lose her again.

The desperate words crammed up my throat, but the Holy Spirit got there first. *Let her talk.*

I shut my mouth and met her eyes again. This time, she was the one who looked away. "And what am I supposed to do? Tell you I never want to see you again? I need you to hack Dad's tube. I need you, and I hate that I need you, but I don't have a choice. I *have* to forgive you."

No, she didn't. She didn't have to do anything. This never-ending game of guilt and obligation was stopping right here, right now. It died with me.

"No, you don't," I said, making sure each word was clear and understood. "I'll do everything I can to save your dad whether you forgive me or not. But if you're going to forgive me, I need you to mean it. I need you to give me the opportunity to earn your trust."

She slowly looked up. "And what if I don't?"

Her voice was cold, and for a moment, I was convinced she meant it. Maybe she couldn't forgive me. Maybe she wouldn't.

Then I remembered who she was. This was the girl who kept asking if I was safe after I'd left her in an alley to die. This was the girl who had begged me with tears to come back to camp. This was the girl who had been my friend since the first grade—even when I was annoying, disinterested, and cruel.

Suddenly, I understood where I'd messed up. I'd spent the past month avoiding this conversation because I was afraid she wouldn't forgive me, but that was never the problem. She wouldn't be sitting here, sobbing her guts out, if she didn't want to forgive.

I took a deep breath and gave her what she really needed: a choice. "Then I guess I'll have to live with that. But at least I asked."

She stiffened. She stared at her hands again, this time in awe—as if she finally realized just how much power she had over me.

I gave her one last chance to end it all. "I'm giving you my weapons, Phil. If you're going to shoot me, do it. But don't say 'I forgive you' if you don't mean it. I can't live that way. Not with you."

I hadn't meant to say it—not now, not like that. But it was out, and with it all the feelings I'd never been able to put in a text message.

I braced myself for the familiar sting of rejection, but it never came. She sucked in her breath, a question flashing across her eyes—and that's when I knew there was hope.

Things are going to be different.

"Philadelphia," I said, this time with confidence, "will you forgive me?"

"Yes, I will," she replied gently, and in that moment, the girl I'd grown up with came back from the dead.

There was so much more I wanted to say, but I wasn't going to do it now, with her father lying frozen between us. So, I mumbled an excuse about needing to get back to work, and she took the hint.

It wasn't until later, after the competing waves of elation and nervousness had faded, that I found the courage to stare into the bathroom mirror and admit the truth.

I love her.

8

John and Dowe kicked me out of the cafeteria soon after, saying they had a riot to organize. My job was to go to work in the morning, pretend like nothing was wrong, and wait for the signal. They didn't give me any other details.

This time, I didn't ask for any.

I went back to my cell and spent the night praying. I had no idea what the time conversion between Rott and Beijing was, but I knew they were ahead of us. That meant Operation Blue Fire was already happening, and Philadelphia, if she was still in China, was at the frontline of a war.

I stared at the stains on the concrete floor and tried to conjure an emotion—any emotion. The world could be ending *right now.* The United could be crumbling as millions of civilians resisted their control—or we could be losing the war. Asia had compromised a lot of the underground, and Blue Fire's reputation was hanging by a thread. The government could be crushing our friends one by one as Asia used the unrest we started to seize power.

I wished I could say without a shadow of a doubt that Operation Blue Fire would succeed. But if someone had pinned me to the wall, I'm not sure I could say that I ever really believed in the operation. I didn't believe in Jael, or Data, or even Blue Fire herself—the flashy, fierce version of Philadelphia they put on TV.

I didn't believe in Blue Fire—but I did believe in God, who had very obviously put her there. I didn't know why, and I didn't know when, but I knew God had a purpose for giving Philadelphia authority. And *that* purpose—whatever it was—would succeed.

That's what I should have been praying for. I should have been interceding for our allies across the world—and I did, sort of. But at some point in the night, I ended up screaming into the floor as I begged God for forgiveness.

I didn't want to be angry. I didn't want to be violent.

I don't want to be like my dad.

I don't remember falling asleep. All I remember is jerking awake when the morning alarm sounded. I was still lying on the floor, Tommy curled up on top of me.

John and Dowe weren't at breakfast, which I hoped was a good sign. I went through the motions and then took up my station in the factory. Lev stayed close by. Every time our supervisors weren't looking, he would snatch a tool or part off the assembly line and stash it in the satchel he'd hidden under the machine.

The first hour passed without incident. I noticed a few of our coworkers were mysteriously absent, but nothing else seemed amiss. Another hour passed, and I began to grow fidgety.

Lev was even more so. He slid up next to me and dropped his voice to a whisper. "What is taking them so long?"

I was wondering the same thing, but I wasn't about to screw this up. "Just wait for the signal."

"Did they say what the signal was?"

I hesitated when I realized that was the one question I probably should have asked. "We have to trust them. But I'm pretty sure we'll know it when we hear it."

I wasn't wrong. At precisely noon, right before shift change, I noticed a bad smell permeating the factory. And I mean *bad* literally—it smelled like cow manure.

And considering there were absolutely no animals on this island, I knew who was responsible.

Two seconds later, the alarm went off.

I jumped as the factory was engulfed in flashing red light. All the prisoners stopped what they were doing. There was chatter on the guards' radios, and then the door burst open.

A young lieutenant leaned over the railing and waved his arms. "All units, topside, now! There's a riot!"

Several guards groaned. The officer nearest to me didn't even look up from his device. "Let me guess. John Dowe?"

"Yessir."

The officer scrolled on his screen. "Who's winning?"

"Sir?"

The officer slid his device back in his pocket. "Last time it was a baking contest. The time before that, a dance off. So, who's winning?"

The lieutenant glanced at the open door behind him. "It kind of looks like they're roping cattle, but I'm not—" He caught himself. "Look, would you just get up here? Please?"

I started to laugh and barely caught myself.

The officer shot me a glare as he stood up. "Everyone, back to your cells. Now!"

Lev nudged my arm. He discretely slung his satchel over his shoulder and joined the line of grumbling prisoners trudging out of the factory. I kept my head down and followed.

The guards herded us out of the factory and around the back of the building. The stench was even worse outside; the whole island reeked like a barn. I couldn't see the main yard, but I heard cheering, country music, and a pig squealing.

I kept my eyes straight ahead. *Don't ask questions.*

Two officers stood at the barrack doors, prodding people inside with their guns. Lev held back until we were at the end of the line—then grabbed my arm and yanked me around the corner. We crouched in the shadows while the guards shoved everyone else inside, latched the doors, and ran for the yard.

"Follow me," Lev whispered.

After checking both ways, we darted across the path to the administration building. We scrambled up the service ladder and crawled across the roof, staying out of sight of the guard towers. The commotion was louder now, and I swore I heard John and Dowe singing some country ballad—and doing a halfway decent job at it.

Lev reached the rooftop vent. He pulled a screwdriver from his satchel and unscrewed the grate, setting it aside silently. Then without a word, he crawled inside and disappeared.

I glanced over the edge. The pipe was narrow, dark, and coated with dust. "Lev, I don't think—"

"Hurry!" he hissed back, his voice tinging off the metal pipe.

I shuddered. *Oh Jesus, don't let me get stuck.* Grasping the roof of the vent, I swung my legs over the edge and dropped in.

The gross walls dragged against my arms as I slid to the bottom, and I swallowed way more dust than I wanted to. I hacked and spit, but I doubted the taste was ever coming out of my mouth.

"This way!" Lev called.

I flattened myself on the floor. He was already a few yards ahead of me, army crawling through the pipe. He made it look easy—but he was half a foot and a couple dozen pounds smaller than me.

I grunted and struggled to keep up. "Wait up!"

He didn't and shimmied around a corner. I focused on not having a panic attack as I put one arm in front of the other. Weak light peered through the vents every few yards, leaving most of the pipe in shadow. I scraped my hands on exposed screws at least five times.

Just think, this'll be a great story to tell Phil, I coached myself.

I finally caught up to Lev. He'd ripped a panel off the side of the vent and was rooting around in the ceiling.

"Did Jayde also teach you how to break into a building through the ventilation system?" I panted.

"I taught myself," he replied, his voice muffled by the insulation. "There was nothing to do on base, so... I learned how to wire electricity."

I imagined him crawling around in the walls on base like a mouse and couldn't decide if that mental picture was hilarious or terrifying.

I pushed myself up on my elbows. "Look, Lev, there's something I need to say."

He grunted an acknowledgment.

I sighed. Now was probably the worst time to be doing this, but if this mission went wrong, I might not get another chance. "I want to apologize for what happened yesterday."

He looked over his shoulder at me.

I met his gaze. "I'm sorry. I shouldn't have hit you, and I shouldn't have yelled."

I felt like there should be more—I'd *smacked* the guy—but I couldn't find the words.

He, apparently, hadn't lost any sleep over the incident, because he just shrugged and stuck his head back in the wall. "It's fine. I'm used to it from Jayde."

I winced. Of all of Jayde's attributes I wished I could emulate, his cruelty was not one of them. "Was he abusive?"

"No, he was just very strict with the discipline. I need the snips." He gestured at his satchel that was on the floor beside him.

I inched forward and reached into the bag. "If you weren't military, I would say that's the same thing." I passed him the tool.

He chuckled. "He didn't treat me any differently than any other soldier. He just... gets very upset when things don't go his way."

"So, why'd you stay?" *Wow, asking all the personal questions today, are we, Stanyard?*

The was a pause. "He was all I had," Lev stated, but blandly, as if he'd long since cauterized all the grief attached to that statement.

"I'm sorry," I mumbled.

He shrugged again. "I thought about leaving. But I had food and a place to stay... and it was just easier to learn the rules and not make him angry."

I knew exactly what that was like. I'd done the same thing with my dad, my sister, even Philadelphia, at first. I'd seen Lev do the same thing with Jayde time and again—except for one crucial incident.

"Why didn't you shoot me?" I blurted.

He glanced back with a frown.

"When Jayde told you to kill me if Phil didn't go through with the mission." I gestured, as if they were both crammed in the pipe with us. "Why didn't you?"

He shook his head. "I couldn't."

That's what he'd said the last time, but I didn't believe it. I'd seen how ruthless he could be on missions. I knew he had no fear of guns or dead bodies. No, I had every reason to believe that if Lev had wanted to kill me, he would have.

"Lev, we both know that's not true," I prodded.

He looked away.

I spelled out all the broken pieces I couldn't explain. "Jayde's the closest thing you have to family—he saved your life. You don't know me. I'm just a stranger."

Lev and I had been strangers at the time. We'd done a couple of runs together, installed some server racks on base and whatnot, but nothing that would constitute friendship. We were only connected because of Jayde. Lev hadn't known anything about me.

He still doesn't, I realized with some regret.

Lev sighed and gave me the answer I'd been expecting all along. "I did it for Blue Fire."

"But why?" I insisted. "You've spent even less time with her. And if you wanted to the rebellion to win, you should have gone through with the assassination."

That was the part I didn't understand, the part where all my preconceived notions about Lev and Jayde and the whole revolution fell apart. I knew how Jayde thought, and I'd seen Lev follow his lead time and again. There was nothing more important to Jayde than ending the United, by any means necessary. If Lev wanted revenge on the government that slaughtered his people, he should have let Phil go through with the mission— even if it meant pulling the trigger on me.

I knew I was beating a dead horse, trying to find meaning where there was none, but I had to know. I had to know why he'd chosen Phil—and by extension, me—over the only "relative" he had.

"Why, Lev?"

He knotted his brow and glared at the hole in the ceiling. "Because..." He groped for words, then closed his eyes and rattled off something in Russian.

He looked back up at me and self-translated. "Jayde is doing this because he hates the United. Blue Fire... isn't."

He was right. Of all the people who had a reason to hate the government, Philadelphia didn't—or, at least, she didn't act like she did. I remembered how she had spared Clint, the commander of our old containment camp, when everyone—including me—was telling her to shoot. She'd also had the perfect opportunity to assassinate the General Secretary of the United, and she'd walked away at the risk of her own life.

Lev fingered one of the wires dangling out of the wall. "Blue Fire didn't go to China because she wanted revenge. And I..."

"...didn't want to be the reason that changed," I finished for him.

He nodded. "I don't want to follow someone like Jayde. I want to follow someone... like her."

We stared at each other, as if he, too, realized how insane that sounded. That the one person who *didn't* want revenge on the government was the person we'd all chosen to lead the war. Philadelphia was the exact opposite of the person you'd want to start a revolution. She'd lose the war to save a few lives, and she'd let her enemies walk away when she had every means to kill them. And when some of them came crawling back, begging for forgiveness—like me, Nic, and so many others—she always, always said yes.

She was the exact opposite of the person you'd want to lead a war. And yet, maybe, that's exactly why we'd chosen her.

It was certainly why *I'd* chosen her.

Lev cut the wire with the shears. "That should take care of the cameras. Hurry."

He rolled over. With a swift kick, he knocked the nearest grate open and jumped down into the hall.

I tossed the satchel to him, then followed—much less nimbly. I almost twisted my ankle on the landing. Every muscle was cramping, but I'd never been so grateful to stand upright on my own two feet.

Lev led the way to the office at the far end. Another unscrewed panel, another snipped wire, and the door hissed open.

"I see why they call you Watts," I commented.

He grinned and gestured me inside.

I grabbed his shoulder. "Lev, listen... thank you. If I ever freak out again, hit me upside the head, okay?"

He cocked an eyebrow like he didn't understand the phrase.

"I don't want to be like Jayde." *Or my father.* "I want us to be friends. So, if I'm ever out of line, you have permission to tell me. Smack me in the face if I'm not listening."

He glanced at my chin, as if judging the trajectory. Then he looked into my eyes and smiled. "Yes, boss."

The warden's office was lined wall-to-wall with computers and security monitors. I walked over to his desktop computer and tapped the screen. A quick toggle of the settings menu proved I was right—the device was connected to the internet, but of course it was password-locked.

No matter—*this* was wiring I could do.

Lev pulled John and Dowe's broken laptop out of his satchel and passed it to me. I crawled under the warden's desk. With a few swapped cables, I wired the laptop into the modem. I knew all the activity on the connection could be monitored, but hopefully the guards would be too busy cleaning up after John and Dowe's rodeo to notice.

Lev stood guard at the door, a screwdriver clenched in his hand like a knife. "Make it quick."

I sat cross-legged on the floor and went to work. Half of the laptop's screen was pixelated, but it booted quickly enough as I downloaded a messaging app and logged in with my old credentials. The program accepted my password without complaint; thankfully, Asia hadn't changed my login.

I scrolled through the homepage. As I feared, my network had gone dark. Most of my saved contacts were gone, the accounts "no longer available." A few had outright blocked me. My entire chat history was grayed out—except for one conversation.

BLUE FIRE

I frowned at the screen. Philadelphia hadn't changed her contact information, which somewhat surprised me. The risk was probably low. Jael was managing her online security, which meant that Blue Fire was, unironically, the one person who could go online and not leave a trail. But Asia would have known about the account after she'd stolen my phone. She could have easily created her own username and contacted Phil.

Maybe that's why Jael left it open.

I pushed aside the gruesome thought and clicked on our chat.

I was more than a little disappointed to see there were only a few unread messages. Sure, there had been no reason for her to text me; she knew I was offline.

But that had never stopped me from texting her.

I swallowed the ugly feeling and read the messages. The oldest was a missed call—from the exact day and time the base was raided.

I cringed when I realized what that meant: Phil watched me get arrested on live TV. Asia no doubt streamed it on the news. Philadelphia must have called me in a panic—and, for the first time in our short relationship, I hadn't answered.

Oh, Phil, I'm so sorry.

Our chat went silent for over a week, and then she'd sent two short texts:

HEY. I KNOW YOU WON'T SEE THIS FOR AWHILE, BUT I WANT YOU TO KNOW THAT I'M PRAYING FOR YOU.

I KNOW GOD IS GOING TO PROTECT YOU.

That was it. Simple, innocent, and full of faith—just like she always was.
I smiled.
"Hurry," Lev hissed. "I don't hear the sirens anymore."
I quickly typed the message I'd composed in my head, cramming all the information Phil needed to know into one text.

I'M ALIVE. WE'RE ON ROTT. JOHN DOWE AND WATTS ARE WITH ME. THE ENTIRE ISLAND IS OFF THE GRID—ALL THE PRISONERS ARE REGISTERED AS DEAD. SEND HELP.

I knew spelling out our location in a text was a risk. Asia and who knows how many of her underlings still had access to my accounts. But hopefully, Operation Day had given them bigger problems.
I hit send, then added:

GOD ANSWERED YOUR PRAYER. YOU WON'T BELIEVE WHAT HAPPENED.

There was more I wanted to tell her, but I had to cast my net wide if we had a chance of surviving. I copy-pasted the message to all of my contacts that weren't grayed out. I knew several of them were shots in the dark—especially Nic and my dad—but the more people who saw the message, the better.
Suddenly, a door banged—at the same time Lev cursed in Russian. "They're in the stairwell!"
I slammed my laptop shut. Lev dragged the office chair to the middle of the floor and climbed on top of it. With a couple quick twists of the screwdriver, he had the ceiling vent open.
I ran underneath him and gave him a shove. He scrambled into the vent, then held his hand down to me. "Hurry, boss!"
Shouts echoed in the hall. There was no way I could hoist myself into the vent—not in time. "No, you get out of here!" I ordered. "I'll take the blame."
"But—"
"Do it!" I shoved the laptop at him.
He mercifully obeyed. He snatched the laptop and yanked the grate shut, then scuffled down the pipe. I kicked the chair to the opposite end of the room.

Lev's thumping faded around the corner—just as the warden burst into the office. "Don't move!"

I obligingly lifted my hands. Not that there was anywhere to run.

The two guards he had with him aimed their rifles, just in case. "How did you get in here?" the warden demanded.

"The door?" I pointed.

He growled and abandoned the question in lieu of a more pertinent one. "What are you doing?"

"Well, I wanted to call my girlfriend, but your computer was locked," I said, which was almost the truth.

"Let me guess." He folded his arms. "You asked John Dowe to turn my front yard into a pigsty to give you cover."

"I knew nothing about the pigs," I said with completely honesty, "but basically, yeah."

He sighed and tried to brush off his jacket sleeve. It was crusted with mud, straw, and a brown substance that probably wasn't dirt. "I guess I shouldn't have expected any less from a friend of John Dowe's."

I grinned. "No, you shouldn't have."

9

They locked me in solitary confinement while they cleaned up John and Dowe's mess—which took almost three days to do. On the second day, they sent me a pork chop for dinner. I thought it was a weirdly fancy meal to serve a prisoner, but the guard informed me that meat was currently the most plentiful food source on the island—and probably would be for a month.

After they'd finally gotten a handle on things, the warden dragged me into his office, cuffed me to a chair, and interrogated me. Well, he didn't so much interrogate me as he did sit across the table and glare at me in annoyance for five minutes straight.

"I'm not sorry?" I offered when the silence had gotten torturous.

"I know you were messing with my modem," he grunted.

I flinched and looked appropriately terrified.

"But, as near as I can see, you didn't send any messages, and there's been no update on your file. So, I'm assuming you didn't get very far."

I tried to keep the relief off my face. The messaging app encrypted its data. It wasn't uncrackable, but it was designed to slip right past the algorithm—and that would be my saving grace.

Thank you, Jesus.

"That means that, as of right now, you and I are the only ones who know about your little indiscretion," the warden continued. "So, I don't feel obliged to tell my boss what happened. Which is quite lucky for you—otherwise, this conversation would have gone very differently."

He pulled his gun from its holster and laid it on the table for emphasis.

"What are you going to do with me?" I finally got the courage to ask.

He leaned back in the chair. "Well, Mr. Dass, it might surprise you to know that I don't make those decisions. My boss decides who comes and who goes from this island. So, unless he—"

As if in answer, the intercom buzzed.

The warden glanced past me to the door. "What do you want?"

It opened to reveal a nervous guard holding a tablet. "Urgent message from the government, sir. Criminal Services."

"Just what I needed." The warden preemptively pinched his temples. "Well, what is it?"

The guard held the tablet up. "They're ordering that John, Dowe, Lev, and him," he gestured at me, "be deported immediately to the mainland for questioning."

I sat up straight. *It worked! Philadelphia got the message!*

The warden slapped his hand on the table. "Really?" he grunted at me.

I couldn't keep the grin off my face. "It worked last time, didn't it?"

"And you think I'm going to fall for it again? No, you're not going anywhere."

"Sir," the guard interrupted, taking a shaky step forward, "they said it's urgent. They're sending a transport tomorrow—"

The warden shot him a glare. "You don't really think that's a legitimate order, do you?"

The guard squinted at the tablet. "It's got a signature…"

"I'm demoting you." The warden snatched the tablet and scanned the screen. "Care to explain how your friends know you're here, Mr. Dass?"

I shrugged.

He took a heavy breath through his nose. His gaze shifted back and forth between the tablet and the gun, as if debating whether he'd rather just end me right here and be done with it.

I clenched my fists and prayed.

He threw the tablet on the table. "Well, forged or not, this piece of paper gives me an alibi and an excuse to get rid of you, so I'm going to let you go."

I let out the breath I'd accidentally been holding. *Praise God!*

"However, a warning." The warden shoved his chair back and stood up. "What happens on Rott stays on Rott. All of the prisoners here are legally dead. Give him a reason, and my boss won't hesitate to make it official."

I shuddered—the fact that the other inmates might suffer because of my stunt was a consequence I hadn't considered. *Jael will know what to do.*

The warden gestured at the guard. "Keep them in solitary until the transport arrives. I want handcuffs and snipers on them until that plane is out of our airspace, understood?"

"Aye, sir." The guard released me from the chair and shoved me towards the hall.

"Mr. Dass," the warden called.

I paused in the doorway and glanced back.

He frowned. "Don't come back."

I smiled. "I won't."

*

Our transport—a sleek fighter jet not unlike the one we'd lost in the ocean—arrived at dawn. True to his word, the warden cuffed us all and escorted us across the yard with an entourage of no less than twelve soldiers. One of them carried Tommy in a cage—an arrangement he was *not* happy about.

As usual, John and Dowe were not at all bothered by the situation. They called goodbyes to prisoners and guards alike, waving like they were in a parade.

Two United soldiers met us at the plane. I was hoping I'd recognize them, but both were wearing full combat suits and helmets that completely hid their faces. Neither of them acted like they knew us as they roughly herded us onto the plane with their guns.

The taller one shoved Lev up the ramp. Lev tripped over the threshold and landed on his face, scraping his hands on the metal floor.

"Move!" the soldier snarled. He kicked Lev in the ribs—and hard. Lev choked on a cry of pain.

"Hey!" I shouted.

"Being a bully is *not* cool," Dowe chided.

The shorter guard put his finger on the trigger of his pistol. "Keep moving," he warned, his voice warped and metallic through the helmet's speakers.

I grasped Lev's arm and helped him stand. "It's okay. It's all for show," I whispered in his ear, and desperately hoped I was right.

The hatch shut, sealing us in the darkness of the plane. The taller soldier pointed at his partner. "Strap them in. And then *please* shoot that dumb cat—I don't want any incidents."

He kicked Tommy's cage. The animal howled and scratched at him.

The shorter guard lifted his pistol. "That won't be necessary." He turned—and shot his partner.

We all stared while the soldier's smoking body slumped to the floor. The shorter guard holstered his weapon. "Don't worry, it was set on stun."

"Are you...?" I ventured.

For an answer, he reached into his uniform and pulled out a dog tag. Etched on the back was the thunderbird symbol.

I grinned. *We're going home!*

The guard pulled a key from his pocket and freed me, then pressed the fob into my hand. "Cuff him to the wall, then strap in. We're going to have to make a break for it."

I hastily released the others—and Tommy—while the guard claimed the pilot seat and started maneuvering controls. The floor thrummed as the copter on the bottom whirred to life. Slowly, we lifted from the sand.

Lev helped me cuff the unconscious guard to an equipment rack, then we claimed the nearest seats and buckled in. Tommy crawled onto my shoulder and wrapped himself around my neck.

I petted him reassuringly and stole a glance out the cockpit window. The sniper rifles in the guard tower seemed to follow us as we glided out over the water.

The radio crackled. "Hawk Unit A, this is ground control. What's your status?"

Our pilot grabbed his handset. "This is Hawk Unit A. Prisoners secured, all systems go. Preparing to enter hyperspeed. Over."

"Roger. Bear west at mark seven—we'll provide cover until you're out of airspace."

"Actually, I need to go the opposite direction."

"What?"

The pilot snapped the handset back on the dash. "Brace yourselves," he ordered, and grabbed a lever.

I did just that and prayed under my breath.

There was shouting on the radio. "Hawk Unit A, you're ordered to turn around—"

It cut off in a fizzle of static as we shot to hyperspeed. The engine shrieked, and all other sound was drowned out by the terrific roar of air as we tore through space. The impact slammed me into my chair and crushed the wind from my lungs. I felt gravity invert and saw stars and was convinced I was going to pass out. The only thing I could feel was the cat's claws digging into my shoulder. Vaguely, I registered John and Dowe whooping.

And then, suddenly, everything stopped. The plane leveled out, and the rush of air quieted to a manageable grind. Oxygen and gravity came back to me, and my head slowly stopped spinning.

The cat relaxed his grip. I looked around and saw that Lev was lightheaded but alert. John and Dowe were completely unfazed, of course.

"Stealth mode activated!" John announced proudly as he unbuckled his harness.

"Hopefully," the guard grunted. He dragged his finger over the navigation panel. "They'll have a hard time tracking us after that sprint. They'll try, but if we take the scenic route, they won't intercept us."

I slumped in the chair and finished the prayer I'd started earlier. *Thank you, Jesus.*

"You good, Aurelius?" The pilot glanced back at me, the light reflecting off his faceless helmet.

"Yeah." I unclipped my harness and sat up. When the world stayed upright, I stood and walked over to the cockpit. "Thank you."

"Anything for Blue Fire," the pilot returned.

I gripped the back of his chair. "Where is she? Is she safe?"

He put his hand up. "Calm down. She's fine. Last I heard, she'd arrived on Mars."

"She went back to *Mars*?" Lev exclaimed, joining us.

"Without us?" John or Dowe added.

"And her cat?" the other echoed.

The boyfriend part of my brain was happy to hear that Philadelphia was safely off-planet, even as the rest of me admitted that was the *last* place she should be right now. "But what about Operation Blue Fire? What happened? Did it work?"

"That's a loaded question," the pilot grunted. "Maybe just wait until we get back to base. Jael will be able to explain better than I can."

I supposed, after surviving prison, hijacking a plane, and getting dredged off a forgotten island, I could accept that explanation for a few hours. "Did Jael send you?"

"Not... exactly."

His hesitation was palpable, even through the speakers. Lev squinted at him.

I tensed. "Was it Data?"

The pilot shook his head. "It's a long story. Let's just say Jael has a lot on her plate right now. So, when I saw that you'd texted Phil, I decided to take care of this little problem myself."

There were two very important pieces of information in that sentence. One, he had access to Philadelphia's accounts, and two, he'd called her Phil—a nickname normally reserved for close friends.

I leaned over. "Do I know you?"

Lev apparently did. He jerked back and spat something that, had I been able to speak Russian, I probably wouldn't have wanted to repeat.

For an answer, the pilot pulled his pistol from its holster and held it over his shoulder. "If you want to shoot me, do it."

Lev snatched the weapon and looked prepared to do just that.

The pilot's hands returned to the yoke. "Just know that if you knock me out, you're going to have to fly this thing."

"Flying I can do," Dowe offered. "No promises on the landing."

I grabbed Lev's arm to stop him. "Who are you?" I demanded.

The pilot reached up and unclipped his helmet, the pressure releasing with a hiss. He tossed it on the seat beside him, then shook out a shock of red-orange hair and turned to face me.

It was Jayde.

TO BE CONTINUED...

ANNIVERSARY EDITION
RED RAIN
OMNIBUS VOLUME 1
RACHEL NEWHOUSE

OMNIBUS VOLUME 2
RED RAIN
RACHEL NEWHOUSE

WANT EXCLUSIVE BONUS SCENES?

Become a Patron and get access to **exclusive bonus scenes** for this series! Plus, you can get digital ARCs, signed paperbacks, collector's edition hardbacks, and merch, or read my WIP as I write it!

Become a Patron at:
patreon.com/rachelnewhouse

Or sign up for my newsletter and be the first to hear about new releases—plus get sneak peeks of upcoming books, cover art, and more!

Sign up at:
rachelnewhouse.com/subscribe

DID YOU LOVE THIS BOOK?

Please consider leaving a review! It's one of the most important things you can do to support an indie author. Thank you!

HI FROM RACHEL

Rachel Newhouse is an author, wife, secretary, and Sunday school teacher from Kansas City, Missouri. Her obsessions are sci-fi, dystopian, and kid lit. When she's not writing, she's cooking Asian food, growing chilis that are too spicy to eat, and watching wildly age-inappropriate shows like *My Little Pony* and *Gravity Falls* with her husband, Joe. She also really likes glitter. You've been warned.

Connect with Rachel:
bio.site/rachelnewhouse

9 781957 432502